Solomon Caesra Malan

Philosophy or Truth?

Remarks on the First Five Lectures by the Dean of Westminster

Solomon Caesra Malan

Philosophy or Truth?
Remarks on the First Five Lectures by the Dean of Westminster

ISBN/EAN: 9783742811820

Manufactured in Europe, USA, Canada, Australia, Japa

Cover: Foto ©Andreas Hilbeck / pixelio.de

Manufactured and distributed by brebook publishing software
(www.brebook.com)

Solomon Caesra Malan

Philosophy or Truth?

PHILOSOPHY, OR TRUTH?

REMARKS

ON

THE FIRST FIVE LECTURES BY THE DEAN OF WESTMINSTER ON THE JEWISH CHURCH;

WITH

OTHER PLAIN WORDS ON QUESTIONS OF THE DAY,

REGARDING

Faith, the Bible, and the Church.

BY THE

REV. S. C. MALAN, M.A.,

OF BALLIOL COLLEGE, OXFORD; AND VICAR OF BROADWINDSOR, DORSET.

" Beware lest any man spoil you through philosophy and vain deceit, after the tradition of men, after the rudiments of the world, and not after CHRIST."—*Colos.* ii. 8.

Μέγιστον τοίνυν κτῆμά ἐστι, τὸ τῶν δογμάτων μάθημα, καὶ χρεία νηφαλίου ψυχῆς· ἐπειδὴ πολλοί εἰσιν οἱ σφαλλόμενοι διὰ τῆς φιλοσοφίας καὶ κενῆς ἀπάτης· καὶ οἱ μὲν Ἕλληνες, διὰ τῆς εὐγλωττίας παρασύρουσι.
S. Cyril of Jerusalem. Catech. IV.

LONDON:
JOSEPH MASTERS, ALDERSGATE STREET,
AND NEW BOND STREET.
MDCCCLXV.

LONDON:
PRINTED BY JOSEPH MASTERS AND SON,
ALDERSGATE STREET.

PREFACE.

For some time past earnest men in England have been alarmed at the spread of certain loose, rationalistic opinions in matters of Religion connected with the Bible, and they have wondered at it—justly, perhaps; since irreverence and unbelief seem out of keeping with the good sense of the English character. Yet, the cause—or, may be, the causes—of the present falling away from the Faith appear natural enough, and not far to seek. One is of native growth; the other is foreign.

I. As to the English side of the present state of things—antagonism between honest Churchmen and Free-inquirers, Free-thinkers, Rationalists, and so-called Philosophers; alarm in the mind of some, in-indifference in that of others; a growing scepticism, and, in consequence, also a lower tone of morals in society in general—it is only the fruit of former errors and short-comings.

The Church—the best and purest form of the Catholic and Apostolic Church on earth—was, as a national Church, intended by God to be the nursing Mother of a great and good people. Equally free from the errors and absurdities of Rome,[1] and from the narrow-mindedness of a meddlesome sectarianism, she framed her wide[2] Formularies[3] on the Word of

[1] " Ea vero omnia, quæ aut valde superstitiosa, aut frigida, aut sparsa, aut ridicula, aut cum meris literis pugnantia, aut etiam sobriis hominibus indigna esse videbamus, qualia infinita sunt hodie in papatu, prorsus sine ulla exceptione repudiavimus: quod colimus Dei cultum ejusmodi ineptiis longius contaminari." Apologia Eccles. Anglic. autore J. Juello, p. 22.

" Speaking, in the next place," says Bp. Bull, in his letter to the Canoness of Newbrugh, " of the visibility and succession of pastors in our Church, he (the *Catholic Scripturist*) challengeth your ladyship, as by promise to make it good. And here I make him this fair proposal : Let him, or any one of his party, produce any one solid argument to demonstrate such a succession of pastors in the Church of Rome, and I will undertake, by the very same argument, to prove a like succession in our Church."

" His demand that we should show a succession of pastors in our Church, in all ages, holding and professing the Thirty-nine Articles, is infinitely ridiculous, absurd, and unreasonable : for we ourselves acknowledge, that the pastors of our Church were before the Reformation, involved as well as others, in the corruptions of the Church of Rome. against which our Thirty-nine Articles are mainly directed : or else there had been no need of a Reformation. And let him, if he can, show a constant succession of pastors in the Church of Rome, always professing the decrees of the Council of Trent, in the points of image worship, invocation of saints, &c., and I will promise with heart and hand to subscribe to that Council.—As for ourselves, that which we maintain is this, That our Church and the pastors thereof, did always acknowledge the same rule of faith, the same fundamental articles of the Christian religion, both before and since the Reformation ; but with this difference that we then professed the rule of faith together with the additional corruptions of the Church of Rome ; but now (God be thanked) without them. So that the change, as to matter of doctrine which hath been in our Church, and her pastors, is for the better ; like that of a man from being leprous becoming sound and healthy, and yet always the same man." Vindication of the Church of England ; Works, vol. II. p. 201, sq.

[2] " What next the Romanist saith concerning our notorious prevarication from the Articles of our Church I do not perfectly understand. He very well knows that our Clergy doth still subscribe them.—But possibly he intends that latitude of sense, which our Church, as an indulgent mother, allows her sons to some abstruser points, (such as predestination, &c.) not particularly and precisely defined in her Articles, but in general words capable of an indifferent construction. If this be his meaning, this is so far from being a fault, that it is the singular praise and commendation of our Church." Bp. Bull's Vindication of the Church of England ; Works, vol. II. p. 204—211.

[3] " Because our Church," says Bp. Bull, " finds that a set form of Liturgy is used by all Christian Churches in the world, without any known beginning, she hath hers too, and that a grave, solemn, excellently composed one, conformed as near as she could devise, to the pattern of the most ancient offices. A Liturgy, for its innocence and purity, so beyond all just exceptions, that the

God,¹ and not on the fancies of men; so as to embrace within them the whole flock of CHRIST, which is "the blessed company of all faithful people."² Too wise to drive, and too generous to threaten, she calls, she admonishes, she loves; too great to resent or to chide, she bears and forbears, and she forgives all insults to herself. Yet, her dignity is such, that her sons go to be princes in all lands, and that her Clergy are of more honour than their fellows, in other countries. Her influence is only for good; and the heart of her people is naturally drawn towards her.

II. Such is the Church in herself, and such is her spirit; the spirit by which she lives, and shall live

papists themselves, upon its first establishment, could not but embrace it. And therefore for several years they came to our churches, joined in our devotions, and communicated without scruple, till at last (as an excellent person in our Church rightly expresses it) 'a temporal interest of the Church of Rome rent the schism wider, and made it gape like the jaws of the grave;' nay, it is transmitted to us by the testimony of persons greater than all exception that Paulus Quartus, Pope of Rome, in his private intercourse and letters to Queen Elizabeth, did offer to confirm and establish the Common Prayer Book, if she would acknowledge the primacy and authority, and the reformation derivative from him." Bp. Bull's Vindication, &c., p. 206, sq.

¹ "The Church of England," says Archbishop Laud, "grounded her *positive Articles* upon Scripture; and her *negative* do refute there, where the thing affirmed by you (Romanists) is not affirmed by Scripture, nor directly to be concluded out of it. And here not the *Church of England* only, but all *Protestants*, agree most truly, and most strongly in this, *That the Scripture is sufficient to salvation, and contains in it all things necessary to it.* The Fathers* are plain, the schoolmen not strangers in it. And have not we reason then, to account it, as it is, *the Foundation of our Faith !*"

² Collect before the Doxology, in the Communion Service.

* S. Basil, De verâ et piâ Fide. "Manifesta defectio Fidei est impietate quâcunque eorum quæ scripta non sunt." S. Hilar. L. 2, ad Constant. Aug. "Fidem tantùm secundum ea quæ scripta sunt desiderantem, et hoc qui repudiat, Antichristus est, et qui simulat Anathema est." S. Aug. l. 2, de Doctr. Christian. c. 9. "In iis quæ apertè in Scripturâ posita sunt, inveniuntur illa omnia quæ continent fidem moresque vivendi." And to this place Bellarm. l. 4, de Verbo Dei non Scripto, cap. 11, saith that S. Augustine speaks "de illis Dogmatibus quæ necessaria sunt omnibus simpliciter," of those points of Faith, which are necessary simply for all men. So far then he grants the question.—Relation of a Conference, &c., 3rd ed. London, 1673, p. 51.

evermore. But if she lives in the spirit, she acts
through her members; and these are they that griev-
ously sinned against her in days that are past, when
the fathers ate sour grapes which have now set their
children's teeth on edge. I need not enter into the
details of a notorious state of the Church during a
race of Clergy now all but extinct; when things habitually took place which one would hardly credit, but
for the few eye-witnesses of them that are also passing
out of sight; when the houses of God were allowed to
fall into decay; when duty was seldom heard of, and
clerical functions were too often discharged by strangers
to the flocks that never saw their shepherds. Then,
in sooth, was the spirit of the Church, if not wholly
quenched, at least sorely grieved. Then, while her men
slept, did the enemy come, do his work, and sow the
seed whence have sprung up the rank weeds of error,
of scepticism, and of unbelief, which the nation now
gathers. Then, while the Priest and the Levite passed
by on the other side, careless of their poor brother
who had fallen among thieves, a good Samaritan had
pity on him, and of his poverty planted his little
chapels here and there in the most distant and most
forlorn corners of the land, which the Church has not
yet reached. But then, also, did the Priest and the
Levite lose their brother, and the Church very many
of her children.

III. During that time life in the Church was kept up
by a few earnest and conscientious men, who, by their
efforts in well doing, prevented her spirit from dying
out. After them came the religious movement of
about thirty years ago, that did much to rouse the
Church from her slumber. She awoke—but to a state
of things very different from what she remembered.

She found a portion of her flock gone; Dissent established in many parishes where afore it had never been heard of, and Popery free to stalk in the land, and to make for the coveted prize; the beginnings of a state of alternate wiles and artifice, of hatred and envy, against which to struggle with her enemies on the right hand and on the left—a state, too, that shall never cease. In dismay at these great losses, some of her chiefs—assuredly not the wisest—seeing so many sheep gone, now propose to do for the Church what has already been done for the University, so as to lower both together; and they talk of throwing down her fences, in order, they say, to call back the wanderers.¹ Strange wisdom, that! to rend asunder the net, in order to catch more fish; and because some of the sheep were allowed to go astray, to level the fold with the ground, and let in the wolves upon the remnant that is left! Better, we had thought, follow the example of the Good Shepherd, and go into the wilderness after the sheep that are lost; many, very many, will be found too glad to be brought back to the fold and to better pastures.

Nay, the present trial of the Church is only the fruit of her own doings; of doings, too, that must

<hr>

¹ "To seek reformation of evil laws," says Hooker, "is a commendable endeavour; but for us the more necessary is a speedy redress of ourselves. We have on all sides lost much of our first fervency towards God; and therefore concerning our own degenerated ways we have reason to exclaim with S. Gregory, "Ὅπερ ἦμεν γενώμεθα, ' Let us return again to what we sometime were;' but touching the exchange of laws in practice with laws in device, which they say are better for the state of the Church if they might take place, the farther we examine them the greater cause we find to conclude μένωμεν ἔνπερ ἐσμέν, 'although we continue the same we are the harm is not great.' These fervent reprehenders of things established by public authority are always confident and bold spirited men. But their confidence for the most part ariseth from too much credit given to their own wits, for which cause they are seldom free from error." Eccles. Pol. Bk. v. Dedic. 2. Words that seem written for the present time.

have been visited on a Church so really great, and on
a nation so greatly blessed. "Shall I not visit for
these things? saith the LORD. The prophets prophesy
falsely, and the priests bear rule by their means, and
my people love to have it so; and what will ye do in
the end thereof?"[1] Yet the trial may soon be over,
if the Church will it; on herself depends whether she
shall suffer long from error and disunion within herself, or whether she will come forth the better and the
wiser for what is past. Humanly speaking, however,
it may be that the working of such beautiful machinery
as the English Church and State together, by a people
gifted with so many sterling qualities, would have
brought about results too great and too good for this
world; and that it must, therefore, have got out of
gear. Out of gear, then, it certainly is; the State
seems disaffected towards the Church, and the Church
at variance with it and with herself. All now depends
on her wisdom, energy, and life; and after she has
been sufficiently tried, then on GOD's mercy in healing
her wounds. One thing, however, is certain—it would
be death to the Church to take her ease at present.
If the Church of England slumber again, she is lost.

IV. But, however tried, she lives—she cannot die;
yet, she cannot rest. And rest she must not, until,
with the whole Church of CHRIST, she lays down her
weapons, and then rest for ever. Meanwhile, she owes
much of her present life and energy to the earnest
teaching of certain of her pious, able, and devoted
sons who are still living. Setting aside as not their
fault, and of little or no moment, the flights of some
of their followers, the want of judgment of others, and
the perversion to Romanism of a few more whose

[1] Jer. v. 79—31.

minds were either weak, warped, or wanting in ballast,
the good those men did in the Church will never die.
They poured a new life into the body of Churchmen;
whether love and care for the houses of God in the
land, or untiring energy and manly devotedness to the
work of the ministry on the highest principles, by
teaching that the Church is not a myth, but a reality;
that her doctrines are not conceits, to be held up and
then dropped—to be made and unmade at the will of
men—but that they rest on objective Truths that shall
stand when heaven and earth have passed away; and
that her Sacraments are not the dead letter of by-gone
types, but that they really are "outward and visible
signs of an inward and spiritual grace," and so, "necessary to salvation." Much of this, however, took by
surprise well-meaning but ill-informed men, who then
drifted aside from such teaching; and who, by so
doing, widened the already existing division of the
Church between High and Low. Nevertheless, but
for the earnestness and for the life infused into the
Church some five and twenty years ago and more, we
may doubt whether she could have weathered the
storms lately come upon her.

V. But if the present state of things—in the Church
error and divisions, and in society scepticism and indifference—is to some extent the result of negligence
and of other short-comings during the past generation,
it may also be owing, partly, to the narrow, stiff, exclusive, though haply well-meaning spirit of the so-
called Low Church on the one hand, and on the other
hand to the want of judgment frequently shown by
many of the so-called High Church party. By placing
undue importance on what may, by comparison, be
called trifles, which, however lawful, were not always

expedient, " that have lately sprung up," says Hooker,[1]
" for complements, rites, and ceremonies of church
actions, and are in truth for the greatest part such
silly things, that very easiness doth make them hard
to be disputed of in a serious manner ;" or, by making
too much of mere forms, which at all times are dead
without the Spirit that gives them life, High Churchmen have often needlessly offended opinions or innocent prejudices of many sheep of their flocks, and have
scared them from the fold, instead of rallying them to
it.   By " paying tithe of mint, anise, and cummin,"
and occasionally either omitting, or at least appearing
to omit, " weightier matters of the Law," High Churchmen made honest and sober Churchmanship at times
appear ridiculous ; and thus laid themselves open to
the charge of inconsistency, perhaps even of frivolity
in grave matters, which the practical, " sound, large,
round-about sense," as Locke calls it, of the English
people, could not endure very long.

These two negative eccentricities—each equally opposed to the real spirit and to the teaching of the
Church of England—by repelling each other, left between them a wide, empty space, called ' latitudinarian-
ism' by the sensible, orthodox, earnest men who float
therein between the two extremes ; ' liberalism' by men
either lukewarm or indifferent ; and either ' Broad
Church' or ' philosophy' by latitudinarians themselves.
The several elements of this motley gathering assimi-
late—as of course they must—according to the affinity
of sentiment, leaving the pure metal of the Anglo-
Catholic Faith to shine alone, and above them all.
Yet, had the two extremes agreed to certain timely
concessions on both sides, for their mutual advantage

[1] Eccles. Pol. Bk. v. Dedic. 3.

and for the good of the people, they might, perhaps, have made up a whole, consistent both with the large Scriptural Spirit of the Church, and with the good sense of the nation ; and thus little room would have been left for these apparently new-fangled, yet in reality stale opinions, hostile alike to the Faith, and to the peace of the Church. The fault, then, seems to lie partly with those who, from whatever motive, would rather rend asunder than yield.

VI. And secondly—as to the foreign or German element in the present rationalistic movement, it is easily accounted for. Many obvious reasons may have had, and may yet have something to do with it. But the chief cause of all this Germanism at the University, and through it in the Church is—the need one has to go to Germany for learning, now that real scholarship, and especially Biblical scholarship, are at the ebb in this country, instead of being at the flow, as formerly. Certain philosophers of the day, comparing themselves among themselves and ignoring their giant sires in learning, may, indeed, amuse themselves and others also, by writing essays on the progress and education of the world, and on the restless activity of this nineteenth century—which, after all, is but the fulfilment of the prophecy that in the latter days " many shall run to and fro, and knowledge shall be increased ;"[1] while, others of the same class, evidently on excellent terms with themselves, may even go so far as to ask, if intellect, activity, ability and knowledge or learning are not on their side ?"[2] And yet, in reality, if instead of smiling at such overweening conceit, we chose to take them at their word and to compare with their pretensions, the

[1] Dan. xii. 4.
[2] See the Letter of Anglicans in the Times for March 11.

writings of some of them who, residing at the University and with every facility for study, could have no excuse for either shallowness, or inaccuracy—we should be justified in bidding Oxford write 'Ichabod' on the portal of her schools, and mourn in ashes over the days of English learning; of such men as Walton, Castell, Lowth, Hickes, Hyde, Pococke, Selden, Lightfoot, Bingham, Stillingfleet, Lardner, Hooker, Porson, Hall, Waterland, Bull, Butler, and other such mighty scholars and learned men;—days that are past, and men that are gone, judging from the few successors they have left. For, it is vain to boast; English scholarship and learning no longer hold their own to take the lead as formerly; but they now seem content to move like waiting-maids at the beck of their German masters; though, haply, little to the liking of these—quos illa tandem

      Occidit miseros crambe repetita magistros.

Yet, in sooth, unless native talent and ability have left the land, all this imitation of others and all this borrowing from them, is assuredly a mistake. For, not only is the English character too solid and too original to make good imitators, but German thought does not suit English heads which, stored in their own way and with their own thoughts, would almost always be best for sense and for steadiness. Only read some of the standard English divines, and others who wrote long ere this Germanism became the fashion, and see what greater breadth and power of thought, what better style, and what sounder learning they show than the divines of the present day!

But for this prevalent ignorance or lack of knowledge, the notorious "Essays and Reviews" would not have drawn one tithe of the notice they did. Nor would Dr. Colenso's works on the Pentateuch; only that the interest these might perhaps have created, is greatly diminished by the small respect one feels for the whole thing.'

VII. Neither is it altogether owing to the simplicity of those who think Deans and Professors 'ex officio' right, good and learned; nor yet to the generous confidence in accredited teachers which is natural to the English character, that these free, or rather, loose opinions are allowed to spread. But, the apparent success of this sceptical or rationalistic proselytism is owing, first—to the readiness with which the natural man (ψυχικὸς ἄνθρωπος) will receive a teaching the object of which is to glorify 'self' and self's 'intellect,' fallen and degraded though this be, by lowering the objects of Faith, and with them also Faith itself; in order to set the heart free from the trammels of the fear of God, and to ease the conscience of the warnings of a Judgment to come. Preachers of such doctrine will always command a large audience, and make many disciples among a certain class of hearers; especially if those preachers enjoy worldly advantages; for there

---

¹ "That which all men's experience teaches them," says Hooker, (Eccles. Pol. Bk. iii. ch. viii. 14,) "may not in any wise be denied. And by experience we all know, that the first outward motive leading men to esteem of the Scripture is the authority of God's Church. For when we know the whole Church of God hath that opinion of the Scripture, we judge it even at the first an impudent thing for any man bred and brought up in the Church to be of a contrary mind without cause."

"I did never love," says Archbp. Laud, (Relation of a Conference, &c. p. 31,) "too curious a search into that which might put a man into a wheel, and circle him so long between proving *Scripture by Tradition*, and *Tradition by Scripture*, till the devil find a means to dispute him into *Infidelity*, and make him believe neither. I hope this is no part of your meaning. Yet I doubt this* question, *How do you know Scripture to be Scripture?* hath done more harm than ever you will be able to help by Tradition."

* "Qui conantur fidem destruere sub specie quæstionis difficilis, aut forte indissolubilis," &c. Orig. q. 35, in B. Matt.

are no subjects on which worldly-minded and thoughtless men will sooner hearken to those who flatter them
and who make things easy for them. Even though
they believe it not, they yet like to hear that 'modern
science' having discovered means whereby the blind
have only to look within themselves in order to see
light and to find their way, tells man to do the same
and to look into his intellect for things which, we are
told, " never entered the heart of man,"[1] and which
" he cannot know"—in order to find the way through
life which even Plato could not discover. And as to
what lies beyond, ' philosophy' has, at last, bridged
over the chasm into which we plunge at death, and
has settled that " Judgment," which, we are told,
" follows after death," is a relative term and liable to
various meanings ; and that, somehow, things will
then be amicably arranged. Like children sitting in
state to make laws for the inhabitants of Saturn, these
teachers imagine to settle what is to be hereafter, and
to decide it after their own fashion. But the end of
both teachers and taught is not by-and-by. We shall
all appear at the bar of that awful tribunal, to our
utter amazement ; and in that day shall the work of
every man be made manifest, of what sort it is.

VIII. So also is this lifting up of the head of scepticism
and of unbelief—an unwonted sight in great and good
England—due, secondly, to the circumstances under
which these free opinions are being broached. On the
one hand, they are put forth with a certain show of
what must appear like learning to persons of little or
no information, by men of high position in the Church
and out of it, who enjoy great worldly advantages, and
who being in favour with the great, are also in favour

[1] 1 Cor. II. 9.

with the multitude that values appearance and show.
The accidents of their social position give them a certain influence, though it be only among the class—a
very numerous one, however—both of thoughtless
men who look not below the surface of things, and
leave others to think for them; and of men who,
though not thoughtless, yet lean irresistibly towards
that which pleases their fancy, or agrees best with
their already foregone conclusions. On the other
hand, those upon whom chiefly devolves the duty of
refuting or of resisting error, in whatever shape, are,
as it happens, for the most part either unable or un-
willing to enter the lists against it.

Most of the Clergy, from the very nature of their
calling, are obliged to become 'practical men,' the
moment they enter upon the duties of their sometimes
arduous parishes, in which they soon find enough to
engross their time and their affections. They reason
with themselves that all this scepticism will not reach
them in the country—though many would be surprised
to hear in what out-of-the-way cottages such matters
are discussed—and they draw the natural conclusion,
that, as regards themselves, their readiest way of meeting error is, to teach the Truth; and thus leave to
others the duty of taking an active part in this inevitable struggle between error and the Faith. They
be true men, nevertheless; many, very many of them
noble-hearted, devoted servants of the Church, who
spend and grudge not to be spent as faithful shepherds
of their flocks for their MASTER's sake. What will
become of the people to be looked after, when the
Clergy, who now move in all ranks of society by
virtue of the reverential feeling of the best part of the
people for their office, are no longer taken from the

b

kernel of the nation, and thus no longer possessed of
the admirable qualities found therein? The profession, it is true, raises any man who enters it as he
ought; yet, unless the man adorn, or at least recommend, the profession, he must bring it into discredit
in the eyes of those who only judge of things by their
appearance.

Other considerations weigh with others of the
Clergy. There are among them men who, though
not indifferent to the present state of things—to the
secret workings of Romanism and to the progress of
scepticism—yet feel such confidence in the good sense
of the nation, and so far trust to the fickleness of public
opinion, as to comfort themselves with thinking that
things will right themselves, without interference on
their part. Others, again, who are indifferent to the
turn of the scale—Gallios, who care for none of these
things—find it easiest to call themselves 'liberals;'
without, perhaps, a clearer idea of the meaning of that
term than going with the stream, and being left at
peace. With others the hope or the chance of pre-
ferment, and other such motives which appear mean
in comparison of the importance of the case at issue,
make them lie in harbour, trim their sails, and wait
for the tide. While others, again, unable to judge for
themselves, follow their only guide, public opinion,
and espouse the cause of the man last or most in
favour with the world.

IX. Thus the number of those among the Clergy
whose voice is heard in defence of the Truth is small
compared with the whole. As a body, they seem, in
this respect, to belie their real spirit and life, and look
almost as if they were either indifferent, or cowed by
the assurance with which the Germanizing rationalistic

party—for 'school' it cannot be called—presumes
upon the social position of some of its members, and,
as we have seen, arrogating to them the brilliant gifts
of intellect, ability, and knowledge, assumes an over-
bearing attitude towards those who are either too well
informed, too independent, or too conscientious to
wish for aught of their philosophy. After succeeding in
making both the University and the Church each into
two camps, they then took to threatening;[1] and one
may do them the justice to say, that they have done
and do their best to make good their threat in distract-
ing the Church. They will thus widen the breach,
and provoke honest and stout hearts to endurance, but
to surrender—never; albeit they claim immunity from
all opposition. So that, by a convenient arrangement
of theirs, if we honest Churchmen venture to avail
ourselves of the leave given us to judge of them by
their fruits, we hear at once that "charity thinketh no
evil"—a favourite quotation with sundry newspaper
homilists; if we rebuke ribaldry on sacred things, we
are said to lose our temper; and if again, we demur to
certain arbitrary treatment on their part, and question
their right so to act, we are then told to hold our
peace; because, of course, "charity beareth all things."

So it must. Meanwhile the air resounds with voices
echoing "intellect," "pride of intellect," and the
like, as applicable to the pretensions or to the results
of these new philosophers. But, may we ask, what
can this mean? For, first—light bears witness of itself,
without any apology for it; whereas their scholarship and learning, for the most part like borrowed
feathers, call forth, not argument, but a smile from
men of average reading. Secondly—real intellects

[1] See the last article in the *Times* for March 9th.

never were proud of themselves. Neither Aristotle,
Plato, Newton, Leibnitz, Linnæus, Cuvier, nor other
such were proud of their understanding, which brought
them, as one of them says, only to God's footstool.
Their intellect was too great not to feel its own weakness, or to be proud of it. They knew two well,
that, after all, light is only relative to the surrounding
darkness; and that with Truth, intellect, sense, and
knowledge there is no respect of persons, but that, in
all men alike, pride comes from ignorance, conceit from
shallowness, and pretensions from vanity. "Truth,"
says Locke,[1] "whether in or out of fashion, is the
measure of knowledge and the business of the understanding. Whatsoever is besides that is nothing but
ignorance, or something worse." "Truth is all simple,
all pure, will bear no mixture of anything else with it.
It is rigid and inflexible to any by-interests; and so
should the understanding be, whose use and excellency lies in conforming itself to it."[2] And, we may
add, Truth, as a principle, is sacred; and he who know-
ingly and wilfully either gainsays or perverts it, is mean
and contemptible. Therefore does Truth, by virtue of
itself alone, win the day. "Veritas vincat necesse
est, sive negantem sive confitentem," says S. Augustine.[3] All it wants is, clear heads and honest hearts
to defend its rights. But no one can plead for the
Truth who does not love it.

X. Such a defence, however, is not, as some endeavour to represent it, a mere intellectual passage of arms,
a controversy involving no consequences whatever beyond the defeat of one or other of the opponents. If
it were so, and if the defence of the Truth were a

[1] Cond. of the Und. sect. xxiv.　　　　　[2] Ibid. sect. xiv.
[3] Epist. 174.

mere matter of opinion, to contend for it were unworthy of sensible men. But "Truth," Aristotle tells
us,[1] "cannot be a matter of opinion, since the same
thing tastes to some sweet, and to others bitter."
Truth, τὸ ἀληθὲς, therefore, is independent of man, and
outside him; he does not make it, but he looks for it;
and whether he find it or not, it exists nevertheless.
And 'the Truth,' ἡ ἀλήθεια, as regards ourselves, and
for which Christians have had, have, and will yet have
to contend, consists in certain objective Truths, made
known to us through revelation in the Bible, held and
taught by the Church of England, and therefore also
by the Church Catholic ever since her beginning.
These Truths imply, as Archbishop Laud says, "the
belief of Scripture to be the Word of God and infallible, as a prime principle of Faith;" and are to be received and understood in their plain and natural sense,
as by the Fathers of the Catholic Church and of the
English Church in particular; and not to be distorted
into a non-natural sense, at the will of men, who at
all times have endeavoured not to rise up to the
Truth, but to bring it down to themselves.

Very far, then, from this controversy being of little
or of no moment, on it depends the spiritual life or the
spiritual death of those engaged in it. For it matters
somewhat, I trow, whether a man be, as by Scripture
and the Church, directed upwards to the only way
there is for him to God, that is, through Faith in the
merits and in the Atonement of CHRIST; the Faith
that shows itself in works done out of gratitude and
love for God as for a FATHER reconciled, and acceptable unto Him only as tokens of the reality of the
Faith that brings them forth, yet without any merit

---

[1] See below, p. 5, R. ix. τὸ μὲν γὰρ ἀληθὲς, κ.τ.λ.

whatsoever of their own;' or whether that same man
be told, as by Rome, which claims infallibility in matters of Faith,' that " the way to be saved is to avoid sin,
and to do works of grace,"' without any reference to
CHRIST's Sacrifice, which alone prevails with GOD and
avails for us; or again, whether that man be sent, as
by the philosophers of the day, to wander and lose
himself within the narrow maze of his own reason and
intellect, turning round and round upon himself;
making that the object as well as the subject of his
worship; and thus, in the end, being no nearer GOD
than when he started on his errand.

A controversy of this kind, then, is not of practical
indifference, as some say or make others believe it to be.
Neither can it matter little whether " the Scripture of
Truth," wherein are revealed unto us " great and precious promises" of things on which depends our eternal
salvation, be upheld, honoured, and defended; or despised, reviled, and, as by some, ranked with old stories
and obsolete legends. Yea, it matters much whether
we be hoodwinked by the specious sophistry " that certain books of the Bible may be less inspired than

' " Nullis ergo operibus aut meritis Deum antevertere possumus?—Nullis
plane.—Debita pietatis officia, quæ ex Fide per caritatem operante profici-
enctur, Deo quidem grata sunt; non tamen ipsorum merito, sed quod ille suo
favore ex liberaliter dignetur," &c. Noelli Catechismus, p. 116, ed. Ox.

" Ex his jam locis liquere arbitror, apostolum—hoc imprimis fundamento
niti, quod quicquid boni ad justificationem ac salutem æternam consequendam
a nobis præstitum sit, id totum ex gratiâ Dei, gratis nobis per Christum data,
promanet, ipsique acceptum referri debeat," &c. Bp. Bull, Harmon. Apostolica,
vol. iii. p. 217; præmed. et seq.

' Romana particularis Ecclesia non potest errare in Fide. Bellarm. l. iv. de
Rom. Pont. cap. 4, sec. 1, quoted in Abp. Laud's Conference, &c., p. 3.

' Q. Re unde hganas colemo salakkourebad / R. Tredvedispen unde mo-
chordre, da madlis requeral unde bpanas. " Q. What must a man do to be
saved? R. He must avoid sin, and do works of grace." Dottrina Cristiana,
&c., per uso delle Missioni della Olorgia; Roma, Sagra Congreg. de Propag.
Fide, 2 ed. sect. vi. p. 31.

others," since who is to decide the ' more or less' in this case, except he be himself inspired? every man assuming to be both judge and jury in a matter entirely beyond him—or whether the Truth regarding this be put before us in the manly words of Archbishop Laud: "Now all *Propositions of Canonical Scripture* are alike *firm*, because they all alike proceed from *Divine Revelation*; but they are not alike *fundamental in the Faith*." "For *the belief of Scripture to be the Word of God and infallible*, is an equal, or rather a preceding Prime Principle of Faith, with or to the whole body of the Creed."[1] For "the *charter of foundation*," says Dr. Waterland,[2] "is undoubtedly an *essential* of the covenant; and therefore, of course, the admittance of the sacred *oracles*, which are the *charter* itself (or at least the only *authentic* instrument of conveyance) is essential to the covenant; consequently, to reject or disbelieve the *Divine authority* of Sacred Writ is to err fundamentally." Wherefore it must be evident to all, that the shallow motive of those who deny this is, to leave every man free to choose or to reject what parts of the Sacred Canon he likes, in order to suit his own personal convenience or fancy; so as to fetter himself with little or no Faith, and practically to owe allegiance to no one but to himself.

XI. In this controversy, then, both sides cannot argue either from the same motives, or on the same principle. Whereas what is called 'Truth' by those who gainsay the Bible or parts of it, and the Catholic Truth contained in it, must be, and indeed is, with them a matter of opinion only—since we cannot admit

---

[1] Relation of a Conference, &c., p. 27, 28, ed. 1673. The italics and capitals are Abp. Laud's.

[2] Discourse of Fundamentals: Works, vol. viii. p. 97. The italics are his.

the existence of a principle worthy of Christian men,
and opposed to either the Bible or the Truth—to
contend for this Truth is a matter of principle, of a
deep, unshaken principle, that dwells in the innermost heart of those who uphold both the Bible and
the Truth it teaches.   But 'principle' will never yield
to mere 'opinion,' since principle alone makes the difference between firmness and obstinacy; 'firmness'
being, devotedness to a principle held on good grounds,
and therefore disinterested; while 'obstinacy,' which
is the firmness of weak minds, is but the pertinacity
of individual opinion, and is therefore selfish and interested.

Thus it is on principle that we contend for the
integrity of the whole Canon of Scripture as received by the Church Catholic and by the Church of
England; it is on principle that we keep and will keep
the Prayer Book, not only for its unrivalled beauty
and excellence, but as the Formulary of the Church to
which we belong, framed and cherished by men holier,
wiser, and more learned than are to be found at present; and it is also on principle that we will fight for
the safety of those Truths which are both the walls
and the fences of the Church, and without which no
Church can exist.   Whereas those who attack the
Bible, who work for the alteration of the Prayer Book,
and who fain would throw down the bulwarks of the
Church, so as to make it one broad plain of their own,
do it from selfish or interested motives; for it cannot
be on a right principle.   Therefore do we see that the
struggle between the Truth and error, appears un-
equal; because, whereas he that honestly contends for
the Truth does so as having everything at stake in
this one principle, the other contends only for self, and

for self-opinion, and is thus always ready to shift at any moment either his ground or his mode of attack, without any scruple as to ways and means thereto.

XII. No time, then, now for ignorance or for indifference among the Clergy, if the Truth is to be upheld; and if the Church is to be defended, the laity should be well taught. To that effect a radical alteration must take place in the style of preaching common in the Church; for souls cannot be saved and minds cannot be trained unless the preachers show that not only they are in earnest, but that they also understand what they teach; two qualifications often thought unnecessary. Then, when the Truth is preached more boldly, and thus better understood, there will not be room for so much alarm in the mind of many, who fear lest it should suffer from the repeated attacks of its adversaries. The Truth has ever been, is, and will be attacked as long as the world lasts; but destroyed— never. "Occultari potest ad tempus veritas, vinci non potest," says S. Augustine;[1] for the LORD GOD of Truth, Who said, "Heaven and earth shall pass away, but my words shall not pass away," is He also "who keepeth the Truth for ever."[2]

Therefore shall the Truth stand; and they alone also shall stand who side with it, love it, and defend it. But in order to be loved it must be known; and ere it be known, it must be studied, sought, searched for, and found; it does not come to men intuitively, as some seem to think. If the Church is to stand, her Clergy must be not only well educated, in earnest, and devoted, but learned. As we shall see presently, no great knowledge is needed to see through false philosophy; yet that little should be had; for ignorance

[1] In Psalm. lxi.   [2] Ps. cxlvi. 6.

never won either a blessing or souls to Christ; and
those err greatly who seem to think that almost anything may do for the teaching the laity receive from
the pulpit, "as if the way to be ripe in faith," says
Hooker,[1] "were to be raw in wit and in judgment; as
if Reason were an enemy unto Religion, and childish
simplicity the mother of ghostly wisdom." Far, indeed, from it. As gold is for the sanctuary, so are
the best gifts in man—reason, intelligence, ability, and
learning, never so great and never so good as when
sanctified by being made to minister to the Faith and
to true wisdom. At present, especially, when the enemies of the Church are on the alert,—both those who
openly plot her fall in order to raise themselves on her
ruins, and her false friends from within, who either
try to throw down her fences, or who from ignorance
of what they do, and from small love for their Church
and for their country, play into the hands of Rome—
for friendship with Rome is treason to England—ought
her true friends to be on the watch, and "commend
themselves by the word of truth, by the power of God,
and by the armour of righteousness on the right hand
and on the left."[2]

"Philosophy," says Hooker, "we are warned to
take heed of: not that philosophy which is true and
sound knowledge attained by natural discourse of reason; but that philosophy, which to bolster heresy or
error casteth a fraudulent show of reason upon things
which are indeed unreasonable, and by that mean as
by a stratagem spoileth the simple which are not able
to withstand such cunning. 'Take heed lest any spoil
you through philosophy and vain deceit.' He that
exhorteth to beware of an enemy's policy doth not give

[1] Eccles. Pol. Bk. iii. ch. viii. 1.   [2] 2 Cor. vi. 7.

counsel to be impolitic, but rather to use all provident
foresight and circumspection, lest our simplicity be
overreached by cunning sleights. The way not to be
inveigled by them that are so guileful through skill, is
thoroughly to be instructed in that which maketh skil-
ful against guile, and to be armed with that true and
sincere philosophy, which doth teach, against that deceitful and vain, which spoileth."—" For unto the
word of God," adds the same wise and sound thinker,[1]
" being in respect of that end for which God ordained
it perfect, exact, and absolute in itself, we do not add
Reason as supplement of any maim or defect therein,
but as a necessary instrument, without which we could
not reap by the Scripture's perfection that fruit and
benefit which it yieldeth.'"[2]

XIII. And honestly to strive for the integrity of the
Bible, of the Truth, and of the Church, is not to fight as
beating the air; it is to fight for the safety of the nation.
As the Church can rest on no other foundation than that
is laid, Jesus Christ, so also " is the throne established
by righteousness" only. With Him " who sitteth
upon the circle of the earth," and before whom " the
nations are counted as the small dust of the balance,"
iron-clads and fleets of merchant-men avail very little.
But, when He said: " Them that honour me, I will

[1] Bk. iii. vi. 10.

[2] " For though *Reason* without *Grace*," continues Archbishop Laud, (Relation
of a Conference, &c., p. 48,) " cannot see the way to Heaven, nor believe this
Book, in which God hath written the way; yet *Grace* is never placed but in a
reasonable creature, and proves by the very seat, which it hath taken up, that
the end it hath, is to be *spiritual eye-water*, to make *Reason* see what by *nature*
only it cannot, (1 Cor. ii. 14,) but never to blemish *Reason* in that which it can
comprehend. Now the use of *Reason* is very general; and man (do what he
can) is still apt to search and seek for a *Reason* why he will believe, though after
he once believes, his *Faith* grows stronger, than either his *Reason*, or his *Knowledge*: and great reason for this, because it goes higher, and so upon a safer
principle, than either of the other can in this life."

honour; but they that despise me shall be lightly es-
teemed;" He also bade history show as a warning to
all, that "righteousness exalteth a nation; but that
sin is a reproach to any people;" that real national
greatness depends altogether on national morality, and
national morality on the national Faith and fear of
God. And, without controversy, the Rock on which
England rests, and on which she has reared the solid
edifice of her great power, is—the fear of God; for
He is more honoured, and His Word has hitherto been
more respected in this country than anywhere else in
the world.

But, on either side of this Rock are quicksands
on which England must tread if she swerve either
to the right hand or to the left. Only take away
the mighty, overruling principle of "the fear of the
Lord, which is the beginning of wisdom, and the
knowledge of the Holy which is understanding;" then
cut the reins of Faith by accustoming the public mind
to doubt and scepticism, and to irreverence for the
Bible, whence alone the fear of God flows; and instead of this, give philosophy and reason to the teeming
life and intelligence of the manufacturing towns, and
see by-and-by what has become of this great country,
and in it of order, justice and equity in the due balance
of power. If you wish to know, only look at France
less than a century since. Things are not yet come
to that; and may God in His mercy avert them from
English hearths! Infidelity has not yet swept the
land with desolation; for there is yet faith, hope, and
charity, among the people; neither does ungodliness
yet prevail; God still loves the land, and He is still
loved and honoured in it; nor does open immorality
stalk abroad, for the nation has not lost shame, and is

still virtuous. But there is the beginning of these things which, like a canker, eat into the body of society. Already one may trace unmistakeable signs of a decline from a higher standard; all the more noticeable, as in no other country were the solid principles of Christianity and the relative duties of the several orders of society so well understood and so well observed as in this.

XIV. Those then, love most the nation, who, despite ribaldry, scorn and ridicule, are most earnest in their efforts, through good report and through evil report, to preserve in their integrity the true causes of national greatness—the Bible and the Church. Those, on the other hand, love the nation least, who, whether in the Church or out of it, whether divines or journalists, gainsay the Bible and the Truth it teaches; and attack or ridicule the Church, by ascribing to her inward spirit the weaknesses and other short-comings of her members; for in so doing they sap the foundation of all national morality, religion and order, and thus also of all real national greatness and prosperity. If therefore, we—and by 'we' I mean those alone with whom I either can identify myself, or wish so to do, namely, men educated at Oxford who are sincerely attached to her, and who, with others, honestly love the nation and heartily the Church of which Oxford was the wonted bulwark—if, I say, we would bear in mind that, even though error and scepticism come in like a flood, the cause of the Truth held by the Church must stand and cannot fail, since the Church herself rests on "the everlasting hills," and her LORD is "the LORD GOD of Truth,"—some of us would stand by it with a better heart than they seem to do. For, "if we strive together for the faith of the Gospel, and, in nothing terrified by our adversaries," uphold GOD's Word as it was received, believed, honoured and worshipped by the Church of CHRIST; and if we adhere to the Prayer Book as to the Formulary and framework[1] of the best and purest form of CHRIST's Church on earth to which by the Grace of GOD we belong, we know that in so doing we have GOD, the Truth and the Church on our side; all of more avail, I ween, than "the opposition of a science falsely so called." What more, then, do we want, to give us courage and confidence in the cause we are called to defend, if at the last we wish to be found having done our duty? And we need to do so, if we wish to stand. For we are not about to pass through the Red Sea, that we should sit still in order to "see the salvation of the LORD;" neither are we going up to the storming of Jericho, that we should have only to blow a few trumpets with a more or less uncertain sound. We are members of the Church militant, and soldiers of CHRIST, whose charge we received in 'sacrament' when we vowed to fight manfully under His banner: "Be thou faithful unto death, and I will give thee a crown of life."

XV. True, there is enough to dishearten at the thought of all that is already lost, either through evil counsels, heartlessness or indifference; especially when,

---

[1] "Our Liturgy," says Bishop Bull, "contains the whole religion of the Church of England: this the popes and bishops of Rome themselves offer to confirm and establish. Let me now ask this question, Is our Liturgy in itself a good and safe way of worshipping God, or not? If not, these popes were to blame in offering to confirm it: for no subsequent decree of a pope could make that safe and good, which was not so antecedently. If it were in itself good and safe, then it is so still, though the pope of Rome never confirmed it; and so the whole religion and reformation of the Church of England is safe and good, by the plain confession of the pope himself, the infallible judge of the Roman Church." Vindication, &c. p. 208.

looking round one sees what great results would crown
the joint action for good of so great a nation as this.
For instance, the 'Genius et Religio loci,' more venerable
and better worth having than either Germanism without German scholarship and research, or than Gallican
inklings without French talent or science, have de-
serted Oxford; not because of a few crying abuses set
right, but amazed at her new form ; who will now recall them to their hallowed and wonted haunts ?   The
Church misses whole flocks of her sheep from the
fold, who will now bring them back?   Some, indeed,
may rejoice in the work of their own hands, but the
better part of the nation mourns, and will yet mourn
over greater losses, unless a spirit of wisdom be given
equal to the interests at stake and to the weal of a
great people.   Nevertheless, much evil may yet be
averted, and great good may yet be done by union, by
oneness of motive, by earnestness, and by principle,
in keeping and holding together " things that are ready
to die;" till Faith and godliness again become the
badge of the nation.   For true Religion alone can
hold and bind together into one solid edifice, the precious stones of national energy, valour, honesty, sense,
steadiness, endurance, enterprise, intelligence, firmness,
loyalty, patience, manliness and generosity ; while ir-
religion, irreverence and scepticism, are the dry rot
that may soon reduce all these fine materials into a
ruinous heap.

XVI. To that intent, earnest Churchmen who do not
make light of the gravest matters ought to lay aside small
differences between themselves—what do they signify ?
—and sink all their private feelings and petty motives
into the one common object of defending the Church,
and with her the nation—against those who from within

strive to level her fences; against the encroachment
of Romanism, alive as it is to the present opportunity
of disunion in the Church; and against scepticism and
false-philosophy; and they shall be blessed in their
deed.   All this is no figure of speech; for while union
in the Church and unity of motive would make her
invincible, her enemies know well that if they can
breed divisions and dissensions within her, they may
then rule if they like.   Only compare Jerusalem besieged by the Assyrian host, with Jerusalem besieged
by Titus, and learn that it is no time for small bicker-
ings when the enemy is at the breach; but it is then,
if ever, time to be at one and to defend the City.

And such a City, too! If she were to be built, it
would be an honour even to draw her stones, and to
work at her walls; but she was built long since, on the
Rock which alone shall abide while heaven and earth are
passing away. Yea, we may tell the towers thereof and
watch at her gates; all we have to do is to love and
to defend her. "In confidence," indeed, "and in quiet-
ness is our strength;" but we show our earnestness by
the way we quit ourselves under our MASTER's eye.
"Our help," truly, "is in the name of the LORD;"
but He watches to see what efforts we make to deserve
His help.   And since we have no leaders to look to,
for every day's experience teaches us to "cease from
man,"—our safety lies wholly in the uprightness and
devotion with which we look unto THE CAPTAIN of our
Salvation, "unto the author and finisher of our faith,
who for the joy that was set before him endured the
cross, despising the shame, and is set down at the right
hand of the throne of GOD." We are also "compassed
about with a great cloud of witnesses" who look to see
how we either run the race set before us, or wrestle

for the prize, and win our crown. Let us then, think
of "the Faith once delivered to the saints," to "those
same spirits of just men made perfect," who believed,
who endured, and who now are at rest. Their Faith,
our Faith, changes not with the times, as certain
teachers fondly talk ; albeit times do change; since
we are now come to those foretold by the Holy Apostle,
when "men cannot endure sound doctrine, but heap
unto themselves teachers, having itching ears ; and
turning away their ears from the truth, are turned unto
fables." Yet the Faith abides unchanged; "always
new," says S. Cyril,[1] because it is the Faith of Him
" who is the same yesterday, and to-day, and for ever."

But if leaders fail us, we have bright examples set
before us, by S. Ignatius, S. Athanasius, S. Ambrose,
of the Church Catholic; by Cranmer, by Ridley, by
Jewel, by Hooker, and by other fearless and manly
defenders of their Church. Those men counted the
reproach of CHRIST a greater honour than the favour
or the smiles of their fellow-creatures; their Faith was
indeed to them "the substance of things hoped for,
the evidence of things not seen ;" they suffered, they
even died for it. But we " have not yet resisted unto
blood"—nay, our life is one of ease and of rest compared with theirs; shall our LORD, then, send us persecution, in order to see whether our Faith is to us as
dear, yea, dearer than life, and we, proved worthy of
the trust committed to us ? The blood, the ashes of
those witnesses for the Truth must have left a germ of
their life in the land; a remnant of more than seven
thousand who have not bowed the knee to the Baal of
worldly opinion and scepticism; men who serve GOD

---

[1] ⲉⲥⲡϩⲣⲣⲉ ⲛⲟⲩⲟⲉⲓⲩ ⲛⲓⲙ. S. Cyr. Ep. in Zoega Codd. Sah.
p. 278.

c

and their generation, but not the times; who do not
leave it to others to settle for them what will be hereafter, being too busy to think of it for themselves, but
whose Faith is to them a reality, persuaded as they
are, of what they believe from the Word of God;
who are not "carried about, like children, with every
wind of doctrine," but whose Hope is the sheet-anchor
of their soul, that holds them fast through sorrows and
through storms, to the yet unseen shores of an everlasting Kingdom.   There must be a host of such men,
worthy of their sires in Faith and in courage.   If only
they were as much at one among themselves, to defend
that which ought to be dear to them, as their adversaries
are in striving to wrench it from them—things would
be very different from what they are.   Even now the
united prayers and efforts of honest Churchmen might
yet, perhaps, save the Church, and hand her down
whole to those that shall come after; instead of leaving to them as their probable inheritance to weep
over her ruins.

XVI. Therefore, even though we fail, let us at least
have the answer of a good conscience that we have done
our duty; every one of us for himself. It is not by the
amount of work done that our MASTER measures our
services; it is by the uprightness and honesty with
which we do Him service. Of course, we must suffer
and endure; this is a part of the service, wherein
consists our being "faithful soldiers and servants."
But we are prepared for it. Not only were we warned
long since that "all that will live godly in CHRIST shall
suffer persecution, but the taunts and ridicule with which
we are made daily familiar by men who seem unable to
view things sacred in any but a worldly light, show us
plainly that abuse is harmless; that it is no argument,

but only the sting of misgivings in a bad cause. We will therefore, bear it, if need be; not as being holier and better in our own eyes than those from whom we differ, albeit they falsely say so of us; but as counting most dear that which they do not value, and as acting on an inward, living principle which they care not to have. If then, we be reviled, so was our MASTER before us; if we be hated or despised, He bids us rejoice, for so was He also; if at times we feel disheartened or cast down, let us think of Him saying for our sakes: My soul is exceeding sorrowful even unto death—and take courage. And if none of these things move us; if we be manly, faithful, and seek "not to please men, but to be servants of CHRIST;" if for the sake of His glorious Name we quit ourselves according to our strength, like men, "making full proof of our ministry," and save at least a portion of a noble and generous people, from error and unbelief, and from the low morality that follows, we may then look for our MASTER's return and for His reward. And since the contention to which we are subject is not a battle of human opinions, but a controversy between the Truth and those who gainsay it, let us bear and forbear, as men serving GOD and not their own selves, and avoid mixing up individuals with the sentiments in them which we disapprove; that our antagonism be one of principle and not of party spirit; and so that our conscience may acquit us of every feeling save that of an honest wish to defend the Truth for CHRIST's sake; not only because it is our duty so to do, but because of the people committed to our charge "as having to give account."

XVII. Such is my motive in offering a few remarks on a work by the Dean of Westminster which has given

rise to contention in the Church. I have chosen it
with preference to every other, not only because it
has higher claims than others to our attention and respect for the sake of its author, from whom no one
would wish needlessly to differ, but also, because treating, as it does, of the History contained in the Bible,
and being addressed to candidates for Holy Orders, it
must, of course be at once, the most important, the
most earnest, and the most accurate book of the sort;
and therefore fittest for the study of the philosophy
which is now the fashion, and which we are told to
reconcile with the Bible; "the sooner the better for
the clergy of the land."

At all events, we hear so much of this philosophy, that since, after all, the teachers thereof do
not tell us wherein it consists, we are left, in self-
defence, to try and find it out for ourselves. The
more so, indeed, as it seems to be the key-note of
all intellect, ability, and knowledge of the present
day; so that it is worth our while to examine it
and see, whether we too must adopt it, or, whether
we may not still keep to our own primitive Faith and
to our old-fashioned love and reverence for the Bible,
without for all that, finding ourselves outside the pale
of intelligence or of common sense. I therefore bring
together as a starting point, a few principles common
to all kinds of philosophy, both ancient and modern;
to which my readers may turn occasionally in order to
compare them with the new teaching offered; without
a constant reference to them on my part. And having
done so, I consider in a few plain words how much
of this new doctrine our own philosophy, sense and
experience allow us either to receive or to reject, according to what we read "in the Scripture of Truth."

My intention was to have reviewed the whole book, in answer to several inquiries from strangers as well as from friends, who had been alarmed or startled at some of the Dean's assertions; but I found so many more things to notice than I had expected, that I have been obliged to limit myself to the first five lectures only. These, however, will suffice to show that the Truth has nothing whatever to fear from such 'free inquiry;' and that it requires at all times far less earnestness to differ from the Bible than to agree with it.

And if in this work, written entirely for the occasion, and, I honestly confess, with grief at having to vindicate Truths dear to our innermost hearts and souls from the insinuations of a high dignitary, as well as with mortification for the credit of my own University at having to correct, in many simple matters, the teaching of one of her Regius Professors, I have myself fallen into error, I shall be truly obliged to any one who will point it out to me, in an honest and manly spirit. The cause at issue and the interests at stake are both so far above any personal considerations, that I shall be satisfied if the Truth be established, and I proved in the wrong; though, of course, only by men who will fairly read this book, study the subject, and then judge of it for themselves. At the same time I am well aware that in this case I may seem to some to write to little purpose. To some, perhaps; but not to all. To many, whose manly spirit raises them above the meanness of prejudice, the Truth is yet greatest; and fair play still a jewel. I write for them; and if I can reclaim only one mind from doubt to Faith, and from scorn to reverence and worship for the Bible, I shall have worked to good purpose; for I write to help Christians in doubt to set

themselves right, and not to refute infidels and scep-
tics, of whose state of mind I can form no idea whatever.
Truth, we know, did not at first prevail on the plain
of Dura; and Shadrach, Meshach, and Abednego had
no chance of being heard while the cornet, sackbut,
and dulcimer sounded, and the shouts of the multitude
rang the praises of the golden image King Nebuchadnezzar had set up. Yet, whether heard or not, they
were in the right; and, strong in that feeling, they
would rather abide true to their Faith, alone, and only
three, and that too, in the fiery furnace in company
with the Son of God, than wait with a crowd around the
king's table. They believed, they trusted, they won;
because they feared Him most at Whose Word even
the King of Babylon trembled. And He still is the
Living God.

For, as there was then, so also now there is, the
same principle holier and deeper, the same Faith more
precious, and the same Hope more sure and steadfast, than anything this world can either promise or
give.

S. C. Malan.

Broadwindsor,
December 20, 1861.

CONTENTS.

PHILOSOPHY, OR TRUTH?

Aristotle in his Metaphysics tells us that—

I. The part of a philosopher is to inquire into the real nature, or truth, of whatever comes under his consideration : τῷ ὄντι ᾗ ὄν ἐστι τίνα ἴδια, καὶ ταῦτ' ἐστὶ περὶ ὧν τοῦ φιλοσόφου ἐπισκέψασθαι τἀληθίς.[1]

But since—

II. The absolute term ‘ to be’ is said in various ways, either as an accident, or, as real essence, the several modifications or acceptations of this term, form the several categories of ‘ what,’ ‘ what sort,’ &c. : ἀλλ' ἐπεὶ τὸ ὂν τὸ ἁπλῶς λεγόμενον λέγεται πολλαχῶς,[2] ὧν ἓν μὲν ἦν τὸ κατὰ συμβεβηκός, ἕτερον δὲ τὸ ὡς ἀληθές, καὶ τὸ μὴ ὂν ὡς τὸ ψεῦδος, παρὰ ταῦτα δ' ἐστὶ τὰ σχήματα τῆς κατηγορίας, οἷον τὸ μὲν τί, τὸ δὲ ποῖν, τὸ δὲ ποσόν, τὸ δὲ ποῦ, τὸ δὲ ποτέ, καὶ εἴ τι ἄλλο σημαίνει τὸν τρόπον τοῦτον.[3]

The real philosopher then, ὁ ὄντως φιλόσοφος studies πῶς λέγεται τὸ ὂν how ‘ to be’ is either predicated, or understood of every single category, without confounding one with the other, since—

III. His object and purpose is, to occupy himself with good sense in the contemplation of truth : βούλεται περὶ φρόνησιν εἶναι καὶ τὴν θεωρίαν τὴν περὶ ἀλήθειαν.[4] And this, too, whatever be the particular branch of philosophy to which he devotes himself ; whether to the ἠθικὸν, φυσικὸν or διαλεκτικὸν μέρος, to the moral,

---

[1] Metaph. iii. 2, 12.

[2] πολλαχῶς μὲν, ἀλλ' ἅπαν πρὸς μίαν ἀρχήν, variously indeed, but always with reference to one and the same principle, id. iii. 2, 3.

[3] Metaph. v. 2, 1.

[4] Eth. Eudem. i. 4, 3.

natural, or dialectic branch thereof. But in none is the real philosopher more in earnest in his search after Truth, than in theology, which is the first of all kinds of philosophy; for—

(a) There are three branches of contemplative philosophy, mathematics, physics, and theology. Of all sciences the contemplative are preferable; and of these, theology is the first : ὥστε τρεῖς ἂν εἶεν φιλοσοφίαι θεωρητικαί, μαθηματικὴ, φυσικὴ,[1] θεολογικὴ—αἱ μὲν οὖν θεωρητικαὶ τῶν ἄλλων ἐπιστημῶν αἱρετώτεραι, αὕτη δὲ τῶν θεωρητικῶν.[2]

The search after Truth, then, of whatever kind, is the delight of the real philosopher; for his occupation, φιλοσοφία—

IV. Philosophy is, according to Pythagoras, a desire, a longing for Truth, and as it were the love of wisdom :[3] ὄρεξις καὶ οἱονεὶ φιλία σοφίας, of wisdom, which is but the science of what is true in the essence of things ; σοφίαν δὲ ἔλεγεν εἶναι ἐπιστήμην τῆς ἐν τοῖς οὖσι ἀληθείας.[4]

Since then—

V. Wisdom, ἡ σοφία, may be termed the most exact (or accurate) of all sciences, ἡ ἀκριβεστάτη ἂν τῶν ἐπιστημῶν εἴη,[5]—it is of all sciences—

(a) The one most to be chosen for its own sake, and for the sake of a clear perception, τὴν αὐτῆς ἕνεκεν καὶ τοῦ εἰδέναι χάριν αἱρετὴν οὖσαν[6]

(b) Said to be ' understanding with science,' ὥστ' εἴη ἂν ἡ σοφία νοῦς καὶ ἐπιστήμη[7]—ἐξ ἐπιστήμης καὶ τοῦ συγκειμένη[8]

(c) A science relating to certain causes and principles, περὶ τινὰς αἰτίας καὶ ἀρχάς·[9]

---

[1] " As a tree that bears no fruit is useless," says Philo, (De Nom. Mut. p. 1056,) " so also is physiology of no use unless it be the means of acquiring virtue ; for this is the fruit thereof, μεταβαντάς ἀπὸ τῆς περὶ τὸν κόσμον θεωρίας πρὸς τὴν τοῦ πεποιηκότος ἐπιστήμην, to proceed from the contemplation of the world, to the knowledge of Him Who made it." A hint, or a rebuke, to sundry naturalists of the present day.

[2] Metaph. v. 1, 10.

[3] Although σοφία and ' wisdom' have no etymological affinity, and do not exactly render each other, they must yet be taken in their popular relation, the one to the other.

[4] Iamblich. de V. Pythag. xxix. p. 57, ed. Müll.

[5] Eth. Nicom. vi. 7, 2.   [6] Metaph. 1. 2, 3.

[7] Eth. Nicom. vi. 7, 2.   [8] Eth. Magn. 1. 35, 11.

[9] Metaph. 1. 1, 17.

(d) Of the understanding searching into the principles of things; νοῦς ἐστι τῶν ἀρχῶν,[1] that is, περὶ τὰς ἀρχὰς τῶν νοητῶν καὶ τῶν ὄντων,[2] into the principles of things of the intellect and essential.

So then—

(e) Philosophy contributes towards the acquisition of wisdom, since it is the cultivation of wisdom; and wisdom is the science of things divine, of things human, and of the causes relating thereto: φιλοσοφία (συμβάλλεται) πρὸς σοφίας κτῆσιν. ἔστι γὰρ φιλοσοφία ἐπιτήδευσις σοφίας, σοφία δὲ, ἐπιστήμη θείων καὶ ἀνθρωπίνων καὶ τῶν τούτων αἰτίων.[3]

VI. Therefore is the well informed philosopher bound to perceive, not only what may be deduced from principles, but also, to ascertain the truth as regards the principles themselves: Δεῖ ἄρα τὸν σοφὸν μὴ μόνον τὰ ἐκ τῶν ἀρχῶν εἰδέναι, ἀλλὰ καὶ περὶ τὰς ἀρχὰς ἀληθεύειν. So also—

(a) The more accurate a man is in his knowledge of causes, and the better able he is to teach them, the better informed do we also think him, whatever be the science he treats: ἔτι τὸν ἀκριβέστερον (ὑπολαμβάνομεν) καὶ τὸν διδασκαλικώτερον τῶν αἰτίων σοφώτερον εἶναι περὶ πᾶσαν ἐπιστήμην.[4]

(b) For it is the part of a well educated man to investigate everything after its kind, as accurately as the nature of it will allow: πεπαιδευμένου γάρ ἐστιν ἐπὶ τοσοῦτον τἀκριβὲς ἐπιζητεῖν καθ' ἕκαστον γένος, ἐφ' ὅσον ἡ τοῦ πράγματος φύσις ἐπιδέχεται.[5] On the other hand—

(c) The proof of a want of education is, not to be able to discern what belongs to a subject from what does not: ἀπαιδευσία γάρ ἐστι περὶ ἕκαστον πρᾶγμα τὸ μὴ δύνασθαι κρίνειν τούς τ' οἰκείους λόγους τοῦ πράγματος καὶ τοὺς ἀλλοτρίους.[6]

VII. Wherefore, it behoves him who is best informed on a subject, to be able to give the most solid principles thereof; as it also befits him who studies the essence of things, to be able to state the most solid general principles; for such is the philosopher: προσήκει δὲ τὸν μάλιστα γνωρίζοντα περὶ ἕκαστον γένος ἔχειν λέγειν τὰς βεβαιοτάτας ἀρχὰς τοῦ πράγματος, ὥστε καὶ τὸν περὶ τῶν

---

[1] Eth. Nicom. vi. 7, 3.   [2] Eth. Magn. i. 35, 11.
[3] Philo de Congr. Quær. p. 435.   [4] Metaph. i. 2, 2.
[5] Eth. Nicom. i. 3. 4.   [6] Eth. Eudem. i. 6, 6.

ὅταν ᾗ ὄντα τὰς πάντων βεβαιοτάτας.   Ἐστι δ' οὗτος ὁ φιλόσοφος·[1]
and—

(a) We then know best, when the subject of our investigation cannot possibly be otherwise than we make it out to be: καὶ τότε μάλιστα ἴσμεν ὅταν μηκέτι ὑπάρχῃ τοῦτο ὅτι ἄλλο.[2] Whence—

(b) The proof that we really know a thing is, that we are able to teach it; ὅλως τὸ σημεῖον τοῦ εἰδότος τὸ δύνασθαι διδάσκειν ἐστίν.[3]

VIII. Therefore is it necessary that he, who investigates like a philosopher, should know scientifically what is true, that is, the Truth, as regards the subject he considers; lest, consulting his own opinion, and trusting unreasonably to the words or to the reasons of others, without examining for himself into the truth of them, he, at the same time, either miss his object, or be obliged to wander from one subject to another: ἐπειδὴ τῷ φιλοσοφοῦντι—ἀναγκαῖόν ἐστιν ἐπιστημονικῶς γινώσκειν, τί τὸ ἀληθές, ἵνα μὴ, δοξαστικῶς αὐτοὺς προσβάλλων, καὶ ἀλόγως τοῖς λέγουσιν πιστεύων ἄνευ μαθήσεως, ἅμα μὲν διαμαρτάνῃ, ἅμα δὲ ἄλλοτ' ἐπ' ἄλλῳ μεταβαίνειν ἀναγκάζεται.[4]   For—

(a) A wise, that is, a well-informed man or philosopher, ought not to be imposed upon by others, but rather to influence them; neither should he be easily persuaded; since it is rather for him to persuade others less informed than himself: οὐ γὰρ δεῖ τὸν ἐπιτάττεσθαι τὸν σοφὸν ἀλλ' ἐπιτάττειν, καὶ οὐ τοῦτον ἑτέρῳ πείθεσθαι, ἀλλὰ τούτῳ τὸν ἧττον σοφόν.[5]

(b) This, however, requires great discretion. For there are men who, because it looks philosopher-like to say nothing at random, but everything with reason, often say unwittingly many things foreign to the purpose and empty. They do this either from ignorance or from vanity. Δεῖται μέντοι τοῦτο πολλῆς εὐλαβείας. Εἰσὶ γάρ τινες οἱ διὰ τὸ δοκεῖν φιλοσόφου εἶναι τὸ μηδὲν εἰκῇ λέγειν ἀλλὰ μετὰ λόγου, πολλάκις λανθάνουσι λέγοντες ἀλλοτρίους λόγους τῆς πραγματείας καὶ κενούς. Τοῦτο δὲ ποιοῦσιν ὁτὲ μὲν δι' ἄγνοιαν ὁτὲ δὲ δι' ἀλαζονείαν.[6]

The real philosopher then searches after the true principles

---

[1] Metaph. lib. 3, 6, 7.   [2] Anal. Post. i. 24, 7.   [3] Metaph. L. i, 12.
[4] Simplic. Comm. in Epict. Enchir. p. 326, ed. Salm.   [5] Metaph. L. 2, 3.
[6] Eth. Eudem. i. 6, 4.

of things, not only because he loves Truth, τὸ ἀληθές, for its own sake, but because Truth, τὸ ὂν ᾗ ὂν, which is an unchanging principle does not, as some seem to think, depend on the opinion of men. For—

IX. What is true, cannot, with reason, be decided by the opinion of the many, or of the few; since the same thing when tasted, appears to some sweet, and to others bitter : τὸ μὲν γὰρ ἀληθὲς οὐ πλήθει κρίνεσθαι οἴονται προσήκειν οὐδὲ ὀλιγότητι, τὸ δ' αὐτὸ τοῖς μὲν γλυκὺ γευομένοις δοκεῖν εἶναι, τοῖς δὲ πικρόν.[1]

(a) So little trouble will most men take in searching after truth; but will, rather, turn aside to what is ready at hand : οὗτος ἀταλαίπωρος τοῖς πολλοῖς ἡ ζήτησις τῆς ἀληθείας, καὶ ἐπὶ τὰ ἕτοιμα μᾶλλον τρέπονται.[2] "Nam sic est vulgus, ex veritate pauca, ex opinione multa æstimat."[3] For such is the multitude ; it judges of things seldom according to what they really are, but chiefly by the opinion of others. Wherefore—

(b) The judgment of ten good men is more weighty and of more consequence, than that of a whole multitude without experience : "Gravior et validior est decem virorum bonorum sententia, quam totius multitudinis imperitæ."[4] For—

(c) Custom serves for the opinion of the multitude ; but wise and well-informed men speak according to nature and according to truth : ὁ μὲν γὰρ νόμος δόξα τῶν πολλῶν, οἱ δὲ σοφοὶ κατὰ φύσιν καὶ κατ' ἀλήθειαν λέγουσιν.[5]

(d) But Truth, in its practical influence over a man, is judged by his works, and by the tenour of his life ; for, in these, it should be supreme : Τὸ δ' ἀληθὲς ἐν τοῖς πρακτοῖς ἐκ τῶν ἔργων καὶ τοῦ βίου κρίνεται· ἐν τούτοις γὰρ τὸ κύριον.[6] And then, it shows itself in more ways than one. In scholarship, the man who loves Truth for Truth's sake, will be painstaking, and, as far as in him lies, accurate ; and he will not meddle with what he cannot ascertain for himself. In learning he will be sound ; in statements, correct and trustworthy ; in his reasonings, conscientious ; and in his conclusions, straight-forward. He cares little for appearance ; he loves reality. Not so, however, with him who has not the love of Truth. In his scholarship, he will

[1] Metaph. iii. 5, 8.   [2] Thucyd. i. 20.
[3] Cic. pro Rosc. Com.   [4] Id. pro Planc.
[5] Sophist. Elench. 12, 9.   [6] Eth. Nicom. i. 8, 12.

be slip-shod and careless; in his learning, shallow; in his statements, uncertain; in his reasoning, hasty; and in his conclusions, crooked. So that he be not found out, but have the
reputation of having the gifts in which he is lacking, he cares
little for the result. Such a man knows not what this means—
to sacrifice everything to the highest and most sacred principle
in man—the love of Truth.

It is this love of Truth, nevertheless, that distinguishes the
real philosopher, ὁ ὄντως φιλόσοφος, from the sham or made up
one, ὁ πλαστῶς φιλόσοφος, and from the sophist, σοφιστής, who is
γοητής καὶ πολυκέφαλος, as Plato calls him.

X. And this is evident; for both dialecticians and sophists
put on the same outward appearance as the philosopher (for
sophistry is but apparent philosophy.) Sophistry, we see, and
dialectics take up the same subjects as philosophy; but real
philosophy differs from the one in the measure of power, and
from the other, in the relative object of life. For dialectics
attempt and discuss the subjects which philosophy seeks to know
thoroughly; and sophistry has only the appearance, but is not.
Σημεῖον δὲ· οἱ γὰρ διαλεκτικοὶ καὶ σοφισταὶ ταὐτὸν μὲν ὑποδύονται
σχῆμα τῷ φιλοσόφῳ (ἡ γὰρ σοφιστικὴ φαινομένη μόνον σοφία ἐστί.)
— Περὶ μὲν γὰρ τὸ αὐτὸ γένος στρέφεται ἡ σοφιστικὴ καὶ ἡ διαλεκτικὴ τῇ φιλοσοφίᾳ, ἀλλὰ διαφέρει τῆς μὲν τῷ τρόπῳ τῆς δυνάμεως,
τῆς δὲ τοῦ βίου τῇ προαιρέσει· Ἔστι δὲ ἡ διαλεκτικὴ πειραστικὴ
περὶ ὧν ἡ φιλοσοφία γνωριστική, ἡ δὲ σοφιστικὴ φαινομένη, οὖσα
δ' οὔ.[1]

For, as with some men it is more to their purpose to appear
to be wise than to be such in reality, without the appearance of
being so, (for sophistry is only sham wisdom, without any
reality; and the sophist is but a trafficker in feigned philosophy,)
it is, clearly, of importance to those men to appear to be doing
the work of a philosopher, rather than really to do it without
having the mere appearance of being thus engaged: 'Ἐπεὶ δ' ἐστί
τισι μᾶλλον πρὸ ἔργου τὸ δοκεῖν εἶναι σοφοῖς ἢ τὸ εἶναι καὶ μὴ δοκεῖν
(ἔστι γὰρ ἡ σοφιστικὴ φαινομένη σοφία οὖσα δ' οὔ, καὶ ὁ σοφιστὴς
χρηματιστὴς ἀπὸ φαινομένης σοφίας ἀλλ' οὐκ οὔσης) δῆλον ὅτι ἀναγ-
καῖον τούτοις καὶ τὸ τοῦ σοφοῦ ἔργον δοκεῖν ποιεῖν μᾶλλον ἢ ποιεῖν καὶ
μὴ δοκεῖν.[2]

---

[1] Metaph. iii. 2, 19—21.   [2] Sophist. Elench. i. 6.

But, a man must have a very high opinion of his own attainments, as well as a very mean idea of wisdom, σοφία, of knowledge and of science, who calls himself a philosopher. For, ὁ σοφὸς θεωρεῖ—ὅσω ἂν σοφώτερος ᾖ μᾶλλον, he who loves wisdom, contemplates in order that he may become yet wiser; and he goes on advancing, προκόπτει. Yet, the more he advances, the more also does his horizon widen, or recede from him; and the space he has measured is, to him, as nothing compared with what lies before him. The more he knows, the less he thinks so. For, in searching after Truth, τὸ ἀληθές, the abstract principle applicable to all things, or after the Truth, τὴν ἀλήθειαν, as regards ourselves—the knowledge of God as He is, infinite, is inaccessible to the intellect of man left to its own resources; and the knowledge of God as He revealed Himself to us in His Word is fathomless; so that the work of the philosopher, whether heathen or Christian, never ceases. As his object is infinite, so is his progress endless, and it ceases only in death. In this sense, then, it is true that—οὕτω τὸν ἔτι προκόπτοντα, φιλόσοφον λέγειν, ψεῦδος, it is false to say of a man, who is still advancing in knowledge, that he is a philosopher,[1] albeit he may be called such for his love of study and of learning—τό γε φιλομαθὲς καὶ φιλόσοφον ταὐτόν,[2] being φιλόσοφος τὴν φύσιν, a philosopher by nature. The honest search after Truth, then, makes the philosopher; the object of his life being, in the highest sense, according to Plutarch's definition of Aristotle's doctrine—[3]

(a) To contemplate the things which are real, and to practise what he ought: θεωρητικὸς εἶναι τῶν ὄντων καὶ πρακτικὸς τῶν δεόντων. And his philosophy becomes—

(b) The constant practice, or exercise, of an art suited to the acquisition of wisdom, ἄσκησις τέχνης σοφίᾳ ἐπιτηδείου—wisdom being, according to the Stoics—

(c) The science of things divine and of things human, θείων καὶ ἀνθρωπίνων ἐπιστήμη.[4]

XI. Men's opinion, then, affects but little the real philosopher. Φιλοσοφῶν γὰρ ἤδη ἅμα μὲν, τὴν σεαυτοῦ ἔνστασιν φυλάξεις

---

[1] Simplic. Comm. in Epict. Ench. c. lxix. p. 310.
[2] Plato, Rep. β. 16, ed. Lond.
[3] De Placit. Phil. Lib. i. Proem. vol. ix. p. 469, ed. Reiske.
[4] Ibid. p. 469.

τἰς ἱαυτὸν ἱπιστρϑμμένος, ἅμα δὶ καὶ κριτὴν σιαυτοῦ σεαυτὸν ἕξις, μαλλίοτα τῶν πολλῶν. By thinking in earnest, and as it becomes a philosopher, he will at the same time keep up his own way of life, and being concentrated within himself, he will become his own judge; a far better one than all the rest.[1]

But as regards πλαστὰς φιλοσόφους, sham philosophers, they are very soon satisfied with their own progress, with their knowledge, and with themselves. Their horizon is bounded by their own conceit, and they soon come to their journey's end, in their search after Truth. As they love their own selves more than tho sacred, unchangeable, eternal principle of τὸ ἀληθἐς, Truth—so also they value their own opinion and that of others above real wisdom. Μὴ οὖν τι πλημμελήσομεν φιλοδόξους καλοῦντες αὐτοὺς μᾶλλον ἢ φιλοσόφους; shall we then be far wrong, asks Plato, in calling them lovers of men's opinion rather than lovers of wisdom? Τούτους γὰρ τὸ φιλόδοξον καὶ ἐπιδεικτικὸν ἐποχλεῖ πάθος, yes, such men are hindered by their passion for men's opinion of them and for show.[2] The noise of the multitude around them drowns the soft whispers, the faint but sure echoes of a land unseen; true messengers from a world to come, to which the ὄντως φιλόσοφος loves to listen within, in secret, and far from the noise of men.

The difference, then, between true and sham philosophers in general, depends not only on their respective ἀρχαὶ principles, and on the στοιχεῖα, the elements of their respective studies, but also on their respective προαίρεσις τοῦ βίου, on the course of life they propose to themselves. Hence the various sects, αἱρέσεις, of philosophy in olden times; hence also the difference between the greatest men of allied schools; as, for instance, between Aristotle and Plato; the former of a vast, powerful, but hard intellect, from which he would withhold nothing, treating of theology, as he would of physics—οὐ γὰρ ἄδηλον ὅτι εἴ που τὸ θεῖον ὑπάρχει ἐν τῇ τοιαύτῃ φύσει ὑπάρχει,[3] instead of making like Plato and Philo, his φυσιολογία a step towards the knowledge of God. The latter, of an intellect equally marvellous, but more refined, and that did exercise a greater influence over his moral character; was in so much a greater man than Aristotle,

---

[1] Simplic. Comm. in Epict. Ench. c. xxx. p. 141.
[2] Simplic. Comm. p. 310.   [3] Metaph. τ. 1, 10.

as he saw and acknowledged how far his intellect alone could take him; confessing he saw but dimly what his spirit did long to penetrate—ἀφαιρείτω, εἴτε βούλεται τὴν ἀχλὺν εἴτε ἄλλο τι, ὡς ἐγὼ παρισκεύασμαι μηδὲν ἂν φυγίω τῶν προσταττομένων—εἴ γι μέλλοιμι βελτίων γινέσθαι. "Let him who cares for me, remove the dimness, or whatever else it be, from my mind; for I am ready to shrink from nothing he may command, if only I may be made a better man thereby."[1] A lasting proof of how true is the record of Socrates: ὅτι ἡ ἀνθρωπίνη σοφία ὀλίγου τινὸς ἀξία ἐστὶ καὶ οὐδενός, "that human wisdom is worth very little, even nothing at all;"[2] and one that justifies S. Paul in the eyes of even men of the world, for asking, "Where is the wise?—hath not God made foolish the wisdom of this world? For after that in the wisdom of God the world by wisdom knew not God, it pleased God by the foolishness of preaching to save them that believe."[3]

Not even Plato's mind could make light out of darkness, nor find out that which "no man can take unto himself except it be given him from heaven," namely, "the grace of God that bringeth salvation, and hath appeared unto all men, teaching us that, denying ungodliness and worldly lusts, we should live soberly, righteously, and godly in this present world; looking for that blessed hope and the glorious appearing of the great God and our SAVIOUR JESUS CHRIST, Who gave Himself for us that He might redeem us from all iniquity, and purify unto Himself a peculiar people, zealous of good works."[4] He came and by His appearing "He brought life and immortality to light through the Gospel," and He thus placed philosophy upon a new footing. Καταργήσας τὸν θάνατον, He laid low the king of terrors, of which even Socrates said, he wist not which of the two it was τὸ τεθνάναι, to be dead, whether a sleep or a transmigration of his soul; albeit he reckoned it θαυμαστὸν κέρδος, a wonderful gain, to look upon death as only one night.[5] And our LORD JESUS CHRIST φωτίσας ζωὴν καὶ ἀφθαρσίαν, having brought life and immortality to light, for ever scattered the gloom that brooded over this benighted world, ere He rose as

---

[1] Alcib. sec. 23, ed. Lond.

[2] Apol. Socr. par. 9, ed. Lond.

[3] 1 Cor. i. 20, 21.

[4] Tit. ii. 11—14.

[5] Apol. Socr. par. 62, ed. Lond.

Sun of Righteousness, bidding His beloved rejoice in the healing beams of His heavenly Light.

To that Light He bade them turn their eyes, telling them
that, as in Him and through Him alone there is now no more
death, so also they ought no longer to look for the living among
the dead ; but to rise heavenwards on the wings of Faith and of
Hope in His promise of Eternal Life through Him.   He told
them to set their affections on things above, and " in patience
to possess their souls," until He come to open the gates of
Heaven, and bid them enter in and take possession of the inheritance which He purchased for them at the price of His precious Blood.

Therefore, if a man be in Him, he is indeed a new creature ;
old things are, for ever, passed away ; behold all things are
become new.   A new faith, ay, a faith in Him which is "the
substance of things hoped for, the evidence of things not seen"
—was, at His coming, given to those who were straying in doubt
or in despair ; and a new and glorious hope was also set before
them, " as an anchor of the soul, sure and stedfast," to bind the
frail bark of their existence on earth to the yet unseen shores of
Eternity.   Thus did men receive new principles, καινὰς ἀρχάς,
and new materials καινὰ στοιχεῖα, wherewith to begin here on
earth the building of their house not made with hands, eternal
in the heavens, beyond the reach of waste and of decay ; all of
which result from καινὴ αἰτία, from a cause new to them, "to
wit, that GOD was in CHRIST reconciling the world unto Himself,
not imputing their trespasses unto them."

It is therefore evident that, since heathen philosophers were
searching after the Truth in which the Christian philosopher
lives, he finds himself in another state of things ; and far beyond the uttermost point at which his heathen teachers could
ever bring him.   He may, indeed, avail himself of the same framework of thought, as far as that will serve, and thank them for
their help thus far ; but he cannot start from the same principles
as those from which they started, either in his θεωρία τῶν ὄντων,
in his contemplation of things that be, most of which are become
new ; or in his πρᾶξις τῶν ἑόντων, in his practice of duties which
ought now to be performed on far higher grounds than heathens
could ever have dreamt of,—without his denying the Faith, and

acting in a manner derogatory from his character of a Christian ;
thus going back to what may truly be called by comparison,
τὰ ἀσθενῆ καὶ πτωχὰ στοιχεῖα, " the weak and beggarly elements"
of a state of things past long ago. In so doing, the Christian
philosopher plays false to his ἔνστασις, to his position as believer
in a Revelation which he cannot deny without forfeiting altogether his Christian character ; and he places himself relatively
to the ὄντως Χριστιανὸς φιλόσοφος, to the real Christian philosopher, exactly in the position of a sophist, whose philosophy
Aristotle or Plato tell us, is a mere pretence ; and whose sophistry consists in making a false application of the principles
adopted by the real Christian philosopher, who alone is earnest
in his search after the Truth.

Having thus laid down these few general principles of philosophy, we will examine how far they are observed in Dean
Stanley's Lectures.

LECTURES ON THE JEWISH CHURCH.

PREFACE.

I. At the beginning of his Preface Dean Stanley reminds us
that these Lectures were " actually or in substance, addressed to
his usual hearers at Oxford, chiefly candidates for Holy Orders."
We must, therefore, consider them as intended by him for this,
the most important class of his hearers ; for, we cannot for a
moment suppose, that a Regius Professor delivering Lectures on
so sacred a subject, to men whom he taught what to believe and
what to teach others also, would not make these men his first
object, and sacrifice to them the tastes or the interests of the
other and less important part of his audience. We are, therefore, justified in taking these Lectures as a kind of text-book—
if not, why were they published ?—intended for the rising generation of clergy. We will look at them chiefly in this light, and
I will, as far as I can, point out fairly the merits as well as the
defects I see, mindful of Locke's good advice : " Let not men
that would have a sight of what every one pretends to, desirous

to have a sight of truth in its full extent, be yet narrow and blind in their own prospect. Let not men think there is no truth but in the sciences that they study, or the books that they read. To prejudge other men's notions before we have looked into them, is not to show their darkness, but to put out our own eyes."[1]

II. "In the first place," says Dr. Stanley,[2] "the work must be regarded not as a history, but as *Lectures*," a mode of instruction which appeared to him "specially adapted to the subjects of which he was to treat;" and which, "while it avoided the necessity of a continuous narrative, enabled him to select the portions most susceptible of fresh illustration and combination," &c. There can, of course, be no objection to this form of teaching, so that, without being a consecutive narrative it may yet present a compact whole, an accurate, true view of the subject in hand, and not merely a string of short essays on the topics best suited to the fancy of the writer. We will, therefore, charitably lay much of what appears superficial or shallow, if not actually trifling, in Dr. Stanley's writing, to the common acceptation of the term "Lecture," by which is too often meant an opportunity of saying much about little, and little or nothing about much that ought to engross our attention. Yet, Lectures should borrow their character from him who delivers them; who, if he have duly studied his subject, so as to be impressed with it, will always endeavour to treat it worthily and adequately, be the form of his teaching what it will; according to R. vi. p. 3. δεῖ ἄρα τὸν σοφὸν, &c.; and ib. (b) πεπαιδευμένου γάρ ἐστι, &c.

III. Dr. Stanley excuses himself for thus dwelling principally on certain prominent objects in Jewish History, by referring his readers for fuller information to the History of the Jews by Dean Milman, to whose scholarship he pays a just tribute of praise; adding, however, somewhat presumptuously:

"whose name has been made dear to all who know the value of a genuine love of truth and freedom, combined with profound theological learning and high ecclesiastical station."

Manus manum fricat, and the Dean of Westminster's meaning

<hr>

[1] Conduct of the Understanding, Sect. III.

is very plain; but unfortunately, it is a contradiction in terms.
For since 'freedom,' ἐλευθερία, ἐλευθέρωσις, is the condition of the
ἐλεύθερος ἀπ' ἄλλων, of a man free or freed from others,—ἐλεύθερον
δὲ καὶ ἴσον τὸ ὅ τι ἂν βούληταί τις ποιεῖν,[1] who can do what he
likes, it is evident that, when dealing with the Bible, and when
thus searching into the Truth contained in it, we cannot go to
work our own way, but we must needs keep within certain
limits, and follow certain principles, οὐ μέντοι ἔξω τοῦ γένους,[2]
so as not to wander from the right path; since to roam at will,
is not 'to seek.' The pointer is not free from restraint though
it run across the cover; it is bound by an invisible spell to a
certain track which it follows warily. "Scrutatur vestigia
atque persequitur, comitantem ad feram inquisitorem loro tra-
hens."[3] Hence it is called κυὼν ἰχνευτής[4]—"canis natus ad
indagandum," according to Cicero,[5] who uses this term to explain the search after Truth.[6] "Omne quod honestum est, id
quatuor partium oritur ex aliquâ; aut enim in perspicientia
veri sollertiaque versatur—in qua sapientiam et prudentiam
ponimus, inest indagatio atque inventio veri." Hence, too,
does he style true philosophy which acts according to certain
settled principles which it follows—"virtutis indagatio."[7] Freedom, then, wanders—and often astray; while true philosophy—
seeks, and often finds.

Our search after Truth, especially after the Truth, cannot be
free, that is, unrestrained; for, we can come at the Truth only
by following the track that leads to it, and not one of our own
choosing; ἀλλ' ὅμως εἰ μέλλομεν εὐδαιμονήσειν, for if we wish to
succeed in our search, says Plato,[8] ταύτῃ ἰτέον, ᾗ τὰ ἴχνη τῶν
λόγων φέρει, we must go in the way the track of analogy leads
us; treading warily on such a hallowed field as that of abstract
Truth. But when our search is about the Truth contained in
the Bible, then, let us, if we be Christians, put off our shoes
from off our feet, for the place whereon we stand is holy ground.
Let alone, then, common sense, reverence, and faith; the instinct of an animal shows us, that when searching after Truth,

[1] Arist. Polit. v. 15.
[2] Anal. Post. II. 13, 2.
[3] Plin. N. H. lib. viii. 61.
[4] Arrian. de Ven. xxi. 1.
[5] De Finib. ii. 39.
[6] De Off. ii. 5.
[7] Tusc. vi. 69.
[8] Rep. Lib. ii. 8, ed. Lond.

free, unrestrained, that is, ungoverned inquiry on our part, may, indeed, be a proof of our self-will, but, most assuredly, not of our philosophy.

IV. Dr. Stanley's view of free inquiry leads him, p. viii., ix., to say, speaking of the change wrought of late years in the histories of Rome and of Greece, that—

"The same change was in a still higher degree needed with regard to the history of the Jews. Its sacred character had deepened the difficulty already occasioned by its extreme antiquity. The earliest of Christian heresies—Docetism, or 'phantom worship'—the reluctance to recognise in sacred subjects their identity with our flesh and blood—in our own time has as completely closed its real contents to a large part both of religious and irreligious readers, as if it had been a collection of fables. Many who would be scandalised at ignorance of the battles of Salamis or Cannæ, know and care nothing for the battles of Beth-horon and Megiddo. To search the Jewish records as we would search those of other nations, is regarded as dangerous. Even to speak of any portion of the Bible as 'a history' has been described, even by able and pious men, as an outrage upon religion."

Does Dr. Stanley really consider this a fair and candid statement of the case? He may wish to put Jewish history on a par with Greek or with Roman records, in his mode of treating them, thus reasoning from one category to another against H. ii. p. 1. But, whereas τὸ ὄν, ' to be,' is said πολλαχῶς, in more ways than one of these several histories, ἀλλ' ἅπαν πρὸς μίαν ἀρχήν, though with regard to one common principle, that of each being ' a history'—yet the τάξος οὐσίας,[1] the accident of the Jewish history being that of a people chosen from among all other nations for a particular purpose, makes its history so distinct as to place it in a category of its own. It cannot, therefore, on sound principles, be treated like either the Greek, the Roman, or any other history whatsoever. So that, while greater knowledge, deeper research were, and are yet, needed in order to throw more light on the history of the Jewish people, no such change is required in it as in the histories of Greece and of Rome ; for in these the change needed, and the change made was, from

----

[1] Metaph. iii. 2, 3.

fable or fiction, to something like tangible reality; whereas
there is neither fable nor fiction in the 'history' contained in
the Bible; but only ignorance on our part as to sundry details
thereof.

It is, therefore, in Dr. Stanley's words, "dangerous to search
Jewish records as we would search those of other nations,"
simply, because it is unphilosophical to treat alike subjects of
such widely different categories. In this, as in everything else,
the work (ἔργον) depends on the habit of mind (ἕξις) and on the
preference or choice (προαίρεσις) of him that does it. We may
handle Josephus or Thucydides as we please; and no greater
harm will probably result from it than some fault or other found
with our scholarship; and it really is also a matter of profound
indifference to the world at large whether the nymph Egeria did
or did not teach old Numa; or whether, as S. Augustine will
have it,[1] he practised 'hydromantia,' or water-magic. But the
man who would handle the history of the Old Testament as he
would handle that fable, would show how little he cared to rest
his search after Truth on the soundest sense, according to R.
iii. p. 1. βούλεται περὶ φρόνησιν—and how far he had forgotten
Aristotle's precept: ἐν ἑκάστοις τὸ πρέπον· οὐ γὰρ ταὐτὰ ἁρμόζει
θεοῖς καὶ ἀνθρώποις.[2] "Propriety in everything; the same things
are not suitable for gods and for men."

V. However plain to Dr. Stanley, it is not easy to see the
connection between the Gnostic heresy of the Docetæ; the peculiar disposition of certain great but singular men; and the
present ignorance of events told in the Bible. The Docetism
of the present time consists in worshipping 'phantoms' in the
shape of men, rather than in that of abstract ideas. Ὦ οἵα
κεφάλη κ.τ.λ. "Oh! what a head," &c., exclaim the worshippers. Philo and Origen were, indeed, fanciful men, and so was,
in some respects also, S. Augustine; who, nevertheless, expresses
himself rightly when he says: "Mihi autem sicut multum
videntur errare, qui nullas res gestas in eo genere literarum
aliquid aliud præter id quod eo modo gestæ sunt significare
arbitrantur: ita multum audere, qui prorsus ibi omnia significa-
tionibus allegoricis involuta esse contendunt."[3] But we may

---

[1] De Civ. Dei, lib. iv. c. 27.　　　[2] Eth. Nicom. iv. 5, 17.
[3] De Civ. Dei, lib. xvii. c. 3.

rest assured, that none of those men are accountable for the
preference shown for the battles of Salamis and of Cannæ, over
those of Beth-horon and of Megiddo. The cause of this lies
elsewhere: first, in the indifference the natural man feels for
GOD and for His Word; and next, in the education at some
schools, where boys often used to learn more of the religion of
Rome or of that of Greece, than of their own. Whether things
be different at present, I know not; but I am told, the time was
when, at certain schools, a false quantity or a slip in the pedigree
of a nymph, was likely to be visited more severely than greater
faults; and when Greek and Roman Histories were, of course,
taught accurately, but Christian history, any how, or not at all.

As Dr. Stanley moves in a wider world than I do, he may
possibly be a better judge than I am, in saying what, otherwise
would sound very clap-trap; namely, that—

"even able and pious men described as an outrage upon religion,
to speak of any portion of the Bible as a history."

This, I confess, takes one quite by surprise; for we had
thought that even Dr. Watts' "Scripture," or "Bible History,"
and other such works, had long been in the hands of people of
all sorts of religious opinions.

VI. Dr. Stanley, however, wishes to correct himself "in pro-
testing against this elimination of the historical element from
the sacred narrative,"—a thing, which indeed, no right-minded
scholar ever dreamt of doing—when he says

"I shall not be understood as wishing to efface the distinction
which good taste, no less than reverence will always endeavour to
preserve between the Jewish and other histories."

This very proper feeling is incompatible with doing for the
Jewish history, what Niebuhr did for that of Rome. But, if
ably carried out with regard to the history contained in the
Bible, it would indeed be, as says the Dean, "a sign of returning healthiness" in such studies; for we can only gain, as he
justly remarks, by becoming acquainted with the actual scenes
of events with which we are already familiar in writing; with
the language, the poetry, the habits of the people recorded in
the Bible. It took me several days to realise the fact that I

was actually at Jerusalem; that the hill I trod was the Mount
of Olives; and that the peaceful village below, was Bethany.
I felt, therefore, somewhat astonished, when an English traveller
accosted me while I was studying the old olive trees of Geth-
semane, and asked me how long I was going to stay; for
that he had been there three days, had "done" it all, and
was off.

And, it would be well if one of these healthy signs were a
return to the study of Hebrew, which is all but ignored in this
country; and yet, without a sound knowledge of it, a man must
be at the mercy of any one somewhat acquainted with it who
pretends to gainsay the Bible. Let no one think he has read,
or can read, the Old Testament, leastways the poetry thereof, in
any other language than Hebrew; assuredly not in Greek; for
—only comparing language with language—the Hebrew idiom
is caricatured by being rendered into Greek; neither can it be
fully rendered into any other language, since a real translation
of a language into another is a thing simply impossible; and is
at best, a paraphrase. A clergyman, therefore, if he be in
earnest, and have both leisure and ability, cannot forego so important a study as that of the language in which the greater
portion of the Bible is written. If he have neither time nor
ability, let him keep to the Authorised Version; it is a safer and
a better guide than the Septuagint.

VII. Lastly, Dr. Stanley reminds us (at p. xi.) that these
Lectures are strictly "ecclesiastical;" and only about " the
Jewish *Church*;" although, he does not, as he might have done,
in this place, define what "a Church" is; or what he understands thereby. However, he—

" has never forgotten that the literature of the Hebrew race is also
the Bible—the sacred Book or Books of Christendom."

That is not saying much. For how else could an utter
stranger to either "Christendom" or to the Bible, express himself, than as Dr. Stanley does? as if he were himself outside
that Christendom, or was fain to own divided allegiance to the
"Sacred Book or Books" of the Christian Religion? With
every due deference to his position, I beg to say that, the more
manly way of putting it would have been : " I never will forget

(the future being, in this respect, a safer tense than the past) that the literature—is also the Bible, the sacred Book or Books, to which we, Christians, owe allegiance as to the Revealed Word of God." For, this is both true and according to common sense; that we cannot be Christians without holding certain objective Truths, revealed to us in the Bible; and we cannot hold them, without bowing, submitting ourselves, and giving our allegiance to them.

VIII. Dr. Stanley then, guards himself (at p. xi., xii.,) and guards us also, against running into the extreme of finding types of the New Testament in every part of the Old. If I understand him, he would limit "types" to such as have "an historical basis," that is, to mere facts in the history of the Old Testament; wherein he is right. For, a type must be the visible figure or likeness of what it is meant to represent; so that, neither allegories, parables, nor prophecies can be "types;" neither are certain facts "types," but only "examples," unless they bear a distinct reference to their antitype. On the whole, then, our best way is not to multiply "types," however safe we be in profiting by the facts recorded as "examples," or, in trying to trace in the Old dispensation, the outline of the shadow of things that were to come, "the body of which is of Christ." Bearing in mind, that, in reality a shadow has an exact relation to the object that casts it, however little we may succeed in tracing its perfect outline, owing, either to the dimness of our sight, to the faintness of the shadow, or to the unevenness of the ground on which it falls. But a shadow has a certain life of its own, which he knows best, who understands the light that makes it. So also, but for the dimness of our intellectual vision, but for the faint outline of the shadows cast over the varied and uneven ground of the Old Covenant by the coming events of the New, we should be able to trace exactly under the Law, the outline of all that to which the Law was intended to bring us.

The study of types requires the profound study of a mind well qualified for it; and no one will blame the Dean of Westminster for preferring reserve to rash dogmatism on the subject. His meaning, however, is not so clear, when he includes questions of "the limits drawn between the natural and the supernatural," among those on which, as on chronology, physics or statistics, he intends to touch but seldom,—"natural and supernatural" being—

"distinctions which to the sacred writers, were for the most part alien and unknown."

Does Dr. Stanley mean that when GOD wrought signs before Moses,[1] and said to him, (v. 17): "Thou shalt take this rod[2] in thine hand, wherewith thou shalt do signs." Moses did not know they were signs, wonders or miracles, and therefore supernatural? No, not even after that "the LORD said unto him, When thou goest to return to Egypt, see that thou do all those wonders before Pharaoh, which I have put in thine hand."[3] Why then did Moses flee from before the serpent into which his rod was changed, if he was used to such a wonder? What about the sign on the dial of Ahaz, granted to Hezekiah?[4] Or, the crossing of the Jordan, "a wonder wrought by the LORD?"[5] &c. If Dr. Stanley meant to say, that "natural" and "supernatural" are only relative terms, we join issue with him. It is perfectly true that what appears supernatural to our fallen nature, would be natural to this same nature if it were not now fallen below the level at which it stood when man was created by GOD after His own image and similitude. A state of existence and certain powers were natural to Adam before his fall, which would now be impossible, or, at least, appear supernatural. The second Adam, our LORD JESUS CHRIST, came to restore by a miraculous union of our human nature with His Divine essence, not only the state of things anterior to the fall, but one even better, and we now have the power, gotten through Him, of being ultimately restored in our humanity to a glorified state, —that is, to a state free from sin, and in the enjoyment of the faculties Adam had ere he sinned. Meanwhile, and as long as we are in bodies not yet freed from sin and glorified, that is, while we are in this life, things and powers that will be natural

---

[1] Ex. iv. 3.

[2] "The rod of GOD." v. 17, and ch. xvii. 9, which he used "in all the signs and wonders, which the LORD sent him to do in the land of Egypt," Deut. xxxiv. 11.

[3] Ex. iv. 21.   [4] 2 Chron. xxxii. 24.

[5] Josh. iii. 5.

to us hereafter, for the present appear supernatural, as, indeed,
they must. The writers of the Old Testament, writing as men
and for men, though taught of GOD, wrote as they believed, of
what was to them signs, wonders and miracles, wrought in order
to attest the power and immediate presence of GOD, without
Whom, a learned doctor of the Law told our SAVIOUR Himself,
these signs and miracles could not be wrought.[1] Of course, we
all know the habit of mind of Dr. Stanley's German authorities,
who wish to explain away some miracles, if not all of them.
On the one hand they might as well deny the presence of GOD
among His people, or in the Universe as Ruler thereof, as to
deny He could not do what works He pleased; and on the other
hand they might as well affirm that our present state is not
fallen, as to deny that signs, wonders, and miracles, are not
supernatural, relatively to it.

IX. On all secondary matters of this kind, Dr. Stanley tells
us (at p. xiii.) he "is content to rest on the researches of others
and to refer to them." This seems a pity; for he thus mars
his work; and hence also arise the several mistakes he makes;
against R. vi. p. 3, ὅτι ἄρα τὸν σοφὸν, κ.τ.λ. A man who loves
Truth for the sake of it, never takes for granted on another
man's witness, what he may ascertain for himself; for second-
hand scholarship is never worth much. But he examines for
himself, according to R. vi. (b) p. 3, πεπαιδευμένου γάρ ἐστιν, κ.τ.λ.,
it is the part of a well-educated man to ascertain as accurately
as he can his subject matter to the full extent thereof; since it
behoves him ἔχειν λέγειν τὰς βεβαιοτάτας ἀρχάς to be able to
give the soundest principles of what he treats, R. vii. p. 3.
If not, and if he trust to others without ascertaining for himself
independently of them, ἅμα μὲν διαμαρτάνῃ, κ.τ.λ. R. viii. p. 4,
he is liable to miss his object, and to make other mistakes.

X. Dr. Stanley is, however, quite right in saying (p. xiii.)—

"that in proportion as such inquiries are pursued by those who
are able to make them, will be gain both to the cause of Biblical
science and of true Religion,"

although he is wrong in saying "fearlessly pursued." For

---

[1] S. John iii. 2. Likewise, did the prophets know that the LORD spake
through them. "As the LORD liveth," said Micaiah, "what the LORD saith

Aristotle, who, we all agree, was a man of great sense, tells us, that if one should fear nothing, εἰ μηδὲν φοβοῖτο, εἴη δ᾽ ἄν τις μαινόμενος ἢ ἀνάλγητος, "he must be either mad or past feeling."[1] Moreover, good taste and respect, to say the least, if nothing more, would make a man wish to approach God and whatever relates to Him, "acceptably," and that is, "with reverence and godly fear." For, if ever, it is assuredly in the case of purblind, ignorant, and fallen human beings, attempting to look into the mysteries of God's attributes, or even into the burden of His Word, that these words are true : "Happy is the man that feareth alway : but he that hardeneth his heart shall fall into mischief."[2] But, perhaps, Dr. Stanley does not really mean all that his words imply. Even he must see, that to enter upon such a study otherwise than with awe and in a devout spirit, is to act the part of rash and inconsiderate men ; for Aristotle warns us again[3] that ὁ δὲ θαρρῶν ὑπερβάλλων περὶ τὰ φοβερὰ, θρασύς· δοκεῖ δὲ καὶ ἀλαζὼν εἶναι ὁ θρασύς, "the man who is over-confident where he ought to fear, is rash ; and that such a character looks very much like a braggart."

XI. Then follows the just praise of Ewald, Dr. Stanley's "Magnus Apollo," for his profound scholarship and extensive learning,

"who has," it appears, "fulfilled the desire expressed twenty-seven (now twenty-nine) years ago by 'Arnold and Bunsen,' in writing his 'History of the people of Israel.' "

We all know that Dr. Arnold was, and is yet, the "grande decus" of the school of which he was Master ; but he too, made a mistake in logic if he classed "Judea," the land of the Bible, with Rome or with Greece. And if he wished that Niebuhr's wholesale dealing with Roman history should be followed towards the contents of the Old Testament, he too, seemed in this instance at least, to care but little for τῷ ὄντι ἦ ὄν, and not much for his categories. Ewald is, indeed, a very remarkable scholar ; but so was Gesenius, and so are other Germans, who seem to

unto me, that will I speak ;" " and Micaiah said, If thou return at all in peace, the LORD hath not spoken by me." (1 Kings xxii. 14, 28.) Even prophets like Balaam, knew themselves to be used at times as instruments in the hands of GOD. " And the spirits of the prophets are subject to the prophets." 1 Cor. xiv. 32.

[1] Eth. Nicom. iii. 7, 7.   [2] Prov. xxviii. 14.   [3] Eth. Nicom. ibid.

come into the world already knowing what others have to learn
during the first half of their life. But Ewald has, of course, his
own peculiar views, which make him, like Ch. Bunsen, a guide
no one dares to follow, without looking well to his going.
Although Ewald's star is no longer in the ascendant in his own
country, his writings are a mine of learning, which, however,
must, like every other ore, be examined and tested with Truth,
ere it is passed off as current coin. But great, and greatly learned
as he is, it is very possible he might differ from Dr. Stanley,
and think " the constant reference to his writings throughout
the new ' Dictionary of the Bible,' " a very doubtful compliment ;
and himself sometimes little honoured by the " intellect, ability,
and learning," of some of his companions.[1]

XII. Dr. Stanley, however, very properly says, (p. xv.) —

" But, in fact, my aim has been not to recommend the teaching
or the researches of any theologian however eminent, but to point
the way to the treasures themselves of that History."

For, in fact, no study is worth anything that is not first-hand ;
and no writer should be taken wholly upon trust ; leastways
those to whom Dean Stanley alludes—

" excellent men who disparage the Old Testament, as the best
means of saving the New ;" and " others who think that it can
only be maintained by discouraging all inquiry into its authority
and contents."

We cannot say much for their discernment. But, " rightly
dividing the Word of Truth," we find that the Old Testament
was a dispensation of types, and " a shadow of good things to
come ;" in which even prophecy glimmered only " as a light in
a dark place, until the day dawned and the Day-star arose."
And we also do, what many do not, we distinguish between a
shadow and shade ; and however little we may succeed, we seek

---

[1] I do not wish to speak disparagingly of a work I do not possess, and which
I have not examined. But knowing, as I do, how and by whom some of the
articles were written, I can feel no great confidence in it. I have consulted it
three times at a friend's house, but never without finding one or more mistakes.
It seemed to me to be as Ovid says—

" congestaque eodem
Non bene junctarum discordia semina rerum."

nevertheless, to trace the objects themselves in the definite outline of their shadows, which the coming Light did cast before
them.   The men who lived in those shadows had to gather the
outline of the objects that cast the shadows from the shadows
themselves; at best a difficult task.   But we, who have the
Light, see the objects themselves; and albeit we may be less
careful of the shadows than of the light; yet these finish the
picture of God's dispensation which, like the finest picture ever
drawn, has both light, lights and shadows.   For as there is no
light without a shadow, and no shadow without light; so also
there would be no New Covenant if there were not also the Old
one, neither could this be " old and done away," unless another
was made to take its place; or, rather, to fulfil it.   Thus then,
however much we may rejoice in the Revealed Light of the
Gospel, we, nevertheless, value the shadows of the Law asa set
off to the Light, with which they make up a whole well-arranged;
we embrace the New Testament to which the Law was meant to
bring us; and we keep the Law with gratitude for having
brought us to it; for had there been no Old Covenant there
would assuredly be no New one.

With regard to the Old Testament then, Josephus says rightly,[1]
that in it, " all things are well arranged according to the nature
of its several parts, τὰ μὲν αἰνιττομένου τοῦ νομοθέτου δεξιῶς, τὰ δὲ
ἀλληγοροῦντος μετὰ σεμνότητος, our Lawgiver cleverly implying
certain things, and adopting dignified allegories to mention
others : τοῖς μέντοι βουλομένοις καὶ τὰς αἰτίας ἑκάστων σκοπεῖν, πολλὴ
γίνοιτ' ἂν ἡ θεωρία καὶ λίαν φιλόσοφος ; so then, he who will look
into the causes of each, will derive from his study a contemplation alike varied and most philosophical."

——— ———

INTRODUCTION.

Dean Stanley divides the History of the Jewish Church into
three periods : (1) from Abraham to Samuel ; (2) from Samuel
to the Captivity of Babylon ; and (3) from that to the destruc-

[1] Antiq. Lib. I. proœm.

tion of the Temple by Titus, and of the independence of the
nation by Hadrian.   The first of these periods, he tells us,
is "often called, though somewhat inaccurately, Theocracy,"
though he does not say why it is thus "inaccurately" described.
He refers to other Lectures; but in these I fail to find the
reason; so that he leaves his readers, as he probably left his
hearers, without a distinct idea on the subject.

Theocracy, θεοκρατία, is a term apparently first introduced by
Josephus,[1] when saying that—whereas the rule of government
had been by some made to consist either in monarchy, in oli-
garchy, or in democracy, ὁ ἡμέτερος νομοθέτης, our lawgiver
(Moses) he adds, εἰς μὲν τούτων οὐδοτιοῦν ἀπεῖδεν, had regard to
none of these forms; ὡς δ' ἄν τις εἴποι βιασάμενος τὸν λόγον, θεο-
κρατίαν ἀπέδειξε τὸ πολίτευμα, but, as some might say, straining
the term, instituted Theocracy as a form of government; whence
it appears that Josephus looked upon Moses as the founder of
the Theocracy.

Yet, looking as we ought, at the whole of God's dealings with
His people, that was to be an emblem of His Church called out
of the world, while living therein, until it be perfected in
Heaven, we find that (1) the call of Abraham was a more complete example of God's free grace, of His will and of His power,
in making this one man, through his firm faith in objective
Truth and implicit obedience to it, the pattern of those that
should believe; than would have been the call, say, out of
Egypt, of the nation which repeatedly turned aside, disobeyed
and murmured, and even worshipped a molten calf, while the
Law was being given to Moses on Mount Sinai.   Therefore did
God first call His Church in the person of Abraham, and not
in his posterity, in order to make him the father and pattern
not only of His Church under the Law but also of His Church
under the Gospel; therefore did God make the promise to him
first, and therefore did He bring about the Exodus of Abraham's
posterity from Egypt in ratification of that very promise.   But
(2) in order that God's people should be brought out of Egypt
according to His purpose, it was ordered that the seventy
children of Abraham that went down to Egypt, should there and
then settle and multiply into a people, to be rescued from the

[1] Contra Ap. ii. 16.

bondage to which they were to be reduced, with signs, wonders, types and miracles, meant as figures of what should follow. And when (3) we consider the various stages through which the children of Israel were made to pass after leaving Egypt, their baptism in the Red Sea as death unto Egypt and a new birth unto God's government of them as His people; the desert, the law, manna, their many warnings and punishments, even through types, as that of the brazen serpent; the crossing of the Jordan under Joshua or Jesus the son of Nun; then the taking possession of the promised Land, and the period of the Judges during which "the LORD ruled over the people;"[1] after that, their having a king so far of God's appointment, that God had foretold him,[2] and that his successors were called "the LORD's anointed," to show that God still held supreme Rule over the nation: then the idolatry, the captivity, and the sceptre not departing from Judah until the coming of Shiloh,[3]—we may be right in agreeing[4] with Bishop Warburton,[5] when he says: "Most writers suppose Theocracy to have ended with the Judges; but scarce any bring it lower than the Captivity. On the contrary, I hold that in strict truth and propriety, it ended not until the coming of CHRIST." Then follow proofs given by that learned and plain spoken[6] divine, to show that Theocracy ended not with the Judges, but continued during the Monarchy, and until the destruction of the national independence of the Jewish people. With him agrees Jahn,[7] and apparently Gesenius, who says that "prophets were but heralds of Theocracy; and oracles only declarations of Theocratic sentiments towards nations not their own."[8]

It seems proved by one institution, that of the Jubilee, when

---

[1] Judg. viii. 23. [2] Deut. xvii. 14, 15.

[3] עַד כִּי יָבֹא שִׁילֹה ד יָתֵי מַלְכָּא מְשִׁיחָא "Until the time when the King Messiah shall come." (Targ. J. B. Uzziel, in Gen. xlix. 10, 11.) וְדִילֵהּ הִיא מַלְכוּתָא "For of Him is the kingdom," (Targ. Hieros. Ibid.)

[4] "Sed cantb," as Carpzov says of him, Appar. Histor. criticus, p. 7.

[5] Divine Leg. of Moses, vol. ii. p. 280, sq.

[6] "I believe it will not be easy to find, even in the dirtiest sink of free-thinking, so much falsehood, absurdity, and malice, heaped together in so few words," speaking of Voltaire's Opinion of the Jews. Div. Leg. vol. ii. p. 239.

[7] Archæol. Bibl. par. 221, Engl. Transl.

[8] Comm. in Is. Einleit. p. 27, sq.

every man was to return to his possession,[1] that the Theocracy
lasted, properly speaking, from the call of Abraham to the
coming of Shiloh; when the FATHER, in a figure, made over
afresh to the SON, the government of His people chosen from
the world, and brought out of it. The year of the Jubilee was
intended to keep up, not only the memory, but the actual and
tangible fact of a Theocratic government, which lay chiefly in
this—that the children of Israel were GOD's servants, His property, as chosen by Him. From the first GOD said to the
children of Israel, " the land shall not be sold for ever; for the
land is Mine; for ye are strangers and sojourners with Me."[2]
" I am the LORD your GOD which brought you out of the
land of Egypt to give you the land of Canaan, and to be
your GOD."[3] " For unto Me the children of Israel are servants; they are My servants whom I brought forth out of the
land of Egypt. I am the LORD your GOD."[4] The land was
then given them to possess, but only in trust; every tribe was
identified with the soil allotted to it; so that the people and the
land went together as GOD's own; and in order to keep up as
much as possible this state of things, the basis and the conditions of Theocracy, every man was to go back to his possession
in the year of Jubilee that came round every fifty years, as a peri-
odical return, restitution, or restoration to the original Theocratic
state under Joshua; a kind of new birth for the people of Israel.[5]

But the children of Israel were reminded daily of the presence of GOD among them as their Supreme Ruler, to Whom
even their kings obeyed, by the intercession at the כַּפֹּרֶת or
mercy-seat, where GOD met Moses, and after him the High
Priest. This was the real seat, the Theocratic throne of GOD in
Israel. There did He make both His presence felt and His will
known, as Ruler, Protector, and Guide in small matters as well
as in great ones. For He not only said He was the LORD their
GOD, and that their kings were His anointed, but He also
styled Himself the LORD of hosts, יְהֹוָה צְבָאוֹת, Who led to
battle His people, στρατηγῷ μὲν αὐτοκράτορι χρώμενοι τῷ Θεῷ
ὑποστράτηγον δὲ χειροτονήσαντι ἵνα τὸν ἀρετῇ προύχοντα, " that took

¹ Lev. xxv. 10.   ² Ib. v. 23.   ³ Ib. v. 38.   ⁴ Ib. v. 55.
⁵ For fuller details see Bahr Symbolik. vol. ii. p. 317, 604, sq.

Him for their Commander in Chief, and appointed under Him some one of excellent courage."[1] J. D. Michaelis[2] differs from the above writers, and V. Bohlen[3] advances the futile opinion that circumcision was the "ächt theokratischen Bund," the real bond or covenant of Theocracy ; if so, it must also have been the case with Egyptians, and with other nations which adopted that rite. For, whereas Theocracy no longer exists in the sense here given to it, circumcision still obtains among the Jews, and among other nations. Everything, however, tends to show, what seems most conformable to the general tenour of God's dispensation towards His Church, both under the Law and under the Gospel, that Theocracy—that is, the government of the FATHER—lasted under the Old Covenant, until MESSIAH came, upon Whose shoulder the government of Grace was put, to remain there for ever.

II. Speaking of the second period (p. xxxii.) of the Jewish history, Dr. Stanley tells us that

"it comprehends the developement of the Jewish Church and Religion through the growth of the Prophetic Order," &c.

How does he understand this growth, in number or in importance ? Prophets were, indeed, sent from time to time to recall the people from their evil ways, and to teach God's will to men ; yet it is said of Moses not only "that there arose not a prophet since in Israel like unto Moses, whom the LORD knew face to face,"[4] but the LORD said also unto Moses, "I will raise them up a prophet from among their brethren like unto thee, and I will put My words into his mouth, and he shall speak unto them all that I shall command him."[5] Since then, on the one hand, no prophet like Moses arose in Israel either before or after him ; and since, on the other hand, the promised SAVIOUR was compared unto him, an honour which no other prophet received, it is hardly correct to speak of "the growth of the Prophetic Order" without specifying how this is to be understood. For the Prophetic Order did not grow in power, in miracles, or in gifts, but Prophets were multiplied as the circumstances of

[1] Joseph. Antiq. Lib. iv. c. 8, 41.   [2] Mos. Recht. Pt. I. p. 180—188.
[3] Genes. einleit. clxxxviii.   [4] Deut. xxxiv. 10.
[5] Deut. xviii. 18 and 15.

the people seemed to require; and their burdens were given
them accordingly.

III. Still less intelligible is Dr. Stanley when he says that
the third period of the Jewish history—

"is distinguished by the last and greatest development of the Prophetic Spirit, out of which rose the Christian Church, and the
consequent expansion of the Jewish Religion into a higher region."
—P. xxxii.

What can all this mean? The Christian Church being the
Church of CHRIST, and called after Him, began with Him, Who
established her on a new covenant and a new order of things;
but not on a "development of the prophetic spirit," chiefly
given to foretell His coming; since the gift of prophecy, granted
to very few even in the Apostolic times, ceased altogether after
them. Moreover, since our LORD CHRIST, Who built His
Church on "the foundation of the Apostles and Prophets," is
compared to Moses, the first of the Prophets, if we except
Enoch and Jacob, it does not appear how this Church of CHRIST
is owing to the development of the prophetic spirit, as such;
unless we call a house the development of the foundation
thereof. It was the fulfilment of prophecies that had gone
before; it was the rising of the Sun of Righteousness after a
long twilight; but it was no more a development of existing
things, than the light of the sun is, practically, for us, a development of the light of the stars; since the word of prophecy is
compared to "a light that shineth in a dark place, until the day
dawn, and the Day star arise."[1]

IV. So also, what is this "expansion of the Jewish Religion
into a higher region" of which Dr. Stanley speaks? How
can a shadow expand into a substance? "the shadow of things
to come" into the body which is of CHRIST? Since we are
told that in Him is neither Greek nor Jew, circumcision nor
uncircumcision, Barbarian, Scythian, bond nor free, but "CHRIST
is all in all,"[2] and "they are all one in CHRIST JESUS,"[3] "the
Mediator of a better covenant,"[4] "Who taketh away the first
that He may establish the second;"[5] "therefore, if any man be

[1] 2 S. Pet. i. 19.   [2] Col. iii. 11.   [3] Ib. iii. 18.
[4] Heb. viii. 6.   [5] Ib. x. 9.

in CHRIST, he is a new creature; old things are passed away;
behold, all things are become new."[1]   If Dr. Stanley means
that Jewish rites and ceremonies expanded into that which they
were meant to represent, and their sacrifices into that of CHRIST,
or into that sacrifice on our part " which is (our) reasonable service," τὴν λογικὴν λατρείαν (ἡμῶν), it was, to say the least, a strange
kind of expansion.   For " expansion" is, of necessity, the exten-
sion of the same thing or substance; now these rites, ceremonies, and sacrifices under the Law " were a shadow of things
to come ; but the body is of CHRIST."[2]

V. Then, speaking of the main bulk of the authorities for his
history, which are " contained in the Canonical Books of the
Hebrew Scriptures," Dr. Stanley goes on to say—

" It has been at various times supposed that the Books of Moses,
Joshua, and Samuel were all written in their present form by
those whose names they bear.   This notion, however, has been
in former ages disputed both by Jewish and Christian theolo-
gians, and is now rejected by almost all scholars.   It has no foundation in the several Books themselves, and is contradicted by the
strong internal evidence of their contents.   To determine accurately the authorship and the dates of these and the other sacred
writings is a question belonging to the same Biblical criticism,
which has thus modified the opinion just mentioned ; and to those
who are called to enter into the details of such inquiries I gladly
leave the solution of the problem."—Pp. xxxii., xxxiii.

If the Dean of Westminster thinks it generous and considerate
on his part to raise doubts in the minds of his younger hearers
on subjects on which their minds should be settled and satisfied, without allaying the doubts he thus raises, many of his
readers will differ from him.   He referred his hearers to other
critics ; but he must be well aware that by far the greater part
of the students who heard him would not go to other critics,
but would rather follow his opinion ; willing and ready as most
young men are, in order to save time and trouble, " jurare in
verba magistri," to swear by their teacher.   And yet, talking of
philosophy, Cicero says[3] to the point : " Est igitur ridiculum,

1 2 Cor. v. 17.   2 Col. ii. 17.
3 Pro L. Murena. 68, ed. Ern.

quod est dubium, id relinquere incertum :—Atque id decernitur omnibus postulantibus candidatis : ut ex senatus consulto, (oratione), neque cujus intersit, neque contra quem sit, intelligi possit." Likewise, Aristotle teaches that ἔστι δὲ τοῖς εὐπορῆσαι βουλομένοις προύργου τὸ διαπορῆσαι καλῶς, those who wish to have their minds settled on a given subject must first of all begin fairly to doubt about it; then follows the settling of the question which is the solution of previous doubt, adding, however, truly, λύειν δ' οὐκ ἔστιν ἀγνοοῦντας τὸν δεσμόν, that it is impossible for those who have no knowledge to loosen the knot. Ἀλλ' ἡ τῆς διανοίας ἀπορία δηλοῖ τοῦτο περὶ τοῦ πράγματος· And this shows itself in the hesitation of a man's thoughts on the subject; he is like one bound hand and foot, who can make no progress either way.[1]

VI. Since, however, Dr. Stanley leaves his readers as he left his hearers, in a kind of doubt which, judging from the tenour of his writing, seems to suit best his habit of mind and his feelings on the subject, I must beg leave to remark that—no criticism can determine accurately from internal evidence alone the exact date and authorship of a Book of the Bible. The critic is not yet born who can, or will, ever say—except through pitiable arrogance—this Book was written by such a one, and by none else; at such a time, and at no other; for such evidence is chiefly negative. All he can do is to 'think so,' that is—to presume. Hence the great variety both of critics and of criticism. If this internal evidence were so plain, some at least would agree upon it; whereas in this, perhaps, more than in any other case, 'doctors' do differ—simply because they pretend to do what they cannot accomplish. For the sake of Dr. Stanley's readers, therefore, or rather for that of his hearers, I will give as briefly as I can, one instance out of many, that may serve for most of the rest, of the ignorance, of the shallow scholarship, if not of the bad faith—which is worse than either—of such 'free-inquirers,' or free-thinking critics as regards the Bible, and show how worthless are their pretensions to settle the age and the authorship of a book from what they call the "internal evidence" thereof.

Von Bohlen, one of the authorities to which Dr. Stanley

[1] Metaph. ii. 1. 2.

refers candidates for Holy Orders,[1] and whose translator, if I
mistake not, once petitioned Parliament for a new version of the
Bible, on the strength, I suppose, of what he had found in that
German work, tells us gravely[2] that the mention of the vine by
the chief butler, as seen in his dream,[3] shows that it is of a later
date, certainly not anterior to the time of Josiah ; because (1) Herodotus says[4] that Αἰγύπτιοι—οἶνῳ δ' ἐκ κριθέων πεποιημένῳ διαχρέων-
ται, οὐ γάρ σφι εἰσὶν ἐν τῇ χώρῃ ἄμπελοι· "the Egyptians make use
of wine made of barley, for that there are no vine-plants, (Wein-
stöcke, as V. Bohlen renders it) in their country;" because (2)
Hecatæus makes Osiris the inventor of this barley-wine, whereas
the Greeks invented the fable of his planting the vine at Nysa,
out of Egypt;[5] because (3) Herodotus again speaks of[6] the wine
brought by Greeks from Phœnicia once a year in earthenware
jars, to be consumed only by Greeks; for (4) true Egyptians,
says Plutarch,[7] looked upon wine as the blood of the enemies of
the gods, and therefore neither drank it themselves nor offered
it to their gods before the time of Psammeticus. Therefore the
history of Joseph is a tale of a later date, and at least that part
of Genesis was written some time towards the end of the kingdom of Judah !

Let us now look at the facts—stubborn things at all times.
First, as to the character of Herodotus for truthfulness, which
by these freethinkers is thought of greater authority than the
Bible; it did not rank very high among his Greek friends.
Ἡρόδοτος ὁ πολυπράγμων, says Diodorus,[8] ἠκολουθηκὼς ἀντιλεγομέ-
ναις ὑπονοίαις εὑρίσκεται, "Herodotus, the busybody, turns out to
have followed conjectures and fancies which contradict one another;" φλυαρεῖ, "he talks nonsense," says Strabo;[9] πολλά
ἐλεγχόμενος τῶν Αἰγυπτιακῶν ὑπ' ἀγνοίας ἡπατημένος, "being convicted of having told many stories about Egyptian matters, from
sheer ignorance," writes also Josephus.[10] No wonder, then, if,

[1] Lect. L p. 24, &c. I refute not V. Bohlen, who is dead, but his spirit, which
yet lives.
[2] Comm. in. Genes. p. 373, sqq.
[3] Gen. xl. 9, sqq.   [4] Lib. ii. c. 77.
[5] Diod. Sic. xvi. 15.   [6] Lib. iii. c. 6.
[7] De Is. et Osir. c. 6. p. 392, ed Reiske.
[8] Lib. I. c. 37.   [9] Lib. xvii. 1.
[10] C. Ap. Lib. i. c. 14, p. 1350, ed. Huds.

as Plutarch says in his treatise περὶ τῆς Ἡροδ. κακοηθείας, on the
evil disposition of Herodotus,[1] τοῦ Ἡροδότου πολλοὺς μὲν—καὶ ἡ
λέξις, ὡς ἀφελὴς—ἐξηπάτηκε, "the simple style of Herodotus
should have taken in many men, who have allowed themselves
to be led by his good nature. But not only, as Plato says, is
it ἐσχάτης ἀδικίας, μὴ ὄντα δοκεῖν εἶναι δίκαιον of the last unrigh-
teousness for one to pretend to be righteous when one is not,
but it is, κακοηθείας ἄκρας ἔργον, the part of the utmost maliciousness to show oneself intolerable through the feint of a
simple, easy temper." So much for Herodotus and his friends.

Yet, to do Herodotus justice, V. Bohlen through his ignorance of Greek, makes him out a greater story-teller than he
really is ; and makes him say what he never meant. Herodotus
says there were in Egypt no ἄμπελοι, that is no "vineyards,"
which V. Bohlen understood and rendered wrongly, "Wein-
stöcke," "vine-plants," so as to make Herodotus say what even
he never could have said, viz. that "the vine" did not grow in
Egypt. If Herodotus had meant that, he would have used the
singular—οὐ γάρ σφι ἐστὶν ἐν τῇ χώρῃ ἄμπελος, according to the
Greek idiom, which in this respect, is much like the English,
viz. to put the genus in the singular, and the species of that
genus, or several genera, in the plural. Thus τὸ ῥόδον, τὸ κρίνον,
'the rose,' 'the red lily,' in general ; ἡ ἄμπελος, 'the vine,' or
'the vineyard,'[2] τὰ ῥόδα, τὰ κρίνα, 'the roses,' the lilies either of
different kinds, or many of the same sort ; e.g. φύεται ἐν τῷ ὕδατι
κρίνεα πολλὰ τὰ Αἰγύπτιοι καλεῦσι λωτόν, "when the Nile over-
flows, there grow in the water a number of lilies which the
Egyptians call lotus."[3] So that, not only could ἄμπελοι never

---

[1] C. 1.   [2] Hence the various renderings of S. John xv. 1, sq.

[3] Herod. II. c. 92. So also κέραμοι εἰσάγεται, 'earthenware is brought ;' ὁ κεράμων, 'one jar,' which in the pl. would have been τὰ κεράμια, if Herodotus had mentioned several jars, though he alludes to πάντα κέραμον, 'the whole of the earthenware,' (Lib. III. 6.) Likewise, τὰ μὲν λεπτόφλοια καθάπερ δάφνη, φίλυρα, τὰ δὲ παχύφλοια καθάπερ δρῦς, "some trees have a thin bark, like the laurel, the lime; others a thick one, like the oak." (Theoph. Hist. Pl. I. c. 5, &c.) "The bark of others is imbricated like that φιλύρας, ἐλάτης ἀμπέλων λυκοστάφου πρασίων, of the lime, of the pine, of the vine, of the broom, and of onions," in the plural; all onions being alike in this respect. And, "whereas plains are most suitable ἐλαίῳ μὲν καὶ συκῇ καὶ ἀμπέλῳ to the olive, to the fig, and to the vine, ἐν πλείστῃ δὲ ἐν εἴσην διαφορᾷ τὸ τῶν ἀμπέλων ἐστὶν ὅσα γάρ ἐστι γῆς εἴδη τοσαῦτά τινές φασι καὶ ἀμπέλων εἶναι· the several kinds of vines differ widely one from another ;

mean 'vine-plants' in the sense of 'the vine' said absolutely, as
V. Bohlen thought, but Herodotus could not have meant it, and
he must have meant 'vineyards,' since he speaks of ἀσταφίς,
'raisins,' used in embalming the cows sacred to Isis,[1] which
imply the growth of the vine in Egypt, as does also the wine
drunk in the days of Rhampsinitus;[2] the wine given as daily
ration to the king's bodyguard,[3] and the οἶνος ἀμπέλινος, 'wine
of grapes,' given to the priests daily,[4] even before the time of
Psammetichus.

Neither is Herodotus much to blame for saying he had seen no
vineyards in Egypt. He might have said it in comparison with
his own country, which is a land of vineyards ; whereas the whole
of Egypt, from the nature of its soil, could never be a 'wine
country,' although such wine as was grown there was celebrated,
on account of the climate which ripened the grapes. The vine
cannot grow well in a wet, watery, rich soil like that of Egypt :
it loves best a more dry and sandy soil ; in Egypt therefore
what vineyards there were, and what vineyards there are now,
are planted on the sandy soil of the Hajer, on the borders of
the alluvial land, at the foot or on the slope of the hills. Herodotus saw but little of Egypt, and chiefly Lower Egypt ; and as
in his day, the vineyards of Marea were probably not planted,
and as he did not go through Antyllis, he might travel from the
sea-shore to Memphis without seeing a single vineyard, albeit
those of Kakem (Κωχώμη) were at no great distance on the hills
westward ; and others were growing elsewhere in Middle and in
Upper Egypt.

For, the vine grew in Egypt from the beginning of what is
called history. Not only is the vine used as a determinative
symbol in hieroglyphics, but as far back as the IVth Dynasty[5] do

Indeed, they say there are as many kinds of vine as there are of soils." (Ib. lib.
ii. 5.) And again, χαλεπώτατα δὲ καὶ ἀμπέλῳ καὶ τοῖς ἄλλοις συκῇ καὶ ἐλαίᾳ,
" the fig and the olive are most injurious to the vine and to other plants ;
χαλεπὸν δὲ καὶ ἡ ἀμυγδαλῆ—so is the almond; αὐτοὶ φυτεύουσί τινες ἐν ταῖς
ἀμπέλοις, yet some people plant it in their vineyards," &c. (Ib. De Caus. Pl. lii.
c. 10, 6, and c. 11, &c.)

[1] Lib. ii. 40.
[2] Lib. ii. c. 121.
[3] Ib. ii. c. 168.   [4] Ib. c. 37.
[5] Leps. Denkm. Abth. ii. Pl. 3, 5, 11, 19, 23, 35, 38, 44, 45, 49, 53.

D

we find wine, in Egyptian ⲁⲡⲏ Copt. ⲏⲡⲏ,[1] mentioned, of
several sorts, white wine, wine of garden-vine, wine of the
north country, wine of Lower and of Upper Egypt; in stated
measure, or measures, and forming part of offerings to the gods:
but in the tomb of Eimei,[2] ⲥⲣ ⲡⲭ ⲛⲣ-ⲁⲁ ⲁⲁⲡ-ⲏⲓ who was
the chief butler, or superintendent of the Great or Royal house,
long before the time of Joseph, we find the whole process of the
vintage, from the gathering of the grapes, to the pressing and
boiling of the wine, into the details of which I cannot now
enter. Again in the VIth Dynasty[3] we find both ⲉⲕ, ζύδος,
barley-wine (beer), mentioned with wine, as an offering to the
gods; and in pl. 69, in the tomb of Manofre, under King Assa,
we have this οἶνος κρίθινος, and five different kinds of οἶνος ἀμπέλινος, (as also in pl. 70, 71); and in pl. 61, that gives the wine
account of the ⲁⲁⲡ-ⲏⲓ, the butler, or bailiff, thirteen servants
are represented bringing him jars of wine on their shoulders;
and that there should be no mistake, the word ⲁⲡⲏ, 'wine,' is
engraved between every one of the servants, to specify the contents of their jars.

For wine not only was drunk by the Egyptians, but it always
formed a part of their offerings to the gods, despite what Plutarch says; as Herodotus tells us,[4] and as we find engraved or
painted in the earliest tombs of Lower and of Upper Egypt; on
the votive monuments of every Dynasty; in Hieratic MSS.; and
in the Ritual of the Dead, where the deceased often says: "I
take offerings on the altars, and I drink wine."[5] So that Plutarch's story of no wine being offered to the gods and V. Bohlen's
faith in it, go for nothing. It was offered as we have seen,
before Psammetichus, and also after him, as proved not only
by the monuments of the Ptolemies, but also by an Aramæo-
Egyptian papyrus, in which we have a detailed account of
the cost, measure, and quantity of חמר צידן קלוי wine
from Sidon, boiled; מצרין קלל Egyptian wine, common; and
קדם אפתח אלהא מצרין קלוי Egyptian wine, boiled; offered

---

[1] Whence ἴρπις—ἴρπις τὸ ῥίζιον, Lycophr. Alex. 579, and note ed. Potter.
ἴρπις θεοῖς οἶνος. Sappho ap. Athen. II. c. 2, ad fin. and Casaubon's note ad l.
Eustath. ad Odyss. 359, ἴσται δὲ ἴρπις Αἰγυπτιστὶ ὁ οἶνος.

[2] Leps. Denkm. Abth. II. Pl. 49, 53.

[3] Ib. 38, 44, 61, 66, 67.

[4] Lib. II. c. 39.

[5] Champ. Gr. Eg. p. 392.

רבא before Phtah, the great god, and לנקדה קדם אסיר for a lustration before Osiris, or לשרותא for the service (or banquet) of the house, &c.[1] All this agrees with what Herodotus says of the festival of Diana (Basht or Paaht) in Bubastis, οἶνος ἀμπέλινος ἀναισιμοῦται πλέον ἐν τῇ ὁρτῇ ταύτῃ ἢ ἐν τῷ ἅπαντι ἐνιαυτῷ τῷ ἐπιλοίπῳ, that more of grape wine was consumed at that festival than during the whole year besides,[2]—assuredly not by Greeks only, as V. Bohlen tells us.

The existence of the vine, the vintage and process of making the wine, long anterior to Joseph, are thus proved beyond doubt by paintings and inscriptions in the tombs of Thebes, of Beni Hassan, and of Ghizeh. We there see the vine trailed on forked sticks, χάρακις, or against a trellis-work, in gardens, and out of them, as at the present day. And this is sufficient to prove that the chief butler need not have lived in the days of Josiah.

But since V. Bohlen quotes even French travellers of the last century, to prove that but few vines exist in Egypt, I may also be allowed to quote other authors to whom he does not allude. Hellanicus, who was twelve years older than Herodotus, tells us that, ἐν τῇ Πλινθίνῃ πόλει Αἰγύπτου πρώτῃ εὑρεθῆναι τὴν ἄμπελον, "the vine was first discovered in the town of Plinthine,"[3] in the Mareotic Nome,[4]—εὐοινία τέ ἐστι περὶ τοὺς τόπους, ὥστε καὶ διαχρεῖσθαι πρὸς παλαίωσιν τὸν Μαρεώτην οἶνον, "where there are localities yielding excellent wine, especially the Mareotic wine that improves by keeping."[5]

> "Sunt Thasiæ vites, sunt et Mareotides albæ,
> Pinguibus hæ terris habiles, levioribus illæ."[6]

Is this too, a Greek legend, like that of Osiris finding the vine at Nysa, according to V. Bohlen?

---

[1] Papyrus Aramæo-Egypt. A. Barges, 1862. Indeed we find that this rite was continued until Christian times; for, in the life of S. Pachom, (Zoega Codd. Memph. p. 77.) we read that his parents having given him to drink ϩⲉⲛ ⲡⲏⲣⲡ ⲉⲧⲁⲧⲟⲩⲱⲧⲉⲛ ⲉⲃⲟⲗⲛϩⲏⲧϥ ⲛⲛⲓⲇⲉⲙⲱⲛ of the wine of which they had offered libations to their gods, he threw it up.

[2] Lib. II. c. 60.

[3] Athen. lib. i. c. 25, p. 34, ed. Cas.

[4] Ptolem. Geog. lib. iv. a. v. 8, p. 251, ed. T. Scylax Caryand. Peripl. p. 307, ed. G.

[5] Strab. xvii. c. l. 14.

[6] Georg. ii. 91, and Hor. Od. i. xxxvii. 4.

This Mareotic wine was κάλλιστος, λευκός τε γὰρ καὶ ἡδύς,
"excellent, white and sweet."[1] The Mareotic wine, however,
was inferior to the Tæniotic grown in that neighbourhood near
the sea, according to Athenæus; who adds that there were vines
all along the Nile, ἡ δὲ περὶ τὸν Νεῖλον ἄμπελις, πλείστη μὲν αὐτὴ,
ὅσος καὶ ὁ ποταμός.[2] Of all these vineyards he tells us that
those of Antyllis were the best; and that the wine of the Thebaid
was light, and had other valuable properties. Much wine was
also made in the Arsinoïte Nome, says Strabo,[3] who adds respecting the oasis of Ammon that it has εὔυδρός τε καὶ εὔοινος,
good water and good wine.[4] To these wines S. Clement of
Alexandria adds the Mendæian,[5] Μενδήσιος νέκταρ,[6] while Diodorus gives his testimony to the goodness of the Egyptian grape
when he says: "that the Egyptian vine being watered regularly,
δαψίλειαν οἴνου τοῖς ἐγχωρίοις παρασκευάζει, yields a rich abundance of wine to the inhabitants."[7] These wines were, as we
have seen, exported to Greece and to Italy, and also eastward
to the coast of Arabia.[8] Then Horapollo tells us, that, if the
hoopoe should be heard frequently πρὸ καιροῦ τῶν ἀμπέλων
before the season of the vines, it was a sign of plenty of wine;
and that on this account the Egyptians represented this abundance through a hoopoe. The author of Joseph and Asenath
tells us that Ἀσεννὶθ ἐχάρη—ἐπὶ τοῖς οἴνοις—rejoiced over the
wines (vineyards) and the harvests of her father.[10] Abulfeda[11]
speaking of Esne in the Thebaid says that it لها نخيل وكروم
"has palm-groves and vineyards." Makrizi[12] in his description
of the convent of El-Cosseir, quotes Khoshâdim, who praises the
wine made there. So also the convent of Tamweih[13] was sur-

---

[1] Athen. lib. l. c. 25. It is alluded to as Μαρεώτδος ἱερὸς ἔρρησε by Nonnus,
(Dionys. xl. 509, comp. also xxix. 247, sq., and xxxvi. 290, with Odyss. i. 197,
Euripid. Cycl. 141, sq., and Diod. Sic. i, 16, 20,) by Pliny, "in Ægypto nas-
citur—Thasia, ætalo, peuce," &c. (Hist. Nat. xiv. 4, 9.)

[2] Athen. ib.   [3] Lib. xvii. c. l. 35.

[4] Lib. xvii. c. l. 42.   [5] Pædag. ii. p. 156, ed. Col.

[6] Alciphron, Ep. lib. iii. ep. 5, ed. Seil.   [7] Lib. i. c. 36.

[8] Anonym. Peripl. M. Erythr. c. 24, in Geogr. Min. ed. Müller.

[9] Hierogl. lib. ii. c. 96, ed. Leem.

[10] Fabr. Cod. Pseud. V. T. p. 85, sq.

[11] Ægypt. p. 73, ed. J. D. Mich.

[12] Hist. Copt. p. 37.   [13] Ib. p. 40.

rounded by palm-trees and vineyards, that yielded delicious wine.[1] In a Sahidic fragment given by Mingarelli,[2] we read of the A. Matthew planting vines around his convent; S. Macarius himself an Egyptian mentions τὴν γεωργίαν τῆς ἀμπέλου,[3] γεωργεῖν οἶνον,[4] as things with which he and everybody else in Egypt was familiar. So likewise the old Copt mentioned by Masudi,[5] when describing the beauties of Lower Egypt and the lake of Tinnis, said there was no place equally beautiful on account of its جنّاتها وكرومها "gardens and vineyards," which he thought had lasted since the beginning of the world. We also read in Cosmas Indopleustes, Lib. xi. of his Cosmographia[6] and in the Acts of A. Benofer, Sinuthius, Matthew,[7] &c., of the vine, of vineyards, of the vintage, and of making the wine, as usual occupations in Egypt,[8] all of which are confirmed by the still more recent accounts of Prosper Alpinus,[9] Forskal,[10] Sir. G. Wilkinson,[11] A. T. Stamm,[12] Nordmayer[13]—"Vites plantandi vel amputandi mos est, mense Mechir (Febr.), p. 77. Mense Mesori (Augusto) etiam uvas in tota Ægypto maturari," &c., p. 57. "Vindemia in montibus prope Cahiram, mense Julio." Likewise Schems ed-din Abilsoroor,[14] "en Mechir, tailler les vignes; en Mesori on presse le raisin."

The statements of which I have just given a mere outline, and to which I may add my own personal knowledge of the existence of the vine in Egypt, from one end of the country to the other, show not only the utter worthlessness of this freethinking criticism, though it be covered with a show of learning sufficient

[1] See also what Makrizi says concerning wine and Egyptian grapes in De Sacy's Chrestom. Ar. Vol. I. p. 62, and 104, 105.

[2] Ægypt. Codd. Reliq. Gr. x. p. 265.

[3] De Cust. Cord. a. ls.

[4] Ib. a. xl. De Charit. a. xxxi., De Orat. a. v., and Homil. xxvi. 11.

[5] Masudi ar. a. vol. I. p. 374.

[6] In Coll. Nov. PP. Mifcon, vol. II. p. 336.

[7] Zoega Codd. Memph. p. 16, Codd. Sahid. p. 433, sq., and p. 539, &c.

[8] For which prayers are offered in the Churches of Egypt, ⲦⲰⲂⲈ,— ⲈϪⲈⲚ ⲪⲀ. ⲚⲒϢϢⲎⲚ ⲚⲈⲘ ⲪⲀ. ⲚⲒⲈⲖⲖ Ⲛ̄ ⲀⲖⲟⲖⲒ Pray for all trees, all vineyards, &c. (Missale Copt. Ar. p. 50.)

[9] De Med. Æg. p. 15, Ven. 1591.   [10] Flora Æg. p. lii.

[11] Mod. Eg. i. p. 463.   [12] De Præs. Stata Agris. Æg. 20, p. 61.

[13] De Calend. Ægypt. Œconom. p. 16, Gott. 1792.

[14] De Sacy's tr. in Notices et Extr. des MSS. I. p. 352, sq.

to take in the unlearned and the unwary, but they also make
evident the 'animus' of men, who would rather risk their reputation for scholarship than not carp at the Bible, and not gainsay
the Truth contained therein. But what must become of those
who will follow such blind guides, but that they should "both
fall together into the ditch?"

Yet this is not all. Had V. Bohlen shown himself a real
scholar by searching out the Truth, and not merely what suited
his own way of thinking and his own purpose, he would have
quoted fairly, and from the same page in Athenæus, what Dion
Academicus says, viz: φιλοίνους καὶ φιλοπότας τοὺς Αἰγυπτίους
εἶναι, that the Egyptians being fond of wine and of drink, εὑρεθῆναι τὶ παρ' αὐτοῖς βοήθημα, invented a contrivance whereby
those who were too poor to drink wine, τὸν ἐκ τῶν κριθῶν γινό-
μενον πίνειν, might drink wine made from barley. From this
statement, therefore, wine from barley seems to have been invented after wine had been brought into use. And this fond-
ness of the Egyptians for drink is confirmed (1) by several passages from MSS. papyri.[1] In the ᛒᚷᚾ or palace of Ramses,
wine and bak, οἶνος κρίθινος, abounded,[2] ρ ⲦⲎⲠⲞⲦ ρ ⲞⲨⲈ-ⲦⲞⲨ
ⲈⲔ, "but how carefully this bak should be avoided," said a
scribe to one of his clients.[3] And (2) by representations on
their tombs. But as to the "Greek legend," as V. Bohlen calls
it, of Osiris having discovered the vine about Nysa—one of the
many towns of that name—σχεδὸν Αἰγύπτοιο ῥοάων, and having
taught men to plant it,[5] it is, to say the least of it, worth as
much as the statement of Hecatæus,[6] that the Egyptians, τὰς
κριθὰς εἰς τὸ πῶμα καταλούουσιν, brew barley into drink; for Diodorus also tells us that the Egyptians made of barley a drink
that is little inferior to wine, ὃ καλοῦσι ζῦθος, which they call
'beer,'[7] taught, as they had been by Osiris, not only to grow the
vine, but also to sow the seed of barley and of wheat.[8] This is
true as far as Egyptian accounts go, since in the Turin MS. of

---

[1] Chabas, MS. Harris, p. 68, note.   [2] Chabas, MS. Egypt. p. 50.
[3] Pap. Anastasi iv. in Mél. Egypt. p. 83.
[4] 'Hard by,' not 'ausserhalb,' 'outside,' i.e., anywhere, as V. Bohlen renders it.
[5] Diod. Sic. Lib. i. 15, 17.   [6] Athen. Lib. x. 4 and 13.
[7] prop. "fermented liquor."   [8] Diod. Lib. i. 17.

the Sacred Book of the Egyptians Osiris says of himself,
ⲀⲚⲞⲔ-ⲠⲈ ⲊⲞⲠⲈ-ⲈⲢⲦ ⲈⲢⲠⲰ ⲤⲞⲦⲰ ⲘⲖⲞⲦⲢ ⲞⲚⲰⲞⲦ
ⲊⲰⲦⲈ ⲈⲘ ⲚⲈ-ⲀⲦ ⲤⲞⲦⲦⲚ ⲬⲰⲢ (מָצוֹר) ⲚⲔⲒⲦⲨ ⲂⲀⲔⲒ,[1]
"I am he that causeth to be, wine, wheat, sheaves, grinding,
flour, in the borders of the king of the strong, the beautiful city
(Egypt)." And both accounts given by Diodorus are further
confirmed by the fact that ⲈⲔ 'beer,' and ⲀⲠⲚ 'wine,' are
almost always mentioned together among offerings made to the
gods; and that they also both, as well as ⲈⲔ ⲚⲈⲬⲈⲖⲖ 'sweet
beer,' form a part of the remedies prescribed in medical books
which passed among the Egyptians for having been written by
Thoth, or Taaud, himself.[2]

Thus are quotations inaccurately given, and surmises broached
with authority in the face of glaring facts that refute them;
and a psalm,[3] that stands in their way, is ascribed to the
time of the Maccabees, if by any means the Bible, the witness
of the Truth it contains, and its power over the heart of man,
may be set aside. And this, translated, eagerly received, puffed
off, and retailed by men yet less learned, is the kind of 'philosophy' we are told to reconcile with the Bible. Can human
presumption, ignorance, and arrogancy go further? Such men,
however they may arrogate to themselves the intellect, the
ability, and the learning of the day, must nevertheless see how
ridiculous they make themselves by their empty boasting.

VII. Whereas, looking at this same narrative with true philosophy, ἡ βούλεται περὶ φρόνησιν εἶναι καὶ τὴν θεωρίαν τὴν περὶ ἀλήθειαν,[4] which is inseparable from good sense, and concerns itself
with the contemplation of Truth, we find in it touches of truth
which attest the authenticity of the writing. We have just
seen that the chief butler did not invent his dream. If we now
compare ver. 11 and ver. 13, we find that whereas the cupbearer says to Joseph, וָאֶתֵּן אֶת-הַכּוֹס עַל-כַּף פַּרְעֹה, 'and I
placed the cup upon the palm of Pharaoh's hand,' Joseph says

---

[1] As given, somewhat freely, by Seyffarth, Theol. Schriften, p. 8.
[2] Chaba. Mél. Egypt. p. 72, 73. Brugsch. Monum. vol. II. pl. cl. L. 3, and
p. 115.
[3] Ps. lxxx. V. Bohlen. Gen. p. 374.
[4] Eth. Eudem. L. 4, 8, 2, E. III. p. 1.

to him, וְנָתַתָּ כוֹס־פַּרְעֹה בְּיָדוֹ, 'and thou shalt put Pharaoh's
cup into his hand:' according to the Hebrew idiom כּוֹס בְּיָד,
Ps. lxxv. 9, Jer. li. 7, Ez. xxiii. 31; but never עַל־כַּף. This
idiom is owing, most likely, to the shape of cups generally used
of old in Palestine, and probably not unlike the pot of manna
stamped on the shekel, which is very much like a goblet, that
was taken and held with the hand. Whereas the cup used by
Pharaoh was most likely flat, like the golden cup of Thothmes
III. in the Louvre,[1] and like those given in Rossellini's great
work,[2] and exactly like the metal كَأس, כּוֹס, in daily use among
Arabs in Egypt and elsewhere. So that the cupbearer, speaking with a knowledge of his office which Joseph could not have,
speaks more correctly according to Egyptian usage; which was,
judging from what I often observed in the East, to place this
flat cup, or saucer, upon the palm of the king's left hand, for
him to take it thence with his right hand, and thus carry it to
his mouth; for it could not be safely passed from the cupbearer's hand to that of the king in any other way.[3] And that
עַל־כַּף, 'upon the palm of the hand,' is the right expression as
regards Egyptian customs, is proved by the use of the same expression at v. 21, where we read that the cupbearer placed the
cup upon the palm, עַל־כַּף, of Pharaoh's hand at the public
banquet.[4] Such touches of truth preserved by Moses, who lived
probably at the court of Ramses II., with the princes Sha-em-djam
and Auf-amen, two of the king's sons, and who, therefore, had
opportunities of becoming acquainted with the duties of the
king's cupbearer, show the authenticity of the writing. We

[1] See Sir G. Wilkinson's "The Egyptians in the time of the Pharaohs,"
p. 98.

[2] Monum. Civ. Tab. lvii. fig. 5, 6.

[3] Joseph and the cupbearer both spoke Egyptian; but Joseph spoke it with a
Hebrew turn, saying something like ⲀⲨ ⲦⲀ-Ⲕ Ⲛ-ⲈⲂⲦ ⲀⲀ ⲦⲀⲦ ⲀⲀ
Ⲛ-ⲀⲡⲀⲀ (or rather, as he used the Memphitic dialect, Ⲫ-ⲀⲡⲀⲀ) rendering יָד by ⲀⲀ ⲦⲀⲦ, albeit these two idioms are not an exact counterpart
of each other; whereas the cupbearer expressly said, ⲀⲨ ⲦⲀ-ⲚⲀ Ⲛ-ⲈⲂⲦ
Ⲉⲣ (rather Ⲉⲓ) ⲦⲀⲦ ⲀⲀ Ⲫ-ⲀⲡⲀⲀ, "And I placed the cup upon the
king's (Pharaoh's) hand."

[4] Compared with בְּיָד said by the cupbearer himself, when he held the cup
in his left hand (v. 11), to press the grapes into it with the right hand.

see, then, with what caution should be read some of the authorities to which Dr. Stanley referred his hearers; and how little
it will do to believe, and to take everything for granted on
the testimony of another man; but rather, if we be in earnest,
ought we to search and to examine for ourselves, especially
when our search is into the Word of God.

VIII. After giving the good advice of comparing one Book of
the Bible with another—a thing done by every intelligent and
earnest student of the Bible ever since Tatian wrote his διὰ τισ
σάρων—Dr. Stanley reminds us that

"the Books of the Old Testament, in their present form, in many
instances are not, and do not profess to be, the original documents
on which the history was based. There was (to use a happy expression employed of late) 'a Bible within a Bible,' an 'Old Testament before an Old Testament was written;' as, e.g., Gen. xiv.,
fragment of a song in Numb. xxi., and quotations from the Book
of Jasher in the Book of Joshua and the First Book of Samuel."—
p. xxxiv.

Wherein the 'happiness' of the expression "a Bible within a
Bible" consists does not, assuredly, appear. Anyhow, it is incorrect; for we have no more right to call those fragments
either "a Bible" or "parts of one," than we have to speak of
'a Thucydides within a Thucydides' when speaking of his reference to the records of Hellanicus, or to his quotations from
Homer. We call "Thucydides" the history that goes by his
name, and we accept on his authority all the speeches, allusions,
and extracts from previous histories he gives, as part and parcel
of his work. We do not think him the less trustworthy, nor the
less a most manly and satisfactory writer, because he chooses to
quote from others; but such is our respect for him as an historian, and so great is our pleasure in reading his terse and
chaste style, that the fact of certain authors—may be, otherwise little known—being quoted by him prejudices us at once
in their favour, on account of their introduction to us through
him. And does he not tell us at the outset[1] that he made use
of ancient documents which seemed to him most trustworthy,
ὡς ἐπὶ μακρότατον σκοποῦντί μοι πιστεῦσαι ξυμβαίνει; for he did not
believe everybody, since he questions Homer's account.[2]   Like-

[1] Lib. i. 1.   [2] Lib. i. 10.

wise Herodotus, despite what Josephus, Plutarch, and Strabo
may say, professes[1] to repeat only what he heard, ὅτιφ τὰ τοιαῦτα
πιθανά ἐστι, as far as it was to be believed; for his plan throughout his history was to write what he heard, and state from
whom.[2] Neither do we find fault with Tacitus because, "ex-
trema tradit," he only gives the chief events concerning Au-
gustus; nor yet with Livy, because he chooses to follow Polybius
in some of his statements; neither yet much with Sulpicius Se-
verus, for making free with several authors, both Christian and
profane. On the contrary, we like to trace in his writings the
thread of the annals of Tacitus, and remnants of other authors.

As we do not think of allowing these quotations to invalidate
our opinion of these heathen authors, neither ought we to allow
our faith in the Bible, and our love for it, to be in the least
degree shaken by a few allusions to anterior documents which
are known to us and entitled to our respect, only through their
being thus quoted. This "happy" expression, "a Bible within
a Bible," seems to imply that a Bible existed formerly, out of
which our Bible was made up; than which nothing can be more
erroneous. "The Bible," or "The Book"—for "Bible" means
"Book"—is "Holy Scripture, that containeth all things necessary to salvation; so that whatsoever is not read therein, nor
may be proved thereby, is not to be required of any man, that
it should be believed as an article of the Faith, or be thought
requisite or necessary to salvation. In the name of Holy Scripture we do understand those Canonical Books of the Old and
New Testament, of whose authority was never any doubt in the
Church," (Art. VI.,)[3] as having been either spoken or written
by "holy men of GOD, who spake as they were moved by the
HOLY GHOST."[4]

This being the case, we have yet to learn, what difference it can
possibly make, either in the authenticity or in the credibility of
their writings, that they should be moved to write fresh matter
from end to end of their Books, or be directed to choose some
fragment of pre-existing documents deemed by the directing

---

[1] Lib. ii. 123.   [2] Comp. also Lib. vii. 152; ii. 44, 99.
[3] No wonder these philosophers should be anxious to dispense with the sub-
scription to the Articles.
[4] 2 S. Pet. i. 21.

Spirit, sufficient for the purpose, and thus fit to be inserted as
part of the Book. In either case direction, or inspiration, is precisely the same; and the authority of the Book thus partly written
and partly compiled is precisely the same also; since the authority
comes not from the letter, but from the Spirit that inspired or
directed the framing of the whole. Take, for instance, two histories of the same nation, by two different authors; the one
inserts into his history pre-existing documents or fragments of
them, as he found them, because they appeared to him worthy
of credit; the other writes the whole history in his own style,
and as Thucydides says, perhaps, ἐπὶ τὸ προαγωγότερον τῇ ἀκροάσει
ἢ ἀληθέστερον, rather so as to write agreeably for the sake of
being read, than truthfully, for the sake of telling the Truth
alone; to which of these two authors should we be most willing
to give credit for the greater honesty? Clearly to the one who
had taken the trouble to quote accurately the words of others
suited to his purpose. So also, and *a fortiori*, in Books
written under the direction of God's Holy Spirit. In short, if
a Prophet or an Evangelist, was led by the HOLY GHOST to
adopt certain records or fragments of them, this choice being
thus overruled and directed, constitutes those fragments part and
parcel of the Book, and entitles them to the same respect, faith
and worship, as the parts of the Book written immediately by
the Prophet or the Evangelist; for, assuredly, if these fragments
or records were not deemed worthy of credit, they would not
have been chosen; but since they were chosen they are then
worthy of all credit. Yet, as they are entitled to credit, only
because they are found in the Bible, it is not logical to speak of
them as of "a Bible" within a Bible; for they would be nothing
without the Bible in which they occur; and therefore they are,
of themselves alone, no "Bible" at all.

This appears the only fair and real view of the question lately
revived in this country, though long since settled and almost
forgotten in others—the apparent arbitrary use of El, Elohim,
and Jehovah, in the several books of the Pentateuch, but especially in Genesis. Those who either deny Inspiration, or who at
least explain it away, make of Genesis a patchwork of writing,
to which we cannot wonder themselves decline to assent. But
admitting, or rather believing in Inspiration as it exists, and

seeing clearly that, whether Inspiration told a prophet what to write or what to choose, the Inspiration was the same, Genesis and the rest of the Pentateuch forms a whole alike authentic and worthy of our implicit faith and of our profound reverence.

IX. After recommending the study of Hebrew, now so much neglected to the great hindrance of true Biblical scholarship, Dean Stanley goes on to say—

"The Hebrew text, however, is not our only source of information as to the original materials of the Sacred History. Without arguing the relative merits of the Hebrew and the Septuagint texts, we have no right to set aside or neglect such an additional authority as the Septuagint furnishes, (p. xxxv.) But to us who feel what the Septuagint was in the hands of the Apostles, as the means of spreading the knowledge of the Old Testament through the Gentile world"—"who feel what a bulwark this double version of the Old Testament furnishes against a too rigid or too literal construction of the Sacred History—the Seventy Translators, if not worthy of the high place which the ancient Church assigned to them, may well be ranked amongst the greatest benefactors of Biblical Literature and Free Inquiry."

This is exactly the language to be expected from a man of Dr. Stanley's sentiments, who is not acquainted with the Hebrew text ; it is, nevertheless, wrong throughout.

First—it is not clear what Dr. Stanley means by his "double version of the Old Testament ;" does he reckon, perhaps, the Hebrew original as a "Version" ? for he cannot here allude to one of the many Greek versions of the Old Testament besides the Septuagint.

Secondly—it is vain to talk of the "additional authority the Septuagint furnishes." Authority cannot be divided, especially in matters of faith. Either the Hebrew text is the original one, and is, as such, the highest and last court of appeal—or it is not. As it is the original, and as the Septuagint is only a Version, under whatsoever circumstances it may have been made, it is but a servantmaid to the Hebrew text. We cannot owe divided allegiance to the Hebrew and to the Septuagint, and make one whole of the two; such a mode of reasoning is unsound. We may and ought to value the Septuagint as perhaps the oldest version from the Hebrew, and consult it as such ; but

also, to let it go whenever it differs from the Hebrew original.
We must not be deceived by the undue importance some men,
especially in this country, are apt to give to the Septuagint,
which proceeds from the fact that—so very few study Hebrew,
that, finding themselves comparatively at home in the Septuagint through their classical education, they like to invest the
Greek Version with a kind of original character and authority.
But, in fact, it is perhaps the most corrupt translation of any of
the ancient ones of the Old Testament; at all events, the text
thereof is in a hopeless state.   So that, as no sound critic would
venture to abide by the Septuagint against the Hebrew, it is
difficult to see how the Septuagint can be a "bulwark against a
too rigid construction" of the Hebrew text, since, after all, we
must come to the Hebrew; nay, even in questions of chronology, we may reckon, if we will, according to the Septuagint,
without for all that, giving it the authority of the original.
So that—

Thirdly—it is not easy to see in what way

"the Seventy Translators may well be ranked amongst the greatest
benefactors of Biblical Literature and Free Inquiry."

Free indeed, but what about? about the lump of pitch, of fat,
and of hair with which Daniel made the dragon burst asunder?
or about what fish it was, the heart and liver of which made the
devil flee away when he smelled the smell thereof?[1] A man must
indeed have a large organ of credulity who believes all he reads
in the Septuagint.   And nothing tends more to show how little
this Version is to be trusted than the pains at which its greatest
apologist, Bishop Walton, is to prove the contrary, in his, as yet
unrivalled, Prolegomena.[2] For, since it is now generally acknowledged, says De Wette,[3] that the story of Aristeas is a
fable, the oldest account we have of this Version is, perhaps, from
Philo.[4] He tells us that Ptolemy Philadelphus taken with a
love and desire for the Jewish laws, εἰς Ἑλλάδα γλῶτταν τὴν
χαλδαικὴν μεθαρμόζεσθαι διενοεῖτο, determined to have these laws
translated into Greek from the Chaldaic (Hebrew) tongue.   He

---

[1] Bel and the dragon—Tobit iii.   [2] Prol. ix. 1—66.
[3] Einleit. in D. A. T. p. 56.
[4] De Vita Mos. lib. l. p. 658, sq., ed. Par.

therefore sent to Eleazar the high priest at Jerusalem, request-
ing him to send him for the purpose able men equally learned
in Greek and in their own tongue.   Philo says nothing of the
number of these men ; but Josephus,[1] who tells us that Ptolemy
wrote to Eleazar at the instance of Demetrius Phalereus, librarian
of Alexandria, also says that Eleazar wrote to him[2] he had
chosen ἄνδρας ἐξ ἀπὸ φυλῆς ἑκάστης, οὓς πεπόμφαμεν ἔχοντας τὸν
νόμον, six men out of every tribe,[3] whom he sent having the
Law.   They delivered to the King of Egypt the parchments
on which the Law was written in letters of gold ; and he placed
the men in the island of Pharos[4] in separate cells, ἰσαρίθμους τῶν
ἑρμηνευόντων εἰσίσκους μικρούς, repeats Justin Martyr, after
Aristeas[5] of which, however, neither Philo nor Josephus say a
word ; albeit Josephus B. Gorion, whatever his authority be
worth, tells us[6] ויתן להם תלמי המלך שבעים בתים ויבדל
איש מרעהו that Ptolemy the king gave them seventy[7] houses,
and separated every man from his fellow, χωρίσας αὐτοὺς ἀπ᾽
ἀλλήλων.[8]   S. Clement of Alexandria simply says,[9] κατ᾽ ἰδίαν
ἑκάστην ἑρμηνεύσαντες, "that they translated everyone his own
version separately"—ἑκάστῳ ἴδιον οἶκον ἀπονείμας·[10] while Abulfeda, I know not on what authority, says,[11] that "such was the
eagerness among the learned men of Jerusalem to obey the
summons of Ptolemy, that Eleazar was obliged to choose six

---

[1] Antiq. lib. xii. c. 2, p. 506, ed. Hud.

[2] This correspondence is also given at length in Eusebius, Præp. Ev. pp.
350, sq.

[3] Epiphanius (De Mens. et Pond. is, p. 168, ed. Petav.) says Eleazar chose
six men out of every tribe in order not to create jealousies.   And Irenæus Adv.
Hær. lib. iii. c. 25, ed. Grabe, gives the names of the seventy-two from Aristeas.

[4] Ib. 12, p. 515 ; Philo l.c. p. 659.

[5] Ad Græc. Cohort. p. 13, 14, ed. Col.

[6] Lib. iii. c. 2, p. 174, ed. Breith.

[7] שבעים ושנים seventy-two, Massech. Sopherim, apud Lightf. Opp. ii. p. 934,
ed. fol. Rot.   So also S. Athanas. Syn. S.S. Opp. ii. p. 156, ed. Col., Euseb.
Præp. Ev. lib. viii. p. 354, ed. Col. from Aristeas, and S. Cyril. Hieros. Catech.
iv. p. 36, ed. Morel.

[8] Euseb. Hist. Eccles. lib. v. c. 9, p. 174, ed. Mentz ; and Iren. Adv. Hær.
lib. iii. c. 24, p. 255.   κατὰ διαφόρους οἴκους ἀλλήλων μὴ συνιέντες.   S. Cyril.
Hieros. l.c.

[9] Strom. i. p. 342, ed. Col.

[10] S. Cyril. Hieros. l.c.

[11] Hist. Ante isl. p. 54, sq.

out of every tribe.[1] And Justin Martyr[2] declares that he had
seen τὰ ἴχνη τῶν οἰκίσκων ἐν τῇ Φάρῳ—ἔτι σωζόμενα, the
traces of these cells still preserved in the island of Pharos.
This, however, may but show that he, like many other travellers,
was very simple to believe all he was told; I too, have seen the
place whence was removed through the air the cell which is now
at Loretto !

We are then told that these thirty-six or these seventy-two
translations were all finished in seventy-two days, and that they
agreed wonderfully together, not only ἐν νοήμασιν, ἀλλὰ καὶ ἐν
λέξεσιν,[3] not only in sentiments but also in expressions. The
king was greatly struck and pleased; he then placed a copy in
the library at Alexandria and sent others through Egypt. When
the Alexandrian Library was burnt, Epiphanius tells us that
copies of the Version that had been preserved were then placed
in the Serapeum.

Whatever truth and fable be mixed up with these accounts,
great difference of opinion did exist as to what books were then
translated from the Hebrew into Greek. Josephus tells us
plainly,[4] οὐδὲ γὰρ πᾶσαν ἱκεῖνος ἔφη λαβεῖν τὴν ἀναγραφὴν, ἀλλ'
αὐτὰ μόνα τὰ τοῦ νόμου παρέδοσαν οἱ πεμφθέντες ἐπὶ τὴν ἐξήγησιν εἰς
τὴν Ἀλεξάνδρειαν, "that the king did not succeed in obtaining
the whole copy of Scripture, but the men sent to Alexandria
to translate, only brought him the books of the Law." So that
either these words mean nothing, or it is in vain that Bishop
Walton and others bring to bear upon this what is also true, viz.
that νόμος is also said of the Psalms, of Isaiah and of the Pro-

---

[1] These men were sent to Ptolemy who صيرهم ﺗﺎ وﺛﻠﺜﻴﻦ ﻓﺮﻗﺔ
وﺧﺎﻟﻒ ﺑﻴﻦ اﺳﺒﺎﻃﻬﻢ واﻣﺮﻫﻢ ﻓﺘﺮﺟﻤﻮا ﻟﻪ ﺗﺎ وﺛﻠﺜﻴﻦ ﻧﺴﺨﺔ ﺑﺎﻟﺘﻮراة
divided them into thirty-six pair, classing them according to their tribes, and
commanded them to translate for him thirty-six copies of the Law. (Ibid.)

[2] Cohort. ad Græc. p. 14.

[3] S. Cyril. Hierus. l.c. συνέντευσαν αἱ πᾶσαι ἑρμηνεῖαι συναστιβληθείσαι
—καὶ τὰς διανοίας καὶ τὰς λέξεις, (S. Clem. Al. l.c.) τὰ αὐτὰ ταῖς αὐταῖς λέξεσι,
(Iren. Adv. Hær. l.c.) all this, θείᾳ δυνάμει (Justin M. l.c.) in the same words
and in the same thoughts; a thing that could not have been, says Philo, but that
the translators, as if inspired, prophesied, not every one different things, but all
the same names and the same words, ὥσπερ ὑποβολεὺς ἑκάστοις ἀοράτως ἐπη-
χοῦντος, as if an unseen prompter told everyone of them what to write.

[4] Antiq. lib. i. 3.

phets in general; for here Josephus distinguishes νόμος from πᾶσα ἀναγράφη, by which he does not surely mean the Apocryphal writings; applying νόμος to the Canonical Books.[1] And the internal evidence of which we hear so much for other Books, certainly seems to confirm all this; for the style of the Pentateuch differs much from that of the other Books, and is better than that of most of them, some of which show a later and less exercised hand. Josephus B. Gorion, however, says that the seventy-two elders and priests among which Eleazar himself explained to the king הַתּוֹרָה וְאֵת שְׁאָר סִפְרֵי הַמִּקְרָא כ׳ד the Law and the rest of the twenty-four Books, التوراة وغيرها "the Law and the rest of it," says Abulfeda, l.c. But Epiphanius, l.c., goes beyond these authors, and says that they sent to the King of Egypt from Jerusalem, κβ′ μὲν τὰς ἐνδιαθέτους, ἑβδομήκοντα δύο δὲ τὰς ἀποκρύφους, twenty-two Canonical and seventy-two Apocryphal Books.

This Version, such as it was, was then deposited in the Library in the Bruchium, and after that in the Serapeum. There Origen consulted it, and on it he worked at his Hex or Octapla. Hence too, the Versions of Eusebius and of Lucian, to say nothing of those of Aquila, of Symmachus, of Jericho, and of Neapolis, together with that of Theodotion; all of which have more or less contributed to the Version of the LXX. as we now have it. So corrupt had the text of Origen already grown that Lucian and Hesychius began a recension of it, of which nothing now remains. This Version of Lucian, as S. Athanasius calls it, is the seventh of those he enumerates.[2] Further particulars concerning what use Origen may or may not have made of the Version of Theodotion,—the Eusebian Revision used in Palestine,—S. Jerome's opinion[3] of the work of Origen, and other such questions would be here out of place; suffice it to say that, albeit some MSS. may be more correct than others,

[1] Philo also (l.c. p. 660) mentions only τὸν νόμον and τὰς γραφάς, as S. Clem. Al. also does; and he speaks of three translators as prophets and as hierophants, οἳ ἐξηγοῦντο συνδραμεῖν λογισμοῖς εἰλικρινέσι τῷ Μωσέως καθαρωτάτῳ πνεύματι, "to whom it was granted to seize and to render in the truest terms the real spirit of Moses," without allusion to other portions of Scripture.

[2] In Synops. S.S. Opp. vol. ii. pp. 156, 157.

[3] Ap. Hartlinæ, in Origen. Opp. vol. i. p. 254—263.

as e.g. that of the Vatican reprinted in Bishop Walton's Polyglot, yet so uncertain is the text of the LXX., so many are the discrepancies, and so great is the mixture and the confusion in it that De Wette[1] says the criticism on the LXX. can be brought no farther than the collecting of various readings; and that not one of the editions yet published, gives a text either pure or trustworthy.[2] L. Bos, than whom few men have been better judges in the matter, enumerates the real uses of the Septuagint, saying:

"Magnam etiamnum habet utilitatem Versio Græca: nam primo multa facit ad Novum Fœdus recte intelligendum—secundo magnum hodieque usum habet Versio Græca ad indagandum verum Sp. S. sensum in codice Hebræo," &c.—"At verò cavendum etiam, ne nimium hanc Versionem extollamus, et plusquam par est, ei fidamus: ne æquiparemus eam veritati Hebraicæ, nedum præponamus. CONFERRE EAM OPORTET CODICI HEBRÆO, NON PRÆFERRE."[3]

---

[1] Einleit. l.c.

[2] While L. Bos, (Proleg. in ed. LXX. Franeq. 1709, 4to.) says: "Confectam esse Versionis hujus partem nullus dubito primis Ptolemæi Philadelphi annis—ejus sive jussu, sive potius sponte sua sacros Libros ex lingua Hebraica in Græcam converterunt Judæi Alexandrini, qui Græcè sciebant. Nequaquam ad illorum accedo sententiam, qui Aristeæ Historiam veram esse agnoscunt.—Falsos autem Alexandrinos Interpretes illos, ex dialecto colligi potest, neque fuerunt illi homines divino numine afflati;—non etiam tot homines, quot vulgo feruntur, nimirum LXX. vel LXXII. hoc opus aggressi falsos videntur; sed pauciores numero, et forsan uti ego quidem existimo, quinque tantùm.—Atque hi homines non transtulerunt omnes libros sacros, quod multi opinantur, sed Pentateuchum solum.—Quod ad reliquos libros attinet, illi deinceps sunt translati, non simul eodemque tempore, neque ab uno, sed a diversis hominibus, diversisque temporibus.—Librum Josuæ serius et quidem post Ptol. Euergetæ Junioris translatum fuisse colligit Doctissimus Hodius ex vocabulo γαῖσος, quod occurrit c. viii.—Diversam a Pentateuchi stilo esse stilum librorum Judicum, Ruthæ et Regum variis exemplis demonstrare possum.—Qui Paralipomena transtulit, rursus alius fuisse videtur Interpres.—Eodem modo se res habet cum versione Esræ et Nehemiæ—Esthera liber conversus fuit in linguam Græcam non Ptol. Philad. tempore sed Philometoris, uti observavit eruditissimus Usserius. (De LXX. Interpret. p. 21.) Diversus iterum Interpres Jobi. Is Poetas Græcos legit. (The Greek Version of Job is treated of at length in J. D. Michaelis Einleit. In die gottl. Schriften des A. Bundes, p. 123—129: he says of it, "ganz unebrecklieb Interpolirt," &c.) Qui Psalmos et Proverbia transtulerunt, periti atque diserti fuerunt.—Diversi etiam Interpretes fuere Ecclesiastæ, Cantici, atque Prophetarum.—Quod vero attinet ad Danielis versionem, qua nos hodie utimur, Theodotionis est," &c.

[3] L. Bos, Prolog. c. 1.

Lightfoot also closes his dissertation on the LXX.[1] and on
the value put upon it by the Jews, with affirming that "five"
and not "seventy" were the men who made it; mentioning also
many of the omissions, interpolations, and other defects in the
Greek Version, and he ends with these remarkable words:

"In his quæ dixi de Versione Græca, atque ejus non-lectione
inter Hellenistas, contra-sentientes novi me habere viros doctis-
simos, et olim quidem ipse fui in contraria sententia. Unde
facilius, uti spero, persuadebitur lectori, me non hæc ex studio
contentionis dixisse; sed ex quanta quanta possum acria rei
disquisitione, cogitationibus sæpiùs iteratis, atque intimo desi-
derio investigandæ veritatis."

An opinion thus formed and thus given by so real and so
learned a scholar, shows the true philosopher, the man who is
in earnest about the Truth of his subject; such opinion, therefore, is of greater weight than a random and popular vote of
thanks to these pretended seventy or seventy-two, "benefactors
of Biblical Literature and Free Inquiry."

X. For, one can apply no other term than 'puerile' to
some of the criticism these 'free inquirers' bring to bear on
the Septuagint. For instance, they do not stop to consider that
this Greek Version being made in Egypt, and in Egypt at
Alexandria, most likely by Jews of that place for Jews of that
place also, it is a local Version, that is, a Version which renders
many terms, allusions, &c., in the Hebrew text, in a way to be
understood by residents in Egypt. Neither do these 'free
inquirers' trouble themselves to look at the map, to see that Palestine and Egypt lying at right angles to each other, and therefore very differently as regards both the Red and the Mediterranean Seas, are each liable to physical and to meteorological
phænomena of wind, rain, &c., which differ almost toto cælo in
each country; as I have found, not only by my own experience,
but by the still higher authorities of Cl. Ptolemy's meteorological
calendar for Alexandria and for Lower Egypt,[2] and from a series
of Observations made by the French Expedition at Cairo in
1800, 1801, and given in their work on Egypt.[3]

[1] Opp. vol. ii. pp. 929—940, fol.
[2] φάσεις ἀπλανῶν, ed. Halma, vol. iii. p. 47, sq.
[3] Descript. de l'Eg. vol. ii. p. 322, sq.

Thus, reasoning *a priori*, we find, what is actually the fact, that in Palestine, the two principal currents of air are easterly and westerly, owing to the situation of the land as regards the sea on the one hand, and the deserts of Arabia on the other; and that in Egypt, these two principal currents of air are from the same causes, northerly and southerly. As I have already treated this subject with some detail,[1] and as I shall have to recur to it when I refute one of Dr. Stanley's expressions respecting the passage of the Red Sea, I will at present only mention that—

First—Whereas, from physical causes, the רוּחַ קָדִים 'east wind' in Palestine, is the most violent and fearful in its effects on animals and on vegetation, that same east wind in Egypt, being checked and cooled by its passage over the Red Sea, is نافِع "wholesome and favourable," as Abdollatif tells us.[2]

Secondly—That from physical causes also, the effects peculiar to the east wind in Palestine belong in Egypt exclusively to the southerly winds.

Thirdly—That, whereas the term יָם, ιοτᴀᴧᴧ, ιοᴛᴧ, is said both in Palestine and in Egypt of any local sea, lake, or river, yet, that when said absolutely with regard to Palestine in general, יָם is הַיָּם הַגָּדוֹל "the Great Sea," or the Mediterranean, Ezek. xlvii. 20, &c., and is used for "west," Josh. xi. 3, &c. But in Egypt "the sea," ἡ θάλασσα,[3] is the "north sea," ἡ βορηίη θαλάσσης,[4] "the Great Sea."[5] And the same local definitions obtain there at the present day; البحر "the Sea" is بحر الرُّوم "the Sea of Roum" or Europe; بحري "maritime" is used for "north," as نِبلي "fronting," i.q. קָדִים in Palestine, is used for "south."[6]

The Alexandrian translators living in a country so differently

[1] Vindication of the Auth. Vers. pt. i. p. 96, sq.

[2] Æg. p. 11, ed. Wh.   [3] Scyl. Per. p. 61, ed. Müll.

[4] Herod. ii. 159, &c.

[5] ⲟⲩⲁⲝ-ⲟⲩⲉⲣ as e.g. in ⳨ⲁ-ⲛⳠ-ⲟⲩ ⲛ̄ϯ ⲅ̄ⲣ ⲥⲏⲧ ⲟⲩⲁⲝ-ⲟⲩⲉⲣ ⲡ ⲉ̄ⲗⲗ ⲗⲗⲏⲛⲧ (ⲛ-ⲧⳤ-ⲛ̄) ⲁⲕ ⲛ̄ϯ ⲡ ⲡ̄ⲛ̄-ϥ ⲡⲁⲕϯ
"the Greeks that (dwell) on the border of the Great Sea (or Great Water-basin!) on the western side of the Saitic nome; the name of which (place) is Raketi (Alexandria.)" (Brugsch Geog. Denkm. i. p. 40, and pl. v. 262.)

[6] Khalîl Dhaher. in De Sacy, Chrest. Ar. p. 70, sq., &c.

situated from that whose Books they were translating εἰς τὴν κοινὴν διάλεκτον, into the vulgar tongue, and so as to become, as Philo says, κοινωφελής of common use, were obliged to translate so as to be understood of those for whom they wrote. They, therefore, very properly, rendered יָם by δυσμή, δυσμαί, where it means "west," said absolutely: had they rendered it by θάλασσα it would have meant "north," said absolutely. Likewise, when translating from the Hebrew the effects of the קָדִים "east wind," they were obliged, in order to make sense in the Greek of Alexandria, to render that term by νότος; and the effects of the קָדִים by those of the νότος, as βίαιος, καύσων, &c. In this case, they, living at Alexandria could no more render קָדִים "east" and "east wind" by ἀπηλιώτης or ἀνατολή, than they could have rendered יָם when meaning "west," by θάλασσα, which, in Egypt, means "north." Free inquirers, however, are not restrained even by the points of the compass; and, therefore, take no account of these local details. But they argue that since "east" in Hebrew is rendered "south" at Alexandria, it therefore means "south" and not "east;" and they afford us the amusing sight of a Professor (V. Bohlen) teaching "that the wind that cleft the waters of the Red Sea must have been a south wind," and his pupil, a writer in the Journal of Sacred Literature, maintaining that it was a "north wind;" because neither will have it as the Hebrew gives it, "east." When, however, any sober-minded and real scholar finds קָדִים "east," predicated of צָפוֹן "north," תֵּימָן "south," or עֶרֶב "west," then will קָדִים lose the sense of "east" which is inherent in it; and the רוּחַ קָדִים "east wind" may then blow from north to south.

Sound criticism and common sense, therefore, grant to the LXX. no more authority than it deserves. As to the Canonical Books, no scholar will set aside the Hebrew text for the Greek Version; and as regards the Apocrypha, wherein the chief authority of the LXX. consists, S. Cyril of Jerusalem warns his catechists, saying: "μοὶ μηδὶν τῶν ἀποκρύφων ἀναγίνωσκε, read me naught of the Apocrypha; for, why should he who ignores the Books received by all, disquiet himself in vain concerning those that are doubtful? ἀναγίνωσκε τὰς θείας γραφὰς, τὰς εἴκοσι δύο βίβλους τῆς παλαιᾶς διαθήκης τὰς ὑπὸ τῶν οβ´ ἑρμηνευτῶν ἑρμηνευθείσας, but read the Holy Scriptures, the twenty-two books of the Old Testament, translated by the seventy-two Interpreters, καὶ ταύτας μόνας μελίτα, and meditate on these only."[1]

For, the degree of authority granted to the Septuagint, from the fact of our LORD having, perhaps, and His Apostles having certainly, quoted from it, amounts to very little after all. Their quoting from the Septuagint sanctioned it, first—only as being the one Version generally available; that is, they sanctioned *the use of a Version from the original*, the main point, to which I shall presently return. Secondly, in quoting the LXX. they sanctioned only the passages they quoted; for, to argue, that their quoting certain passages sanctions the whole Version and all the things contained therein, is very much like saying—I have picked this ripe pear off that tree, therefore all the rest are ripe—a kind of argument which not only shows little philosophy, but which refutes itself.

As to our SAVIOUR quoting the Septuagint—the place brought forward as an example S. Luke iv. 17, 18, is by no means conclusive. For S. Luke might himself give the quotation from the LXX. as his wont was, he not being a Jew. Nay, it is far more likely that the Lesson was then read by our LORD in Hebrew; for had it been in Greek "the eyes of all" would not have been "fastened on Him," except in astonishment at what He could mean; inasmuch as Justin Martyr tells us[2] plainly, that the LXX. πανταχοῦ παρὰ πᾶσίν εἰσιν Ἰουδαίοις, οἳ καὶ ἀναγινώσκοντες οὐ συνίασιν τὰ εἰρημένα, "is everywhere among the Jews, who, however, do not understand what is said therein." Neither is it reasonable to suppose that the Jews then showed less respect for the Hebrew text of the Law than they do at present, when in every little synagogue they read it in Hebrew; albeit not ten persons present, perhaps, can understand what is read, until it is explained in the vulgar tongue. Hence the origin of the Targums in former times. For as to the boasted passage from the Talmud Hier. Lib. Sota c. 7, given by Buxtorf,[3] of R. Levi having heard them in the synagogue of Cæsarea, reading in

---

[1] S. Cyril. Hier. Catech. iv.   [2] Pro Christ. Apol. p. 72.
[1] Lex. Chald. p. 104, s.v. תרגם.

Greek the Lesson out of Deut. vi., Lightfoot[1] proves that it was not 'reading' but 'reciting ;' and not out of the Book of the Law, but that it was said only "de recitatione periocharum phylactericarum."[2] Nay, we dare not press the point of our SAVIOUR's quotations from the Septuagint, lest we make Him out far less accurate than His Apostle. For instance, He is said at S. Matt. xvi. 27, to have quoted καὶ τότε ἀποδώσει ἑκάστῳ κατὰ τὴν πρᾶξιν αὐτοῦ. either from Ps. lxii. 13, ὅτι σὺ ἀποδώσεις ἑκάστῳ κατὰ τὰ ἔργα αὐτοῦ ; or from Prov. xxiv. 12, ὃς ἀποδίδωσιν ἑκάστῳ κατὰ τὰ ἔργα αὐτοῦ, which S. Paul quotes far more correctly thus : ὃς ἀποδώσει ἑκάστῳ κατὰ τὰ ἔργα αὐτοῦ. Rom. ii. 6.

Of course, we cannot for a moment suppose that this has reference to Sir. xxxv. 21, ἕως ἀνταποδῷ ἀνθρώπῳ κατὰ τὰς πράξεις αὐτοῦ ; we may rather perhaps, infer from this pretended quotation in S. Matt. that it is no quotation at all. For we have in Ps. lxii. 13, כְּמַעֲשֵׂהוּ and in Prov. xxiv. 12, כְּפָעֳלוֹ both sing. and in the LXX. κατὰ τὰ ἔργα, both pl.; yet ἔργον might have been used in the sing. ; for although it somewhat differs in idiom from τὰ ἔργα, as does ' a man's work' from 'a man's works ;' yet this difference is far from being always observed in the LXX.: and the pl. כְּמַעֲשָׂיו would have been quite as idiomatic as the singular. But פָּעַל which is used chiefly in poetic style, differs nearly as much from עָשָׂה as πράττειν does from ποιεῖν. Such a passage as מִי פָעַל וְעָשָׂה[3] shows the difference, and shows that פָּעַל in Prov. xxiv. 12, is better rendered through πρᾶξις,—περὶ μὲν οὖν πρᾶξιν καὶ τὰ πρακτὰ ἡ φρόνησις, περὶ δὲ τὴν ποίησιν καὶ τὰ ποιητὰ ἡ τέχνη.[4]—compared with בַּעֲשֹׂת צְדָקָה לַיְהֹוָה[5] wherein we see clearly that πράξεως μὲν οὖν ἀρχὴ προαίρεσις'—διὸ οὔτ' ἄνευ νοῦ καὶ διανοίας οὔτ' ἄνευ ἠθικῆς ἐστὶν ἕξεως ἡ προαίρεσις'—ἡ γὰρ εὐπραξία τέλος, ἦ δ' ὄρεξις τούτου.[6] Whence we may safely conclude that our SAVIOUR's words are not a quotation from the Sep-

---

[1] Opp. vol. ii. p. 397.

[2] And as Selden farther says: "Nimirum erant formulae sacrae quibus ex Ebraeorum scitis uti licuit etiam lingua qualicunque utenti nota, veluti Adjuratio Uxoris suspectae, Preces, Benedictio mensae, &c. Sed vero dubitari nequit, lectionem illam ezadi του in Gemara ac sic memoratam, ac Hellenisticam dictam, ipsam fuisse Graecam Deuteronomii Versionem," &c. (J. Seld. Comm. in Eutych. Pat. Alexandrini Orig. Eccl. p. 162.)

[3] Isa. xli. 4.   [4] Eth. Magn. l. 35, 9.
[5] Prov. x. 16.   [6] Eth. Nicom. vi. 2, 4.

tuagint; but whether they be His or S. Matthew's, they are an exact translation—לְאִישׁ being well rendered ἑκάστῳ,—of the Hebrew of Prov. xxiv. 12; and far more correct than either of the other renderings of the Septuagint.

So much is made of these, so called, quotations from the LXX., said to be found in the New Testament, that a little cool reasoning on the subject may not be here out of place. In fact, most of these said quotations bear about as much resemblance to the passages from which they are said to be taken, as e.g. this expression in Shakspeare:

" Be wary; best safety lies in fear;"[1]

bears to, " Happy is the man that feareth alway;"[2] or as—

" Give every man thine ear, but few thy voice,"[3]

bears to, " Let every man be swift to hear, slow to speak;"[4] or, again, as—

" This spirit dumb to me, will speak to him,"[5]

bears to, " if a spirit or an angel hath spoken to him,"[6] &c., not one of which can be called a quotation from the words of Scripture. Yet this, and worse than this, is done with regard to the LXX. We are gravely told e.g. that, μὴ ἰδεῖν θάνατον, S. Luke ii. 26, Heb. xi. 5, is a quotation from τίς ἐστιν ἄνθρωπος ὃς ζήσεται καὶ οὐκ ὄψεται θάνατον;[7] whereas they both are Hebraisms, to which Philo[8] alludes when speaking of the use of ἰδεῖν in Holy Scripture; λέγεται γὰρ ὅτι πᾶς ὁ λαὸς ἑώρα τὴν φωνήν, οὐκ ἤκουϊν, et sq. Likewise, πορεύου εἰς εἰρήνην, S. Luke vii. 50, is said to be quoted from 1 Sam. xx. 42; but this too is the Hebrew idiom, לֵךְ לְשָׁלוֹם; so also ἐλέησόν με Κύριε υἱὲ Δαβίδ, S. Matt. xv. 22, is another such quotation from Ps. vi. 3, חָנֵּנִי יְהֹוָה ἐλέησόν με Κύριε. So, again, κατευθύναι τοὺς πόδας ἡμῶν εἰς ὁδὸν εἰρήνης, S. Luke i. 79, is said to be taken from καὶ ὁδὸν εἰρήνης οὐκ οἴδασι, Isa. lix. 8; εἰρήνη ὑμῖν, from Judg. vi. 23, which is the Hebrew שָׁלוֹם לְךָ; forgetting that—if these and other like expressions given by the Evangelists be called ' quotations,' that is, the very words spoken by those of whom they

[1] Hamlet, act i. sc. 3.
[2] Hamlet, ib.
[3] Hamlet, ib.
[4] Ps. lxxxix. 47.
[5] Prov. xxviii. 14.
[6] S. James i. 19.
[7] Acts xxiii. 9.
[8] De Migr. Abr. p. 395.

are told, and not a translation of their words into Greek, then
both our Saviour, the Syrophenician woman,[1] the blind beg-
gars,[2] blind Bartimeus,[3] Thomas,[4] the man possessed of the
devils,[5] our Saviour to His mother,[6] the lepers to Him,[7] the
rich man to Abraham,[8] must all have spoken Greek, and that
too, quoting the Septuagint; an assertion, I trow, few will
venture to make.   Nay, even Herod addressing the daughter of
Philip,[9] must have remembered exactly the words of Ahasuerus
to Esther, as given in Esth. v. 3; the angel coming in to
Mary,[10] is made to repeat the words said by the angel to
Gideon;[11] and both are also made to speak Greek.   This
system of quotation, that would hold good in no other case, and
which also cannot hold good in this, makes the oddest compari-
sons, as e.g. between the mustard-tree,[12] and the tree mentioned
in Daniel iv. 9, "that reached unto heaven;" the parable of the
vineyard[13] is also thus taken from Isa. v. 1, 2 ; the final gathering of God's elect mentioned in S. Matt. xxiv. 31, is made to
refer exclusively to the Jews;[14] the battle of Armageddon which
is yet to be fought[15] is thus made to be either the battle of
Megiddo lost by Josiah[16] or the other won there by Barak nearly
seven hundred years before ; ἐν ἀρχῇ ἦν ὁ λόγος[17] is derived from
τῷ λόγῳ τοῦ Κυρίου οἱ οὐρανοὶ ἐστερεώθησαν ;[18] yea, even our Lord's
Prayer is made to be partly taken from David's thanksgiving for
the offerings to the temple.[19]

But, in all this there is neither scholarship, philosophy, nor
sound criticism.   On the other hand, common sense tells us that
men speaking and writing in the same language, and on the
same subject, which they all draw from the same source, must
of necessity often agree in thought and in word.   Accordingly,
we find that the Apostles and the Evangelists having to preach

[1] S. Matt. xv. 22.
[2] S. Mark x. 47 ; S. Luke xviii. 38.
[3] S. Matt. viii. 29 ; S. Mark v. 7 ; S. Luke viii. 28.
[7] S. Luke xvii. 13.
[9] S. Mark vi. 22, 23.
[11] Judg. vi. 12.
[12] S. Matt. xxi. 33.
[15] Rev. xvi. 16.
[17] S. John i. 1.
[19] 1 Chron. xxix. 10—13.

[8] S. Matt. xx. 30.
[4] S. John xx. 28.
[5] S. John ii. 4.
[9] S. Luke xvi. 24.
[10] S. Luke i. 28.
[13] S. Matt. xiii. 33.
[14] Deut. xxi. 4.
[16] 2 Chron. xxxv. 22.
[19] Ps. xxxiii. 6.

and to write in the same language as that of the LXX., and
having to refer not only to the same original of which the LXX.
is but a translation, but also to treat of the same subjects, it
is impossible that they should not make use of some of the
same expressions as the LXX., be they Hebraisms, idioms, turns
of phrase, &c.; all of which may be more or less modified according to the character or to the birthplace of the writer. And
this is precisely what happens. We find e.g. that S. Matthew
who was of Galilee, is more Hebrew in his Greek—I pass by the
question of a Hebrew original of his Gospel, for the present—
than S. Luke who, most likely, was not a Jew. Thus S. Matthew gives quite correctly, according to the Hebrew and to the
LXX. οὐ φονεύσεις, לֹא תִּרְצָח &c., οὐ μοιχεύσεις, οὐ κλέψεις,[1]
whereas S. Mark and S. Luke give μὴ φονεύσῃς, μὴ μοιχεύσῃς,
&c., which agree neither with the Hebrew nor with the LXX.;
but which are, perhaps, more common Greek.

If, therefore, we understand by 'quotations from the LXX.'
that which alone can be called such, viz. the exact repetition of
the words given, we shall find that real quotations from the
LXX. to be found in the four Gospels are very few. Out of
one hundred-and-four such quotations which I have carefully
examined, I have found only thirty-six literal. Of these, twenty-
seven need not be quotations, but may be looked upon as translations from the Hebrew, which could not be rendered otherwise
either by the LXX. or by the Evangelists; so that these twenty-
seven quotations prove nothing. There remain nine concerning
which I will not now do more than say that, in general, S. Luke
quotes less fully than S. Matthew, who sometimes differs from
the Septuagint, but agrees with the Hebrew, as e.g. in ch. ii. 15,
where he read לְבָנִי; and not with the LXX. לְבָנָיו τὰ τέκνα
αὐτοῦ; whereas S. Luke keeps to the LXX. in ch. iv. 17—19,
where he gives καὶ τυφλοῖς ἀνάβλεψιν, which is not found in the
Hebrew.

So that when we look at things as they are, we fail to discover
wherein lies much of this vaunted excellence of the LXX. as
"a treasury of Biblical criticism." For, as to its having been
read habitually in the synagogues of Palestine, like the question

----

[1] Ch. xix. 18, and v. 21.

of our SAVIOUR's usually speaking Greek, I can only refer the
reader to Mr. Rogers' work,[1] where he will find reasons ' why ;'
and then to the work of Salmasius, one of the greatest scholars
the world ever saw,[2] for reasons ' why not ;' with which, I own,
I most agree.

All these questions of authenticity, interpolation, recension,
corruption, &c., as regards the LXX.,—questions, too, which will
never be set at rest,—show plainly that the main point, the main
object of the Greek Vulgate, is independent of them.   With all
these imperfections, that Version did much good at the time, and
is yet doing much good where it is used.   What, then, was the
object for which it was allowed to be made at the time?

Whatever might have been the King of Egypt's intention,
whether it was to enrich his national library, or to make himself acquainted with the laws of the Jews, who were living in
great numbers in his dominions,—or whether this Version was
made for the Hellenistic Jews, or, as it appears, for the Gentile
world in general,—matters not.   It was then made by the will
of GOD, in order that the Scriptures, which until that time were
known only " μόνῳ τῷ βαρβαρικῷ γίνει to a race called ' barbarian' by the Greeks," as Philo says,[3] should thenceforward
become κοινωφελής, of common use: thus "gratiâ Dei inter-
pretatæ sunt Scripturæ priùs quam Dominus noster descenderet,
et antequam Christiani ostenderentur,"[4] and so as to prepare
the world for His coming.   The translation of the, then, only
Revealed Truth, from the sealed volumes of the Hebrew Canon,
into a language spoken wherever civilisation did reach, and the
publication through such means of prophecies then known only
of the nation to which they had been delivered, was virtually
for the heathen world the dawn of day, that glimmered immediately before the rising of Him Who is the True Light.   No
wonder, then, if He was expected when He did come; if even
oracles would no longer speak, awaiting the appearing of Him
Who is the Way the wise of this world could not find, the Truth
they sought in vain, and the Life they yearned after, without
ever obtaining a sure and certain hope of it.   Therefore, con-

[1] Dissertations on the Gospels, London, 1862.
[2] Funus Hellenisticæ L.
[3] De V. Mos. p. 658.   [4] Iren. Adv. Hær. Lib. iii. c. 26.

sidering the place this Version occupied, it was in a certain sense the "door unto Christ," as S. Chrysostom says,[1] εἰκότως δὲ θύραν τὰς γραφὰς ἐκάλεσεν, for those who could read the Old Testament in no other tongue. And this being done through a Version from the original, sanctioned for ever the use of translations in the preaching of the Gospel; and by so doing, taught a practical lesson on the subject of Inspiration, which we shall consider elsewhere more fully.

Taken, then, at its due worth, and used intelligently, the Septuagint—although no "bulwark against too rigid or literal a construction of the Sacred History," since it can have no absolute authority as a last appeal in difficult or in doubtful questions with a real scholar, who, of course, would never dream of leaving the Hebrew text for the Greek, yet—is valuable as a help for the criticism of the Canonical Books of the Old Testament. On such terms—but on such only—may we accept, even gratefully, the services of this Egyptian bondmaid to her Hebrew mistress—the Hebrew Scriptures—that must ever remain the original and the literal text of the Old Testament.

XI. Dean Stanley then mentions another class of authorities for Sacred History—"heathen traditions," which he very properly does not seem to overrate; although we must always, with him, recognise with pleasure in heathen writers any allusion, be it ever so faint, to the Sacred Narrative. In this respect heathen traditions are of greater interest, as appearing, as it were, at a greater distance from the people of God than the legends told in Rabbinical or in Mohammedan writings. Even these, however, oftentimes deserve some notice on account of their very absurdity; but authority they can have none, not even though they bear on the history of an "inspired people." This is, again, one of the 'happy expressions' the Dean of Westminster so much likes, but which, it must be owned, is far from being as clear or as clever as it seems to him.

XII. Many will, I doubt not, agree with me that it must at least be difficult to see wherein lay the 'inspiration' of a people that murmured against God, that disobeyed Him, so that Moses exclaimed, "Would God that all the Lord's people were prophets, and that the Lord would put His Spirit upon

[1] Hom. lviii. in S. John, p. 324, ed. Migne.

them!"[1] that served Baal and Ashtaroth, until only one prophet
was left to the seven thousand men who had not bowed the
knee to those idols; and a people that brought down upon
themselves well-merited judgments for their wickedness. But
we may perfectly understand that being a 'chosen people,' they
were, even during their waywardness, the object of God's especial care, shown in many ways, but chiefly in His raising among
them from time to time 'inspired men,' as speaking witnesses
to His rule, and as heralds of His coming judgments.

XIII. Dr. Stanley next (p. xxxvii.) raises the interesting
question of Eastern traditions relating to the Jewish people, and
how far some of them have "a substantial existence of their
own," independently of the Coran and of the Old Testament.
Such a question can be fully answered only by one who, like
Burkhardt, would spend the better part of his life among the
wild tribes of Arabia, from Yemen to Tadmor and Damascus,
and converse freely with them; then comparing the oral lore
thus acquired with the Targums, the Talmud Babylonicum, and
other ancient Rabbinical works, and then with the Coran, in
order to see whence Mahomet derived his knowledge of facts
not mentioned in Holy Scripture. We find, indeed, both in
the Coran and in the writings of Ash-sharestáni, Abu'l-feda,
Abu'l-faraj, Es-soyuti, Abi'l-sorur, and others, accounts of the
idols worshipped by the Arabs during what they call الحال
الجاهلية "the time of their ignorance," i.e., before Islamism.
Some of those idols had names as nearly connected with a
Hebrew origin as others mentioned by Sanchoniaton in his
Phœnician history; such as the goddess Allat, اللات, Οὐρανίη
Ἀλιλάτ;[2] مناة, מני, Meni, Μήν; هبل, הבל, Hobal, ὁ βήλ;
نسر, Nasr, Nisroc, &c.[3] Some of those idolaters, says Abu'l-faraj,
يقول بالمعاد, even talked of (i.e., believed in) the resurrection or
'return;' a statement repeated by Chrysanthus, Patriarch of
Jerusalem,[4] who renders معاد 'return,' by قيامة 'resurrection.'
This sounds very much like an echo of the Patriarchal Creed,

---

[1] Numb. xi. 29.   [2] Herod. iii. 8.
[3] Pococki Spec. Hist. Ar. p. 4 and 95, sq.
[4] In his treatise on Religions, ed. Beirut. p. 7.

"I know that my Redeemer liveth, and that He shall stand at the latter day upon the earth; and though after my skin, worms destroy this body, yet in my flesh shall I see GOD, Whom I shall see for myself, and mine eyes shall behold, and not another,"—especially when brought from the land of عوض 'Awas, or Us, from the dwellings of his children the Adites, to whom هود Hûd (Heber) was sent as prophet.[1]

Yet we ought to receive such statements very cautiously; for both Abu'l-faraj, and after him the Patriarch Chrysanthus, borrowed their information most likely from certain verses preserved by Al-Kaxwîni,[2] found engraved on ancient ruins in Hadramaut, in the neighbourhood of Aden,[3] wherein we read[4]

يقيم لنا من دين هود شرايعاً
ويؤمن بالايات والبعث والنشر

"Our kings," say the Adites, "establish for us sacred laws after the religion of Hûd, and we believe in signs, and (in) the Resurrection, and (in) the Life." But, in the original Hymiarite inscription found in 1834 at Hian Ghorâb, not a word is said of all this, added, no doubt, by the Arabic translator who engraved the Arabic inscription, in accordance with the Arabic traditions found in the Coran,[5] according to Mr. G. Hunt,[6] who reads, (p. 4):

"As to us, we coerce the abandoned, the seditious, and the slothful, but we strongly love the orderly and the steady. And the base we stigmatise.

"Our strong camels fit for travelling sweep on proudly and are lean [i.e., hardy]. And the bow-twang sounds sharply, and the sword-clash is frequent. And the smart [soldier] is made welcome, but the disapproved—"

Verses thus interpreted by Mr. Forster:[7]

"Over us presided kings far removed from baseness, and

---

[1] Abu'l-feda. Hist. Ante Isl. p. 16 and 18.

[2] Vol. II. p. 43, ed. Wust. and afterwards reprinted by A. Schultens in his Monum. Vetust. Arabia, Lugd. Bat. 1740, p. 67, sq.

[3] Forster, Geog. Arab. vol. II. pp. 81—106; and 351—408.

[4] V. 7, Al-Kazw. and A. Schult.

[5] As, e.g., Sur. xliii. 34, sq.; xxvi. 122, sq.; xlvi. 23, sq., &c.

[6] Hymiaric Inscr. Plymouth, 1848.

[7] Geog. Ar. vol. II. p. 350.

stern chastisers of reprobate and wicked men, and they noted
down for us according to the doctrine of Húd,

"Good judgments written in a book to be kept, and we believed in the miracle-mystery, in the resurrection-mystery, in
the nostril-mystery."

Both these renderings cannot, of course, be right. Mr. G.
Hunt commends his reading by his greater exactitude and his
better knowledge of Arabic; but he is radically wrong in taking
no account of the small rings that separate the words, after the
true Ethiopic and Abyssinian fashion,—a fashion akin to that
of the Samaritans, and of the Assyrian inscriptions; thereby
making words according to his own notion. Mr. Forster is
right in observing the division of words recorded on the inscription; but his reading is so unscholarlike, so arbitrary, and
so fanciful, that one can place no confidence in it.[1]

XIV. Yet, however interesting be such dim, uncertain remnants of olden memories of GOD's people, cherished among the
sons of the East, they are but faint echoes, after all, of the history of that people whose "influence irrespective of the Scriptures," and outside the Covenant, must be compared to the
indistinct sound of voices in which men outside a building can
catch but a few words. It is not likely that a nation, called
from all the rest and set apart, if not cut off from them by peculiar ordinances—νόμιμα—πολὺ τὸ παρηλλαγμένον—πρὸς τὰ τῶν
ἄλλων ἀνθρώπων,[2] that were held "instituta sinistra, fœda, quæ
pravitate valuere;"[3] of all nations, μόνους—ἀκοινωνήτους εἶναι τῆς
πρὸς ἄλλο ἔθνος ἐπιμιξίας, the only one that would not mix with
any other, παραδόσιμον ποιοῦν τὸ μῖσος τὸ πρὸς τοὺς ἀνθρώπους, and
that handed down hatred for men as an inheritance to her chil-
ren,[4] "adversus omnes alios hostile odium;"[5] a nation whose

---

[1] In these two lines he reads arbitrarily ﻝ for ﻭ, or takes no account of either;
ﻙ for ﺯ ﺥ for ﺱ, ﻭ for ﻱ and ﻱ for ﺍ ﺭﺕ for ﻱ and ﻱ for ﺏ and ﺹ
omits ﺍﻥ reads ﻭ for ﺯ; omits ﻱ, omits two letters in a word of five;
inserts ﻙ where it is not; reads ﻱ for ﺭ, and reads ﺥ for ﻱ or ﻙ.
I have not Rödiger's work on these inscriptions; and I regret I cannot speak
of them with more certainty; but in order to work on them I should require
a trustworthy copy of them, and books of reference which I have not.

[2] Diod. Sic. Fragm. in Stroth. Ægypt. II. p. 35.

[3] Tacit. Hist. v. 5.   [4] Diod. Sic. ibid. p. 369.   [5] Tacit. ibid.

Acropolis (Jerusalem) was saved from being looked upon, ὡς τυραννίον, as a seat of tyrants, ἀλλ' ὡς ἱερόν, but was looked upon as a sanctuary only by the honour in which it was held; since their institutions were said to be τῶν τυραννίδων τὰ λῃστήρια, "the robberies of tyrants," some of whom, ἱκάνουν καὶ αὐτὴν (τὴν χώραν) καὶ τὴν γειτνιῶσαν, laid waste their own land as well as that of their neighbours;[1]—it was not likely, in short, that a nation that sank through untold vicissitudes from a short glory to the most abject state of poverty and contempt,

"Judæi, quorum cophinus fœnumque supellex,"[2]

should exercise any but a trifling influence on her neighbours, who were utterly foreign to her commonwealth.

Had we therefore, only the accounts of the Jews left us by Tacitus, Strabo, Diodorus, Justinus, and others, we could not know they were so great a nation, albeit Dr. Stanley thinks we should; nay, we must have had a far more exalted idea of Persia and of Assyria, while the second book of Herodotus on Egypt alone would outshine them all. Neither was it intended that the Jewish people, as a people, should influence much other nations with which it was taught, for a particular purpose and for a certain reason, to have nothing in common. But chosen of God as it was, to be His peculiar people, the visible image and the first beginnings of His Church, of His "family which in heaven and earth is named," God's purpose would not have been answered, neither would the Hebrew people have exercised its rightful influence over those without whom "it should not be made perfect," if its birth, bondage, deliverance, baptism, wanderings, murmurings, punishments, conquest of the Promised Land, and subsequent waywardness, trials and repentance, and overwhelming judgments, which happened to them for ensamples, had not been "written for our admonition, upon whom the ends of the world are come." The Old Testament, therefore, was not written, as it were, by accident, in connexion with the Jewish people; but the writing thereof was as much an integral part—and thus as much a necessary result—of the existence of the Jewish nation as 'the chosen people,' as the

---

[1] Strabo, Lib. xvi. c. 5. 35, sq.   [2] Juv. Sat. III. 14.

Old Covenant made with them was intended to be a harbinger of the New.

XV. As to other writers, such as Josephus, and whatever other collateral histories we may like to read, such as that of Josephus B. Gorion, we may or may not believe them, or part of them, according to their greater or less claims to our belief; for they are entirely independent of the record given in the Bible. To them we may grant belief; to this we owe the allegiance of Faith. I shall elsewhere show the real, practical, and popular difference between belief and Faith; and if I am called, as no doubt I shall be by some, 'old fashioned' for thinking so, Truth, I answer, is also very old fashioned; and by it I will abide.

XVI. "Such are the main authorities," says Dr. Stanley, of the Hebrew text, the Septuagint, Heathen and Eastern traditions, and Josephus.

"In using them for these lectures," says he, "it will sometimes happen that they hardly profess, or can hardly be proved, to contain the statement of the original historical facts to which they relate. But they nevertheless contain the nearest approach which we, at this distance of time, can now make to a representation of those facts. They are the refraction of the history, if not the history itself—the echo of the words, if not the actual words."—p. xl.

Granted, as regards the Septuagint, Josephus, and the traditions; but does Dr. Stanley really mean that the history told in the Hebrew text is only a "refraction of that history" and "the echo of the words," but not the actual words? If such be his sentiments, he cannot assuredly be envied for them. For my part I believe, and I will go on believing, that the history therein told is the history itself, in so far as it was seen good in God's sight that I should know it. Moreover, I also believe that, were I able, I should understand why such and such things, and not others, are told in that history; as well as why thus much of them, and no more, is made known to me. But as regards that history and that Book, to inquire 'why' and 'wherefore' would be sheer folly and arrogance on my part. I therefore abstain from it. I receive that Book as it is given

me, for the Giver's sake; and as I endeavour to study it, I find
that the deeper I go the deeper it is, and that it is far beyond
my understanding.   I cannot say "I have seen the end of all
perfection," but I can say, in sooth, that I have seen the end of
some; since I have read nearly all the writings of Confucius,
Meng-tsze, and of Lao-tsze in their own wonderful tongue, for
it is idle to think one can read a man's thoughts in any translation of his works.   I have sought for wisdom among the
Buddhists of Tibet and of Ceylon, and in the peerless lore of
India and of Aryâna vaêja; Plato, Aristotle, and Cicero are my
friends; yet "I count all these but loss for the excellency of the
knowledge of Jesus Christ my Lord—that I be found in
Him, not having mine own righteousness, but that which is
through the faith of Christ, the righteousness which is of God
by faith."   And I find him as he was said to be, the wisest of
these wise men of old, who owned that—ἡ ἀνθρωπίνη σοφία ὀλίγου
τινὸς ἀξία ἐστὶ καὶ οὐδενός—human wisdom is worth but little,
yea, nothing at all; but also that the Psalmist is yet wiser in
saying, "Thy commandment is exceeding broad."

--- ---

THE PATRIARCHS.

LECTURE I.—THE CALL OF ABRAHAM.

After sowing broadcast over the last page of the Introduction sundry expressions about "errors in chronology," "in
numbers," "contradictions between different narratives," to
which I shall recur in another place, Dean Stanley opens his
first lecture with telling us that "the Jewish Church or nation
has its origin from Moses," but that the Patriarchal age is the
prelude to it.   So that the first event in this period, the migration or call of Abraham, according to whether we look at its
human or at its divine side, "may fitly be treated as the opening of all ecclesiastical history."

So far so good; with this one exception, however, that there
is no 'human' side to Abraham's leaving his native plains for

F

the hills of Canaan, except for such as look at everything
divine and spiritual from a human point of view. Abraham
' migrated,' it is true; but, for a man in his position, for a po-
tentate, as it were, in wealth, in lands, and in very much cattle
among the اهل البلد, the inhabitants of a city of Chaldea,—to
leave all this, taking with him his wife and servants, in order to
go " he knew not whither," would, from a human point of view
only, appear little else than madness.   But Abraham, being
called by GOD, migrated in obedience to that call, by faith in
certain objective Truths then set before him by GOD; and his
obedience to that call, whatever his kinsmen might think of it,
" was imputed unto him for righteousness, and he was called
the friend of GOD."   So that his migration was only the public
act by which he showed his obedience; and thus, by his works,
made his faith perfect.

The 'human and the divine' side of Abraham's migration are
not, therefore, as Dr. Stanley says, " set before us in the Biblical
narrative, as if in unconscious independence of each other,"—a
somewhat flippant way of speaking of it.   For how can this
be, after that " the LORD had said unto Abram, Get thee out of
thy country, and from thy kindred, and from thy father's house,
unto a land that I will show thee ?"[1]   One feels almost hurt at
having to call a Dean's notice to the evident consciousness of
purpose throughout this grand example of GOD's call and of
man's obedience to it; for Terah did not, either by accident or
unconsciously, take Abram from Ur of the Chaldees; neither
did Abram and all he had leave Haran to wander at random
over the boundless plains of Shinar; but he left Ur, and then
Haran and all that he had, in order to ' walk towards' the great
and precious promises which GOD did set before him as objects,
which Abram 'saw' by faith—as he did the day of CHRIST—
and which he reckoned more true than the world in which he
lived, and of more value than all he left behind.

He did so by the will and at the bidding of Him Who said
to him, " I am the LORD thy GOD that brought thee out of Ur
of the Chaldees."[2]   And this was believed among his posterity:
" Thou art the LORD GOD," said Nehemiah,[3] " Who didst choose

---

[1] Gen. xii. 1.   [2] Ib. xv. 7.   [3] Ch. ix. 7.

Abram, and broughtest him forth out of Ur of the Chaldees, and
gavest him the name of Abraham." For, "the GOD of glory
appeared unto our father Abraham when he was in Mesopotamia,
before he dwelt in Charran, and said unto him, Get thee out of
thy country and from thy kindred, and come into the land which
I shall show thee," adds S. Stephen.[1] Not as ' a tradition' according to Dr. Stanley, for if S. Stephen had wished for a tradition he would have chosen one of the traditions generally received in Edessa itself; but he said it, as taught of GOD, in
order to explain and to place beyond doubt that which being
well known of all Abraham's kindred, was taken for granted in
the first mention of Abraham's call from the land of his birth.
For, his origin and his call were known even to the heathen
neighbours of his children; since Achior, the captain of the host
of Holofernes told him that " this people are descended of the
Chaldeans, and they sojourned heretofore in Mesopotamia—many
days; then their GOD commanded them to depart from the
place where they sojourned, and to go into the land of Canaan."[2]

Better, by far, and more straightforward to deny the whole
thing, than to make a history of Abraham of our own. Thus
Dr. Stanley, in order to support his own view of the case quotes
Gen. xii. 5, " And Abraham took Sarai his wife," &c., as part of
what he calls the ' external' or ' human' side of the migration;
whereas this is said of Abraham, and Abraham did it, after what
GOD had said unto him at v. 1, of the same chapter, and in
consequence of that very verse which Dr. Stanley gives as the
opening of the ' divine' side of Abraham's movements; thus, in
fact, taking v. 5, in a ' human,' and v. 1, in a ' divine,' point
of view—but by what authority? and thus himself also showing
unconsciously though it be, that the ' divine' and the ' human'
sides of Abraham's migration are so blended together as to be
inseparable; since he takes of the one in order to prove the
other.

II. Dr. Stanley, therefore, asserts too much when he further
says that—

" there was nothing outwardly to distinguish Abram and his family
from those who had descended from the Caucasian range into the

---

[1] Acts vii. 2, 3.   [2] Judith v. 6, sq.

plains of the South in former times, and who would do so in times
yet to come."

There was this to distinguish them from all other such wandering tribes; (1) the irresistible impulse, ἐνθουσιασμός, of their
chief, who led them, not like other clans or families, to wander
about in search either of pasture for their flocks, or of an abode
for themselves, but, under God's guidance, to a land He had
promised, and which was their hope, the lode-star to direct their
march until they actually came there. And (2) they were distinguished from (other) Caucasian tribes, in that they were
Syrians, אֲרַמִּים Deut. xxvi. 5, Gen. xxiv. 4, sq., xxxi. 20, 24,
and not Chaldees, and that most probably no tribes from what
we may rightly call the Caucasian range, ever found their way
to the plains of the South. For, even if the Chaldees, Chasdim
or Chaldeans from among whom Abraham was called, could be
proved to have been Χαλδαῖοι, οἵτινες τὸ παλαιὸν Χάλυβες ἀπημά-
ζοντο, the Chaldeans which were formerly called Chalybes,[1]—
a very doubtful question—they lived either in southern Colchis,
or, as some of them did, among the hills of Pontus, too far from
the Caucasus to be called "the Caucasian range." For this
range did not extend indefinitely, even unto the northern parts
of India, which were not συνάπτοντα τοῖς Καυκασίοις ὄρεσιν, as
Patroclus, whom Strabo[2] corrects, did think; but the Caucasian
range, properly speaking, is as Strabo tells us,[3] ἔστι δ᾽ ὄρος
τοῦτο ὑπερκείμενον τοῦ πελάγους ἑκατέρου τοῦ τε Ποντικοῦ καὶ τοῦ
Κασπίου, διατειχίζων τὸν ἰσθμὸν τὸν διέργοντα αὐτό, "that Caucasus,
the mountain which overhangs both the Euxine and the Caspian
Seas, stretching across the isthmus that confines it." Strabo
further limits the breadth of this range as he had the length
thereof; and lest we should ascribe to it any of the hills properly belonging to Armenia, or the high table land therein contained, he goes on stating that the spurs or buttresses ἀγκῶνες,
of the Caucasus embrace Iberia, καὶ τοῖς Ἀρμενίων ὄρεσι συνάπ-
τουσι, and join on to the mountains of Armenia; and he adds:
ταῦτα δ᾽ ἐστὶ μέρη τοῦ Ταύρου πάντα, τοῦ ποιοῦντος τὸ νότιον τῆς
Ἀρμενίας πλευρόν, κ.τ.λ. "these are all parts of the Taurus, that

[1] Strabo, lib. xii. c. iii. 18, 19, 28.   [2] Lib. ii. 2.

[3] Lib. xi. 15.

forms the southern side of Armenia, as it were somewhat detached northwards and stretching on towards the Caucasus and
to the shore of the Euxine."

III. But since so much is made of tradition, we may adopt
one respecting the original land of the Chaldees that recom-
mends itself by its probability, and that is followed by the Targum of Onkelos and by other Chaldean authorities. We read
there[1] that the ark rested עַל טוּרֵי קַרְדּוּ "on the mountains of
Cardu;[2] Τοῦ δὲ πλοίου τούτου καταπλεύσαντος ἐν τῇ Ἀρμενίᾳ, says
Berosus, ἔτι μέρος τι (αὐτοῦ) ἐν τοῖς Κορδυαίων ὄρεσι τοῖς Ἀρμενίας
διαμένει—"that ship having rested in Armenia, a portion of it
is said to be still remaining on the Corduæan mountains of
Armenia."[3] "These mountains," says Indjidjean in his Armenian Antiquities,[4] "are like a belt, and compass the land of
Armenia as it were on four sides reaching even unto Mount
Masis, on which, according to the Armenian tradition, the ark
did rest; so that, Arab authors, who, unable to pronounce accurately the word 'Gortus,' call these hills Djûdi, may yet
mean Mount Masis," (Mount Ararat,) &c. The Armenian,
however, makes a mistake; for these hills are called قردى
Cardü in the version of Saadias, and جبل القرون Djebel el-Carûd,
Mount Carûd in the version published by Erpenius; Arabs also
say كرد pl. اكراد Curd, pl. Acrâd.[5] This range of mountains

[1] In Gen. viii. 4.

[2] ܩܪܕܘ ܒܛܘܪܝ Pesch. and S. Ephr. in Gen. viii. Opp. L. p. 53 and 153.
"The ark," says the Mendæan writer of the Lib. Adami, iii. 72, "descended
ܩܪܕܘ ܕܛܘܪܝ ܥܠ upon the mountains of Cardon, and rested there." And
the names of these mountains according to the Targ. B. Uzziel, are קרדו
Cardonia and ארמיניא, Irminya.

[3] Berosus, ed. Richt. p. 58; Georg. Syncell. Chronogr. p. 53, ed. Dind.
These mountains are called Καρδούχια ὄρη, (Xen. Anab. iv. 1, 2), "Carduchi
quondam dicti, nunc Corduæni," (Plin. N. H. lib. vi. 17 ;) որք են կորդուացւոց
"which is Cardu," lit. "Gortus," says Indjidjean, in quoting this passage of
Pliny, (Indjidj. Ant. Armen. Vol. i. p. 79); Γορδυαίων χωρία, (Strabo, lib. xvi.
24); and called by Armenian writers լերինք կորդուաց "the mountains
of the Cardu;" (Moses of Chorene, lib. ii. c. 33 ; i. 13); and the valleys
thereof; (Mich. Tchamtchean, vol. ii. p. 854,) &c.

[4] Vol. i. p. 81.

[5] The name Djudi, الجودي is given to the mountains on which the ark

called جودي ظاغ Djŭdi Dâgh by the Turks, is tipped with snow
during the greater part of the year. It bounds the plains of
Mesopotamia looking north from Mosul, and the view from the
top of those mountains over these same plains, with the bill of
Sinjâr (Sbinar?) far on towards the horizon, and the Tigris
meandering below, is one of the most beautiful and one of the
most interesting of panoramas; since we may think that, in all
probability, it can differ but little from the view Noah had when
he came out of the ark.

Where Mount Sarendib be on which the ark is said in the
Samaritan version to have rested is not known, though it be
rendered by Mount Ararat; and it cannot be in any way connected with the tradition given by Bar-Hebræus,[1] of the ark
resting in Apamea chief city of Pisidia.[2] But the Arabic account of Mount Djŭdi, is evidently borrowed from the Targums,
that give a local tradition which has much to recommend it.
Yet, I should be the last to bring it forward if it were in any
way opposed to the witness of Scripture; but it is not. The

rested, in the Coran, Sur. xl. 44; and thence by all Arabic writers, who sometimes write it جودي ' Djordi;' "male pertinaci errore," says Schultens, (in
Lex. Geogr. ad fin. Vit. Salad.); who pleads for Mount Ararat (Mount Masis),
not being aware of the meaning given to the 'Montes Gordyæi' by Armenians
themselves. Al-Kazwini, however, determines the part of the hills on which the
ark rested, saying:

جبل الجودي جبل مطل علي جزيرة ابن عمر
من الجانب الشرقي "Mount-Djŭdi is the mountain which overshadows
Djezīret Ibn-Omar on the eastern side;" من ارض الموصل "of the land of
Mosul," adds Ab'al-fada, (Hist. Ant. I. p. 16.) "The ark of Noah, on whom
be peace! rested on it, as the Most High God said: (Cor. Sur. xl. 44) 'And it
rested on the Djŭdi,' and Noah, on whom be peace! built on it a place of worship which subsists unto this day, and unto it people resort. There remained on
that mountain timbers of the ark unto the time of Beni Abbas." (Al-Kazwini,
vol. l. p. 157, ed. Wüst.) The Geographical Lexicon quoted by Schultens, gives
nearly the same words, though it says nothing, either of the place of worship,
or of the timber; but it speaks of two "towns Kardy and Basydy by the side
of El-Djudi in Mesopotamia, and near to the town of Themanin, where Noah's
ark rested;" wherein Schultens sees רתיב 'the eight' saved by water, &c.

[1] Chron. p. 7.
[2] Bar-Hebræus here uses the Greek word ܐܦܡܝܐ κιβωτὸς; the whole subject is treated at length in J. Bryant's "Vindication of the Apamean Medal;"
Anc. Mythol. vol. v. pp. 296—313; and Cellar. Geog. Ant. vol. II. p. 136, 168,
sq. 'Απάμεια Κιβωτὸς of Ptol or 'Ατ. Κιβωτὸς. But the legend is of a later date.

words of the Hebrew text הָרֵי אֲרָרָט Gen. viii. 4, simply mean
'the mountains of Armenia proper,' Jer. li. 27, and not Mount
Ararat, now called in Turkish Allah Dágh, 'the Mountain of
God,' and in Armenian, Mount Masis in particular;[1] however
strenuously Armenians contend for their Mount Masis, with its
many names, as for the Mount Ararat meant in the Hebrew
text.[2] The plain or province of 'Ararat' situate in the north of
Armenia and a royal prerogative, took its name, Moses of
Chorene tells us,[3] from Aræus who fought there against Semi-
ramis, was defeated, and left it the name *ւյրարրատ* 'shame'
or 'defeat of men.' But Indjidjean[4] tells us the name
արարատ 'Ararad,' was never used for the whole nation among
Armenians, although it was so used among foreign nations ; as
well as that of 'Aram' or 'Armenia.'[5] Since then the mountains of Cardu, or Djúdi, were reckoned to Armenia, Onkelos
and the tradition which he followed only specify the range of
mountains on which the ark did rest, in the country mentioned
in the Hebrew text.

After having stood on the top of that range, and seen the
plains of Mesopotamia below, and then travelling through the
whole of Armenia which is as mountainous and intricate as
Switzerland or the Tyrol, it struck me that the tradition prevalent in Chaldea and preserved by Tg. Onkelos, by Mendean
writers, and in the Coran, was very plausible. Had the ark
rested on Mount Masis or Ararat, Noah and his immediate descendants would have lost themselves ere they found their way
through the narrow winding valleys and over the high and pre-
cipitous passes of the whole of Armenia into the plains of Shinar.
Whereas, if we admit that the ark did rest on the mountains of
Cardu, Noah and his family would have only to descend from

---

[1] Moses Choren. lib. i. c. 11 ; Indjidj. Ant. vol. i. p. 54, sq.
[2] Μάσιυ ὄρυς, Strabo, lib. xii. c. 4 ; Indjidj. Antiq. Arm. p. 58.
[3] Lib. i. 14 ; ii. 21.   [4] Antiq. vol. i. ch. i. 3, p. 7.
[5] Moses of Chorene, lib. i. c. 11, derives 'Armenia' from Aram, son of Haik,
great grandson of Japhet ; for the Syrians call it 'Armen,'—which certain learned
but fanciful men derive from יֵרֵחַ הַר 'mountain of the moon,' in allusion to the
shape of the ark, one of the first objects of worship—and Persians call it 'Ar-
menigk ;' wherein Strabo lib. i. p. 2, 34, says : τούτο γὰρ ὑφ' ἡμῶν Σύροισι καλοῦ-
μένους ὑπ' αὐτῶν τῶν Σύρων ('Αρμενίους και) 'Αραμμαίους καλεῖσθαι.

the hills on which they stood when coming out of the ark, into
the wide plain spread at their feet below ; and there form their
earliest settlements under the lea of those hills. For it is but
reasonable to think that the first families of mankind after the
Flood did not, at once, wander very far from what was to them
in fact the cradle of their existence, and that they gradually
spread and peopled the plain of Shinar, until after the dispersion at the Tower of Babel ; when they were sent forth to people
the Earth.

IV. Where, then, was "Ur of the Chaldees ?" and who were
those Chaldees, or Chasdim ? The man would render a great
service to history, both sacred or profane, who could 'settle' this
question. But, if we can bring forward no proof, we may,
nevertheless, glean a few facts that may help us towards a right
knowledge of the subject. Strabo, who from his birthplace
must have written with good knowledge of the geography of
Pontus especially, tells us,[1] that τῆς δὲ Τραπεζοῦντος ὑπέρκεινται
καὶ τῆς Φαρνακίας Τιβαρηνοί τε καὶ Χαλδαῖοι καὶ Σάννοι, above Tra-
pezuntus and Pharnacia, are both the Tibarenians, the Chaldeans, and the Sannians ;[2] οἱ δὲ νῦν Χαλδαῖοι Χάλυβες τὸ παλαιὸν
ὠνομάζοντο, "but these Chaldeans of to-day were formerly called
Chalybes," and celebrated for their silver and iron mines, and
for the manner in which they wrought those metals.

—τῶν δ' ἄγχι πολύρρηνες Τιβαρηνοί·
τοῖς δ' ἔτι καὶ Χάλυβες στυ‡ελὴν καὶ ἀτερπέα γαῖαν
ναίουσιν, μογερού βεδαηκότες ἔργα σιδήρου.[3]

"Hanc prope sunt Chalybes, durissima rura colentes ;
Quos labor exercet sævus ferrique metalla."[4]

Whence 'chalybs,' steel. "Ergo Chalybes et Chaldæi iidem,
eorumque regio ferri dives," says J. D. Michaelis ;[5] and on this
he builds his opinion that the כַּשְׂדִּים were those Chalybes ;
proving it as he thinks, from Jerem. xv. 12, "Shall iron break

[1] Lib. xii. c. 3, 18, 19.

[2] Τιβαρηνοὶ καὶ Χαλδὴ καὶ Σαννοί, (Menippi Fragm. in Marciani Heracl. in
Geogr. Minorum, Vol. I. p. 573, ed. M.)

[3] Dionys. Perieg. v. 767, ed. M.

[4] Prisc. Perieg. 744, ed. M. ; et Avieni Desc. O. T. v. 947 ; Scylax Car. 68,
p. 65, ed. M. ; Xen. Anab. v. 5, 1 ; Arriani Peripl. P. Eux. c. 27, 31, ed. M., &c.

[5] Spicil. Geog. II. 78.

northern iron and steel !" said of these Chalybes. He further
shows from Jerem. i. 14, iv. 6, vi. 1, x. 22, xiii. 20, Ezek.
xxvi. 7, that the Chaldæans or Chasdim, were to come from the
north; and in reply to those who said that anyhow, coming
from Babylon they must reach Jerusalem from the northward,
he brings forward Jerem. vi. 22, הִגֵּה עַם בָּא מֵאֶרֶץ צָפוֹן
"behold, a people cometh from the *north country*;" and x. 22,
" behold—a great commotion out of the *north country*, to make
the cities of Judah desolate," &c.[1] He thinks that "interjecto
Jesaiam inter et Jeremiam tempore, fortassis Manasse in Judæa
regnante, Chaldæos Septentrionales ex antiqua patria magno
agmine erupisse," these northern Chaldees left their ancient
abode, during the time that elapsed between Isaiah and Jeremiah, and after successive victories took possession of Babylon
and of the country round; as either described or foretold by
Habakkuk i. 6, "For lo, I raise up the Chaldæans, that bitter
and hasty nation, which shall march through the breadth of the
land, to possess the dwelling places מִשְׁכָּנוֹת that are not
their's." But J. D. Michaelis makes no allusion whatever to the
Χαλδαῖοι mentioned by Xenophon,[2] which were also on the borders
of Armenia, but on the south-east, adjoining the Καρδοῦχοι.[3]

[1] Gesenius (Comm. in Is. c. xxiii. 13, vol. ii. p. 749,) attempts to refute
J. D. Michaelis with Es. xxvi. 7, which rather confirms what Michaelis says;
and with Jer. xxxix. 5, and lii. 9, that prove nothing, by showing that Nebuchadnezzar was at Riblah; for he might have been there, whether coming from
Babylonia or from elsewhere eastward of the Euphrates. But Gesenius did not
see that he contradicted himself in attacking J. D. Michaelis; since himself applies the words, "who raised up the righteous man from the east," Is. xli. 2,
and "calleth a ravenous bird from the east," xlvi. 11, to Cyrus. (See Comm. in
Is. l. c.) If, therefore he understands ' the east' literally of the land where Cyrus
dwelt, surely J. D. Michaelis had the same right to take the terms ' north' and
' north country' as literally, when said of the Chaldees.

[2] Anab. lib. iv. c. 3, 4; v. c. 5, 17: Cyrop. lii. c. 1, 34; c. 2, 1, 7; vii. c. 2,
5, &c.

[3] Even the passage Anab. vii. c. 8, 25, Καρδοῦχοι δὲ, καὶ Χάλυβες, καὶ Χαλδαῖοι, which some propose to alter to ἢ Χαλδαίοι, without any authority whatever,
shows these Eastern Chaldæans to have been distinct from the Chalybes or so
called Northern Chaldæans; since while among the Chalybes, (Lib. v. c. 5, 1,)
he speaks of the Καρδοῦχοι, καὶ Χαλδαίοι, whom he had made enemies by forag-
ing among them; showing that when Xenophon was there and when he wrote
(b. c. 400) the Chalybes were not yet called Chaldæi, as in the days of Strabo,
b. c. 30.

We have every reason to suppose, however, that the name Χαλδαίος was given by the Greeks, with their usual ignorance of foreign names, and κατά τινα λέξεως παραφθοράν ἢ παρανοήσιν, (Eustath.) to the Χάλδοι, inhabitants of the Χαλδία, χώρα τῆς Ἀρμενίας,[1] owing to the similarity of Χαλδία and Χάλδοι, that were little known compared with γῆ Χαλδαίων, Χαλδαίοι, known of all the then civilised world. Eustathius therefore, is probably quite right in saying,[2] Χώρα δὲ Ἀρμενίας ἡ Χαλδία, ἧς μέχρις ἡ Ποντικὴ βασιλεία. Τοὺς δὲ ἐκεῖσε Χάλδους ἐπικρατεῖ ἡ συνήθεια δισυλλάβως, οὐ Χαλδαίους. Χαλδαῖοι γὰρ τρισυλλάβως οἱ ποτὲ μὲν Κηφῆνες, κ.τ.λ. Λέγονται μέντοι παρά τινων καὶ οἱ περὶ τὴν Κολχίδα Χάλδοι Χαλδαῖοι τρισυλλάβως κατὰ Δικαίαρχον. "Chaldia is, indeed, a province of Armenia, to which the kingdom of Pontus reaches. But the custom prevails to call those people Chaldi (disyllabic) not Chaldæi. For the Chaldæi (trisyllabic) are those who were descended from Cepheus, &c. Yet the Chaldi, who join on to Colchia are by some called Chaldæi (trisyllabic) as Dicæarcus tells us." These Χάλδοι, Chaldi, * խաղբդի-ք,* 'Khaghdi-k,' or 'Khaldi,' are always carefully distinguished by Armenian authors from the Chaldæi, *քաղդեա-ցիք,* 'Chaghtyai-k,' or 'Chaldyai.' Thus Moses of Chorene,[3] says Colchia was divided into four provinces, the southernmost of which was *Ճանիք որ են խաղդիք* "the Djani (Sanni), which are the Khaldi."[4] These were conquered by Valarsaces,[5] and are named *Ճանիք պոնտացւոց, որ են խաղդիք* "the Sanni of Pontus, which are the Khaldi," among whom Tacitus was slain.[6]

Even in Xenophon's time, the Chalybes occupied more than one tract of country; since some of them ἀλίγοι ἦσαν καὶ ὑπήκοοι

[1] Steph. Byz. s.v. p. 453, ed. Dind.

[2] Comm. in Dionys. Perieg. v. 767, p. 350, ed. Mull.

[3] Geog. p. 356, ed. Wh.

[4] J. D. Michaelis, who evidently knew nothing of Armenian, and trusted entirely to Whiston's translation, quotes this and other passages from Moses of Chorene to show the existence of these Chaldæans of Pontus. But in every one of these instances Moses Chor. speaks of the *խաղդիք* 'Khaldi,' which he distinguishes from the *քաղդեացիք* 'Chaldæans' in Lib. i. c. 4.

[5] Moses Choren. Hist. Lib. ii. c. 4.

[6] Ib. c. ll. iii.

τῶν Μοσυνοίκων, "were few and subject to the Mosynœci," whereas[1] others were αὐτόνομοι, "independent."[2]

We see then that Χαλδία is not a corruption of Χαλδαία, as Müller thinks,[3] albeit he is right in saying " de Chaldæis Armeniæ in hisce Ionicis h. l. cogitare nequit," if by " Chaldæi Armeniæ" be understands the Χαλδαῖοι of Xenophon ; for the Χάλβοι were severed by the whole of Armenia from these eastern Χαλδαῖοι. And there can be no difficulty in making Χάλβοι, Chaldi, Chaldees, out of խաղդէբ, for the Greek χ is made to answer for the ք 'cha' in Χαλδαῖοι, and for խ, in Χάλβοι ; and again ք stands for Ⴍ in 'Cardu,' Καρδούχια ὄρη, Carduchi montes ; and the Armenian ղ which is pronounced 'gh' in the throat, like a certain vulgar way of pronouncing 'r' in French,

[1] Anab. Lib. v. c. 5, 1.

[2] Ib. vii. c. 8, 25. They were all, however, identified with the Χάλβοι, Khaldi, and these again with the "gens Armenochalybes ultra Trapezuntem, à majore Armenia xxx mill. passuum distans," (Plin. H. N. Lib. vi. 4,) and with the "Armenochalybes qui et à latere Colchicarum solitudinum ad Cerauniæ habitant et Moschorum tractus ad Iberum amnem in Cyram defluentem," (Ib. c. xi.) mentioned by Indjidjean (Antiq. Arm. vol. i. p. 337, and 327), where he quotes several fathers of the Armenian Church, to prove the intercourse which existed from the first with Colchis through the Armenochalybes or Chaldi. Among them from the first ՚ի սկզբան անդ ծաղկեալ ուսմանց flourished sciences, զի բանք Փորմալէոնի այնպէս գուցանեն թէ առաջին նախահարք բաղդէացւոց բնակեալ էին ՚ի Ձորս կովկասու առ պոնտոսիւր և կոչէին բաղդիք, քաղիբք, իսկ մեզ խաղդիք. " For the words of Phormaleon go to prove that the first ancestors of the Chaldeans dwelt in the valleys of the Caucasus towards Pontus ; they were called Chaldi (Khaghdi-k), Chalybes (Chaliv-k), and by us Khaldi (Khaghdi-k), and came and settled on the other side of the Euphrates, which was called the land of the Chaldeans. They, at first Chaldi or Khaldi, խաղդիք կամ խաղդիք, որք էին կողքիացիք who were Colchians, had from the first astronomical tables engraved on stones in Colchis, whence they were taken to Greece," &c. Likewise Michael Tchamtchean (Hist. Arm. vol. i. p. 209, and ii. 66, 78, &c.) speaks of the խաղդիք կամ երկիր խաղդեաց ՟ արևմտակողմ սայոց և ՚ի Շիւսիսոյ բարձր Շայոց " Khaldi, or land of the Khaldi, on the western side of the Dsu, and to the north of the Highlands of Armenia."

[3] Note ad Marc. Heracl. Epitome Peripl. Menippei, Geogr. Min. vol. i. p. 572.

and sometimes also in English, answers in very many words for
'l;' as e.g. աղւանք, Aghvan, Alban(us). So that, even though
Schultens says: "Unde الكرا Curdi nostri? A Gordyæo monte
dicerem si اتراد scriberetur," we should have ready to hand the
etymology of כַּשְׂדִּים Chasdim, Chaldees, if we wished to handle
it as coolly as does Gesenius. He thinks that כַּשְׂדִּי and Χαλδαῖος "haud difficulter conciliari possunt. Statui enim potest,
nativam formam fuisse כֶּרֶד, quæ in Curdorum nomine الكرد
servata ab Hebræis et Chaldæis in כַּשְׂדִּי (ר et ש permutatis) à
Græcis contra in Χαλδαῖος mutata sit,"[1] (Gol. ad Alfrag.)

But, in sooth, 'ר' et 'ש' non sic permutantur, without proof
thereof; and Schultens is right when remarking on these same
words of Golius, "Cl. *Gol.* p. 17, ad *Alfrag.* autumat *Curdorum*
appellationem reliquias esse *Chaldæorum* ut ex كلدانيون *Chaldæis,* non tantum كسدانيون *Chasdæi,* sed et كردانيون *Chardei,*
Chærdæi sint conformati, iidem cum veterum quoque *Gordyæis.*"
He adds, "Hæc mihi quidem non magnopere rident."[2]

Neither does Gesenius' offer[3] to make Arphaxad אַרְפַּכְשַׁד
father of the כַּשְׂדִּים (as Josephus does) and to derive it from Ar.
ارف pl. ارفة 'border,' and כֶּשֶׂד for כַּשְׂד, so as to mean
'border of Chesed,' or 'land of Chesed,'[4] commend itself to
exact scholarship; nor yet Ewald's emendation, in making ارف
i.q. ارب 'to make fast,' so as to read in אַרְפַּכְשַׁד 'the fortress
of Chesahed.'[5] But, besides the arbitrary way of making 'Arphaxad' the name of a people in Gen. x. 22, and even at 24, and
as it must be, the name of a man, in ch. xi. 10—18, without
any ground for so doing,[6] the "allgemeine Lautgesetze," the

---

[1] Thes. L. S. s.v. כֶּשֶׂד.

[2] A. Schult. in Lex. Geog. ad V. Salad. s.v.

[3] Gesenius borrowed this etymology from J. D. Michaelis (Spicil. Geog.
ii. p. 76) without acknowledging it, although he loses no opportunity of refuting
him if he can. It only shows how the scholarship of to-day subsists on that of
others; and that there would be but little of it, if it were not for the giants in
learning of the last two centuries. After all, Vitringa is better worth reading
than Gesenius on Isaiah; and J. D. Michaelis is a safer man than Ewald, and
quite as learned, if not more so.

[4] Comm. in Jos. vol. ii. p. 743.   [5] Gesch. Volk. Isr. i. p. 405.

[6] Reland. Palæst. p. 62, sq., is worth reading on this subject.

universal laws of articulation, of which Ewald speaks, in order
to twist כֶּשֶׂד into כַּשְׂדִי, *kshad* into *kard* or *kasdi*, and this out
of *kard* or *kurd*, are far from clear or trustworthy, without proofs,
which he does not give. Granted שׁ changes into תּ and ס,
' Schibboleth' into ' Sibboleth,' and ' r' into ' l;' but ' r' or ' l'
into ' s' is not so easily done on grounds that are neither fanciful
nor arbitrary. Shemitic dialects may be called one family ; but
like brothers and sisters, they all have their own individual
characters ; and it is not always safe to explain the peculiarities
of a brother by those of another. So also these Arabic-Hebrew-
Shemitic terms are seldom logical, and so, do not always hold
good ; witness Simonis' etymology of אַרְפַּכְשַׁד which he renders, " *diffusio* (familiæ) *maxima*," and brings it from Arab.
אֲרֵי *fudit*, Heb. פָכָה *manavit, effudit se*, and Chald. and Syr.
שְׁדָא *fudit, effudit* ! [1] Yet, will it not do to find much fault
with him, as he is still a great authority with the scholars of to-
day whenever it suits their purpose. Why do such etymologists
not at once see in אַרְפַּכְשַׁד, ارفاكساد, ' Urfa of Chesed,' i.e.
' Ur of the Chaldees ?' it would have the advantage of connecting the present name with the former one of Ur !

Moreover, the Armenian word աղբակ, which Ewald brings
forward to support his etymology, rather destroys it. աղբակ,
աղբագ or Հաղբակ, ' Aghbag,' ' Aghpak' or ' Haghbag,' also
' Albac' and ' Alhacia,' [2] is the name of two districts of Armenia.
աղբակ փոքր, ' Lesser Aghbag,' in the province of Gordjaik,
was also called կորդուք, or աղբակ կորդուաց, ' Gortùk'
or ' Aghbag of the Gortùk,' or ' Curds ;' and forms a portion of
the hilly country that extends to the north of Nineveh, and between the lakes Van and Urumiah. It is the part of Assyria
adjoining Armenia, which Ptolemy[3] says, καλεῖται ἡ μὲν παρὰ τὴν
Ἀρμενίαν Ἀρραπαχῖτις, was called ' Arrapachitis.' The other
Aghbag, աղբակ մեծ, the ' Greater Aghbag,' is a part of the
Province of Vashnragan, to the north of the Lesser Aghbag.[4]
Those, then, who fancy they find the ' traces of Arphaxad' in

---

[1] Onom. Vet. T. p. 438.   [2] Moses Chor. Geog. p. 360.

[3] Lib. vi. c. 1, 2.

[4] See Michael Tchamtchean, Hist. Armen. vol. ii. p. 806, i. 998, and map.
Indjid. Antiq. Armen. vol. ii. p. 64, &c.

'Aghpag' and in 'Ἀρφαραχῖτις, must not divide the word into
אַרְפַּ כְשַׂד as they do; but, according to the supposed radicals,
into אַרְכַּד שַׂד; then, as J. D. Michaelis remarks, what becomes of שַׂד? Thus it is by no means proved that Arphaxad
was the father of the Chasdim; and even if he were, nothing would
be gained as regards the birthplace of Abraham, who was not a
Chaldee, but himself a Syrian as well as his grandson, "the
Syrian ready to perish;"[1] and like his nephew Laban, the Syrian
of the city of Nahor.[2]   Neither were these nations taken one
for the other, since Jeremiah (xxxv. 11) mentions expressly
חֵיל רַפְּשֻׂדִים and חֵיל אֲרָם, "the army of the Chaldees and
the army of the Syrians."

Thus, then, we are now no nearer actual certainty than when
we started on this inquiry; "imo potius," says the learned Vitringa,[3] "an non tot incerta et confusa tradita magnas menti
offundunt tenebras?" We have, however, acquired greater knowledge, chiefly from local geography,—(1) respecting the Χάλδοι, Chaldi, which were twofold: those inhabiting Pontus, and
workers of metals, that could not be reckoned to the "Caucasian
range;" and those inhabiting Colchis, that might be reckoned
to the Caucasus, but were not workers of iron, and therefore
could not be the כַשְׂדִים alluded to in Jer. xv. 12. And (2) we
see that these Χάλδοι, whether of Pontus or of Colchis, were always distinct from the Χαλδαῖοι, Chaldæi. We also find that the
Χαλδαῖοι of Xenophon were close to the Καρδοῦχοι, but not the
Χάλδοι; inhabiting the same, or nearly the same, tract of country
they do at present, mountain fastnesses, they share with the
Curds, who are thus called by the Turks كرد from their wild
and 'wolfish' indomitable nature; and whom, although not alike
in features, they resemble in their predatory disposition, as in
the days of Job, i. 17. But this is a Turkish etymology. We
must rather look to their name as a remnant of מִם, קַרְדֹו,
whom Ah'ul-faraj makes a son of Shem, but which, at all
events, is a very ancient name of the mountains on which, from
time immemorial as it appears, the Ark is said to have rested.

[1] Deut. xxvi. 5.   [2] Gen. xxiv.
[3] Comm. in Jer. vol. i. p. 412.

While the 'Chaldi' ֆաւֆաիւգ have almost disappeared, the 'Chaldæi' subsist in great numbers at the present day, and speak nearly the same language as formerly; not, however, in the land they conquered in the south of Mesopotamia, but in the land of their birth in the north of it. They are now reduced to their original state זֶה הָעָם לֹא הָיָה, as a people that was not, until the Assyrians יְסָדָהּ לְצִיִּים established it into a powerful nation for them that dwelt in the wilderness around,[1] as Isaiah said of them prophetically. Whence, then, were they called Χαλδαῖοι? ἀπό τινος Χαλδαίου.[2] If so, from כֶּשֶׂד Chesed, a son of Nahor (Gen. xxii. 22), one of Abraham's line; and thus speak of 'Ur of the Chasdim' per πρόληψιν, as Vitringa, and Bochart, and Ditmar,[3] and Hyde[4] think, though not J. D. Michaelis? And why—a singular fact—are they called כַּשְׂדִּים, Chasdim, by the Hebrews, and ܟܠܕ̈ܝܐ, Chaldāye, by the Syrians, both Hebrews and Syrians being originally from the same country? It is best to say nothing of what one does not know.

V. Where, or what then, was אוּר כַּשְׂדִּים, 'Ur of the Chaldees?' I know not what Bayer says in his work, which I have never seen; but I feel sure that neither he nor any one else can answer this question with certainty. From what has been said, however, we must in all probability, look for it in the north, and not in the south of Mesopotamia; and we must again resort to tradition, which we may receive as we like. We read in the Kufale,[5] that in the thirty-fifth jubilee, and in the fourth year of the third seven years thereof, Ragu took to himself a wife whose name was Ura, daughter of Ur, daughter of a son of Chesed, and to him was Serug born. Then began men to commit all manner of violence, and to build fenced cities. And Ur,[6] the son of Chesed, built Arābä, which is of the Chaldees, አራ : አየተ : ከአፈወን : (Cheledewon), which he called after his own name, and after that of his father, &c. There dwelt Serug, and after him his son Nachor, to whom he taught the

---

[1] Isa. xxiii. 13.

[2] Steph. Byz. s. v. p. 455, sq., and Euseb. Chron. Armen. vol. i. p. 11.

[3] VaterL. der Chald. p. 4.   [4] V. R. Pers. p. 75.

[5] C. xi. p. 45, ed. Dillm.   [6] Or, Ud, according to other MSS.

magical arts, &c. ;¹ and to him was born Sarah. On the other
hand, Michael Tchamtchean, in his history of Armenia,² gives a
very modern origin to Ur, which he says was the name of a governor, of Parthian origin, appointed 'ի միջագետաց յերկրին
եդեսացւոց there in Mesopotamia, in the land of Edessians,
by Valaraces; and who gave his name to the city which some
call Orhe, but which afterwards was called Urha.³ Indjidjean,
however, tells us⁴ "that from all antiquity the science of the stars
flourished in the city of Ur, whence some derive the word
Uranus, Οὐρανός, and that there the teaching concerning the
sun brought about the worship of fire, called հուր, húr, in old
as well as in modern Armenian; and the city of Ur, which is
Urha and Edessia, is in Mesopotamia, adjoining the land of
Armenia." While Matthew of Edessa alone of all Armenian
writers says that Edessa was built by Tigranes; but he does not
say whether it be Tigranes I. or II.⁵

But how comes it, if Edessa, which is Urhoe, be Ur, neither
S. Ephrem nor Jacob of Edessa once alludes, so far as I know,
to its being either 'Ur of the Chaldees' or the birthplace of
Abraham? One would think they would have mentioned so
high a distinction of their own famed city. S. Ephrem simply
speaks of ܐܘܪ ܕܟܠܕܝܐ Ur of the Chaldees, and says⁶ that Nimrod
ܐܡܠܟ ܒܐܪܟ ܕܐܝܬܝܗ ܐܘܪܗܝ "reigned in Arech, which is
Edessa."⁷ A. Ezra, R. S. Jarchi, R. S. Ben Melech, in Miclol

¹ P. 46.   ² Vol. I. p. 216, sq.
³ The Patriarch Dionysius (Assem. B. Or. vol. I. p. 388, note 1) alludes to
this in his Chronicle (fol. 16), where he says that, in the eighteen hundred and
eightieth year of Abraham (B.C. 136), ܐܡܠܟ ܚܠܐ ܐܘܪܗܝ ܡܠܟܐ ܩܕܡܝܐ
ܒܐܘܪܗܝ ܫܢܝܐ ܚܡܫ—ܘܡܢܗ ܗܘܬ ܡܕܝܢܬܐ ܐܘܪܗܝ ܕܐܬܩܪܝܬ "Orhoe, first king of Urhoe
(Edessa) began to reign there, and reigned five years; and from him was the
city called Urhoe." If so, why not Orhoe? "Then began the kingdom of
Urhoe, which lasted from Olymp. 161 to Olymp. 249 (B.C. 136 to A.D. 217)."
⁴ Antiq. Armen. vol. I. p. 38, sq.
⁵ Notices et Extr. des MSS. by Ch. Cirbied. 1822, p. 22.
⁶ On Gen. ix. vol. I. p. 58.
⁷ But in another place (p. 154) he says ܐܪܟ ܕܐܝܬܝܗ ܐܘܪܗܝ "Arech
which is Urhoe;" a statement repeated by Ab'ul-faraj (Chron. p. 9), who, like
other Syrian authors, always uses the term ܐܘܪܗܝ and ܐܘܪܗܝܐ, 'Urhoe'
and 'Urhojo' for 'Edessa' and 'Edessenus.' It would be interesting to trace

Jophi, say nothing on the subject. The Midrash Rabba[1] only explains אוּר by the story, found in the Coran, Abu'l-feda, and elsewhere, of Nimrod casting Abraham into a furnace of fire, whence he came forth unhurt. R. D. Kimchi[2] explains אוּר by בִּקְעָה, 'vale,' or 'valley,' and proves it, as he thinks, through Isa. xxiv. 15, "Wherefore glorify the LORD בָּאֻרִים in the fires." The LXX. renders אוּר through χώρα, which, however could not be from אוּר changed into עִיר, 'a city,' a 'township,' as Chwolson says.[3] Abarbanel,[4] who is justly commended for his learning, says that "Ur Chasdim אֵינוּ אֶרֶץ כַּשְׂדִּים אֶלָּא שֵׁם מָקוֹם is not the 'land of the Chaldees,' but the 'name of a place' on the other side of the River Euphrates, in the kingdom of Aram. Several cities were taken by Assur, and the fairest of them was the one called 'Ur of the Chasdim,' because the Chasdim took possession of it." He then alludes to R. D. Kimchi's opinion; and he mentions that of others who say that the Chasdim הָיוּ עֹבְדִים הָאֵשׁ וְאֵת הַשֶּׁמֶשׁ were worshippers of fire and of the sun there, and that on that account it was called 'Ur, fire and light of the Chasdim ;' סוֹף דָּבָר "the end of it, however," says Abarbanel, "is that Ur Chasdim was a city on the other side of the River;" and thus he leaves us where we were.

He is right, nevertheless, in saying that אוּר is the name of a place, and cannot be the name of a country, nor yet a euphemism; for cities are not so called. We never read of عروس المدن 'the bride of cities,' said for Damascus, although this epithet often follows the name of that city; neither is "the joy of the whole earth" said without 'Jerusalem;' nor yet عروس الشام 'the bride of Syria,' for Ascalon, unless that city be

---

the link in Syriac between ܐܘܪܗܝ and ܐܘܪܗܝ. 'Ur of the Chaldees' and 'Urhoi.' This can only be done by looking into Syriac MSS. anterior to the names Mallukho and Edessa. And it seems as if 'Urhoi' must be derived from 'Ur,' rather than, as one says, of its Arabic name الرها , 'Roha,' 'Erroha,' from the Greek 'Callirrhoe.'

[1] Fol. 42.
[2] Sepher Shoresh. s. v.
[3] Die Ssab. I. 313, note 4.
[4] Comm. in Pent. ed. Ssab. fol. 42, verso.

named, any more than ὀμφαλὸς γῆς without Dodona, &c. Neither
does Gesenius' derivation of אור from the Sanscrit, without
proofs of this being the case as regards Ur Chasdim, do more
than make one lose confidence in such etymologists; like
'Agupta-s' for Ægyptus, and 'Nila-s' for Nilus. These are assertions that require proof, without which they are worthless.
Bochart, who is yet unrivalled for his multifarious learning—
"undequaque doctus"—says[1] rightly, "saltem Ur Chaldæorum
ubi Abrahæ majores habitarunt, Gen. xi. 28, non procul erat à
Corduenâ, in qua substiterat Arca Noæ. Res patet ex Ammiani
Marcell. Lib. v. Itaque Ur circa Nisibin, Tigri propior et Cor-
duenæ duabus nimirum stationibus." He, like Gesenius, however, leans in favour of Eupolemus,[2] who puts Ur whence Abraham came forth ἐν πόλει τῆς Βαβυλωνίας Καμαρίνη ἥν τινας λέγειν
πόλιν Οὐρίην· "Sic enim Ur Chaldæorum erit Ura de qua Plinius,[3]
quod putaverim Chaldæos אור scripsisse, id est Auran; unde
apud Ptolemæum in Babyloniæ descriptione, παράκειται δὲ τῷ
Εὐφράτῃ ἡ Αὐρανῖτις χώρα." Yet he sums up in favour of the
"Ur mentioned by Ammian, as Abraham's birthplace, because
the way thence to Canaan lay through Haran; whereas, if he
had started from the (now called) Babylonian Ur (Werka?), his
route lay through a large expanse of desert on his way northwards, and he would have to come south, thus crossing twice
the Euphrates. Moreover, Abraham's ancestors did not share
in the common dispersion, but lingered around the mountains
of Cordyena on which the Ark rested." Josephus[4] leaves the
matter in doubt. "Aran (Ἀράνης)," he says, "ἐν Χαλδαίοις ἀπέ-
θανεν ἐν πόλει Οὐρῇ τῶν Χαλδαίων λεγομένη, died among the Chaldeans, in a city called Ura of the Chaldeans; and his sepulchre
is shown unto this day." Abu'l-feda,[5] alluding to the doubt
that exists as to Abraham's birthplace, says, "Some put it in
الاحواز El-ahwâz, and others بابل وهي العراق in Babel, which
is 'Irâk." On which Ibn Batûtah,[6] speaking of the cave on
Mt. Casius, near Damascus, where Abraham first saw the star,
&c., says, "Yet I saw in 'Irâk قرية تعرف ببرص a village known

[1] Phaleg. Lib. i. c. 10.   [2] Euseb. Præp. Ev. lix.
[3] Lib. v. c. 24.   [4] Antiq. Lib. l. c. 6.
[5] Hist. Ante Isl. p. 20.   [6] Vol. l. p. 231.

as Born, between El-Hillah and Baghdad, in which they say
مولد ابراهيم بها Abraham was born. It is near the town of
Dhoulkefl,[1] and Abraham's tomb is found there." Hyde[2] is of
this opinion, and takes 'Ορχόη in Babylonia[3] to be Ur, though
he is at great pains to show that it is the same word as Urhoe,
Roha, Erroha, and Callirrhoe.

As regards this name given to Edessa, in common with many
other places in Epirus, in Macedonia, at Tyre, in Moab, &c.,
Pliny[4] says, " Arabia supra dicta habet oppida, Edessam quæ
quondam Antiochia dicebatur, Callirrhoen a fonte nominatam."
Hence the Arabian رها or الرها Rohe, or Errobe, " the name of
which ادانا بالرومية in Rum (Greek and Latin) is Edessa."[5]
'Αντιόχεια—ὀγδόη ἡ ἐπὶ τῆς Καλλιρρόης λίμνης,[6] the which, compared with 'Έδεσσα, πόλις Συρίας διὰ τὴν τῶν ὑδάτων ῥύμην οὕτω
κληθεῖσα,[7] leaves no doubt as to the city, and to its situation;
albeit it gives Cellarius[8] and Berkelius[9] some little trouble to
reconcile these statements with Strabo, who, after saying[10] that
the Euphrates is crossed at Anthemusia, in Mesopotamia,
ὑπέρκειται δὲ τοῦ ποταμοῦ, σχοίνους τέτταρας διέχουσα, ἡ Βαμβύκη,
ἣν καὶ 'Έδεσσαν καὶ 'Ιερὰν πόλιν καλοῦσιν, ἐν ᾗ τιμῶσι τὴν Συρίαν
θεὸν τὴν 'Αταργάτιν, " beyond the river, (coming hither from Mesopotamia,) at about four schœni, is Bambyce, which they call
Edessa and the Holy City, in which they worship the goddess
Atergatis."

On this I may remark—(1) that as to Edessa (Oorfa), Stephanus Byz. errs in saying that it was so called ' from the gush
of waters there.' He meant Καλλιρρόη; for, from want of a
more certain etymology, we may think 'Edessa' not far from
Heb. הֲדַסָּה ' myrtle,' i. q. אָסָא, Pers. آس تر ' green myrtle,'

---

[1] A ' faithful' man, known for his fasting, &c., Cor. xxi. 85, mentioned together with Enoch and Ishmael; by some said to be Job, but by Abu'l-feda (Hist.
A. i. p. 26) said to be the name given to Bishr, Job's son, whom God sent to
preach to his countrymen after Job's death.

[2] De V. R. Pers. p. 73.

[3] Ptolem. Geog. Lib. viii. 20, 29; and v. 20, 8.

[4] N. H. Lib. v. c. 24.

[5] Lexic. Geog. ap. Schult. V. Salad. s. v.

[6] Steph. Byz. s. v. vol. i. p. 64, ed. Dind.

[7] Ibid. p. 171.   [8] Geog. Antiq. Lib. iii. c. xv. 25.

[9] Not. in Steph. Byz. s. v.   [10] Lib. xvi. 1, 27.

a name given to beautiful women,[1] and thus also probably to
cities in green and beautiful localities, such as that of جنّة,
Edessa. Thus Damascus is styled by Abu'lhosain جنّة الشرق
"the garden of the East," "where the myrtle من آسها لكبت
جنّة لا تنقضى offers a garden that never ends," and where every
orchard on the river banks is ever green; عريس المدن "the
bride among cities" ظلّ ظليل وماء سلسيل "embosomed in thick
foliage and watered by bubbling streams."[2]

2. Although Bambyce and Edessa cannot both be true of the
same city, yet there is this to account for Strabo's ascribing
Edessa to Syria. In Lib. xvi. 1, 2, he says, δοκεῖ δὲ τὸ τῶν Σύρων
ὄνομα διατεῖναι ἀπὸ μὲν τῆς Βαβυλωνίας μέχρι τοῦ Ἰσσικοῦ κόλπου,
ἀπὸ δὲ τούτου μέχρι τοῦ Εὐξείνου τὸ παλαιόν. "Formerly Syria
seems to have extended from Babylonia to the Gulf of Issus,
and thence to the Euxine." He may thus reckon Edessa to
Syria, where Ibn al-Wardi places it, when, speaking of Aleppo,[3]
he says, "Here is Errboa, also a large city, fenced and defended
by a wall, وبها العين التي نبعت للخليل ثم حين رمى
المنجنيق, and in it is the fountain of the Prophet, that sprang
up to Abraham (El-khalil) when he cast the engine against the
temple of the idols. There are several towns around it, and all
these belong to the province of Haleb."[4]

3. Although Strabo either said 'Bambyce' of Edessa, or
'Edessa' of Bambyce by mistake, yet he may be justified in
calling Edessa Ἱερὰ πόλις.[5] For Edessa had, from the days of
Adæus or Thaddæus, her apostle, a character for sanctity. Josue
Stylites, a native of Edessa, who wrote a history of all the vicis-

---

[1] Esth. viii. 7, 10, 11.   [2] Ibn Batûtah, I. p. 188.
[3] P. 26, in Rosenmüll. Anal. Ar.
[4] For "Syria" was a very comprehensive term, Pliny says (Lib. v. 18),
"Syria—Palæstina vocabatur, et Judæa, et Cœle, dein Phœnice, et quæ recedit
intus Damascena: ac magis etiamnum meridiana, Babylonia. Et eadem Mesopotamia inter Euphraten et Tigrin: quaque transit Taurum Sophene; citra
vero etiam Comagene."
[5] We must distinguish between Ἱερὰ πόλις, i. e., πόλις Ἱερά, and Ἱεράπολις,
although the two may have originally been identical. The first means a 'holy
city,' πόλις Ἱρή, Ἱρὴ πόλις (Luc. de Dea Syr. throughout), and belongs to Hierapolis in Syria, or Mabug, celebrated for the worship of Atergatis. The other
is given to Hierapolis in Phrygia (Colos. iv. 13), of which more presently.

situdes of his own city from A.D. 495 to 507, says that, " the
Persians were not then able to take the city, although pressed
on all sides, in fulfilment of the promise made by CHRIST
to Abgarus, the faithful king, saying, ܪܘܩ ܘܣܐ ܘܩܪ
ܣܣܟܣܐ ܣܐ ܟܟܟܣ, Thy city shall be blessed,
and the enemy shall not have dominion over it for ever."[1]   And
S. Ephrem in his Testament[3] alludes to this in these words :
ܪܣܚܣܟܐ ܐܣܐ ܘܣܐܘܐ ܣܗ ܟܪܟܐ ܗܪܣ ; " Blessed is
the city in which ye dwell, Urhoe, the mother of wise men :
the city that received the blessing from the mouth of the SON
Himself through His disciple.   This blessing, then, shall rest
on her unto the coming of the Holy One ; on her, ܣܐܘ
ܘܣܣ ܟܣܘ ܘܘܣܣ ܟܣܪܟܐ ܐܣܪܟ, on Urhoe, the blessed city of
Mesopotamia."[3]   Theodoritus, also,[4] speaking of the passage of
Julian through his favourite place, Harao, says that τὴν Ἔδεσσαν
ὡς εὐσεβείᾳ κοσμουμένην εὐώνυμον κατέλιπεν, "that he passed
Edessa on his left, as being a city adorned with piety,"[5] ἐπὶ
ἀρχῆθεν παιδημεὶ χριστιανίζειν ἔλαχεν ἥδε ἡ πόλις, "because that
city happened to have been Christian from the beginning ;"
for, from the preaching of Thaddeus τῇ τοῦ Χριστοῦ προσανά-
κειται προσηγορίᾳ· " Edessa continues faithful to her Christian
name."[6]   Thus, then, Strabo might place Edessa in Syria, and
call her Hierapolis ; but the name ' Bambyce' never belonged
to her : it was the name of Ἱερὰ πόλις, Mabug, or Mambej, in
Syria proper, chief city of the Cyrrhestica, under the Romans.[7]

---

[1] Assem. B. Or. i. p. 261, and 262.　　　[2] Ibid. p. 111.

[3] Acta S. Ephremi, p. xxxii.

[4] Hist. Eccl. Lib. iii. c. 26, and iv. 18.

[5] " Out of hatred for her inhabitants," says Sozomen, Hist. Eccl. Lib. vi. 1.

[6] Euseb. Hist. Eccl. Lib. ii. 1.

[7] Although, probably from want of books, I cannot find that Bambyce " sei
eine baumwollen stadt," &c., ' a cotton town,' as Forbiger (Alte Geogr. vol. ii.
p. 643, note) says, yet I cannot help suspecting some confusion between this
and the Hierapolis of Phrygia.   For if Bambyce, Βαμβύκη, come from βόμβυξ,
bombyx, then Hierapolis was a ' silk,' and not a ' cotton' growing city : but of
this especial distinction I can find no trace.   And if Βαμβύκη be, as indeed it may
be, a Hellenized form of the Arabic name منبج, manbedj, (though not of
منبض manbis, ' a bow for beating cotton,') then it has nothing to do with
silk, but rather with the great pile of wood συρή, " lighted," as Lucian tells us,
δαρτίων δὲ πασέων—μεγίστων τοῦ ὀλαφος ἀρχομένοις ἐντελέουσι· καὶ μὶν οἱ μὶν συρῆν

The Ur mentioned by Ammianus Marcell. might, from its situation have been the birthplace of Abraham; but the same reasons make Edessa quite as eligible; and since tradition fixes on that spot, we may keep to it till we have reason to change. It was, indeed, a city of many names, but not as Dean Stanley gives them: namely—

"Orfa, Roha, Orchoe, Callirrhoe, Chaldæopolis, Edessa, Antioch of the far East, Erech, Ur."—p. 6.

For Orchoe, 'Ορχόη, and Chaldæopolis belong to the supposed Ur of Babylonia, and not to Edessa; and Antioch could not be " of the far east," unless Antioch in Mygdonia (Nisibis) were called ' Antioch of the farther east.' Moreover, Dr. Stanley omits, I know not why, two names which did belong to Edessa,

---

ἐν τῇ λαμπάδι ἐκλίσει, " at the greatest of all feasts, that of the opening of spring, which some call a wood-pile, but others a beacon or lamp, from the large pile set on fire in honour of Juno or Atergatis." (Luc. de Dea Syr. vol. iii. p. 126, ed. Dip.) So also at Aphaca, near the temple of the Ἀφροδίτη Ἀφακῖτις—κατὰ μὲν οὖν τὸ ἱερόν—τῇ ἐν τοῦ ἀέρος λαμπάδος ἢ σφαίρας φαίνεται δίκην κ.τ.λ. (Zosim. Hist. in Aurel. p. 32, ed. Steph.) And Abu'l-feda (Tab. Syr. p. 127, sq. ed. Koehl.) quotes the author of Al-Ansab, who says that Manbed] was built by Coaru, who called it Munbeh منبه, and who raised therein بيت نار a 'fire-house' or 'fire-temple.' From منبه ' Manbeh,' the generic term for 'fire-place' or 'house,' came the Arabic 'Manbedj.' It is called Mabug ܡܒܘܓ in Syriac, and ܡܒܘܓ Hierapolis, 'the priestly city,' (Assem. B. Or. ii. 22) and is often mentioned as the seat of an Episcopate celebrated through Xenaias or Philoxenus (Assem. B. Or. p. 11, sq.); and also as a town given to idolatry, of which James, Bishop of Sarug, in his treatise on Idols (Assem. B. Or. ii. p. 327, sq.), says that "the devil made Mabug ܡܠܡ ܕܐܠܗܐ a city of priests of goddesses, and named it after himself, in order that it should go astray for ever."

Lastly, whatever claim Hierapolis of Syria—l. c., Mabug—may have to the name ' Bambyce,' certain it is that Hierapolis of Phrygia (Colos. iv. 13) is, to this day, called ' Pambuk qalæsi,' i. e., ' Castle of cotton ;' owing to the tepid thermæ, hot mineral springs, that made it famous in olden times ; that leave a white deposit which has accumulated for ages past, and which from Laodicea (Strabo, Lib. xiii. c. 1, 14) looks exactly like a waving sheet covering a part of the hill on which stand the ruins of Hierapolis. From the theatre, which commands a beautiful view of Khozan dágh, the mountain of Colossæ, and of the range of Mount Cadmus, with the ruins of Hierapolis on the foreground, this white sheet is hardly visible ; but from the bottom of the hill, and coming from Laodicea, and from that part of the vale of the Meander, this ' Castle of cotton' forms a very remarkable object.

namely, her own name Urhoe and Urhâ, and that of 'Justino-
polis,' given her by Justinus.[1]　It was the capital of Abgarus,
who, however, never was 'Akhar,' as Dr. Stanley says, "Abgarus, Agbarus, or Akbar," (p. 6,) misled, I trust, by Hyde;[2]
for 'Abgar' was a name which, like 'Cæsar' at Rome, 'Pharaoh' or 'Ptolemy' in Egypt, and 'Antiochus' in Syria, was
given to all the Governors of Edessa; a list of which is preserved in the Chronicle of Dionysius.[3]　After Abgar, and in
consequence of his reported letter to our SAVIOUR and the reply
he received from Him, Edessa became as we have seen celebrated for her faith; and then as a school to which men flocked
from all parts of the East, drawn alike by her reputation for
wisdom and for learning, and by the beauty of her situation.

V.　This is equally striking whether you come from the north,
down the green slopes of the lower hills of Armenia, or from
the rich pastures and the waving cornfields that spread far and
wide on to the horizon looking towards Haran.　But the most
beautiful picture this city presents is, perhaps, from the pass in
the steep hill at the back of the town.　After a dreary journey
of several hours over a barren table land,—the luxuriant foliage
of the walnut-trees, and the dark green cypresses which rising
above the city walls, stand like gaunt sentinels around the sacred
tank and by the Mosque of Abraham, on the foreground—the
city itself as it were embraced by rugged rocks and steep hills
on the right and on the left, with its churches, its white mina-
rets and numerous cupolas, detached from the green plains of
Mesopotamia that stretch beyond unto the foot of the blue hills
of Mardin—forms a picture only second to the view of Damascus coming from Dara at the foot of Anti-Lebanon.

I will not enlarge on my feelings at this sight; though it be
far inferior to Haran in interest.　I have visited many places of
renown, even the most holy; yet the plains and the hills of the

---

[1] μετεκλήθησαν τοίνυν ὑπὸ τοῦ αὐτοῦ Ἰουστίνου Ἔδεσσα καὶ Ἀνάζαρβαι, καὶ
τούτων ἐκάτερα τῇ αὐτοῦ προσηγορία κατεκοσμήθησαν. (Evagr. Hist. Eccles.
Lib. iv. c. 8.)　"Both Edessa and Anazarbus had their names changed by Justinus, and each was adorned with his name."

[2] De Vet. R. P. p. 74.

[3] 'Abgar' in Syriac means 'lame.' "Ali," continues Assemàn, (Bib. Or.
vol. I. p. 261, note,) "Augarum, Abagarum, Abbarum, Agbarum, vel Acbarum
proferunt: sed non rectè; a Syriaca enim radice recedunt," &c.

land of the Patriarchs seemed to be of other hues than the rest;
the air they breathe is fresher from the East, and they seem to
tell in plainer language the truth of their ancient history.   But
once inside the walls of the town and past the sacred spring, all
illusion ceases.   I tarried not, therefore, until I reached a high
spot, within the upper walls, whence I could see, far to the
southward, the mound and ruined tower of Haran, as a distant
landmark on the boundless plain of Padan-Aram.   As in travelling in the East I put faith only in the unchanging and unchanged features of the landscape and of the scenery around
the sacred spots I visited, and dwelt on that chiefly, I confess
that the sight of those plains from the hills of Ur, interested me
much more than the grated hole in which I was told Abraham
was born.   I would rather feast my eyes and refresh my mind
by studying the peculiar expression and language of the hills
and of the plains which I knew Terah and Abraham and Nahor
must have trodden, and on which they must have wandered
with their flocks, certain as I felt, that I then beheld some of
the landscape they must have seen; and that it could not be
very different from what it was in their time.   This, indeed, is
the real charm of Eastern travel; for as to the stories you hear,
they are a waste of time and a burden to the memory.

The fish in the tank, however, a pretty kind of cyprinus, with
bright orange fins, whether sacred to the memory of Abraham,
as Hyde tells us from an Arabic author, or rather, as it appears
to me, a remnant of the same heathen worship[1] as that of the
fish at Hierapolis sacred to Atergatis—were, I found, very much
like other fish.   Some days, a shoal of them would follow me
round the tank even if I threw them nothing to eat; as those
did of which Lucian speaks at Hierapolis, οἵτινες ἔρχονται καλεό-
μενοι, "that came when called;" at other times I could not
evoke them from their depths with handfuls of peas sold for the
purpose.   My philosophy availed me nothing; but I found that

---

[1] So remarkable a spring as that at Oorfa, could hardly fail to be the seat of
some idolatrous worship in olden times—chiefly that of Juno, Venus Syria, Der-
ceto, or Atergatis, to whom fish were sacred.   Not only do we find the lake and
the fish at Hierapolis, but also at Aphaca between Heliopolis (Baalbek) and
Byblos (Gebail), καθ᾽ ὃ ναὸς Ἀφροδίτης Ἀφακίτιδος Ἦρυται. τούτου πλησίον
λίμνη τίς ἐστιν, κ.τ.λ.   Zosimi Hist. lib. I. in Aurel. p. 32, ed. Steph.

whether at Ur of the Chaldees or elsewhere, fish will not rise when you like; and that, do what you will, you must abide their pleasure.

VI. The objects at Oorfa which I found of far greater interest than either the fish, the Mosque, or Abraham's cradle, were ancient sepulchral caves hewn out of the live rock at the back of the hill[1] on which the city is partly built. No sepulchres I saw before or since gave me so good an idea of what Machphelah מַכְפֵּלָה, "the double cave,"[2] must be, or must have been; several of these, that bear witness to the wear and waste of ages past, must have been hewn at a great cost; and bespeak the wealth and the importance of those for whom they were prepared. The first chamber, or hall, of some of these sepulchres might measure from twenty-five to thirty feet in length by fifteen or twenty in width and as many in height. The entrance into this hall was originally small enough to be closed with one or with two stones; and at the end of this first chamber, opposite the entrance, is another opening that leads into an inner chamber around which the dead lay in niches cut on three sides of it. On one of these I found traces of colour laid on the mortar with which it was coated after the manner of Etruscan tombs in the neighbourhood of Clusium, or of Greek tombs near Delphi. This may have been Terah's place of burial; this hollow cave may have re-echoed the rolling of the stone at the entrance, as Terah's last farewell to the son he buried ere he left this city for the plains of Haran.

Hence, from the hill in which these ancient dwellings of the dead were made, and looking towards Haran we may follow the course Terah, Abraham, and Nabor took on leaving Ur, and fancy them, their families and their flocks, wending their way across the plain to the southward towards the low mound then called חָרָן as now, حران, Haran.

"Was it," asks Dr. Stanley, "as according to Josephus, the grief of Terah over the untimely death of Haran? Was it, as according to the tradition followed by Stephen, that the higher call had already come to Abraham?"—p. 8.

---

[1] Now called Top-dagh, طاغ توب; not 'Top-dag' as Dr. Stanley says.

[2] From כ 'to double;' hence Κεφαλληνία, from the shape of that island. Bochart, Phaleg. p. 464.

And the same pen answers, " we know not."

VII. So then Dean Stanley seems to admit, that for him, Stephen's statement is only a tradition which carries with it no convincing proof or certainty. Thank God, we know better. We know that it was God Who brought Abraham, first—not out of Haran, but out of Ur of the Chaldees, (Gen. xv. 7.) And, lest there should be any doubt about it, the statement made in Gen. xi. 26—32 was, to use the language of the present day, written by an Elohist ; whereas, Gen. xv. came from the pen of a Jehovist. So that it appears that both Moses and his so-called anterior documents, agree in saying that Abraham left Ur of the Chaldees at God's bidding ; and for no other reason.

We know, further, that for those who receive the Bible as they ought, the fact that a man gifted with a wisdom and with a spirit which his adversaries could not resist, (Acts vi. 10,) whose face when he spake was like that of an angel ; who, just before his death saw the heavens opened and the Son of Man standing on the right hand of God—saying, at that same time : "the God of glory appeared unto our father Abraham when he was in Mesopotamia, before he dwelt in Charran," takes this statement out of the category of 'tradition.' Tradition is but the worn out selvage of Truth. But this is Truth itself. True, by reason of the time, of the facts, of the person who said it, of the person who wrote it, and of the Book in which it is written.

For, as to the quibble raised respecting Ur of the Chaldees not being ' in Mesopotamia,' it is unworthy of real scholars ; since we have seen, that before the time of Stephen, the limits of Syria and of Mesopotamia were far from fixed, and that at the time of Stephen, Ur or Edessa was reckoned to Mesopotamia proper according to the strict division and meaning of that term. For even when conventionally reckoned to Syria, Edessa as well as Haran, must always have been, geographically speaking, in Mesopotamia, in Padan-Aram, in Aram of the two Rivers ; a country, which from the very first, was physically and not conventionally, determined. Secondly,—since we admit that we do not exactly know where Ur of the Chaldees was, or what it really means, is it not idle to contend that it was not in Mesopotamia ? And thirdly,—admitting that Ur of the Chaldees was Edessa, and a city of the Chaldees, might it not be in

Mesopotamia, in אָרָם נַהֲרַיִם as well as, Apamea, Nicephorium, and Callinicum, founded by the Seleucidæ, ἐν τῇ μέσῃ τῶν ποταμῶν, as Zosimus calls Mesopotamia?¹ or as well as a settlement of Argives in Cilicia, of Phoceans in Gaul, or of Dorians in Caria and in Sicily?

VIII. But if, for argument's sake, we talk of 'tradition,' which of the many traditions did S. Stephen follow? Here, in sooth, may we say, "We know not." Dean Stanley refers us to Josephus, Antiq. Lib. i. c. vii. 1, but it is at c. vi. 5, that he mentions Terah's departure from Ur, μισήσαντος τὴν Χαλδαίαν διὰ τὸ 'Αράνου πένθος, "his having taken a dislike for Chaldea on account of his mourning for Aran; and they all came to Haran in Mesopotamia;" wherein we see that Josephus had no clear idea of the site of Ur, Οὔρη τῶν Χαλδαίων; but he took it for a city of Chaldea, instead of for a settlement of the Chaldees. Had he dreamt of Edessa being Οὔρη, he never would have drawn the limits of that Chaldean territory somewhere between Oorfa and Haran, a distance of not twenty miles, especially seeing both are in the heart of Mesopotamia. But, had Dr. Stanley read carefully the statement of Josephus to which he refers us, he would have seen, that Josephus ascribes Abraham's departure from 'Chaldea' to obedience to God's order, and that καταλείπει τὴν Χαλδαίαν—τοῦ Θεοῦ κελεύσαντος εἰς τὴν Χαναναίαν μετελθεῖν—πισθεὶς τοῖς ἀπροσωμένοις, "he left Chaldea—at God's bidding to come to Canaan—believing what he was told." So that, whatever Terah's private feelings may have been, we see that both Josephus and S. Stephen agree in saying that Abraham left Ur of the Chaldees in obedience to God's call; the very thing "God said unto him: I am the Lord that brought thee out of Ur of the Chaldees, to give thee this land to inherit it." (Gen. xv. 17.)

IX. Since then, their departure from Ur of the Chaldees was "to go into the land of Canaan;" and was not 'for Haran,' to which "they came" on their way, and "dwelt there;" the move cannot have originated with Terah, although he, being at that time the head of the family, is represented as "taking Abram his son" and his near of kin, to lead them forth from that land.²

¹ e.g. Lib. i. p. 28, ed. Steph.
² 'Ur of the Chaldees' is said at Gen. xi. 28, to be "the land of Haran's

But the move must have begun with Abraham; καίτοι τίς ἕτερος οὐκ ἂν ἠχθίσθη, "for, indeed what other man," says Philo,[1] "would not have been grieved, not only at leaving his own home, but at being driven from one town to another, into difficult and intricate wildernesses? Who is he that would not have turned back, giving up his object and the hope of it, hastening from his present difficulties, and thinking it folly to choose acknowledged evils for goods as yet unseen?"

And this first call of Abraham at Ur, and his instigating his father Terah to leave it with him, may possibly be veiled under the manifold traditions left us on the subject. S. Ephrem, for instance,[2] tells us that the "Chaldeans in Thare's (Terah) time having forsaken the knowledge of God gave themselves up to the worship of a god of their own, Cainan,[3] to which they had built a splendid temple. Meanwhile crows were sent to lay waste their land, as a punishment. One day, Abraham was sent by his father to his field to drive them away; but, unable to succeed, he exclaimed: O God, ܐܠܗܐ ܒܚܡ ܚܙܠܐ ܐܘܟܕܐ ܟܪܝܪܐ Maker of Heaven and Earth, help me! God heard him, and at once the crows flew away. Abraham astonished went home and told his father what had happened, and insisted on their all giving up the worship of Cainan. Terah, however, declined.[4] So Abram set fire to the temple, and Haran having

---

nativity." But this says nothing against the fact of Abraham and his family being ' Syrians' and not Chaldees. For (1) Haran might have been born there, and not his brothers; and (2) Ur of the Chaldees, being, probably, a 'settlement' only of the Chasdim in Mesopotamia, Abraham might be born there, and yet be a Syrian, אֲרַמִּי.

[1] De Migr. Abr. p. 352.

[2] Collectan. S. Ephr. and Jacob. Edess. in S. Ephr. vol. i. p. 158.

[3] ܡܟܐ ܕܡܐܝ ܚܡܠܐ ܡܘܟܚܘ, ܚܢܙܝ ܟܠ ܚܟ ܚܡܠܐ, Libra Zodiacalis, ܟܠܟܡܐ ܡܚܠܡܚܡܕ܆ ܚܡܐ ܘܚܡ ܚܡܠܐ ܚܢܙܝ ܗܘ ܗܘ ܗܘ "At the voice given by Caino (the Balance) were produced all things brought forth by the waters, that are hurtful and by which the world is injured." (Lib. Ad. i. p. 232, ed. Nork.) The constant worship of water as a part of that of fire, may be seen in many instances: a long dialogue between ܐܘܪ Ur, called the ' king of darkness,' as destroying it, with his mother ܟܐ ܟܘܡܐ, the Chaotic water, is found in the same book. (I. p. 390, sq., and II. 306, sq.)

[4] Terah, called أَزِر ' Azar' in the Coran, Sur. vi. 75, &c., is said to have made and sold idols, at Beit Iláhiyah, east of Damascus (Ibn Batút. vol. i. p.

come to put it out, or at least to save the idol, was consumed
in so doing. Then followed a persecution against Terah on the
part of the Chaldeans, who required that he should give up
Abraham. He refused, and was then made to leave Ur with all
that he had." This tradition is not found either in the Greek
or in the Armenian Versions of the works of S. Ephrem; and
the story of the crows[1] is the only particular Abulpharaj gives
respecting Abraham;[2] but it is told at even greater length in
the Ethiopic Kufâle. There, we are informed that "at seven
years of age Ahram could read books, and that he ran away from
Terah's house because he would not worship idols." Then follows the story of sowing time and of the crows, which is here
said to have happened when he was fourteen; of the fire set to
the temple of idols, of Abram's knowledge of the heavenly
bodies, &c. In the Targum J. B. Uzziel on Gen. xi. 28, we read
that Nimrod "cast him לְאַתּוּנָא דְּנוּרָא into a fiery furnace,[3]
because Abraham preached against idols. Haran said he would
be on whichever side did win. Abraham was not hurt by the
fire; but it fell from Heaven and destroyed Haran in presence
of his father." But, enough of these stories.

X. At every step from Oorfa on the way to Haran, which now
lies as it did of old, at about six hours' march from Ur, the hills
on the right and on the left of the plain recede farther and farther, until you find yourself fairly launched on the desert ocean
—a boundless plain, strewed at times with patches of the brightest flowers, at other times with rich and green pastures, covered

---

237) and آمس علي كفر "was attached to his unbelief," says Ab'al-feda,
(Hist. A. I. p. 20.) He is thought of differently in the Abyssinian Church, that
calls him ࢶࢳࢽ : "faithful" (J. Lud. Lex. s.v.) Yet Abraham had to get
him out of hell, "as a good son ought to do to his father." (Perikta Sota, in
Eisenm. Endekt. Jud. ii. p. 359, &c.)

[1] It is said to have happened when Abraham was fifteen years old. The word
ܩܡܨܐ S. Ephr. and ܩܡܨܐ Abulph. is rendered 'locusts,' by the translator of S. Ephrem; but wrongly. J. D. Michaelis saw in it adpazas, and
Bruns and Kirsch so rendered it, rightly. For in the Ethiopic Kufâle where the
same story is told, c. xii. p. 47—49, we read, ቆᎾᎩ : ፁᎶᎸ : "a cloud of
crows." Locusts, however, laid bare the same country more than once, as e.g.
a. n. 952, after a famine. (Matth. of Edessa, in Notices et Extr. des MSS.
vol. ix. p. 21.)

[2] Chron. p. 11.   [3] Cor. Sur. v. 20, and Masûdî. c. iv. vol. i. p. 85.

with flocks of sheep and of goats feeding together, here and there a few camels, and the son or the daughter of their owner tending them.   One can quite understand how the sons of this open country البدو 'el-badu'—the Bedaweens—love it, and cannot leave it : no other soil would suit them.   The air is so fresh, the horizon is so far, and man feels so free, that it seems made for those whose life is to roam at pleasure, and who own allegiance to none but to themselves.   But by far the chief interest for any one who visits such a land for what the land has to give, is—not to look for Roman spear-heads lost by Crassus, nor yet for the ruined tower of a Christian Church, neither for the shrines of Bosin, of Del-Shemein, of Barnemro Tarhato, and other gods of which Jac. Sarugensis speaks,[1] and which are said to exist in the neighbourhood, as remnants of " the gods of Haran ;"[2] but the chief interest lies in the associations of patriarchal life among which he finds himself at once.

The village of Haran itself consists of a few conical houses, in shape like beehives, built of stones laid in courses one over the other, without either mud or mortar; these houses let in the light at the top, and are clustered together at the foot of the ruined castle built on the mound, that makes Haran a landmark plainly visible from the whole plain around.   The principal inhabitants of the place are the Bedaween tribes, which haunt the neighbourhood in search of pasture.   One of their tribes, the Anazees, had spread their tents of black goats'-hair at the foot of the mound, between that and Rebekah's well; and I pitched my tent among them.

That same day I walked at even to the well I had passed in the afternoon coming from Oorfa; the well of this the city of Nahor,[3] " at the time of the evening, the time that women go out to draw water."   There was a group of them, filling, no longer their ' pitchers,'—since the steps down which Rebekah went to fetch the water are now blocked up,—but filling their water-skins by drawing water at the well's mouth.   Everything around that well bears signs of age and of the wear of time; for as it is the only well of drinkable water there, it is much resorted to.   Other wells are only for watering the flocks.   There

[1] Assem. B. Or. vol. i. p. 327.   [2] 2 Kings xix. 12.
[3] Comp. Gen. xxiv. 10, xxviii. 5, 10, xxix. 4.

we find the troughs of various height, for camels, for sheep, and for goats, for kids and for lambs; there the women wear nose-rings, and bracelets on their arms, some of gold or of silver, and others of brass or even of glass. One of these was seen in the distance bringing to water her flock of fine patriarchal sheep; ere she reached the well, shepherds, more civil than their bre-thren of Horeb, had filled the troughs with water for her sheep. She was the sheikh's daughter, the "beautiful and well favoured" Ladheefeh.

As the shadows of the grass and of the low shrubs around the well lengthened and grew dim, and the sun sank below the horizon, the women left in small groups; the shepherds fol-lowed them, and I was left alone in this vast solitude. Yet not alone: the bright evening star in the glowing sky to westward seemed to point to the Promised Land, as when Abraham took it for his guide; the sky overhead, clear and brilliant as when he gazed on it, and the earth, the ground on which he trod,—all spake a language heard nowhere else. The heavens whis-pered and the earth answered, "Walk by faith," "stagger not at the promise of God through unbelief," but do as Abraham did, "be strong in the faith, giving glory to God," and "by thy works make thy faith perfect." There is, also for thee, a Promised Land—thy home. Keep thine eye thereon, and thou, stranger and pilgrim on the earth, believe Him that pro-mised, as Abraham did; "seek," as he did, "a better country, that is, an heavenly," and it shall be "counted unto thee for righteousness."

These words, breathed in the silence of the night, and in presence of Abraham's witnesses, the same stars and the same heavens which he saw, carried home to my heart a reality I had never felt before. Mean and foolish did the strife of tongues of the outer world then appear; vain did the pretensions of its wisdom seem, and futile the opposition of a science falsely so called—here, by the well of Haran, within hearing of God's promise to Abraham, within sight of Abraham's faith in that promise, and of his obedience to Him that promised, Whom he counted faithful. That was real philosophy. His life was—our life is—practical; πρᾶξις—τοῦ δέοντος. Reason upon it, then, as you will, this was the ἔργον, the work of Abraham's faith—to

go whither God called him; not seeking for motives or for
fancies within himself, but obeying God.   One step of his from
Ur towards Canaan was worth all that philosophy ever did
devise.   In accepting to walk by faith as his condition through
life, and in making proof of his faith through his obedience,—
giving up self and self-will to God,—Abraham was a wiser and
a greater man than all the wise men of Greece; for he denied
himself, and trusted God.   So, then, "his faith wrought by
his works," and his reward for it was, to be "called the Friend
of God"—at peace in this life, and at rest in Heaven.

I went back to my tent: it was beset with visitors, who, with
genuine Eastern hospitality, bade me welcome among them, and
we soon became friends.   I spent several days with them and
in the neighbourhood, but chiefly by the well of this "city of
Nahor," to which Eliezer came for Rebekah, and Jacob for
Rachel.   Among my hosts I noticed especially one called El-
khalil, a venerable old man, whose likeness I drew several times;
for it could only be that of Abraham.

XI.   But—to return to the world—Dean Stanley says that

"for the highest spirit of the Patriarchal family Haran could not
be a permanent abiding-place."   "Two days' journey brought
him to the high chalk cliffs which overlook the wide western
desert.   Broad and strong lay the great stream beneath and between.   He crossed over it, probably near the same point where
it is still forded—at Zeugma; the ancient passage was a little
west of the present passage at Bira."—pp. 0, 10, and note.

Yet all we know for certain of Abraham's journey from Haran
to Canaan is what we read in Scripture: "And Abraham took
Sarai his wife, and Lot his brother's son, and all their substance
that they had gathered, and the souls that they had gotten in
Haran; and they went forth to go into the land of Canaan; and
into the land of Canaan they came."[1]   There is no sign of
delay in this; but from it we must gather, with S. Ambrose,[2]
that "paruit itaque mandato Abraham, nec ulla legitur mora
intervenisse.   Egressus perambulavit usque ad Sichem."   Everything else not mentioned in Scripture concerning Abraham's
journey south is legendary, from Aleppo to Mecca.   One legend

---

[1] Gen. xii. 5.   [2] Vol. iv. p. 173, de Abr. Patr.

is as trustworthy as another; and we need not, therefore, believe
Justinus, Nicholas of Damascus, Berosus and others more than
the traditions or the legends sown broadcast over the East
through the Talmud and through the Coran.

I have never seen "Beer's Leben Abrahams," to which Dr.
Stanley refers; but Nicholas of Damascus,[1] it is true, says, according to Josephus,[2] that Ἀβράμης ἐβασίλευσε Δαμασκοῦ ἔπηλυς
σὺν στρατῷ ἀφιγμένος ἐκ τῆς γῆς ὑπὲρ Βαβυλῶνος Χαλδαίων λεγο-
μένης· "Abraham reigned in Damascus a stranger, who had
come with an army from the land called 'of the Chaldeans'
beyond Babylon." And Justinus[3] also tells us, "Judæis origo
Damascena, Syriæ nobilissima civitas:—nomen urbi a Damasco
rege inditum—post Damascum Azelus, mox Adores, et Abraham, et Israhel reges fuere." But one thing in this statement is as true as another; Abraham was King of Damascus
according to Justinus as much as 'Israhel;' so Jacob, too, must
have reigned there. And when Dean Stanley, who seems to
put faith in the story told by Justinus, and to wish to see Abraham 'King of Damascus,' further draws, as he thinks, a proof
of it from a certain play upon the words Eliezer of 'Damascus,'
as having been brought thence by Abraham, he ought also to
maintain, on precisely the same grounds, that Potiphar 'had
reigned in Dothan,' since the steward of his property was
Joseph his servant, a Hebrew, who came from thence, and was
lord of all his house; and that Sarah must have been 'Queen of
On,' or of Tanis, since she had an Egyptian maid.

Let us see, however, what all this is worth. And first about
this play upon the words: וּבֶן־מֶשֶׁק בֵּיתִי הוּא דַּמֶּשֶׂק אֱלִיעֶזֶר,
'And (the son of possession of) he that looks like the probable
heir to my house, (is) this Eliezer of Damascus;'[4] whereon it is
argued that מֶשֶׁק, being ἅπαξ λεγ. for מֶשֶׁק, 'possession,' was
chosen by the writer—the fifth historian ! says Ewald[5]—to alli-
terate with דַּמֶּשֶׂק, in a kind of proverbial form, that points to
an older history, &c.,—a fond conceit, truly.

For, what of that ? Alliteration is almost peculiar to Shemitic
languages in all ages; only take the first page of an Arabic

[1] P. 114, ed. Orell.   [2] Antiq. Lib. i. c. 8.   [3] Hist. Lib. xxxvi. c. 2.
[4] Gen. xv. 2.   [5] Volk. Isr. i. p. 446, note.

poem, and read.' Besides, it is difficult to see how this pretended play on הַמֶּשֶׁק and the term בֶּן־בֵּיתִי (verna mens,
οἰκίτης μου), v. 3, can possibly even show that Abraham ever was
at Damascus, much less that he reigned there. For, by comparing together Gen. xii. 4, xvi. 16, xxi. 5, and xxiv. 20, we find
that Abraham was seventy-five years old when he left Haran;
eighty-six when Ishmael was born of Hagar, that is, one year
after Sarah had given her to Abraham, that, again, being ten
years after Sarah had had Hagar for a maid (Gen. xvi. 3). Now
"Sarai Abraham's wife took Hagar her maid, the Egyptian,
after Abram had dwelt ten years in the land of Canaan" (ib.);
that is, of course, the same year that he left Haran to come to
Canaan, whence he went straight to Egypt, on account of the
famine; and there either Sarah bought Hagar, or, as the story
goes, Pharaoh gave Hagar to Sarah, grieved that she should
have to wait upon herself.

Clearly, then, Abraham arrived in Egypt within less than
a twelvemonth after his departure from Haran. This, it must
be seen, leaves very little time for his conquest of Damascus and
for his reign there, if he ever went near the place. Moreover,
Eliezer, if born in Abraham's house at Damascus, that is, the
same year Abraham left Haran, must have been sixty-five years
old when Abraham sent him into Mesopotamia (Gen. xxiv. 1—3)
to fetch Rebekah, since Isaac was then forty, and Abraham one
hundred and forty years old; therefore Eliezer could not be
more than thirteen or fourteen years of age when Abraham
spake of him as of בֶּן־בֵּיתִי or בֶּן־מֶשֶׁק בֵּיתִי, in ch. xv. 2—a
very young 'steward' indeed. But, rather, the fact that he
could not be a 'steward' at this early age proves (1) that
בֶּן־מֶשֶׁק cannot be rendered 'steward,' but as Gesenius rightly

---

¹ Thus, for instance, we find a 'real' play upon this very word مشق,
دمشق, in Ahmed Arabsiad. V. Tim. c. xcvi. vol. ii. p. 909; where, speaking
of Timur's soldiers at Damascus, he says: ولها رحلوا عن دمشق وقد
"when مشقوا اوراق نعمها من اغصان وجودها أي مشق that
they departed from Damascus دمشق, and after they had 'combed' مشقوا
the leaves of her beauties off the branches of her wealth أي مشق, ay, a
thorough 'combing.'" This is alliteration indeed, the other is fancy.

renders it in the sense of "'the presumptive heir' to my house."
This is also the meaning given to בֶּן in this place by Abarbanel,[1]
who remarks that, when sent to fetch Rebekah, Abraham does
not call him 'son,' but only 'elder servant.' And as to his
name 'Eliezer,' it was given him, says the Midrash Rabbah,[2] on
account of his help to Abraham in defeating Chedorlaomer and
his allies; the Targ. J. B. Uzziel and Targ. Hieros.[3] putting
into Abraham's mouth these words, "The child of my house,
הוּא יְדֵי אֶתְעֲבֵדוּ לִי נִסִּין בְּדַמֶּשֶׂק, through whose assistance
(hands) wonders were wrought by me (or, for me) in Damascus,
thinks he is to inherit of me!"

Be this as it may, it is very clear that we have not "in this
play on the name of Abraham's faithful slave," as Dean Stanley
says, "a guarantee of the close tie which subsisted between the
Patriarch and his earliest conquest;" a mere assumption, without a shadow of proof, that is no guarantee whatever of what
cannot have happened, if we look attentively at the text of
Scripture. And as to the fame of Abraham, which ἔτι καὶ νῦν ἐν
τῇ Δαμασκηνῇ—δοξάζεται, "is still great about Damascus," says
Josephus,[4] as another guarantee of Abraham's reign there, his
fame is still greater in the Hedjâz and at Mecca; so he must
have reigned there also.

XII. Nothing, therefore, is less likely than that Abraham
should have followed the route Dr. Stanley marks out for him.
First, the 'Zeugma' he mentions as having been a little to the
south of Bîr, or El-Bireh, البيرة,[5] (and not 'Birs,') Turkish,
'Beredjik,' was so called τὸ ζεῦγμα τοῦ Εὐφράτου, because of the
bridge, said to have been built by Alexander the Great, which
did there span the river, deep and rapid as it is, and united the
two opposite banks. This Ζεῦγμα, however, was either of the
Comagene, according to Pliny, or of the Cyrrhestica, according
to Ptolemy.[6] It was, therefore, to the north of Haran, and not
on the way to Canaan; whereas Abraham's direct route to
Canaan lay straight from Haran to the other and older Zeugma,

[1] Comm. in Pent. p. 46, verso, ed. Bash.
[2] Fol. 45, verso.   [3] Ed. Walton, l.c.
[4] Antiq. Lib. I. c. 7.
[5] Abu'l-fed. Tab. Syr. p. 127, ed. Koehl.
[6] Cellar. Geog. Ant. vol. ii. p. 341, sq.

near Thapsacus, πρὸς τὸ πάλαι τὸ κατὰ τὴν Θαψακόν,[1] which Dr.
Stanley seems to have overlooked. This would bring Abraham
in a straight course also to Tadmor, and thence, somewhat out
of his way, to Damascus, if he then visited that place. But, inasmuch as the small town of Sichem is the first station mentioned
in Holy Scripture after Haran, it is most probable that Abraham followed, on his way from Haran to Canaan, the same route
which Jacob took on his way from Canaan to Haran, and which
Dr. Stanley himself marks out for him at p. 63; that is, from
Haran to Tadmor, and thence, through the Haurán, to the
fords of Jordan, near to Salim, or Salem. His course would,
naturally, be as straight as possible, and shaped according to
the wells or other watering stations for his flocks. It is idle to
suppose him conquering Damascus or any other territory while
bent on reaching the land to which God was leading him,[2] which
he traversed, and through which he reached Egypt, within less
than a twelvemonth of his leaving Haran.

XIII. We may, then, think what we like of the story told by
Ibn al-Wardi,[3] of Abraham being moved by God to leave his
country with his family for Schaubet-el-beidha, 'the white city,'
whither the angel Gabriel was sent to guide him to the 'white
mound' باتل الابيض, on which the citadel of Aleppo stands.
Ibn Batútah[4] calls it 'الشهبا, the 'grey' rock, and goes on to
say that Haleb, Aleppo, takes its name from "Abraham's 'new
milk' حلب ابراهيم the milk of his flocks, which he gave to
the poor," &c. When he left Aleppo, Ibn al-Wardi says that he
prayed for all sorts of blessings on the town; so that now, whoever visits that city never leaves it without shedding tears of
regret. My experience was different from this: I was, on the
contrary, very glad to leave it. This story is also told by El-
kazwíni;[5] nevertheless, even Arab writers are not agreed upon
the subject: "nam aliqui *Arabum* volunt eum tetendisse nimis
australiter per *Meccam*, sic alii eorum nimis borealiter per Haleb
quæ Aleppo: sic *Ibn al-Mallá Halebensis*, qui dicit Haleb

[1] Strabo, Lib. xvi. c. 1. 23.

[2] ἵετο δὲ ἐσσύμενος—"he hastened on his way thither, putting his readiness
to obey God on a par with his arrival there."   Philo. De Abr. p. 358.

[3] Tab. Syr. ed. Koehl. p. 189.   [4] Trav. vol. I. p. 148.

[5] Vol. ii p. 122, ed. W.

fuisse ex locis ad quæ peregrinatus est Abraham, qui ibi aliquan-
diu substitit post discessum suum ab Haran. Prob nugæ !"[1]

XIV. But we should never have done if we rehearsed half of
what is told of Abraham in Jewish and in Arabic writers. There
is nothing he could not either know or do. בן ג׳ שנים הכיר
אב׳ את בוראו. "At three years of age Abraham knew his
Creator," says R. Bechai;[2] though here, again, authors differ,
since Masudi[3] quotes Cor. xxi. 52, to show that قد اوتی رشده
"the first inward guidance had been given him," ere he came
out of the cave on Mount Casius, near Damascus, where he had
been hidden.[4] And no wonder, since R. Menachem tells us[5]
that רבו של אב׳ צדקיאל, "Zadkiel was Abraham's tutor;"
and many more absurdities of this kind, which would make up
a large volume of most unprofitable matter.

XV. After giving us a pretty description of Damascus at
p. 10, Dean Stanley proceeds to a fuller account of Abraham's
character, and says—

"Not many years ago much offence was given by one, now a
high dignitary in the English Church, who ventured to suggest
the original likeness of Abraham by calling him a Bedouin
sheykh."

One can hardly picture to oneself the state of innocence that
could take offence at such a thing; but, that it can be true,
being said by the Dean of Westminster, is assuredly no compliment to his countrymen. Yet the same thing is repeated by a
reviewer friendly to the Dean in the "Edinburgh Review"
(Jan., 1864, p. 137)—reviews are often strange things—who
there can bring himself to say that—

"Dr. Milman's greatest crime (as Dr. Stanley has observed), without which his other offences would scarcely have been noticed,
was that he ventured to let in the light of common day upon
ground which was popularly considered too sacred for the sun to
shine on. It was thought an unpardonable familiarity with holy
things, a dangerous and profane liberty, to speak of Abraham as a
Sheikh or a Bedouin chieftain; of the Israelites after their occu-

[1] Hyde, De V. R. P. p. 74. [2] Par. Vajer. fol. 29, col. 3.
[3] Vol. I. 84.
[4] But 'born,' according to Ibn Batutah, vol. I. p. 231.
[5] Par. Schemoth, fol. 80, in Eisenmeng. End. Judenth. I. 523, ii. 375, &c.

pation of Canaan as an 'independent yeomanry, residing on their
hereditary farms;' of the Levites as a 'learned nobility ;' of Israel
itself as a 'confederacy of separate republics' or of 'scattered
cantons.' "—pp. 137, 139.

Of course, the ἰδέα of all this is self-evident—it is to make
party capital out of what is really too claptrap to find its way
into manly writing. The ὄντως φιλόσοφος, the real philosopher,
would not condescend to such trickery. He would not try to
catch the ear of the multitude—"vulgus, quod ex veritate
pauca, ex opinione multa, æstimat"[1]—in making it appear that
light is on his side only, and that others are yet in gloom, at
such a trifling price. Yet what light? to call Abraham a Bedouin Sheikh. One cannot refrain from a smile at such childish
criticism, nor from wondering at what the state of minds must
be that can call this "the light of common day." Their own dimness it appears is not yet removed; and ere they operate on their
brethren's eyes, themselves need indeed see well enough to do it.
At the same time, we may question the fairness of fathering
upon the venerable Dean of S. Paul's, commonplace expressions,
which he is much too learned ever to have considered as "light"
thrown upon the subject. Whatever be his religious opinions,
of which I am no judge, he at all events is a scholar, and very
superior to those who now run for shelter under his wings.

The fact is that Abraham was neither a 'Bedouin' nor a 'Bedouin Sheikh ;' for in those days—at least in those parts—such
terms as البدو and البداويين, 'bedu' and 'Bedaween,' were
not in use. But, by belonging to those who, in polite Arabic,
are called اهل الوبر, 'the family of men dwelling in tents made
of black hair,' to the 'Scenitæ' of Latin authors, Abraham was
more likely to be what in Syriac might be ܒܪ‌ܒܪܐ, 'Bar-baro,' a
'son of the open country,' a 'barbarian,' the father, too, of a
'barbaric race,' βαρβαρικοῦ γένους.[2] He was 'Paganus,' or
better still, 'a heathen,' even while he was "the Friend of God"
and "the Father of the faithful ;"[3] since 'heathen' comes from
'heath,' the Gothic ჰᲐᲘΨ, a 'field,' adj. ჰᲐᲘΨGᲘ, A, 'of

<hr>

[1] Cic. pro Rosc. Com.   [2] Philo, De V. Mos. Lib. I. p. 684.
[3] Rom. iv. 11, 16.

'the field,' a man or a woman living in the fields or country ; a 'heathen,' שָׂדֶה אִישׁ. It is not the light of day, τὸ σαφηνές, the plain Truth, that is to be dreaded, since Truth in itself—but especially Truth as regards the Bible—is the hallowed principle, the sacred object to be desired, to be searched for, and to be put forth at all cost when requisite. But 'Truth' is too often disfigured by those who give themselves for its apostles. Thus, to compare Abraham to an Arab Sheikh is so natural and so simple, that it need not be thought of twice; but to make it appear as an effort of genius, as a proof of the 'philosophy' of a particular party, is not creditable. What is it, according to Plato, that distinguishes the ὄντως φιλόσοφοι, 'real philosophers,' from the πλαστῶς φιλόσοφοι, 'sham philosophers,' but φιλοδοξία μᾶλλον ἢ φιλοσοφία, but " the love of praise or the love of men's opinion, rather than the love of truth?" And what does separate the philosopher φιλόσοφος from the sophist σοφιστής, but the ἦθος, the 'moral habit,' and the ἔθος, the 'manner or custom' of each in setting forth the Truth, honestly or not ?

It stands to reason that, the more we become acquainted with daily life, but especially with patriarchal life, in the East, the better we understand the narrative of Scripture, and the more also we can enter into the spirit of it. We then judge better of distances, of allusions, and of the relative position of places, if we have visited the land of the Bible; and if we have not visited it, but only know the languages of the Old and of the New Testament, and something of the language at present spoken in Palestine, we are able to understand expressions and the force of terms which are all but a dead letter to us if we do not. If we have visited the Holy Land, we then see the various events of which we read in Holy Scripture, as it were, painted on a real background.

No one, for instance, can have seen as I did, the striking of tents and the moving of a whole Arab encampment at sunrise, with flocks and herds that spread for miles over the high table land that separates the hills of Moab from the vales of Rabbath-Ammon, without being able for ever after to feel more at home in reading the history of Abraham's journeyings, of Isaac, and of Jacob with his two bands, returning from Padan-Aram. The reality of certain narratives contained in the Old Testament

can only gain by such experience; and the more it is multiplied
the better. But as regards those for whom such accounts are
written by eye-witnesses, it all depends on how things are put
before them. The events and the scenes recorded in the Bible
may be treated like ordinary events and ordinary scenes, even in
a jocular way; or with reverence and worship, as it is meet they
should be; as events and scenes of a land which, although it
be now "trodden down of the Gentiles," is, nevertheless, the
sanctuary of the whole earth.

"What then," asks Dean Stanley, "is the position which has
been accorded to Abraham by the general witness of history?"—
"We see it best by considering the two names by which he is
known in eastern traditions, 'Friend of God' and 'Father of the
Faithful.'"

XVI. Although we cannot, of course, talk of the general
witness of history to a man who is only one great subject
of the most peculiar and especial history in the world, and shut
out from all others; a subject only second to the great object
of that history, to Him "Whose day Abraham saw and rejoiced,"
yet Dr. Stanley has a few very good and pertinent remarks on
the first of these names at pp. 13, 14. The name El-Khalil,
'the Friend,' 'the intimate Friend' of God, obtains in Mohamm-
medan countries only from the use made of it in the Coran.
Whoever has studied the spirit of the Meccan impostor, as shown
throughout his life, may see at once why he fixed principally
upon this title of Abraham. It was necessary for him that he
should claim friendship with, and praise him who was 'the
Friend of God;' and of whom, on that account, he tells many
wonderful and absurd stories. For the same reason of self-
interest, did he hold up other characters of the Old and of the
New Testaments; even our Lord Himself; so that he might
embrace and gather all, Jews as well as Christians, in the meshes
of his crafty, barefaced imposture. There can be no doubt
about it; since فاتاد جبريل نعلّمه دينه واصطفاه الله نبيه وخليلا
"Gabriel came and taught Abraham true religion"—Islamism,
of course—"and God chose him for His Prophet and for His
Friend."[1]

"Abraham was, indeed, chosen by God, as he was called by

God," says Dr. Stanley, who, however, seems to have a somewhat indistinct idea of his subject, when he adds:

"Although in the word 'ecclesia,' in its religious sense, the etymological meaning, of an assembly *called forth by the herald*, is lost in the general idea of 'a congregation,' yet this original meaning gives a fitness to the consideration that he who was the first in the succession of the 'ecclesia' or 'church,' was so by virtue of what is known in all subsequent history as his 'call.'"—p. 14.

XVII. For the etymological meaning of ἐκκλησία, 'ecclesia,' is hardly "an assembly *called forth by the herald ;*" if so, and if the 'being called by a man' constituted the ἐκκλησία, then the congregation called by the muezzin to the mosque from the minaret, would, to a certain extent, be an ἐκκλησία; though not according to the idea of it received at Athens. The 'herald' was clearly, only an accident, a form of calling. The ἐκκλησία must be called ; so a herald was sent to call every member to the place of gathering; but what constituted the ἐκκλησία was, of course, not the 'herald' himself, since a message might have been sent in some other way than through him, but the νομίμη ἐκκλησία consisted both in and of the gathering together of certain citizens only, called from the rest, as being duly qualified to become members of that 'ecclesia,' ἐκκλησία; the first of those qualifications being that of citizenship, for foreigners were not eligible; next, that of age, birth, character, &c. Those citizens thus qualified and then called, were said to be ἐκκλητοί, called out from among the rest, by virtue of certain rights they had ; for those rights entitled them to the calling, not the calling to the rights ; they were called, only to certain duties, which entailed rewards, &c.

Nothing could be less like what is termed 'a congregation,' a motley gathering of people, of animals and of things inanimate, than the ἐκκλησία—'a chosen assembly of free citizens duly qualified,' whose parents were also free, and who themselves were not otherwise disqualified by crime or by defamation. Very far from being a 'congregation' only, it was held in the public square, ἀγορά, where the space marked out for the 'ecclesia' was fenced off by hurdles, γέρρα, in order to keep out strangers, who could not be admitted until after the votes had been taken.   And it was on account of all these distinctive features of ἐκκλησία, 'ecclesia,' that this term, and no other, was chosen by the HOLY GHOST, from among other generic ones, such as : ὅμιλος, ὁμήγυρις, σύναξις, σύνοδος, συναγωγή, σύγκλησις, ἀθροισμός, ἀλία, εἰρία, πανήγυρις, συνηλυσία, σύλλογος, ἄγερσις, ἐπάγερσις, ἄγυρις, ἀγορά, συλλογή, θάμυρις, ἀνάκλησις, ἀγελή, πολίμνιον, &c., and from other specific terms, such as : βουλή, κατάκλησις, &c.

The ἐκκλησία then consisted of citizens called out from among the rest, by virtue of certain rights they had, for certain purposes, functions, &c.   The 'purpose,' be it deliberative or what not, of the 'ecclesia' was the 'object' proposed to every citizen thus called; and that brought him to the assembly.   God called Abraham, as being ἐκλεκτός, 'chosen,'[1] and He set before him promises " afar off," yet true, for the sake of which, Abraham came out of Ur, and walked towards the Land of promise.   Without such an object he would not have gone; but that object thus set before him, and real, though unseen, because true by virtue of Him Who promised it, and Who set it before Abraham, not only brought Abraham out of Ur, but kept up his strength of purpose through his long journey towards Canaan.   And he thus represented the Church which could not exist without objective Truths and promises which she holds and cherishes—but does not make.

Except this apparent oversight as to the real meaning and character of ἐκκλησία, 'ecclesia,' the whole remainder of this paragraph in Dr. Stanley's book is well worth reading.   I will only remark that the story of Abraham and of the sun, moon and stars, related by Dr. Stanley at p. 17 as told by Ibn Batútah, is incorrectly given.   It runs thus :[2] " From this cave, Abraham saw the star, the moon and the sun ; as the sublime Book says."   There[3] it is thus told: " When the night fell over him he saw a star ; he said : This is my LORD : but when it did set, he said : I do not like those that set.   And when he saw the moon excelling in brightness, he said : This is my LORD : but when it set, he said : Surely, unless my LORD guide me I shall be among them that live in error.   But when he saw the sun, yet brighter than the moon ; he said : This is my LORD ; this

[1] Rom. xi. 28.   This is again treated elsewhere.
[2] Ibn Bat. vol. I. p. 231.   [3] Cor. Sur. vi. 76, sq.

is the greatest. But when it set, then he said : O my people, I
am indeed innocent of that which ye do in common (i.e. idolatry.)
For my part, I have like an orthodox turned my face towards
Him who created the heavens and the earth ; for I am not of
those who join together (to worship idols.)" This story is often
told by other authors ; as e.g. by Masudi,[1] who, however, gives
it only in part.

XVIII. Then follow (pp. 18, 19) other excellent remarks on
Abraham's faith as shown by his works, if so be I understand
Dr. Stanley right. We will not discuss together " the paradox
of the reformer," as he calls it ; but if he mean by what he
says that Abraham's faith was not in words but in works, and
that by his works it was made perfect, for that without works
faith is dead—then I agree with him, and we both agree with
S. James. Yet what does he mean by, " was counted to him ?"
I understand it to mean, that Abraham was accounted righteous
by God, for believing Him, even so far as to hope against hope ;
—his hope being the very work—τὸ ἔργον, though not in this
case, τὸ τέλος—of the faith that wrought it ; so that " he stag-
gered not at the promise of God through unbelief." And as he
gave proof of his faith through works which showed his faith
to be implicit and sincere, thus acknowledging that God, as
God, had full right to bid him walk by faith and not by sight,
his works were accepted ; yet only as tokens of his faith.
Through works which his faith made him do, he showed himself
to be ' righteous,' that is ' doing right' in giving up ' self,' and
in giving himself up to do God's will only, body soul and spirit.
Yet, as naught of this could be wrought in him and by him,
unless he had first believed and trusted God, it is clear that his
' righteousness' consisted, not in the works themselves as works,
but in the faith that wrought them. Abraham was ' righteous,'
not in leaving Ur or Haran ; but in leaving these cities at God's
bidding ; believing and trusting Him.

In other words, the object, or objects, set before him by God,
the Land of Promise,[2] and the day of CHRIST, were Truths and
' the Truth,' for Abraham. That Truth set before him as the one
object to which he looked by faith—faith, being as we shall see,

[1] Vol. I. p. 84.

[2] προσδέχει—προσοτέρω σημείοις δηλούμενα.   Philo. De Abr. p. 358.

both intellectual, belief, and moral or spiritual, trust in GOD
and in His promises—brought him out of Ur and made him
walk towards Canaan: as the lode-star of his course. Fancy
him looking, as some now teach, for the Truth within himself;
would he ever have left his father's house, to go he knew not
whither ? or, had he been called, and had he not believed the call,
would he have forsaken everything in order to obey that call ?
But, so little have Truth, faith and obedience altered since Abraham's time, that he is said to be the " father of them that believe ;"
and they that " are of faith are blessed with faithful Abraham."
Nay, it is hard to understand, how a well constituted mind; can
do otherwise than see clearly, that Abraham's righteousness
consisted in his faith in certain definite Truths set before him,
and towards which he walked, being led thither by that faith.
Truth was for him objective; the only subjective Truth he knew
was the conscience of his having obeyed GOD; by coming out
of Ur at GOD's call, to look for a land as yet only promised, but
promised by GOD. No wonder, then, if Dr. Stanley seems to
find it difficult to reconcile all these plain facts, and all this
plain teaching, with that of the so-called philosophy of the day,
that confounds ' faith' with ' belief,' that is, belief and trust in
things spiritual and peace of mind withal, with belief and misgivings in things intellectual, and no peace of mind withal, only
for the sake of escaping from the inevitable surrender of ' self'
to objective Truth—the only Truth there is—and therefore from
obedience to aught but to ' self' also. Yet, " without faith it is
impossible to please GOD," and " faith without works is dead,
being alone."

So thought, so did, so teaches Abraham. Therefore was he
also called the " Father of the Faithful"—not only as father of
the chosen people which, whatever may its sins of idolatry, of
stubbornness have been, was nevertheless ' faithful' compared
with other nations; but Abraham was called the ' Father of the
Faithful,' as being the pattern for them to follow who wish to
be blessed with him in his ready, whole and entire obedience to
objective Truth, to GOD's call and promises; both the type and
the seed of the Church militant in the earth. Yet, for all that,
Abraham was not the " first believer," (p. 19,) as Dr. Stanley
says: at least S. Paul did not think so. For, he tells us plainly,

that "by faith Abel offered unto God a more excellent sacrifice than Cain, by which he obtained witness that he was righteous, God testifying of his gifts;" " by faith Enoch was translated that he should not see death"—" for before his translation he had this testimony, that he pleased God. But without faith *it is* impossible to please *him* : for he that cometh to God must believe that he is, and *that* he is a rewarder of them that diligently seek him—τοῖς ἐκζητοῦσιν αὐτόν. By faith, Noah being warned of God of things not seen as yet, moved with fear prepared an ark to the saving of his house ; by the which he condemned the world, and became heir of the righteousness which is by faith." (Heb. xi. 1—7.)

This would be more than enough, even if we had not the Epistle to the Romans, to show that " faith with S. Paul" was not as Dr. Stanley says, " almost synonymous with the admission of the Gentiles." Righteousness that is by faith is not applied by wholesale to nations ; but to every individual heart, that makes objective Truth, so to speak, subjective, by receiving it through faith, and then acting upon it, according to the strong or to the weak nature of that faith, more or less as it did in Abraham's heart. Dr. Stanley's intention, therefore, is not clear when he says :—

" In modern ages of the history of the Church it has too often happened that the doctrine of 'faith' has had a narrowing effect on the conscience and feelings of those who have strongly embraced it."—p. 10.

What can this mean ? Dr. Stanley does not think, assuredly, that it is possible for man to believe, that is, to trust his Creator too much ? Abraham, at least, did not think so. " Hath not the potter power over the clay ?" and " shall the clay say to him that fashioneth it, What makest thou ?" Or does Dr. Stanley allude to the weakness of human nature, which often would restrict the grace of God, either to mere outward forms of worship, of dress, of rites, or of ceremonies not positively contrary to the Word of God ? Or does he mean men who judge others in the matter of eating, drinking, and the like ? For, he cannot wish to say, that the definite creed of those " who are ready to give a reason of the hope that is in them," narrows their conscience or their mind in thinking that those who are not able to give reason of such a hope, because, perhaps, they have none, are to be pitied? All that can be said is, that "those on whose conscience the doctrine of faith has a narrowing effect" do not understand it aright.

They know nothing of the real "doctrine of faith" who say: 'I believe,' and stop there, careless of their works; neither do those, who think that their own works—that is, "their own righteousness which is of the law," and but "filthy rags" at the best, will avail them, by virtue of a dreamy, indefinite, general and unmeaning belief they have in God, understand "the doctrine of faith." Still less do those who hold and who teach that men may believe or not, may accept or reject as they like, the witness God giveth in His Word, and who treat that Word the Bible, with even less reverence than they would one of their favourite heathen authors; who thus throw off all and every kind of restraint which 'faith' imposes on the heart, and yield allegiance only to what falls within the narrow scope of their limited intellect—have an idea of what is meant by "the doctrine of faith." Those alone understand "the doctrine of faith," who do as Abraham did; who, denying themselves, by crushing within them the conceit and the puny pride of their own intellect, give up their own will to God, and accept His terms —to walk through life as did those "of whom the world was not worthy," by faith in Him, moved by their obedience to His will, and not to their own. "The doctrine of faith" consists in "receiving the kingdom of Heaven as little children," who feeling their own weakness believe what they cannot understand, and trust him that speaks, because their heart is too fond to doubt him. "The doctrine of faith" is to say with Samuel: "Speak, Lord, Thy servant heareth"—and to do it.

S. Paul is clear enough on this point. Writing to Gentiles he speaks, of course, of their admission "into the household of God," and that too, through faith in Him Who wrought out for them their admission, by "breaking down the middle-wall of partition," and "nailing to His Cross, the handwriting of ordinances that was against them." But, so far from thinking that "faith was almost synonymous" with that, S. Paul says to these same Gentiles: "The Gospel of Christ is the power of God, παντὶ τῷ πιστεύοντι, to every one that believeth;"—(and not ἑκατέρῳ τῷ πιστεύοντι to each of the two, Jews and Gentiles;) but, in order,—" to the Jew first and also to the Gentile;"[1] and, " CHRIST is the end of the Law for righteousness to every one that believeth," παντὶ τῷ πιστεύοντι, for, " with the heart man believeth unto righteousness."[2] " So then they which be of faith are blessed with the faithful Abraham."[3]

XIX. " His very name implies this universal mission," says Dr. Stanley. His name, truly; but not the name Dr. Stanley gives him thus—

" 'The Father,' (Abba): 'The lofty Father,' (Ab-ram): 'The Father of multitudes,' (Ab-raham): an abbreviation of *rab-amon* (*hamon* = multitude, as of the drops of rain, the swelling of springs, the voice of singers). Gesenius, *Lexicon*, 281."—p. 20.

First—'Abba' or 'Abbô' is the Syriac term for 'father' in the emphatic form, which never entered into the composition of 'Abraham.' In that form which properly means 'the father' it is used like ὁ πατήρ, in the vocative, Abba, 'Father,' 'our father,' 'my father,' &c.[4] But in Hebrew, the voc. 'father,' in the sense of 'my father' is אָבִי,[5] shortened into אֲבִי, when forming proper names given by one man to another, such as אֲבִימֶלֶךְ 'Abimelech,' &c., (i.e. 'O father, O my father king,') 'father, king;' אֲבִיאֵל (O father, my father strong,) 'mighty, father.' But when such names were given absolutely, as for instance, by GOD to Abraham, and not relatively, the proper name was then formed with אָב, אַב, 'father,' and not with אֲבִי 'my father.' The few other proper names thus formed besides that of Abraham, prove the rule; such as אֲבִינֵר and אֲבִישַׁי אַבְנֵר; and אַבְשָׁי each of a different meaning; as well as אֲבִידָם[6] and אַבְרָם, and as altered by GOD, אַבְרָהָם.

Secondly—Gesenius' Lexicon from which Dr. Stanley quotes must, probably, be the English translation which I do not

---

[1] Rom. i. 16.   [2] Rom. x. 4, 10.   [3] Gal. iii. 9.

[4] S. Mark xiv. 36 ; Rom. viii. 15 ; Gal. iv. 6.

[5] The same idiom obtains in Arabic and in other Shemitic dialects e.g. يا عمي ' O my uncle,' a familiar address to men, يا أمي ' O my mother,' to elderly women, &c.

[6] Numb. xvi. 1, 2, &c.

know; for Gesenius treats of אֲבְרָם at p. 11 of his Lexicon,
ed. 1833, 8vo., and at p. 10 of his 'Thesaurus L. Sanctæ,' 4to.,
and "p. 281" seems very far in the book for a term beginning
with אַב except it be mentioned at רָם. But in the editions
I have there is assuredly nothing said about "*amon*" and
"*hamun*." Gesenius who, in general, is a sound scholar, tells
us that in אַבְרָהָם, רָהָם may be compared with Ar. رهام
'a large number;' but he does not say a word in either Lexicon
about *rab-amon*; and since the root רדם does not exist in
Hebrew, we can only compare it with the Arabic term. Simon,
however,[1] proposes אַב רַב הָם '*pater multitudinis turbæ*,' μέγας
πατὴρ πλήθους ἐθνῶν (Sir. xliv. 19), and says that others have proposed אַב רָם הָם *pater excelsus multitudinis*; an etymology
which is much like this one given by Dr. Stanley in another
note, p. 20:

"According to the Persian tradition, his name, before his conversion, was Zerwan, 'the wealthy.' Hyde, *Rel. Pers.* 77."

Here again Dr. Stanley seems to take everything for granted;
although he is, perhaps, hardly to blame for not knowing that
here Hyde is not quite correct.

XX. It is true that زروان Zerwán, زرهوان Zerbwán, and
زربان Zerbán, are given in Persian dictionaries as names of
Abraham,[2] in like manner as the same names were given to
Shem, according to Moses of Chorene;[3] and no doubt Abraham
is so mentioned in the book quoted by Hyde, which I have not;
yet all these are but legends, like the rest. For in the very
quotation "e libro Zend" given by Hyde,[4] and from prayers
contained in the Khorda-Avesta, Zerwan does not refer to 'King
Abraham' as Hyde infers, but to King Zerwán, 'Old Father
Time;' and not to any real king of that name; for no such a
king is to be found in the Tarikh Jehan Ara that gives all the
kings of Persia before Islamism. A like passage occurs in the
Yesht-Sáde:[5] "Be ye as long-lived as King Zerwán;" and

[1] Onom. vol. I. p. 451.   [2] As e.g. in the Borhán-i-qáto', s. vv.
[3] Hist. lib. I. c. 5, p. 17, ed. Wh.
[4] Rel. V. P. p. 77. The quotation is not in Zend, but in Pa·zend or Parsi.
[5] xxix. and xxxii. vol. I. pt. ii. p. 154, sq. ed. Kleuker.

elsewhere,[1] " be ye as immortal as Kai-Khosrú." This 'Zerwân' or 'Zerbân' when said of Abraham, does not as far as I
can find, (I have however, very few books to help me) refer in
any way to Hyde's etymology 'auri custos,' which is out of the
way and far fetched.

But there can be very little doubt, I think, that all these
terms are one and the same, and derived from the Zend 'Zar-
vâne akarana,' or qadhâta, uncreated or self-existent Time, repeatedly mentioned in the Zend Avesta; as e.g. in the Vendi-
dad XIX.[2] nizbayañuha. tú. zarathustra. thwâshahâ. qadhâ-
tahe. zrvânahe. akaranahe. "Call, O thou Zerdhust, upon the
heavenly, uncreated, self-existent Time;" to which Zerdhust
answers:[3] nizbayemi. thwâshake. qadâtahe. zrvânahe. akaranahe.
" I call upon the heavenly self-existent, uncreated Time," &c.
This must be the real origin of Zervân or Zeruân of Berosus,
quoted by Moses of Chorene,[4] as having reigned after the Flood,
but before the Tower of Babel, with Titan and Japethostes, &c.,
and mentioned also by Mariba of Catina who had found at
Nineveh a book translated into Greek by order of Alexander the
Great, in which he read that " all history begins with զրւ-
ուաննււււււււււււււււււււււււււււււււ Zerwân and Titan
and Apetostes."[5]

This same Zerwân is also mentioned by Eznig, in his refuta-
tion of heathen sects,[6] who, when speaking of the Parsi worship,
says: "The Parsis say that, before there was anything, either
of things in heaven or of things in the earth, զրււււււ նՁ
ււււււ ֆր. one existed whose name was Zerwân, which means
either 'fate' or 'glory.' From him were born Ormizt[7] and
Armen, the two principles of good and of evil," &c. Michael
Tchamtchean[8] quotes from Moses of Chorene and from other
authors, the Sibyl of Berosus, which he says was Berosus' own
daughter, repeating what I have quoted from Moses of Chorene

[1] Spiegel Z. Av., Abth. III. p. 233.
[2] Id. p. 176.
[4] Moses Chor. lib. I. c. viii. p. 23.
[7] Hormozd and Ahrimân. Mich. Tchamtchean relates a dialogue of Zerwân,
concerning his son Ormizt, about the creation of the world, &c. Hist. Arm.
vol. ii. p. 26.
[8] Hist. Arm. vol. i. p. 57.
[†] Vol. I. p. 175, ed. Spieg.
[‡] Hist. lib. I. c. v. p. 16.
[§] Lib. ii. i, p. 113, ed. Ven.

respecting Zerwän; but he adds[1] that "Shem having migrated
to the north-west, called the hill on which he dwelt Sim, after
himself; and other places after the names of his sons, as e.g.
the hill Zerwän, after his son Zerwän." Indjidjean also[2] repeats
the same things, and has a whole chapter devoted to show, that
Shem was Zordasht or Zoroaster; and that "what the ancients
relate զման նախկին զրուածայ պարզել իմանալ զման
սեմայ concerning the first or primitive Zerwän, is to be understood of Shem." This 'primitive' or 'great Zerwän,' Shem
of the Armenians, is the زروان بزرگ 'the great Zerwän' of the
Persians; a title they give to Abraham; every nation thus
making the most of its favourite ancestor, as Egypt of Menes,
Thebes of Cadmus, and the Rhodians of Jove, εἴτινς ἐκ Διὸς
εὔχοντο.

XXI. "There is yet," says Dr. Stanley—but this time, he
speaks hesitatingly—"a more certain and enduring memorial of
this side of Abraham's mission,"

"if we may trust the ingenious conjecture of a distinguished
writer that—whereas 'Elohim' is a plural and means 'gods,' and
therefore, must have been coined in a polytheistic age—Abraham,
instead of looking upon these gods as so many devils, looked upon
these 'Elohim' as so many names invented with the honest purpose of expressing the various aspects of the Deity, though in time
diverted from their original intention."—p. 23.

In short, if I understand him aright, whereas Abraham was
accustomed in his idolatrous days, to see 'gods,' 'Elohim,'
worshipped, and to worship them himself, he perpetuated his
turning from these idols to the true God, by still keeping to the
term 'Elohim,' but using it with a verb in the singular; as e.g.
instead of saying, as formerly, 'the gods have done it;' he now
said, 'the gods has done it,' &c., and he thus introduced
Monotheism.

"Abraham," continues Dr. Stanley's authority, "saw that all
the Elohim were meant for God; and thus Elohim comprehend-
ing by one name everything that ever was or ever could be called
Divine, became the name by which the Monotheistic age was
rightly inaugurated: a plural conceived and construed as a sin-

[1] Ch. ii. p. 59.   [2] Antiq. Armen. vol. i. p. 285, 286.

gular. From this point of view the Semitic name of the Deity,
which at first sounds not only ungrammatical, but irrational, becomes perfectly clear and intelligible. It is at once the proof that
Monotheism rose on the ruins of a polytheistic faith, and that it
absorbed and acknowledged the better tendencies of that faith."
—p. 23.

It matters little who said this; it means absolutely nothing.
Had Abraham been the first to use 'Elohim' with a singular
verb, and had he never used any other term for 'God,' this
'conjecture' would hardly be one; it would carry its own proof
with it, and be evident. As it is, however, we can only look
upon it as written for writing's sake, as another specimen of that
'philosophy for the million,' that looks somewhat learned, perhaps; but is not so.

First—a conjecture in order to be 'ingenious' must be probable; but this is not; for—while we cannot prove that Abraham did set the example of using 'Elohim' with a singular verb,
we can prove that he did not.

Secondly—the use of אֱלֹהִים which is a 'plural of majesty'
only, with a sing. verb, is an idiom of the language; either of
servile and abject reverence for kings and superiors, inherent in
the Eastern character; or, of partitive construction of nouns in
the plural with a verb, a pronoun or an adjective in the singular, as e.g. אֲדֹנִים 'lords'—i.e. 'lord,' 'master,' אֲדֹנִים קָשֶׁה
'a hard master,' lit. 'domini durus.' Is. xix. 4. אֲדֹנָיו הַמִּצְרִי
(his lords) 'his lord the Egyptian,' Gen. xxxix. 2, Ex. xxi. 6,
8, 29, &c.¹ בְּעָלֶיהָ Job xxxi. 39, her husband, lit. 'her lords;'
בְּעָלָיו 'his lord;' lit. his lords or masters; all of which are
not relics of polytheism; but are simply idiomatic.

Thirdly—if so be that אֱלֹהִים 'Elohim,' with a sing. verb or
a sing. adjective, be a token of Abraham's Monotheism, how
comes it that the same expression is used for one idol? e.g.
Dagon אֱלֹהֵינוּ our god; (lit. 'our gods;') 1 Sam. v. 7.
Baal-zebub, אֱלֹהֵי the god (lit. 'the gods') of Ekron, 2 Kings

¹ Danz Thargum. p. 26, 149, 150; Ewald Hebr. Gr. p. 326, sq., and 541.
Gesen. Lehrgeb. p. 662, sq.

i. 2; and the molten calf, Ex. xxxii. 1, xxiii. 32, said to be
אֱלֹהִים 'gods,' for 'a god.' We grant that every one of these,
was the personification of some property or of some quality of
Nature,—will anyone maintain that Dagon as well as Baalzebub,
and Baalzebub as well as Mnevis, "comprehended in himself
everything that was or that could be called Divine," so that
whether Dagon, Ashtaroth, Baal, Moloch, or Baalzebub, they
were all one and the same thing, without distinction or difference? For, if the conjecture holds good in the one case it
must also hold good in the other. But—

Fourthly—as a proof of how futile is this supposed "more
certain and more enduring memorial" of Abraham's Monotheism
—we have only two instances on record of Abraham using the
word אֱלֹהִים 'Elohim,' viz. Gen. xx. 13, and Gen. xxii. 8.
In the *first* instance Abraham used 'Elohim' with a verb *in the
plural*; and in the *second* only, with one *in the singular*. Moreover, the first passage, הִתְעוּ אֹתִי אֱלֹהִים was written by a
so-called Elohist; and the second אֱלֹהִים יִרְאֶה־לּוֹ by a Jehovist. So that according to the showing of these philosophers,
and to use their language, Abraham grew but slowly[1] out of
his Polytheistic habits into Monotheistic expressions, and seems
to have been a long time making up his mind on the subject;
since the first time he is recorded to have used 'Elohim,' and
that too, with a verb in the plural, he had left Haran nearly
five-and-twenty years. It was only, perhaps, twenty years later,
and after that God had said to him: "I am the Almighty God,"
אֵל שַׁדַּי, Gen. xvii. 1, that Abraham used 'Elohim' with a verb
in the singular. Nay, all we can gather from this "ingenious
conjecture," and from the facts I have brought to bear upon it
is, that Abraham used the term 'Elohim' very much in the
same way as Socrates uses θεός and θεοί, thus: οὐ τοίνυν μόνον
ἤρκεσε τῷ θεῷ τοῦ σώματος ἐπιμεληθῆναι—ἀλλὰ τὴν ψυχὴν—ἀν-

---

[1] These are almost the words of Ewald, Hebr. Gr. p. 641, who speaking of
אֱלֹהִים says: that "nachdem der mosaische Monotheismus eingeführt war," after
that the Mosaic (not Abrahamic) Monotheism was introduced, אֱלֹהִים gradually,
"almählig," grew to be construed with a verb in the singular. We see, as we
shall again see, that in this 'philosophy' the master and the disciples are not
always at one.

ἐφυσε. "But verily, it did not suffice to God to care for the body of man, He also created within him the soul;" τίνος γὰρ ἄλλου ζῴου ψυχὴ πρῶτα μὲν θεῶν τῶν τὰ μέγιστα καὶ κάλλιστα συνταξάντων ᾔσθηται ὅτι εἰσί; τί δὲ φῦλον ἄλλο ἢ οἱ ἄνθρωποι θεοὺς θεραπεύουσι; &c. "For the soul of what other animal owns the first feeling concerning the gods who have ordered everything so beautifully, namely, that they exist? What other race but that of man worships the gods?"[1] We must all admit, that it is not saying much for Abraham, to hold that he was not in advance of Socrates in his knowledge of GOD.

XXII. Hitherto, and until "the light" of the "common day philosophy" gleamed upon the pages of Holy Scripture, one had thought that the knowledge of the true GOD which Adam, Abel, Enoch, Noah, Shem, and his children must have had, was by them perpetuated among the early patriarchs. Even in the days of Enos, הוּחַל לִקְרֹא בְּשֵׁם יְהֹוָה, Gen. iv. 26, men began to call upon the name,[2] not of 'JEHOVAH' itself, since it was not then made known to them, but upon the Name of the LORD,— of Him Who afterwards revealed Himself as JEHOVAH. Enoch הִתְהַלֶּךְ אֶת־הָאֱלֹהִים "walked with GOD," (Gen. v. 22,) and we are told that those who then pleased Him pleased Him only by their faith in Him. (Heb. xi.) This 'conjecture,' then, is not sound, neither is it περὶ φρόνησιν καὶ ἀλήθειαν, (R. iii. p. 1); and Abraham was not the first to introduce the use of the verb in the singular with 'Elohim,' for Eve did so before him when she said: כִּי שָׁת־לִי אֱלֹהִים זֶרַע (Gen. iv. 25), "For GOD hath appointed me another seed instead of Abel."

XXIII. But, inasmuch as there is only one straight road, that of Truth, of τὸ ἀληθές—τοῦ ὄντος ἢ ὄν—all those who will not walk therein must go astray. This very subject is a fresh proof of it. We have heard one Professor telling us that the 'Elohim'

---

[1] Memorab. Socr. lib. iv. 13, also 5, 7, 18, 19, &c.

[2] The rendering of the Authorized Version is correct; albeit the Targ. Hieros. and J. B. Uxriel, the Midrash Rabbah (p. 27, verso), Miclol Jophi (p. 3, note), and R. S. Jarchi l.c. explain it to mean, 'They called other gods by the name of the LORD.' i.e., they made themselves idols: a meaning Targ. Onkelos seems to think right, as it renders הוחל hoph. 'corptum est,' by יְהֹוָה, 'the sons of men ceased from calling upon the Name of the LORD.' Neither Abarbanel nor A. Ezra allude to it.

of Abraham showed his Monotheism; which, however, Moses must have introduced, says another;[1] while a third devotes two whole volumes, not wanting in ratiobalistic learning, such as it is, to prove the *Polytheism* of Moses. "Voici ma pensée," says this philosopher,[2]

"je crois que—le premier chapitre de la Genèse, est le programme de six actes cosmogoniques que l'on jouait devant les initiés dans les mystères Egyptiens;—que Moïse met en action dans le Pentateuque un grand nombre de divinités subalternes, bien qu'il ne permette d'adorer que Jéové, l'Adoni, le maître, le chef suprême, l'Autos, le lui, qui domine tous ces Alloï, tous ces autres, dits en Hebrew Aloïm ou Aleïm,—Je crois, au contraire que le Polytheisme de Moïse, avoué enfin et bien compris, serait un salutaire exemple de tolérance religicuse, et que la scène qui se passe dans le Jardin d'Eden est relative à l'initiation Egyptienne."—Pref. pp. vi., vii.

Being very much in advance of the age, he traces the successive improvements in the Hebrew alphabet, which was originally taken from the Zodiac,[3] to that of Peleg, or Pelasgian, at the tower of Babel, which he frames in his own way; he then dates the first reading from the days of Enos, interpreting the passage (Gen. iv. 26) אָז הוּחַל לִקְרֹא בְּשֵׁם יְהֹוָה

"AE ZOVEL L-QBA B-CUM JEOVE, *alors on commença à lire par le nom* AEI; et commencer à lire par le nom AEI, revient a la façon de parler, commencer à faire usage de l'ABC."—p. 130.

After that he gives pictures, drawn from Egyptian figures, of these "Aleïm de Moïse," which he calls "dieux Amonéens" from 'No-Ammon,' in Egypt, and then he proceeds to give, in vol. ii., a literal and verbal translation of the first three chapters of Genesis, in this wise:—[4]

"LA GENESE.

CHAPTER I.

Sens Vulgaire.	Texte.	Sens Intime [et Rationnel.[5]]
Dieu	ALEIM	Les Forces, les Dieux (Amonéens, Demiourgues, Artistes ou Fabricateurs du monde)

[1] Ewald, above, p. 114, note.
[2] Lacour, Aleïm, ou les Dieux de Moïse, 1839.
[3] Vol. i. p. 107, sq.   [4] Vol. ii. p. 21, sq.   [5] Vol. i. p. 281.

créa	BRA	taillaient, formaient, sculptaient,
au commencement	BRACHIT	en commencement-d'être, en ébauche
	AT	la substance
les cieux	ECUMIM	des signes célestes, du ciel stellé, des cieux,
et	UAT	et la substance
la terre	HARTZ	de la terre blanche et aride."

Verse 2.

" était	HITH	était, était faite,
informe	THOU	un signe pyramidal ou obéliscal, une borne figurant l'être informe et sans vie positive,
et confuse,	UBBOU	et un ove figurant l'enveloppement compressif de l'être informe et sans vie positive ;
et l'obscurité était	UHCHR	et il y avait des ténèbres compressives faisant empêchement
sur	OL	sur
la face	FNI	la surface
de l'abîme	THOUM	des signes tumulaires pyramidaux figurant l'être informe et sans vie positive.
et l'esprit	UROVE	Mais le souffle, l'esprit dilatant et libérateur
de Dieu	ALEIM	des Forces, des Dieux,
se mouvait	MRHPUT	planait avec amour, couvait, incubait pour réchauffer et féconder
sur	OL	sur
la face	FNI	la surface
des eaux	HMIM	des eaux, des semences, des êtres."

This kind of Hebrew and the translation thereof is what this philosopher calls "*le sens intime* ou *rationnel*, de RATIONALIS, raisonnable, conforme à la raison."[1] Can human conceit and folly exceed this; and need we any further proof of the extremes of unreasonableness to which Rationalism will go? If such senseless exhibition does not convince men, nothing will.

We then come in Dr. Stanley's book (pp. 23—26) to a well-

---

[1] Vol. I. Introd. p. xxiii.

written and interesting account of God's covenant with Abraham, upon which I have to make the following remarks.

XXIV. At page 24 Dr. Stanley, after saying correctly that—

"Abraham was bidden to prepare as if for the peculiar forms of sacrifice which for centuries afterwards, in his own country, were used to sanction a treaty or a covenant,"—p. 24,

refers us to V. Bohlen's note on Gen. xv. 10. I trust Dr. Stanley does not take for granted all V. Bohlen says; it would indeed be ἀλόγως, without reflexion. (R. viii. p. 4.) For the German critic tells us there, nothing new, certainly; but in a parenthesis he states that בָּתַר, the term used in this passage of Genesis for dividing the victim, is a word of later date, which occurs in the Song of Solomon, ii. 17, Jer. xliv. 18, and that the victims were chosen after the Levitical institution, &c.; evidently meaning to imply that this narrative was written later than we believe it to have been, and that the writer, be he Moses or any one else, did not give the facts as they actually took place, but that he arranged them in his own way. Now, what is this worth?

He tells us dogmatically that בָּתַר, which he writes without points—thereby intending to speak in general of the 'root' בתר, and not of the verb בָּתַר in particular—is of a later date. The fact is that the verb בָּתַר is ἅπαξ λεγ. here, and that the derivatives בֶּתֶר, בִּתְרוֹן are found in two other places. However, not only does it often happen that derivatives are used later than the verb or the root, but this is the usual way in spoken languages; and all languages were spoken at some time or other. But for this, what would become of the 'formation' and gradual improvements, or, at all events, alterations in languages? According to V. Bohlen's reasoning, we have good reason to say that these lines of Cædmon—

> leoht þær æþere .
> þunh þpihtnes þonb .
> bæᵹ ᵹenemmeb[1] .

are of a later date, because in Milton[2] we read—

[1] Cædmon, Par. ii. 35, p. 8.   [2] Parad. Lost. Bk. vii.

> "God saw the light was good;
> And light from darkness by the hemisphere
> Divided: light, the day, and darkness, night,
> He named."

seeing 'leoht' is 'light,' 'bæg,' 'day,' 'ʒenemmeb,' 'named,' &c. Or we might as well say that Chaucer and Herbert both lived together, because each wrote a 'Country Parson,' one in verse and the other in prose, and each happens to use some words alike.

If Homer, or any other favourite author, such as Pindar or Thucydides, were thus treated, there would be little left in them that their friends would care to read; for the interest lies, not only in the story they tell, but also in the style, through which we love to be carried back to the time when they severally wrote. Let us take, for instance, this line :—[1]

$$\text{ἦμος δ' ἠέλιος μετενίσσετο βουλυτόνδε}$$
$$\text{καὶ τότε δὴ Κίκονες κλῖναν δαμάσαντες Ἀχαιούς.}$$

Homer never wrote this: we know better. First of all, Homer never existed; settle where he was born, whether on the banks of the Meles or on the slope of Pelinæus, and we will believe you.

Secondly, and to begin with the first word: ἦμος, it is true, is of Ionic origin; so that, for that matter, Homer might have written it; but as we do not know where he was born, we do not believe in him. Then, again, the author of the Iliad, indeed, always writes ἦμος in protasi; but the apodosis sometimes begins with τῆμος, and sometimes with καὶ τότε, δὴ τότε or τότε δή. Now, we know that in the best style of all well-ordered languages, both East and West, the protasis and the apodosis are always observed, with the relative adverbs or particles; 'when'— 'then ;' ὅτε—τότε, &c.: ἦμος—τῆμος, therefore, is more correct, and of a better age, than ἦμος—καὶ τότε, &c. So, then, such lines as

$$\text{ἦμος, φίλαι, κατ' οἶκον κ.τ.λ.}$$
$$\text{τῆμος θυραῖος ἦλθεν—}$$

must be older than Sophocles, though found in his plays ;[2]

---

[1] Odys. ix. 38.   [2] Trach. 531, sq.

no doubt from some anterior document handed down among
the Heraclidæ; although there can be no doubt that Sophocles
himself wrote such a line as

εὖ γὰρ οἶδ᾽ ὅτι
κάτοιδεν, ἧμος τὸν Κιθαιρῶνος τόπον,
ἐπλησίαζον[1]—

where ἧμος stands alone, without the apodosis.

Likewise, when we find in the Iliad[2]

ἧμος δ᾽ ἥλιος κατέδυ, καὶ ἐπὶ κνέφας ἦλθε
δὴ τότε κοιμήσαντο—

we call such lines 'Smyrnean,' from Quintus Smyrnæus, who
wrote the Posthomerica; but when, on the other hand, we read[3]

ἧμος δ᾽ οὔτ᾽ ἄρ᾽ πω ἠὼς, ἔτι δ᾽ ἀμφιλύκη νύξ,
τῆμος ἄρ᾽ ἀμφὶ πυρὴν κριτὸς ἔγρετο λαὸς Ἀχαιῶν,

we reckon these to Homer, if he ever lived—at least, we call
them Homeric. But when ἧμος and τῆμος are separated from
each other by more than one line, as in Il. λ′ 80—90, such lines
may safely be thought pre-Homeric; we therefore call them
'Meonian,' from 'Meone,' the mother of Homer, although we
do not exactly know who she was. As to ἥλιος, it may be Homeric; but with regard to μετενίσσετο, it is doubtful. For we
find it, e.g. in Apollonius Rhodius,[4] said of a wild beast 'coming,'
not 'going,' as it is here said of the sun; so that they cannot
both be right. And as regards βουλυτόνδε, it must be taken
from these lines of Apollonius—

ἧμος δὲ τρίτατον λάχος ἤματος ἀνομένοιο
λείπεται ἐξ ἠοῦς, καλέουσι δὲ κεκμηῶτες
ἐργατίναι γλυκερόν σφιν ἄφαρ βουλυτόν ἱκέσθαι,
τῆμος ἄρ᾽ ἤροτο νειός[5]—

inasmuch as it is not usual to derive a noun from an adverb,
but rather the contrary; the noun being the origin of the adverb—βουλυτόνδε found in Homer must be of later date than
βουλυτόν found in this passage of Apollonius. This line of the
Odyssey, therefore, must be either an interpolation, or of a
much later date than Apollonius. Altogether, these two lines
may be considered spurious.

[1] Œd. Tyr. 1134.   [2] π′ 475.   [3] Il. η′ 433.
[4] L 1245.   [5] iii. 1339, sq.

Sed hæc nugæ. It is only to show that the same kind of
criticism that would rightly be called contemptible, or rather no
criticism at all, regarding books which, however favourite, have
done no moral good, is yet called 'philosophy' when applied to
the one Book which, through its influence, is alone the power of
God unto salvation. And why? Simply because men hate
the light of that Book, and try to darken it in every way they
can. Yet, it shines. The sun cares very little for all the
awnings put up in order to shut him out. He shines, and continues to shine, and will continue to shine unto the end, though
not on those who purposely hide themselves from the wholesome effect of his rays. Such are critics of V. Bohlen's school.
The spirit of their criticism shows itself at once; nothing is too
paltry for them; so that they beguile unwary and ignorant men
into shutting themselves up at mid-day, lighting the candle of
their own intellect, and calling that the sun.

It is impossible not to smile at their absurdity,—at the absurdity, for instance, of deciding that בָּתַר, a genuine Hebrew,
and no 'foreign' term, is of a comparatively modern date, because, besides being seldom used, two of its derivatives are found
in later books. But we have seen what this is worth as regards
terms belonging to the language itself; for when these terms
are clearly foreign, the case is different. At this rate, why not
ascribe the writing of Genesis to Isaiah or to Jeremiah? for
בָּדוּ, 'emptiness,' occurs first in Gen. i. 2, and after that in
Isa. xxiv. 1, Jer. iv. 23; בָּהוּ, then, is of Isaiah's or Jeremiah's
time, and the first chapter of Genesis may come from the pen
of either of them,—most likely from that of Isaiah; since we
have no means of proving that all ἅπαξ λεγόμενα, and that all
terms rarely used were not invented, 'pro re natâ,' by some
author of credit who then set the fashion.

Thus also פָּחַד occurs in Genesis, in Judges, in Zephaniah,
and in Jeremiah: which wrote the others? Did the Elohist
write Jeremiah, or Jeremiah the Elohistic passage? In this
case the 'verb,' which is found in Judges and in Zephaniah, is
youngest, and the derivative פַּחַד is oldest, occurring, as it does,
in Genesis; while in the case of בָּתַר, which was written by a
'Jehovist,' the 'verb' is oldest and the derivatives youngest.
Are these relative peculiarities of the Elohistic and of the Jeho-

vistic styles, to derive the verb from the noun, and vice versâ?
Again, מרח occurs twice, in Lev. xxi. 20, and in Isa. xxxviii. 21:
which was first written?   And since מרץ is found only in Job,
in 1 Kings, and in Micah, Job may, or must have been, written
by Ezra.   So much for this 'rational' criticism, which has one
distinctive mark beside that of absurdity, to be inconsistent; and
therefore it is no criticism at all, but simply the expression of
certain men's minds—so far, then, of little worth.

On a par with this is V. Bohlen's assertion that Abraham dis-
posed the victims after the Levitical pattern.   This is sophistry.
For God, Who ordered the Book of Leviticus, might, I trow,
tell Abraham how to arrange them.   Of the two, the Levitical
pattern was rather after this.

XXVIII. The second remark I have to make is on Dr. Stanley's calling this covenant with Abraham "the first covenant, the
Old Testament." (p. 25.)   At first it seems as if Dr. Stanley
overlooked 'the first covenant,' "the everlasting covenant" made
by God "with man and with every living creature," the bow that
joins earth to heaven in token of peace, and which is now as
beautiful as when the sun of heaven drew it on the retreating
storm of the Flood.   Yet, even if Dr. Stanley calls this 'the
first covenant' not absolutely, but relatively, to the 'New,' it
then excludes Abel, Enoch, Noah, and others who walked by
faith; so that, even thus, it is hardly a correct expression, for
assuredly God's covenant with Noah is, and will still continue,
binding, as long as the world lasts; and this covenant is anterior to that which God made with Abraham.

XXVI. Thirdly, Dr. Stanley, in a note (p. 25), speaking of
the boundaries of the land promised by God to Abraham, says—

"Gen. xv. 18—21. The 'River of Egypt' (here only) is the
Nile.   It is inserted, evidently, as the extreme Western limit of
Jewish thought and dominion."

Was the Regius Professor sure of what he stated; or did he
state it only on the authority of others, without any research of
his own into τὰ πρῶτα στοιχεῖα of what he asserts? thus perhaps, committing himself.   He tells us that the "'river of
Egypt' means (here only) the Nile;" but—

First, why "here only?" for נהר must be said of the Nile in

Isa. xix. 5, where הַיָּם is said of the river when it πελαγίζει, is like a sea.[1] In this verse, however, נְהָרוֹת is said of the canals of Egypt, as in Exod. viii. 1,[2] whereas יְאֹרִים, pl. of יְאֹר, the 'river,' is always said of the 'rivers,' the 'branches' of 'the river.'[3] Here, then, יְאֹרֵי מָצוֹר cannot be said of the 'canals' made by Ramses II. (Sesostris), who ἀπὸ Μέμφεως ἐπὶ θάλασσαν ὤρυξε πυκνὰς ἐκ τοῦ ποταμοῦ διώρυγας, "dug many canals from Memphis to the sea, in order to facilitate the transport of merchandise— τὸ δὲ μέγιστον, πρὸς τὰς τῶν πολεμίων ἐφόδους ὀχυρὰν καὶ δυσέμβολον ἐποίησε τὴν χώραν—but who chiefly by these means made the country safe against the incursions of enemies, and difficult to invade;"[4] a fact that bears directly on the sense given to this expression in 2 Kings xix. 24, and Isa. xxxvii. 25, but which I cannot discuss here. And the reason for which נָהָר in the singular is here said of the Nile, and in the plural נְהָרוֹת, of 'canals,' is plain. נָהָר is the generic term for 'a stream of water flowing in a bed either natural or made with hand;' and therefore is the Nile, the נָהָר, the 'water-stream,' κατ' ἐξοχήν, of Egypt, and therefore also is it to be understood of the 'River' when in connection with Egypt; although, when said absolutely, it applies to 'the River,' the largest and the nearest to the first

[1] Ἐν δὲ ταῖς ἀναβάσεσι τοῦ Νείλου καλύπτεται πᾶσα (Αἴγυπτος) καὶ πελαγίζει πλὴν τῶν οἰκήσεων—πισθέοσται κατὰ τὴν σύμπασαν ὄψιν—"in the inundations of the Nile the whole of Egypt is covered with water, and is like a sea, in which the towns and the villages appear at a distance like islands" (Strabo, Lib. xvii. 1, 4); τότε—ὁ Νεῖλος—πέλαγος ἐξαίφνης ἔκασαν τουτί τὴν Αἴγυπτον—"then the Nile suddenly makes a sea of the whole of Egypt." (Himer. Orat. xiv. 8, 9.) Whence Diodorus says (Lib. I. 19, 4), τὸν δὲ ποταμὸν ἀρχαιότατον μὲν ὄνομα σχεῖν Ὠκεάνην, ὅς ἐστιν Ἑλληνιστὶ Ὠκεανός, that "the River from the first was called 'Okeane,' which in Greek is 'Okeanos,' (Ocean)."

[2] And in Inscr. Rosett. l. 14, ed. Kosegart. in Prisca Æg. Lit. t. iv.

[3] That צוֹר can apply to nothing else is proved by the whole context of Ezek. xxix. 3—5, where the king of Egypt is compared to a dragon or to a crocodile, הַתַּנִּים, the symbol of Egypt, as we shall see hereafter, in the midst of 'his rivers.' And to show that these 'rivers' cannot apply to 'canals,' but that they must be taken for the 'branches' of the Nile—whether five or seven—three times does the prophet speak of דְּגַת יְאֹרֶיךָ, the 'fish of thy rivers.' But the fish lived first in 'the rivers,' whence they passed into the 'canals,' dug, and fed by 'the rivers,' long after these were formed by 'the River.'

[4] Diod. Sicul. Lib. I. 57.

settlements of the descendants of Shem, that is, to the Euphrates.

נָהָר may also perhaps, be said of the Nile in Is. xi. 15; yet, only, ' perhaps;' for Gesenius[1] and before him Vitringa,[2] T. Onkelos, Jarchi, Abarbanel and Kimchi, Vatablus and others, understand it of the Euphrates; whereas S. Cyril, S. Jerome, Theodoret, Hyde, &c., think it is said of the Nile. Gesenius, in order to support his opinion, takes a hint from Vitringa and quotes Peritsol[3] to show that לְשׁוֹן יַם־מִצְרַיִם הוּא יַם סוּף "the tongue of the sea of Egypt is the Red Sea."[4]

But, in sooth, where did Gesenius ever see against the voice of antiquity יַם־מִצְרַיִם said of the ' Red Sea,' which is always called יַם־סוּף, Copt. ⲫⲓⲟⲙ ⲛ̄ϣⲁⲣⲓ, and in old Egyptian the ' tank of Arabia,' ⳝⲏⲓ אַגַם פּוֹיִנְט, in which the ' Tesem' god was doomed to live ?[5] Ἐρυθρὴ θάλασσα, Ἀράβιος κόλπος ἐπὶ τῇ Ἐρυθρῇ θαλάσσῃ, always distinguished from ἡ θάλασσα, or ἡ Βορηίη θάλασσα,[6] ' the sea ' of Egypt, τὸ Αἰγύπτιον πέλαγος ;[7] بحر الروم الذي هو بحر الشام ومصر "the sea of Roum (Mediterranean) which is also the sea of Syria and of Egypt."[8]

In the Hebrew text we have two terms in use,—נָהָר מִצְרַיִם

---

[1] Comm. in Jes. vol. I. p. 442.   [2] Vol. I. p. 359, sq.

[3] Aggereth Orach. Olam. p. 106, 107, ed. Hyde.

[4] But this is, most probably, a mistake borrowed from Jarchi, and which Hyde, in a note on this passage (ibid. p. 191), sets right thus : " Male statuit *Mare Ægyptium* esse *Mare rubrum*. Nam ex Isa. xl. 15 [this very verse], plane constat quod per *linguam maris Ægyptiaci*, intelligatur ea Mediterranei pars Ægypto proxima in qua septem Nili ostia exonerantur. Propheta enim in eam exitium hoc modo denuntiat, *anathematizabit Dominus linguam maris Ægypti*; et agitabit manum suam super *Fluvium*, quem percutiet in septem rivis suis. Mari autem rubro quod ab Ægypto distat, aliquid indixisse, certè nec Ægyptum nec ejus fluvium tetigisset, nec ad eam allo modo spectare potuit. Dicat autem quod velit ὁ πλέων; non ad alta properabimus."

[4] Ritual of the Dead, ch. xvii. l. 66, ed. Leps.

[6] Herod. ii. 158, 9, 11.   [7] Strabo, lib. xvii. c. 1, 4, 35, &c.

[8] Masudi, vol. I. c. viii. p. 195; and el-Kazwini, vol. I. p 119, sq. Gesenius simply asserts that יַם־סוּף is here the ' Red Sea ;' and Vitringa (Comm. p. 358) only says, " Hoc *Mare* rectè dici possit *Ægyptium* ;" but neither gives a proof thereof, so that their joint testimony goes for very little. A. Ezra explains here שִׁיחוֹר by הוא נהר מצרים הנקרא שיחור, " the river of Egypt called Shihor ;" and he applies נהר to the Euphrates; but neither he nor R. S. Jarchi explains what is meant by ' the seven streams,' to which Gesenius does not even allude. These are understood of the ' seven branches' of the Nile, and נהר of the Nile

and נַחַל מִצְרַיִם the 'River of Egypt,' and the 'torrent of Egypt,' and two names for those rivers, הַיְאֹר, יְאֹר, and שִׁיחֹר. Of these יְאֹר, is the Egyptian ⲒⲞⲨⲢ, ⲖⲞⲨⲢ, Sabid. ⲈⲒⲞⲢ, ⲒⲞⲢ, Memph. ⲒⲀⲢⲞ and with the article ⲪⲒⲀⲢⲞ 'the River,' the only river in Egypt, never called by any other name, either in the enchantments practised in the days of the Ramessides,[1] or in the prayers of the Churches of Egypt;[2] and by comparison, the same term is used in Daniel for 'the River' of Babylon. Then שִׁיחֹר, 'Shihor' from שָׁחֹר 'black' is said by some to be a name of the 'Nile,' because it is called Mi-Aṣr, as Egypt is Χημία, from ⲔⲀⲘⲈ, 'dark,' 'darkness,' and 'Egypt;' and by others it is said to be the name given to the 'torrent of Egypt' which empties itself into the sea at El-Arish. If it be so, it cannot be the appellative of the Nile; for a name applicable to two objects is no special or proper name at all.

But נָהָר has a wider meaning than נַחַל 'a torrent,' which is a נָהָר only under the circumstances of a narrow, a rocky or a sandy bed, of a valley, of a sudden rise and fall, of overflow and drying up, &c.[3]

---

itself, by many critics ; but Vitringa remarks rightly that it is not said the river should be smitten 'in the seven streams,' נְהָרִים, but 'into seven streams,' נְהָלִים, that is, in order to effect its rapid decrease and drying up.

[1] Chabas, Pap. Harris, throughout.

[2] Missale Copt. Ar. p. 41, &c.

[3] Thus a נַחַל is in a valley, وَادٍ, Job xxi. 33 ; xl. 22, Isa. lvii. 6 ; 'over-flows,' Amos v. 24, Isa. xxx. 28 ; 'dries up,' Job vi. 15 ; and is thus fitly said of 'tears' that gush out, flow, and dry up when grief ceases, Lam. ii. 18. Thus we read of נַחֲלֵי אֵיתָן, 'never-failing streams,' Ps. lxxiv. 15, which only dry up with the sea, Job xiv. 11, like נַחַל, Jonah ii. 4 ; said in Job xiv. 11 to be dried up by miracle, by the same power that made a torrent נַחַל אֵיתָן, Amos v. 24, 'never fail' in the wilderness of Tekoah. These characteristics of נַחַל make it the only fit term for 'the river' mentioned in the vision of Ezekiel xlvii. that runs rapidly, and then subsided at once. Hence it was a new thing indeed to create נְהָרוֹת וִיאֹרִים, Isa. xliii. 19, 20, such streams or rivers in a dry land, for נְחָלִים were there already ; so that the converse of this image is equally correct and true : "I will turn streams or rivers into a wilderness," Isa. l. 2, Ps. cvii. 33. This relative meaning of נָהָר and of נַחַל is beautifully set forth in Job xx. 17, נַחֲלֵי נַחֲלֵי דְּבַשׁ וְחֶמְאָה, 'canals or branches, rivers and torrents of honey and of butter.'

These and like instances show that there is a meaning or an intention in the very letter of God's Word: for the prophets and the holy men of old did not write at will, but as they were moved. As regards נָהָר and נַחַל in particular, they show that נַחַל could never be said of the Nile in Lower Egypt; and it might be said of the Nile in Upper Egypt, פַּתְרוֹס, only under certain exceptionable circumstances of scenery, nature, &c., as about Silsileh, where 'the river' flows between high cliffs; and then נַחַל could only be said of the Nile in poetry. But as regards 'the river of Egypt' promised as boundary to the land of Israel, all we can say is, that it is yet to come; though indeed it may.

But it has never yet been so. Aben Ezra says of נָהָר in this place " הוא שיחור ולא היאר " here is meant Shihor, and not the river Nile." Abarbanel also[1] says that " it is not אינו נילוס the Nile, for the Nile is יאר and not נהר; but from the נהר מצר to the Euphrates shall be the frontier of Israel." And on Numb. xxxiv. 5, where we have נַחַל מִצְרַיִם mentioned as the limit, R. S. Jarchi says that " it means the river that flows before Egypt," to which A. Ezra says: it is the river of Egypt, ואינו היאר, " but it is not the river Nile." With this agrees the Samaritan Arab. Version of Abusaïd that says on نهر مصر هو وادي العريش بعد الشام من تلك, נחל מצרים الجبهة ' river of Egypt,' " the river of Egypt is Wâdy el-Arish on the frontier of Syria from that side;"[2] ἕως Ῥινοκορούρων τῆς ὁριζούσης Συρίαν κατ' Αἴγυπτον καὶ τὴν ἐρυθρὰν θάλασσαν; " as far as Rhinocorura, the limit of Syria towards Egypt and the Red Sea."[3] And in the division of the land of Canaan recorded in the Samaritan Book of Joshua (Chronicon Samaritanum), p. 22, where the frontiers stated in Joshua xv. 4, 47, are given, we are told that " at first and until fear prevented them, they thought of extending their border (l. 110), الى ان ياتي نيل مصر وهو الوادي unto خروجة البحر الذي يمتد ساحله من مصر الى فلسطين

---

[1] Comm. in Pent. fol. 50. recto.
[2] De Sacy Mém. de Literat. p. 149.
[3] Geo. Syncell. Chron. p. 86 ex Abyd.

the Nile; but that frontier is the Wâdy or torrent that opens and empties itself on or into the sea, the shore of which extends from Egypt to Palestine."[1]   This was נַּבַל מִצְרַיִם ' the frontier of Egypt,' 2 Kings iv. 21, 2 Chron. ix. 26, from which Solomon's kingdom reached unto the Euphrates; and this is further made plain by 2 Kings xxiv. 7, " and the king of Egypt[2] came not again any more out of his land : for the king of Babylon had taken from the river of Egypt unto the river Euphrates all that pertained to the king of Egypt."

But the frontiers of Egypt eastward, were always at a considerable distance from the Pelusiac or easternmost branch of the Nile. For, east of that branch, that is, towards the land of Canaan, were the Sethroïte, Bubastite, Phagrariopolite and the Heroopolite nomes, with the cities of Ramesses, Pithom, Baal-zephon, Migdol, &c., extending with the name ' Arabia,' answering to الخوف الشرقِ which was distinct from the Egyptian possessions in the peninsula of Sinai, more or less in a straight line from the gulf of Suez (Heroopolites Sinus) to the corner (לְשׁן יַם־מְצְרַיִם r) of the Mediterranean sea towards El-Arish. So that the king of Babylon could not take from the king of Egypt what had always been his own; but Nebuchadnezzar took from Nechao II. all that which former kings of Egypt, especially Thothmes and Ramses II., had taken by conquest from the ' River of Egypt' unto the Euphrates. This is again confirmed by a hieroglyphic inscription given in Lepsius' Denkm. Abth. iii. 31, and quoted by Brugsch,[3] ⲡⲣ Ⲙⲗⲟⲩⲁⲧ ⲕⲗⲗ ⲡ̅ⲛⲁ ⲟⲩⲁ ⲡ̅ ⲛⲉⲣⲡⲓⲛ (ⲛⲉⲟ)

[1] This passage seems akin to another in Epiphanius, (Adv. Hæres. Lib. Ⅱ. Tom. ii. p. 703,) where we are told that "the earth was divided between Shem, Ham, and Japhet, the lots being cast in Rhinocorura, δι καὶ ἐν ἀκολουθίᾳ ἔχει, καὶ οὐδὲν ἀσαφέστερον, ἀλλ' σαφεστερον μᾶλλον, Ρινοκόρουρα γὰρ ἑρμηνεύεται Νεὰλ, καὶ οὕτω φύσει οἱ ἐπιχώριοι αὐτὴν καλοῦσι, ἀνὰ δὲ τὴς 'Εβραΐδος ἑρμηνεύεται κλῆρος· as it appears from what followed, and is no vain report nor fictitious. For Rhinocorura is interpreted Neàl (נחל) and thus do the natives of the land call it ; (' quem antiqua proprie fontem barbari Dara nominant, ceteri vero accolæ Nachal, vel Nahal, vocant,'—Onomil lib. l. p. 13, ed. Col.) ; but in Hebrew it means ' lot,' of ' inheritance.' Although we cannot derive ' Nile' from (נחל), yet it is very possible that the Samaritan tradition and Epiphanius' story hold each other by the hand. Nay, we find נחל and נהר, yet more intimately related, as etymologies of Νηρεὺs and of Νηλεὺς respectively ! (Nork. Bibl. Mythol. pt. I. p. 302.)

[2] Nechao II. Brugsch. Hist. Eg. p. 254.

[3] Geogr. Inschr. vol. i. p. 54, and pl. vii. 303.

K

" from the waters of Egypt unto Nehrin" (Mesopotamia), show-
ing (1) that in the days of Thothmes II., the " waters of Egypt"
formed the boundary of the land of the Pharaohs towards
Canaan; and (2) that these " waters of Egypt" can be nothing
else than the נַחַל מִצְרַיִם which falls into the sea at El-Arish
(Rhinocorura); for, neither ' the River,' called in Egyptian
' Atur' or ' Aur' when in its bed, and ' Hapimnau,' ⲠⲀⲘ-
ⲘⲞⲨⲀⲧ, when covering the land, nor the Great Sea, ⲞⲨⲀⲝ-
ⲞⲦⲈⲣ, nor yet the Red Sea, ϢⲎⲓ Ⲛ̄ ⲠⲞⲦⲚⲦ, could be styled
in Egyptian, " the Waters of Egypt."

Moreover the limits ascribed by monuments to Egypt on the
side of Palestine, agree with those given to Canaan and to Palestine in Holy Scripture. Thus Ex. xxiii. 31. " And I will set
thy bounds from the Red Sea even unto the Sea of the Philistines, and from the desert unto the river," told more in detail
in Numb. xxxiv. 4, 5, and Josh. xv. 4, " And your border shall
fetch a compass from Azmon unto the River of Egypt, and the
goings out of it shall be at the sea;" and Amos vi. 14, " But,
behold, I will raise up against you a nation, O house of Israel,
saith the LORD GOD of hosts; and they shall afflict you from
the entering in of Hamath unto the river (or ' valley') of the
wilderness," i.e. " Sihor which is before Egypt," Josh. xiii. 3,
the borders of Judah. For " David gathered all Israel together,
from Shihor of Egypt even unto the entering of Hamath," as
stated in 1 Chron. xiii. 5.

Comparing these passages together it seems that the frontiers
meant, are the same throughout, that is, either strictly defined
by the ' torrent of Egypt,' generally called ' Shihor,' (El-Arish,)
or indefinitely and generally drawn from the northern extremity
of the Gulf of Suez to the corner of the sea at Rhinocorura
(El-Arish). Hence we may conclude that if GOD's promise to
Abraham is yet to be fulfilled נְהַר מִצְרַיִם may mean the Nile,
seeing we know not what may yet take place. If, however, we
are to consider this promise as fulfilled when the kingdom of
Israel reached its widest extent under David and under Solomon,
then the ' torrent of Egypt' called ' Shihor' by A. Ezra and
R. S. Jarchi in contradistinction to ' Nilus,' is the limit meant
in Gen. xv. 18, where נָהָר is used as a generic term, of which

נַחַל is the species. Since, whereas נָהָר מִצְרַיִם may be said of the ' Shibor' נַחַל מִצְרַיִם could never be said of the Nile where the Nile is supposed to be meant as the utmost limit of Israel in Lower Egypt : still less likely could נַחַל be the etymology of 'Nile,' as Vitringa thinks. So that unless Dr. Stanley has more proofs to bring forward than I can find, he cannot say as he does, " the ' river of Egypt' (here only) the Nile."

LECTURE II.—ABRAHAM AND ISAAC.

THE Dean of Westminster begins this lecture with the remark, that the present state of Palestine may, to some extent give one an idea of what it was in the days of Abraham—less, however, all that now makes it different from what it then was. We may wish it were so. We wish one met here and there some of the Canaanites who were then in the land ; that one could see them at their worship, and know more about the very few traces left of their former existence in the land ever consecrated by their name. As it is, however, most of such relics are to be sought for elsewhere. So utterly have the people of Canaan perished, that the most perfect and most interesting remains of Canaanitish worship and building may yet be seen, not in Canaan proper, but elsewhere, as for instance, in Malta.

I was returning from Egypt and from India in 1840 when, at my passage through Malta, I visited the Hdjâr Cham, Qim or Qima, the ' stones of Cham' or of ' Qim,' (worship or veneration) as they are called, which had just been cleared of the soil which had accumulated around and within their enclosure for perhaps more than three thousand years. For, the fact of their being situated on the upper part of a hill, where no alluvial soil could possibly reach them, shows that the several feet of earth with which they were filled, must either have been thrown in purposely or, rather, that this earth was the slow but regular accumulation of decayed vegetable substance and soil during a

long range of centuries. The groundplan of the building
showed in the rudest and simplest fashion, the outer and inner
courts and the sanctuary or νεώς of the actual temple, formed of
large unhewn stones several feet high for the outer wall, and
lined inside with a course of smaller stones more or less worked
by hand. The passage from one such a hall to another was
through doorways cut in solid stones, of a rude Egyptian or
Etruscan outline, i.e. wider at the bottom than at the top. In one
hall, which seemed to be the temple, and at the east end formed
in a kind of apse, were several niches in which female figures
were found with monstrous limbs, but with the smallest hands
and feet ; most probably the oldest figures of Ashtaroth of the
Syrian Venus in existence. In front of these niches were stone
seats and altars rudely carved ; and in another room, or rather
enclosure (for the worship was there performed in the open air)
the altar carved with the palm-tree—the Phœnician or Cartha-
ginian symbol—was yet standing where it was left after the last
sacrifice, close to the seat of the high-priest, on the back of
which were carved two serpents and an egg—two other Eastern
symbols. In what we might call the 'ash-pit,' behind that stone
seat were found horns of sheep and of goats, and the ground
was yet strewn with ashes.

Of all the remains of antiquity I ever saw, none struck
me as so ancient ; and none of that probable date ever appeared so perfect. I was more interested in it, as a genuine
monument of the oldest times, than even in the splendid remains of Thebes ; and I visited Hdjâr Qim or Cham more
than once during my stay, to sketch it as it was found. I have
visited it again since, but the ruthless bands of visitors—one
cannot call them travellers who travel without a traveller's mind
—have more injured these precious tokens of a real antiquity
than the unsparing hand of Time has done during perhaps more
than thirty centuries. In the absence of all inscription or clue
to the date of these two temples or Casal Crendi, we may probably assign them to the time when according to Suidas[1] the
Canaanites fled from before Joshua, first to the coast of Egypt,
whence they were driven to the coasts of Africa, where they left
on record in inscriptions on stone the reason for their having

[1] S. v Χαναάν.

left their country.[1] The passage from the nearest coast to
Malta is very short, and might have been crossed easily even in
those early days. At all events, and judging from the shape,
the construction, the stone figures, the carved palm, serpent, and
egg, and the skeletons found each with a stone egg in one hand,
show these remains to be of Phœnician origin, and ancient
enough to date from the time when Canaan and Phœnicia were
accounted one and the same.

II. One wonders what those Canaanites could have been like;
although we have a correct idea of the warrior Hittites of which
we hear so much in Egyptian annals. For these were the
principal tribe of Southern Canaan in Abraham's time; a tribe
always more or less on bad terms with their neighbours of
Tanis or of Avaris; until either they alone, or they and some
of their friends could resist the temptation no longer, fairly took
possession of that coveted land and reigned there. And when
driven away, they ceased not to give the Pharaohs trouble; for
Rameses II. thought it worth his while to sit in state in his
town of Rameses, built for him by the Israelites, and then to
read a lesson to the great king of the Chetas (Hittites) Cheta-sar
שֶׁר הֲרִתִּים son of Marou-sar, son of Sapalulu, and there to
make with him a treaty graven on tables of silver, adjuring him
by his god Sutech to stay within the limits of his territory, and
there to keep the peace. As regards the name of this powerful
tribe, nothing but ‘terror’ is to be got out of its etymology, if
it be Hebrew.[2] But being always mentioned with the Perizzites as distinct from them, even unto the days of Solomon who
put them under tribute, it does not appear why Dr. Stanley

---

[1] These inscriptions, says Suidas, (also mentioned by Procopius, Vandal. c. ii.
10), εἰσὶ μέχρι τοῦ νῦν ἐν τῇ Νουμιδίᾳ περιέχουσαι οὕτως· “ Ἡμεῖς ἐσμὲν Χαναναῖοι, οὓς
ἐδίωξεν Ἰησοῦς ὁ λῃστής,” are yet to be found in Numidia stating: “ We are
the Canaanites which have fled from before Jesus the Robber.”

[2] But of this J. D. Michaelis (Spicileg. Geogr. pt. ii. p. 10), says rightly,
“ Quod de etymo nominis habent, a terrore ducto, non alii solum, sed ipse
Bochartus (l. iv. c. 36, p. 304) meum non facio. Nescio, unde dicti Chetwei,
plerumque veri non dissimiliores commiscet etymologias ponerem, prout ـــــ
sive ـــــ conferre luberet, sed pudori est. Indoles Gentium non ex nomi-
nibus æstimandæ, quæ et earum sortiantur, ab urbe, a terra, a flumine, &c., et
honorifica sibi samere contenti atque imbelles remanent.”

should say " the Perizzites, or as they are usually called, the
Hittites ;" since פרז and חתת are no synonyms. The Periz-
sites rather seem to have answered in the days of Abraham to the
اهل الوبر 'dwellers in tents,' of later days, the pagani, Bedouins
or gipsies of Palestine who wandered without allegiance to any
one, free and lawless, from the lowlands of Canaan to the hills
of the Amorites, and into the wilderness of the south ; wherever they pleased.

We may be sure that Abraham could never have passed without hindrance through the land in which he had no right even
to 'set foot,' occupied as it then was by those motley tribes
almost always at war among themselves and living on plunder,
but for the protection of Him Who was his "shield and his
exceeding great reward." The Arkite, the Canaanite, or the
Perizzite, would have stopped his march from Damascus, if he
came thence ; and if he journeyed through the desert, may be the
Girgashites would have disputed the fords of Jordan, and the
Hivites his settling to rest under the oaks of Moreh ; bidding
him move on to some more friendly tribe of the south ; unless
some forlorn Perizzite family had made friendship with him and
had escorted him to their border, or to the ' tryst' of their clan,
to some wide-spreading oak by the side of a spring. Even at
the present day, when surveying the land from some high ground,
these evergreen oaks, or ilexes (for terebinths are not now
common) dot here and there the landscape with their dark, stal-
wart masses,—the trysting-trees of wandering Arabs.

III. There are several terms used in the Old Testament for these
three kinds of trees : 'the oak,' the 'ilex,' and the 'terebinth,' viz.,
אֵיל אֵילָה אֵלוֹן אֵלָה אַלּוֹן which come from different roots.
These terms are sometimes interchanged ; yet, as Gesenius says
correctly in a learned criticism on all these terms[1]—I have examined every passage in which they occur—"אֵלוֹן nusquam
terebinthus redditur, nisi Jud. iv. 11, à Syro. Contra quercum
magna constantia habent vet. VSS. (planè enim nauci est planities[2]) אֵלּוֹן denique, magna constantia veteres quercum reddunt ;

---

[1] Thes. L. S. p. 50.

[2] 'Planities' however is the rendering given by Onkelos, Samar. sometimes
Jonathan B. Uzz., A. Fars, R. S. Jarchi and R. B. Melech in Michlol Jophi,
p. 6, recto.

quod etiam mirè confirmatur duobus locis, Jes. vi. 13, Hos. iv.
13." From my own observation, I should feel inclined to take
אֵלָה for a 'terebinth,' אַלּוֹן for an 'oak,' and אֵלוֹן for an 'ilex.'
But, inasmuch as 'oak' is a generic term for the 'ilex' (Quercus
ilex, L.), and some sixty more species of oak, several of which
(e.g., q. ægilops, ballota, &c.) grow in Palestine, these several
terms may well have been used in a wide sense, as was δρῦς,
which originally meant only 'a tree' (draksha). Thus, albeit
the terebinth (Pistacia terebinthus, L.) is in many respects as
different a plant from the oak as the hemp, the hop, or the
spinach, yet, as the colour of its foliage, its shape, and sometimes its size, somewhat resemble those of the ilex, these trees
may have been alluded to under the general term of אֵלָה, and
of its derivatives. The 'oak' of Shechem was most likely an
ilex, the sire, may be, of some fine specimens yet to be seen in
sundry nooks and corners of Palestine; as, e.g., in the narrow
winding wâdy leading from Lubbân to Seilûn (Shiloh), under
which were, when I visited it, the remains of a very ancient
sanctuary, built of large stones; evidently of a very great age.
But the ilex of Shiloh is the finest and oldest looking tree of the
kind I ever saw; its gnarled roots clench the ground as if they
had been wedded to it from everlasting, and its hoary, crooked
boughs droop over the remains of the old building hard by, as
if that building had been reared, had lasted its time, and then
had crumbled into ruins under the eternal shade of that giant
witness of olden times. The rustling of its leaves seems to
murmur 'Heli,' 'Elkanah,' and 'Samuel,' and to sigh over
what followed. It is a fine representative of Ὠγύγη καλουμένη
δρῦς, 'the oak called Ogygian,' under which Josephus[1] tells us
Abraham dwelt at Hebron. On the other hand, the אֵלֹנֵי מַמְרֵא
Gen. xiii. 18, may have been a grove of ilexes; but, more likely,
of other oak trees, like those which now grow in abundance on
the hills to the east of Hebron.

The following sentence (p. 30), therefore, reads rather oddly
from the pen of a Regius Professor:—

"As a rock or a palm-grove in the desert, so in Palestine itself
was the isolated terebinth or ilex, the most massive and majestic

---

[1] Antiq. Lib. I. c. s. p. 26, ed. Huds.

of its native trees, and therefore legitimately, though not quite
correctly, rendered by the English parallel of 'the oak;'"

as it conveys the impression that Dr. Stanley considers the terebinth and the ilex as one and the same. If not, he would have
written, 'so in Palestine itself was the isolated terebinth or the
isolated ilex; and' (unless 'mass and majesty' be inseparable)
'the most massive and most majestic of its native trees, and
each therefore,' &c. He seems, however, indifferent as to which
tree it was, or whether those trees at all differed from each
other; for at page 29 he refers us to Gen. xii. 6 for "the terebinths of Moreb," where mention is made of only one אֵלוֹן מוֹרֶה
which at page 30 he calls "the oak of Moreh."

IV. Then, anticipating Abraham's return from Egypt while
on his way thither, Dr. Stanley describes Abraham's second
visit to Bethel and his parting from Lot; and he thus moralises
on this "the first *controversy* that divided the Patriarchal
Church:"—

"It was the first instance of 'agreeing to differ,' in later times so
rarely found, so eagerly condemned; and yet not less suitable to
all times, because of the extreme simplicity of its early application."

Quite so; and nothing could be more desirable than this patriarchal style of agreeing to differ by parting either to the East
or to the West. Unfortunately the two cases are not parallel,
and the world is not now so wide as it then was. The patriarchal difference was about wells and pasture land, and was
soon settled by Lot continuing to differ and going elsewhere—
by far the better way; whereas the differences of the present
day, to which the Dean of Westminster seems to allude, are
about wells and pastures of another sort. They are about principles too sacred to be touched; about the integrity of the Bible,
which is to us the Word of Life; about our holy and most precious Faith, that rests thereon; about the Truth as it is held by
the Catholic Church, and by the Church of this country. Those
differences are also about the rights, the fences, and the formularies of this Church, Queen of princes in all lands, and nursing
Mother of a great and good people; and for the sake also of this
Church and of her sons, there are also differences about the

University, once famous everywhere for sound learning, and in this country for the religious, sterling, and wholesome English education she was wont to confer on all well-bred sons committed to her charge.

And these differences exist between those who could make themselves happy with things as they were, and those who either could not or would not; between those who venerate, love, and worship the Bible, as being the Word of God revealed to them, and those who ridicule, slight, or gainsay it; between those who live by Faith, who would sooner lose all than part with the Hope as the anchor of the soul sure and steadfast which that Faith in the Word of God gives, and those whose faith reaches no further than their intellect; between those who wish to uphold and to maintain the Truth taught by the Church Catholic as the Rule of Faith, and those who will neither have a Rule nor, perhaps, a Church, and who will make the Truth for themselves; between those who love the Church of the nation for her own sake and for that of the people, who will therefore uphold and defend it, and those who rather try to throw down her fences and to abrogate her formularies; between those who wish, if possible, to keep the University a seat of sound and religious learning, and of the sterling education which no other university ever gave, for the sake of the sons they have to send thither, and those who, having no sons to send thither, have no greater ties to it, perhaps, than the drudgery of lectures and the gossip of the common-room, and yet think themselves alone authorised to have a voice in matters affecting the welfare of the University, and the moral future of the sons of England that are sent thither. These are a few of the wells and of the pastures about which the best thing would be, as we are told, to agree to differ, and part; were it not that, judging from past and present experience, it looks very much as if this agreement meant—that those alone should stay who clamour for a change.

V. What the legend of the Convent of the Holy Cross near Jerusalem be, to which Dr. Stanley alludes in a note at page 32, I know not. But it must be akin to what says S. Ephrem[1] on Gen. xiii. 17: "Then was the Cross distinctly drawn. The Land which had been promised to the early patriarchs in the

---

[1] Vol. I. p. 61.

mystery of the Cross, was by reason of the Cross lost to them, and made over to other heirs."

VI. There is not much to remark in the few following pages, which are a fair specimen of the Dean of Westminster's chaste and agreeable style. One expression, however, causes a smile, when we are told that Abraham's instinct led him to the wilderness of Beer-sheba to see Ishmael, "who recalled to him his own early days,"—when he was eighty-six years of age! The other is—

"where the imperious caprice of the Arab chieftainess forbade Hagar and her son to remain any longer in the tent," &c.—p. 87.

Dr. Stanley, I am quite sure, only wishes to draw a lively picture of what he may have seen in his travels in the East, yet his words give a wrong impression of a transaction which, without excusing Sarah's petulence of temper in itself, was clearly brought about for God's own purposes. First, Abraham was not an Arab, but a Hebrew; names and nations which, although apparently very near each other (עֵבֶר, עֲרָב), have nevertheless each a different origin. Secondly, Sarah was not an Arab chieftainess, but the wife of the "Friend of God," who by faith[1] "bare a son against hope, because she judged Him faithful that promised." Thirdly, it was not imperious caprice on her part, for it was sanctioned by God, Who said unto Abraham, "In all that Sarah hath said unto thee, hearken unto her voice" (Gen. xxi. 12). Fourthly, Hagar and Ishmael did not live in Abraham's tent. She never was there but when waiting on her mistress, and she had a tent of her own close by that of Sarah; or a small compartment of it allotted to her for her own use and that of her child.

Neither was Isaac "the child of laughter and joy" (p. 87), as if it were a laughter 'of joy' only. There may have been joy in Sarah's heart as in Abraham's (Gen. xvii. 17) at the news; but Isaac's birth was, humanly speaking, so improbable and unexpected, that her laughter was rather of doubt (ib. xviii. 12); otherwise she would not have denied that she had laughed (ib. 15). And Isaac may have been so named to remind her of her laughter of doubt; albeit she felt ashamed of having doubted when the angel reminded her of it (ib. 13, 14, 15).

[1] Heb. xi. 11.

VII. In speaking of Abraham's external relations to the Canaanitish tribes among which he sojourned, Dr. Stanley, if I
understand him aright, implies that Abraham was on the best
of terms with them, as worshipping the same GOD they worshipped in a sort of ill-defined, arbitrary manner.

"Abimelech, Ephron, Mamre, Melchizedek, all either worship the
same GOD, or, if they worship Him under another name, they are
all bound together by ties of hospitality and friendship. To overlook the unity, the comparative unity, between Abraham and the
neighbour races of Palestine, would be to overlook one of the
most valuable testimonies to the antiquity, the general Patriarchal
spirit of the record as it has been handed down to us."—p. 40.

We have seen just now the Patriarchal way of "agreeing to
differ," and its obvious advantages; we now come to the Patriarchal way of making "a distinction without a difference,"
and of worshipping or not, all or nothing, after the fashion of
one's neighbours.

Abraham would have been the first to resent such imputa-
tion. He would have replied that, living as a stranger and a
pilgrim in a land occupied by idolatrous and corrupt tribes as
those of Sodom and Gomorrah, in which he had no possession
whatever, not even to bury his dead, until he bought the right
to it, it would have been folly in him to quarrel with them,
even in a less degree than Simeon and Levi (Gen. xxxiv.); but,
while serving the Living GOD among men who worshipped
idols, he treated them with courtesy in all common dealings of
every-day life, though he could hold no communion with them.
He would not take from among them a wife for his son, neither
did he purchase land where he knew he should have no inheritance, no, not so much as to set his foot on; he therefore be-
haved to his hosts as a stranger in their land, as "a pilgrim
towards a better country, even an heavenly."

As regards Melchizedek, we know whom he served and worshipped; but it is probably a mistake to class his GOD and the
worship of that GOD with the worship of the God of Abimelech,
of which, however, we know nothing: whereas we are certain
that Ephron and Mamre, being Hittites, worshipped a very
different god from that of Melchizedek and of Abraham. The

God of the Hittites, who brought the worship of it to Avaris, in
Lower Egypt, even before Abraham's time, or very soon after,
was Seth, or Sutech, often mentioned on Egyptian monuments
and in MSS. Papyri, and represented, either as a man with the
head of an ass, or as an ass with his tail erect, even when styled
'the good god,' nTp nɕp, as he is in the inscription found
on the sphinx of Baghdad ; whence we see that his shape could
have nothing to do with either love or hatred for him.[1]   For,
albeit in later times of Egyptian history his worship was either
suppressed or identified with Typhon, and his images scratched
off the monuments all over the land, probably out of hatred for
the foreign dynasty that had taken Avaris, and for a long time
had reigned there ; yet at first, and while the foreign rule pre-
vailed in Avaris or Tanis, as in the days of Apap or Apophis,
Sutech was the chief divinity worshipped there.   He figures as
an ass with his tail erect in the treaty of Ramses II. with
Cheta-sar, the King of the Hittites already mentioned, and
made not long before the exodus, in the city of Ramesses.[2]
Ramses having come to return thanks to his father, Amun Ra-
Hormachu-Tum of Heliopolis, and to Sutech (figure in the inscription afterwards scratched off) the glorious son of Nut,
mentioned, no doubt, in order to show the Hittite king a bond
of union between them, Cheta-Sar came to sue for peace, and
Ramses framed the treaty cϪp ιpι poτ npⲆ ιpι poτ
coττϪ ⲛ nⲑo ⲛ ⲕⲏⲁⲗⲉ between Ra and Sutech of Egypt
(l. 8), having previously said (l. 7) that this treaty was made
between the King of Egypt and the King of the Hittites, ßⲇ
nⲛⲧp Ϫⲏp ⳦poⲧι poτ oτ oⲧⲧ cⲛ, " that God (nⲛⲧp,
the Deity) should not create enmity between them ;" making
use of a very rare and very remarkable expression, especially in
a treaty of this kind, when mentioning the Deity or God abstractedly as one and the same between them, whatever His
name be.   This would seem at first to favour Dr. Stanley's
opinion, but in reality it does not ; it only shows how utterly
careless and indifferent were those heathens as to the real character of their gods ; assuredly so in Egypt, where in several

[1] Pleyte, le dieu Seth, pl. I. 9, 10 ; lii. 1.
[2] See above, p. 133, and Brugsch. Mon. vol. I. pl. xxviii.

nomes gods were worshipped which in other nomes were either
hated or eaten; and in Canaan, judging from sundry Egyptian inscriptions in which Suteeh and Baal are mentioned, these two
gods may have been worshipped together.

Thus we have the certainty that, whether good or evil, the
chief god of the Hittites in the days of Ephron and of Mamre
was Set or Sutech (whence שָׂטָן, Satan?), the same as in those
of Cheta-Sar, and that it was often coupled with Baal, and represented like him.[1] We cannot, therefore, admit the reciprocal
fraternity of feeling which, says Dr. Stanley, seems to have
existed between Abraham and his heathen hosts; neither can
we reconcile this with the staunch Monotheism he is said to
have introduced.[2]

VIII. Likewise is the note given by Dr. Stanley (p. 40)—

"The God of Melchizedek (Gen. xiv. 18) was not *Eloah* or
Elohim, but *Eliun*, the name given to the God of Phœnicia by
Sanchoniaton (Kenrich, *Phœn.* 288)"—

incorrect, and worth very little. For, first, *Eliun* was not 'the
God,' i.e., the chief divinity, of Phœnicia, but only one of the
gods worshipped there.[3]

Secondly, 'Eliun' was not 'the GOD' of Melchizedek, as Dr.
Stanley says inadvertently. 'The GOD' of Melchizedek was
אֵל עֶלְיוֹן, 'the Mighty Most High,' 'God the Most High;' a
very different thing; and He was 'the GOD' of Daniel (Dan. v.
18, iii. 26, iv. 2) and of Asaph (Ps. lxxviii. 35, 56). For we
may be sure that Melchizedek, who was a figure of the true King
of Righteousness, Who is a High Priest for ever after his order,
had the right faith, and not that of either his Phœnician or his
Canaanitish neighbours.

Thirdly, 'Eliun' עֶלְיוֹן was also 'the GOD' of Balaam

---

[1] Brugsch. Mon. i. pl. xlv. c. 1, 7.   [2] See above, p. 115.

[3] Ἐκ τούτων, says Sanchoniaton (p. 34, ed. Orell, and Euseb. Præp. Ev. L. I.
c. x. p. 37, ed. Col.), γεγόνασι ἕτεροι—κατὰ τούτους γίνεταί τις Ἐλιοῦν καλού-
μενος Ὕψιστος καὶ θήλεια λεγομένη Βηρούθ, οἳ καὶ κατῴκουν περὶ Βύβλον κ. τ. λ.
"After these,"—i. e., Misor, Sydyk, Taaut, the Cabiri, and then another race
which invented medicine,—" were born a certain Eliun, that means ' most high,'
(עֶלְיוֹן, Elîôn, ' high,' ' most high,' adj. Deut. xxvi. 19; xxviii. 1; Josh. xvi. 5,
&c.,) and a female called Bêrûth; and they lived about Byblus," &c. So that
this ' Eliun' was an inferior god of Phœnicia, and not ' the God' of that land.

(Numb. xxiv. 16), of Moses (Deut. xxxii. 8), of David (Ps. vii.
18, and repeatedly in the Psalms), of Jeremiah (Lam. iii. 38),
and of Isaiah (Isa. xiv. 14).

Fourthly, עֶלְיוֹן was the common title of gods and of goddesses at Carthage. Thus, in the Pœnulus of Plautus,[1] Hanno
begins thus: אֲנַת עֶלְיוֹנִים עֶלְיוֹנוּת, ' All hail, gods and goddesses;' and again at l. 4, &c.[2]

Fifthly, besides ' Eliun,' the Phœnicians had also ' Eloim,'
Ἐλοεὶμ, אֱלֹהִים, οἱ δὲ σύμμαχοι Ἤλου τοῦ Κρόνου Ἐλοεὶμ ἐπεκλή-
θησαν ὡς ἂν Κρόνιοι—" Eloim was the name by which the companions in arms of Ilus, son of Cronus, were called, as children
of Cronus," &c.[3] The Phœnicians and Carthaginians also worshipped אֱלִם, ' gods,' plural of אֵל, Ἦλος, ' god.'[4]

So that we learn nothing from Dr. Stanley's note but what
we knew already, viz., that certain Hebrew terms are found in
neighbouring dialects; and since Sanchoniaton wrote a correct
account, even of the Jews, εἰληφὼς τὰ ὑπομνήματα παρὰ Ἱερομβάλου
τοῦ ἱερέως θεοῦ τοῦ Ἰευώ—" having received the principal heads of
his narrative from Hierombal, priest of the God Jevo,"[5] who,
whether Jerubbaal,[6] that is, Gideon, or not, must have been a
worshipper of the true God, as priest of Jevo, or Jehova,—it is
not singular that he should make statements akin to facts mentioned in cotemporaneous history of the Old Testament. But
this proves nothing to the purpose; and since Dean Stanley
makes the story of Joseph and of Asenath a canonical Book of
the Old Testament in the Armenian Church,[7] I almost wonder he
did not draw his information about Phœnician matters from the
complete history of Sanchoniaton published by Wagenfeld and

---

[1] Act. v. sc. 1.

[2] Judas L. Phen. p. 10—12, sq. Movers Pun. texte, p. 73, where he differs
from Bochart, and from Gesenius. Mon. Phœnic. p. 363, sq.

[3] Sanchon. p. 29, ed. Orell. Ewald, Weltschöpf. Sanch. p. 43, sq.

[4] Inscr. de Marseilles, A. Bargès. Paris, 1847, l. 16, et p. 56.

[5] Sanchon. p. 2, ed. Orell. Euseb. Præp. Ev. Lib. i. c. 6.

[6] Bochart (in Geogr. Sacra. Opp. vol. i. col. 774) makes Ἱεράμβαλος i. q.
' Jerubbaal,' the name given to Gideon by his father Joash, i.e. יְרֻבַּעַל; but
Movers (Phœn. vol. i. 434) makes it a name of the Tyrian Heracles, or ' archal,'
mentioned in Palmyrenian inscriptions—but θεοῦ Ἰαριβάλου, i.q. ' Jarbas,' or
Jerubbesheth, another name of Gideon. 2 Sam. xi.21. (Gesen. Mon. Phœn. p. 229.)

[7] Lect. iv. p. 76.

Grotefend a few years ago, with even a facsimile of the MS. from which it is translated.[1]

IX. Dr. Stanley, however, very wisely declines to discuss who was the Pharaoh that received Abraham at his court. No one has yet 'settled' it, despite the many surmises on the subject; and no one ever shall, unless some more explicit information comes to light, in the shape of monuments or of papyri, than we yet possess. Until then we cannot speak with certainty. Eupolemus[2] does not mention the Pharaoh, but only says that Abraham taught the Egyptians astrology.[3] S. Ephrem[4] does not, either, mention the Pharaoh's name, but only says Abraham went to Egypt to learn that his posterity should not leave that land, but after great judgments foreshadowed in the detention of Sarah at Pharaoh's court. Josephus[5] calls him only Φαραώθς, and Joseph. B. Gorion[6] mentions him as הָרְעֹה, Pharaoh. Marsham[7] calls him Ameris; Africanus[8] calls him 'Ramessemeno;' Abu'l-feda[9] says he was سلوان بن علوان وقيل طوليس 'Selwán,' son of 'Alwán,' or as others call him, 'Túlis;'[10] and he adds that, indignant at Sarah waiting upon herself, he gave her Hagar for a maid.[11] Lesueur

---

[1] Sanchuniathon's Urgesch. d. Phön. ed. Wagenfeld; mit einem Vorw. von Dr. G. F. Grotefend, Hanov. 1836; and again in Greek and Latin, Bremæ, 1837.

[2] Quoted by Alex. Polyh. in Euseb. Præp. Ev. Lib. ix. c. 16, p. 419, ed. Col.

[3] On which subject Mr. Osborne, who calls that Pharaoh 'Achthoes,' of the Eleventh Dynasty, has a great deal to say (Mon. Egypt, vol. i. 374, sq.) But what he says cannot command much attention, if he can find 'Adam' (p. 262) and the worship of him in 'Atúm' or 'Túm,' the evening sun, worshipped especially at On, which he calls 'Athens' (at p. 334); Noah or 'Nu,' in 'Num' or 'Nun;' Ham, in 'Amun;' Iris in 'i-sha,' אשה; Misraim, son of Ham, in 'Osiris,' which he derives from שר, 'a potter!' and makes מצרם the dual thereof!!! Phut, son of Ham, in 'Phtah' (p. 327, sq.); and other marvellous etymologies (found at p. 86, sq., vol. ii., and throughout the work), which one can hardly understand a man bringing himself to write deliberately.

[4] In Gen. vol. i. p. 80 and 158.
[5] Lib. vi. c. 38, p. 741, ed. Breith.
[6] In Geo. Syncell. Chr. vol. i. p. 189, ed. Dind.
[7] Antiq. Lib. i. c. 8.
[8] Chronic. p. 73.
[9] H. A. Isl. p. 20, sq.
[10] A name given him also by other Arabic writers.

[11] The accidental omission of the end of Gen. xvi. 3, at p. 98, where mention is made of Hagar, renders that passage somewhat confused. The point proved is, not that Sarah had had Hagar ten years when she gave her to Abraham, though this be probable, but, that she gave her to Abraham when he had been ten years in Canaan, dating evidently, from his arrival there from Haran.

brings Abraham into Egypt under Ramesse Meno, fifth king of his fifteenth Theban dynasty B.C. 2499.[1] Brugsch gives no opinion in his 'Histoire d'Egypte.'[2] Bunsen makes Abraham visit Egypt during the first half of the old kingdom, B.C. 2900; and Champollion-Figeac[3] places Abraham's visit in the sixteenth dynasty, somewhere about Ouserteseu; but a man who, to show the pastoral government of Egypt at that time, says, "les Hé- breux s'uniaaient en mariage avec les Egyptiens; Agar, femme d'Abraham, était née en Egypte," &c., can deserve very little respect for what he says. Chabas,[4] a very safe and equally able and learned Egyptian scholar, places Abraham under the Hyksôs, about 1,900 B.C., concluding, from the similarity of manners at the court of Abimelech and at that of Pharaoh, that the two kings were of the same race: such doings, however, were, and are, common at most other courts also. At last; Lepsius[5] places Abraham under Thuthmosis IV., or under Amenophis III., in the eighteenth Dynasty, after the expulsion of the shepherd kings, and not during their reign.

All these computations, which vary by more than a thousand years, show how utterly hopeless it is for the present to wish to fix Abraham's visit at the court of Pharaoh.

X. His "craft," as Dr. Stanley calls it, however, is thus ex- plained by S. Ephrem :[6] "He called her his sister as a preserva- tive; for she was daughter of Haran his brother. Wherefore he said to Lot, We are men, brothers. So also Moses: Men, ye are brothers. And Abraham said to Abimelech, She is my sister, daughter of my father, though not of my mother; making her daughter of Terah, albeit she was his son's daughter."

XI. On this transaction at Abimelech's court Dr. Stanley says in a note (p. 42) :—

"The English Version is afraid of saying that Sarah was the wife of Pharaoh—'I might have had' for 'I had.' Gen. xii. 19."

wherein he is right; for there is no reason for rendering אֶקַּח otherwise than 'I took,' as in ch. xl. 11; Numb. viii. 16;

[1] Chron. des Rois d'Eg. p. 322.   [2] Æg. Stelle, vol. v. pt. 1, p. 356, 468.
[3] L'Egypte, Univers, p. 293, sq.   [4] Rev. Archéol. xv°. année, 1 livr. p. 7.
[5] Æg. Chron. p. 388.   [6] Vol. L. p. 157.

Deut. i. 15, &c. Of all the old versions, the Vulgate, which has 'ut tollerem,' is the only one that renders it differently.

XII. Then Dr. Stanley, after giving us a lively description of Abraham's pursuit after Chedorlaomer and his confederates " to the scene of Abraham's first conquest, Damascus," comes to speak of "the mysterious appearance of Melchizedek on the scene," saying (p. 45) :—

" No wonder that when, in after times, there arose One whose appearance was beyond and above any ordinary influence of time and place, the author of the Epistle to the Hebrews could find no fitter expression for this aspect of his character than the mysterious likeness of Melchizedek."

Dr. Stanley, it seems, is afraid of committing himself by calling S. Paul the author of the Epistle to the Hebrews. In this, however, he might be more likely to have right on his side than in many assertions he confidently makes. But had he forgotten David's expression, " The LORD hath sworn, and will not repent, Thou art a Priest for ever after the order of Melchizedek ?" (Ps. cx. 4.)[1] Dr. Stanley ought not to have omitted this, especially while dwelling on Melchizedek's office, if he had remembered what we read of Him Who is our High Priest, " set on the right hand of the throne of the Majesty in the heavens," " the King of kings," to Whose dominion there shall be no end, and Whose redeemed people are to be " kings and priests" for ever. For this is the greatest and the real interest of the likeness drawn by the HOLY GHOST between Melchizedek, who was both priest and king, and our LORD JESUS CHRIST, Who is also Priest and King for ever ; albeit Dr. Stanley thinks

" there is enough of interest if we merely confine ourselves to the letter of the ancient narrative."

'Interest' there is, if we will but look into the question and compare Melchizedek's office with that of kindred rulers in other countries, and at the same time too, such as the פ֫ךֵ אֵ֫ן, the כֹהֵן אֹן 'priest of On' in Egypt, a man like Potipherah, a title of which even the Ramses were proud and which they added to their regal epithets as a kind of 'Defender of the

---

[1] And Heb. vi. 20 ; vii. 21.

Faith;' during the whole of their reign; a title and an office
with which we may compare that of خان 'Khân,' among the
Tartars. But this is not the place for details, for there is not
"enough of interest" in this subject when it relates to Melchizedek.

"That title of Divinity" (Eliun), continues Dr. Stanley—

"also appears for the first time in the history; and we catch from
a heathen author a clue to the spot of the earliest primæval sanctuary where the Supreme Name was honoured with priestly and
regal service: tradition told that it was on Mount Gerizim Melchizedek ministered."—p. 45.

Tradition, forsooth! we have seen that 'Eliun,' as Dr. Stanley gives it, was no "title of Divinity" in the mouth of Melchizedek; for this word 'Eliun' עֶלְיוֹן is only the adjective
that qualifies אֵל 'the Mighty God,' called by Melchizedek
אֵל עֶלְיוֹן 'the Mighty God Most High;' it is this title, and
not 'Eliun' עֶלְיוֹן alone, that does appear in this place for the
first time. And as to Gerizim, does Dr. Stanley not know that
the mountain at present called Mount Gerizim may, after all,
have been Mount Ebal? It is impossible to determine from
Deut. xi. 20, the real position of these hills. For as they stand
north and south relatively to each other, they would both be
"by the way where the sun goeth down" for the children of Israel
when, and where Moses spake these words. After the return
from the captivity, the Samaritans built for themselves a temple
on Mount Gerizim to rival that of Jerusalem; and from that time
date all the stories they tell of its sanctity; such as—that
Abraham and Jacob worshipped and that Isaac was offered on
it; that it never was even wetted by the waters of the Flood, that
it is the holiest spot on earth, &c. So also they, as everybody
knows, changed 'Ebal' into 'Gerizim' in their own Samaritan
version, as well as in the Hebræo-Samaritan text of Deut. xi. 4,[1]
to make it appear that the Levites stood, and that the altar was
built on Mount Gerizim and not on Mount Ebal, as Moses
commanded and as Joshua did, Josh. viii. 33; and they added

[1] A fraud some of their descendants admitted when I taxed them with it in
their own city.

the substance of Deut. xi. 8, 4, after the 10th commandment in both Ex. xx. and Deut. v.

Hence did Eupolemus borrow the account to which Dr. Stanley seems to give credit, but which bears traces of a Samaritan origin. Speaking of Abraham Eupolemus, as quoted by Alexander Polyhistor,[1] says that, ἑνισθῆναί τε αὐτὸν ὑπὸ πόλεως ἱερόν, Ἀργαριζὶν, ὅ ἐστιν μεθερμηνευόμενον ὄρος Ὑψίστου, παρὰ δὲ τοῦ Μελχισεδὲκ ἱερέως ὄντος τοῦ Θεοῦ καὶ βασιλεύοντος λαβεῖν δῶρα, " he was hospitably received within the temple of the city, Argarizin, which is interpreted ' Mountain of the Most High,' and that he received gifts from Melchizedek who was both King and Priest of God." Now, first, Ἀργαριζὶν is the Samaritan הרגריזם/ארגרזים Argarizin, هرجرزيم, always written thus in one word in the Samaritan Pentateuch, and sometimes in the Samaritan Chronicle, instead of being written in two words like the Hebrew הַר גְּרִזִים. Secondly—Ἀργαριζὶν does not mean ὄρος Ὑψίστου; for גְּרִזִים may, after all, be the pl. of גְּרִזִי, ' Gerizite' or ' Gerzite,' 1 Sam. xxvii. 8, as Gesenius[2] justly remarks; so that הַר גְּרִזִים would mean the ' mountain of the Gerizites ; but ὄρος Ὑψίστου comes from the names of holiness given to it; such as طور بريك the ' Blessed mountain' as it is called throughout the Samaritan Chronicle.[3]

Moreover, the connexion between Melchizedek and Mount

[1] Euseb. Præp. Ev. Lib. ix. c. 17, p. 419.   [2] Thes. L. S. s.v.

[3] And in Masudi (vol. I. ch. v. p. 115,) who says : " the Samaritans call Nablûs by the name of بيت المقدس ' the Holy House,' (Jerusalem,) where they have a mountain طور بريك called by them the ' Blessed Mountain.'" (The editors of Masudi who were not acquainted with the Samaritan Chronicle, give طور بريد ' Cold Mountain ;' but De Sacy, Chrestom. Ar. I. 342, gives the right reading طور بريك.) Likewise Mahrizi (De Sacy, Chrestom. Ar. p. 111 and 303) tells us how Sanballat asked of Alexander leave to build a temple on طور بريك the ' Blessed Mountain ;' then Sanballat built there a temple after the model of that of Jerusalem, and tried to draw Jews to it by telling him that ' Tor-barik' or the ' Blessed Mountain,' was the place spoken of by God when He made mention of it في التورية بقوله فيها اجعل البركة على طور بريك in the Law saying : " Put the blessing on the Blessed Mountain."

Gerizim appears nowhere else. Most of conspicuous mountains
were at some time or other either consecrated to some god,
chiefly to Jupiter, as the Olympi of Thessaly, of Bithynia, of
Mysia, &c.; or they were honoured with some kind of worship;
we may, therefore, suppose that Mount Tabor, which is far more
conspicuous than Mount Gerizim, might have, at least, as good
a claim as Mount Gerizim, to be considered the altar of the land
of Canaan in the days of Abraham. Accordingly S. Athanasius
in his history of Melchizedek[1]—which I am surprised the Regius Professor does not mention,—says nothing whatever of
Mount Gerizim, but makes Melchizedek reside on Mount Tabor.
It was in the temple of idols on Mount Tabor that he was
brought to the knowledge of the true God; and it was there
also that ἐν τῷ δάσει τῆς ὕλης ἐλθὼν, ἡμέρασεν ἐκεῖ ἔτη ἑπτά, going
into the thickest of the forest[2] he continued therein seven years.
It was there that Abraham came to him, in obedience to a voice
that said to him, ἄνελθε ἐν τῷ ὄρει Ταβὼρ καὶ κράξον τρεῖς φωνάς·
ἄνθρωπε τοῦ Θεοῦ, "go up to Mount Tabor and cry three times:
O man of God! and a man of wild appearance will come out.
Fear not; but cut his shaggy hair, pare his nails, clothe him,
and he will bless thee. Abraham obeyed, and went to Mount
Tabor; Melchizedek met him; and having come down from
the mountain took a horn of oil, and setting to his seal that
God's word was true, καὶ ἐπισφραγίσας τῷ ῥήματι τοῦ Θεοῦ, he
blessed Abraham saying: εὐλογημένος εἶ τῷ Θεῷ τῷ ὑψίστῳ, καὶ
τὸ λοιπὸν καλεῖται τὸ ὄνομά σου τετελειωμένον· Blessed be thou of
the Most High God, and let thy name from henceforth be called
' Perfect,' " &c.

S. Ephrem,[3] however, tells us a different story; he says that
ܘܗܿܘ ܡܠܟܝܙܕܩ ܡܢ ܫܝܡ ܗܘܐ "This Melchizedek was Shem,
who was both king and priest, and lived, not only in the days
of Abraham, but also in those of Esau and of Jacob; that Rebekah went to consult him and heard from him that she should
bear twins, and that the elder should be subject unto the
younger." And S. Ephrem adds " that she never could have

[1] Hist. Melch. vol. I. p. 74.
[2] There is yet an extensive forest of oak, of Q ægilops, ballota, and other trees,
at the foot of the mountain, above Chazulloth.
[3] In Genes. c. xlii. vol. i. p. 61.

left her husband, to go and consult Melchizedek, had she not heard of his greatness from Abraham." Neither would Abraham have given tithes to Melchizedek if he had not thought him so much above himself.[1] It is only in deference to Aristotle's saying, διὸ καὶ φιλόμυθος ὁ φιλόσοφος πῶς ἐστιν,[2] "the philosopher is, in a way, fond of stories," that I have given these traditions, and to show those who follow them, that they will hardly thus arrive at the Truth.

In this case we have nothing to go by on which we can rely, but the narrative of Scripture; and we may rest assured that, if it had not been intended by God that Melchizedek should appear as it were "without father, without mother, without descent, having neither beginning of days, nor end of life: but made like unto the Son of God,"[3] for purposes into which it is impertinence on our part to pry, we should know more about him than we do. We neither know where he lived nor where he reigned; whether the Salem of which he was king was the Salem or Salim, nigh unto which Jacob pitched his tents, and John baptized,—or Jerusalem; but we know that it means 'Peace' and that Melchizedek, as type of Christ, was King of Peace as well as King of Righteousness; and this is worth to us more than many traditions.

Moreover there is against even the possibility of Eupolemus' story, the fact that—not once in the whole Samaritan Book of Joshua (or Sam. Chronicle) is Melchizedek alluded to. I have found Mount Gerizim mentioned as طور بريك the 'Blessed mountain,' in ch. xix., xxi., xxiv., xxv., xxvii., xxix., xxxviii., xlv., xlvi., and xlvii., and in ch. l. it is styled هر جرزيم and جبل جرزيم 'Har Djerizim' or Djebel Djerizim, or Gerizim,[4]

---

[1] And S. Ephrem ends with a singular reasoning, that ܡܛܠ ܕܝܢ ܕ [Syriac text] ܣܘܡܦܘܢ ܘܡܠܟܝܙܕܩ ܚܡܫܐ ܚܠܒ ܫܢܝܐ ܘܗܘܐ .ܗܘ ܘܗܘܐ ܐ[Syriac]ܐ : ܘܡܠܟܝܙܕܩ ܡܠܟܐܡܠܟ "Inasmuch as the years of Melchizedek extended up to the years of Jacob and of Esau, therefore is it said with probability that he was Shem."

[2] Met. i. 2, 10.   [3] Heb. vii. 1—3.

[4] And so it they apply Gen. xxii. 2; xxx. 20; Ex. xv. 17, and Deut. xxxiii. 15. Ash-Shahrestani, in his account of the Samaritans, calls Mount Gerizim جبل يقال له غريم the mountain called 'Gharim,' evidently a mistake for 'Gharizim,' which he says is the 'Qiblah of the Samaritans,' near Nablous. Ash-Shârest. vol. ii. p. 170.

but no allusion is made to Melchizedek; a circumstance hardly probable if the Samaritans had felt they had the slightest right to claim him for one of their worthies. So that "the smooth rock and natural altar" as relics of Melchizedek on Mount Gerizim, on which Dr. Stanley dwells, are, I fear, a fond conceit; and of a much later date than Melchizedek himself.

XIII. Still less credible is what follows:

"But what is now the last relic of a local and exhausted, though yet venerable religion, was in those patriarchal times the expression of a wide, all embracing worship, which comprehended within its range the ancient chiefs of Canaan and the Founder of the Chosen People."

So that, on the strength of that tradition of Eupolemus which, as we have seen, has no probability whatever, we are to believe that, while Abraham who was a Shemite, and who, living among Shemites, nevertheless worshipped idols from which he was divinely 'called' to establish the service of the true God (in Canaan, of course, since he left his own country immediately after his call)—the Hittites, the Canaanites, and other tribes which were even then destroyed by fire from Heaven for their evil deeds, had preserved among themselves the knowledge of God so far as to be on a par with Abraham after he had been called from his idols, and had become (as we are told) the founder of Monotheism! The consistency of this either with what Dr. Stanley said before, or with what we know of Hittite and of Canaanitish worship does not appear: still less of real philosophy is there in—

"The meeting of the two in the 'King's Dale' personifies to us the meeting between what, in later times, has been called Natural and Revealed Religion; and when Abraham received the blessing of Melchizedek, and tendered to him his reverent homage, it is a likeness of the recognition which true historical Faith will always humbly receive and gratefully render when it comes in contact with the older and everlasting instincts of that religion which the Most High God 'Possessor of Heaven and Earth' has implanted in Nature and in the heart of man, in 'the power of an endless life.'"

First, the inference Dr. Stanley draws from the meeting of Melchizedek with Abraham in 'the king's dale,' looks very

much like a touch of that same 'Docetism' with which he re-
proaches,[1] as being a 'phantom worship,' those who do not take
the history of the Bible literally, and venture to draw either
allegories or fanciful inductions from bare facts.

Secondly—which was the 'Natural' and which was the 'Revealed' religion? For, Dr. Stanley has just told us that Abraham, Melchizedek, Ephron, Abimelech, Mamre, and others
formed a kind of 'happy Patriarchal family' bound together
"by a wide, all embracing worship." So that, they, according
to the Regius Professor, must have all agreed on the same
"wide, all embracing" principles; since we cannot conceive a
worship without a faith nor a faith without a principle. Granted
then, that what we read in Rom. i. 18—32 be said of those
among the heathens who wilfully "held the truth in unrigh-
teousness" (ver. 18), of the bulk of those who were thus brutalised, and not of the wise among them, who like Plato and others
did their best to make good use of their reason,—what, then,
about these? Simply that: "the world by wisdom knew not
God," and since "by wisdom it knew not God it pleased God
by the foolishness of preaching to save them that believe;"[2]
"for therein (in the gospel of Christ) is the righteousness of
God revealed from faith to faith: as it is written, The just shall
live by faith."[3] Since then, "without faith it is impossible to
please God,"[4] and since this Faith must rest and does rest on
revelation, either immediate, as to Abraham, Moses and others,
or mediate, as to us, in the Bible—whosoever had that Faith,
must have had it through revelation; that is, through a direct
communication from God with his heart. For, since "faith is
a fruit of the Spirit," it never could grow spontaneously in the
heart of man; inasmuch as "the natural man (ψυχικὸς ἄνθρωπος)
receiveth not the things of the Spirit of God: for they are
foolishness unto him; neither can he know them, because they
are spiritually discerned."[5] Therefore, even if we were to understand "from faith to faith," Rom. i. 17, to mean 'from
Natural to Revealed Faith or religion,' must this (so called)
Natural faith or religion if intended to please God, be revealed
from Heaven to man. And, since there are not two means of

[1] Pref. p. ix.   [2] 1 Cor. i. 18, 19.   [5] Rom. i. 17.
[4] Heb. xi. 6.   [3] 1 Cor. ii. 14.

salvation and of reconciliation, but only one—" to wit, that GOD was in CHRIST reconciling the world unto himself,"[1] those who, being apparently outside the covenant, did please GOD " through faith"—men whom He raised from time to time as witnesses for His Truth, as lights in a dark place—must have pleased Him through Faith, more or less strong, in the reconciliation without which they must have continued at enmity with Him.

So then, in like manner as Abraham, whom we must take to represent ' Revealed religion' in Dr. Stanley's view of the case, "did see the day of CHRIST and rejoiced," must also the patriarch Job, for instance, of whom we know so little as to be justified in putting him with Melchizedek on the side of Natural Religion according to Dr. Stanley's estimate of each, have looked also forward to the same day and even beyond it, when he said : " I know that my Redeemer liveth, and that he shall stand at the latter day upon the earth." So with regard to Melchizedek : " consider how great this man was, unto whom even the patriarch Abraham gave the tenth[2] of the spoils."[3] For he was both King and Priest ; and, so far, not only greater than Abraham, but also the living type of Him in whom Abraham believed, and to whom, therefore, he paid honour and worship. And this, through ' revelation' to Abraham, but ' naturally' to Melchizedek ? One grieves to have to point out such things to a Regius Professor of Ecclesiastical History, and to have to tell him that this supposed " meeting of Revealed and of Natural religion in the king's Dale" is pure Docetism, and a dream.

XIV. It is very easy thus to make ' Revealed Religion' do homage to ' Natural Religion,' and to make it appear as second and inferior to that, but it is neither philosophical—τῷ ὄντι ἤ ὅν—nor manly. It is not philosophical to speak of Melchizedek as personifying Natural Religion, and at the same time to admit, as Dean Stanley must needs do, that he was a type of our LORD CHRIST, who came into the world only because ' Natural

---

[1] 2 Cor. v. 19.

[2] In a note p. 46, Dr. Stanley quotes " Jerome, *Epist. ad Evangelum*, § 6, who justly remarks that the narrative leaves it ambiguous whether Abraham gave tithes to Melchizedek or Melchizedek to Abraham." But Jerome seems to have forgotten his Hebrew (see p. 139.) And Dr. Stanley overlooked Heb. vii. 4, where S. Paul tells us that Abraham did give tithes to Melchizedek.

[3] " And without all contradiction the less is blessed of the greater." Heb. vii. 4, 7.

Religion' was, and is, unavailing; and powerless to save man. It is a contradiction in terms. And it is not generous, it is neither kind nor right to mystify such vital truths. The intention of it seems obvious. It is, of course, as easy as it is likely to be popular, to teach and to preach with the apparent authority of an accredited position—this "wide, all-embracing worship," that sets before man Truths so hazy that they cannot be distinguished from the mist in which they are put; that imposes no burden of a positive Faith in positive promises; and that binds the conscience with elastic bands; that takes in Abraham, Melchisedek, Hittites, and Canaanites together, without distinction, or, at all events without difference; that seems to be everything and nothing, abrogating all ideas of a 'narrow way' and of a 'broad road,' and making it all one level plain where Revealed and Natural religion and any other creed may disport themselves and claim a footing on equal terms.

But it is not according to Truth. It is not according τῷ ὄντι ἢ ὄν, καὶ τῇ ἀληθείᾳ, that, "historical faith"—by which we must, I presume, understand faith in our SAVIOUR's death and sacrifice as a fact in history—

"will always humbly receive and gratefully tender recognition when it comes in contact with the older and everlasting instincts which 'the Most High GOD, Possessor of Heaven and earth,' has implanted in nature and in the heart of man."

What instincts? "the law written in their hearts," may be. When? before the first promise of a SAVIOUR? ere GOD said to the serpent: "I will put enmity between thee and the woman, and between thy seed and her seed; it shall bruise thy head, and thou shalt bruise his heel?"[1] These "instincts" therefore, and this "historical faith," are very much of the same age; and if "historical faith" comes in second in the history of man, it is only because it was not wanted while man yet shone with the glory of GOD, whom he then knew as he was known of Him. But, after that this brightness had left Adam's form through his fall, after that his innocence had ended in guilt, and that his knowledge of GOD, his intimate communion with Him, his spiritual life in GOD, had left in him only shame, regret for what he had done; only faint echoes of the voice he once heard,

[1] Gen. iii. 15.

and fading memories of what he once enjoyed; when, in short, all that remained of his first divine image, was, a body doomed to return to dust instead of fulfilling a higher destiny; and 'instincts' only of his former estate, instead of the full brightness of his nature, erst pure and godly,—then at once did Faith step in: Thou art lost, said God to Adam, and driven from My Paradise, and thou shalt die. But there is in My realms One Who "is alive for evermore," Who has the keys of hell and of death, and Who will set thee free. He alone is the Way, the Truth, and the Life. Believe in Him, and thou shalt live.

XV. "The power of an endless life" therefore is not in the "everlasting instincts" of this natural religion, as Dr. Stanley says, if I understand him aright. For I do not know what he means by "implanted in Nature and in the heart of man." If he meant man's nature, he would have said: 'in the nature and in the heart of man;' and as to the 'everlasting instincts' of nature,' i.e., of creation, it is difficult to see what they can be. Taking, however, 'nature' here to mean 'man's nature,' how can the instincts of a nature that fell and was doomed to die, the body into dust, the soul away from God, have any "power of their own of an endless life?" They tend upwards, it is true, in token of their origin, and they may rise even beyond the limits of the intellect; yet not higher than the thoughts of man; which, being human and earthly, can never, of themselves, soar to those things which "eye hath not seen nor ear heard, neither have entered into the heart of man, things which God hath prepared for them that love Him."[1] Only ask Plato if his instincts rose higher than his thoughts, high as these were, and if he did not yearn after what he felt was yet higher —too high for him to attain unto. From want of the sure witness of a Revelation, the flight upward of these 'instincts' in him was hindered, dragged downwards, by the weight, the short tether of his reason, that could not reach beyond a certain point, immeasurably short of God, as God is. And as regards "the heart of man, which is deceitful above all things and desperately wicked,"[2] it is, indeed, difficult to see whither its natural instincts can tend, except to what is evil. "The power of an endless

_____
[1] 1 Cor. ii. 9.   [2] Jer. xvii. 9.

life," then, is not where Dr. Stanley seems to put it, but where S. Paul declares it to be[1]—in Him Who alone is "the Life and the Light of men;" "Whom to know is life eternal," and Who hath power to give eternal life to whom He will.[2]

XVI. After alluding to the destruction of Sodom and of Gomorrah (p. 46, 47), Dr. Stanley goes on to treat of the sacrifice of Isaac, which he very properly calls "an act of faith"—

"that marks at least one critical stage in the progress of true religion. There have been in almost all ancient forms of religion, in most modern forms also, two strong tendencies, each in itself springing from the best and purest feelings of humanity. One is the craving to please, or to propitiate, or to communicate with the powers above us, by surrendering some object near and dear to ourselves. This is the source of all sacrifice."

Does the Dean of Westminster really think this to be "the source of all sacrifice?" If so, he seems to take the figurative or derived sense of 'sacrifice' for the literal meaning of the term. He might as well render this passage of Tacitus,[3] "cunctos qui aderant, in verba Vespasiani adigit; mittitque legatos ad duas legiones, 'ut idem sacramentum acciperent,'" 'that they might receive the same sacrament,' as to overlook the true source and origin of 'sacrifice,' and place it in the acceptation of this term which is derived from the institution of the rite.

Regarding, however, the very first sacrifice or oblation offered, we are expressly told that "by faith Abel offered unto God a more excellent sacrifice, πλείονα θυσίαν, than Cain, by which he obtained witness that he was righteous, God testifying of his gifts, and by it he, being dead, yet speaketh."[4] "We are therefore, led to consider," says Archbishop Magee,[5] who wrote in the days of English learning, and to whose work it is a real satisfaction to turn—"whether we are not warranted by Scripture in pronouncing the entire rite to have been ordained by God, as a type of that ONE SACRIFICE, in which all others were to have their consummation." "Let us, then, examine the circumstances of the first sacrifice offered up by Abel.

---

[1] Heb. vii. 16.   [2] S. John i. 4; xvii. 2, 3.   [3] Hist. iv. 21.
[4] Heb. xi. 4.   [5] Atun. and Sacr. vol. i. p. 47, sq.

"It is clear from Scripture that Abel's sacrifice was accepted, and that of Cain was rejected. Now, what could have occasioned the distinction? If we look to the writer to the Hebrews, that the ground on which Abel's oblation was preferred to that of Cain was, that Abel offered his in faith, the meaning then is, that by faith Abel offered that which was much more of the true nature of sacrifice than what had been offered by Cain. Abel, consequently, was directed by faith, and this faith was manifested in the nature of his offering. What, then, are we to infer? Without some revelation granted, some assurance held out as the object of faith, Abel could not have exercised this virtue; and without some peculiar mode of sacrifice enjoined, he could not have exemplified his faith by an appropriate offering. The offering made was that of an animal. Let us consider whether this could have a connection with any Divine assurance, communicated at that early day.

"It is obvious that the promise made to our first parents conveyed an intimation of some future deliverer, who should overcome the tempter that had drawn men from his innocence, and remove those evils which had been occasioned by the fall. This assurance, without which, or some ground of hope, it seems difficult to conceive how the principle of religion could have had place among men, became to our first parents the grand object of faith. To perpetuate this fundamental article of religious belief among the descendants of Adam, some striking memorial of the fall of man, and of the promised deliverance, would naturally be appointed. And if we admit that this scheme of Redemption by the death of the only-begotten SON of GOD was determined from the beginning; that is, if we admit that, when GOD had ordained the deliverance of man, He had ordained the means; if we admit that CHRIST was *the Lamb slain from the foundation of the world*; what more apposite memorial could be devised than that of animal sacrifice? exemplifying, by the slaying of the victim, the death which had been denounced against man's disobedience: thus exhibiting the awful lesson of that death which was the wages of sin, and at the same time representing that death which was actually to be undergone by the Redeemer of mankind; and hereby connecting in one view the two great cardinal events in the history of man,—the FALL,

and the RECOVERY; the death denounced against sin, and the
death appointed for the Holy One, Who was to lay down His
life to deliver man from the consequences of sin."—"Abel, in
firm reliance on the promise of GOD, and in obedience to His
command, offered that sacrifice, which had been enjoined as the
religious expression of his faith; while Cain, disregarding the
gracious assurances that had been vouchsafed, or, at least, dis-
daining to adopt the prescribed mode of manifesting his belief,
possibly as not appearing to *his reason* to possess any efficacy or
natural fitness;—in short, Cain, the first-born of the fall, ex-
hibits the first-fruits of his parents' disobedience, in the arrogance and self-sufficiency of reason rejecting the aids of Revelation, because they fell not within *its* apprehension of right.
He takes the first place in the annals of Deism, and displays, in
his proud rejection of the ordinance of sacrifice, the same spirit
which, in later days, has actuated his *enlightened* followers in
rejecting the sacrifice of CHRIST."[1]

XVII. "The other tendency," continues Dr. Stanley,

" is the profound moral instinct that the Creator of the world cannot
be pleased, or propitiated, or approached by any other means than
by a pure life and good deeds. On the exaggeration, on the contrast,
on the collision of these two tendencies, have turned some of the
chief corruptions, and some of the chief difficulties, of ecclesiastical
history. The earliest of these we are about to witness in the life of
Abraham. There came, we are told, the Divine intimation, 'Take
now thy son,' &c.; but the form taken by this Divine trial or
temptation was that which a stern logical consequence of the
ancient view of sacrifice did actually assume, if not then, yet certainly in after ages, among the surrounding tribes, and which
cannot therefore be left out of sight in considering the whole historical aspect of the narrative. Deep in the heart of the Canaanitish nations was laid the practice of human sacrifice—on the
altars of Moab, of Phœnicia, of Carthage, &c.,—this almost irre-

---

[1] Aton. and Sacr. vol. I. p. 50—53. I recommend those of my readers who
may not know Archbishop Magee's work on the subject, to read it; they
will find, in his sound and manly English style, a wholesome restorative, after
the mawkish, diluted Germanism to which we are being treated 'ad nauseam
usque.' They will also find, in Carpsovii Mantissa de Sacrificiis, Appar. Crit.
pp. 699—725, a full statement of the Divine Institution of Sacrifices, with all
the arguments brought for or against it.

pressible tendency of the burning zeal of a primitive race found its terrible expression. Such was the trial which presented itself to Abraham."—pp. 48, 49.

Would not this have been called 'a sophism' by Aristotle? But ere we consider it, let us look at the note Dr. Stanley gives on Abraham's trial or temptation. It runs thus (p. 48):

"That this temptation or trial, through whatever means it was suggested, should in the sacred narrative be ascribed to the over-ruling voice of God, is in exact accordance with the general tenor of Hebrew Scriptures. A still more striking instance is contained in the history of David, where the same temptation, which in one book is ascribed to God, is in another ascribed to Satan: 'The Lord moved David to say, Go, number Israel' (2 Sam. xxiv. 1). 'Satan provoked David to number Israel' (1 Chron. xxi. 1)."

First, I must vindicate Dr. Stanley from the great offence some people seem to have needlessly taken at his calling God's command to Abraham "a trial or temptation." 'Trial' and 'temptation' have the same meaning; only 'trial' is Anglo-Saxon, and 'temptation' is originally 'infimæ Latinitatis' for 'tentatio.' In daily use these terms have come to be said, the one for trial of strength, of patience, of faith, &c., and the other for solicitation to sin; but in either case it is a 'trial,' whether of strength or of spiritual life in resisting the voice of the tempter. When grace within is the stronger of the two, temptation becomes only a trial; if, however, sin within is stronger than grace, then the trial ends in a breaking down. In Hebrew נָסָה, as in Greek πειράω, are used to express both 'trial' and 'temptation.' So that, when we read "that God did tempt Abraham" (Gen. xxii. 1), it means simply that God did try Abraham's faith. So also, when said of man towards God, as in לֹא תְנַסּוּ אֶת־יְהוָה אֱלֹהֵיכֶם,[1] οὐκ ἐκπειράσεις Κύριον τὸν Θεόν σου, LXX., "Thou shalt not tempt the Lord thy God," it is said of trying God's patience and His forbearance towards us, &c. And this, doubtless, is Dr. Stanley's meaning in saying "trial or temptation;" for he cannot have forgotten, "Let no man say when he is tempted, I am tempted of God;

----
[1] Deut. vi. 16.

for God cannot be tempted with evil, neither tempteth He any man."[1]

And this, secondly, bears directly on the two passages Dean Stanley compares together, in one of which (2 Sam. xxiv. 1) the Dean, who overlooks the Hebrew, understands the words "he moved David against them" to apply to "the Lord," the subject of the preceding sentence, but, against idiom and grammar; whereas, in the parallel passage (1 Chron. xxi. 1), Satan is expressly said to have "stood up and provoked David to number Israel." If Dean Stanley had looked at the marginal notes of his English Bible, he would have found there, in 2 Sam. xxiv. 1, the shortest and best commentary on "he moved David against them," viz., "Satan, see Chron. xxi. 1, Jam. i. 13, 14." And to show that this comment is correct, the omission, or rather, the ellipsis of 'Satan' before "he moved," is strictly according to the Hebrew idiom, which often omits the subject or noun, when plainly understood from the context. Thus, in Gen. xiv. 20, וַיִּתֶּן־לוֹ מַעֲשֵׂר מִכֹּל, "And he (i.e., Abraham, proved by Heb. vii. 4) gave him the tenth (or tithes) of all."

Likewise Gen. xli. 13, אֹתִי הֵשִׁיב עַל־כַּנִּי, "Me he (i.e., Pharaoh) restored into mine office."

Again, 2 Sam. iii. 8, "And Saul had a concubine whose name was Rizpah, וַיֹּאמֶר, and he (i.e., Ishbosheth, which the Authorized Version rightly introduces into the text) said unto Abner," &c. This passage alone would prove the rule; for if these words referred to Rizpah, we should have וַתֹּאמֶר fem. instead of וַיֹּאמֶר masc.

A like instance occurs in 1 Kings i. 6: וְאֹתוֹ יָלְדָה, "And she bare him after Absalom;" 'she,' i.e., Haggith, who bare him (Adonijah) after Maacah had borne Absalom, as stated in 2 Sam. iii. 3, 4.

So also in Job iii. 3: "Let the day perish wherein I was born, and the night in which אָמַר (a man) said," &c. Also at v. 20, יִתֵּן is said of 'God,' Who alone giveth light.

Again, Ps. cv. 40: שָׁאַל וַיָּבֵא שְׂלָו, "he (i.e., the people) asked, and He (i.e., God) brought quails," &c.

[1] S. Jam. i. 13.

It would be useless to multiply examples of an idiom which occurs frequently.[1] These will suffice to show that Dr. Stanley could never have called the apparent discrepancy between 2 Sam. xxiv. 1 and 1 Chron. xxi. 1, "a striking instance," had he consulted the Hebrew. As it is, he seems to trust to others; and therefore, like everybody else who takes statements second-hand, he is liable to make mistakes. For instance, the ignorance of Hebrew grammar that applies וַיָּסֶת "he moved" to 'the Lord,' simply because this happens to be the subject of the foregoing sentence, will do strange things with history; it will make Josiah וַיֵּלֶךְ יֹאשִׁיָּהוּ—וַיְמִיתֵהוּ kill Pharaoh-Necoh at Megiddo (2 Kings xxiii. 29) instead of Pharaoh Josiah; nay, it will make life death; for "when they arose, early in the morning, וַיַּשְׁכִּימוּ בַבֹּקֶר behold, they were all dead corpses," כֻּלָּם פְּגָרִים מֵתִים, (2 Kings xix. 35; Isa. xxxvii. 36).[2] This case, however, is very plain. The writer of 2 Sam. xxiv. 1, writing when the event he described was still fresh in the memory of the people, and never dreaming any body would ever do else than allow the Lord the same authority over Satan as in Job ii. 6, much less impute to Him the moving of David to sin, left out the subject 'Satan' before וַיָּסֶת, 'and he moved;' whereas the writer of 1 Chron. xxi. 1, who wrote much later, supplied the subject 'Satan' as being the real author of the sin David committed, and of the calamity that followed.[3]

XVIII. I have said that, according to Aristotle's definition (R. vi., p. 10), Dr. Stanley's way of alluding to human sacrifices in Canaan and elsewhere, in connexion with the sacrifice of Isaac, would be called 'a sophism;' because this bringing together of these sacrifices of Isaac and of the Canaanites has only a specious appearance of truth, without any regard whatever to τὰ ἴδια τοῦ ὄντος ἢ ὄν, to the peculiar circumstances that

---

[1] See Gesen. Lehrgeb. p. 803; Ewald, Heb. Gr. p. 644, sq.; Glassii Philol. Sacra, vol. i. p. 609, sq.

[2] Something like this occurs also in Greek; e.g., ὁρῶντες—βλέποντα Πλάτων —δι᾽ ἢ λέγονται ἔχοντα—καθέλοντι—is said of the Jews, and ἔθηκαν εἰς μνημεῖον of Joseph of Arimathæa and of Nicodemus, &c.

[3] "Nam aliter Deus tentat, aliter Diabolus. Diabolus tentat ut subruat, Deus tentat ut coronet." S. Ambros. de Abrah. Lib. i. Tom. iv. p. 184.

distinguish this sacrifice from all others. Since, in fact, the sacrifice of Isaac, though it took place in Canaan, had no more to do in intention, in spirit, in motive, in the object and in the subject of it, with the passing of children through fire to Moloch or to Adrammelech, than with the Irish La Baal tejnne, or with the broiling of human hearts on the altar of Huitzilopochtli and Tezcatlipok.[1]

For, first, even Dr. Stanley admits that this practice of human sacrifices "laid deep in the heart of Canaanitish nations,"— showed itself "if not then, at least in after ages." Abraham, therefore, did not follow the example of others, but he set it to them—a very different thing indeed, since his sacrifice of Isaac is the first of the kind on record; and the sacrifice of Iphigenia (such as it was); of a man yearly to Chiun or Saturn in Phœnicia and at Rhodes; to Aphrodite in Cyprus; to Bacchus at Chios and in Tenedos; to the sun at Heliopolis; to Mars at Lacedæmon; to Saturn at Carthage; to Jupiter at Megalopolis, in Arcadia; of a boy to Wadd in Arabia, and other such, are all of later date than that of Isaac.[2]

And secondly, not only was Abraham not a Canaanite, and thus not only could he not have much in common with the thirst for human blood laid deep in the heart of the Canaanites, but, according to Dr. Stanley's own showing, he was on the best of terms with them, bound to them by a "wide, all-embracing worship," of which, he also tells us, human sacrifices formed as yet no essential rite. How then could "this almost irrepressible tendency of the burning zeal of a primitive race" be "the trial which presented itself to Abraham!" especially when, as we know, these same human sacrifices which these Canaanites may have copied from him, were among the abominations that brought "the iniquity of the Amorite to the full," that made those nations accursed, and doomed them to utter destruction?

But I will hope that Dr. Stanley is less to blame than those he takes as guides, for thus "darkening counsel by words without knowledge," as regards the most awful and the most touching type in the Old dispensation; a type so plain, so solemn, as

[1] Help's Conq. of Amer. vol. ii. p. 335, sq.
[2] Euseb. Praep. Ev. p. 155—163; Id. Theophan. Syr. Lib. ii. 54, sq.

M

to make us pause ere we even speak of it, while we look on this bright picture of faith unfeigned and of obedience on Abraham's part—of mercy, of pity, and of love towards us on the part of the FATHER, Who wrought out the sacrifice, and of the SON, Who gave Himself up for it on our behalf when He was stretched on the wood of the Cross laid on this earth, His Altar. I therefore pass by the Rabbis as either not to the purpose or absurd, and by the voice of the Church in all ages as unanimous on this point, only to say that even Mahomedan writers mention this sacrifice of Isaac as one of the three things التي ابتلي الله ابراهيم بها نقيل هي هجرته عن وطنه والختنان وذبح ابنه وقيل غير ذلك " through which GoD did prove the faith of Abraham; that is, his flight from his native land, circumcision, and the sacrifice of his son; though others say differently."[1] And Mahomet himself says of it,[2] " Verily, this ان هذا لهو البلا المبين was for him a trial no one could mistake.[3] Wherefore we have left for him among the posterities, ' Peace on him !' ' Peace on Abraham !' Thus do we reward them that do well."

XIX. Dr. Stanley then brings us to what he thinks was the scene of the sacrifice :—

" It was not the place which Jewish tradition has selected on Mount Moriah at Jerusalem ; still less that which Christian tradition shows, even to the thicket In which the ram was caught hard by the Church of the Holy Sepulchre ; still less that which Mussulman tradition indicates on Mount Arafat at Mecca. Rather we must look to that ancient sanctuary of which I have spoken, the natural altar on the summit of Mount Gerizim. On that spot, at that time the holiest in Palestine, the crisis was to take place. One, two, three days' journey from ' the land of the Philistines'—in the distance the high crest of the mountain appears," &c.—p. 49.

The Dean seems very certain of what he asserts ; but, first— where the ' land of Moriah' might be we know not. A. Ezra l.c., Abarbanel,[4] R. S. Jarchi l.c., Midrash Rabbah,[5] wherein the

[1] Abu'lf. Hist. A. S. p. 22.   [2] Sur. xxxvii. 107.

[3] Almost in the words of S. Ambrose: " Denique Deus probatus sibi tentat. Et sanctum Abraham probavit ante et sic tentavit, ne si ante tentaret quam probasset, gravaret." De Abrah. Lib. i. t. iv. p. 184.

[4] Comm. In Pent. fol. 61, verso.   [5] Fol. 61, sq.

opinion of many Rabbis is found, all concur in applying the
term ' Moriah' either to the hill mentioned in 2 Chron. iii. 1, on
which the Temple was built, or in rendering מוֹרִיָּה by ' vision,'
in allusion to God appearing there to Abraham.[1] Although
nothing is said of the sacrifice of Isaac either in the Samaritan
Chronicle, the Samaritan Hymns and Letters published by
Gesenius and by Cellarius, yet it is well known that the Samaritans apply Gen. xxii. 2 to Mount Gerizim.[2]

Secondly—the claim the Samaritans put in for Mount Gerizim to be Mount Moriah dates, as we have seen, only from
after the captivity.[3] " However this may be," continues Michaelis, " the Samaritans were not at enmity with the Jews
before the building of the Temple on Mount Gerizim, and until
then they would have common interests and common worship."[4]
But, after the Temple was built by Alexander's leave on Mount
Gerizim, on the site of the small place of worship that existed
there before that time, the Samaritans of Sichem arrogated to
their city the title of ' the Holy Place,' بيت المقدس, in op-

---

[1] But מוֹרִיָּה could never come from רָאָה. The Targ. Onkelos and Targ. J. B.
Uzziel and Hieron. render it מוֹרִיָּה, ' land of worship ;' LXX. εἰς τὴν γῆν
τὴν ὑψηλήν ; Pers. and Saadias كَانِدَا أَصْنَاف, ' into the land of the
Amorites ;' Samar. [Samaritan script], ' in terram visionis,' Vulg. ; so
that interpreters are far from being agreed either on the meaning of the term
or on the site of the mountain.

[2] Gesen. De Indole Pentat. Sam. p. 33.

[3] " Judaei," says J. D. Michaelis (Supplem. ad Lex. Heb. p. 1553) " montem
Moriam pro loco immolationis Isaaci destinato habuerunt ; ac nisi fallor et
Samaritani. Adscribo versionem Chaldaicam Chronicorum : in monte Morie, in
loco, ubi coluit et adoravit Abraham nomen Domini : Iste locus est terra cultus,
ubi coluerunt Jehovam omnes generationes, ibi quoque oblaturus erat Abrahamus
filium suum in holocaustum, liberavit vero eum verbum Domini, et oblatus est
aries loco ejus : ibi oravit Jacob, cum aufugeret ab Esavo fratre, ibi denique
adparuit angelus Domini Davidi. Haec est traditio seu sententia si vera ac
certa, aliquid sane facerent ad litem Samaritanorum et Judaeorum de loco cultus
divini Deo placente, de qua mira tradit Josephus, Ant. xiii. 3, 4, in jure Mosaico,
§. 168, exposita, deliberata, dubitata."

[4] And according to Makrizi اتفق طوائف من اليهود وصلوا به وصاروا " crowds of Jews
يحجون الي هيكله في الاعياد ويقربون قرابينهم فيه
came to it to pray there ; they made pilgrimages to the temple on Mount Gerizim, and offered their sacrifices in it." (De Sacy, Chrest. Ar. vol. i. 112 and
301, sq.)

position to Jerusalem; and afterwards they connected Mount
Gerizim with Abraham and with his sacrifice.[1]

The Samaritans called Mount Gerizim not only طور بريك
'Blessed Mountain,' as we have seen, but also جبل البركات
'the Mountain of Blessings,' جبل الفرايد 'the Mountain of
the Commandments;[2] ‏ ᛎᛈᛚᚡ·ᚪᚢᚦᛏ, 'the Hill of Eternity;'
‏ᛎᚪ·ᚪᛗᚦᚦ 'Beth-el;' and in one of their letters to this country[3]
the Samaritans call it 'The Mountain of Inheritance,'[4] where
the presence of the Divine Majesty dwells; the great and
chosen place, which God did choose; the Gate of Heaven.[5] All
this is on a par with the story already told, of Mount Gerizim
not having been even wetted by the waters of the Flood; and
other like absurdities, for which there is not the slightest foundation.

XX. Thirdly—according to Arabic writers, Isaac never was
sacrificed "on Mount Arafat at Mecca," as Dr. Stanley says.
Abu'l-feda tells us[6] that "after Hagar's death at Mecca, God
commanded Abraham to sacrifice unto Him his son; one is
doubtful whether it was Isaac or Ishmael, but God redeemed him
with a ram. Those who think it was Isaac who was offered in
sacrifice place the spot in Syria at two miles علي ميلين من
‏ميلين من (or leagues) from Ælia, which is Jerusalem. Those, however, who think it was Ishmael يقول ان
‏ذلك كان بمكة say the sacrifice took place at Mecca." And
Masudi,[7] after telling of the dismissal of Hagar, goes on to say

---

[1] As we find from Asclepiodorus, who, speaking of Marinus, a philosopher,
native of Neapolis πρὸς ὄρει—τῷ 'Αργαρίζῳ καλουμένῳ near to the mountain
called 'Argarizus,' is called by Damascius θεοσεβὴς καὶ φιλοσοφίαν, 'impious
and blasphemous,' for adding that he saw on that mountain a temple Διὸς
ὑψίστου of Jupiter Most High ᾧ καθιέρωτο 'Αβραμος ὁ τῶν πάλαι Ἑβραίων
πρόγονος, to whom Abraham, the father of the ancient Hebrews, was devoted
(as priest); and he adds; ὡς αὐτὸς ἔλεγεν ὁ Μαρῖνος, "as Marinus himself relates." (Damasc. ap. Phot. Bibl. p. 1055, ed. Roter.) This same Marinus, at
first a Samaritan, afterwards combated the Samaritan opinions, ἅτε εἰς καινοτο-
μίαν διὰ τῆς 'Αβραάμου θυσίας, ἐκφθείσας, as being innovations from the sacrifice of Abraham."

[1] This, however, is said also of Mount Sinai in the Samaritan hymns.
[2] Epistola Samar. ad Job. Ludolph. Cizæ. 1688, p. 1, 6, &c.
[4] Deut. iv. 20, sq.
[5] Jaynb. Comm. in Chron. Samar. p. 247.
[6] Hist. A. l. p. 22.   [7] Morondj es-zahab. vol. i. p. 87.

that "GOD commanded Abraham to sacrifice his son, whom GOD did redeem with a precious victim.[1] The sacrifice of Abraham has given rise to different opinions: some say it was Isaac, others that it was Ishmael. If the command was given to Abraham at Mina, then Ishmael was sacrificed, الى اسحاق لم تدخل الحجاز for Isaac never entered the Hedjâz; but if the command came in Syria, then it was Isaac, الى اسمعيل لم يدخل الشام for Ishmael never entered Syria."

XXI. Fourthly—Dr. Stanley pretends to fix the distance from "the land of the Philistines" to Mount Gerizim, by "one, two, three days' journey." But he must, first of all, fix where this land was; whether it was the land of the Philistines during their first or second settlements, and whereabouts in that land Abraham was, that he should take three days to go to Mount Gerizim. For unless we know the starting point, we shall find some difficulty in measuring the distance. We read that, after Abimelech and Phichol had made their covenant with Abraham at Beersheba, Abimelech and his captain "returned into the land of the Philistines,"[2] i.e., to Gerar, his kingdom,[3] between Kadesh and Shur, further south than Beersheba. If so, then, Beersheba could hardly be in 'Gerar,' where Abraham dwelt at first;[4] yet, for all that, still in the 'land of the Philistines.' If, therefore, Abraham started from Beersheba for Mount Gerizim, he could not reach it in three days of Eastern travel, he on his ass, and Isaac and his two young men[5] on foot.

As I did not travel for statistics, I never timed myself when once on the march, which lasted every day, except Sundays, from 3 or 4 to 9 or 10 A.M., and from 3 or 4 to 7 or 8 P.M.; I therefore borrow from Dr. Robinson's Itinerary[6] the following distances:—

		Hours.	Min.
From Bir es-seba' (Beersheba) to Hebron	. .	11	10
„ Hebron	„ Jerusalem	6	15
„ Jerusalem	„ Nâblûs . .	14	30
		33	55

[1] Cor. Sur. xxxvii. 10.   [2] Gen. xxi. 33.
[3] Gen. xx. 2. Hitzig. Philist. p. 116, sq.   [4] Gen. xx. 1.
[5] Eliezer, who was then fifty-five years old, and Ishmael; according to tradition.
[6] Res. vol. iii. pp. 66, 67, 81.

There are, then, thirty-four hours' march by the shortest route from Beersheba to Shechem, or to Mount Gerizim; that is, at the rate of a little over eleven hours a day. But, since "on the third day Abraham lifted up his eyes and saw the place afar off," went thither and returned to where he had left his servants, he, being at least a hundred and fifteen or twenty years of age (one hundred and thirty-six according to tradition), must have journeyed from Beersheba to Mount Gerizim at the rate of at least fourteen or fifteen hours a day, so as to accomplish the distance from Beersheba to where he left his young men, thence to Mount Gerizim, and back to them in three days—a thing simply beyond the bounds of probability. And if we suppose Abraham to have started from somewhere else than Beersheba in the land of the Philistines, which at that time extended, possibly, from Gerar to Ekron over the Philistine Pentapolis,[1] we can, of course, form no idea either of the distance or of the situation of the mountain God did show Abraham; for, as we have seen, Mount Tabor, or Little Hermon, might have at least as good a claim as Mount Gerizim to be classed among the earliest places of worship in the land of Canaan.[2]

XXII. Then follows another of Dr. Stanley's careless expressions :—

"The sacrifice was accepted—the literal sacrifice of the act was repelled. On the one hand the great principle was proclaimed that mercy is better than sacrifice," &c.

Where is that 'principle' proclaimed? Nowhere do we find that "mercy is better than sacrifice," leastways that this is a 'principle;' for not only was 'sacrifice' in the case of Christ necessary, and mercy could not then be shown, but 'sacrifice of ourselves' is also required of us ere we can be acceptable unto God. Did Dr. Stanley think of " Behold, to obey is better than

[1] Josh. xiii. 3.

[2] The real fact is that it is idle to speculate on the site of the mountain, on which the sensible and profoundly learned J. D. Michaelis says (Supplem. ad Lex. Heb. p. 1551): "Totam denique historiam Gen. xxii. perlegenti videbitur sacrificio Isaaci locum desertum destinatum fuisse, dumis horrentem, ubi nemo illud spectaret, aut opem ferre posset : at mons Moria in vicinia Hierosolymæ, quæ Abrahami jam tempore regem, et vero Dei veri sacerdotem, habebat, Melchisedecum."

sacrifice, and to hearken than the fat of rams "?[1] that is to say,
the offering of 'self' unto GOD, in obedience to His will, is the
real 'sacrifice' He looks to; and being the 'real' offering, it is
better than the mere outward rite and worship without a willing
or an obedient heart, wholly given up to Him. For 'mercy'
is GOD's prerogative; 'obedience' and 'sacrifice' are man's part
and duty. Therefore does GOD say, חֶסֶד חָפַצְתִּי וְלֹא זֶבַח,
"I have taken pleasure in (or 'I delight in') mercy, and not in
sacrifice:"[2] that is, He delights in exercising His prerogative of
gracious Sovereign, of tender and compassionate FATHER, whenever it can be done without warping the eternal rule of justice.
He delights in showing mercy and pity for our infirmity, and in
not being "extreme to mark what is done amiss" in us, whenever He finds an 'honest' and 'sincere' heart wholly given up to
Him; for "He knoweth whereof we are made." And in this
sense is Hos. vi. 6 quoted in S. Matt. ix. 13, and xii. 7, as proved
by the context.

It is in displaying this power of showing mercy and pity whenever justice allows, that GOD delights, rather than in victims,
since He says, "I will take no bullock out of thy house, nor he
goats out of thy folds; for every beast of the forest is mine, and
the cattle upon a thousand hills."[3] But since mercy on GOD's
part presupposes a willing and obedient heart, though, may be,
with weak efforts or slender means on our part to work out our
intentions, 'showing mercy,' though inherent in GOD's nature,
becomes practically an accident as regards our being the objects
of it; since we can hope for no mercy at His hands unless we
have first made a whole sacrifice of our 'self,' body, soul, and
spirit unto Him, which is our reasonable service. This spiritual
sacrifice being indispensable, and mercy only dependent on it,
very far from "mercy better than sacrifice" being a 'principle,'
the only 'principle' in this case, both ἀρχή and στοιχεῖον, is that
of 'sacrifice of ourselves unto GOD.' Dr. Stanley's expression
is an oversight; for had he carefully considered the matter, he
would have seen that in this case GOD showed Abraham mercy,
saying, "Because thou hast obeyed my voice;" for without this
obedience there could have been no mercy shown him. Yet

---

[1] 1 Sam. xv. 22.   [2] Hos. vi. 6.   [3] Ps. l. 9, 10.

Dr. Stanley's expression, misunderstood, might lead shallow
thinkers to the practical view of the words "mercy is better
than sacrifice" which Mahomedans take. They preface acts of
the grossest sin with الله كريم, 'God is generous and merciful!'

XXIII. On the Phœnician sacrifices Dr. Stanley has this
note :—

"According to the Phœnician tradition, 'Israel, king of the
country, having by a nymph called Anobret ["the Hebrew fountain"] an only son, whom they called Ieoud, the Phœnician word
for an only son [so applied to Isaac, Gen. xxii. 2], on occasion of
a great national calamity adorned him in royal attire, and sacrificed him on an altar which he had prepared.'—Sanchoniathon :
see Kenrick's Phœnicia, 288."

Whereon I may remark, first—that this king was Saturn, called
'Israel' by the Phœnicians. Secondly—that 'Anobret' cannot
mean 'Hebrew fountain.' If so be ἀν is (?) for עין (rather ab,
Ἀἰὼν for עַיִן), 'Hebrew fountain' would be 'Ανιβρία, עין עברית,
in Phœnician as in Hebrew.' Thirdly—as to 'Ιεοῦδ, Ewald[2]
says, very correctly, that it may be meant for 'Judah' rather than
for Isaac. Fourthly—that we have no reason to feel certain
this passage is from Sanchoniaton. It may be Porphyrius' own
composition. He was either from Tyre or from Batania (Bashan), and is said to have been well versed in Jewish matters.

In the two following pages Dr. Stanley speaks of the object
of the sacrifice of Isaac, but in a manner on which I can only
remark, that it is far below the dignity and greatness of the
subject. He does not warm up to it; what he says is timid,
cold, and lifeless, on the very subject of Life itself. And he
ends this lecture with these words, which are not quite so
clear :—

"Questions have often arisen on the meaning of the words
which bring together in the Gospel history the names of Abraham
and of the true and final Heir of Abraham's promises. But to
the student of the whole line of the Sacred History, they may at

_____

[1] Gesen. Mon. Phœnic. p. 443. Bochart (Phaleg. p. 712) proposes to read it
עֲנֹת מ, Annobret, i.e., "ex gratiâ concipiens." Gesenius, however, "quam
donavit concypiris." But then, what comes of ח? (Mon. Phœnic. p. 400.)

[2] Weltshöpf. Ganch. p. 52.

least be allowed to express the marvellous continuity and community of character, of truth, of intention, between this, its grand beginning, and that, its still grander end."

Will Dr. Stanley know what this "marvellous continuity and community of character, of truth, of intention" come from ?—from Faith in the objective Truth of God's promises, in obedience to His will.

LECTURE III.—JACOB.

I. Dr. Stanley opens this Lecture, which is generally speaking, well written and interesting, with an outline of Jacob's character that calls only for one remark :

At p. 54 we read :

" Esau—caught—by the sight of the lentile soup—' Feed me, I pray thee, with the 'red, red pottage,' &c.' (Gen. xxv. 30, in the original.)"

The original does not say : " with the red, red pottage." הַלְעִיטֵנִי נָא מִן־הָאָדֹם הָאָדֹם הַזֶּה, Gen. xxv. 30, means, " support" or " feed me, I pray thee with this red pottage," ' this here red pottage,' or ' this very one ;' for I am faint, and cannot wait for another. The article repeated twice, and the second time with the demonstr. pron. gives it no other sense whatever ; and shows that the stress was laid by Esau—not, as Dr. Stanley makes him do, on the colour—' red, red,' but—on his being hungry and on his wishing to have at once the pottage that was being made for others, who might then wait for theirs. It is a pity that Dr. Stanley, apparently no Hebrew scholar, did not consult some one able to advise him better ; or at least, that he did not avoid quoting the original, which, it is evident, he does not understand.

The Authorised Version, however, renders well this passage, given more literally in the marginal note.

This first paragraph of Lecture III. ends with an excellent remark :

" There is a nobleness in principle and in faith which cannot be
wholly destroyed, even though it be marred by the hardness of the
Jew, or the Jesuit, or the Puritan."—p. 50.

It is well Dr. Stanley should acknowledge this. May we all
bear in mind that ' principle and faith' may appear in others
than Jacob, and may show themselves as much in an honest
opposition at the University to dishonest statutes, and question-
able divinity, as to the wiles of a Syrian father-in-law.

II. We now come to Jacob's progress through life; beginning with his departure from Beersheba to go to Haran. " Was
the migration of Abraham to be reversed?" asks Dr. Stanley.
How could it be ? But as Abraham though 'on such 'friendly
terms' with the Hittites and with the Canaanites, would not
take for his son a wife from among nations accursed, so also did
Jacob leave the daughters of Heth to his brother Esau, who
sold his birthright—and such a right, too—for a pottage of
lentiles; whatever happened, and at any cost of toil or of journey, Canaanitish blood could not intermingle with the children
of the Promise; for the Canaanites were doomed to be thrust
out of the land they had defiled, in order to make room for the
lawful heirs to it. It was God's; and He gave it to His people.

The first halt of Jacob mentioned was at Bethel.

" On the hard ground he lay down for rest, and in the visions
of the night the rough stones formed themselves into a vast staircase, reaching into the depth of the wide and open sky, which,
without any interruption of tent or tree, was stretched over the
sleeper's head."—p. 59.

Could Dr. Stanley be in earnest when he wrote this? It
certainly never occurred to me, when I was at Bethel, neither
does it now, while I am looking at the sketch I took near 'Ain
Yebrûd, that the stones and rocks lying about could ever be
made into " a vast staircase reaching into the depth of the wide
and open sky." It must be a dream indeed, not of Jacob, but
of Dean Stanley. There is not, anywhere near there what may
be called ' a rock' of any height. The ground is, indeed, rocky;
as much like some parts of Cornwall as rocks of transition or of
secondary formation can be like primitive ground of that kind ;
but there is not any where near, a single rock even like that of

Selah, which stands on the right, going from Michmash to
Anathoth. The ascent or descent of such a staircase as Dr.
Stanley makes out would have been very difficult indeed; even
for angels.

III. Also the stone set up by Jacob, was not, as Dr. Stanley
insinuates, at p. 60, a building to be compared with "the walls
of Tyrins, or with a cromlech of Wales or of Cornwall." It
was a single stone, and that too, not a very large one, since he
had used it for a pillow; it must have been a stone somewhat like
the stone "Samuel set up between Mizpeh and Shen, which he
called Eben-ezer," 1 Sam. vii. 12; it was, and could have been
no 'building;'[1] assuredly not like the walls of Tyrins I saw
and sketched, in which the stones are roughly cut to fit, very
much as in the walls of Volterræ; leastways like a cromlech of
Wales or of Brittany, most of which were made up of stones too
large for one man to rear. Of all existing monuments I saw
that combine Nature with the most primitive workmanship, are
the 'Hdjàr-Cham,' or 'Qima,' already mentioned at Malta.
They are real cromlechs[2] that deserve all the attentive study of
men fond of antiquity.

IV. The whole of this paragraph pp. 60, 61, is worth reading; albeit Dr. Stanley, while speaking of Bethel, gives his
readers no details respecting the Phœnician βαιτύλια, λίθους
ἐμψύχους, 'animated stones,' wrought out by the god Οὐρανός,
Uranos.[3] These stones βαιτούλια or βαιτύλια, according to Damascius, were seen in numbers by Asclepiades on Mount Liba-
nus, as well as by Isidorus.[4] The account given by Damascius,

[1] Whatever might have been 'the altar' Jacob built there afterwards, Gen.
xxxv. 3.

[2] 'Crom,' bending in worship, 'lench,' stone; i.q. 'hadjar,' stone, 'hdjàr,'
stones, 'qima,' (of) worship.

[3] Sanchon. p. 30, ed. Orell.

[4] He probably alludes to the Phœnician legend in adding ἱερὰ γεννᾶ καὶ
ἑαυτὴν διίζη βίου θεοφιλῆ καὶ εὐδαίμονα, "that this sacred race of animated stones
led by itself a happy and religious life," (Damasc. vit. Isid. Ap. Phot. Bibl. p.
1049.) They are, however, of an erratic nature; for Damascius says he once
saw, τὸν βαιτύλιον διὰ τοῦ ἀέρος κινούμενον, the Baetulion that moved through
the air, carried by a physician, whose name was Eusebius, and who, when one
night he felt a sudden impulse to go out of Emesa towards the mountain—he
saw a globe of fire fall from heaven—he ran to it, to put out the fire, καὶ καταλαβεῖν αὐτὴν οἶσαν τὸν βαιτύλιον, and he took it, and lo, it was a Baetulion,

however, by no means settles the case of the Bætulia; for others
make them to have been square stones representing the world,
which of old was thought to be of that shape.[1]

From Bethel Jacob went on towards Haran, the city of Nahor.
The simple narrative of Scripture brings fresh to my memory
many scenes I witnessed when in Mesopotamia, and this side
'the River.' As, e.g., the large stones which in certain parts of
Syria, as at Dara near Aleppo, cover the mouth of wells, and
which are as spherical as rough hewing can make them, so as
to be 'rolled away,' (Gen. xxix. 2, 3,) though not by one man;
for they are too heavy; this being intended as a security against
water being stolen and strange flocks watered; for whereas it
might often so happen if one individual alone could remove the
stone, it is less likely to be done when it requires several men
to help one another. I am also reminded of "Rachel coming
with her father's sheep," (Ib. v. 6,) by a sketch made on the
spot of the sheikh's daughter feeding her father's sheep, with
the well at which Eliezer tarried and the ruins of the city of
Nahor in the distance,—touches of Truth that tell more than
volumes of description. And, besides the figure of El-khalil, I
may fix on some other sons of that desert as fit representatives
of Bethuel, of Laban, of Laban's shepherds with their flocks,
around the well's mouth or abroad on the plain. One sees ever
and anon, in that land, Laban with Jacob, and Jacob with Leah
and with Rachel, not only at Haran, but starting with his
camels and numerous herds and flocks lowing and bleating, indifferent to the bustle of the men who strike the tents, put
them up and lade the camels with them. Jacob's interview with
Esau is being acted every day in that country; and the excite-

and he asked it of what god it was, and it replied, of the god Gennæus of Heliopolis. He then describes it as a globe, whitish, about a span in diameter, more
or less, and sometimes reddish, &c. Καὶ γράμματα ἀνθρώπων ἡμῖν ἐν τῷ λίθῳ
γεγραμμένα, on which he showed us letters written. When he inquired of it
the stone gave an oracle—which he considers divine, but Isidorus thinks it
rather of the demon order. Εἶναι γὰρ τῶν δαίμονα, τὸν κινοῦντα αὐτόν. For it
must be some demon that sets it going, and Eusebius says that some Bætulia
belong to certain gods as to Saturn, to Jupiter, to the Sun, and other such stones
belong to other gods." (Damasc. ibid. p. 1062, 1063.)

[1] See Nork, Bibl. Mythol. p. 345—348, for his account of Jacob's ladder;
and in general, for a marvellous explanation of what he calls 'Biblical Mytho-
logy.'

ment produced in the camp, by the news that a hostile band is at hand, is amusing when not carried too far.

It so happened to a friend of mine and to myself when among the hills of Gilead, on our return from Rabbath Ammon; a horseman arrived at full speed during the night of one of the most fearful storms I ever experienced bringing the tidings that a tribe with which my hosts were not on friendly terms was in the neighbourhood. At dawn a council of war was held—a most picturesque scene and among scenery then seldom visited —a hundred horsemen were sent in one direction, and the sheikh of the tribe under whose protection we had placed ourselves, took us by another way than he at first intended, to the steep banks of the Jabbok, which we forded at what I must call 'Mahanajim,' i.e. two camps of a few black Arab tents that were there on either side the torrent. A march of an hour or two then brought us to the ruins of Djerash (Gerasa) which are said to be more extensive and better worth visiting though less interesting than those of Palmyra; but these relics of Roman art and splendour were as nothing, compared with the beauty of the forests of Bashan and of the fine oaks, aged sons of the earth in that land—among which we journeyed for a whole day on our way to Gadara, the Jordan, Bethshan, and to Mount Gilboah.

I thought of Jacob, of his troops, and of his meeting with Esau, every moment of the days we spent between the heights of Gilead, the downs of Ammon, and the ford of the Jabbok. The women looked like Leah, Rachel, and Deborah; the men too, must have been the picture of Esau—wild-looking, dark and shaggy, djerid in hand, flashing light from their piercing eyes that whirled hither and thither from under their kafieh, with long tresses of jet black hair they often wear, like women, on each side the face—Samson's locks, probably, (Judg. xvi. 14,) giving them a fierce and very remarkable appearance; though rough, yet harmless, civil and trustworthy if you place yourself at their mercy, and converse with them yourself; but very much the reverse if you do not, and if you hold intercourse with them through an interpreter; then hope for nothing, and trust them in nothing. I travelled in the length and breadth of the land with no other weapon than my pocket-knife; I never took ex-

corts but from among themselves, I went where I liked, and,
as independent as a patriarch, I pitched my tent and tarried at
pleasure where I listed; and from 'Dan to Beersheba' I never
lost a thing, but on the contrary, I met every where with the
greatest civility; most of all at Samaria itself, where, I was told
before I went, I should be murdered. I had interviews with
many an Esau; but being myself a 'plain man,' dwelling in a
tent, and my servants like Jacob at Bethel, in the open air, we
always parted good friends—possibly, I own, because they judged
from my mode of travelling—the only one enjoyable—that I
was not a prize worth having.

Jacob's journey to Haran and his return thence through
the desert and the hills of Gilead to Salem or Salim, not far
from the banks of the Jordan, and thence again to Shechem,
Bethel, Hebron, and yet further south, become a reality for
such as have visited that 'Holy Land,' as they ought to visit
it, with their heart interested in it, their mind alive and their
eyes open—and themselves able to hold intercourse with their
hosts in their own tongue. For travelling among men with
whom you can hold no communication, is like visiting a gallery
of statues. This is often an advantage, I admit, when travelling
in Europe; but it is a very great loss in the Land of all Lands,
the one best worth visiting; where at almost every step you are
reminded of some incident in the Book you ought to love best;
if so be you travel with intelligence and with a devout mind.

V. I feel satisfied, after having seen the patriarchal sepulchres
of Oorfa and others in the neighbourhood of Tyre, and beyond
Jordan at Heshbán, that I have a far more correct idea of what
the cave of Machpelah must either have been or at present be,
than travellers who, having been at Hebron, did not after all
see it. Judging then from the conformation of those sepulchral
caves, several groundplans of which I have by me, Dr. Stanley
may, I think, be right in understanding Gen. l. 5, "the grave
which I have digged for me in the land of Canaan," to mean
"'the cell' that Jacob had digged for himself in the primitive
sepulchre of his fathers," p. 74. It is, however, very possible,
and even probable, that these words of Joseph to Pharaoh, especially when compared with ch. xlvii. 29, may simply be an
Egyptian idiom. An Egyptian of Joseph's rank at the court of

Pharaoh, would naturally speak of 'hewing' or 'digging a cave for himself,' as the wont of great and wealthy men was who during their lifetime prepared for themselves the sumptuous abodes, where their bodies were to rest in state until the final transmigration of their souls.[1]

The procession which went with Joseph to Hebron is also thoroughly Egyptian. It was doubtless a testimony of respect on the part of the Egyptians, if not to Jacob himself, at least to him as father of so great a man as Joseph. But this host was also intended as a safeguard against the Hittites, and against also, perhaps, the Amalekites, with which Egypt must have been at war then, as it was at most other times; if not, the caravan would have taken the shortest and best route, "by the way of the land of the Philistines,"[2] and not, as it did, partly by the way Moses led the children of Israel eastward of the Dead Sea. This route taken by Joseph, is by no means free from difficulties; or rather, uncertainties, which shall never be cleared unless some Egyptian authentic Papyrus, not yet discovered, and bearing on the subject, be brought to light.

LECTURE IV.—ISRAEL IN EGYPT.

I. "THE appearance of Joseph in Egypt," says the Dean of Westminster,

"is the first distinct point of contact between sacred and secular history, and it is, accordingly, not surprising that in later times this part of his story should have become the basis of innumerable fancies and traditions outside the limits of Biblical narrative. The feud of the modern Samaritans and Jews is carried up by them to the feud between Joseph and his brethren."—p. 76.

Dr. Stanley quotes Dr. Wolff as his authority in this case. It is doubtless correct, since the Samaritans claimed Jacob for their father, (S. John iv. 12,) reckoned themselves of the tribe of Ephraim, and have the sepulchre of Joseph and his portion

----

[1] Diod. Sic. Lib. i. 91; Herod. Lib. ii. 148, sq.   [2] Ex. xiii. 17.

of land among them; I can, however, find no allusion to this statement in the authorities I have at hand.

II. Dr. Stanley further says:

"The history of Joseph and Asenath is to this day one of the canonical books of the Church of Armenia."

This is again one of those statements that show Dr. Stanley's carelessness about his authorities. Suspecting he might have mentioned the subject in his Lectures on the Eastern Church, I borrowed the book, and, accordingly, I found at p. 8:

"Their (the Armenians') canonical Scriptures include two books in the Old and two in the New Testament acknowledged by no other Church; the history of Joseph and Asenath, the Testament of the Twelve Patriarchs, the Epistle of the Corinthians to S. Paul, and the third Epistle of S. Paul to the Corinthians,"

where "Curzon's Armenia, 225," is given as Dr. Stanley's authority. It is, however, far from satisfactory. A writer who, like Mr. Curzon, publishes a list of birds so full of mistakes as he does at p. 150 of his work on Armenia,[1] shows, at least, that he cannot be very particular in ascertaining the truth of what he states; since, in a list of 176 birds of Armenia, there are no less than 47 mistakes.[2]

III. The canonicity of a Book that rests upon a statement twice endorsed by a Regius Professor of Ecclesiastical History at Oxford, is of sufficient importance to justify my giving in full his authority for so doing.

"Among the Armenians," says Mr. Curzon, p. 225, "the Holy Scriptures contain more books than those of the Western Churches.

---

[1] Murray, 1854.

[2] To say nothing of such errors as "Insepores" for "Incessores;" "Palmepedes" for "Palmipedes;" "Dentirostres" for "Dentirostres;" "aquila fulvus" for "fulva," &c., that betray great ignorance of even the rudiments of Latin. But, such names as "F. Ossion" for "F. Œsalon;" "great strike, red-backed strike, small strike," for "great shrike," &c.; "curruca cineria" for "C. cinerea;" "Phœn. tilkys" for "Phœn. tithys;" "Phœn. succica" for "Phœn. suecica;" "Troglod. euaopærur" for "Troglod. europæus;" "Lin. montalm" for "Lin. montium;" "Corr. frugeleus" for "Corr. frugilegus;" "Œdicnemus" for "Œdicnemus;" "Lin. melanolenas" for "Lin. melanoleuca;" "A. albifrous" for "A. albifrons," &c., not only shake one's confidence in other things found in the book, but also show how books are got up for the season and for the public.

In the Old Testament, after the Book of Genesis, occurs the Testament of the Twelve Patriarchs, the sons of Jacob; then the History of Joseph and his wife Asenath," &c.—"The Testament of the Twelve Patriarchs, is well known; but I am not aware that the Book of Asenath has been printed in any European language.[1] This curious book was translated into Italian, from an ancient Armenian manuscript of the Bible in my possession, by an Armenian friend, and translated from the Italian into English by myself: this I presume to be the only copy of the Book of Asenath in the English language. It is a work of considerable length and is interesting, not only from the place it holds in the estimation of a numerous body of Christians, but also from the picture it presents of the manners and customs of Egypt, at some remote period when it was written," &c.

This is, indeed, a very slender foundation upon which to rest the canonicity of any Book. We must, however, do Mr. Curzon the justice to see that he does not say the Book is held for 'canonical;' but simply that the Holy Scriptures of the Armenian Church "contain more books" than those of the Western Church. The canonicity of the book rests on Dr. Stanley's construction of Mr. Curzon's statement. Dr. Stanley must, therefore, also on the same principle, hold the Epistle of Barnabas, Hermas, &c., for canonical, since they are sometimes found added to the canon of Scripture; as e.g. in the Sinaitic MS. At this rate the canon of Scripture may evidently be enlarged almost to any extent.

But the history of 'Joseph and Asenath,' forms no part of the Canon of the Armenian Scriptures. It is not even mentioned either in the list of Canonical Books prefixed to the standard and critical edition of the Armenian Bible printed by the Mechitarists at Venice in 1805, for which the very best MSS.—thirty in number for the New Testament—were used, or in the preface to it, in which the books are mentioned in detail, and reasons given for rejecting 'the Book of Sirach,' although it forms a part of the Greek Scriptures. Neither is 'Joseph and Asenath' alluded to in the edition of the Armenian Bible published in

---

[1] Mr. Curzon may be forgiven for not knowing that the Book of Joseph and Asenath is given in Greek and in Latin in Fabricii Cod. Pseudep. Vet. Test. Vol. ii. p. 85—102; and Vol. i. p. 774—784. But we might expect Dr. Stanley to have alluded to the fact.

N

1817 at S. Petersburg under the patronage of S. Ephrem of Estchmiadsin, Catholicos of all Armenia; as the order of the Books differs in each list, I give them both.

VENICE, 1805.　　　　S. PETERSBURG, 1817.

The Books of the Old Testament.

Genesis.	Genesis.
Exodus.	Exodus.
Leviticus.	Leviticus.
Numbers.	Numbers.
Deuteronomy.	Deuteronomy.
Joshua.	Joshua.
Judges.	Judges.
Ruth.	Ruth.
Book of Kings I.	Book of Kings I.
„ „ II.	„ „ II.
„ „ III.	„ „ III.
„ „ IV.	„ „ IV.
„ Chronicles I.	„ Chronicles I.
„ „ II.	„ „ II.
Ezra I.	Ezra I.
„ II.	„ II.
Nehemiah.	„ III. (Nehem.)
Esther.	Tobith.
Judith.	Judith.
Tobith.	Esther.
Book of Maccabees I.	Book of Maccabees I.
„ „ II.	„ „ II.
„ „ III.	„ „ III.
Psalms.	Job.
Proverbs.	Psalms.
Ecclesiastes.	Proverbs.
Song of Songs.	Ecclesiastes.
Wisdom of Solomon.	Song of Songs.
Job.	Wisdom.
Isaiah.	Ecclesiasticus, or Sirach.
Hosea.	Isaiah.
Amos.	Jeremiah.
Micah.	His Lamentations.
Joel.	Baruch.
Obadiah.	Ezekiel.
Jonah.	Daniel.

Nahum.	Hosea.
Habakkuk.	Joel.
Zephaniah.	Amos.
Haggai.	Obadiah.
Zechariah.	Jonah.
Malachi.	Micah.
Jeremiah.	Nahum.
Baruch.	Habakkuk.
Lamentations of Jeremiah.	Zephaniah.
Daniel.	Haggai.
Ezekiel.	Zechariah.
	Malachi.
	Prayer of Manasseh.
	Ezra IV.

The Books of the New Testament.

S. Matthew.	S. Matthew.
S. Mark.	S. Mark.
S. Luke.	S. Luke.
S. John.	S. John.
The Acts.	The Acts.
Ep. of S. James.	Ep. to the Romans.
„ S. Peter I.	„ Corinthians I.
„ „ II.	„ „ II.
„ S. John I.	„ Galatians.
„ „ II.	„ Ephesians.
„ „ III.	„ Philippians.
„ S. Jude.	„ Colossians.
Ep. to the Romans.	„ Thessalonians I.
„ Corinthians I.	„ „ II.
„ „ II.	„ Timothy I.
„ Galatians.	„ „ II.
„ Ephesians.	„ Titus.
„ Philippians.	„ Philemon.
„ Colossians.	„ Hebrews.
„ Thessalonians I.	Ep. of S. James.
„ „ II.	„ S. Peter I.
„ Hebrews.	„ „ II.
„ Timothy I.	„ S. John I.
„ „ II.	„ „ II.
„ Titus.	„ „ III.
„ Philemon.	„ S. Jude.
Revelation of S. John.	Revelation of S. John.

VENICE, 1805.

Additional Books.

Sirach.
Words of Sirach.
Ezra III.
Prayer of Manasseh.
Ep. of the Corinthians to S. Paul.
Rest (death) of S. John.
Supplication of Euthal.

The Books called 'additional' in the Venice edition, are not considered Canonical; and at the end of the list in the S. Petersburg copy there is a note stating that the whole of the Old Testament consists of forty-eight books, of which three, viz. Ezra i. and iv., and Maccab. iii., are outside the Canon.[1]

Seeing how much the two standard editions of the Armenian Scriptures vary in the list of their Canonical Books, and that neither one nor the other even mentions the history of 'Joseph and Asenath,' whether as Canonical or as Apocryphal, the fact of its being placed after Genesis in Mr. Curzon's MS. copy can have no weight whatever, unless we know of what age is that MS., and by whom revised and sanctioned. I should, therefore, on this ground alone, consider the evidence conclusive against the canonicity of 'Joseph and Asenath.' Yet, in order to get at the truth—worth obtaining at any price—I wrote to the Archbishop Hormus, General Superintendent of the Mechitarists of S. Lazarus at Venice, for further information respecting the canonicity of 'Joseph and Asenath.' He replied thus through his secretary in a letter dated Venice, April 6th: "L'Histoire de Joseph et d'Asenath n'a jamais été rangée par l'Eglise Arménienne dans les livres canoniques; au contraire, elle est connue comme une légende, dont on ne connaît pas même le temps de la traduction." I wrote at the same time to a friend of mine at Constantinople, an excellent Armenian scholar, asking him to get me the best information he could on

---

[1] The order of the Books in the Georgian Bible, Moscow, 1743, fol., is as follows: The five Books of Moses, Joshua, Judges, Ruth, Kings I. II. III. IV., Chronicles I. II., Ezra I., Nehemiah, Ezra II. III., Tobith, Judith, Esther, Job, Psalms, Proverbs, Ecclesiastes, Song of Songs, Wisdom of Solomon, Sirach, Isaiah, Jeremiah, Lamentations, Baruch, Ezekiel, Daniel, Twelve Minor Prophets, and Maccabees I. II. III. The order of the Books in the Slavonic Bible, from which the Georgian list seems taken, is the same; except that in it Ezra III. is placed after the Maccabees.

the subject. He writes in a letter dated Constantinople, April 16th : " I have made the inquiry which you requested in regard to the Apocryphal books (Test. of the Twelve Patriarchs and Joseph and Asenath) and in order to secure an answer from the highest authority, I called on the Armenian Patriarch and directly asked him whether they were regarded by the Armenian Church as canonical books. He replied that they were not ; said he had seen them in MS., but that they had never been printed." This is, I trust, conclusive as to the claims of these two Books, to a place in the Canon of Scripture of the Armenian Church.

But Dr. Stanley falls yet into another error, when he says, that these "two Books of the Old Testament are acknowledged by no other Church."[1] The Syrian Church received ' Joseph and Asenath' as much, or as little, as the Armenian Church ; for among the Books of Ebed-Jesu, either of the Old Testament, or about it, we find,[2] ܩܨܬ ܐܨ ܐܟ ܕܐ ܐܣܚܢ ܕܐܝܢ ܐܣܚܐ ܩܨܬ " The Book of Asiath wife of Joseph the just, son of Jacob."[3]

Lastly, the original of this legendary tale of Joseph and of Asenath, is probably the Greek of it given by Fabricius in Vol. II. of his Codex Pseudepigraphus V. Test., to which Dr. Stanley might have referred his hearers, both for this book and for the Testament of the Twelve Patriarchs.[4] There they would find the particulars of the day of Joseph's marriage, and of Asenath's disposition and appearance, &c. She was in no respect like Egyptian women ; but altogether like Hebrew ones: μεγάλη οὖσα ὡς Σάρα, καὶ ὡραία ὡς 'Ρεμβίκα, καὶ καλὴ ὡς 'Ραχιήλ, " tall as Sarah, fair as Rebekah, and as handsome as Rachel."[5]

IV. Not more certain than this canonicity of ' Joseph and Asenath,' is Dr. Stanley's opinion, that—

"To the description of the loves of Joseph and Zuleika in the Koran, Mahomet appealed as one of the chief proofs of his inspiration."

[1] Lect. on the Eastern Church, p. 6. I have looked in vain in Dr. Stanley's work for an account of the Georgian Church. Can he have overlooked it ? I hope shortly to publish a translation from the Russian of the history of that Church. That translation is now nearly finished.

[2] Assem. B. Or. Vol. iii. p. 7.

[3] On which Assemani says : " Hujus libri quem Sobensis Josepho tribuit, nemo veterum meminit ; nec quale fuerit opus, divinare possumus, quum nulla id Bibliotheca, quod sciam, repræsentet. Suspicor, historiam cum originis gentorumque Asenathæ uxoris Josephi filii Jacob Patriarchæ, ex fabulosis Judæorum narrationculis commentatam, Flavioque Josepho, aut certe Gorionidi tributam."

[4] As well as for the history of Melchisedek.   [5] Vol. ii. p. 86.

I wish Dr. Stanley had stated his authority for this; inasmuch as I can find no traces of it. Sûra XII. of the Coran is called سورة يوسف "The Sûra of Joseph," because in it is related what Mahomet calls احسن القصص "the best of stories," the history of Joseph told after Mahomet's own fashion, which he received in the revelation of the Coran. In the whole of that Sura, the name of Zuleikha زليخا is not once mentioned; neither can I find it any where else in the Coran. It is, I believe, a name of Persian origin, become celebrated through the poems of Nazâmi and of Jâmi. Zuleikha is, indeed, said by the Persian author of the Borhan-i-qâte', s.v. to have been زن عزيز مصر "the wife of 'Aziz of Egypt;" but the Arabic historian Abulfeda[1] who tells us that this 'Aziz who bought Joseph was the intendent of the public granaries, calls his wife هزينه وراودته عن نفسه 'Râ'êl,'[2] and says that Râ'êl showed an unlawful passion for Joseph, whose innocence was proved in the end; and he was put into the office which 'Aziz held. Mahomet, however, does not draw from this story a greater proof of his inspiration than from that of Abraham, of Noah, or of our LORD Himself; he simply says that in the Book revealed to him the story he tells is found. As we believe our history of Joseph because it is found in the Bible, and do not believe the Bible because it tells us of Joseph, so Mahomet laid higher claims than that to his inspiration. He never forgets to tell us that he received it from the angel Gabriel and from GOD Himself,[3] in a tissue of falsehoods which are loathsome to read, although written in a magnificent tongue.

V. Speaking of Egypt, p. 77, Dr. Stanley has this note :—

"The Biblical names of Egypt are *Mizraim* (possibly from the *two* banks, or the *upper* and *lower* districts) and *Ham* (dark). Traces of both remain—the one in the Arabic name of Cairo *Misr*: the other in the word 'alchemy,' 'chemistry,' as derived from the medical fame of ancient Egypt."

There are in the Bible two more names for Egypt, מָצוֹר and, possibly, רַהַב Ps. lxxxvii. 4, lxxxix. 11, Is. li. 9.[4] מָצוֹר

---

[1] Hist. A. I. p. 28.

[2] Not 'Rachel,' راحيل.

[3] Sur. xxxv. and liii., &c.

[4] According to Bochart, Phaleg. col. 259, ed. Leyd., who trusting to a Greek

the name of Egypt, occurs in 2 Kings xix. 24, Is. xxxvii. 25, xix. 6, &c.[1] The etymology is uncertain and the meaning is therefore doubtful. It may allude to the division of Upper and of Lower Egypt, constantly mentioned even in some of the oldest monuments of Egypt. But Upper Egypt in Hebrew is פַּתְרוֹס Pathros, ⲡⲁⲑⲟⲩⲣⲏⲥ, 'the land of the south wind;' and we can hardly suppose the dual of the Hebrew term מִצְרַיִם to refer to the two banks of the Nile, inasmuch as in Lower Egypt which was the real מִצְרַיִם, there would have been ten or fourteen such banks, two to every one of the five or of the seven branches of the Nile, every one of which is a יְאֹר.[2]

But 'Ham,' חָם, does not mean 'dark,' as Dr. Stanley says. It only means 'hot.' The native name for Egypt was ⲕⲁⲙⲉ, ⲭⲁⲙⲉ, with the symbol of a crocodile's tail, the meaning of which is 'dark,' in allusion to the colour, μέλας, of the soil of Egypt; hence called by Plutarch Χημία, of the colour of the pupil of Egyptian eyes.[3] It is therefore very possible that the two terms חָם and ⲕⲁⲙⲉ or ⲭⲁⲙⲉ might have been mixed up together, from the similarity of sound.[4]

etymology for the name 'Ἄφριβις in Lower Egypt, will connect ' Rahab' with it, and will find in ' Athribis' the Coptic ⲣⲏⲟ ⲡⲓⲁⲓ, and in ⲡⲓⲁⲓ, חָם, which he renders ' pear,'—the shape of Lower Egypt; he also sees in the Arabic ريف الريف—a name of Egypt. All this erudite structure, however, falls to the ground from the simple fact, that there is no word in Coptic like ⲡⲓⲁⲓ for ' pear.' And the etymology ⲡⲏ-ⲟⲩⲁⲃ for ' sacred to the sun' offered by Forster (in Jablonski Opp. vol. i. p. 228) is against the rules of the Coptic language; for it means ' sacred sun,' and not ' sacred to the sun.' But ' Athribis' comes from the goddess ' Athor,' whose name is coupled with the standard of the Athribite nome. (Brugsch. Geog. Denkm. i. p. 250.) So that חָם for Egypt must be looked for elsewhere.

[1] It is by some derived from צוּר and from צַר, ' to fortify,' and ' to restrain or confine;' and by others from צרר, so as to make מֵצַר, מֵצָר, מְצָרֵם; for the dual of מָצוֹר from צַר, or from צָר must be מְצָרֵם and not מְצָרַיִם.

[2] This is not the place for more particulars than to refer the student chiefly to Rödiger's art. יְאֹר in Gesen. Thes. L. S.; to Bochart, l.c., to Gesenius in v. מִצְרַיִם, to J. D. Michaelis' De חָם Ægypto Grammatica; Spicil. Geog. Pt. 1. p. 157, and to Reland's Palæst. p. 62, sq.

[3] De Is. et Osir. per. 33, p. 58, ed. Parth.

[4] Hence, perhaps, χημεία, ἱερὰ τέχνη ἡ τοῦ ἀργύρου καὶ χρυσοῦ κατασκευή Suidas s.v.—Ἀρχημία; nam ἀπὸ τῶν χυμῶν ἢ χυμάτων; potius à χέω, i.q. χεύματα; vel à χέω vel Χήμι prophetæ artis apud Ægyptios? (Vide sis celeb.

VI. In describing the officers of Pharaoh's court at p. 78, Dr. Stanley mentions the 'chief of the gaol,' whereon he says in a note :—

"'Chief of the round tower' or 'castle;' hence 'chief of the gaol.'"

It is not surprising that Dr. Stanley should here, again, fall into error on the proper rendering of a Hebrew term; but 'round tower' for בֵּית הַסֹּהַר in Gen. xl. is bad grammar; even if סֹהַר were an adjective, and not, as it is, a noun for 'tower,' 'castle,' 'round building,'—'round house' would not be בֵּית הַסֹּהַר, but בֵּית סֹהַר, and 'the round house' would be הַבֵּית הַסֹּהַר. For the description of Hebrew 'adjectives' through a noun in construction with another, thus, בֵּית הַקֹּדֶשׁ, 'house of holiness,' i.e., 'holy house,' is, to say the least, a clumsy contrivance to bend the genius of Shemitic construction to Western ideas; for 'house of holiness' and 'holy house' differ. Here, then, בֵּית הַסֹּהַר can only mean the 'house' or 'place of the tower' or of the 'castle;' if so be סֹהַר is a Hebrew term. For A. Ezra says, l.c., לא נדע אם הוא לשון הקדש או לשן מצרים, "it is not known whether this be a Hebrew or an Egyptian word."[1] But, whatever be the case as regards

Salmasius in Quaest. Plin. in Solinum, p. 772, sq., et Bochartum, Phaleg. col. 206, sq.) If it comes from χυμος χέειν, it must be written 'chymistry,' and it has nothing to do with colour, but only with the pouring out of juices; if, however, it come from the Egyptian word, it must be written 'chemistry,' and means 'the black art.' But why? These are interesting questions which it would be foreign to my purpose further to discuss at present.

[1] The Egyptian etymology, however, offered by Jablonski (vol. i. p. 321) such as ϭⲱⲛϩⲁⲡⲉϩ, which is contrary to all rules and neither Coptic nor Egyptian, is rightly condemned by J. D. Michaelis who says: "Verum haec sors, hic morbus philologorum est quo minus linguae notam sit, eo plus et audacius etymologiae indulgeant;" for the Coptic has indeed suffered at the hands both of men who knew it not, and of others who, even now-a-days, make it answer every purpose of the most ungrammatical etymologies. Without affirming that סהר be an Egyptian term, it is impossible not to compare the words that follow הַסֹּהַר viz. קְדֹשׁ אֲשֶׁר אֲסִירֵי הַמֶּלֶךְ אֲסוּרִים "the place where the king's captives were bound," added, it seems, by way of explanation —with ⲥ̄ⲭ̄ⲡ and ⲥⲉⲡ, frequent expressions in Egyptian. Speaking of

the etymology of סֹהַר, we see that בַּיִת is construed with it, exactly as it is with הַכֶּרֶם, הַיַּעַר, the vineyard, the forest, &c., in בֵּית־הַיַּעַר, 'the house of the forest or wood,' not the 'wood-house'; the 'house of the vineyard,' not the 'vine-house,' &c. בֵּית הַסֹּהַר, therefore, must be rendered 'the house of the tower,' or the 'castle,' and not "the round house."

VII. Dr. Stanley, I am happy to say, does not, like V. Bohlen, attempt to deny the authenticity of the chief butler's dream, as being opposed to a disputed passage of Herodotus respecting the existence of the vine in Egypt; but he mentions "the vintage" as it is seen represented on the walls of several tombs in Upper and in Lower Egypt.

VIII. In speaking of the "peculiar Hebrew name" for the Nile, however, he says:—

"'Ior' and 'Sichor' (*Sinai and Palestine*, Appendix, § 38.) In Egyptian it was 'hapi-mu,' the genius (*Apis*) of the waters (mu.) The word 'Nile' is derived from an Egyptian word signifying 'blue.' Wilkinson, v. 57; Sharpe, 145."

Before I examine Dr. Stanley's statement, let me vindicate Sir G. Wilkinson from an oversight he is too learned to commit. There is no 'Egyptian' word, as Dr. Stanley says, but there is a Sanscrit one, 'nilas,' that means 'blue.' Accordingly, Sir G. Wilkinson[1] says:—

the enemies of the Sun or of Osiris, we read in the Ritual of the Dead, ch. xix. l. 13, ⲁⲟⲧ ⲭⲩⲧ-ⲟⲧⲩ ⲛⲃ ⲭⲣ ⲥⲭⲣ, 'and then all his enemies (were) smitten down,' with the determinative of a man thrown down like a prisoner of war; so that, whether we take ⲥⲭⲣ to be one term, (as Mr. Chabas does, MS. Harris, Glossary s. v. and p. 21, 34, &c.) or to be ⲭⲣ with the causative ⲥ prefixed—reading ⲭⲣ ⲥⲭⲣ in the idiomatic way of קִרְקַר־קֶסֶף may be akin to שׁב and שׁב to ⲥⲭⲣ, a captive, a prisoner, or an enemy defeated and taken prisoner. See for ⲥⲉⲣ, 'abigere,' with the determinative of a man condemned to death, &c., De Rougé's Et. d'une Stèle, pp. 17, 18, 106, 107, &c. But I mention this only as a coincidence which may deserve attention. The same expression, and others akin to it, occur in Ritual ch. xv. l. 35, xlx. l. 6, xxx. l. 4, &c., and MS. Harris, p. l., l. 3, 11, ii. l. 9, &c.

[1] Anc. Egypt, 2nd Series, Vol. ii. p. 57.

"It is remarkable that the name Nilus accords so aptly with
the colour given him by the Egyptian artists. Nil, or neel, is the
word which still signifies *blue* in many Eastern languages. The
*Nil*ghaut, or '*blue* mountains;' the *Nil*ab, or '*blue* river,' applied
to the Indus; *neeleh*, the name of indigo in Egypt and in other
countries—suffice to show the general use of this word; and its
application to the river of Egypt was consistent with the custom
of calling those large rivers *blue*, which from the depth of the
water frequently appear of that colour."

The name 'Nile' is, and must be, foreign, for it is never
called thus either in Coptic or in Egyptian; a fact that shows
how vain are Jablonski's, and, after him, Champollion's[1] efforts
to derive it from the Coptic ΠΕΙ — ΑΛΗΙ "certo et determinato
tempore adscendens;" seeing a name is not likely to be derived
from a language in which it never occurs.

IX. There are three foreign etymologies for Νεῖλος: the Greek,
proposed by Herodotus and Diodorus Sic., derived from an
Egyptian king of that name; which is very improbable, seeing
Νεῖλος is not an Egyptian name. There is yet another, given
by Tzetzes,[2] Τρίταν, ὁ Νεῖλος, ὅτι τρὶς μετωνομάσθη. πρότερον γὰρ
Ωκεανὸς ἂν ἐκαλεῖτο· δεύτερον Αετός, ὅτι ὀξέως ἐπέρρευσε· τρίτον
Αἴγυπτος· τὸ δὲ Νεῖλος νέον ἐστι,[3] ἐτυμολογούμενον ἀπὸ τοῦ νέαν
κατάγειν ἰλύν, καὶ χερσοῦν τὸ πέλαγος, γέγονε Νεῖλος, κατὰ συναι-
ρεσιν Νεῖλος κ.τ.λ. "'Triton' is the name given by Lycophron
to the Nile, because its name was changed three times. It was
first called 'Okeanos,' next Αετός, eagle, because of its rapid
stream; then Αἴγυπτος, Egypt. (masc.) But the term 'Nile' is
more modern; derived as it is from its bringing down fresh mud,
and turning sea into land, it became Νεῖλος, and by contraction
Νεῖλος."[4]

The next etymology is the Sanscrit 'nilas,' 'dark blue,' 'black

---

[1] Jabl. Panth. Æg. pt. ll. p. 157; Champ. Eg. sous les Phar. l. p. 136.

[2] Ad Lycophron. Alex. 119, ed. Pott.

[3] The name Νεῖλος is not mentioned in Homer; but Hesiod (Theogon. 338)
says:—

       Τηθὺς δ' Ωκεανῷ Ποταμοὺς τέκε δινήεντας

         Νεῖλόν τ' Ἀλφειόν τε καὶ Ἠριδανὸν βαθυδίνην.

[4] Tzetzes, however, explains it a little differently at v. 576, and J. Lydus says
(De Mensib. iv. 68, ed. Creuz.) that Ἰλλὶ was ὄνομα τῷ Νείλῳ πρότερον, then
Αἴγυπτος, Χρυσορρόας, and lastly, Νεῖλος, from a king of that name.

blue;' but I leave others to derive 'Nile' from 'nilas,' Egypt
from 'ăgupta-s,' and, as do Hitzig and other German scholars
of the present day, a host of Phœnician and other Shemitic
names, from the Sanscrit. Once it was the fashion to make
Hebrew the mother of Latin, of course of Greek, and even of
Anglo-Saxon; but that is naturally given up, and Sanscrit
now fulfils the office of Alma Mater to a very large family.
Her own children, however, are numerous enough, without her
being saddled with the responsibility of half the languages of
mankind. But etymologists, like all other 'ists,' will have their
hobby; and, like all other hobbies, etymology is often ridden
very hard indeed.

The last foreign etymology offered for 'Nile' is, as we have
seen, the Hebrew נַחַל, Nuchal, Nahul, Νεῖλ. But, seeing this
Hebrew term could not apply to the Nile in Lower Egypt, and
only by poetical licence, and under certain circumstances, to the
Nile in Upper Egypt, this etymology is not more satisfactory
than the others: so that we must be content to ignore it for the
present. As J. D. Michaelis says, speaking of מִצְרַיִם, "non
multum ignorabo si id unum ignorem, unde nomen habeat."

X. Likewise יְאֹר, 'Ye'or,' 'Ior,' is not "the peculiar He-
brew name" for the Nile, as Dr. Stanley tells us, but it is the
Egyptian term for 'river,' adopted into the Hebrew language.
The word ⲀⲦⲞⲨⲢ, ⲀⲞⲨⲢ, 'atur,' 'aur,' occurs in very old
Papyri, as, for instance, in the ancient fragments of the Ritual
of the Dead, in the Papyri d'Orbiney, Sallier, Anastasi, and
Harris, and on stone monuments. This ⲀⲞⲨⲢ is the Sahidic
ⲈⲒⲞⲢ, ⲒⲞⲢ, whence יְאֹר, and the Memphitic ⲒⲀⲢⲞ, and with
the article ⲪⲒⲀⲢⲞ, "the River," κατ' ἐξοχήν, the only name by
which "the River" is mentioned by Egyptians, from the old
kingdom to the litanies of the Coptic Church. Unless we hold
—but who would?—that before the Hebrews had intercourse
with the Egyptians, 'the River' had no name in Egyptian, the
term יְאֹר must be Egyptian, and not Hebrew.[1] Its Egyptian
origin, however, is proved by the fact that in Hebrew יְאֹר is

[1] Unless it be brought from the Vêdic 'ir,' 'ara,' or from the Zend, 'yare'!

said only of 'the Nile,' and the plural יְאֹרִים only of the
branches of it, except in the Book of Daniel, where, for very
obvious reasons of custom, of time, and of place, several Egyptian
terms such as יאר, רב־דסמבחיא, חרטמיא, and others were
adopted by the author of that Book. And it is interesting to
see, from the common idiom of Egypt, how 'the river' was
identified with everything belonging to the people; thus, e.g.,
ⲭⲓⲟⲟⲣ, lit. 'take the river,' means 'to cross' even the sea;[1] and
with them ⲓⲟⲙ, 'sea,' and ⲫⲓⲟⲙ, 'the sea,' were said not
only of the Northern Sea, but also of 'the river' when spread
over the land.[2]

XI. It was chiefly thus, as Parent of the Land, as the Maker
and Giver of Egypt, which was δῶρον τοῦ ποταμοῦ, "a gift of the
River,"[3] that the Nile was worshipped by the Egyptians. He
was then styled ⲡⲁⲡⲓ-ⲙⲟⲟⲩ or ⲙⲟⲩⲁⲩ, 'Hâpi-môu' or
'mûau,' from ⲡⲁⲡⲓ, to 'cover,' or 'covering,' and ⲙⲙⲱ,
ⲙⲙⲟⲟⲩ, or ⲙⲟⲩⲁⲩ, 'water.' As such he was said to be

---

[1] As in Acts xxi. 2, &c.

[2] As יְאֹר is the Egyptian (not the Hebrew) name of the Nile, so is שִׁיחוֹר,
שִׁחֹר, and שִׁחוֹר, 'Sihor' or 'Shichor,' said by Rödiger (Thes. L. S. s. v. p. 1393)
to be the Hebrew for it. He derives it from שׁחר, 'black,' and connects it with
Μέλας, Melo, &c., well-known epithets of the Nile. But (1.) שׁחר has other
meanings, e.g., 'to open,' 'burst,' &c.; whence שַׁחַר, 'the dawn,' &c. (2.)
שִׁיחוֹר, in Josh. xiii. 3, which Rödiger says means the Nile, as in Gen. xv. 18, is
given as the southern limit of the tribe of Judah, which Reland properly remarks (albeit Rödiger overlooks it) never reached unto the Nile. 3. The authority Rödiger adduces of the Arabic of Saadias rendering שִׁיחוֹר in Josh. xiii. 3, by
نيل مصر 'Nile of Egypt,' must be compared with the Samaritan authorities
given (p. 129), which he also ignores. (4.) שִׁיחוֹר, likewise, is said of the Belus,
near Aco, שִׁיחוֹר הַ Josh. xix. 26, 'fluvius vitri,' "lente currens et limosus."
And (5.) 'Sihor,' or 'Shichor' is by A. Ezra, Abarbanel, &c., always applied to
the 'torrent of Egypt,' at El arish, &c. For more particulars compare Isa. xxiii.
3, Jer. ii. 18, Josh. xiii. 3, and 1 Chron. xiii. 5, and the commentators and Targums. One thing is clear, that it is not the exclusive name of the Nile, since it
is said of two other streams, Josh. xiii. 3, and xix. 26; and that it may be related to the sense of 'bursting forth,' as torrents in the wilderness, as well as to
that of 'muddiness;' especially as the Nile is muddy only during a portion of the
year.

[3] Herod. ii. 5, 10; Strab. i. 29.

ⲛⲟⲩⲛ, νοῦν, "the waters of the beginning," ἄβυσσος;[1] ϩⲁⲡⲓ-ⲙⲱⲟⲩ-ⲧϥ ⲛⲉⲧⲉⲣ-ⲟⲩ,[2] 'the covering water,' Hâpi-mōou, 'father of gods' (of certain gods only), such as frogs, fishes, crocodiles, &c., and 'father of the gods' when identified with Ra, the sun, and thus also with the worship of Osiris, who regulated its rise and overflow; ⲥϫⲁⲟⲩ-ⲛϥ ϩⲁⲡⲓ-ⲙⲱⲟⲩ ⲙ̄ⲙⲛ ⲙⲁⲁⲧ-ⲟⲩϥ, "who, though unseen, yet gave orders to Hâpi-mōu[3] to go, spread abroad and fertilize the land." As such, the Nile, ὁ Αἴγυπτος, was worshipped as father in one sense, and in another sense as husband of the land, ἡ Αἴγυπτος. "What else is Egypt," asks Strabo,[4] ἡ Αἴγυπτος—πλὴν ἡ ποταμία, ἣν ἐπικλύζει τὸ ὕδωρ, "but the land on each side the River, which the water overflows?" ὁ θεὸς—φὰς Αἴγυπτον εἶναι ταύτην τὴν ὁ Νεῖλος ἐπιὼν ἄρδει, "the god having declared that 'Egypt' is the land which the Nile waters during the overflow."[5]

Therefore did they call τὰ ἔσχατα τῆς ὕλης, the utmost borders of the fertile soil, Νέφθυν καὶ Τελευτήν, 'Nepthys' and 'the end;'[6] and thither repaired those who left the world, whether captives to the quarries, or saints to their cells. One of these, living at ϣⲓⲏⲧ, Shièt, near to the Natron lakes, and thus not far from the cultivated soil, ⲁϥⲃⲱⲕ, "went," as we are told,[7] ⲉⲕⲏⲙⲉ ⲉϣⲓⲃϯ ⲛⲟⲉⲓⲕ, "into Egypt to exchange his stale bread for new loaves." So true it is that, even to this day, Egypt proper is physically that which is covered by the Nile during the overflow; and no more.

No wonder, then, if the Great Dragon, הַתַּנִּים הַגָּדוֹל, the Crocodile, which by a singular coincidence is called in Arabic فرعون 'Phra'ūn,' crouching among his rivers in Lower Egypt,

[1] Horap. Lib. I. 21, ed. Leem.

[2] Leps. Götter Kr. p. 22, id. Vier Elem. p. 165, 207.

[3] Ritual of the Dead, c. xvii. l. 69.

[4] Lib. I. c. 26.

[5] Plut. de Is. et Os. c. 18. In the popular worship Hâpi-mōu was identified with Osiris, and the land with Isis; ὡς δὲ Νεῖλον Ὀσίριδος ἀπορροήν, οὕτως Ἴσιδος σῶμα γῆν ἔχουσι καὶ νομίζουσι, "for as they look upon the Nile as flowing from Osiris, so also do they call the land the body of Isis; οὐ πᾶσαν ἀλλ' ἣν ὁ Νεῖλος ἐπιβαίνει σπερμαίνων καὶ μιγνύμενος; not the whole country, however, but that only which the Nile overflows and fertilises." (Ib. c. 33.)

[6] Zoega Codd. Sahid. p. 310.

[7] Plut. de Is. et Osir. c. 69.

should say, " My river is mine own, I have made it," alluding
to the canals he had dug;[1] that the proud Ptolemies should receive this boon of the River's overflow at the hand of their gods,

T̄A-A P̄K P̄P̄ĀṂI-ṂṂ OṪP P̄ P̄ṂĀṂE T̄P-Ч.

" I (Chnuphis) grant thee, Ptolemy Euergetes, an abundant
Hâpi-môu every year ;"[2] and that to this day the people should
every year be told to pray for it on bended knees in the churches
of Egypt.[3]

XII. The popular worship of Egypt did connect, as we have
seen, the rise of Hâpi-môu with Râ, the sun, or Osiris ; since the
rise of the River begins about the summer solstice, and falls
about the autumnal equinox. And the Egyptians chose among
the beasts of the land the kine, as living, every-day emblems of
their local worship. The bulls they consecrated, one to Ptah,
the other to Osiris, and the cows to Isis ; chiefly, however, in
Lower Egypt, where these animals and the green pastures on
which they feed are more common than in the Thebaïd. Wherefore we find a bull on the standard of four nomes of Lower
Egypt, where KA-KEE, the ' Black Bull,' was as much honoured
as the EPE-T TAYP, the ' Red Cow,'[4] that was also sacrificed
to Typhou ; while the hawk takes that place on the standards of
Upper Egypt. Even to this day the kine of ‎خيس‎ Khais, in
the district of El-Hauf, near to Bilbeis and to Wâdi Tumîlât,[5]

[1] Ezek. xxix. 3, 9 ; xxvii. 2.
[2] Champ. Gr. Eg. p. 399.

[3] TWBP, ēxe ПXIṂEĀOГI ēПGIWI N̄TE ПIIAPWOT
ĀṂṂWOT ḤEП TAI POṂṂI ӨAI N̄TE ПХC ПEПП̄OṪ
CṂOT EPWOT N̄TEҶEПOT EПGIWI " KĀTĀ ПOTGI "
N̄TEҶT ĀṂ ПOṪПOҶ ĀṂ П̄P̄O ĀṂṂKĀP1 " П̄TEҶGIĀ-
ПOTGITEП ḤĀ ṂIGIKP1 N̄TE ПIPWṂEĀ " N̄TEҶT
ĀṂФOP̄EЛЛ N̄ ПITEBṂWOT1 N̄TEҶX̄A ПEПП̄OB1
ṂĀṂ EBOЛ. " Pray for the rise of the rivers of water (in) this year, that
CHRIST our GOD will bless them, and bring them up, according to their mea-
sure ; that He will spread the joy they give all over the land ; that He will sup-
port us and the children of men ; that He will save alive our cattle, and forgive
us our sins." (Miss. Copto-Ar. ed. Rom. p. 133.)
[4] Rit. ch. 148 ; and 141, l. 17.
[5] Possibly the Land of Goshen.

are celebrated as البار الحلوة, 'the kine of Hauf,' for their
beauty and their fat. They are the living images of their prototypes, black, white, and red, painted on the walls of Prince
Mourhet's Tomb at the Pyramids;[1] or on those of Menophre's,
where we have the fat kine marked as ⲈⲰ ⲚϭⲢ, ⲤⲦⲚ ⲢⲎⲨ,
"good kine, king's houses, No. 43, 86," &c. ;[2] or in those of
Menophth at Beni-hassan, where the ⲢⲚ ⲈⲰ ⲚϭⲢ "name of
each good kine" is given.[3]

Throughout Lower Egypt especially Hāpi-mōu was represented and worshipped in the symbol of a bull, with special
rites as Hāpi, or Apis, at Memphis; and with other local differences as Men, or Oer-meri, Mnevis, at On. The bull Apis was
styled ⲀⲠⲨ ⲀⲚ⳰-ⲢⲀⲀ Ⲛ ⲠⲦⳘ, ⲤⲦⲚ Ⲛ ⲦⲈⲂⲚⲰⲞⲨ ⲚⳘ
ⲚⲦⲢ, "Apis, the new life (incarnation) of Ptah, sovereign of
all cattle, divine;"[4] and 'Men, Oer meri,' Mnevis, had for his
distinctive epithet ⲀⲚ⳰-ⲢⲀⲀ Ⲛ ⲠⲀ, 'Second or new life (incarnation) of the Sun.'[5] Whatever differences might at first
exist in the honours paid to these two bulls, owing to the sway
of Ptah at Memphis and to that of Atum or Osiris at On, they
had so many features in common, that, among the people especially, these differences were by degrees lost in the practical,
popular worship of Hāpi-mōu connected with Osiris in the form
of a bull, and in that of the land, or Isis, in the form of a
cow.[6]

[1] Osburn, Mon. Eg. vol. ii. p. 456.
[2] Rosellini, Mon. Civ. vol. i. p. 243, sq. pl. xxvi.
[3] Rosell. id. pl. xxxviii.
[4] Brugsch. Mon. i. pl. ix. and p. 17.
[5] De Rougé, Etude d'une Stèle. p. 65.
[6] Thus we find worship paid to ⲀⲤⲓⲠ⳰-ⲀⲠⲨ, Osiris-Apis, (Brugsch. Mon.
i. pl. ix., Sir G. Wilk. 2nd Series Vol. iii. pl. 31,) who is also called ⲔⲀ-ⲔⲀⲀ
'Bull of Egypt,' (Rit. of the D. c. exiii. l. 19,) as well as to Ptah-Sokaris-
Osiris, and to Osiris adorned with the Nilometer, the distinctive badge of
Ptah, (Sir G. Wilk. ib. pl. 23, 25, 33,) for "most of the priests," says Plutarch,
εἰς τὸ αὐτό φασι τὸν Ὄσιριν συμπεριπλέχθαι καὶ τὸν Ἆπιν, ἐξηγούμενοι καὶ διδάσ-
κοντες ἡμᾶς ὅτι εἰκονικὸν εἴδωλον χρὴ νομίζειν τῆς Ὀσίριδος ψυχῆς τὸν Ἆπιν,
"say that Osiris and Apis are woven into one, explaining and teaching us
thereby to consider Apis as a beautiful image of the soul of Osiris." (De Is. et
Osir. 29.)

The cows sacred to Isis were seven in number; whether from the number 'seven' being sacred, especially in Egypt, or from the seven planets revolving round the sun, Ra, Osiris, Osiris-Apis, or Hâpi-(mōu). It is impossible to follow all the details of this worship, the broad features of which are very plain,—so plain as to point out at once the object of Pharaoh's dream. But I may be forgiven, perhaps, if I mention the delight, as well as the surprise with which, in my study of the Ritual of the Dead, I turned over the leaf that revealed to me Pharaoh's dream itself, the seven sacred cows with the divine bull, from an original drawing made, may be, before Pharaoh did dream of them.[1] It is, indeed, as I afterwards read in V. De Rougé's outline of the Ritual,[2] "une touche de couleur locale," a stroke of native colouring; a voice, assuredly from the dead, bearing witness, as in the case of the vine and of other facts, to the Truth, to the accuracy, and to the trustworthiness of the Sacred Text; and despite all the garbled statements, all the mock scholarship, that 'free inquirers' bring to bear against it.

And it is no dead letter. There are the names of the seven sacred cows (all of which I am not yet learned enough to read safely), and the list of gifts of bread, haq, geese, &c., offered to all the eight—ⲧⲁ-ⲧⲛ, "given you," says the soul in transmigration through the realms of Atum.[3]

The dreams Pharaoh dreamt were so thoroughly Egyptian in all their particulars, as well as in their bearing, that they would have had little or no significance for one who was not an Egyptian. This might be an additional reason to make one

[1] Dr. Stanley thus alludes to these cows in a note, p. 78, "There were seven sacred cows in the Book of the Dead, c. 148."

[2] p. 30.

[3] Atum is thus addressed in behalf of that soul (Rit. ch. cxlviii. l. 9.) ⲁⲛⲧ-ϩⲣⲕ ⲣⲁ ⲛⲧⲣ ⲛⲥⲧ ⲙⲙ ⲁⲧⲛ-ϥ ⲁⲛϫ ⲛϩⲣ ⲙⲙ ϫⲟⲩ ⲁⲟⲩ ⲁⲟⲩϥⲁⲛϫ ⲙⲙⲁ ϫⲟⲩⲧ ⲣϫ ⲣⲛⲕ ⲁⲟⲩ·ϥ ⲣϫ ⲥϫϥ ⲕⲉⲟⲩⲁ ⲉϩⲉ-ⲟⲩ ϩⲛⲁ ⲕⲁ ⲁⲣ ⲧⲁ ⲧⲁ-ⲟⲩ (ϩⲛ) ⲟⲉⲓⲕ (ϩⲛ) ϩⲕ ⲛ ⲁⲛϫⲟⲩ-ⲟⲩ. "Hail! thou sun-God, brilliant in his own orb. Life appearing on his mountain! this soul also (Aufanch P. N.) declared just, knew thy name; this soul knew the seven cows with the Bull, to give them bread and haq, among the living."

doubt the commonly received opinion, mentioned by Syncellus,[1] ὅτι ἐπὶ Ἀφώφιος ἦρξεν Ἰωσὴφ τῆς Αἰγύπτου, "that Joseph was Ruler of Egypt in the days of Aphophis," that is, during the Shepherd Dynasty. Yet, even if this Aphophis, or Apophis, be the Apepj mentioned in the Papyrus Sallier as reigning at Auar (Avaris) in the days of Ra-seqenen Tau-aa-qan, who worshipped no other god but Set or Sutech, he might have imbibed Egyptian notions and be well acquainted with Egyptian worship, seeing he was the fourth king of his dynasty. Yet there are other reasons in favour of the Pharaoh of Joseph not having been of the Shepherd race; and, after all that has been written on the subject, all opinions for and against are little better than surmises; so that we must wait for other documents than those we possess ere we can speak of it with certainty.

XIII. In mentioning the seven years of famine (p. 79), Dr. Stanley quotes Mr. Osburn's opinion that it was caused by the bursting of an inland lake, of which he even gives a map,[2] and to which Orosius[3] alludes, although not distinctly. The cause of a famine, when it occurs in Egypt, is, we know, either the too great or the too small elevation of the waters at the time of the inundation: from fourteen to sixteen or eighteen cubits at Cairo is the limit, beyond or below which the inundation cannot take place without injury to the land and to the inhabitants.[4] Therefore the famine foretold by Joseph must have been owing to one or to the other of these, probably to the latter; and all other famines that have taken, or that will yet take place in Egypt, must have the same cause; from the first on record under Ouertesen (or Usertesen) I., (not Sesortason I.), c.c. 2800 ? B.C. to the last famine heard of. But although the famine itself was brought on by what are called 'natural causes,' yet the foretelling of it was from God, to Whom Nature and all causes obey. Orosius, following the opinion commonly received in his day, tells us, " fuit itaque hæc fames magna sub rege Ægyptiorum Diapolita, cui nomen erat Amasis quo tempore Balæus Assyrios, Argivos Apis regebat,"[5] very near the time of Ra-seqenen Tau-aa-qan who defeated Apepj, during whose reign we

[1] Chronogr. vol. I. p. 115, 204, ed. Dind.
[2] Monum. Eg. vol. ii. p. 133.
[3] Hist. Lib. i. p. 13.
[4] See Sir G. Wilk. Modern Eg. vol. I. p. 280—282.
[5] Hist. Lib. I. p. 33.

have seen that Syncellus says all agree to think Joseph came to
Egypt.

XIV. After describing Joseph's investiture with the golden
necklace—a ceremony which took place after every signal service
rendered by a man to the state, as, e.g., by Ahmês, who was re-
warded seven times with it[1]—with the golden ring and with the
state robe of fine linen, not necessarily white in the highest
officers of state,[2] Dean Stanley continues—

"Before him goes the cry of an Egyptian shout (*Abrech !*), evidently resembling those which now in the streets of Cairo clear
the way for any great personage driving through the crowd of
man and beast."

The Dean then tells us to compare about the "Egyptian shout"
"Wilk. ii. 24," where we read in a note :

"The word abrek אַבְרֵךְ is very remarkable, as it is used to the
present day by the Arabs when requiring a camel to kneel and
receive its load."

We need not, however, in this case, appear to apply to
men what is said of camels. For, even though Sir G. Wilkinson be of opinion that "when they kissed the firman, they
also bowed the knee," yet the only application of אַבְרֵךְ by
him is to camels, wherever these be loaded, whether in the
desert or in the khan ; whereas Dr. Stanley refers it to the
shout of those who cry in the streets of Cairo—or indeed of any
other Eastern city—to make way for some one on horseback.
It certainly never occurred to me, when I said أبرك, 'abrok,'
i.e., 'bend the knee,' to the camel I rode across the Egyptian
desert, to compare this order to kneel with the shout of the
herald going before Joseph's chariot. Neither do I think it
need be compared. It is just such a coincidence as the Arabic
أبيب 'Abib' and אָבִיב, between words which have nothing to
do with each other, as I shall show regarding these terms.

The Arabic برك, like the Heb. and Chald. בּרך, is said especially of a camel bending the knee to drink or to be loaded.[3]

[1] Tomb. d'Ahm. Inscr. 1, 2.
[2] See Sir G. Wilkinson, Anc. Eg. vol. III. p. 347, sq.
[3] e.g., in this play upon the word برَكة, Barakat or Baraka, the name of a

So also בָּרַךְ in Hebrew, whence בְּרֵכָה, 'a place where camels kneel to drink,' 'a pool;' the meaning of 'blessing' being secondary. But אַבְרֵךְ cannot be a Hebrew form of בָּרַךְ; therefore does V. Bohlen[1] try to make it an inf. hiph. for הַבְרֵךְ, substituting א for ה after the Chaldee; and he refers us to Gesenius,[2] who seems inclined to agree with V. Bohlen, and who compares אַבְרֵךְ with a like form, אַשְׁכִּים, Jer. xxv. 3. In his Thes. L. S. s. v., however, he is more in favour of an Egyptian etymology. It would lead me too far to demonstrate the futility of V. Bohlen's criticism in this case; but it is all of a piece with what he says in the same page concerning the gold ring, the gold collar, the robe of fine linen put upon Joseph,— "that they are articles of luxury which betoken a much later date." One wonders at a man, who valued his reputation for learning, lowering himself to write in this wise. As if we had not engraved records, as we have seen, of Ahmès, who lived under Uertesen, long before Joseph's time, being honoured seven times with the golden collar; and as if we did not possess the gold ring of Shuphu (Cheops) and the golden cup of Thothmès III.; to say nothing of a multitude of Egyptian gold ornaments adorned with precious stones, tokens of luxury of a still greater antiquity, discovered and published long before V. Bohlen wrote his work.

Of course, the intention of V. Bohlen and of Gesenius, in endeavouring to make out אַבְרֵךְ to be a Chaldaism, is, to try and lower the date of Moses' writings. But as we have seen above (p. 120), with regard to בָּתַר, this argument concerning ἅπαξ λε-

---

town built by a sultan of that name in Tartary, a traveller there says (V. Timur. c. xlv. vol. i. p. 376):

صحرا' تعزي الي سلطانها بركة
تد كنت اسمع ان الخدير يرجد في
بركت ناقه ترحالي ببجانبها
فما رايت بها في واحد بركة

"Having heard that good was to be found in the deserts called after their sultan Barakat, I made the camel on which I travelled to kneel (barraktu) by that place; but there I did not look on a single blessing (barakat)."

[1] Genesis, p. 386.   [2] Lehrgeb. p. 319, note 2.

γέμετα is utterly worthless. And the unfairness of classing a word found in Genesis—a word, too, which Gesenius[1] himself thought never likely to be satisfactorily explained—with a similar form occurring in Jeremiah, who lived in the time of the captivity, must strike even the most superficial inquirer. What would be thought of the Greek scholar who ascribed the Iliad to the time, if not to the pen, of Quintus Smyrnæus, because there are certain forms common both to the Homerica and to the Post-homerica? Even 'free inquirers' would disown him then, albeit they welcome him when he does the same, or a worse thing, towards the Bible. For, in order that, according to common sense and to fairness of dealing, such argument hold good, as affecting the age of a book, words of another date must occur in it, not once, as in this case, but repeatedly, as in the writings of Ezra, of Nehemiah, and of others. And V. Bohlen's attempt to strengthen his position by bringing פֶעֶנֵחַ from the unknown Shemitic פֶעֶן, and taking no account of the ח added by him to this imaginary word, only shows to what shifts 'free inquirers' scruple not to resort, in order to allure the unwary. Yet, whatever be their creed, they should be—honest.

The most probable etymology for אַבְרֵךְ is the one offered by De Rossi,[2] vis.: ⲁⲡⲉ-ⲡⲉⲕ, 'ape-rek,' 'bow the head.' Both these words are found in ancient Egyptian; and I thought I had met with an illustration of this passage in Brugsch's Monum. Egyptiens, vol. i. pl. xlvii. f., reading it in his translation "Abaisse la tête, O Roi d'Egypte," &c. But I cannot read and render the original text otherwise than ⲁ-ⲟⲩⲭ ϩⲣ-ⲕ ⲥⲧⲛ ⲛ ⲕⲙⲉ (ⲡⲕⲁϥⲓ), &c.: "Ah! let thy face shine, O King of Egypt," &c. There is, however, a yet better example in Sharpe's Egyptian Inscriptions, pl. 40, l. 21,[3] which M. Chabas[4] quotes as the etymology of אַבְרֵךְ, and which he renders "ape-rek, tête basse!" There, four gods and two goddesses, Isis and Nephtys, stoop with their hands down, and bowing their heads, thus explained in the hieroglyphic text, ⲛⲛ ⲛⲧⲣ-ⲟⲩ ⲙⲙ ⲥϫⲡ ⲟⲩ ⲛⲛ ⲁ-ⲗⲟⲩ-ⲥⲛ (ⲥⲛⲁⲩ) ⲙⲙ ⲡⲕ ⲁⲡ-ⲟⲩ-ⲥⲛ, &c.:

---

[1] Thes. L. S. s.v.   [2] Etymol. Ægypt. p. 1, and 339.
[3] And also pl. 64, first series.   [4] Pap. Prisse, p. 6.

"these gods here represented (in this drawing) with their two arms bowing their heads," &c.[1]

XV. " His (Joseph's) Hebrew name," continues Dr. Stanley—

"disappears in the sounding Egyptian title, whichever version of it we adopt, Zaphnath Paaneach, 'Revealer of secrets,' or Psonthom Phanech, 'Saviour of the age,' or 'Peteseph.' "

The Dean of Westminster has a way of solving difficulties by cutting them, which is more expeditious than philosophical. I was not aware, until now, that these renderings were settled; and I thought that the fact of there being more than one rendering of the same title shows that the meaning of that title was not yet ascertained.

Some, like Jablonski, think that the LXX. must have read צפנת פענח aright in rendering it Ψονθομφανήχ, or Ψοθομφανήχ, on which L. Bos gives, from an Oxford MS., ἔστιν σωτὴρ κόσμου. ὁ Σύρος ἔχει ὁ εἰδὼς τὰ κρυπτά. Philo, κρυπτῶν εὑρετής, ἢ ἀπεροκρίτης, which means, 'Saviour of the world.' The Syriac version has, 'He who knows hidden things.' Philo, 'revealer or discoverer of secrets.' Both the Hebrew and the Greek texts have tried to the uttermost the ingenuity of critics, and will try it yet longer. For the Syriac reads, ܕܓܠܐ ܠܗ ܟܣܝܬܐ "to whom secrets are revealed," i.q. Targ. Onkelos, דְּטְמִירָן גְּלָן לֵיהּ. But Targ. Jon. B. Uzziel has דִּטְמִירָן מְפָרְשָׂה, "who explains secrets."[2] The Vulgate omits the Egyptian name, and gives "Salvatorem mundi." The Samaritan has ⲦⲓⲘⲓⲢⲧⲓ ⲅⲁⲗⲁ either 'Timirti gala,' 'he discovered my secret,'[3] or better, and with a different reading, 'Timirtè galè,' 'discoverer of secrets.' The Arabic of Saadias follows the Samaritan, Chaldee, and Vulgate, and reads مُعْبِر الخَفَايا, "revealer of things hidden;" whereas the Arabic published by Erpenius has, with nearly the

---

[1] In another and anterior work (Ioarr. Histor. de Seti Ier. p. 36) M. Chabas renders this text thus: " Ces dieux-ci, dans ce tableau, ont leurs mains baissées devant leurs faces," &c. But with deference to that excellent scholar, they are 'hands,' and not 'faces;' moreover, how is ⲁⲁ ⲠⲔ ⲀⲠ-ⲞⲨ-ⲤⲚ to be rendered "baissées devant leurs faces?"

[2] Compare Dan. ii. 18, 27, 28.　　　[3] Pfeiffer, Dub. Vex. p. 1074.

same meaning, كاشف الأسرار, "revealer of secrets;" while the Version of Abu Said renders it كنز العلم "treasury of science." And lastly the Persian follows the Hebrew without rendering the term; while the Ethiopic, Armenian, and Slavonic Versions follow the LXX., and the Georgian reads " Psom-panis."

Philo,[1] speaking of Joseph, says the king changed his name for one in the tongue of the country, ἀπὸ τῆς ὀνειροκριτικῆς, relating to his interpretation of dreams; and elsewhere[2] he adds, ὁ δὲ Ψονθομφανὴχ τοῦς ἐστι θεασόμεθα, 'let us see what this Psonthomphanech means:' it means, then, ἐν ἀποκρίσει στόμα κρίνον, 'a mouth discerning in giving an answer.'[3] Another author, quoted by Eusebius,[4] mentions Joseph as

Ἰωσὴφ, ὃς ὀνείρων
θεσπιστής, σκηπτοῦχος ἐν Αἰγύπτοιο θρόνοισι.

"Joseph, who was interpreter of dreams, ruled over Egypt." Josephus[5] says that the king gave him the name Ψοθομφανήχ, on account of his own wonderful intelligence; for this name σημαίνει—κρυπτῶν εὑρετήν, means 'discoverer of things hidden.' According to Jablonski,[6] Origen[7] renders it ᾧ ἀπεκαλύφθη τὸ μέλλον, "he to whom the future has been revealed;" and S. Chrysostom[8] explains it τῶν κρυπτῶν γνώστης "a man who ascertained things hidden;" and Theodoret,[9] who read it Ψομθομφανήχ, says that he was thus called τῶν ἀπορρήτων ἑρμηνευτήν, "Interpreter of Secrets," as having made known unto the king his dreams.

It is evident that these several interpretations of Ψοθομφανήχ are one and the same, copied from one another originally, perhaps, from an allusion to Dan. ii. 47, v. 11, 12, and thence through the Chaldee paraphrase and the Peschito. For we shall see presently that the LXX. Ψοθομφανήχ or Ψονθομφανήχ is no transcription of the Hebrew צָפְנַת פַּעְנֵחַ, of which Bochart[10] says, "Septuaginta interpretes qui versionem suam in Ægypto ediderunt illud scribunt Ψοντομφανήχ (sic) Salvatorem mundi, interpretatur Hieronymus. At alii quos defendit numerus junc-

[1] De Josepho, p. 543, ed. Par.
[2] Prov. xxiv. 26.
[3] Ant. Lib. ii. c. 5, p. 59, ed. II.
[4] Hes. vol. i. p. 48.
[5] Vol. i. p. 106, ed. Seb.
[6] De Nom. Mutat. p. 1058.
[7] Præp. Ev. p. 430.
[8] Opp. vol. i. p. 207.
[9] Vol. iv. p. 606, ed. Montf.
[10] Phaleg, Opp. vol. i. col. 59.

læque umbone phalanges, occultorum interpretem, vel futurorum revelatorem."[1] But F. Nork,[2] who makes out Joseph's history to consist wholly of mythic events, explains "*Zaphnath Phenech*" to mean "Verborgen seyn des Phönix," "disappearance of the Phœnix," and Asenath to be a daughter of Dinah by the god Suteeh! If this be the kind of 'modern science' and of 'modern philosophy' we are expected to reconcile with the Bible, our task is hopeless. Although not quite so far gone, Van Bohlen denies that there be any Egyptian element in the history of Joseph, but asserts that all "fremdartige Wörter," all foreign expressions in it are Aramaic; he therefore derives[3] צָפְנַת from צָפַן, *verbergen*, 'to hide,' and well known; and פַּעְנֵחַ from פַּע, *eröffnen*, 'to open,' which, however, exists nowhere but in his imagination, despite what Castellus says.[4] Yet, not only does V. Bohlen derive פַּעְנֵחַ from a fanciful verb, but he does so against all rules of grammar, by adding ח, which is no suffix in Hebrew, or in any other Shemitic tongue; and he then proposes to derive *aiôn* from *snh*, the Coptic ⲉⲛⲉϩ, 'age,' (as being contained in פַּעְנֵחַ); thus taking off, in this instance, the same aspirate which he adds in the other! This is indeed what Germans call 'Willkühr,' arbitrary self-will; but neither criticism nor scholarship. It is 'free inquiry' with a vengeance; so free that, as we have seen that in another instance,[5] it will not be fettered even by the points of the compass, so also in this it frames etymologies in which we may truly say that 'consonants go for very little, and vowels for nothing at all'—anything, it matters not what, so long as the Bible is attacked.

---

[1] Others, like Vitringa (Obs. Sac. L I. dis. L c. 6) endeavour to explain it through צָפַן, 'to hide,' and נֵחַ, which is not Hebrew; or like Simon, (Onom. v. L p. 601, sq.) who says of צָפְנַת פַּעְנֵחַ "quod occulti revelatorem, sc. indicem significat, consentientibus omnibus VV. Or. et Paraphrasis, à quorum consensu non esse discedendum, rectò judicat Grotius." Dogmatic, but not logical. "Nomen נֵחַ ut proprium et צָפְנַת פַּעְנֵחַ per *Intiamum Pheneaehi* (regis, qui Profanis *Apachus*) exponit Kohlreisgius. Singularis quoque est sententia H. Horchii in Textuum S. Fasc. L p. 19, cui פַּעְנֵחַ idem est cum Hebræo נֵחַ *respondens, responsor*, posito ﬨ pro ﬦ ejusdem organi, sicut רֹעֶה sit pro רֹעֶה, *pastor*, Metaphor. *res*; et ﬣ pro ﬤ ut in בֵּס pro נֵס, נֵחַ pro נֵחַ." 'Singularis,' indeed, yet worthless.

[2] Biblische Mythol. vol. L p. 404, sq.   [3] Gram. p. 387.

[4] Lex. Heptagl. s.v. col. 3075.

[5] See above, p. 50.

But real Hebrew scholars know better; and A. Ezra[1] says rightly of צפנת פענח, "if this expression be Egyptian, אם זו המלה מצרית לא ידענו פירושה, we know not the meaning thereof; ואם היא מתורגמת לא ידענו שם יוסף, and if it be a translation, we do not know Joseph's name." Abarbanel[2] renders it 'Revealer of secrets,' adding, it is true, לא הספיק לו זה, "there is no doubt of it;" but he gives no proof of this, so that S. Jarchi is a better teacher when, explaining it also "Revealer of secrets," he adds nevertheless, לא לפענח דמיח במקרא, "there is no example of פענח in the Hebrew text;" and R. S. Ben Melech,[3] who compares צפנת פענח (which he says is Egyptian) with the names Nebuchadnezzar gave Daniel and his companions[4] in Aramean, says also that "some have indeed tried to explain it through the Hebrew," but adds, very sensibly, תמה הוא איך קרא שם בלשון הקדש פרעה, that "it is a wonder Pharaoh should have called him by a Hebrew name."

Of those who have looked for the meaning of Ψονθομφανήχ in the Coptic, Kircher[5] says that ΨΟΝΘΟΛΛ means 'future,' and ΠΑΝΗΚ, 'an augur.' But he gives no proof of what he asserts, neither can he; for these terms, like others of his own making, do not exist in Coptic. Pfeiffer[6] justly finds fault with him, and offers either ΠΙΘΤΟΛΛ ΠΑΝΗΚΑ, a term that does not exist; or ϹΟΠΑΠ ΔΙΘΕΒΕΝ, which he renders "desideratorum augur," but equally absurd.[7] A. Gutbier[8] proposed ϬΕΠϤΑΤ ΠΙΟΝΘ, which he renders 'relaxatio vitæ;' but ϬΕΠϤΑΤ in Coptic means 'a kick,' and not 'refreshment,' and the combination of these two terms is against grammar. A. Müller[9] proposed ΠΙϹΟΠΤ, 'creation,' or 'mankind;' "inde. Ψονθομφανήχ esse Salvatorem hominum." Forster[10] offers a yet less

---

[1] L. c. Comm. ed. Buxtorf.
[2] Comm. in Pent. fol. 90, vo.
[3] Michol Jophi, p. 14.
[4] Dan. I. 7.
[5] Prodrom. Copt. c. v. p. 126.
[6] Dub. vex. p. 167.

[7] So also in his Exercit. quinta, p. 105, sq., he proposes ϬΟΠΑΠ ΠΑΠΙΚΑ, also an offspring of his imagination. Indeed, at p. 1070, sq., he shows evidently, by the way he wrote both Armenian and Coptic, that he knew nothing whatever of either language.

[8] Ibid. p. 1073.
[9] Ibid. p. 1073.
[10] Mantissa Æg. in his De Bysso Ant. p. 101, sq.

probable etymology, viz., ⲥⲁϧⲛ̄ⲛⲟⲩϯ ⲛ̄ⲁ-ⲉⲛⲉϩ-ⲓϧ, i.e.,
(as he fancies) 'the scribe of the divine, eternal Spirit.' But besides
that this term is simply an impossible compound, and against
all grammar, ⲓϧ Eg. ⲁⲓϧ, very far from being only 'spirit,'
means 'evil spirit;' and thus it is always used for δαίμων and
δαίμων; in the New Testament, and for 'pestilence' in Ps. xci. 6.[1]
La Croze thought that ⲭⲱϥ ⲛ̄ⲧⲉ ⲛⲉⲛⲉϩ, which he renders
"caput sæculi," would do; but ⲭⲱϥ, 'his head,' is inadmissible in this place, the suffix ϥ not being according to grammar
in such a case. Lastly, Bernard and Jablonski[2] propose a better
etymology for Ψονθομφανήχ, viz., ⲛⲥⲱⲧ ⲁ̀ⲉ ⲫⲉⲛⲉϩ, "'salva-
tio' vel 'salvator sæculi';" and Gesenius[3] another for Ψονθομφανήχ,
viz., ⲛⲥⲟⲛⲧ ⲁ̀ⲉ ⲫⲉⲛⲉϩ, "'sustentator' seu 'vindex mundi,'
vel sæculi," &c.

But first—the meaning of the name given by Pharaoh to
Joseph is to be sought for, not in the language spoken under
the Ptolemies, but in that of the earlier Pharaohs. So true is
this, that

Secondly—the LXX. Ψοθομφανήχ and Ψοντομφανήχ are no
correct transcription of the Hebrew letters. Allowing that
φανήχ renders ΠΥΝ, ψοθον or ψοντον does not express ΠΥΣ;
for no really Coptic term begins with Ψ, since ΨΟΙ for ⲛⲥⲟⲓ,
ⲯⲁⲥⲣⲉϥ, for ⲛⲥⲁⲥⲣⲉϥ, &c., date from the time when such
words as ⲛⲓⲁⲟⲥⲝ for 'ὁ dux,'[4] found their way into Egypt;
but the real equivalent for Ⲩ in Coptic is Ⲭ, and 'ⲧ' or 'ⲧⲓ' in
ancient Egyptian.

Thirdly—it stands to reason, that, if the Coptic translator or
translators had recognised in Ψοθομφανήχ an Egyptian or a Coptic
term, or terms, they would have corrected it accordingly; as they

[1] Forster, however, offers a still more monstrous term, made up of ⲛ-ⲟ̇ⲟⲛⲧ
"vel coalescerate scilicet ⲛ articulo et sequente ϩ, ⲫⲟⲛⲧ, [how and
when? since we find ⲛⲣⲟⲛⲧ ⲛ̄ⲱⲛ, 'the priest of On,' in this very
verse, and not ⲫⲟⲛⲧ]; et adeo Josephum, ut Iyciam honori consuleverat, ap-
pellarent ⲛⲣⲟⲛⲧ ⲁ̀ⲉⲫⲁⲉⲛⲉϩ-ⲓϧ ⲥⲁⲥⲥⲥⲥ sacerdotem Spiritus
æterni." But ⲁ̀ⲉⲫⲁⲉⲛⲉϩ means, not 'evil,' but 'evil mel.'
[2] Opp. vol. i. p. 213.   [3] Thes. L. S. s. v. ⲛⲥⲭⲥ, p. 1181.
[4] Zoega Codd. Memph. p. 84.

did in other instances. Instead of only transcribing the Greek
which they, evidently, could not make out, they would have re-
solved ψ into ΠC, since this ψ is said to be for ΠC in ΠCⲰT ;
but he or they, neither saw ΠC in ψ, nor CⲰT or CⲟⲚT in
ψⲟⲑ, or in ψⲟⲩⲧ ; still less Ⲁ̀ in ⲟμ, or ΠⲈΠⲈⳉ, ⳘⲈⲚⲈⳉ,
in ⳨ⲁⲛⳈⳊ. This seems to prove that we look in vain for the
meaning of Ψⲟⲑⲟμ⳨ⲁⲛⳈⳊ among Coptic etymologies ; for were
it to be found there, the Coptic version would have done so, and
would have told us what it meant in Coptic, instead of transcribing literally a Greek word without meaning. For it is not
reasonable to try and draw etymologies for a word from a language the native writers of which could make nothing of that
word.

Fourthly—it is singular that one and all of the above etymologists have overlooked the ' α ' in ⳨ⲁⲛⳈⳊ ; for this ' α,' Copt.
Ⲁ, is the hinge on which the whole name turns, and may be an
additional proof that Pharaoh, who alone could either create a
minister or give him a name, did so in gratitude for himself.
Admitting, for argument's sake (though it be not so really,) that
ⲈΠⲈⳉ, ' age,' forms a part of ⲠⲩⳊⲲ it could not be ΠⲈΠⲈⳉ,
' peneh,' as all these etymologists propose, with the def. art.
only ; but it should be with the relative or with the possessive
article ΠⲀ, both ὁ τοῦ and ὁ μοῦ ; so as to read ' paeneh,' a
word which renders and expresses better the Hebrew sounds,
and which means ' my age,' or ' of the age.' If it is to be
' Saviour,' it must be ' Saviour of my age,' and not of ' the
age ;' for Ⲁ̀ ΠⲀ (art. relat.) i.e. τοῦ ὁ τοῦ, would hardly be
grammatical.

But since we have, at least, the Hebrew letters which represented the Egyptian name, when they were written, and since
we see the Greek Ψⲟⲑⲟμ⳨ⲁⲛⳈⳊ is not an exact expression of those
Hebrew letters, it seems that the only safe ground to work
upon, is the name as it stands in the Hebrew text. Now we
find that, as I have said, the Egyptian letter and articulation
best answering to Ⲩ is t́, tj, Ⲭ, hierogl. a snake ; as e.g. ⲬⲈⲦⳌ,
ⲬⲈⲦ, ⲬⲀⲦⳌⲓ, ⲬⲈ, ⲬⲞⲦ, &c.[1]

_____

[1] Champ. Gr. Eg. p. 40, id. Dict. Eg. p. 174; De Rougé, T. d'Abus. p. 37,

And as to ע, not only is it acknowledged on all hands that it stands for à, as in רעמסס Râmesses, פוטיפרע Potiphera (and not 'rab'), but better Potiphrà, ΠΑ-ΤΙ-ΠΡΑ or ΠΡΗ, ΦΡΑ or ΦΡΗ; צען 'Tsan,' rather than 'Tso'an,' Tânis; כנען hierogl. Kânanâ, &c.,[1] but also, the syllable מע in מעשה shows clearly, that this term cannot be Hebrew; for the syllable מע is almost impossible in Hebrew. It shows, therefore, that since we find the simple Sheva, against analogy, placed under the ע only, I may say, for the look of Hebrew orthography, but to show the absence of a real vowel, the ע here must be pronounced à as in Râmesses רעמסס where the ע has a patach only because two shevas could not follow each other; רע being râ'â i.q. râ. We may then distribute the letters of צפנת פענח with their Egyptian equivalents, thus:

ת	נ	ע	פ	ן	נ	פ	צ
ⲐⲬⲈ	ⲛ	ⲁ	ⲛⲫϥ	ϯⲧ	ⲛ	ⲫⲛϥ	ⲭⲩⲓ

which might be read according to the above etymologists; Memph. ⲬⲪⲞ-ⲚⲦⲈ-ⲪⲈⲚⲈⲢ, Sahid. ⲬⲠⲞ-ⲚⲦⲈ-ⲠⲈⲚⲈⲢ, 'born,' 'offspring of eternity,' 'Heaven-born;' or 'possession,' 'boon,' 'treasure of the age;' ⲬⲪⲞⲒ-ⲚⲦⲈ-ⲪⲈⲚⲈⲢ, 'arm,' 'support of the age,' or 'world;' but inasmuch as the second word must begin with Pâ, it cannot be ⲠⲈⲚⲈⲢ the 'world' or 'the age;' but rather ⲠⲀⲚⲬ 'the life,' or ⲠⲀⲀⲚⲬ 'my life;' so as to read, ⲬⲪⲞⲒ-ⲚⲦⲈ-ⲠⲀⲀⲚⲬ, 'arm or stay of my life;' or yet Memph. ⲬⲒ-ⲪⲚⲞⲨϯ-ⲠⲀⲀⲚⲬ, Sahid. ϬⲒ-ⲠⲚⲞⲨⲦⲈ-ⲠⲀⲀⲚⲢ, Anc. Eg. ⲬⲀⲨ-ⲚⲚⲦⲢ-ⲚⲀⲚⲬ, or ⲠⲀⲀⲚⲬ or ⲬⲀⲨ-ⲚⲚⲦ-ⲚⲀⲚⲬ 'God has taken up, preserved, or restored my life,' or 'the life'—of the people. Or

sq., and the sign read tje, more suitable to certain inscriptions. (Champ. Gr. Eg. p. 547, et Dict. Eg. p. 180, but best explained by De Rougé, T. d'Abm. p. 185, sq.) The relative value of these letters is proved by several proper names, e.g. Heb. צען Tso'an, or Ts'an, Copt. ⲬⲀⲚⲈ or ⲬⲀⲚ, hierogl. ⲦⲀⲚⲨ Tanis; צידון Copt. i.q. Greek ⲤⲒⲆⲰⲚ, hierat. tji(dn)ne Sidon; צר Copt. i.q. Greek ⲦⲨⲢⲞⲤ, hierat. tjer, Tyre; צרפה hierogl. tjarpta, Zarephath, or Sarepta, &c. Brugsch. Geogr. Denkm. vol. iii. p. 25, 42, 43, 44; vol. i. p. 10.
[1] Brugsch. id. p. 10.

again, Memph. ⲭⲏϥ-ⲛⲟⲩⲧ (for ⲭⲏϥ ⲫⲛⲟⲩⲧ) ⲡⲁⲁⲛⲟ̄
'GOD has redeemed, or, is near to, my life;' if ⲭⲏϥ might be
construed without ⲟⲩⲁ, for ϥ is the equivalent for ⲟ and also
for ⲟ suff.; or still, Memph. ⲭⲫⲟ-ⲛⲟⲩⲧ-ⲡⲁⲁⲛⲟ̄, Sah.
ⲭⲛⲟ-ⲛⲛⲟⲩⲧⲉ-ⲡⲁⲁⲛⲟ, 'gignit Deus vitam meam,' vel ' vitam' sc. populi, &c.

I do not of course attach any great importance to these etymologies; although they are according to grammar and, more
or less, to analogy. They are only meant to show that the
LXX. Ψοθομφανήχ or Ψοντομφανήχ does not, and cannot represent פשׁנת עפנת, since ψ is not צ, neither by conversion nor
otherwise; and ψοθομ is not עפנת. Whence we gather that
the LXX. did not rightly understand the meaning of a term
which they rendered in their own way, into a word that does
not exist in the language in which it is assumed to have been
spoken. This is further proved by the Coptic version making
no sense out of what is given by the LXX. as Coptic or
Egyptian; whence it appears that neither the LXX. nor the
Coptic translators understood it aright. Our only chance, therefore, is to get at it through the letters of the Hebrew original.

Brugsch, I am happy to find, sanctions my reading of פענח;
and refers it to the district of Memphis called anch-ta, or Ta-
pa'nch פענח(ת) and proposes to read the name thus:
ns-pen-ta-p.anch, which he even gives in hieroglyphics,[1] and
renders it, "dies ist der Gouverneur von Tapanch," ' this is the
Governor of Tapanch,' i.e. 'of the district of life.' In this
etymology, however, that great and thorough scholar, is at a
loss to account for צ, which he owns "ist schwer zu sagen" is
hard to tell. It must be hard, indeed, if he, who shall live in
his works as long as Egyptian is studied, cannot find it out.[2]

On the other hand, M. Chabas, who is also as deep as he is

---

[1] Geogr. Denkm. vol. I. Tab. xliii. 1114, and p. 237.

[2] He wrote thus in 1857; but in 1850 he looked for the Egyptian words in
Ψοθομφανήχ which he divided thus: " ψο-(ν)-θο-φανχ. p.m-a-ta-p.anch, c'est
à dire, ' princeps mundi vitæ.' Le nom mundus vitæ m 5t encore de les textes
hieroglyphiques; c'est lci où le soleil couchant (Tmen, Atmou) se cache. C'est
ainsi qu'on lit dans le rituel funéraire de Turin (c. 15, col. 43) Djet.f em ankm
Tmen holy.f em (to) anch, &c., dicit (mortuus Osiris) ad celebrandum Deum
Tm occultantem se in mundo vitæ," &c.　(Lettre sur un MS. bilingue, p. 53.)

conscientious and safe a guide in Egyptian lore, explains only the first word רַעֲנֵשׁ which he gives thus: "ϪⲈⲚⲈⲒⲐ 'les délices de Neith.' Le nom donné à Joseph est ainsi parfaitement en harmonie avec la sagesse dont il avait fait preuve."[1]

Thus, of these two great scholars, one hesitates about the first word, which the other finds quite easy, saying nothing of the second word, which is the only one the first scholar explains. Surely this is enough to show how worthy, on the one hand, are the efforts of those who labour honestly to arrive at the Truth of the subject they treat, and, on the other hand, how unworthy is the frivolity with which others treat that same Truth. See R. ix. (d) p. 5, sq. Τὸ δ' ἀληθές, κ.τ.λ.

In conclusion, we remark as regards "Zaphnath-Paaneah" that (1) the LXX. Ψονθομφανήχ, renders not the Hebrew words; nor yet Coptic or Egyptian terms; since the Coptic translators did not recognise any, in the rendering of the LXX. (2) That we must look to the Egyptian as rendered by the Hebrew words, for the etymology thereof. (3) If we read the Hebrew with the vowel points, it might be ϪⲀϤ-ⲚⲀⲦ-ⲠⲀⲈⲚⲈⲢ, Zaph-nat-paeneh ('paeneah' as expressed in Hebrew), 'the God of the age has possessed him.' But (4) inasmuch as ⲠⲀⲈⲚⲈⲢ, is doubtful as an Egyptian term, we had better take the Hebrew letters alone at their real value, which is, either ϪϤ ⲚⲦ-ⲚⲀⲚϪ, 'Zaph-nat-panch,' 'the God of Life has taken, or inspired him,' i.e. 'taught by the God of Life;' or (but not so well) ϪϤ ⲚⲦ ⲚⲀ-ⲀⲚϪ, 'taught, inspired by the God of the House of Life.'[2] Such an epithet is as much in Egyptian style, as that of ϪⲚⲤ ⲢⲀ-ⲚⲦ-ⲚⲂ̅, 'Chons-ha-nat-neb,' 'Chons, chief of all gods," the name of the High Priest or prophet of Chons, in De Rougé's Et. sur une Stèle, p. 19, &c.

As to the other Egyptian name of Joseph, Πετεσήϕ, Peteseph, which Dr. Stanley does not explain, mentioned by Chaeremon[a] in his account of the Exodus under the leadership of Moses and of Joseph, whom he calls ἱερογραμματεύς, it is not easy to deter-

---

[1] Pap. Prisse, p. 6, 7.   [a] Or, 'sacred college.'
[2] Chaerem. Alex. in Fragm. Hist. Gr. ed. Müller, vol. III. p. 495, sq. Cory, Fragm. p. 182, Jos. c. Ap. Lib. i. 32, p. 1358, ed. Huds.

mine the probable etymology of it. We may, however, compare this name which in Egyptian means, 'He of the Sword,' ΠΕΤΕ or ΠΕΤ-Ε-CHϘ, (like ΠΕΤ-Ε or ΠΕΤΕ-ΦΡΑ, 'He of the Sun,') in token, perhaps, of his office, with what Plutarch says of Darius Ochus that the Egyptians ἐκάλεσαν (αὐτὸν) μάχαιραν—ὀργάνῳ φοινικῷ ταριχάζοντις, called him 'a sword,' (CHϘ or CIϘI, 'Seph,' or 'Siphi,') likening him to a bloody instrument, as having killed many, even the god Apis.[1] The same reason cannot apply to Joseph; but the sword was also an emblem of rank, of justice, and of authority; so much so, that a certain kind of sword or dagger, is constantly used in hieroglyphics as a symbol of priority—ϷΟΥΕΙΤ.[2]

XVI. Then Joseph—

"Becomes son-in-law of the High Priest of the Sun-God in the sacred city of On, Petephre or Potipherah ('he who belongs to the Sun'). He and his wife Asenath, the 'servant of' the goddess 'Neith' (the Egyptian Athene or Minerva), may henceforth be conceived—looking—as in an Egyptian tablet, the type of the solemn happiness of calm and stately marriage."—p. 81.

This connexion was, at that time, the highest Joseph could have made, next to marrying one of the king's daughters; but he could not do this, not being either of royal blood or an Egyptian. In marrying the daughter of ΠϷΟΠΤ Ν ΑΠ the High Priest of the city sacred to Atum, the Evening Sun, the Sun of Amenti, Joseph at once stood firm in the high station to which GOD and Pharaoh had raised him. As to On or Ān it was then, and it continued until the downfall of the Egyptian kingdom, to be the most celebrated city of Egypt, not so much in the world at large as in Egypt itself. I am not writing the history thereof, for this would be out of place at present; I will only say that, not only did the Rameses bear, as we have already seen, the title of ϷΚ ΑΠ, 'governor of On,'[3] but the sacred character of the city was so interwoven with the history

---

[1] Plut. de Is. et Osir., c. xi. p. 10 and 53, ed. Parth.

[2] Champ. Dict. Eg. p. 338, sq., Gr. Eg. p. 242.

[3] Of this On, ΑΠ ΑΑϷΤ, the Northern On, Heliopolis, not of On, ΑΠ-ΡΗC the Southern On, Hermonthis, near Thebes.

and with the associations of the people of Egypt, that one can
hardly read a page of an Egyptian MS. or a column of an
inscription, without some allusion to On, the city of Atum, the
most sacred Sun; the Sun of the Lower World.

There, at On, he was worshipped with the greatest pomp,
with the most devoted homage, and with all the learning of the
Egyptians; there, were his praises sung, and prayers offered to
him for the souls in transmigration through his realms of light
—in strains full of stern, manly thought and beauty; and often
so like passages from the Rig or from the Sáma-vêda to the
praise of Agni, as to show the unity of worship in days of yore
—proclaimed even from the abode of the Egyptian dead. I
will not now further allude to this interesting subject, bound as
I am not to swerve from the matter in hand; especially as I
hope at some future time to publish parallel passages from both
Aryan and Egyptian lore, bearing on the Truth contained in
the Word of God—the Bible.

We have already had occasion to notice the regal dignity of
the High Priest in those days, when speaking of Melchizedek.[1]
Here, Potipherah is styled כֹהֵן ἱερεύς only; but this is merely a
generic expression, to mark his office, as devoted to the service
of Atum, ἀρχιερεύς being here meant by ἱερεύς: in the same way
as Chæremon, speaking of Moses and of Joseph, calls them both
γραμματεῖς, 'scribes;' but Joseph especially, ἱερογραμματεύς,
' a sacred scribe.'[2]   The ἱερεῖς were of different degrees, as e.g.
ⲡⲟⲩⲁⲃ ϩⲣⲁⲓ ⲛⲉⲁⲛϣⲱⲟⲩⲛ, ⲛⲉϥⲁⲓⲉⲁϣⲓⲣ, &c., the priest
of the altar, of the censors, &c.; but they were all inferior in rank
to the προφῆται; ⲛⲧⲣ-ϩⲛ-ⲡⲟⲩ, who were also of the first,
second, third, or fourth degree.[3]   They married, as we find
from the paintings and from the inscriptions of some of the
richest tombs of the Thebaid, hewn out by prophets of Amun-

---

[1] See above, p. 145, sq.   [2] See above, p. 205.
[3] Thus we read in the tomb of Icheñion at Thebes (Champ. Gr. Eg. p. 242, sq.)
ⲛⲛⲧⲣ-ϩⲛ or ⲛϩⲛ ϩⲟⲩⲉⲓⲧ ⲛ̄ ⲁϭⲓⲣⲓ ⲟⲩⲛ-ⲛⲟⲩⲣ ⲁⲗⲁ
ⲭⲟⲩⲧ. ⲛϩⲛ ⲛⲁⲁϩ ⲃ ⲛ̄ ⲁⲁⲉⲛ-ⲣⲁ ⲛⲥⲧⲛ ⲛ ⲛⲧⲣ-ⲟⲩ
ϥⲁⲓⲛⲟⲩⲣ.   "Ounnophre, declared just, first prophet of Osiris. Phaïnophre
second prophet of Amun-ra, Sovereign of the gods;" and others mentioned in
the same description as third and fourth prophets.

Ra: thus Petarphre says of himself, ⲀⲚⲔ ⲈⲚ ⲤⲒ Ⲛ̄Ⲉ̄Ⲛ ⲞⲨⲚ-Ⲁ ⲈⲚⲀ ⲈⲰⲢ ⲒⲀ ⲈⲂⲦ (ⲦⲂⲀⲔⲒ) "I prophet son of prophet, am with Horus rejoicing in the city of Abydos."[1] And on an inscription of the Palace at Karnak,[2] we read ⲀⲚⲔ ⲚⲤⲒ Ⲛ̄Ⲉ̄Ⲛ-ⲚⲞⲦ ⲚⲀⲀⲦ Ⲛ̄ ⲀⲀⲈⲚ ⲈⲒ ⲦⲀⲀⲀⲨ ⲤⲒ ⲚⲞⲨⲀⲂ, "I am son of great prophets of Amun, and son of a priest on my mother's side," mentioning both the ιερεύς and the προφήται, who were appointed by the king as supreme; and who exercised their priestly functions in families, handing their office down from father to son.[3]

We have among several documents, an interesting one bearing directly upon this subject. On a 'stèle' erected to the memory of Bak-en-Khensu,[4] we read that he was ⲞⲨⲀⲂ 'priest' at sixteen; Ⲛ̄Ⲧⲡ-ⲀⲦ̄Ⲥ̄, 'holy father' at twenty; Ⲛ̄Ⲧⲡ ⲈⲚ ⲚⲀⲀⲈ Ⲧ̄, 'third prophet' at thirty-two; Ⲛ̄Ⲧⲡ ⲈⲚ ⲚⲀⲀⲈ Ⲃ̄ 'second prophet' at forty-seven; and at fifty-nine he rose to the highest rank of Ⲛ̄Ⲧⲡ ⲈⲚ ⲀⲠⲈ, 'head' or 'chief of the prophets'—probably ἀρχιερεύς, Ⲛ̄Ⲧⲡ ⲈⲚ ⲚⲈⲞⲨⲈⲒⲦ Ⲛ̄ ⲀⲀⲈⲚ, Ⲛ̄Ⲧⲡ ⲈⲚ ⲀⲠⲈ Ⲛ̄ ⲀⲀⲈⲚ-ⲢⲀ ⲤⲦⲚ Ⲛ̄Ⲧⲡ-ⲞⲨ, "first prophet of Amun, chief prophet of Amun Ra, Sovereign of the gods." The years of office of these High Priests, who were also comptrollers of the king's household, and chiefs of other public departments, were recorded together with those of the king under whose reign they lived.[5]

Dr. Stanley seems to consider 'Petephre' and 'Potipherah' as one and the same name, since he adds, "he who belongs to the Sun," as qualifying both alike. But he may be forgiven for so doing, since a master in the art of 'Free Inquiry' makes a worse mistake. I give his note on this subject, as another example of worthless scholarship, if not of wilful perversion of facts—which is far worse than either carelessness or ignorance.

XVII. He says:—

"On the identical form (Gleichförmigkeit) of פּוֹטִיפֶרַע (Potipherah) with Potiphar, Jablonski (Opusc. II. p. 210—read 215)

[1] Champ. Gr. Eg. p. 248.
[2] Champ. Gr. Eg. Ibid.
[3] Diod. Sic. Lib. i. c. 73.
[4] Rev. Archéol. Janv. 1863.
[5] See e.g. Etude sur une Stèle, p. 184, sq.

explains Potipherah through Π—Δονт—φρη *Priest of the Sun;* and indeed, this name might be known, since the Jews had a temple of their own at Heliopolis. V. Bohlen, Genes. Comm. p. 887."

He then refers us to his commentary on ch. xxxvii. 36, where, speaking of פּוֹטִיפַר, he ridicules those who wish to bring to Egyptian etymologies, names like these, which he says, are after all, the offspring of late and degenerate idioms; witness פּוֹטִיפַר which he, after Gesenius, takes to be an abbreviation of 'Potipherah;' and of even a later date.

The spirit of all this is plain enough; it is to lower the Bible in every possible way. If this were done with real learning, it would command attention; but done as it is, with rash and incorrect statements that go to prove the evil disposition of the writer, it can only repel an honest mind.

First, then—will any honest scholar maintain that these names were first known when the Jews had their temple built at On, at the instance of Onias, and by Ptolemy Philometor's leave?

Secondly—Jablonski never once hints at Potiphar, and Petephre, or Potipherah being the same; neither s.v. Petephre,[1] nor s.v. Potiphar,[2] nor yet under Potipherah.[3]

Thirdly—V. Bohlen could know very little of Coptic if he thought Jablonski's Π-ϱ,ΟΠϮ-φρη *P-hont-phrè,* a fit etymology for פּוֹטִיפַר or for פּוֹטִיפֶרַע *Potipher,* or *Potipherah.*

Fourthly—his resting his criticism on the fact that the LXX. renders both 'Potiphar' and 'Potipherah' by Πετεφρής is worth no more than the authority of the LXX. in other like cases—that is, nothing at all. For as Πετεφρής is the Hellenized form of an Egyptian name probably in use at the time of the Ptolemies, the LXX. seems to have thought it would be as good an equivalent for 'Potiphar' and 'Potipherah,' as ψοντόμ or ψοθόμ for צֹעַן; Πηθώ for פִּתֹם and Σεπφώρα for both שִׁפְרָה 'Shiphrah,' and צִפֹּרָה 'Tsipporah;'[4] and so, indeed, it is; but quite as incorrect.

---

[1] Opp. vol. l. p. 203.   [2] Ibid. p. 205.
[3] Diss. vIiL de T. Gosen, c. 4. p. 209—215; Panth. 138.
[4] Ex. i. 11, 15, ii. 21, &c.

P

According to these free etymologists, the syllables פַּר, פֶּרַע,
and פַּרְעֹה phar, pherā, phar'oh, or par'oh, in the three names
פּוֹטִיפֶרַע, and פַּרְעֹה, mean 'the Sun,' and are each
the Egyptian pᴀ or ᴘʜ, with the art. Φ, ᴨ; פַּר phar, they say
is the short of בֶּרַע, pherā, and פַּרְעֹה, par'oh, is the long of it,
and their disciples wonder. But there is probably no example
on record of ΦᴀⲢ being transposed into Φᴩᴀ, since it cannot
be; still less of Φᴩᴀ being lengthened into Φᴩᴀᴀ; the Egyptians had too much respect for the name of their God to deal
thus with it. Not one instance of this occurs in the six hundred
and ten proper names given by Brugsch in his list;[1] neither
among the many names found in his Lettre sur un MS. bilingue; nor yet in his 'Sammlung Demotischer Urkunden."
Greeks did indeed mangle the names of the gods both of their
own country and of Egypt; but Egyptians, never.

As a proof thereof, let us examine this Πετεφρής of the LXX.
Πετι is, properly, the Memphitic relat. pron. or adj. with the
def. article, ᴨ-ⲈⲦⲈ, ᴨⲈⲦⲈ, 'is qui,' vel 'is quem,' (sc. dedit,
amat, &c.); and Φρης is the Memph. Φᴩᴀ or ΦᴩH 'the sun,'
with the Greek ending ς. Such a compound as 'is qui sol,'
'is quem sol' means, of itself, nothing without a complement.
ᴨⲈⲦⲈ, therefore, which in Sahidic would be ᴨⲚⲦ, and in Old
Egyptian ᴨⲚⲦⲒ cannot be the relat. pron. ᴨⲈⲦⲈ in Πετεφρής.[2]
This, I believe, is proved to demonstration by the very examples
Champollion gives[3] to show the contrary. At p. 306, sq., he
gives the various forms of ᴨⲚⲦⲒ in hieroglyphic and in hieratic
characters, and at p. 310 he gives what he calls the contracted
forms of ᴨⲚⲦⲒ used in the construction of proper names; viz.
ᴨⲦ, ᴨⲦⲞⲨ, in which, however, he introduces the new symbols
of the so-called 'level' and of the 'hand holding it,' without

---

[1] Demotisch. griech. Elgen. 1851; and Parthey, Ægyptische Pers. nam. 1864.
[2] We might, indeed, read ᴨⲈⲦ-Ⲉ-ΦᴩH which is grammatical, for lit. 'is
qui ad Solem' i.e. 'Soli' (sc. deditus est); but such a combination hardly seems
probable. This name is also written sometimes Πετεφρής. This in Coptic
would be ᴨⲈ-ᴨⲦⲈ-Φᴩᴀ or ΦᴩH 'He of the sun.'
[3] Gr. Eg. p. 310.

accounting for this supposed 'contraction' occurring only in
proper names, and only with these symbols. Now, it so happens
that these two symbols, in their symbolic as well as in their
phonetic capacity, always express ⲧⲁ or ⲧⲓ 'to give' or 'gift;'
M. Chabas,[1] it is true, seems to enlarge on Champollion's assertion in his Gr. Eg. p. 310; but, I think, by an oversight,
since most of the examples he gives prove my position, that—
since the 'level'[2] generally stands at the head of inscriptions for
'I give' or 'I offer,' or 'gift,' 'offering,' &c., and that either
alone or 'in the hand' it means and reads, 'to give' or 'gift,'
or even 'gifted,' as in ⲧⲁ-ⲁⲛϧ 'gifted with life,' said of kings,
&c.—This said 'contraction' of ⲛ̄ⲧ̄ⲓ into ⲛ̄ⲧ̄ by means of
these two symbols, is no contraction at all; but reads ⲛ-ⲧⲁ
or ⲛⲉ, ⲛⲁ-ⲧⲓ, 'the gift' (of), or 'the given' (of); so as to
read פּוֹטִיפָרַע ⲛⲁ-ⲧⲓ-ⲫⲣⲁ, 'he whom the sun has given;'
M. Chabas himself seems to think so; for he gives in hieroglyphics[3] ⲛⲉⲧⲓ-ⲫⲣⲁ "Peti-phra, don de Phra, Héliodore,"
as the Egyptian for פּוֹטִיפָרַע.[4]

Yet, this etymology is not altogether satisfactory; for the י
is not well represented by the Eg. 'a' (the arm). This long
vowel י, however, shows (I) that we must look for the equivalent of פֹ in the Eg.[5] ⲛⲁ or in some other long vowel, and not
in the indefinite sound of ⲛⲉ, or ⲛⲉⲧ, ⲛⲉⲧⲉ; that, therefore,

[1] Inscr. d'Ibsamboul, Rev. Archéol. XV' Ann. p. 709.

[2] If so be it is a 'level,' and not a kind of bread, offered to the gods at funerals
and at other seasons, in loaves, called κολλύραντ or κολλάραντ, (Athen. Lib. x.
c. 4, p. 418, 447, ed. Cas.; and Lib. iii. c. 30, 80, ll. 77.) Eg. ⲕⲣ or
ⲕⲗ-ⲁⲥ-ⲧⲓ, i.e. 'cake-worthy,' or 'devoted—gift,' or 'funeral gift,' or 'offering,' ⲕ̄ⲗⲁⲥ-ⲧⲓ (Ritual c. xvii. l. 7, and Dict. Eg. p. 450); further proved
by the Inscr. of Thothmes III. (Brugsch. Mon. vol. i. Pl. xlii. l. 4, near the
bottom,) where we have apparently one of these loaves, είς δξὸ ἀνηγμένον,
'brought to a point,' which Αἰγύπτιοι κολλύραντ ἐνὸμαζεν the Egyptians called
'callistès,' (Jul. Poll. Onom. vi. 73, p. 246, ed. Bek.) together with other kinds
of bread offered to Amun. If, however, it be not a κολλύραντ, but really a
'level,' its symbolic meaning must be 'equity,' in offering suitable gifts either
to the gods or to men.

[3] Papyr. Prisse, p. 7.

[4] See also Roselll. Mon. Civ. Vol. i. p. 117.

[5] Champ. Gr. Eg. p. 188, 264.

(2) the Greek Πετεφρἡς for 'Potiphar' and 'Potipherah,' is of no more weight than the Greek rendering of 'Shiphrah' and of 'Tsippôrâh' by Σεπφώρα, or that of 'Αμενρύτιος for 'Amun-Hor;' for the LXX. could not render פוטע by Πετε except through carelessness or indifference.[1]

Granting that פרע is the Memphitic ϕρ⳾—for there were dialectic idioms in those days as well as later—פר in פושׂפר cannot be the same word. But, and until a better etymology can be offered, 'Phar' in 'Potiphar' may be, again in Memphitic, ϕⲁⲣ—for we are now dealing with events in Lower Egypt, for ⲡ·ⲣⲁⲣ, 'the Har,' Horus; (like ϕⲏⳋ for ⲡⲣⲏⳋ, ϕⲟⲟⳋ for ⲡⲣⲟⲟⳋ, &c.) e.g. 'Αρῶηρις ⲣⲣ-ⲟⳋⲉⲣ, 'Har, the elder' or 'the great;' thus 'Potiphar,' פושׂפר would mean, 'he that is given by Horus;' ⲡⲁ-ⲧⲓ-ⲡ·ⲣⲁⲣ, or ⲡⲁ-ⲧⲓ-ϕⲁⲣ. And, so far as the dignity of the epithet went, there was not much to choose between 'Potiphar' and 'Potipherah,' since Har, Horus, the sacred Hawk of Egypt, was often identified with the Sun, and was only another name for it. So much, at all events, for the "Gleichförmigkeit," or 'like construction,' as 'free inquirers' call it, of these two proper names.

XVIII. V. Bohlen having thus made out to his satisfaction, that 'Potipherah' and 'Potiphar' being one and the same (as proved by Πετεφρἡς) were first talked of when Onias had built his

---

[1] The above was already written when I received M. Chabas' "Mélanges Egyptologiques, 2ᵈᵉ Série," and found therein at p. 26 the proof of what I have just said, as to the carelessness of the LXX. in rendering proper names not of Greek origin. For in a quotation he gives from Letronne's Recherches pour servir à l'histoire d'Eg. p. 341, we find the proper names Πετεενῶϕις, Πετεενῶϕις, Πετερμῶφρες, &c., that show that—when the relative ⲡⲉⲧ, ⲡⲉⲧⲉ is made part of a proper name transcribed in Greek, it takes the ⲛ̄, ⲣ, without which it would not form a grammatical term; e.g. Πετε·ρ·εϕτιι, for ⲡⲉⲧⲉ·ⲛ̄·ⲥⲁⲧⲉ, &c. So that, the LXX. Πετεφρἡς, must either be, as I have said, for ⲡⲉⲧ·ⲉ·ϕⲣⲏ, 'is qui soli,' (sc. deditus est), a compound term which does not recommend itself, or it must be for ⲡⲁ·ⲧⲓ·ϕⲣⲏ, 'Ηλιόδωρος, which is more probable; since ⲡⲉⲧ·ⲉ·ϕⲣⲏ in the language of the Pharaohs would be ⲡⲡⲧ·ⲁⲁ·ϕⲣⲁ or ⲡⲡⲧ·ⲁⲁ·ϕⲣⲁ. Pati, or Pat·m·phra; less flowing than ﬡﬡﬠ Pa-ti-phra. Yet, how little we know about it?

temple at Heliopolis, not two centuries before our SAVIOUR's birth, he does not actually, like Nork, make Asenath the daughter of Dinah by the ass-headed god Sutech, but he nevertheless, like Nork also, brings אָסְנַת not from the Egyptian, but from the Aramean. And with Nork, he quotes a passage of the Talmud also given by Buxtorf,[1] wherein it is said that at weddings the custom was to throw some barley brought from the granary, אִסָּנָא *isanyā*, into a cup or vessel called אָסִינְתָא *asinthā*, saying : "Grow and multiply like this barley"—which when it had grown, was afterwards brought back to the married pair, &c. We may, at all events, thank these 'free inquirers' for affording us innocent amusement. Would they were always as harmless, as when they tell us that Asenath, daughter of Potipherah, Priest of On, was named after an iron or a copper saucepan into which her Jewish parents cast a handful of barley at her wedding! Free, very free indeed.

The etymology alluded to by Dr. Stanley, however, is nearer the truth. 'Asenath,' daughter of Potipherah, was like her father, and in true Egyptian style, called after some divinity. Asenath, possibly ' As-neith,' ⲁⲥ-ⲛⲉⲓⲑ, " *le mérite de Neith,*" as M. Chabas interprets it,[2] was so called, as being, if not sacred to that goddess, at least under her patronage. This name is connected with Neith, in like manner as Ae-ḉai ⲁⲥ-ⲏⲥⲓ is with Isis.[3] Jablonski who offers ⲥⲟⲩⲉ-ⲛⲉⲓⲧ for the etymology of ' Asenath' compares it with *Hatirvir*, (Gift of Neith) the name of a priest of Neith.[4] Seiffarth[5] offers ⲁ.ⲛ.ⲁⲓⲧ-ⲭⲟⲣ ' power of Neith,' but like many of his renderings, it is far from satisfactory as regards ⲭⲟⲣ. Ublemann, however, who belongs to the same school, derives ' Asenath' from ⲁⲙⲉ-ⲛⲉⲓⲟ ' Asheneith,' and gives to ⲁⲙⲉ the same meaning Champollion gives to ⲁ.ⲥ.[6] But the ס ' s ' in אָסְנַת can no more be transcribed by ש ' sh,' than ס in רַעְמְסֵס Rámeses ; for they both render the hierogl. *s*, or ' crook ;' so that even ⲁⲙ-ⲛⲉⲓⲟ ' worshipper

[1] Lex. Chald. col. 167.   [2] Pap. Prisse, p. 7; but better, ⲁⲥ-ⲛⲁⲧ.
[3] Champ. Précis S. Hier. Tab. p. 28.
[4] Opp. Vol. ii. p. 209 ; Panth. p. 56.
[5] Theol. Schr. Æg. p. 100.
[6] Isr. u. Hyksos. p. 45, et de Vet. Æg. Ling. p. 25.

of (i.e. 'caller upon') Neith' cannot be thought of for 'Asenath ;'
and M. Chabas' etymology, 'merits of Neith,' i.e. 'like Neith,'
must be received as best for the name of the daughter of the
High Priest of On, Pa-Tum, the Holy City of Egypt. She
might be much of what her Greek biographer tells of her,[1] a
damsel of high repute, as daughter of the greatest man in the
land, and second only to the king, ere Joseph was raised by GOD,
'to fill the heart of his sovereign,' ⲙⲁⲣ̄ ⲉ̣ⲏⲧ ⲛ̄ ⲥⲟⲧⲧⲉⲛ
in the language of his day, as πρῶτος φίλος, as his Counsellor
and as Ruler of his land. He was blessed as GOD alone blesses ;
and his progeny was compared as Dr. Stanley says very well,
and much to the point—

"not to the stars of the Chaldean heavens, or to the sand of the
Syrian shore, but to the countless fish swarming in the great
Egyptian river."

XIX. After some good remarks, p. 81, the Dean of Westminster treats briefly of the stay of the Israelites in Egypt, and
of the different length of their sojourn there, according to either
the Hebrew, the Greek, or the Samaritan texts ; but he wisely
abstains from giving a decided view on questions which neither
Lepsius, De Rougé, Bunsen, Brugsch, Uhlemann, Chabas,
Knötel, Koch, Henry, Lesueur, Poole, Sharpe, Nash, Sir G.
Wilkinson, nor as many others as have written on the subject
have yet been able to settle. Neither will I, assuredly, offer
an opinion ; but I will only give the points I find sufficient for
my purpose, in endeavouring to fix landmarks in that broad
and hazy distance.

1. The Israelites can never have been the Hyksös of which
Manetho speaks. He says[2] that 'Hyk' in the sacred tongue
means 'King ;' τὸ δὲ ΣΩΣ ποιμήν ἐστι καὶ ποιμένες κατὰ τὴν
κοινὴν διάλεκτον, "but σὸs means 'shepherd' and 'shepherds' in
the common dialect" Not only is such an unusual combination
of the sacred and of the common idiom in one word, most suspicious, but Josephus himself was not sure of it ; for he says a
little after, that in another copy οὐ βασιλεῖς σημαίνεσθαι διὰ τῆς
τοῦ Ῡα προσηγορίας, ἀλλὰ τοὐναντίον αἰχμαλώτους δηλοῦσθαι ποι-

---

[1] Bios Ἀσενέθ in Fabricii Cod. Pseud. V. T. Vol. i. 774, sq., ii. 85, sq.
[2] Joseph. C. Ap. Lib. i. c. 14.

μίνας, not "'kings' but 'captive shepherds' were described by
the term 'Hyk ;' τὸ γὰρ Τκ πάλιν Αἰγυπτιαστὶ καὶ τὸ Ακ δασυνό-
μενον, αἰχμαλώτους ῥητὰς μηνύει· for that 'Hyk' again in Egyptian and Ak aspirated, really mean 'captives.'" All this is
correct. 'Hyk' or 'Hak' occurs very frequently for ' governor,
ruler, or petty king,' as e.g. of the nomes of Egypt; 'Hak An,'
the ' Governor of On,' also a title of Ramses ; and ' Hak' also
means ' captive ;' but though these two words be pronounced
alike they differ so completely in hieroglyphical, and therefore
also in hieratic writing, that neither Josephus nor Manetho
could have consulted the original copy. And as to ΣΩΣ, sös,
it answers to the Coptic ϢⲰⲤ, rendered in Sahidic, ⲈϤⲢ̄ⲞⲞⲚⲈ
Ⲛ̄ⲚⲒⲈⲤⲞⲞⲨ " he who tends the sheep,"[1] but the equivalent for it
has not yet been found in the old language. Sös has been
identified by some with the Sasū, a Nomadic people often mentioned in Egyptian documents ; but they were of Arab descent.
So that, there may be some truth in the Arabic tradition recorded by Abulfeda[2] that the Pharaoh under whose reign Joseph came to Egypt was Er-Rajjan son of El-Walid, رجل من
العماليق من ولد عملق بن سام بن نوح " a man from among
the Amalekites, who draw their origin from Amlak, son of Shem,
son of Noah ;" and elsewhere (p. 16) he reckons among the
many sons of Shem, طم وعمليق الذي هو أبو العماليق ومنهم
كانت الجبابرة بالشام والفراعنة بمصر " Tasm and Amlēk, who
is the father of the Amalekites ; and from them descended the
Giants (רפאים) of Syria and the Pharaohs of Egypt." So
that, whether 'kings' or 'captives' the Sasū could not be the
Israelites ; not to mention the probable time of the two Hyksos
or Shepherd Dynasties, which could never be made to agree
with the thread of history to which the sojourn of the Israelites
in Egypt belongs.

But the real name for these ποιμένες was 'Mena-u,' (Copt.
ⲘⲞⲞⲚⲈ ' to tend,' ⲘⲞⲞⲚ, ⲘⲀⲚ-ⲈⲤⲞⲞⲨ 'tend-sheep,' ' shepherd,') and they are thus mentioned in several instances, as,
e. g., by Ahmès, who went to Avaris (?) with Ra-sqenen Tau-na-
qen, fought and took it from Apepj II., and brought away thence

<hr>

[1] Zoega Codd. Sahid. p. 316.   [2] Hist. A. I. p. 28.

a man and three women prisoners, &c.[1] These Arab pastors were long remembered and mentioned in Egyptian writings as the 'pest' or 'plague,' Aat-u.

2. The Israelites are mentioned as Hebrews, 'Aperi-u,' or 'Aberi-u,' in several places in the Leyden Papyri, which I have not, and cannot verify. I quote this on the safe and good authority of M. Chabas.[2]

3. Following the letter of Scripture, that is, of the Hebrew for the Old, and of the Greek for the New Testament, I find that God said unto Abraham, Gen. xv. 13, "Know of a surety that thy seed shall be a stranger in a land that is not theirs, and shall serve them; and they shall afflict them four hundred years;" and that this statement is again repeated by S. Stephen, Acts vii. 6, to show that not the 'sojourn,' but the 'affliction' of Abraham's posterity was to last four hundred years. For "now the sojourning of the children of Israel, who dwelt in Egypt, was four hundred and thirty years," Exod. xii. 40; a statement which is further confirmed by S. Paul, Gal. iii. 17, where he speaks of the Law being given four hundred and thirty years after God's covenant with Abraham and with his seed; clearly reckoning from the time the validity of that covenant began as regards the children of Abraham, that is, from the day they set foot in the strange land of Egypt.

4. From the tenour of the last chapter in Joseph's history (Gen. l. 14—26), it is very evident that the Pharaoh of whom he asked leave through his ministers to go and bury his father (v. 4) was not the same who had given him his ring and had clothed him in fine linen. Joseph, though still a great man in the land, was, it would seem, no longer in office; while his last words to his brethren, "God will surely visit you and bring you out of this land," read not like the expression of faith only, but also like the foreboding of coming sorrow, and like a feeling of solitude in a land of strangers, and without a home anywhere. Joseph, then, was seventeen years old when sold into Egypt; thirty years old when he stood before Pharaoh (Gen. xli. 46); and thirty-nine (ch. xlv. 6) when Jacob and his family came to Goshen; and as he died "a hundred and ten years old" (ch. l.

[1] De Rougé, T. d'Ahmès, p. 171; Chabas, Mél. Egyptol. p. 34, sq.
[2] Mél. Egyptol. 1ère série, p. 42, sq.; et 2de série, p. 143, sq.

26), he had spent ninety-three years of his life in Egypt, and
had seen, we may be sure, more than one Pharaoh on the
throne. The 'affliction' of Abraham's seed I therefore take to
have begun from the death or from the expulsion of the Pharaoh
who raised Joseph to honour; when Joseph's influence at court
either fell or ceased altogether, and with it the favour shown to
his family. This is the more probable if we place the coming
of Joseph into Egypt according to the prevalent tradition under
Apophis, i.e., Apepj II., the last of the Arab, Sású, or Ama-
lekite Dynasty, about the beginning of the XVIIIth Diospolite
Dynasty. And the new Pharaoh, who began the 'affliction' of
the children of Israel, may have been the Ra-seqenen Tau-aa-qan
whom Ahmès accompanied to Avaris, where Apepj II., whom
he deposed, had reigned, thirty years after the coming of Jacob
to Goshen, when Joseph was about seventy years of age. All
this would thus have taken place in the eighteenth century
before CHRIST, according to probability, and to the chronology
of the Authorized Version, of Chabas and of Brugsch—no mean
witnesses in such matters. These are, I know, mere surmises;
yet they are better than many others rather taught as dogmas
than offered as mere opinions. Moreover they have this great
advantage, that they agree with the letter of Scripture, and with
the probable history drawn from Egyptian documents.

XX. "The land of Goshen," continues Dr. Stanley, "was
the frontier land, reckoned as in Arabia rather than in Egypt."
And on this he has the following note:—

"El-Arish is the traditional scene of the overtaking of Joseph's
brethren by Pharaoh's officers. (Denon. ii. 90.)"—p. 84.

What officers, and where? Dr. Stanley does not surely
mean, by "Pharaoh's officers," Joseph's steward, whom Joseph
sent after his brethren "when they were gone out of the city,
and not yet far off." (Gen. xliv. 4.) This tradition, however,
has so little to recommend it, that one does not see (1) what
could induce Dr. Stanley to record it; and (2) still less what
connexion there can be between these said "officers of Pharaoh"
pursuing Joseph's brethren, and the 'land of Goshen.' Such
confusion of ideas only creates error.

For, first—Joseph was at the seat of government; and if it

was not Memphis, it was assuredly Tanis or Avaris. But this, the easternmost city that ever was a royal city in Lower Egypt, was at several days' march from the site of El-Arish.

Secondly—the whole transaction of the steward following after Joseph's brethren soon after dawn, when they were "not yet far" from the city—their return to Joseph "who was yet in the house" (v. 14), and not gone out to his public business, from which he generally returned "at noon" (ch. xliii. 25)—his making himself known unto them, and Pharaoh's interview with him about them—all took place the same day (xliv. 3—xlv. 24).

Thirdly—Goshen never reached to El-Arish. Jablonski wasted a vast erudition in eight dissertations,[1] to try and show that Goshen was Κωχώμ or Κωχών, that is, the Heracleopolite nome; Κωχώμ being, as he thinks, ΚΑϤ-ΧШΑΑ, the 'land of the strong,' i.e., Hercules. A great number of far better etymologies might easily be offered; but it would lead to no result beyond what is already obtained, viz., that the land of Goshen was probably in the most fertile district of Lower Egypt, called Wâdi Tumîlât, in the neighbourhood of Bilbeis, on the ancient canal that joined the Nile with the Red Sea at Heroopolis, that formed, as it were, the entrance town into the valley from the desert side, and was also, possibly, the meeting-place (לְגֹּשְׁנָה) of Jacob and Joseph. (Gen. xlvi. 28.)[2]

XXI. An interesting representation[3] of what—but for the date thereof—might be taken for a family of Israelites coming into Egypt, is found in the tomb of Chnumhotep at Beni-Hassan. It is dated the sixth year of Usertesen II., that is, some say, about a thousand years before the time of Joseph. The countenance of both men and women is Shemitic, and they wear tunics embroidered in plain, formal patterns, that remind one of the later expression, כְּתֹנֶת פַּסִּים, the coat of many colours, of coloured embroidery or patchwork, Jacob gave Joseph. But, unless the commonly received opinion regarding the Dynasty under which this painting was made be

---

[1] Opp. vol. ii. p. 77—234.

[2] See Brugsch. Geogr. Denkm. vol. i. p. 265, 298 ; Champoll. L'Eg. sous les Pharaons. vol. ii. p. 87, sq.

[3] Rosellini, Mon. Real. pl. xxvi., xxvii. ; Brugsch. Illst. d'Eg. p. 63.

altogether at fault, it can serve as no direct illustration of a
Scriptural narrative. We have,[1] however, a scene of captives
ⲉ̄ⲕⲧ ⲀⲚ Ⲛ̄ ⲅ̄Ⲛ̄ⲕ̄ ⲣ̄ ⲕⲀ-ⲦⲞⲨ Ⲛ̄Ⲧⲣ-ⲅ̄Ⲁ ⲀⲦ̄ⲫ̄-ⲫ ⲀⲉⲉⲚ
taken and brought to Thebes by Thothmes III., building a temple
for his father Amun. Among them are, evidently, Shemites; and,
seeing the children of Israel had been about two hundred years
in Lower Egypt, where they were enduring affliction, when this
building of Thothmes III. took place, there is nothing to hinder
us from recognizing in these Jewish faces some of the same
people who, two hundred years later, were evil-entreated by
Ramses II., and made to build for him his treasure-cities
Pithom and Rameses; for the scribe Keniamen[2] writes to his
master, an overseer of the household of Ramses-Meriamun, "that
he had given grain to the soldiers and to the Aperi-u (Hebrews)
who were drawing stone for the house of Ramses, south of
Memphis." In another Papyrus[3] we have a description of the
Bekhen, or treasure city of Rameses; and in another[4] Pithom is
plainly alluded to. Yet these scraps only make one long for
more. It seems to us that at every line we must alight on
some familiar name, which, like a sunbeam on the dim page
of the history of those days, would guide us aright as to the
time, and link at once the heathen with the Sacred Records.
But, hitherto, we have only just evidence enough of this kind
to whet our inquiry and to try our patience; showing, as it
does, that we might have had it full, had not the very monuments we possess perished in part. A scrap of Papyrus is either
worn away or torn off in the midst of a sentence or of a name
which we long to see either finished or complete, and yet
cannot; because we must be reminded at every step that, even
as regards the letter of the Word of God, we are to walk by
faith, and not by sight. If we had everything made so plain as
to require no searching, our Saviour would not have said,
"Search the Scriptures;" for then we should walk, as it were, by
sight, and our faith, and with it our obedience, would be little
tried, because little required. But God wishes to see in us the
faith that searches His Word as an act of worship, and not as

---

[1] Brugsch, Hist. d'Eg. p. 108.
[2] Papyr. Leyde, I. 349, Chabas, Mél. 2ᵈᵉ Série, p. 144, sq.
[3] Anastasi II. and iv.   [4] Anastasi vi.

an effort of doubt. He has a right to require of us such homage. If we render it, His Word bears us witness of itself; but if we deny Him that obedient worship, our evil conscience there bears us witness of the truth of that Word.

XXII. After giving a description of On that reads oddly while one has present to the mind the sanctity of that City of the Sun, and the profound veneration with which it is always mentioned in Egyptian lore, as among the living on earth, so also by the dead in Amenti, Dean Stanley says:—

"How important was that worship (of the sun) may be best understood by remembering that from it were derived the chief names by which kings and priests were called—' Pha-raoh,' ' The child of the sun,' ' Potiphe-rah,' ' The servant of the sun.' "— p. 89.

This statement contains several oversights. First—even if there were such a term as ' Pha-raoh,' ' pha' does not mean ' the child,' nor ' raoh' ' of the sun.' Secondly—if there were such a word as ' Potiphe-rah,' ' potiphe' does not mean ' the servant,' neither does ' rah,' strictly speaking, mean ' of the sun.'

We saw,[1] when speaking of the etymology of ' Potipherah,' that, according to these ' free inquirers,' the three words פַּר, פֶּרַע, and פַּרְעֹה Phar, Phera, and Par'oh are said to be one and the same term for "the sun." Disciples of Hermogenes— ὅτῳσι δοκεῖ ὅ τι ἂν τίς τῳ θῆται ὄνομα, τοῦτο εἶναι καὶ τὸ ὀρθόν· καὶ ἂν αὖθίς γε ἕτερον μεταθῆται—οὐθὲν ἧττον τὸ ὕστερον ὀρθῶς ἔχειν τοῦ προτέρου κειμένου, ὥσπερ τοῖς οἰκέταις ἡμεῖς μετατιθέμεθα²—" who think that whatever name we give to a thing, even though we change it as often as that of our servants, that name be, nevertheless, the right one." To whom Socrates: ὦ παῖδες 'Ιππονίκου, παλαιὰ παροιμία "ὅτι χαλεπὰ τὰ καλά ἐστιν ὅση ἔχει μαθεῖν" καὶ δὴ καὶ τὸ περὶ τῶν ὀνομάτων οὐ σμικρὸν τυγχάνει ὂν μάθημα· "' Good things,' my children, ' are hard to learn,' said your grandmother; and truly, there is yet something to teach even about names." 'Ορθῶς δή· The sun is represented in hieroglyphic inscriptions as a disc, with or without the ' uræus'; and when the name either precedes or follows the symbol, it is always written RA; in Hebrew letters רע, ra; and the same

---

[1] Above, p. 212.   [2] Cratyl. 3.

thing takes place in hieratic MSS. when the definite article
'pe' or 'pä' is prefixed—in certain constructions only, since RA,
like Ζεύς, is a common as well as a proper noun—we have PE
or PA-RA; Memph. PHE or PHÄ-RA, Heb. פֶרַע, 'the Sun;' and
with the possessive article or pronoun, PA or PHA-RA, 'he of the
Sun,' or 'my Sun.'

As the King of Egypt was styled 'Son of the Sun,' CI-PA
SI-RA (seldom PA-CI), the Sun RA formed part of the name
and of the surname of many Pharaohs, e.g., RA-MSES, or RA-
MESES, 'Sun-horn;' RA-SEQENEN, &c. And they were often
addressed by courtiers and by the people as, " O King of Egypt,
Sun of all nations," &c., as in c̄τ̄н̄ н̄ кнⲗⲗⲉ ⲡⲁ н̄ п̄c̄т̄
н̄т̄т̄-ⲟⲩ¹ said to Sethos I. Chevalier Bunsen, therefore, whom
certain men follow implicitly, makes a mistake when he says²
that kings of Egypt, to whose kingdom RA had set no bounds
but those on which he shines,³ were not addressed as 'Sun,' but
as 'Son of the Sun'; for, again, the messengers sent by the
King of Bekhten to Ramses III., address him thus: "Glory to
thee, ⲡⲁ н̄ п̄c̄т̄ н̄т̄т̄-ⲟⲩ, O thou Sun of all nations, grant
us to live near thee!"⁴ And, again, Ramses-Meriamon is mentioned as п-ⲡⲁ—н̄т̄т̄р ⲁⲁ "the Son, the great God, life,
health, and strength be his! the great Lord Ramses-Meriamon;"⁵ and thus repeatedly.

Some, like Rosellini,⁶ have attempted to draw the term פַּרְעֹה
'Par'o,' Pharaoh, from פֶרַע, 'Phe-rä,' the Sun. So also M.
Chabas,⁷ who gives ⲛⲉ-ⲡⲁ, or ⲡⲣⲁ as the etymology of ' Pha-
raoh;'⁸ while Sir G. Wilkinson⁹ says of " Pharaoh"—

" that it is written in Hebrew Phrah, פַּרְעֹה, and is taken from
the Egyptian word Pire or Phre (pronounced Phra), signifying

---

¹ Brugsch. Mon. vol. i. pl. xlvii. *f.*   ² Æg. Stelle, ii. p. 13.
³ Inscr. of Sethos I. in Brugsch, Mon. vol. i. pl. xiv. *d.*
⁴ Etude sur une Stèle, p. 60.
⁵ Pap. Lee. l. 2, and Pap. Rollin, l. 2, 3, p. 170, 173, in Pap. Harris, ed. Chabas.
⁶ Mon. Stor. vol. i. p. 115.   ⁷ Pap. Harris, p. 173.
⁸ But what are we to think of Mr. Sharpe proposing ⲛⲓ-ⲁ-ⲡ̄н pl.-a-rē, for
the etymology of ' Pharaoh' ? in Rad. of a Vocab. of Eg. Hierogl. p. 68.
⁹ Anc. Egyp. vol. i. p. 43, note.

the Sun, and represented in hieroglyphics by the hawk and globe,
or Sun, over the royal banners. But the word is not derived
from or related to *ouro*, 'king,' as Josephus supposes. Phooro is
like Pharaoh; but the name is Phrah in Hebrew, and Pharaoh is
an unwarranted corruption."

I am sorry to have to differ from Sir G. Wilkinson, whose
opinion on Egyptian matters is worthy of all respect; yet I am
afraid I must lean to the side of Ch. Bunsen, who, while saying[1]
—as we have seen, erroneously—that the kings of Egypt were
not addressed as "O Sun," adds, however, rightly, "Moreover,
the ה in פרעה is not accounted for, if *Phre* or *Phra* be the
etymology thereof. But whether ra, 'sun,' and ouro, 'king,'
were or were not confounded together, certain it is that Pharaoh
comes from the root of *ouro*, and means the 'king.'" And
Ch. Bunsen, I think, is right.

Of those who agree with Ch. Bunsen, Josephus[2] says: ὁ Φα-
ραὼν κατ' Αἰγυπτίους βασιλέα σημαίνει, "Pharaoh means 'king'
with the Egyptians." Geo. Syncellus[3] alludes to this when he
says that the kings of Egypt, τὸ πλεῖστον Φαραὼ λέγονται, are
mostly called Pharaoh, which was an epithet common to them
all. And Cedrenus[4] partly copies it, saying that Pharaoh was
a name common to all the kings of Egypt.[5] Following this
track, Jablonski says:[6] "Fuerunt eruditi qui veteribus, id me-
moriæ prodentibus, fidem denegarent, aut rem in dubium vo-
carent. Sed frustra. Nihil sane verius—communi dialecto
ϕοⲩⲣⲟ regem significat; et Theb. antiquissima ⲡⲣⲣⲟ, quasi
dicas Parro, vel quod Æg. plane idem est ϕⲣⲣⲟ, Pharro."
Brugsch says:[7] "revera vocem Ægyptiacam *p.ara p.arai* fontem
esse Græci ϕαραώ maxime vox congrua Copticæ affirmat, qua
rex ⲉⲣⲣⲟ, ⲟⲩⲣⲟ nominatur." But in his Hist. d'Egypte[8] he

[1] Æg. Stelle, ii. p. 15.   [2] Antiq. Lib. viii. c. 6, 2.
[3] Chron. vol. i. p. 117, ed. D.
[4] P. 73, ed. Bonn. und Mich. Glycas, p. 294
[5] As it is given in a quotation falsely attributed to S. Jerome: "Ægyptiorum
reges omnes tunc Pharaones dicebantur non hoc proprium habentes nomen, sed
pro dignitate reges tunc utebantur hoc nomine, sicut apud nos Imperatores
Augusti appellantur," &c. (Taken from a note at the end of Euseb. Chron.
Armen. vol ii. p. 309.)
[6] Opp. vol. i. p. 374.   [7] De nat. et ind. ling. Æg. p. 24.
[8] P. 156.

swerves from the right path in offering *per-aa*, 'great house,' as
the etymology of 'Pharaoh!' Kosegarten[1] quotes from Champollion's first edition of his *Précis*, p. 72, where he says: "Le
groupe hiéroglyphique qui répond aux mots coptes *prro, prra,
pouro*—se lit simplement *ra*, ou bien avec l'article *pra*, et sig-
nifie *tête, chef*, Bashm. *ra*, Theb. *ro*. Ce groupe pris adjective-
ment veut dire *principal, supérieur, capital*." In his second
edition, however, Champollion altered his opinion for the better
thus: "le groupe[2] hiéroglyphique répondant au mot copte n'est
autre chose que le nom hiéroglyphique phonétique du *Basilic
ou serpent royal*, emblême de la souveraine puissance—dont nous
trouvons la transcription en charactères Grecs, *OTPAI-os*, dans
le texte d'Horapollon. L'image de ce serpent décorait exclu-
sivement le front des rois; c'est là l'origine de l'appellation
ΠΟΤΡΟ *le basilic* donnée aux souverains d'Egypte." Bochart's
etymology for 'Pharaoh,' فرعون 'Phra'ûn,' 'a crocodile,' is
ingenious, like that of J. Simon,[3] فرع, 'Phar'un,' 'chief;'
Olderman's and Perizonius' ΠΙΡϢΜΜΔΙC, i.e., 'excellent,' and
Müller's ΦΔΡΙϢΤΤ, 'patriæ pater,' are absurd; and V. Bohlen's
opinion that[4] פַּרְעֹה appears first distinctly in later history and
in Ezek. xxxii. 2, and is thus formed in Hebrew to agree with
פֶּרַע, 'princeps,' בִּפְרֹעַ פְּרָעוֹת, Judg. v. 2, is specious, false,
and utterly unsound.[5]

But Ch. Bunsen and Champollion are right, the one in
pointing out the fact that those who derive פַּרְעֹה from פֶּרַע,
ΠΡΔ, 'the Sun,' do not account for the ה; and the other for
giving the Egyptian ΔΡΔ, 'basilisc,' the 'emblem of regal
power,' as the etymology of פַּרְעֹה.

In this case it is right to go rather by the letters of פַּרְעֹה,
than by the vowel points, which are of a later date. Those
read PRÂA, or PHARÂA, and seem to express exactly the οὐραῖος,
written ΔΡΔ in Egyptian[6] with the article; so as to make of
פַּרְעֹה, PARÂA, or PHARÂA, ὁ οὐραῖος, i.e., 'the king.' In this

---

[1] De priscâ Æg. Lit. p. 18.   [2] P. 124.
[3] Onom. V. T. p. 355.   [4] Gen. p. 163.
[5] I wonder he never thought of the Burmese 'Phù-rah;' Siamese 'Phrah,'
God, Superior.
[6] Brugsch, Gram. Dem. p. 24.

respect, however, the Hebrew should be written פרעה, in
order to render the two 'a's' ('arms') with which ⲀⲢⲀ or
ⲀⲢⲀⲀ are written. But if it were so, the two עע together
would in Hebrew create an articulation foreign to the Egyptian,
and to the orthography of ⲀⲢⲀⲀ in the old language. So
another letter must be used to supply the place of the second
Ⲁ; and as א would be against Hebrew analogy, ה was adopted
in accordance with it. Thus we have both ע and ה accounted
for.

The fact, nevertheless, abides, that we never find, either in
hieroglyphic inscriptions or in hieratic Papyri, or even in the Demotic monograms derived from the hieratic, the expression ⲚⲀⲢⲀ
or ⲚⲀⲢⲀⲀ for 'the king;' but always ⲤⲦⲚ, ⲤⲞⲨⲦⲈⲚ, 'ruler
or governor.' So that, while we cannot, consistently with fair
etymology, derive פַּרְעֹה from ⲪⲞⲨⲢⲞ or from ⲚⲢⲢⲞ, we may
yet do so from ⲀⲢⲀ, ⲀⲢⲀⲀ, as derived from an older form,
ⲀⲢⲀⲢ; albeit we have not at present any certain clue to the time
when the fem. ⲀⲢⲀⲢ, ⲀⲢⲀⲀ, the symbol of heavenly power
over life and death, and thus of royalty, was used in the masc. for
'king,' and in the fem. for 'queen.' This symbol, however, was
worn by kings in their crown as 'sons of the Sun,' around which
it was coiled when mentioned as 'God'; and thus were they looked
upon as his offspring on earth: for οὐραῖον, says Horapollo,[1]
ὅ ἐστιν Ἑλληνιστὶ βασιλίσκος[2] χρυσοῦν ποιοῦντες, θεοῖς περιτιθέασιν,
"they adorn their gods with an uræus made of gold; αἰῶνα δὲ
λέγουσιν Αἰγύπτιοι διὰ τοῦδε τοῦ ζώου δηλοῦσθαι, for the Egyptians
say that eternity is represented by this animal, which, of all
other serpents, is alone immortal. Wherefore, since it seems to
have power over life and over death, do they put it upon the head
of their gods." Although it is impossible to speak of such etymologies with certainty, yet it seems probable both that the
Greek οὐραῖος, which I can find only in Horapollo, was derived
at Alexandria, from ⲞⲨⲢⲞ, 'king,' and not from οὐρά, 'tail,' and
that ⲚⲀⲢⲀ or ⲚⲀⲢⲀⲀ are the origin of פַּרְעֹה, inasmuch as all
these terms, ara, arar, araa, ourr, rro, ouro, 'uræus,' 'diadem,'
and 'king' seem connected together.

---

[1] Lib. I. c. i. ed. Leem.   [2] Regulus, Plin. N. H. viii. 21, &c.

Anyhow, certain it is that Pharaoh does not mean 'Child of the Sun,' as Dr. Stanley says, but simply 'the king;' for רעה can never be רע; neither does 'Potipherah' mean 'servant of the Sun'; but only 'he whom the Sun gave,' Ἡλιόδωρος.

This divine origin of kings, in which every sovereign of Egypt prided himself, calling upon the Sun as upon his father, kept up throughout the kingdom a feeling of servile and cringing subjection on the part of the people, and of a haughty and absolute despotism on that of the king. "Who is the LORD," said Pharaoh to Moses, "that I should let Israel go? I know not the LORD, neither will I let Israel go;" language worthy of a successor of Ramses II., who δι' αὐτῶν δὲ τῶν αἰχμαλώτων ἅπαντα κατεσκεύασε,[1] employed no Egyptians, but only captives in the construction of his treasure cities; among others, of Pithom and of Rameses. "To please my master, Bek-en-Ptah," said the scribe Kaniser, "I have obeyed the order my master gave me, saying, Distribute rations to the soldiers as well as to the Aperi-u (Hebrews) who draw the stone for the great Bekben (palace or royal treasure city) of King Ramses-Meriamun, lover of justice, who are under the charge of the Madjai Amencman. I give them rations every month according to the excellent directions my master gave me."[2]

This collateral witness to the bondage of the Hebrews is interesting, especially from the hands of one of the נֹגְשִׂים, taskmasters themselves, giving account to one of "Pharaoh's officers" ⲤⲬⲀⲓ-ⲞⲨ, סֹפְרִים, which, in Egyptian drawings, are never absent from a scene of labour, or of corn and of wine harvest. But as the term 'Aperi,' in which we may recognise עברי, pl. 'Aperi-u,' occurs among a colony sent by Ramses IV. into Southern Egypt, after the date of the Exodus, we must in that case suppose that all the Israelites did not leave Egypt with Moses, but that detachments of them were drafted with other captives into the interior of the kingdom. But, whether in Lower or in Upper Egypt, they were both dreaded, detested, and despised, until the hour of their deliverance came. Yet this state of bondage, of a nationality crushed by oppression to

[1] Diod. Sic. lib. l. 56.
[2] Pap. Hierat. Leyd. i. 248, pl. 6, l. 5, in Chabas Mél. Egyptol. p. 49.

the lowest state of degradation, was, if I may say so, a necessary
antecedent to the display of God's power in delivering the Hebrews from the iron yoke of such thraldom, to make them His
people. They were ever reminded of it. As Dr. Stanley says,
they were to let their servants rest on the Sabbath day, because
they themselves had also been slaves; and every fiftieth year
they were to return to their possessions, in token that they
were at first bondmen in Egypt, then God's servants, to whom
He gave the land which is His own.

XXIII. We cannot, therefore, agree with Dr. Stanley that—

" The bare desert and the bold hills of Palestine formed a wholesome and perpetual contrast to the magnificence of Egypt."

The children of Israel, indeed, when in the desert, longed for
the vegetables they had in profusion in Egypt, even in their servitude ; but even these did not grow without their toiling hard
and long for them, as slaves do there to this day. " For the
land, whither thou goest in to possess it," said Moses to the
people, " is not as the land of Egypt, from whence ye came out,
where thou sowedst thy seed, and wateredst it with thy foot, as
a garden of herbs : but the land whither ye go to possess it, is
a land of hills and valleys, and drinketh water of the rain of
heaven : a land which the LORD thy GOD careth for : the eyes
of the LORD thy GOD are always upon it, from the beginning of
the year even unto the end of the year."[1] Never was Egypt
thus spoken of ; neither can we suppose that even the exuberant
growth on the plains of Egypt, that was doomed and destroyed
for the sake of God's people, could ever look like the " Promised
Land," " the land flowing with milk and honey," " which the
LORD careth for." It was enough His eye should be upon it.
His presence alone makes every desert to rejoice and every wilderness to blossom as the rose. Where His presence goes with
His people there He gives them rest.

XXIV. Dr. Stanley then goes on to say—

"There were two other traces of their dependent position in
Egypt ;—one is the disease of leprosy which for the first time
appears after the stay in Egypt ;—the other relic of repugnance
between the two races—is the ass—which was regarded by the

[1] Deut. xi. 10—12.

Egyptians as the exclusive, the contemned symbol of the Nomadic race who had left them."—p. 95, 90.

As regards the leprosy, the fact that it is mentioned only after the stay of the Israelites in Egypt, is by no means conclusive as to its having originated among them while there. For, unless either Abraham, Isaac, or Jacob, or some member of their families had been leprous, there would have been no occasion to mention it during their time. Likewise, unless Potiphar, his wife, or Pharaoh, had been so afflicted, it could not have been mentioned as regards Egypt; unless it had been sent as a scourge, like the plague or famine. But it might exist among the Egyptians in single cases, without being an epidemic; and the Israelites are as likely to have caught it from the Egyptians, or from some other of the captive strangers then in Egypt, as these from the Israelites. Moreover, the several words for 'leprosy' and 'leprous' found in Coptic writings must, probably, have their origin in some term of the Old language we may yet discover, when the unknown diseases mentioned in the Berlin and Leyden Medical Papyri have been ascertained and recognised; or when we get additional evidence on the diseases of Egypt.[1]

XXV. Still less is there to warrant our thinking the contempt with which Dr. Stanley says the Egyptians looked upon the ass, a remnant of their hatred for the 'lepers,' meaning the Israelites, whom Manetho says Amenophis expelled from Egypt. Not only do we find asses forming a part of the stock of farms in the days of Shupho and of Assa before Abraham's time, but we also find both Bâl (Baal) and Sôtech or Seth, the Typhon of Egypt, represented as an ass, with his tail erect, in monuments centuries older than the coming of Jacob's family into Egypt. Dr. Stanley might as well attribute to the hatred of the Egyptians for the Hebrews, the obloquy in which the ass, as an animal, is now, and has been in every country,—yea even in Palestine,—as the contempt the Egyptians are supposed to have had for it. Much rather, were the Hebrews,—perhaps as having at first come to Egypt on asses, or as using them rather

---

[1] One of these Coptic terms ⳠⲰⲂⲢ, or ⳠⲰⲂⲀⲢ, is, indeed, compared with רַחַם; but, besides such a comparison having little to warrant it, were it true, it would refer rather to the itch than to the leprosy.

than horses, during their bondage—connected with Egyptian
ideas, associations and images already ripe and multiplied in
the land when they made their first appearance in it. Plutarch's
authority, which is always quoted in these matters, agrees
thereto :[1] ὅλως τὸν ὄνον οὐ καθαρὸν ἀλλὰ δαιμονικὸν ἡγοῦνται ζῶον
εἶναι διὰ τὴν πρὸς ἐκεῖνον (Τυφῶνα) ὁμοιότητα, " in short, and altogether, do the inhabitants of Busiris (in L. Egypt) and those of
Lycopolis (Sint. U. Egypt), look upon the ass, not as a clean
animal, but as upon one connected with the Evil Spirit (to
which they dedicate it, c. 50) from its resemblance to it." And
to show that, if so be the Hebrews were by the Egyptians connected with the contempt shown to the ass, the Hebrews only
came in for their share with others in that contempt, and were
not the sole objects thereof ; Plutarch tells us (id. c. 31) that
τῶν Περσικῶν βασιλέων ἐχθραίνοντες μάλιστα τὸν Ὦχον ὡς ἐναγῆ
καὶ μιαρὸν, ὄνον ἐπωνόμασαν· " hating Ochus most of all the Persian
kings, as accursed and abominable, they surnamed him 'the Ass ;'
when he, saying, This ass then shall devour your ox—slew Apis
on the spot ; as Demon relates. But those who say that when
after the battle (with Osiris) Typhon fled for seven days on an
ass, and having escaped γεννῆσαι παῖδας Ἱεροσόλυμον καὶ Ἰουδαῖον,
αὐτόθεν εἰσὶ κατάδηλοι τὰ Ἰουδαϊκὰ παρέλκοντες εἰς τὸν μῦθον, begat
his sons Hierosolymus and Judæus, show plainly that their
object is to drag Jewish affairs into this fable."

XXVI. As to the 'points of contact' between the Israelites
and the Egyptians of which Dr. Stanley speaks—there is, of
course, nothing to hinder Moses from having wrought imple-
ments for the Tabernacle after the modified pattern of what he
had seen in Egypt. He was learned in all the wisdom of the
Egyptians, and he would, naturally, turn it to good account, as
a handmaid to his superior knowledge received from GOD.
Many well-intentioned people have taken needless offence at this
idea ; but assuredly, and as S. Paul taught much later, that
every creature of GOD is good—when "sanctified by the Word
of GOD and prayer," so also there was nothing in the Egyptian
designs adopted by Moses that was in itself objectionable. The
use alone to which they were put, made them either good or bad.

XXVII. But as to 'points of contrast' between the Israelites and

[1] De Is. et Osir. c. 30.

the Egyptians to which Dr. Stanley refers, they must have been, as indeed they were, as many and as wide apart, as the grossest idolatry and Revealed Truth can be. And it is hardly the work of an earnest philosopher, whose business is with τῷ ὄντι ἤ ὄν, with the real character of the Egyptian and of the Hebrew worships respectively, to find points of contrast between two religions which can have nothing in common, save the one fact that they each worship something. This system of a "wide, all-embracing worship" is not true, and therefore not philosophical; for how can Truth and error, light and darkness, exist together? Neither can sound philosophy consider it from a Christian point of view, except to see the disagreement of its two principal categories; the one τὸ ὄν ὡς ἀληθές that which is —Truth; the other τὸ μὴ ὄν, ὡς ψεῦδος, that which is not—falsehood.

XXVIII. The following note, therefore, does not say much—

"If it be true that the Egyptian belief in a future state was inseparably united with the belief in transmigration, and that from this sprang the worship of animals, then the exclusion of the true doctrine from the Mosaic theology may have been occasioned by the necessity of getting rid of this false excrescence—a remarkable instance of primeval Protestantism. Bunsen's Egypt, iv. 049."—p. 99.

The Egyptians did believe both in the immortality and in the transmigration of the soul; but their worship of animals was in no wise connected with it; since among the forms of birds and of reptiles the soul in transmigration was allowed to take, several never were worshipped; and other animals that were worshipped are never mentioned as inhabited by a human soul.[2] Thus the Egyptians worshipped the seven sacred cows and the bulls Apis and Mnevis, for reasons we have already seen, as being the abode of the soul of Osiris.[3] The he-goat of

---

[1] Arist. Metaph. iii. 2, 3.

[2] Neither were they worshipped for the sake of their own soul, as Porphyrius tells us, (De Abstin. 10), for at least as far as I know, we have not authentic documents to show that the Egyptians believed that animals had souls, and Porphyrius is often incorrect. But they were worshipped as living emblems of some quality, or of some principle in nature; if not consecrated to some god.

[3] Plut. de Is. et Os. 20, 29, &c., and above. p. 191.

Mendes was worshipped for a very different reason from that of
transmigration; so also with the ram, sacred to Amun and worshipped in certain cities, yet eaten in one of them, as Strabo tells
us; the cat was held sacred for its having slain the serpent enemy
of the sun; as we see in the XVIIth Ch. of the Ritual of the Dead,
and elsewhere repeatedly; the dog was honoured for the sake of
Anubis according to certain legends preserved by Plutarch; the
crocodile, the symbol of Egypt and of darkness, was like the
ram, worshipped in certain cities, yet eaten in others, as Herodotus tells us; the lion and the jackal were also worshipped for
particular reasons; the hawk was sacred to the sun, not because
of transmigration, but because it was thought to consist only "of
blood and of spirit" as Porphyrius[1] tells us; since the soul when
purified, took the form of a hawk, as being then fit to fly upwards
to the source of Light and Life; the ibis was sacred to Thoth,
as frogs were to Kek the god of darkness, and as being thought
the symbols of the first matter ὕλη, of the male principle in
Nature; so were serpents, which represented the female principle; fishes of various sorts were sacred to some god or goddess;
yet so little had they to do with the transmigration of the soul
into them, that one, the oxyrrhinchus, is the constant symbol of
the corpse ϬⲀⲚⲦⲒ or ϬⲀⲚⲦⲞⲦ after the soul and the human
germ have left it, and when lying on a litter; the common
beetle of Egypt, seen on every sand-bank working the ball that
contains its eggs, was sacred to the noonday sun as Cheper,
creator and vivifier, not assuredly, as at any time the abode of
man's soul; and lastly the ass was alternately worshipped, hated,
dreaded, or despised, as the personification of Seth, Suteeh,
and of Baal, and not as being the abode of a human soul.

But the Egyptian doctrine of transmigration such as we find
it taught in their Rituals, however philosophically impossible,
was nevertheless free from the absurdities with which it pleased
the popular conceit of the Greeks to clothe it, as being a doctrine "of barbarians." Yet they were far in advance of the
Greeks; and Plato would, perhaps, never have written his
Phædrus as he did, had he not studied the wisdom of Egypt at
On; for whatever be the errors the want of a Revelation made
them commit, it is certain that in Egypt both the immortality

[1] De Abst. 9. ed. Müll.

of the soul, and the reward of the good, together with the punishment of the wicked at the bar of the tribunal of Osiris, in Amenti, were taught long before the times of Moses or of Joseph, and even before Abraham set foot at the court of Pharaoh.

Even then they taught at On that the world (κόσμος) was divided into Upper and Lower ($\overline{2\rho}$ and $\overline{\chi\rho}$); the Upper world consisted of the upper Nûn, "the waters above the firmament," deified as Nùt, on the back of which, as on the back of his mother, the Sun, Rä at his rising, and Cheper at noon, was supposed to sail in his bark. When he reached the western horizon, he was then called Tum or Atum,[1] and held even more sacred than during his course across the upper heavens; for he was thought to be then passing on from the world of the living to the world of the dead, Amenti, and there to shine over the plains of Hatapham and on the fields of Aalu,[2] ploughed and sown by the souls in transmigration, and watered by their Häpi-môu after the manner of Egypt above. Between these two upper and nether worlds, which were both eternal, was this our earth, then thought immoveable, and everything in it that is liable to change or to decay.

Once free from its earthly body, the 'sekhù'—that is, the soul with the human germ—was received at the gates of Amenti, where it was supposed to reach by slow degrees what was called $\overline{\Pi2\rho}$ ᎭᎭ $2\rho o\tau$,[3] the 'manifestation of day,' that is, the entering into the region of pure Light and of Eternal Life. First was set before him the 'crown of justification' given to those who were proclaimed righteous, which made them friends of the gods; and with that prize before him the sekhù began his journey, beset with dangers from crocodiles, from serpents, and from other monsters, from the lake of fire, from the hillet on which the condemned were beheaded, unto the hall of Osiris, where the soul was put into one scale, Truth or Righteousness into the other, and then weighed, ere it received its reward.[4]

---

[1] The god of On. He was specially honoured there; whence the city was called 'Pa-tum,' ' Of Tum.' This is not the Pithom of Ex. i.

[2] ' Ala' or ' Aoru ı' the possible etymology of ' Elysian.'

[3] Rit. ch. xvii., title, &c.

[4] One of those dead told of a very different journey to S. Coluthus. See Zurga Codd. Memph. p. 43.

During this progress the soul might at a certain point ιρι
ⲭⲡⲣ-ⲟⲩ ⲛ̄ⲃ ⲛ ⲁⲁⲣ-ⲧⲟⲩ-ϥ, assume whatever form it
liked, whether of a golden hawk, of a prince, of a god, of a
lotus-flower, of Ptah, of the Phœnix, or of the egret ; and lastly,
the form under which it is represented hovering over the
mummy of the body it had left, that of the divine hawk with a
human head, when τελία μὲν οὖν οὖσα καὶ ἐπτερωμένη μετεωροπορεῖ,[1]
" being perfected and gifted with wings, it flies upwards" to
Him who gave it, and whence, according to Egyptian notions, it
was to return after thousands of years to inhabit the same body
it once had on earth. Plato, therefore, does not represent correctly the Egyptian doctrine, if he meant for it—ἔνία καὶ εἰς
θηρίου βίον ἀνθρωπίνη ψυχὴ ἀφικνεῖται, καὶ ἐκ θηρίου, ὅς ποτε ἄνθρωπος
ἦν, πάλιν εἰς ἄνθρωπον[2]—that there, at a certain stage of the
migration through φᾶης, Hades, "the soul of man reaches the
life of some beast, and he that was once a man again out of a
beast into a man ;" for, the assuming of these several forms was
at the option of the sekhû. It is therefore more probable that
the soul should then put on the form of some object loved or
honoured during its former life on earth, than that it should first
honour that object during life, in order to inhabit it after death.

The worship of animals, therefore, was not so much connected
with the doctrine of the transmigration of the soul into the
form of an animal, psychologically absurd as it is, as this doctrine
was the result of the worship of animals for powers of nature
they were supposed to represent. We may, therefore, look upon
such stories as the dialogue written by Æneas Gazæus[3] on
transmigration, as the offspring of Greek imagination, or as a
popular and erroneous opinion, rather than Truth, though it
were invented with a good motive.

Theophrastus—"The Egyptians seem to think that the same
soul puts on the body either of a man, of an ox, of a dog, of a
bird, or of a fish ; and so, according to them, now this soul
feeds on the ground like an animal, say an ant or a camel ; νῦν
δὲ εἰς ἰχθὺν ὀλισθήσασα κῆτος ἢ μεμβρὰς γενομένη τὴν θάλατταν ἔδυ,
and then slipping into a fish, and becoming either a whale or a
sprat, it swims away into the sea."

[1] Phædr. 55. ed. Lond.   [2] Ibid. 61.
[3] Bib. Vet. Pat. vol. ii. p. 378, ed. Gall.

Αἰγύπτιος—ἐπὶ τῆς τερατολογίας· εὐδαιμονοίην ἂν εἰ κάμηλος, ἢ μέμβρας, ἢ κολοιὸς γενοίμην. The Egyptian—"For shame! to speak thus of such marvels. Happy should I be to become either a camel, a sprat, or a jackdaw."

Anitheus—"But, O Egyptian, do you laugh? For my part, I wonder that Theophrastus, knowing these things, yet mixes among Egyptians," &c.

XXIX. All this is very much, on the part of the Greeks, like the connexion of the ass with Jews on the part of the Egyptians. Yet, in fact, the Egyptian Rituals of the Dead, and their doctrine of transmigration,—or, more correctly, of their passage through the regions of Amenti, free as it is from all the sensuality of other heathen creeds, stands in bright contrast to them. Some of the chapters of the Ritual of the Dead remind one of like passages in the Rig or in the Sáma Véda; but there is a greater interest attached to these Egyptian Scriptures, in that they place before us the actual creed, faith, and hope of that wonderful people in a distinct and visible shape.

So entirely did a true Egyptian live in the future hope of his safe passage through Amenti to the hall of Osiris, and thence to final emancipation into the realms of eternal light, that, as Diodorus tells us, τὸν μὲν ἐν τῷ ζῆν χρόνον εὐτελῆ παντελῶς εἶναι νομίζουσι, τὸν δὲ μετὰ τὴν τελευτὴν δι' ἀρετὴν μνημονευθησόμενον περὶ πλείστου ποιοῦνται, "they held the time of their present life very cheap, but prized most highly the time after death, if that was to be remembered for virtue's or for merit's sake. Wherefore they call the houses in which men live καταλύσεις, 'lodgings' or 'inns,' on account of their short stay in them; but they look upon their sepulchres as eternal homes for the length of time they are to spend in Hades."[1] This their faith was indeed to them "the substance of things hoped for, the evidence of things not seen;" they made good proof of it by the contrast they established between the houses of their pilgrimage on earth, not one of which subsists at present, and the houses eternal in their heavens, which they prepared for themselves during their lifetime, and which shall endure as long as their land exists. They were, of all heathens, both the most religious and the most practical of their faith.

[1] Diod. Sic. Lib. i. c. 51, 92, 93.

This faith led to their embalming of the body, which the soul was to revisit after thousands of years,[1] and which had prayers said for its preservation during that time.[2] There is something very beautiful in this idea, if we could receive it; but, especially in that which Plato seems to have partly borrowed thence, ἀνάμνησις ἐκείνων ἅ ποτ' εἶδεν ἡμῶν ἡ ψυχὴ συμπορευθεῖσα θεῷ καὶ ὑπεριδοῦσα ἃ νῦν εἶναί φαμεν, καὶ ἀνακύψασα εἰς τὸ ὂν ὄντως, "of the recollection of those things which our soul once saw while it walked with God, and both looked down upon the things we say do now exist, and also looked up towards that which really is,"—Eternal Truth.[3] Whatever truth or error there may be in this, the very slight allusion to the resurrection of the body —if this be what Dr. Stanley means by the "true doctrine"—in the writings of Moses was assuredly not owing to any consideration he might have, one way or the other, for Egyptian ideas. The theocratic government of the people of GOD was so peculiar and so exceptionable, as to account for any deviation from what we might think, à priori, necessary for it. GOD spake unto Moses, wrought wonders, gave His Law amid thunders and lightnings, led His people by the cloud,—in short, was, so to speak, present, though Himself not seen; and being thus present, He required obedience to Him for the time being, and not for the sake of promises yet afar off; so that the economy of the Theocratic dispensation was, as indeed it might be, fully wrought out, without allusion to another and future state, the bliss of which would but be the presence of GOD which they then enjoyed. It is therefore difficult to see what this "primeval Protestantism" of Chevalier Bunsen, mentioned by Dr. Stanley, can possibly mean; since GOD's rule over His people, and His laws for them, had no other reference to Egypt than to bid them forget it, and abjure all they had seen and heard there. It is one of those high sounding sentences, with more wind than weight, that are written only to fill a line or to finish a period. We might as well say, with even more truth, that the Egyptians were the most orthodox Romanists of their time.

XXX. So, also, does Dean Stanley make a very good ending of this lecture, by a description of the winged sun seen under the portal and over the entrance of every temple in Egypt,

---

[1] Rit. ch. 89.   [2] Ibid. ch. 45, 154.   [3] Phæd. c. 61.

which he understands to be an emblem of a beneficent overruling Power—

"a direct expression of the feeling which has been made immortal in the words 'Under the shadow of Thy wings shall be my refuge.'"—p. 100.

I am afraid, however, that this beautiful imagery will hardly hold together, and that the idea of 'protection' is very doubtful, as connected with this symbol; although 'protection' is very plainly indicated through the vulture holding the symbol of life, and overshadowing with his wings the person of the king, as often represented in sculptures;[1] with which may be compared the origin of the ἀετός, ἀέτωμα, or δέλτα of Greek temples, which some Corinthian architect

—θεῶν ναοῖσιν οἰω-
νῶν βασιλῆα ἐθου-
μον[2] θῆκεν[3]

although the symbolism of the vulture and of the eagle respectively be entirely different. But the wings added to the orb of the sun on Egyptian buildings, both public and private, are the wings of the common beetle (scarabeus sacer, L.), sacred to the sun, and an emblem of it at noon, as Creator and Generator of the world. Certain Egyptian paintings[4] show this plainly,[5] as does also the woodcut given by Sir G. Wilkinson.[6] Although the idea of "protection of the Deity," as Sir G. Wilkinson says, might be attached to this symbol, yet, if it was so, it was not to the expanded wings, but to the Sun itself, as 'Cheper' in the middle of the sky, as in the centre of a portal. For the real idea of 'protection' for the Egyptians lay in their idea of 'heaven,' which they represented as a woman crouching to feed and to shelter her offspring—whence heaven is always feminine (ПЄ-Т, ТПЄ); and with the Hebrews such idea lay, individually, in the familiar sight of a fowl, be it a hen or an eagle, sheltering

[1] As, e.g., on the Stele, in V¹. De Rougé's Etude sur une Stèle, &c.
[2] La., one at each end of the building.   [3] Ol. xiii. 29.
[4] Such as Brugsch. Mon. i. pl. xviii.
[5] And plainer yet, when compared with such passages as, e.g., Sama Véda, ii. 6, 3, 7, 2, "garb'hé mátub." Ityádi.
[6] Anc. Eg. vol. v. p. 476.

her young under her wings,[1] and generally in the Eastern idea
of 'heaven' as father and shield protecting the earth, found
from Aryâna to Ultima Thule, "and made immortal," as Dr.
Stanley says, by the words, שֶׁמֶשׁ וּמָגֵן יְהוָה אֱלֹהִים, "The
LORD GOD is a sun and shield."[2]

LECTURE V.—THE EXODUS.

"THE history," strictly speaking, "of the Jewish Church,"
says Dr. Stanley, "begins with the Exodus."

"In one sense, indeed, History herself was born on that night
when Moses led forth his countrymen from the land of Goshen.
(Bunsen's *Egypt*, i. 23.)"

Strange birth, which took place nobody knows when; yet
stranger beginning, which no one can point out! 'History,'
Ιστορία, however, implies neither dates nor an unbroken thread
of events; it is simply the knowledge of facts acquired by personal inquiry, be the facts detached or connected. In this
sense, therefore, was history born long before the date assigned
to it by Chevalier Bunsen; if not, how can he, speaking as he
does, claim our belief in the 'endless genealogies' of his Egyptian gods, heroes, and kings, which he carries some thirty thousand years further back than the 'history' of which he gives
here the beginning, and than that of Genesis? The marvel is,
how there can be men found to follow such a guide, who leads
them backwards and forwards, and who contradicts himself.
Common sense, however, tells us that 'history' begins with
the first authentic narrative of facts we have; and this, as
proved by its origin, by its own intrinsic evidence, and by the
unanimous voice of the Church of CHRIST, is—the Book of
Genesis. Chevalier Bunsen and his school will have long moul-
dered into dust, and their voice will have long ceased to be
heard, when this Word will yet live, and yet speak.

[1] Deut. xxxii. 11; Ruth ii. 12; Ps. xvii. 8; lxiii. 7; S. Matt. xxiii. 37, &c.
[2] Ps. lxxxiv. 12.

I. This, then, is the beginning of our history :—

"IN THE BEGINNING GOD CREATED THE HEAVENS AND THE EARTH."

When?—In the beginning.

"And the earth was without form and void, and darkness was upon the face of the deep. And the Spirit of GOD moved upon the face of the waters."

When?—When the earth was a preparing, both before and according to some, during the periods of encrinites, palms, ichthyosauri, iguanodons, anoplotheria, dinotheria, (Chev. Bunsen's early Egyptian dynasties,) &c.; after the earth had settled in its present shape, while the surface thereof was being prepared for man, and after the last great catastrophe that led to its actual settled condition. Then followed the present creation and arrangement of our system, Gen. i. 3, sq.; when, possibly, the earth, which may have experienced a greater nutation of her poles than at present, and which until then might have moved in a wider orbit, began to revolve around the sun, then made the centre of our planetary system. I am well aware of the difficulties of this explanation; but I find greater ones in other theories. At all events, and until I can find something on which I may rely with greater certainty, I will believe that no display of GOD's Almighty power could be too great, in creating, forming, arranging, and disposing a world like our own, on which He was to place man, created after His own image and similitude, and afterwards even send His own SON.

II. As with the world then, so also with the history of the Jewish Church in the popular acceptation of the term 'History,' we can hardly take for its origin one event more than another, unless we can fix the date thereof, as a beginning. But the beginning must be placed at the origin, and this origin at the first mention of the man who is looked upon as the father of the people whose history we study. The beginning of a stream is the spring thereof, even though the stream disappear underground during some portion of its first course. So also, as regards the Jewish Church, we have seen that, albeit it could not be constituted into a 'church' ere there were people enough born to form it, and until these, again, were ostensibly brought out from among other nations, yet that the Jewish Church, properly speaking, began in Abrabam, who was himself a more perfect type of what the Church of God should be in the world, than even the people of Israel when leaving Egypt. For this coming out of Egypt was but the fulfilment of what God said to Abraham, after he had himself been called out of Ur of the Chaldees. Until Moses appeared as deliverer, the Church of God had been first one man, then a family, and continued as such more or less, until it was finally constituted, after the departure from Egypt and the baptism in the Red Sea; but whether a man, a family, or a people, they were ἐκκλησίαι, 'called out,' separate and distinct, through a special rite, inheritors of God's promises, and walking by faith in them, as well on the way from Ur to Egypt as in the house of Nymphas. Abraham is the pattern of every true member of that Church, walking under God's eye; Moses is the pattern of what every leader in that Church, frail and militant, should be, in faith, in patience, and in long-suffering, for his Master's sake.

III. Passing over the mention of Moses by Strabo, and Diodorus, Dr. Stanley professes to give the history of Moses, "as it appeared to his nation at the time of the Christian Æra," (p. 105, sq.) We should never have done if we tarried by all the traditions about Moses; whether in the ' Life of Moses,' דברי הימים or elsewhere. Keeping, therefore, to the Scripture account as to the only narrative on which we can rely, we come to the name of ' Moses' on which Dr. Stanley expresses himself in this wise :—

"The child was brought up as the princess's son, and the memory of the incident was long cherished in the name given to the foundling of the water's side. Its Hebrew form is *Mosheh*, from *Masah*, 'to draw out'—because I have *drawn* him out of the water. But this is probably the Hebrew termination given to an Egyptian word signifying ' saved from the water.' "

And in a note to this :

"In Coptic, *mo* = water, and *ushe* = saved. This is the explanation given by Josephus (Ant. ii. 0. 0; *c. Apion.* i. 31), and confirmed by the Greek form of the word adopted in the LXX., Μωϋσῆ, and thence in the Vulgate, *Moyses*, &c. Brugsch (*Histoire d'Egypte*, 157, 173) renders the name *Mes* or *Messou* = child, borne by one of the princes of Ethiopia under Rames II., appearing also in the names *Amosis* and Thuth-*Mosis.*"—p. 100.

The Dean, I am sorry to say, makes several mistakes in these few lines.

First—*Mosheh* does not come from *masah*, but from *mashah*.

Secondly—he copies the reading 'I have *drawn*' or 'I drew him out' of the water, which the Hebrew does not clearly mean.

Thirdly—he makes another mistake in giving "Coptic *mo* = water, and *ushe* = saved" as etymology for 'Moses' or 'Mosheh ;' for *ushe* does not mean 'saved.'

Fourthly—Brugsch does not say '*Mes* or *Messon*,' but "*Mes* or *Messou* ;" both passive participles, one by position, the other by termination.

Fifthly—when Dr. Stanley writes "*Amosis* and Thuth-*Mosis*," what does he make of 'A' in 'Amosis,' which he writes as a prefix to 'mosis ?'

The truth is, that, like Φονλομφανίχ, Μωϋσῆς has tried the skill of critics, though hardly more successfully. I will briefly mention the chief opinions. J. Simon[1] remarks very justly that מֹשֶׁה from מָשָׁה can only mean 'drawing' and 'extraction,' but not 'drawn ;' for this would be מָשׁוּי. Bochart[2] contends for this Hebrew etymology on the strength of מְשִׁיתִהוּ which he renders 'extraxi eum,' the more so as מָשָׁה is only said of 'water ;'[3] and he quotes also Is. xliii. 11, which, however, has nothing to do with it.

Glassius[4] says that since מֹשֶׁה means 'extrahens,' this name was given him prophetically, as being he who was to bring the Israelites out of Egypt. And as to an Egyptian etymology he adds, "nugæ hæ sunt." Buxtorf fil.[5] quotes Abarbanel, to show that the etymology must be Hebrew. Hottinger[6] quotes R. Gedalia who taught that Moses' mother gave him the name 'Mosheh.'[7] Hottinger also quotes the Syrian Isa Bar-ali, who says that the name of Moses the prophet means محا من ملكه

---

[1] Onom. V. T. p. 240.

[2] E.g. 2 Sam. xxii. 17, (Lq. Ps. xviii. 17.)

[4] Philol. Sac. l. p. 711, ed. D.

[5] Dissert. Phil. Theol. l. c. 46, ed. 1645.

[6] Hist. Or. p. 76.

[7] But he had many others such as Jared, Jedor, &c., mentioned by S. Jerome, and also in the ספר דברי הימים p. 4. sq.

'taken out of the water;' but, says the same author, he was
also called Paalthiel, Jamehil, &c.

Mahomet, of course, often alludes to Moses in the Coran.[1]
He does not explain his name; but in Sur. xx. 33, sq., he
refers to a revelation from GOD to Moses' mother, in which
GOD commanded her to take and put him into an ark and to
throw him في اليم 'into the sea,' which Abulfeda[2] renders by
في النيل 'into the Nile.'[3] Makrizi,[4] however, mentions the
village of Shabrân, on the eastern bank of the Nile, on the
borders of Tora, as the birthplace of Moses; and that there he
was thrown into the sea (the Nile.) S. Ephrem[5] only alludes
to the meaning of the name 'Moses' with a play upon the words,
very beautiful in the original, but that cannot be translated,

ܒܢܘܗܝ ܒܢܘܗܝ ܕܚܙܐ ܗܘܐ. ܗܘܐ ܗܢܘ ܕܚܙܐ ܡܢ ܥܠܝܗܝ ܒܢܘܗܝ
ܕܢܛܦܐ ܗܘܐ. "He saw the light in the river; he who had
been cast into it to be deprived of light." And S. Ephrem goes
on to give as his opinion that Moses had received his name from
his mother, &c.

As to the probable etymology of מֹשֶׁה J. D. Michaelis[6] mentions some of these opinions, but adds, that "he cannot deny
that an Egyptian etymology is the most probable. It may be,
however, that Pharaoh's daughter did give an Egyptian name
to Moses, which Moses rendered into Hebrew," &c. And on
these lines of the Sibylline oracle,[7]

—ἡγητῆρα καταστήσει μέγαν ἄνδρα
Μωσῆν, ὃν παρ' ἕλους βασίλισσ' εὑροῦσ' ἐκομίζει—

Hottinger remarks: "illud tamen elucet, Judæorum testimonio
parentes Mosi nomen indidisse Hebraicum. Alterum Mose
Ægyptiacum est." In proof of which, Philo[5] says Pharaoh's
daughter gave Moses a name according to etymology, as having

---

[1] Eg. Sur. xix., xx., xxvii., &c.   [2] Hist. A. 1. p. 30.

[3] Upon which Ibn Batûtah enlarges, saying, ليس في الرض نهر يسمى
بحرا غيره "there is no other river in the world called 'sea' but the Nile."
He errs, of course; since the Ganges is repeatedly called 'Gangâ-sâgara,' the
Ganges ocean, &c.

[4] Hist. Copt. p. 37.   [5] Comm. in Exod. vol. I. p. 198.
[6] Suppl. ad Lex. Heb. p. 1562.   [7] Or. Sibyll. p. 305, sq. ed. Gale.
[5] De V. Mos. p. 605.

taken him out of the water, τὸ γὰρ ὕδωρ μῶς ὀνομάζουσιν Αἰγύπτιοι, κ.τ.λ., for the Egyptians call the water 'môs.' And Josephus[1] says, indeed, τὸ γὰρ ὕδωρ μῶ οἱ Αἰγύπτιοι καλοῦσιν, ὑσῆς δὲ τοὺς ἐξ ὕδατος σωθέντας, that the Egyptians called the water 'mô,' and those who are saved out of it 'uses'; but he evidently knew nothing about it, although Dr. Stanley relies on his authority; for elsewhere[2] when refuting Manetho's name for Moses, 'Osarsiph,'[3] he says that this name does not agree with 'Moses,' Μωϋσῆς, as 'saved out of the water,' τὸ γὰρ ὕδωρ οἱ Αἰγύπτιοι μῶϋ καλοῦσω, "for the Egyptians call the water môü;" thus contradicting himself when he says that, 'water' which before he called μω, is now μωῦ; making nothing of σης. Chæremon, however, who was an Egyptian, did not consider Μωϋσῆς an Egyptian name; for, as we have seen, speaking of the Exodus under Moses and Joseph, he adds: Αἰγύπτια δ' αὐτοῖς ὀνόματα εἶναι τῷ μὲν Μωϋσῇ Τισιθὲν, τῷ δὲ Ἰωσήφ Πετεσίφ, "their Egyptian names were for Moses 'Tisithen,' and for Joseph 'Peteseph.'" S. Clement of Alexandria[4] agrees with Philo and partly with Josephus, saying, the princess had given the child the name 'Moses,' for having taken him out of the water, τὸ γὰρ ὕδωρ μωῦ ὀνομάζουσιν Αἰγύπτιοι, "for the Egyptians call the water môü," and he further quotes the poet Ezekiel, who says:

> ὄνομα δὲ Μωσῆν ὠνόμαζε, τοῦ χάριν
> ὑγρᾶς ἀνεῖλε ποταμίας ἀπ' ἠόνος.

"The princess called him Moses, because she rescued him from the marshy bank of the river." This same poet is quoted at yet greater length by Eusebius,[5] who relates the story as told by Artabanus (q.v.) that says, "Moses was called Μουσαῖος by the Greeks, and that he was the teacher of Orpheus," &c. Moses' origin is also probably alluded to in these Orphic lines quoted by Eusebius,[6]

> —ἔστι δὲ πάντως
> Αὐτὸς ἐπουράνιος—
>   —ὡς Παλαγενὴς διέταξεν
> ἐκ θεόθεν γνώμαισι λαβὼν κατὰ δίπλακα θεσμόν.

"He is everywhere, He Who lives in Heaven,—as Hylogenes

[1] Antiq. lib. ii. p. 76, ed. H.   [2] C. Apion. c. 31.
[3] C. 26.   [4] Strom. lib. i. p. 348, ed. Ca.
[5] Præp. Ev. p. 436, sq.   [6] Præp. Ev. lib. xiii. p. 666.

R

(the one born of the mud) has taught in order by precepts, having received them in two tables from GOD." We have seen that Hermann and Gessner[1] apply this ὑλογενής to Adam; but the context clearly forbids it; wherefore some have proposed ὑδογενής and ἰλυγενής in its stead.

Jablonski[2] dwelling on the Greek rendering of מֹשֶׁה Μωϋσῆς alludes to the Coptic etymology mentioned by Salmasius, ⲙⲙⲟⲩⲟⲓ, which he renders, ‘taken out of the water;’ and he offers instead of it ⲙⲙⲟⲩ ϣⲉ, ‘coming out of the water,’ which is no better. Kircher offers ⲙⲙⲟⲩⲧⲥⲕⲥ, which he renders, ‘saved out of the water,’ but ⲟⲩⲧⲥⲕⲥ is not Coptic. A. Müller[3] proposes ⲙⲙⲟⲩ-ⲥⲱϯ for ‘redeemed from the water,’ but no better. Lastly, comes Jablonski's own ⲙⲙⲱ-ⲟⲩⲝⲉ for ‘saved out of the water,’ and, as he thinks, easily made into Μωϋσῆς. But the tongue of the Pharaohs was no more Coptic than Anglo-Saxon is English. Moreover, ⲟⲩⲝⲉ does not exist in Coptic; it is either ⲟⲩⲝⲉⲓ, or ⲟⲩⲝⲁⲓ, ‘to save,’ ‘salvation ;’ and ⲝ is no equivalent for ש, but for ϫ; since ‘Ibsheus’ for ⲡϫⲟⲉⲓⲥ, ‘the Most High,’ ‘the LORD,’ is a common but vicious and vulgar pronunciation. Mingarelli[4] ends his remarks on ⲙⲙⲩⲧⲥⲕⲥ, saying, the name of Moses might be made up of “ⲙⲙⲟⲩ et ⲥⲉ, bibere, aut ϣⲉ ire, abire.” A. Georgi[5] says of ⲙⲙⲩⲧⲥⲕⲥ that it is “vere Ægyptum,” and proposes ⲙⲙⲟⲩⲟⲓ or ⲝⲓ, ‘aquâ sublatus;’ but it is ungrammatical in this sense. Ig. Rossi[6] offers the same, and thinks Moses was written ⲙⲙⲟⲩⲝⲁⲓ vel ⲙⲙⲟⲩⲝⲉ servatus ex aquis. Lastly, Brugsch[7] identifies ‘Moses’ with the Egyptian ‘Mes,’ ‘Messou,’ a word which means ‘child,’ (as he says), and a name borne by one of the seven princes of Ethiopia under Ramses II. in the days of Moses. But the learned German here overlooks the fact that we have this same ‘Mes’ or ‘Messu,’ spelled ⲙⲉⲥ in ⲣⲁ-ⲙⲉⲥ ‘Râ-mess,’[8] so that evidently ⲙⲉⲥ ‘Mess’ is not מֹשֶׁה ‘Mo-

---

[1] Orph. Fr. H. L. 36, ed. Herm.
[2] Gloss. Sac. p. 29.
[3] Pr. Ev. Joh. Præf. p. cxliv.
[4] Hist. d'Eg. p. 187.

[5] Opp. vol. i. p. 151, sq.
[6] Æg. Codd. reliq. p. cclxxl. sq.
[7] Etym. Æg. p. 127.
[8] Ex. i. 11, xii. 37, Gen. xlvii. 11.

sheb;' the less so, as the same hand wrote both these words,
and thus determined the articulation of each term, both in hieroglyphics and in the spoken language, as being respectively
ⲙⲗⲥⲥ and ⲙⲗⲟⲩ, *mes* and *meh*.

To the above terms offered, several others, also in pseudo-
Coptic, might be added, all equally ungrammatical; for in Coptic
there are no such compound terms as most of those above offered as etymologies; but they are formed regularly; e.g.
ⲫⲉⲛⲥⲛⲟⲩ, 'shed-blood,' i.e. 'bloodshed,' &c.[1]

IV. In the word מֹשֶׁה therefore, שֶׁה cannot be a past parti-
ciple, even granting מֹ stands for 'water;' but it must be a substantive. Now ⲥⲓ or ⲥⲉ Memph. ϣⲉ, 'son,' is, in the ancient
tongue, placed either first or last in the compound term; although in Coptic it comes first, as e.g. ϣⲉⲛⲥⲟⲛ 'cousin,' for
ϣⲉ ⲛ̄ ⲥⲟⲛ, ϣⲉⲛⲡ̄ⲁⲡⲟⲛ 'son of Aaron' (prop. name), &c.
Thus in Egyptian we have, ⲡⲁ-ⲥⲓ or ⲥⲓ-ⲡⲁ, 'son of the sun,'
a common epithet of the Pharaohs; ϣⲟⲩ-ⲥⲓ, ⲡⲁ-ϣⲟⲩ-ⲥⲓ,
ϣⲟⲩ-ⲥⲓ-ⲡⲁ,[2] &c.: a good example of this occurs in ⲁⲙⲛ̄-
ⲥⲉ ⲙⲥ ϩ̄ⲣ "Amun's son, born of Horus," said of Chons.[3]

As regards the Egyptian etymology of מֹשֶׁה therefore, the
case seems to be this: (1) as in the matter of Ψοθομφανήχ, so
also in that of Μωϋσῆς, our only authority is not the Greek but
the Hebrew;[4] and this is proved by the conclusive fact that the
Coptic version instead of recognising an Egyptian or a Coptic
word in Μωϋσῆς, simply transcribes the Greek, as it does in the
case of Ψοθομφανήχ, into a term which has no meaning. (2.) The
Sacred Text, Philo, and S. Clement of Alexandria, both of whom
may have known the Egyptian tongue, lead us to find in the
syllable מֹ mō, ⲙⲱ, the term for 'water,' which is ⲙⲱ,
ⲙⲟⲩⲁⲩ, or ⲙⲙⲟⲩ, mō, mūau, or mūu. (3.) Egyptian gram-

---

[1] The only known exception to this rule is in the ancient tongue, in which
the verbs ⲙⲉⲓ, ⲙⲙⲁⲓ 'loved,' ⲥⲱⲧⲡ̄ 'chosen,' and perhaps also ⲥⲱⲧⲡ̄
'devoted' are used as past participles and placed last in the compound; perhaps
also ⲙⲙⲉⲥ 'to be born;' but more regularly ⲙⲙⲉⲥⲟⲩⲧⲧ, 'born.'

[2] Pap. Harris, p. 35.   [3] In Étude sur une Stèle, L. 2, p. 25.

[4] Since the Greek having no ϣ shin, ϣ, changed it into ს sin, or ს, e.g.
'Sharin,' Σαρων, שִׁמְשׁוֹן 'Shimshon,' Σαμψών, &c.

mar and monuments also let us recognise in שׁה the Egyptian
ci, ce, and Memph. ϣⲉ 'a son;' and teach us also that this
ci, ce or ϣⲉ may form a part of an Egyptian proper name.
(4.) As the events recorded in this 2nd chapter of Exodus, took
place in Lower Egypt, we may take the Memphitic or the Bashmuric dialect for a guide; we find accordingly ⲙⲟⲟⲩ for
'water,' and ce or cⲏ 'son,' and ⲙⲟⲟⲩ-ce or ⲙⲟⲟⲩ-cⲏ in
Bashmuric for משׁה. But ce is ϣⲉ in Memphitic, either for
ce or for ϣⲏⲣⲉ 'a son;' so that we have the Memphitic
ⲙⲟⲟⲩϣⲉ or ⲙⲟⲟⲩⲧ-ϣⲉ 'Môshe' or 'Moûshe,' as the Egyptian
for משׁה 'water-son,' or 'child of the water.'

But this Egyptian name does not agree with the reason given
for it כִּי מִן־הַמַּיִם מְשִׁיתִהוּ rendered "because I drew him
out of the water." A. Vers. How then shall we reconcile this
apparent discrepancy? Easily. Moses gives in Hebrew the
words spoken by the princess in Egyptian. She called him
'son of the water,' or 'water-child,' because, said she, I drew
him out of the water; in other words, because he is a foundling whom I saved from the water. His Egyptian name referred, not to his being actually 'taken out' of the water, or
born out of it; but to the fact that the water was figuratively
his mother; and according to this view of the subject, this name
was given by the only one who could give it,—she who had
taken the child out of the river. In this case the coincidence
between the Egyptian ⲙⲟⲟⲩϣⲉ, משׁה, and the Hebrew מְשִׁיתִהוּ
as from משׁה, would be only accidental as regards the pronunciation.

A. Ezra, however,[1] says that משׁה is the Hebrew translation
of the Egyptian מונים 'Monios,' the name given by Pharaoh's
daughter to Moses. But Abarbanel[2] refutes him, saying that
proper names are never translated, even though the verbs from
which they are derived be translated; e.g. the Targ. Onkelos
gives משׁה but renders מְשִׁיתִהוּ by שְׁחַלְתֵּיהּ which bears no
affinity to משׁה; likewise 'Zaphnath-Paaneah' is thus given
and not translated. He further asserts that Moses' name is
Hebrew; and that it was given to Moses by his mother, re-

[1] Ad L   [2] Comm. ad loc. and Job. Bastorfi dl. Dissert. Philol. p. 486.

marking very justly,[1] that מְשִׁיחָתוֹ is not the 1st pers. sing.,
which is never written without a ו after the ת, thus מְשִׁיחְתוֹ,
הִשְׁאַלְתִּיהוּ, נְתַתִּיו, מְצָאתִיהוּ, מְצָאתִיהָ, יְלִדְתִּיהוּ, &c., but
that it is the 2nd pers. sing. fem. like יְלִדְתַּנִי Jer. xv. 10,
לְבַבְתִּנִי Song of Solomon iv. 9; and says "that every feminine
ת in this 10th verse, is said of Jochebed, Moses' mother, who
brought the child to Pharaoh's daughter, and he became her
son.   And she (Jochebed) called his name Mosheh, because she
said, Thou (Pharaoh's daughter) didst draw him out of the
water."   Abarbanel has on his side grammar, which he rightly
calls ' regular,' while Gesenius[2] calls it ' defective;' but both he
and A. Ezra omit to tell us the meaning of מֹשֶׁה in Hebrew.[3]

V.   Leaving aside the traditions given by Dr. Stanley, we read
that, when Moses was grown up, seeing one of his brethren
ill-treated by an Egyptian, he slew the Egyptian; and when this
came to the king's ears, Moses fled from court into the land of
Midian.   Had the quarrel taken place between two Egyptians,
or had Moses been an Egyptian, he himself would have been
liable to be put to death, for not slaying the aggressor, if we
are to believe what Diodorus tells us.   Speaking of the laws of
Egypt,[4] he says that: ἐὰν δέ τις ἐν ὁδῷ κατὰ τὴν χώραν θεὴν φονευ-
όμενον ἄνθρωπον, ἢ τὸ καθόλου βίαιόν τι πάσχοντα, μὴ ῥύσαιτο δυνατὸς
ὤν, θανάτῳ περιπεσεῖν ὀφείλει, " if one saw on the road about the
country a man being killed or at all ill-treated, and delivered
him not, being able to do so, he was to be put to death."   Such
may have been the law in theory; but when carried out it seems
to have been different for the ruler and for the captive.   ' Right
against might,' in writing; but ' might against right' in practice; then, as also very often at present, wherever it may be.

Moses then fled, as it were to await in the grand, awful
scenery of the desert of Sinai the death of Ramses, and the seal
of his own mission.   I cannot follow Dr. Stanley in his beautiful description of a country I was unfortunately prevented from

---

[1] As indeed Pfeiffer (Dub. Vex. p. 214) also does.

[2] Lehrgeb. p. 346, note 5.

[3] We must remark that the question here lies only between the final ת
and ת; for as we saw above (p. 159) the fem. preform. ת of the verbs in this 10th
verse, need not all refer to the same person, according to Hebrew idiom.

[4] Lib. l. c. 77.

visiting; I, therefore, return thence with him and Moses to Egypt. Sent on his errand with his shepherd's staff, which henceforth became "the rod of GOD wherewith to do signs and wonders"—a fit emblem of the utter weakness of the instruments the LORD uses, that the glory be His and not our own—and strong in the Revelation of the Eternal One, (not τὸ ὂν ὄντως according to Plato, but) ὁ ὢν ὄντως according to Truth, ὁ *ΩΝ καὶ ὁ *ΗΝ καὶ ὁ *ΕΡΧΟΜΕΝΟΣ, ὁ ΠΑΝΤΟΚΡΑΤΩΡ, "Which is, which was, and which is to come, the ALMIGHTY"—Moses left his father-in-law and the desert of Horeb to return to Egypt. As S. Paul went into Arabia after his call to the Apostleship, in order to prepare himself for the life of toil, of trial, and of shame —but after that of glory, that awaited him, so also Moses the shepherd was schooled among the stern scenery of that same country for his mission to the king of Egypt.

VI. Hitherto, he had worshipped the GOD of Abraham, of Isaac, and of Jacob, 'El-Shaddaï,' the GOD Almighty, 'El,' the Mighty, 'Elohim,' the Awful, the worshipful One,[1] the Majesty of Heaven; but now GOD had spoken with him; he was now endued with a power, and fraught with credentials at which even the proud heart of Pharaoh, and the gods of Egypt should bend. He was βραδύγλωσσος,[2] slow of speech; but He that made the mouth did send him, and He would teach him how to use it; or, He would make words for him, and a spokesman to utter them;[3] he was a feeder of flocks, although once at court in Egypt, and shy of returning thither; but He that sent him said He would be with him; He would make him God to Pharaoh, and make Egypt tremble at the wave of his shepherd's staff. He was but a plain man after all, but the LORD his GOD was to be with him; and with Him Moses would be the Prophet, the Man of God; the Deliverer at whose bidding the sea would roll back; the Leader of Israel's host at whose in-

---

[1] Dr. Stanley says 'El,' ' Elohim,' 'the strong one,' 'the strong ones,' as if ' Elohim' were the pl. of 'El.' But the pl. of אֵל El is אֵלִים as in Phœnician and in Punic inscriptions; and אֱלֹהִים is, of course, the pl. of אֱלוֹהַּ or אֱלֹהַּ probably a radical term; if not from אָלַהּ laua. 'to worship.'

[2] Ἦν φῶς ἄσβεστον, ἄφθαρτον, ἀκατανόητον—ὅτι ὁ βραδύγλωσσος ἐνεγράφετο; τὴν ἔναρξιν ἐφ᾽ ἕαυτ, οὐρανὸν ἐνδιδούς. Lucian Philopatr. p. 250. vol. ix. ed. Bip.

[3] Aaron—τὸν προφορικὸν λόγον. Philo. De Migr. Abr. p. 400, sq.

stance Amalek would flee; the Lawgiver who should receive his
tables at God's hand, and who should talk with Him as a man
with his friend; at whose word, therefore, the rock poured forth
water, the heavens rained manna, the pestilence came and retreated, and the desert land yielded flesh to eat; whose hand,
in short, nothing could stay—because the LORD was with him.
But the LORD is the same yesterday, to-day, and for ever towards
them that fear Him and trust in His mercy. As He was with
Moses whom He raised for a special purpose, so He is also with
every one of His people who honestly fears and serves Him, not
hindered by the fear of man or by worldly reasons. Yea, the
humblest of His servants may yet sing, in the words of that
same Egypt: ⲁⲣⲓⲉⲙⲓ ϧⲁ ⲁⲧⲫⲏⲭ ⲙ̄ⲡⲕⲁϩⲓ, ϫⲉ ⲫⲧ̄
ⲛⲉⲙⲁⲛ "Know ye even unto the ends of the earth, that the
LORD is with us."[1]

VII. So Moses, and Aaron who had gone to meet him, came
to Egypt; and in Egypt, to Pharaoh. Moses taught Aaron
what to say, and Aaron spake. But, "as time rolled on," says
Dr. Stanley—

"as the first outward impression passed away, and the deep, abiding recollection of the whole story remained, Aaron the prince
and priest has almost disappeared from the view of history: and
Moses, the dumb, backward, disinterested prophet, continues for
all ages the foremost leader of the Chosen People, the witness that
something more is needed for the guidance of man than high
hereditary office or the gift of fluent speech,—a rebuke alike to
an age that puts its trust in priests and nobles, and an age that
puts its trust in preachers and speakers."—p. 116.

Excellent words, that one likes to find uttered and written
by the Dean of Westminster. Would that his and all other
hearers did act up to them; and did hearken to him in this respect, to see that they run not after the glitter of high position
and of fluency of speech, as they would after a will-o'-the-wisp;
but compare what they hear with the only standard there is,
that of God's Word; so that, at the last, they find themselves
having a "good assurance of hope;" and not be led astray.
There is too much at stake in this, to trifle with it; and to seek
man, and not the Truth, in what we hear.

[1] Diara. Copto-Ar. p. 198.

But Moses' words, though plain, were telling, because he sought not his own, but spake as GOD bade him. "Go, stand before Pharaoh, and thus shalt thou say unto him." And when Pharaoh heard it, he trembled, and begged Moses and Aaron to entreat for him the same GOD of whom erst he had said, "Who is the LORD that I should obey His voice?" The message delivered was the message given; it could not be sent and return without effect; but it wrought that whereunto it was sent. And so it does to this day; and so it shall do until no more messages are sent; when the tramp of the archangel shall sound: Lo! He cometh; make ready. Happy the messengers who will then be found to have been faithful, honest and sincere! Happy they whose conscience will not accuse them in His presence, of having sought their own glory, but only the glory of GOD! For that day is coming; the day that shall try the work of every one; of what sort it is.

Therefore, Moses won his place in the goodly company of Elijah, of Abraham, of the LORD JESUS Himself in glory, not because he was a great man, not because he was brought up at court by Pharaoh's daughter; not because he was learned in all the wisdom of the Egyptians; not because he had wrought signs and wonders,—since others will have prophesied and done many wonderful works in the LORD's name, and yet after all be cast out of the Kingdom,[1]—but Moses is now in glory because "he verily was faithful in all his house, as a servant, for a testimony of those things which were to be spoken after." Faithfulness, however, implies faith; for no man can be faithful who seeks his own glory. So then, "by faith Moses, when he was come to years, refused to be called the son of Pharaoh's daughter; choosing rather to suffer affliction with the people of GOD than to enjoy the pleasures of sin for a season; esteeming the reproach of CHRIST greater riches than the treasures in Egypt; for he had respect unto the recompense of the reward"—and he has his reward.

VIII. This is that Moses whom the LORD raised to deliver His people out of captivity, with a mighty hand, and through judgments against Pharaoh, his people, and their gods. Dr. Stanley is much too brief on this subject; and this is not the

[1] S. Matt. vii. 22.

place to supply that which is lacking in him. He certainly
tells us that "it was not an ordinary river that was turned into
blood; it was the sacred, beneficent, solitary Nile"—but he
might have added that the miracle lay, not only in the blood,
but in the time of year. In Epiphi (or June) the Egyptians are
accustomed to see their river blood-red, yet wholesome to drink;
but now, in Tybi (or January) was it, not only blood-red, but
loathsome blood. Yet they were not doomed to perish, as they
must have done if left seven days without water. The blow was
aimed at Hâpi-môn, at the God Nile, ⲀⲦ-ϥ-ϥ Ⲛ Ⲛ̄Ⲧⲣ-ⲞⲨ
'father of gods,' and he alone suffered; but where the water was
not visibly his, on the bed of sand and gravel below the muddy
deposit of the river, was the water good; and there did the
Egyptians dig for it and find it.

"It is not an ordinary nation," continues Dr. Stanley, "that is
struck by the mass of putrifying vermin lying in heaps by the
houses, the villages, and the fields, or multiplying out of the dust
of the desert sands on each side of the Nile valley: it is the clean-
liest of all the ancient nations," &c.—p. 110.

IX. The Regius Professor's ideas about frogs do not seem
very clear, if he classes them with vermin; for, according to the
popular acceptation of the term, frogs are not, like vermin,
either 'noxious or small animals.' They are most harmless, and
some of them are of a large size; especially in the land they
love best—Egypt. But in the days of Moses they were sacred,
not originally to the Sun, as the learned Bochart thought,
making them water-nymphs and prototypes of the Musæ, but
they were sacred to Kek, the god of darkness; i.e., of the
primordial ὕλη, 'earthy matter,' as the male principle in nature.[1]
And albeit the monuments on which they are thus represented
are of the time of the Ptolemies, yet had not the frogs been thus
honoured, other symbols would have been chosen by the Egyptians, rather than those they actually did choose. This seems
proved by the frequent occurrence of the frog as a goddess,
Haqt, nb-t n-Hrur, 'Haqt Lady of Hrur,' a city of the Nome
Sah, in Upper Egypt.[2] She was honoured at Hrur, in connec-

[1] Leps. Gött. lv. El. p. 150, sq.
[2] Brugsch. Geog. Denkm. l. p. 227. I also find this goddess 'Haqt,' repre-

tion with Chmun, there represented as a ram; the heating,
generative power together with the ὕλη, the matter that gene-
rated. In this capacity is the frog also mentioned as a god,
'Ka,' i.q., 'Kek,' as given by Sir G. Wilkinson, pl. 25, 8, fol. 6.

From his explanation, however, at p. 256, 257, vol. iv., he
does not seem to have then read the name 'Hrur' as the city
where Haqt was adored, neither to have known what Lepsius
has shown—that this frog-headed god Ka (as named by the
'arms extended upwards') was the same as 'Kek;' and not
Ptah. Moreover, the legend given by Sir G. Wilkinson himself
reads $\overline{BA}$' ᴀᴛ-ϥ-ϥ $\overline{N}$ $\overline{NTP}$-ᴏᴛ ᴋᴀ, "generative power or
spirit, father of gods, Ka;" and as a proof thereof the 'Cheper,'
or beetle sacred to the Sun as creator, rests on the head of the
frog-god—a very perfect symbolism. As a symbol of the
primordial matter out of which the frog, Aaq-t, $\overline{P}$,ᴋ-ᴛ, so
called from the noise it makes, it was also reckoned a symbol of
regeneration—ἀντὶ ἀναβιώσεως, βάτραχον—on the testimony of
Chæremon;[2] or of coming to life, according to Horapollo,[3] who
tells us that the Egyptians represented by a frog a man as yet
unformed, ἐπειδὴ ἡ τούτου (βατράχου) γένεσις ἐκ τῆς τοῦ ποταμοῦ
ἰλύος ἀποτελεῖται· "since the frog is produced by the mud of the
river, ὅθεν καὶ ἔσθ' ὅτι ὁρᾶται τῷ μὲν ἑτέρῳ μέρει αὐτοῦ, βατράχῳ, τῷ
δὲ λοιπῷ, γεώδει τινὶ ἐμφερὴς, ὡς καὶ ἐκλείποντι τῷ ποταμῷ, συνεκλεί-
πων" "whence it sometimes appears partly frog and partly mud,
which disappears with the fall of the river." Hence the goddess of Epiphi, the month in which the rise of the Nile begins,
had the head of a frog, as in that month the ground seems alive
with them; hence, too, are tadpoles used as the symbol to express
μυριάδας, 'a hundred thousand,' an indefinite number.[4] The
symbolism of the frog at the foot of the palm-branch, used to
represent years and periods of years, is thus evident; both one

sented as a 'frog sitting' in the monuments of the oldest dynasties. (Leps.
Denkm. Abth. ii. pl. xxix., lxi., lxiv., Grab. 45, sq.)

[1] Or $\overline{BAS}$ in connection with the ram.   Champ. Dict. p. 134 and 412.

[2] I give this on the authority of M. Devéria (Notat. des combinus de mille,
p. 5), for I cannot find it in the fragments of Chæremon I have, ed. Müller.

[3] Hierog. Lib. i. 25.

[4] Th. Devéria, Notat. des mnt. de mille, p. 4, sq.   Chabas, Étud. Égypt. 2e.
Mém. p. 10; and Brugsch. Monum. i. pl. xlvi. c.

and the other were emblems of 'renovation,' (Heb. שׁנה, Æg.
ⲣⲣⲙⲛⲉ,) the one of time, the other of existence.

The intention of the plague of frogs, therefore, was aimed,
first, at the worship of those reptiles; secondly, at them, as offspring of the River; and thirdly, the miracle lay in their covering the land in Tybi (January), when there are fewer of them
abroad over the land of Egypt than at any other time, owing to
the low level of the River in that month.

X. Likewise was the plague of lice aimed at the rites and
ceremonies of Egyptian priests, whose name and symbol in
Egyptian, ⲟⲩⲁⲃ, with water above and below, stands for
'purity,' or 'purification.'[1]

XI. So also was the ערב, the mixture or swarms of flies of
all sorts, intended to show the folly of worshipping chafers and
beetles of other sorts; for, however much the learned among the
Egyptians might symbolize the worship of these creatures, the
common people saw no symbols in them, but worshipped what
they saw, whether beetles, bulls, the River, or frogs, fish, and
crocodiles in it.

"It is not the ordinary cattle that died in the field," continues
Dr. Stanley, "or ordinary fish that died in the river, or ordinary
reptiles that were overcome by the rod of Aaron. It is the sacred
goat of Mendes, the ram of Ammon, the calf of Heliopolis, the
bull Apis, the crocodile of Ombos, the carp of Bahneh."

On which Dr. Stanley adds this note:—

"The 'serpent' of Exod. vii. 9, 10, 12 (a different word from
that in iv. 3, vii. 15) is evidently a 'crocodile.'"

XII. The plague of murrain had also a very plain object.
The Bull Apis figures already in tombs of the IVth Dynasty,[2]
under Choufou or Shûfû, long before the days of Moses; so
does Mnevis at On, and Ba-empi at Mendes; they died, as did
the horses, sheep, dogs, cats, and other animals that were
either prized or worshipped, while Egypt was being destroyed.
So also the turning of Moses' rod into a serpent, and that

[1] προτιμῶσι τε καθαρὰ εἶναι ἢ εὐπρεπέστερα. Οἱ δὲ ἱρέες ἑωυτῶν τῶν τὸ σῶμα
διὰ τρίτης ἡμέρης, ἵνα μήτε φθεὶρ μήτε ἄλλο μυσαρὸν μηδὲν ἐγγίνηταί σφι θεραπεύουσι τοὺς θεούς. Herod. Lib. ii. c. 37.

[2] Leps. Denkm. Abth. ii. pl. 15.

again into a rod, had its own meaning. From Apap[1]—the giant
serpent that was slain by the gods, and that still drags its huge
coils with a dagger stuck in each, on every Egyptian drawing—
to Sar, Hunti, Haī, Sapi, Nahavka, Mehen, Neb-hotp,[2] and
other snakes of Egypt and of Amenti, with the 'Araa,' Βασιλίσκος, the symbol of 'God and King,' were aimed at in that
sign. It had a very different meaning from the tricks practised,
then as now, by serpent charmers of Pharaoh's court, as we
read in several parts of the Magical Papyrus published by M.
Chabas;[3] as well as in Zoega,[4] who speaks of one who took in
his hands ⲚⲒⲢϨⲞⲨ ⲘⲚ ⲚⲔⲈⲢⲀⲤⲦⲔⲤ ⲘⲚ ⲚⲞⲨⲞϨⲈ, 'ser-
pents, and cerastes, and asps,' and tore them asunder without
any harm to himself.

XIII. But, although we read in Exod. iv. 3, vii. 15, that
Moses' rod was turned into a 'serpent' נָחָשׁ, and at ch. vii.
9, 10, 12, that it became a 'dragon' תַּנִּין, and that תַּנִּין may
mean a 'crocodile'—it does not follow that they were two distinct signs. But, rather, we may see in this another[5] of those
intrinsic evidences of the authenticity of the narrative, as written
by one who was accustomed to Egyptian ideas and idioms. For,
in Egyptian, the symbol of Apap with its coils and daggers is
the determinative of other monsters of the serpent kind in
Amenti, as Tu-Katen, Ha, Her,[6] &c., though not of 'crocodiles,'
which are always determined by a crocodile.[7] Further, at ch.
cxxv. l. 85 of the Ritual, this same Apap is the determinative of
ⲤⲀⲢϨ-Ⲁ ⲀⲬⲬ-ⲞⲨ, "I drown monsters"—also of the serpent kind; alluded to and represented in the following chapters of the Ritual. But in Hebrew, whereas נָחָשׁ would be
said of a serpent, such as the one which came of Moses' rod,
תַּנִּין alone would be used in good Hebrew, for one of such
huge dimensions as Apap, which so often figures as determinative in hieroglyphical texts. Moses was learned in that lore;

[1] Rit. ch. xxxix.

[2] Pap. Harris, p. 74, 76, 164. Rit. c. xvii. l. 34, 61, c. lxxxvii. l. 33, 38, sq.,
&c. Brugsch. Geog. Denkm. vol. i. p. 277, 281, &c. Leps. Göt. iv. El. p. 164,
224, &c. Sharpe, Eg. Inscr. ii. 61, sq.

[3] Pap. Harris, p. 68, 133, &c.   [4] Codd. Sah. p. 341.

[5] See above, p. 39, 40.   [6] Pap. Harr. p. 61, 75, &c.

[7] Rit. ch. xxxi.—xxxvii.

so that, when he used שְׁרֶץ in Exod. iv. 3, vii. 15, he alluded
to the 'serpent of a particular size;' and when he adopted נָחָשׁ
in Exod. vii. 9, 10, 12, he spake of the 'serpent-kind in general,'
as determined in his thoughts by the תַּנִּין, 'monster' or 'dragon'
Apap, with which he was familiar.

XIV. As to "the carp of Eshneh," it is a myth; and the Regius
Professor is not more fortunate with his fish than with his frogs.
First—Latopolis is not called 'Eshneh,' but 'Esneh,' or rather
'Esnā,' اسنا.[1] Secondly—the fish worshipped there was the λάτος,
'latus,'[2] which seems to have given its Greek name to the city,
since it was not Latona, Λητώ, that was worshipped there, but
'Αθηνᾶ καὶ ὁ λάτος,'[3] 'Minerva and the latus-fish;' unless Strabo
makes a mistake. We do not know for certain what the λάτος
was; but, both from the representation of it in Sir G. Wilkinson's Anc. Eg. v. 253, and from the description of it in Athenæus,[4] where we read that the λάτος was caught "in the sea at
Scylla, as well as in the Nile, of two hundred pounds weight,"
it could be no 'carp.' Among other sacred fish was the so-
called 'lepidotus,' of which Sir G. Wilkinson gives a bronze
figure at p. 252. This, judging from the dorsal fin, would do
very well for 'a carp;' yet this was not the fish worshipped at
Latopolis or Esneh. But for the dorsal fin, one might have
thought of the פָרָה, ἄβραμις, 'bream,'[5] or of the 'benny,'
bynni, البِنّي, Copt. ⲔⲀⲚⲞⲨϢⲒ. But it is impossible to speak
with certainty as to what species was the λάτος, without works
of reference which I have not.

"It is not an ordinary land," continues Dr. Stanley, "of which
the flax and the barley, and every green thing in the trees, and
every herb in the field, are smitten by the two great calamities of
storm and locust: it is the garden of the ancient world," &c.—
p. 119.

XV. The mere destruction of exuberant crops, and with them
of the land of Egypt for that year, is not the point; and Dr.
Stanley ought to have dwelt at greater length on this plague,

---

[1] Abulf. Æg. p. 23, ed. J. D. Mich.
[2] Strabo, Lib. xvii. c. 40.   [3] Ibid. c. 47.
[4] Lib. vii. c. 17, p. 311, ed. Cas.   [5] Champ. Gr. Eg. 74.

which is the nail, as it were, that fastens to all time the month
of the Passover. A work of this kind is not the place to enter
into details, especially as I have already written at length upon
the subject.[1] I must, however, mention a few facts with reference to the plague of hail and to that of locusts, which cannot
be overlooked.

We read in Exod. x. 31, 32, that "the flax and the barley was
smitten; for the barley was in the ear and the flax was bolled,
but the wheat and the rie were not smitten: for they were not
grown up. Heb. *hidden* or *dark*." A. V.

No sooner has the Nile retired into its bed, than the seed is
sown all over Egypt. Prosper Alpinus,[2] who resided long at
Cairo, says "that all crops grow so fast and reach to maturity
so soon, that by the end of November the flax which is sown in
November, in lands on which the water dwells longest,[3] in many
places is in blossom, and the clover is already fit to cut. Cereals
are in the ear generally about Christmas, and the harvest of
them takes place at the beginning of March." He repeats this
at p. 176, adding : "Omnes segetes—toto mense Februario per-
fectam maturitatem nanciscuntur," "all crops ripen during the
whole of February." So also Shems ed-dín Abilsorûr,[4] who
fixes sowing time in Athor (Oct.—Nov.), and in Choiak (Nov.—
Dec.), and the beating of the flax in Pharmuthi (March—April),
says that "barley is sown before wheat and all other crops," and
is reaped "trente jours plus tôt que le blé," thirty days before
wheat.[5] Forskal[6] says, "Hordeum cum mense Februario ma-
turatur; triticum ad finem Martii persistit, barley ripens in
February, but wheat towards the end of March." And Sir G.
Wilkinson[7] says, "Barley and wheat, which are carried, the
former in the fourth, the latter in the fifth month, are sown
about the middle of November; the time, however, greatly depends on the duration of the inundation." And at page 458 he
adds "that some barley is also reaped at the end of ninety

[1] Vindication of the Authorized Version, pp. 11—32.
[2] Hist. Nat. Ægypti, p. 6, ed. 1735.
[3] Flore Eg. in Descr. de l'Eg. p. 11, sq.
[4] Extr. des MSS. vol. i. p. 252.
[5] Flore Eg. in Descr. de l'Eg. p. 11, sq.
[6] Flor. Æg. p. xliii.
[7] Mod. Eg. and Thebes, Append. i. vol. i. p. 456.

days," and that wheat, of which he enumerates five varieties,
"is reaped at the beginning of April." To this I may add my
own experience of Sir G. Wilkinson's accurate statement, and
the conclusive testimony of Philo,[1] who lived in Egypt, and who,
speaking of the season of the Passover, says: "It is placed beyond doubt by the fresh ears brought as first-fruits on the
second day of the feast, as offerings to the priests, ἡ ϛ̔ὰγ
ϕωϑⲁⲃωⲩⲕ ϥωⲣϥⲁⲩⲃⲃ ⲉ̄ : for the spring is the season of
harvest."

XVI. It would be needless to multiply authorities in order to
show, from what I have just said, that the hail which smote "the
barley in the ear, (אָבִיב) and the flax already bolled," (גִּבְעֹל)
must have fallen, in an average year, between the first and the
third week in Mechir, that is, in the early part, or towards the
end of February. Then the wheat (which is always sown and
reaped later than the barley), and the rye? כֻּסֶּמֶת, kurt [?]
(whether ὄλυρα, ζέα, 'durrah,' or sorgho, I do not wish here to
discuss[3]), were not smitten, because they were אֲפִילֹת 'hidden,
dark,' not yet come up, but under ground. It must have been
so, otherwise the hail that smote "every herb of the field"
would have smitten the wheat and the rye had they been above
ground. These two sprouted up after the hail, and ere the
locusts came a few days after to eat them up, until Egypt was
"destroyed." Whether the hail fell a week earlier or not, matters little; it is enough to notice that it happened within a
month's time of the night of the Passover, which was on the
fourteenth moon of חֹדֶשׁ הָאָבִיב, the month of the first ripen-
ing ears; that is, on the fourteenth of the month answering to
our March of that year.[4] For here חֹדֶשׁ הָאָבִיב cannot apply
to the second crop of green ears, i.e., of wheat ears, but it must
apply to the first crop, to the first ears approaching to maturity,

[1] Quaest. in Exod. in Paralip. Armena. p. 444.

[2] Rosell. Mon. Civ. vol. i. p. 376, sq., and pl. lxvii. sq.

[3] See, however, Salmas. Hyleus Iatricus, cp. lvii. p. 68, sq., for ζέα, ἕλυρα, κεγχδαλις, &c.

[4] Μαρτίῳ τὰ πρωτότοκα, τῇ δ' τούτων τοῦ μηνὸς συλλαβόντες τοὺς Αἰγυπτίους ἐξῆλθον, προστάξει Θεοῦ τοῦτο ποιησάντες. Cedrenus, Hist. p. 38; and Mich. Glycas, Annal. ii. p. 290, ed. Bonn.

viz., to barley ears, three weeks or a month before wheat ears
ripen and are gathered.

Since then, when the wheat is אָבִיב, approaching to maturity, but yet green, soft, and succulent, the barley harvest is
over, it is then literally 'harvest time;' for harvest begins with
the first sheaf of barley in February, and lasts until the wheat
is carried, early in April. It stands to reason, therefore, that
since the Passover took place on the fourteenth day of the
month of green or first ripe ears, this is said of barley, and it
must have been within a very short time of the hail, which
did not hurt the wheat that was not grown up. This proves
clearly that, although in the revolution of years this חֹדֶשׁ
הָאָבִיב happened one month earlier or later, so as to necessitate
the occasional intercalation of Veadar, or thirteenth month, yet
that this first Passover did take place—as, indeed, it was meet
the first beginning of a new year, and with it of a new life,
should take place—as early in that year as it ever could do.
This was prepared by a good inundation the year before; for
had it been either too high or too low, the seed could not have
been put in in time, or if put in, would not have prospered.
Thus, while Moses was peaceably feeding his flock in the desert of Horeb, and ere God spake to him in the bush, was the
River rising at God's behest, to brood over the land, so as to
prepare food for His people and for their deliverance. In
Goshen there was no hail; and as the children of Israel had
left Egypt ere the wheat harvest could have set in had there
been no locusts elsewhere in Egypt, the children of Israel must
have made the dough they bound in their kneading troughs,
and of which they baked unleavened cakes, of the barley of that
year, just reaped.[1] The sign of the hail and of thunder, then,
did not consist in the fall of hail at that season in particular,
since Ptolemy, in his Calendar,[2] puts down for the sixth of
Pharmuthi, or March, Νψ ἢ νότος ἢ χαλάζα, "south-west or
south wind, or it hails," as also in the preceding month; but no
such hail had ever before been seen for the ravages it caused.

XVII. Likewise, the locusts are a frequent visitation, but they

---

[1] Compare the 'barley loaves' at the same season; S. John vi.
[2] φας. ἀνδρων, ed. Halma, vol. iii. p. 47.

are in general brought by the south and south-west winds from
the deserts of Libya. They follow in the train of Thueris,
ⲐⲞⲨⲢⲎⲤ, the burning wind of the south, as one of its dreaded
scourges; but this happens later in the year. It was a sign
and a wonder that the 'east wind,' the wind most favourable in
Egypt should bring them, and that a west wind should arise to
send them back whence they came, and cast them into the 'tank
of Punt,' the Red Sea,[1] with other enemies of the land.

XVIII. Thus, if we study the features of these judgments of
GOD, we shall see His finger in every one of them. "It is the
finger of GOD" were the Egyptians constrained at last to say.
Even if we look upon them as aggravated forms of "calamities
natural to Egypt," yet either the aggravation, or the time of
year, or the point of every judgment, showed whence it came.
"Woe unto us!" said the terrified Philistines, "woe unto us!
Who shall deliver us out of the hand of these mighty Gods?
These are the Gods that smote the Egyptians with all the
plagues in the wilderness." (1 Sam. iv. 7, 8.) I cannot, however, agree with Dr. Stanley that the darkness was an aggravation of the "darkness of the sandy wind;" for, first, that
wind never blows before the middle or the end of March, and
secondly, even if it had been such a darkness of sand raised by
the Khamseen winds, how does Dr. Stanley account for wind,
sand, and darkness being only on the Egyptians, and light,
without either wind or sand, on the children of Israel? Such a
miracle would have been, if possible, greater than the "darkness that might be felt" during three days, at the time, too,
when the moon should be bright in the heavens as one eye of
Osiris, the other by day being the sun in all his splendour. Of
all the wonders and of all the judgments wrought or sent to
break Pharaoh's heart and to terrify his people, this last warning was by far the most awful. The LORD's rights, avenged in
the death of the first-born, caused "lamentation, and wailing,
and woe;" but the death of Osiris and of Isis at once, neither Sun
nor Moon seen in the Egyptian heavens for three days, was, in
sooth, the doom of the living and of the dead,—the doom at
once of Isis; of Ra, Cheper, Atum and Shu-si-Ra, Har and

---

[1] Rit. ch. xvii. l. 60. ⲠⲔⲒ ⲣ̄ (and not ⲓ̄ⲧ̄ⲓ) ⲚⲞⲨⲚⲦ: as by a mistake at p. 126.

s

Harmachu, yes, even of Nut his mother; of Osiris, the father
of all gods; the supreme Lord of Egypt and Judge of Amenti.
In vain did the priests of On, astonied at this long night,
pour forth their terror in earnest litanies to their god: "Hail,
O son of Phra! born of Tum himself; self-existent, without
mother; real Lord of Righteousness and Truth, Sovereign Ruler
of the gods !

$$\overline{\text{тр}}\text{-к } \text{ДИТ-ТА сОГТ } \overline{\text{П}}\text{-к ДПК-Т}$$
$$\text{ДА } \overline{\text{ПП}}\text{-к ПОТІ } \overline{\text{П}} \text{ } \overline{\text{тр}} \text{ ДИТ-ТА.}$$

O thou that scatterest the storm, shine, O shine through this
desolation, in thy name of Shent-Ta" (Lord over the storm, lit.,
storm destroyer.)[1] But, whether of Baal on Carmel, or of Atum
at On, there was no voice, no answer; for this was the judgment of the LORD on that god; and "the LORD, He is GOD."

XIX. "There are some days," says Dr. Stanley at p. 120,

"of which the traces left on the mind of a nation are so deep, that
the events themselves seem to live on long after they have been
numbered with the past. Such was the night of the month Nisan
in the eighteenth century before the Christian era."

Thus is the Passover announced! Small praise this from a
herald of Him Who was then ushered in as "a Lamb without
blemish and without spot," until His Church should hear that
He is "the Lamb of GOD, that taketh away the sins of the
world;" fore-ordained even then, but made manifest in these
last times, that our faith and hope might be in GOD. Event,
forsooth ! the type of that for which alone this world was made,
and by which alone it stands. Event, at which angels fall
down and worship, and saints in heaven sing praises around the
Throne: "Unto Him that loved us and washed us from our sins
in His own Blood; and hath made us kings and priests unto GOD
and His FATHER; to Him be glory and dominion for ever and
ever. Amen." It is an 'event' indeed, but one which no heart
that is touched by that event can think of, much less mention,
except in the strains of the deepest and most humble worship.

This event, however, did not take place in the month Nisan,

[1] Pap. Harr. pl. l. L 8, sq. il. 5, 6, 8, 9; and Chabas, Mélanges Egypt. 2de
série, p. 100, sq.

for there was then no such a month. נִיסָן, the origin of which
is uncertain, appears for the first time after the captivity, Neh.
ii. 1; Esth. iii. 7. But, until Moses, the Israelites had no
reckoning of their own; no other than the tropical year of their
masters: even the 'vague year' was beyond them. Therefore
does God call the mouth in which the Passover and the Exodus
took place the "month of the green ear," חֹדֶשׁ הָאָבִיב; and
this He told Moses should be to them רֹאשׁ חֳדָשִׁים, "the head
of new moons," or 'months' (Exod. xii. 2) instead of Thoth, the
first Egyptian month. Their reckoning of time could only date
from their existence as a people; and this, again, only from the
day they were set free from bondage.

Some careless, and other shallow scholars have imagined
they had made a great discovery in the coincidence between the
Arabic ابيب ' Abib,' the tenth month of the Egyptian Calendar,
and the Hebrew word אָבִיב; and heedless of Hebrew grammar,
of facts, and of everything else, some free handlers of the Bible
have thought themselves clever, in attempting to identify
אָבִיב, which they take for a proper name, against all grammar,
with the Copto-Arabic ابيب Abîb, ⲉⲡⲏⲡ, 'Επιφί, Epiphi;
thus either putting the Exodus in the hottest month of the
Egyptian summer, or shifting the place of the month of Epiphi,
Abîb, from where the Copts have ever kept it in their Calendar.
Yet those critics never made a real use of their discovery, neither
have they seen that, if it were true, it would at once give them
the date of the Exodus to within a day. For, if so be אָבִיב
is like ابيب, Epiphi, and is a proper, and not a common
name; and if so be Abîb and Epiphi are the same as אָבִיב, we
have only to follow up Mr. Biot's calculations of the 'vague
year' until Epiphi happened in that part of the Tropical year in
which barley ripens in Egypt, and that will give the date of the
Exodus.

But all that rests on no foundation whatever. In Hebrew,
proper names never take the article, but are placed in construction without it. Thus בֵּית דָוִד, 'the house of David,' &c.,
and not בֵּית הַדָוִד. So with the names of the months, thus:

s 2

חֹדֶשׁ טֵבֵת, בְּחֹדֶשׁ נִיסָן, 'in the month Nisan,' Neh. ii. 1 ; חֹדֶשׁ טֵבֵת,
'the month Thebeth,' Esth. ii. 16 ; חֹדֶשׁ אֲדָר, id. iii. 7, 'the
month Adar ;' חֹדֶשׁ סִיוָן, id. viii. 9, 'the month Sivān ;' יֶרַח זִו,
'the month Ziv,' 1 Kings vi. 37 ; יֶרַח בּוּל, 'the month Bul,'
id. ver. 38 ; viii. 2 ; Neh. i. 1, &c. But when the term 'month'
or 'moon' is in construction with a common term, be it adjective
or substantive, this always takes the article; e. g., בְּחֹדֶשׁ
הָרִאשׁוֹן הוּא חֹדֶשׁ נִיסָן, Esth. iii. 7, where the adjective takes
the article, but the proper name does not. So also חֹדֶשׁ
הַשְּׁבִיעִי, הַשְּׁלִישִׁי, הַתְּשִׁיעִי, 'the seventh, the third, the ninth
month,' &c. ; as with a noun, e. g., לְכֹל חָדְשֵׁי הַשָּׁנָה, 'for all
the months of the year,' 1 Chron. xxvii. 1, where the common
noun in construction with חֹדֶשׁ takes the article. Likewise
חֹדֶשׁ הָאָבִיב, 'the month of אָבִיב,' i. e., 'of green ears,'[1] and
not "the month Abib," as rendered by the A. V. against the
grammar of the language. As I have demonstrated in my Vindication of the A. V. that ابيب, Abib, is simply the Arabic
pronunciation of ЄΠΗΠ, Ἐπέπ, Epiphi, which Arabs could not
pronounce otherwise than 'Abīb,' changing 'p' into 'b' and 'é'
into 'i,' I will only here add, that a convincing proof of the
shallow scholarship of those who identify ابيب with the fictitious 'month Abib,' אָבִיב, is, that the LXX., writing in Egypt,
rendered אָבִיב everywhere by τῶν νέων sc. καρπῶν, which the
Coptic Version translates ΠΙⲀⲂⲞⲦ ⲀⲂⲂΕΡΙ, "the new month."
Now ЄΠΗΠ, 'Ἐπιφ, appears in almost every Greek and Demotic
Papyrus or Greek MS. of the time of the Ptolemies ; anterior to
the time at which it is first mentioned in 3 Maccab. vi. 38. If,
therefore, there were, or could be, any shadow of resemblance
between אָבִיב and ЄΠΗΠ, 'Ἐπιφ, would not the LXX. have
noticed it, and have translated אָבִיב, Abib, by 'Ἐπιφ, and the
Coptic translators by ЄΠΗΠ? If they did not, it is because it
never occurred to them that אָבִיב could be 'Ἐπιφ, or that the
Passover could ever have been in 'Ἐπιφ, Epiphi, the month of
'drought,' and not of 'green ears ;' no, nor indeed to any one

---

[1] As proved by Ex. ix. 31. and Lev. ii. 14 comp. with 2 Kings iv. 42, &c. ;
and explained at length in my Vindication of the Authorised Version. p. 40. sq.

else but to those who are ever casting about for some new subject, be it ever so absurd and unscholarlike, whereby they may
hope to gainsay the Truth of the Bible with an appearance of
learning which they feel confident few will care to look into.

So little did the Egyptian Church look for the Passover in
their hottest summer month, Epiphi, and so utterly worthless
is the assumption of these 'Abibites,' that S. Cyril of Alexandria, speaking in a sermon of the kingdom of CHRIST,[1] says:
ⲡⲅⲁϫⲉ ⲡⲉⲛⲧⲁⲛⲭⲟⲉⲓⲥ ⲭⲟⲟϥ ⲙⲙⲙⲱⲧⲥⲏⲥ, ϫⲉ ⲁⲣⲓϣⲁ
ⲛⲁⲓ ⲛϥⲟⲙⲙⲛⲧ ⲛⲕⲁⲓⲣⲟⲥ ⲧⲉⲣⲟⲙⲙⲡⲉ, ⲁϥⲡⲉϣ ⲧⲉⲣⲟⲙⲙⲡⲉ ⲉϣⲟⲙⲙⲛⲧ ⲛⲟⲧⲱⲛ. ⲁⲣⲓϣⲁ ⲛⲁⲓ ⲡⲉⲭⲁϥ
ⲙⲙⲡⲉⲃⲟⲧ ⲛϣⲣⲣⲉ ⲙⲙⲡⲙⲙⲛⲧⲁϥⲧⲉ ⲙⲙⲡⲟⲟϩ ⲙⲙⲡⲁⲣ-
ⲙⲟⲧⲧⲉ—"The word which our LORD Most High spake unto
Moyses: 'Make Me a feast three times in the year,' dividing
the year into three parts. 'Make Me,' said He, 'the feast of
the first month which is the fourteenth moon of Parmuti.'"
ⲡⲓⲁⲃⲟⲧ ⲫⲁⲣⲙⲟⲧⲉⲓ ⲉϥⲡⲗⲟⲧⲱⲧⲉⲃ ⲉϧⲟⲩⲛ ⲉϯ-
ⲣⲟⲙⲙⲡⲓ ⲙⲃⲉⲣⲓ—"the month Pharmuthi, which passes into
the new year."[2]   Parmuti, Pharmuti, or as the Copts who
speak Arabic pronounce it, 'Barmûdeh,' beginning, according
to the Alexandrian Calendar, on the 27th of Dystrus (Macedo-
Syrian reckoning), and from the 23rd to the 27th of March.[3]
This is sufficient to show that EPIPHI, Copto-Arab. ABIB, never
was the month of the Passover in Syria, or in Egypt where the
first Passover took place; for S. Macarius, himself also an
Egyptian, tells us[4] the children of Israel left Egypt, ἐν τῷ μηνὶ τῶν
ἀνθῶν, ὅτε πρῶτον ἐπιφαίνεται τὸ ἥδιστον ἔαρ, "in the month of
flowers, when sweetest spring begins to break forth."[5]

---

[1] Zoega Codd. Sahid. p. 615.   [2] Id. Codd. Memph. p. 24.

[3] So also Apollinarius, Bishop of Hierapolis in Syria (Halma's ed. of Ptol.
vol. vi. περὶ τοῦ πασχ.): ὁ σωτὴρ ἡμῶν—ὡς ἀληθὴς ἀμνὸς ἐτύθη ὑπὲρ ἡμῶν ἐν
ἡμέρᾳ παρασκευῇ τῇ ιδ΄ τοῦ πρώτου μηνὸς τῆς σελήνης—καὶ ἀνέστη τῇ ιϛ΄ τοῦ
πρώτου μηνὸς τῆς σελήνης ἐν ᾗ καὶ τὸ δράγμα νενομοθέτητο προσφέρειν τὸν ἱερέα·
"Our SAVIOUR—as the true Lamb—was slain for us on the preparation day,
the 14th of the first month of the moon; and He rose again on the 16th of the
first month of the moon, in the which it had been established by law, that the
heave-offering of first-fruits (δράγμα, עמר) should be offered by the priest."

[4] Homil. xlvii. p. 533, ed. Prit.

[5] "In mense maturescentis frugis" (Munster); "Spicarum, i.e., mense quo
spicae exeunt è calamis, nam vox Hebraea עמר propriè calamum in cujus summi.

Therefore was the intercalary month Veadar occasionally necessary, בְּדֵי שֶׁיִּהְיֶה הַפֶּסַח בִּזְמַן הָאָבִיב, "in order that," says Eliah B. Mosheh,[1] "the Passover should always be in the time of the green ears," and also לַעֲשׂוֹת שָׁנָה מְשֻׁלֶּשֶׁת עָשָׂר חֳדָשִׁים עַד שֶׁיִּהְיֶה הָאָבִיב בְּחֹדֶשׁ הָרִאשׁוֹן, "in order to make the year of thirteen months, so as always to manage that the green ears, or first fruits, אָבִיב, be in the first month." And Maimonides:[2] "Wherefore, then, is this Veadar introduced? מִפְּנֵי זְמַן הָאָבִיב. Because of the time of the first fruits; that the first month be in the time of them." And since, from natural causes, the date of the Passover must thus vary within the course of a whole moon, whereas some writers speak of it and of חֹדֶשׁ הָאָבִיב 'the month of green ears,' as generally in April, others, both Jews and Gentiles, place it in March, the date of the first Passover.[3]

But it is like lighting candles to the sun to adduce more proofs of a thing so plain. The Passover was instituted with regard to the season, and not to the month. The breaking loose from a grinding bondage into a new state of existence, into a new being, as a type of another and a better life, could

---

late spica est significat; hoc in terra promissionis fit mense Martio, vel in principio Aprilis." (Fagius et Vatablus.)

So, again, Stephanus Gobarus (in Phot. Bibl. p. 891, ed. Rot.) says that the Annunciation took place ἐν τῷ μηνὶ τῶν νέων—alov ἀκριλλίῳ ἐν οἱ Εβραῖοι νιεὰν καλοῦσι "in the month of the new fruits, that is, April, which the Jews call Nisan;"—the month of the new creation.

And "God," says Philo, (Quæst. i. in Exod. in Paralip. Arm. p. 445,) "distinctly fixed the month of the first-fruits as the beginning of months, but the children of Israel * յեգիպտացւոցն երրեքին՝ խաւեֆաւք յաշխարհին նոցա քաւկուֆեան սովորուֆեաւք խաբեալք*; should return to Egyptian (habits), misled by that to which they had been accustomed during their stay in Egypt."

[1] In Joh. Seldeni Diss. de Ann. Civ. Jud. p. clxi.

[2] De Sanctif. Novil. c. iv. in Ugolini, vol. xvii. p. 253, sq.

[3] Thus Theodorus Gaza (De Mensib. xiv.) says, περὶ τοῦ Παςχαλίου μηνὸς—ὅτι τὴν μὲν ἀρχὴν ἔχει κατὰ τὴν τοῦ Μαρτίου μηνὸς ἡ΄, τὸ δὲ τέλος κατὰ τὴν τοῦ Ἀπριλίου ε΄, "concerning the Paschal month, that it begins on the 8th of March, and ends on the 5th of April." While Josephus (Antiq. Lib. 3. c. 14, 6) says "that the Passover was by God's order prepared from the 10th to the 14th τοῦ Ξανθικοῦ μηνὸς—ὅτι κατὰ μὲν Αἰγυπτίους Φαρμουθὶ καλεῖται, Νισὰν δὲ καθ' Ἑβραίους, of the Macedonian month Xanthicus, which is called Pharmuthi by the Egyptians, and by the Hebrews Nisan."

only take place when nature itself breaks forth into a hymn of
praise unto Him Who made it, for the freshness and for the
beauties of spring. And so it did. No month was then mentioned, because, had it been mentioned by name, the Passover
would often have been in the time of harvest, and not in that of
the very first fruits—as it must have been. The season alone
was stated, the month of the first fruits, whatever the name of
it be; and that month was of course to be the first of months.
New birth, new life, new reckoning, beginning with the new
month, or month of the new fruits; for, in sooth, old things
were about to pass away for ever, and behold, all things were to
be new. "Principium enim omnium," says Procopius Gazæus,[1]
"et in principio omnium esse Christus secundum æternam ex
Patre generationem ab initio ad finem usque sanctificans nos.
Et in mense novorum fructuum celebratur festum. Nam præte-
rierunt vetera, et ecce omnia ut inquit Paulus, nova facta sunt."[2]

Therefore was it not, as Dr. Stanley says, in the month Nisan,
which did not then exist, that the children of Israel kept the first
Passover, but in the first month, the month of first fruits. In
that month, and on that day too, was CHRIST our Passover
sacrificed for us, to redeem us from the thraldom of sin, of the
world, and of death, and to give us everlasting life—a night, a
sacrifice, a deliverance, and a triumph over His and our foes, to
be observed and remembered indeed for ever, even in Heaven.

XX. Therefore, to tell us, as the Dean of Westminster does,
p. 121, that—

"The animal slain and eaten on the occasion was itself a memorial of the pastoral state of the people"—

is to think and to write unlike a philosopher, without regard to
τῷ ὄντι ἧ ὄν of so sacred a type; thus taking a mean view of it.
So the Lamb foreordained, and slain even before the foundation

---

[1] Comm. in Exod. p. 246.

[2] And S. Cyril (Comm. in Exod. Lib. ii. p. 267, ed. Par.), referring it, as of
course, to CHRIST, says, ἀναφέροντες εἰς Χριστὸν, ὁρίζεται τοίνυν ἐν ἀρχῇ τοῦ
ἔτους ἐν τῷ πρώτῳ μηνὶ τῆς ἱερουργίας ὁ καιρός, "the season is fixed at the beginning of the year, in the first month of the religious service; ὥσπερ ἐν μηνὶ
τῶν νέων ἡ πανήγυρις' wherefore is the solemn assembly in the month of the
new fruits, for old things are passed away, as S. Paul says, behold all things are
become new; and man's nature springs and blossoms afresh towards its first
origin in CHRIST." &c.

of the world, was so prepared because Jacob's sons were to be
shepherds! We had thought, on the contrary, and we still
think, that a lamb without blemish was appointed for the
Paschal Sacrifice, as the only fit emblem of the LAMB OF GOD,
without blemish and without spot, "Who knew no sin, but was
made to be sin for us, that we might be made the righteousness
of God in Him." Therefore did thousands of angels around
the Throne say with a loud voice, "Worthy is the Lamb that
was slain to receive power, and riches, and wisdom, and strength,
and honour, and glory, and blessing." And therefore did the
earth answer, "Blessing, and honour, and glory, and power, be
unto Him that sitteth upon the throne, and unto the Lamb for
ever and ever." And under the whole heaven was heard—
"Amen."[1]

XXI. Israel then was ready—if 'ready' may be said of a
rush through the prison gates burst open by a flood or by an
earthquake,—and in that memorable night was the start made
from Rameses,—whether this be Delbeis, according to Makrizi,[2]
or Sedir, Sadr, or Abukesbeid, according to Abussïd and others,
in Wâdi Tumilât, the possible site of Goshen. This is not the
place to treat fully this subject on which volumes have been, and
will yet be, written, every one advocating some fresh discovery
of his, from the downright infidel, who like Dubois-Aimé[3] calls
the cloud "un tourbillon de sable," a 'whirlwind of sand,' and
treats the whole narrative of the Exodus, as "faits dictés par
l'orgueil national"—to the blind or ignorant who think thought
and research unnecessary. I will only point out, that so entirely were the children of Israel under God's guidance, that
Moses at starting did not know what awaited him and the
people; for they started for three days' journey into the wilderness urged by the Egyptians and with Pharaoh's leave, with
their wives and children and with much cattle, to hold a feast
unto the LORD. Moses, therefore, could not and did not, watch
the day and hour of the tide as certain 'philosophers' have
fondly asserted; for it was not until after Moses and the people
were encamped at Etham, that the LORD commanded them "to

---

[1] Rev. v. 12—14.
[2] Mém. Géogr. sur l'Eg. vol. i. p. 61, 62.
[3] Descr. de l'Eg. vol. ii. p. 309, sq.

turn,"[1] and encamp before Pi-ahiroth—a place of herbage and of fresh water—"between Migdol and the sea, over against Baal-zephon." 'To turn' here could not, of course, mean to retrace their steps; but rather, perhaps, to take the usual route from Egypt into Arabia across the sea. Therefore was it told Pharaoh "that the people fled," because they were gone in another direction than either they or himself at first expected; for neither he nor the Egyptians could think they had fled, if they had gone "into the wilderness," as understood by Pharaoh and by his people, i.e. into the wilderness of Egypt, beyond the borders of the cultivated soil, at Etham. Here did the Egyptian host overtake the children of Israel; and here did these "see the salvation of the LORD," who wrought and fought for them. For He commanded Moses saying: "Lift thou up the rod—'the rod of God'—and stretch out thine hand over the sea, and divide it: and the children of Israel shall go on dry ground through the midst of the sea." "And Moses stretched out his hand over the sea; and the LORD caused the sea to go back by a strong east wind all that night, and made the sea dry land, and the waters were divided."[2]

XXII. As I have discussed this subject elsewhere,[3] I will now only briefly remark on these words of Dr. Stanley:—

"Whichever these (routes followed by the Israelites) be, the narrative compels us to look for the passage somewhere near the head of the then gulf, whence the width would be such as to allow the host to pass over in a single night, and the waters to be parted by the means described, namely, by a strong wind, or by the shortness of the distance required for the Israelites to escape the pursuers."—p. 127.

On which Dr. Stanley adds to "strong wind" the note:—

"Not necessarily 'east.' See LXX. (Ex. xiv. 21) and Philo. V. M. i. 82."

Here Dr. Stanley simply repeats what his masters say, unfortunately without caring to search into the truth of it; therefore at a risk. B. viii. p. 4. But, really, such scholarship seems so poor, that one feels it no credit to have to refute it.

[1] שוב, Ex. xiv. 2.   [2] Ch. xiv. 13, 15, 21.
[3] Vindic. of the A. V. pt. 1.

First—We saw above, p. 51, sq., that owing to the difference in the situation and in the physical conformation of Egypt and of Palestine, the meteorological phænomena of wind and rain, &c., are also equally different in each country. In Palestine the 'west wind' or 'wind of the sea' רוּחַ יָם and רוּחַ קָדִים the 'front' or 'east wind,' are the two prevailing and the two strongest currents of air. In Egypt, these are, as indeed they must be, the north and the southerly winds.

Secondly—In Palestine, the east wind, owing to the quarter whence it blows, מִמִּדְבָּר from the wilderness, Hos. xiii. 15, is either 'strong' עַזָּה Ex. xiv. 21; 'hot and soft' חֲרִישִׁית Jonah iv. 8; 'blighting' שְׁדֻפָה Ex. x. 13; Ez. xvii. 10, xix. 12; 'hot and drying-up,' מֵחָרָבָת מִיבְשָׁה Hos. xiii. 15; 'injurious to health,' Jonah iv. 8, and Job xv. 2, from the effect it produces; 'violent, rooting-up,' Job xxvii. 21; Ps. xlviii. 7; Jer. xviii. 17, &c. But in Egypt, this same east wind القبول, الصبا is, on the contrary, ناعنة soft, favourable, and wholesome, according to Abdollatif, who tells us,[1] that

"Upper Egypt suffers from being deprived of this wind, ان الصبا مجربة عنهم بجبلها الشرقي المسمى المقطم فانه يستر عنها هذا الريح النافعة وقلما تهب عليهم حالة اليهم الا نكبا for the east wind is warded off from its inhabitants by the eastern chain of mountains called El-Mokattem; which, indeed, hinders that favourable wind from reaching that land; so that it blows on the inhabitants not with free breath, but as it were sideways. Wherefore the ancient Egyptians chose to fix the seat of government at Memphis, and to remove it so that it be to the west of that eastern mountain; likewise the Greeks chose Alexandria, and avoided the parts about Fostat because it is near to the Mokattem; for that mountain shelters more those who live close to it than those who are farther off—so you will find that those places in Egypt which are exposed to the east wind are more healthy than the rest."

Thirdly—We find from the meteorological calendar of Ptolemy made chiefly at and for Alexandria,[2] that owing to the sea-coast stretching there east and west, this east wind seldom blows

---

[1] Ægypt. p. 10, ed. Wb.   [2] Cf. Ptolem. ed. Halma, vol. iii. p. 47.

at Alexandria; and we also find by comparing that same calendar for every month in the year, with the observations made at Cairo by the French expedition in 1800, 1801,[1] that, as we might expect from the different and more inland situation of Cairo, the climate, and the winds, rain, and meteorological phænomena are to some extent modified.

From all this, however, we gather the facts, that, whereas in Palestine the chief currents of air are east and west because 'the sea,' ἡ θάλασσα, lies north and south—in Egypt, 'the sea,' ἡ θάλασσα, البحر الروم المحيط[2] lying east and west, causes the principal winds to be north and south. The north or Etesian winds are favourable; but the νότος, the south, and λιβάνοτος, and λίψ, the south-west winds are dreadful in their effects. "About the spring equinox," says Mr. Reynier,[3] "a southerly, burning wind called 'Khamseen' blows first for three days, and more or less for fifty, the atmosphere is of a purple tint, all plants and animals suffer much, some even die; the plants, however, suffer more than the animals; if the first gusts happen when the grain is formed and nearly ripe, the wind hastens its maturity; if, however, they happen when the grain is yet unformed, the crops are withered and lost." I can bear witness to such a wind in the second week in April; so violent, and raising such clouds of fine red dust that I was unable to travel for two days, until it had fallen. These winds are called Khamseen, خماسين i.e. 'of fifty' (days) as lasting periodically more or less that time; but by the Copts, they are called المريسي 'Marisi,' i.e. 'southern,' from ⲘⲀⲢⲎⲤ, 'south;' and ⲦⲞⲨⲢⲎⲤ, ⲐⲞⲨⲢⲎⲤ, ⲐⲎⲞⲨⲢⲎⲤ, 'south wind;' possibly Θούηρις of which Plutarch speaks,[4] as of Typhon's concubine, both symbolized by Jablonski[5] into Typhon, the קדים, and Θούηρις, the south wind. But most of his Coptic etymologies are worth very little; and, as to symbolism, it is often made doubtful when, as in this case, it is not clearly defined. It is possible, however, that

1 Descr. de l'Eg. vol. ii. p. 322.

2 Lit. 'surrounding.' but also applied to the Mediterranean in Egypt.

3 Agricult. de l'Eg. in Mém. sur l'Eg. vol. iv. p. 15, sq.

4 De Is. et Osir. c. 19.

5 Panth. Æg. pt. iii. p. 85, sq.

פַתְרוֹס, Pathros, may come from ⲡⲁ-ⲧⲟⲩⲣⲏⲥ 'the parts of the south wind,' the south of Egypt. Be this as it may, we have the same parallelism in the principal winds in Palestine and in Egypt; only from different points of the compass. In Palestine, from the east and from the west; in Egypt, from the north and from the south; and as the west sea-wind is welcome in Palestine, so is also the north sea-wind equally welcome in Egypt; as the Etesian wind ⲛⲓ ⲛⲝⲉⲉ ⲁⲉ ⲙⲉⲣⲧ 'the sweet pleasant, north wind,' as it is called in several inscriptions; the gift of Apis at Memphis, and of Osiris at Thebes.[1] So also in Palestine, is the north wind welcome in summer as blowing from Lebanon; e.g. Song of Solomon iv. 14, "Awake, O north wind; and come, thou south; blow upon my garden." No Hebrew poet would have said: 'Awake, west wind, and come, thou east wind;' for this would have been too warm at Jerusalem, or it would have withered the plants and blighted the fruit.[2]

We see then, again plainly, that the LXX. being written by Alexandrian Jews, and for Jews in Egypt, these were obliged to render קָדִים or רוּחַ קָדִים, not by 'east wind,' but by the effects of that wind in Palestine which belong only to the south wind in Egypt; otherwise the Greek Vulgate would not have been understood, if, rendering the Hebrew literally, it had for instance, told the Egyptians that ears of corn were blasted with the 'east' wind, when that wind in Egypt rather helps them to grow; and is counted a blessing and not a curse. But they were obliged to leave this as it were open, and simply said ἀνεμόφθοροι, leaving the Egyptians to ascribe the effect to their ⲧⲟⲩⲣⲏⲥ or south wind. Hence comes that, as we have already seen, they rendered קָדִים and its effects by βίαιος, καύσων, νότος, &c., and by any thing except the literal term ἀπηλιώτης, or ἀνατολή, which in this case was inadmissible, because it would not have been understood.

---

[1] Brugsch, Monum. i. pl. viii. and xvii.

[2] But, the LXX. were correct in rendering the Hebrew literally in this place: ἐξεγέρθητι Βορρᾶ, καὶ ἔρχου Νότε, καὶ διάπνευσον κῆπόν μου, as the north wind in Egypt is, we see, welcome and agreeable; and the south wind is often fresh, if not very cold, باردة جَنوب. Abdollat. Æg. p. 12.

XXIII. Therefore, conclude these 'philosophers' who trouble themselves very little about τὸ ἀληθές, the truth of this ὂν ᾗ ὄν, particular case and peculiar circumstances—since the LXX. render קָדִים and רוּחַ קָדִים 'east wind' by 'strong,' 'hot,' 'stormy,' &c., and 'south,' therefore does קָדִים 'east,' mean either 'south,' 'strong,' 'north,' 'hot,' or 'stormy;'—with what knowledge, others may judge. Thus we have the amusing sight of two of these 'philosophers' contending about this verse, Ex. xiv. 21,—the one V. Bohlen, who tells us that קָדִים is "eine Irrthum," a mistake![1] and that "sollte Südwind heissen," it should be called south wind;[2] and the other, that it must have been "a strong north-east wind."[3] They lay themselves open to ridicule, and they deserve it. If they were what they profess to be —philosophers—they would see that קָדִים from its etymology and from its use, never loses the meaning of 'fronting,' i.e. 'east.' For when a term is so used as to be capable of only one rendering, that rendering must, of course, be the τὸ ὂν ᾗ ὄν, τὸ ἀληθές, the real, intrinsic, original sense of the term, and all other meanings thereof must be figurative or secondary. Now, in Ezek. xlii. 10, where mention is made of the four winds, רוּחַ קָדִים 'east wind' stands for 'east,' and can be interpreted in no other way. This then must be its real meaning; as real for one who wrote in the Hebrew of Palestine, as that of 'sea' for יָם, יָמָּה when it is used for 'west.'

Local idioms of this kind belong to every country; and if no account is to be taken of them when translating from one text into another for the use of the people, a literal rendering will often be mere nonsense. Thus as we have seen יָם 'sea,'[4] means

[1] Comm. in Gen. p. 381.   [2] Genes. Introd. p. lxxxiii.
[3] Dr. Robinson, Researches, vol. I. p. 83, 1st ed. Journal of Sacred Literature, Oct., 1854, p. 116, sq. So also J. Clericus ad l. Quatremère Mém. sur le lieu où les Isr. traversèrent la Mer Rouge, in Mém. des Inscr. et B. Lettres, 1851, vol. xlv. p. 45, sq.
[4] In Egyptian, ⲒⲞⲦⲘⲘⲀ, Copt. ⲒⲀⲘⲘ, ⲒⲞⲘⲘ 'sea,' was like יָם said of 'the sea' or of 'a sea or lake' with regard to any given locality; thus יָם the sea of Chinnereth or Galilee: and ⲪⲒⲞⲘⲘ ⲚⲦⲈ ⲪⲒⲞⲘⲘ, Egypt. ⲈⲒⲚ-Ⲧ ⲘⲘ ⲚⲒⲞⲦⲘⲘⲀ 'the way of the sea,' whereby is meant the port of Berenice on the Red Sea, for the miners of Radesieh (Chabas, Mém. des

'west' of the land of Palestine; and רוּחַ יָם or 'sea wind,'
means there, 'west wind.' But, in Egypt 'the sea' البحر
means 'north,' and ريح البحرية 'sea wind' means 'north
wind,' ἐτήσιος ἄνεμος, 'northern,' soft, agreeable, and welcome;
likewise تبلي 'fronting' means 'south' in Egypt, because it
is towards the Qibla of Mecca; whereas קָדִים 'fronting'
in Palestine meant 'east,' as being the side towards which
they looked at sun-rise. Again, if these terms are to be
divested of their home-meaning when used in other countries,
what are we to make of, e.g. Numb. iii. 23, where it is said, the
Gershonites were to encamp יָמָּה "towards the sea." What
sea? They had the Mediterranean, or 'western sea,' to the
north, the Heroopolite gulf to the west, and the Ælanite to the
east: and let us suppose that the Egyptian translator had rendered it literally الي البحر 'seawards' (instead of الي المغرب
'westwards') it would mean 'northwards' instead of 'westwards.' Now if we argued from this rendering of יָמָּה by
الي المغرب 'westwards,' that יָם, לְיָם, יָמָּה never meant
'seawards,' but always 'westwards,' we should make strange
sense of such passages as Josh. xvi. 3, 8, 1 Kings v. 9, where
the cedar trees instead of being brought from Lebanon 'to the
sea,' would have to be taken from Lebanon to the coasts of Tar-
shish. Yet this is what they do, who argue from the necessary
meaning given in Egypt to a Hebrew term, that it must have
that same meaning in Palestine also, under totally different circumstances.

But, as they have not the courage to go so far as to render
בְּרוּחַ קָדִים עַזָּה 'by a strong south' or 'north wind,' they
render it as does Dr. Stanley, "by a strong wind," leaving out
קָדִים altogether; and shutting their eyes to these two facts:

First—that since the east wind in Egypt is generally قابلي

Mines d'Or, letter M. on the plan. Pap. Harris, p. 17.) It was also said of the
Nile when περιηγήτης, both in Egyptian, in Hebrew, and in Coptic, as now in
Arabic. But when 'the sea' was thus alluded to without qualification, both in
Hebrew, in Coptic, and in Egyptian, as now in Arabic, it meant the Mediter-
ranean, (see p. 61.)

'soft and favourable,' it was purposely made שַׁוָּה 'strong' by the Divine will; therefore—secondly—that since it was found necessary to employ the wind which is naturally soft, and to make it strong, contrary to its habitual nature, and for a particular purpose, it shows that this wind, and no other, was the one that should do that work.

XXIV. And so it was.   No other wind could have 'cleft asunder' (בקע) the sea; for either the north or the south wind, by blowing upon the length of the gulf instead of upon the width thereof, would have simply pushed back the waters before it, but never so as to make them a wall on the right hand and on the left.   This could be done only by a wind blowing athwart the gulf in one particular spot, so as to make a way in the midst of the sea.   And He Who made it blow could well make it blow how and where He would.   Therefore, and to conclude, not only was it a strong 'east wind,' but, reasonably speaking, it could be no other; and, as I have said, until we find קָדִים predicated of either north, south, or west, we will continue to believe it inseparable from its radical meaning of 'fronting,' that is, 'east;' and, leaving these 'philosophers' to settle between their 'north' and 'south,' we will, with Scripture, take the mean, and hold that God did cause a "strong east wind" to blow all that night, so as to cleave the sea in two, raising on each side the waters כְּמוֹ־נֵד 'like a heap,' as He did at the passage of His people through the Jordan, under Joshua.

For, as in that case it was meet that death, eager to swallow them, should be apparent, and apparently restrained by the command of Jesus the son of Nun, who brought them into the Promised Land; so also in this case it was necessary that, in order to be constituted a Church, a people set apart from the world by a rite of consecration, the children of Israel should be "baptized unto Moses and in the sea."   But they could not have been 'baptized,' i.e., 'buried' unto death to Egypt, and 'come out' of the water in token of their new birth to altogether a new kind of life, had not the waters 'been made to stand,' as the Scripture says, on the "right and on the left," and to rise above the heads of the host passing through them on the dry ground.   Here, then, to talk of ebb and flow, of moon and tides, of north and south wind, of anything,

in short, but what the Scripture of Truth says concerning this
grand miracle, this glorious display of GOD's might in behalf of
His people, is so derogatory from the course a real philosopher
would take in considering τὸ ἀληθές, the Truth of the subject,
that I will only refer my readers to the whole literature there is
written on it from Clericus, Goldsmid, Jurke, Lessing, &c.,
downward; the more so as I have elsewhere exposed the worthless scholarship of one who attempted to gainsay the Scripture
account and the Authorized Version thereof.[1]

XXV. But among sundry good remarks—though not up to
the subject—with which Dr. Stanley closes this lecture, the following words deserve notice, as they might easily be miscon-
strued.   At p. 129 Dr. Stanley says :—

"In later times Religion has been so often and so exclusively
associated with ideas of order, of obedience, of submission to
authority, that it is well to become occasionally reminded that it
has had other aspects also.   This, the first epoch of our religious
history, is, in its original historical significance, the sanctification,
the glorification of national independence and freedom."

The intention of the Dean of Westminster in this passage
is very far from clear.

First—whence does Dr. Stanley derive the term 'Religion;'
'à relegendo,' from vain repetitions, or 'à religando,' from its
holding the heart captive? Secondly—deriving the term 'religion' 'à religando,' we may notice—"that it has been associated with order and obedience" not "in later times only," as
Dr. Stanley teaches, but from the very first. By faith Abel,
Enoch, and Noah obeyed GOD; that was their religion. By
faith Abraham left his home and country, and, in obedience to
GOD, wandered as a stranger in a land not his own, during a
hundred years of his life; that too was his religion. By faith,
also, Isaac and Jacob were led, and did walk in obedience to
GOD, as religious men. By faith, likewise, did Joseph withstand the temptations of Potiphar's house, kept by his religion
from yielding to the solicitations of lust, and thus made to act
in the fear of GOD, and in that only. By faith also "Moses,
when he was come to years, refused to be called the son

[1] Vindication of the A. V. Pt. I. p. 3—162.

of Pharaoh's daughter, choosing rather to suffer affliction with the people of God, than to enjoy the pleasures of sin for a season;" that was his order and his obedience. "Esteeming the reproach of Christ greater riches than the treasures of Egypt, for he had respect unto the recompense of the reward ;" that was his faith. "By faith he forsook Egypt, not fearing the wrath of the king; for he endured, as seeing Him Who is invisible;" that was his subjection to that authority. "Through faith he kept the Passover, and the sprinkling of the blood"—as subject, obedient and religious—"lest he that destroyed the first-born should touch them." "By faith they passed through the Red Sea as by dry land"—subject, orderly and obedient to Him Who led them—"which the Egyptians assaying to do were drowned." Thus deriving 'religion,' not 'à relegendo'—for we have no proof to show that the patriarchs could read—but 'à religando,' we find the best examples of it in good olden times.

Thirdly—looking at "this the first epoch of our religious history," we can find no greater proof of order, of obedience, and of submission to authority, no grander example of entire dependence upon God, and of devoted service to Him, than in this departure from Egypt. It was not "national independence," that is, irresponsibility to any one; neither was it "freedom;" but only escape from bondage. For 'freedom' means, as we saw at page 13, entire independence from others; but in this case the children of Israel only exchanged their bondage to the Egyptians for their service to God. They were His servants, whom He redeemed from servitude to other masters, and whom He made His people when He constituted them into a nation, with Him at the head as King, Who gave them His laws, which He enacted thus: Do this, and thou shalt live; "but cursed be he that continueth not in all the things written in the book of the law, to do them." To which the people answered, Amen.

This does not look much like national independence; neither was it much like 'freedom' to have to receive laws and statutes from such absolute authority. Neither, indeed, was it freedom. It was a state of servitude no longer to the Egyptians, it is true, but to the Lord of heaven and earth, of life and of death,

T

Who gave them His orders, and Who parcelled out to them His land under certain conditions. So thoroughly conditional was their tenure of that land, and so little was it their own freehold property, that they were reminded of it even in their deeds of sale. וְהָאָרֶץ לֹא תִמָּכֵר לִצְמִתֻת כִּי־לִי הָאָרֶץ כִּי־גֵרִים וְתוֹשָׁבִים אַתֶּם עִמָּדִי: "The land shall not be sold unreservedly," said the LORD, "for the land is mine, and ye are strangers and sojourners with me. For unto me the children of Israel are servants; they are my servants whom I brought forth out of the land of Egypt. I am the LORD."[1]

XXVI. Whatever amount of civil statute law there might be mixed up with these injunctions to the Israelites as 'people of GOD,' the principle on which they were made to rest, is the same now as it was then: it is that of absolute and entire subjection and obedience to GOD as Creator, FATHER, and LORD Supreme—subjection not conditional, and obedience not optional, but whole, humble, and devoted. Without this there can be no religion; neither εὐσέβεια, θεοσέβεια, nor even θρησκεία. Cicero, to wit: "Qui sancti? qui religionum colentes? nisi qui meritam diis immortalibus gratiam justis honoribus et memori mente persolvunt."[2] So spake even a heathen of what he called religion and the worship of his gods. What shall we say, we Christians? Even that ἐλευθερωθέντες ἀπὸ τῆς ἁμαρτίας, δουλωθέντες δὲ τῷ Θεῷ, "being made free from sin, and become servants of GOD, we have our fruit unto holiness, and the end everlasting life. For the wages of sin is death, but the gift of GOD is eternal life, through JESUS CHRIST our LORD."[3]

This is our faith, and the hope that is set before us; this is our religion and our bondage. We are free, yet servants; free, in the liberty wherewith CHRIST hath made us free—freedom, indeed, compared with the yoke of bondage to the old ordinances of the Law. Yet, although free, we are "not to use our liberty for a cloke of maliciousness;" but as the servants of GOD. This is the check on our freedom to sin; but it is the charter of our freedom to do good as free citizens of "a better country, that is an heavenly." With it we study to "purify our-

---

[1] Lev. xxv. 23, 55, and 41, 42, sq.   [2] Pro Plancio, 80, ed. Ern.
[3] Rom. vi. 22, 23.

selves, even as He is pure," by obeying Him, and for His sake, those whom He has set over us as lords temporal and spiritual. We therefore honour the Sovereign because we fear GOD; we are "subject to the powers that be as ordained of GOD," whether to the worse, as were the saints at Rome; or to the best, as those in England who love "religion, order, and obedience" are to the Queen.

XXVII. But this religious principle of faith in GOD and of obedience to Him, which is the only foundation of all good present and to come, forbids the setting up of our own will in opposition to His; leastways our arrogating to ourselves either wisdom, intellect, or power apart from Him. Wisdom, indeed! "Where is the wise? Hath not GOD made foolish the wisdom of this world?" And did not he who was said by the oracle to be the wisest of men, not only declare that human wisdom is worth very little, but that the superiority of his own wisdom, such as it was, lay in that—ὅτι ἃ μὴ οἶδα, οὐδὲ οἴομαι εἰδέναι—"he did not pretend to know what he did not know." This ἐποίησι τὸ ὄνομα "made his fame," as he confessed, ἴσως μὲν δόξω τισὶν παίζειν, not without an inward smile.[1] Human wisdom, we see, does not reach very far. Intelligence or intellect, do you say? Who first gave it to man? Yet now, fallen as it is, dimmed and lowered by him to whom it was given for the highest end—to understand GOD—this intellect seeks to set itself free from all allegiance to Him Who had made it perfect, by refusing Him submission and obedience in a path which this intellect is now too dull and too weak ever to find out of itself. Plato felt this when he longed to have the film removed from his vast intelligence, if by any means he might become a better man. Let certain Christians who have the light of the Truth, learn of him who only felt after GOD if haply he might find Him; lest, after all, the first should be last.

And, as to our having any power of our own, apart from GOD—what power had the children of Israel when told "to stand still and see the salvation of the LORD?" Our help, then, is also in the Name of the LORD, "Whose strength is made perfect in our weakness." Our only strength is in the promise,

[1] Apol. Socr. 6, 5, 9, &c.

" As thy days so shall thy strength be. The Eternal God is
thy refuge, and underneath are the everlasting arms."[1]

Feeling, then, as we do, we should indeed be sorry to say or
to think that at any time Religion—that is, true Religion—can
possibly be independent of order and of obedience; neither
would we uphold in unqualified terms "the sanctification, the
glorification of national independence and freedom," lest these
words might be mistaken, and we understood to advocate more
freedom, either ecclesiastical or civil, than is meet and consistent with religion, order, and obedience to authority. For
this is the only safe road to lasting prosperity on earth, and to
happiness hereafter, because it is the only way to it ordained of
God.

We should be afraid to appear as if glorifying our own pride,
our own independence, and our own conceit, more than anything else; as if slackening instead of straitening the bands of
Religion and thus destroying it; and as if throwing down all
fences in the Church, and a good many in the State; always
provided we ourselves might stand. But, rather, we feel persuaded, from all the examples of true Religion we have seen,
that Religion cannot exist without faith, order and obedience to
God in all things, and for His sake to those whom He has appointed to be instruments in His hands, and ministers of His
will in matters ecclesiastical and civil, which hinder neither principle nor the conscience; that is, which do not interfere with
our duty to God.

XXVIII. And here I must take leave of the Dean of Westminster. I have purposely examined the first part of his work, and no
other, lest I should appear to have chosen the portion or portions
most open to criticism. And I have endeavoured to remark
upon it fairly; pointing out the many passages in the work
which commend themselves by their thoroughly good English
taste and feeling, with as much pleasure, as I felt of disappointment at having to advocate with him the cause of Truth against
the invasion of erroneous or foreign teaching. I might say
much; but my respect for the position he occupies in the
Church forbids my doing more than express a hope that, when
he again writes for candidates for Holy Orders, he may bear in

[1] Deut. xxxiii. 25—27.

mind that the nature of their calling and the importance of
their office requires at the hands of their teachers a lore alike
sound and accurate.

No man can reach unto the highest of earthly positions, that
of a real scholar, or of a real philosopher and friend of the
Truth, which is the same thing, if he do not value Truth τὸ
ἀληθές abstractedly, for its own sake, and the Truth, τὴν ἀλήθειαν,
above everything else.   Without this ruling principle within
him, he is constantly in danger of being, as Plato says, φιλόδοξος,
more fond either of his own opinion or of that of others, than
φιλόσοφος, a lover of truth, of the Truth and of wisdom.   This
very motive must often warp his judgment and mislead him into
arguing after the manner of those whom both Plato and Aristotle
called σοφισταί, sophists, because they presented their Truth, and
argued upon it from their own view of it only, and not on true
principles.   But this depends, of course, on the προαίρεσις τοῦ
βίου, on our individual disposition, and on the choice of what
we propose to ourselves as the aim and object of life; whether
to serve and to please men, or to serve and to please God; whether to shape the Truth so as to meet their wishes, or honestly
to labour at it as an act of homage to God, and of worship of
Him Who is the God of Truth, careless of men's wishes about
it; since they neither make Truth nor the Truth.   For Truth
is a gem they are allowed to find by searching for it as for hid
treasures with their limited efforts, in the little World in which
they live; while 'the Truth' is the pearl of great price, for which
we shall seek in vain in the earth; it is given of God from above.

"There is in the world," says Hooker, "no kind of knowledge,
whereby any part of truth is seen, but we justly account it precious; yea, that principal Truth, in comparison whereof all knowledge is vile, may receive from it some kind of light; whether it
be that Egyptian or Chaldean wisdom mathematical wherewith
Moses and Daniel were furnished, or that natural, moral, and
civil wisdom, wherein Solomon excelled all men," &c.,—"to de-
tract from the dignity thereof were to injure even God Himself,
Who being that Light which none can approach unto, hath sent
out these lights whereof we are capable, even as so many sparkles
resembling the bright fountain from which they rise."[1]

[1] Eccles. Pol. Bk. iii. ch. viii. sq.

However much we may grieve or smile at the conceit or at the ignorance of men who treat this Truth as if it were of their own choice or making, and who handle the Bible in which it is revealed to men with less veneration, perhaps, than some of their own writings; we must nevertheless see with satisfaction that, if we are to judge of their learning and scholarship by the samples thereof we have just examined, both the Truth and the Bible are safe from their attacks. If such teaching has a baneful influence, it can only be over the mind of superficial men, who let others think for them, or over that of men who, being neither ignorant nor superficial, trust their accredited leaders with generous confidence, and take all they say for granted; but such lore is utterly powerless over men who know what to believe and what to doubt, who take no statements upon trust, and who, in all matters of intellectual knowledge, require proofs, and not assertions only. This ought, then, to induce the Clergy to revive Biblical studies among themselves; not only that of Divinity, but also the study of Hebrew and of Shemitic literature that bears upon it; for without such knowledge they are entirely at the mercy of the first comer who may attempt to gainsay the witness of the Old Testament.[1]

They can, of course, bestow their energies on no better object than on the study of the original texts, and of the Truth they contain; bearing in mind what the holy Apostle said to a bishop who had no New Testament: "All Scripture is given by inspiration of God, and is profitable for doctrine, for reproof, for correction, for instruction in righteousness; that the man of God may be ἄρτιος, perfect—πρὸς πᾶν ἔργον ἀγαθὸν ἐξηρτισμένος, thoroughly furnished unto every good work—studying to be approved of God; ἐργάτην ἀνεπαίσχυντον, ὀρθοτομοῦντα τὸν λόγον τῆς ἀληθείας, a workman that needeth not to be ashamed, rightly dividing the word of truth;" and withal "shunning βεβήλους κενοφωνίας—or καινοφωνίας—profane and vain—or new-fangled —babblings; for they will increase unto more ungodliness."[2]

---

[1] Every Clergyman need not know Hebrew, for all have not the requisite ability for such study; but there ought at least to be one Hebrew scholar to every five Clergymen, all of whom are expected to have mastered the Greek of the New Testament.

[2] 2 Tim. iii. 16, 17; ii. 15, 16.

And such exist, it appears, in all countries, though with less harm, perhaps, than in this; because there is here in general such solidity of character, such earnestness of purpose, and so much more real religion than elsewhere, that opposition thereto is the more keenly felt.   Even from Egypt we hear—

Murad. "To tell you the truth, I have been in the company of many elderly men whom we call ' ulemâs,' learned doctors and dignitaries ; but never have I heard them say much to the purpose."

Ali. " If, then, our ' ulemâs' do not know what they ought to know, what use do they make of the books they carry about with them, and read all the day long ?"

Murad. "None whatever.   Don't you know the common saying, عمايمهم مثل الابراج واكمامهم مثل الاخراج والعلم عند الله 'Their turbans are like towers, and their sleeves are like hampers, and the learning is—with God' ?"

Ali. " You are right.   Many of them بعمامة ثقيلة يغطوا عقل خفيف hide a light mind under a heavy turban, and carry in their sleeves books they do not understand."

Murad. " Well, they are not all alike."[1]

No; and real "intellect, ability, and learning," with whomsoever they be found, are worthy of great homage for their own sakes, as the brightest and best of earthly gifts.   But light seldom praises itself—it shines.

---

[1] في مخاطبة العالمين in a conversation between two scholars ; Savary's Dial. Ar. d'Eg. p. 448 and 330,

PLAIN WORDS ON QUESTIONS OF THE DAY

RESPECTING

FAITH, THE BIBLE, AND THE CHURCH.

———

I. **We may, then, keep the Bible.**—Yet, the thought must have occurred to others as well as to myself, in hearing all this talk about the philosophy we are told to reconcile with the Bible, though we cannot; what—in the estimation of these philosophers, and if their philosophy be true—is to become of poor, simple-minded and ignorant people, of the multitude, in short, who cannot understand all this wisdom? Or yet, of other plain, straightforward men, whose philosophy goes not beyond common sense, who therefore, will none of this new teaching at any price, but will have plain sound English sense, that they can understand, and sound old-fashioned doctrine withal; not only of the days of Jewell, Hooker, and of other such pillars of the Church, but even older than they—as old as the Apostles, the prophets, and the patriarchs? what is to become of them if this philosophy be the only right thing? Or, have these philosophers, perhaps, "taken away the key of knowledge"—the Word of God[1]—"shutting up the kingdom against men, neither going in themselves nor suffering them that are entering to go in?" Or, is it that they "desire to be teachers of the law; understanding neither what they say, nor whereof they affirm?"—"But we know that the law is good, if

[1] "Claves autem quibus aut claudere regnum cœlorum aut aperire possint, ut Chrysostomus ait, dicimus esse scientiam Scripturarum: ut Eusebius, esse interpretationem Legis: ut Eusebius, esse verbum Dei.—Cumque clavis, qua aditus nobis aperitur ad regnum Dei, sit verbum Evangelii, et interpretatio Legis et Scripturarum; UBI NON SIT VERBUM, IBI DICIMUS NON ESSE CLAVEM." Apologia Eccles. Anglic. J. Juell. p. 15.

a man use it lawfully." We know that there is, and that there
can be nothing better than 'real' philosophy—ἡ φιλοσοφία ἡ
ἀληθής, as S. Chrysostom calls it[1]—which, for a Christian, consists in searching, in thinking and in reasoning, as a Christian
ought to search, to think and to reason, that is—not backwards,
from himself to God, as heathens did, and as certain philosophers
of the day will do; but forwards, from God as revealed in His
Word, to himself. And this Christian philosophy as it is found
in the Gospel of Christ is, at once, so deep that no human intellect can search it out—since even angels desire to look into
it—and yet so simple, that "the common people heard gladly"
THE FOUNDER of that philosophy, when He silenced Herod, re-
buked lawyers, convicted Pharisees, and "preached the Gospel
to the poor." Let us then, for awhile, leave those philosophers
to their philosophy; and talk plain, common sense, for plain
people.

BELIEF AND FAITH.

11. Aristotle tells us that 'good' is the end to which most
things tend, the object most men set before themselves in their
thoughts, and in daily life. They connect this idea of 'good,'
some with one thing, others with another; so that, heathen and
other philosophers did set about trying to find out, both wherein
this idea of good consists, and wherein the 'greatest good' for man
lies. Some placed it in the gratification of the senses and of the
appetites; others in virtue; others, again, like Plato, put the supreme good for man, in drawing as near as in him lies to 'that
which really is,' τὸ ὄν, whereby he understood—God. But those
men not having a Revelation, were so completely in the dark as
to the actual fallen and degraded state of man's nature, that
Marcus Varro[2] reckoned two hundred and eighty-eight different
sects of philosophers, either existing, or possible, whose object
was to set this nature a task to fulfil in endeavouring to better
itself, for which it has neither ability nor power. I need hardly
point out that with those men, as with the philosophers of the
present day, those who either could not or would not receive their
teaching were altogether shut out from all hope of sharing in the
benefits their philosophy was said to confer. The poor, the igno-

---

[1] De Sacerd. lib. i. c. 1   [2] S. August. Civ. Dei. lib. xix. c. 1.

rant, the penitent, therefore, had then, as they now have, no hope whatever, consistently with that teaching, if we are to receive it.

III. But we do not. Common sense alone tells us that our human nature must be of two things one—either sinless or sinful; either in its original state of innocence, or fallen from it. Except we be past feeling or grossly ignorant, however, our own experience, every moment in the day, teaches us, apart from Revelation, that our nature is fallen very low indeed, from its exalted origin, to which it must be restored, or, if not restored, continue as it is, degraded. Our own sense, further, tells us also, that our human nature having thus fallen by depriving itself of certain powers and of certain attributes it had originally, cannot possibly of itself and with its own efforts, regain those lost privileges.—A broken limb cannot set and mend itself; and being of our nature "dead in trespasses and sins," we cannot be further "alienated from the life of God"[1] than we are. Our fallen nature then, must receive from without power to restore itself, that is—from God; and thus be restored by Him.

And here again, simple, unassisted reason teaches also that under such circumstances, a good, merciful, and gracious God, could not and would not so word His offer and promise of eternal happiness, as that few of His creatures could understand it; and so describe the way He has made for the restoration of our human nature to its former estate,—yea, even to a higher one—as that fewer still of those creatures should be able to make out that way and to walk in it; and thus be virtually shut out from the happiness promised. We believe, on the contrary, that, however men may either from conceit, ignorance or self-righteousness darken God's counsel with words without knowledge, God's offer of reconciliation, and His promise of eternal life, must be told in terms so plain, that the simplest and most ignorant may understand and receive them.

IV. And so it is. As "the world by wisdom knew not God, it pleased God by the foolishness of preaching to save them that believe;"[2] thus, practically "making foolish the wisdom of this world,"[3] that is—showing the plain and only way to eternal good, which the joint wisdom of the whole world had not been able to devise or to find out. Even Plato yearned after the very

[1] Eph. ii. 1—3, iv. 18.   [2] 1 Cor. i. 21.   [3] Ibid. 20.

Word which is now preached to the poor, and, in his own way, sought the kingdom promised "to the poor in spirit."

For such is God's plain dealing with His people at all times. While He says: "I am the Lord that maketh all things: that turneth wise men backward, and maketh their knowledge foolish,"[1] He also says: "I am found of them that sought me not;" "to this man will I look, even to him that is poor and of a contrite spirit, and trembleth at my word,"[2] adding, "Blessed are the poor in spirit, for theirs is the kingdom of heaven."[3] And pointing to the way thither, He said, of old—"This commandment which I give thee this day, is not hidden from thee, neither is it far off. It is not in heaven that thou shouldest say, Who shall go up for us to heaven, and bring it to us, that we may hear it, and do it? But the word is very nigh unto thee, in thy mouth and in thy heart, that thou mayest do it. See, I have set before thee this day life and good, and death and evil."[4] And in later times, no longer of shadows, but of light and of realities, those same plain words were made plainer still, and placed within the reach of all by the Holy Apostle, when he says: "The word is nigh thee, even in thy mouth, and in thy heart: that is, the word of faith, which we preach; that if thou shalt confess with thy mouth the Lord Jesus, and shalt believe in thine heart that God raised him from the dead, thou shalt be saved. For with the heart man believeth unto righteousness; and with the mouth confession is made unto salvation."[5]

V. Here, then, is this plain way; not the "wisdom of words," nor "the wisdom of this world," nor yet 'philosophy,' but— "the word of faith," to be confessed with the mouth as an expression of the heart, προφορικός λόγος, and believed with the heart—τῇ καρδίᾳ—"unto righteousness," by simple and gentle, ignorant and learned alike; "for with God there is no respect of persons."[6] Faith,[7] then, πίστις, is this principle brought to

---

[1] Is. xliv. 24—26; 1 Cor. iii. 19, 20.　　[2] Is. lxv. 1, lxvi. 2.
[3] S. Matt. v. 3; Ps. li. 17.　　[4] Deut. xxx. 11—15.
[5] Rom. x. 6—10.　　[6] Rom. ii. 11; 2 Chron. xix. 7.

[7] I use the term 'Faith' throughout—except where otherwise explained—to mean what S. Paul does, "belief with the heart unto righteousness" in objective Truths revealed by God to us in His Word, delivered to the Catholic Church and necessary unto salvation, as distinguished from mere 'belief,' in the sense of—'assent of the intellect to things of the intellect,' νοητά and νοούμενα. Like-

light by the Gospel, that was altogether unknown to the wise
men of heathendom, and new to their wisdom.   Why? because
Faith, which is " a fruit of the Spirit,"[1] and therefore under
' spiritual' influence—or ' spiritual,' as distinct from mere intellectual assent or ' belief,' is said to be " the substance of things
hoped for, the evidence of things not seen."[2]   These " things
not seen," and these " things to be hoped for" then, must be
made known ere Faith in them can exist.   But we are told that
" these are things which eye hath not seen, nor ear heard, neither
have entered into the heart of man, which God hath prepared
for them that love him."[3]   Since then " these things never entered into the heart of man," man's heart or man's intellect would
weary itself, as, indeed, it has ever wearied itself in vain, in trying
either to devise them, or to find them out.   Therefore must they
be made known to man by some one else than himself, ere he
can hear or think of them ; in other words, they must be ' revealed' to him by God who has both prepared and promised
them.   " Wherefore are we told," says Philo,[4] " not that
Abraham saw God, but that God appeared, or revealed Himself
unto him ; for it was impossible that a man should of himself
καταλαβεῖν τὸ πρὸς ἀλήθειαν ὄν, comprehend that which really is,[5]
μὴ παραφήναντος ἐκείνῳ ἑαυτὸ καὶ παραδείξαντος, unless that Truth
(God) had shone in his presence and had shown itself to him."
Therefore also, is Faith said " to come by hearing, and hearing
by the Word of God,"[6] in which God has revealed to man the
things He has prepared for him, and which He promises ; together with the conditions on which His promise is to be ratified
and those good things are to be inherited.

wise are the terms ' spirit,' ' intellect,' ' soul,' and ' body,' taken here throughout in their plain and practical sense : ' spirit' (πνεῦμα), as the feature in our
nature most resembling the image of God, and the means of direct intercourse
and of impressions from Him to us ; and in this respect distinct from the " intellect,' (νοῦς), which consists in our thinking and understanding faculties ; while
the ' soul,' (ψυχή), is understood in Aristotle's sense of it, and also in that of
Philo, to include not only affections, feelings, and passions, but also the intellect ;
and lastly the limb, σάρξ, or the body, σῶμα, as the abode of the spirit and the
soul.

[3] Gal. v. 22.   [2] Heb. xi. 1.
[1] 1 Cor. ii. 9.   [4] De Abrah. p. 361, D. ed. Par.
[5] Whereby Philo, like Plato, understood God, ὁ ὤν.
[6] Rom. x. 17.

"For," says S. Cyril of Jerusalem, "we may neither deliver nor maintain the least part, τὸ τυχόν, of the mysteries of the Faith without the Holy Scriptures; nor yet misrepresent them either through bare probability, or with wisdom of words; neither oughtest thou to believe me teaching thee these mysteries, unless thou canst draw from the Holy Scriptures proof of what I say. Ἡ σωτηρία γὰρ αὐτὴ τῆς πίστεως ἡμῶν, οὐκ ἐξ εὑρεσιλογίαν, ἀλλὰ ἐξ ἀποδείξεως τῶν Θείων ἐστὶ γραφῶν. For the very preservation of our Faith does not depend on the witty inventions and on the wisdom of men's words, but it rests on proof given by the Holy Scriptures."—Catech. iv.

VI. But, inasmuch as "the things which God hath prepared for them that love Him," partake of the nature of Him Who 'is Spirit;' they are not of the intellect, intellectual, but of the spirit, spiritual, and are therefore, "spiritually discerned."[1]

And here, in order the better to understand this, yet without entering into the scientific details of a subject which only shows we are, in sooth, "fearfully and wonderfully made," and a mystery to our own selves[2]—let us bear in mind S. Paul's plain and practical distribution of our nature into "spirit, soul, and body;"[3] 'the body' of the earth, earthy, and for a time the abode of 'the soul,' which according to Aristotle, to Plato, Philo, &c., consists of the intellect, understanding, or mind, and its faculties, such as reason, the will, &c., of feeling and of lust or desire;[4] and the spirit which is the best part of man, since it is that in which he bears the greatest resemblance to the image of God, "Who is Spirit." Man's nature then, may be practically represented by three circles intersecting one another at the centre; the one uppermost in this figure being the ruling power in man for the time being; whether it be the spirit over the

---

[1] 1 Cor. ii. 14.

[2] Delitzsch, die falsche u. die wahre Trichotomie in Bibl. Psychol. p. 64, sq.

[3] 1 Thess. v. 23.

[4] Τρία δ' ἐστὶν ἐν τῇ ψυχῇ τὰ κύρια πράξεως καὶ ἀληθείας, αἴσθησις, νοῦς, ὄρεξις.—Πράξεως μὲν οὖν ἀρχὴ προαίρεσις, ὅθεν ἡ κίνησις ἀλλ' οὐχ οὗ ἕνεκα, προαιρέσεως δὲ ὄρεξις καὶ λόγος ὁ ἕνεκά τινος· διὸ οὔτ' ἄνευ νοῦ καὶ διανοίας οὔτ' ἄνευ ἠθικῆς ἐστὶν ἕξεως ἡ προαίρεσις—διὸ ἢ ὀρεκτικὸς νοῦς ἡ προαίρεσις ἢ ὄρεξις διανοητική, καὶ ἡ τοιαύτη ἀρχὴ ἄνθρωπος, κ.τ.λ. (Eth. Nic. vi. 2, 1, sq.) Τρισσεύουσι ἡμῶν τῆς ψυχῆς ὑπαρχούσης, τὸ μὲν νοῦς καὶ λόγος, τὸ δὲ θυμὸς, τὸ δὲ ἐπιθυμία καλεῖσθαι λέγεται. (Philo de Confus. Ling. 9, p. 323.)

soul and body; or the soul over the body and spirit, or yet the
flesh or body over the soul and spirit; the soul in this, being
wonderfully connected with the body by means of the blood;
with the spirit through its intellectual and moral faculties; and
the spirit being thus joined with it, and with the body by dwelling therein.

VII. In man's original state of innocence, the spirit with
which Adam held intercourse with God, had dominion over both
his soul and body; and Adam was thus a spiritual man; that
is, his body and soul were under the influence of his spirit.
But, by sin he upset that fabric, which then fell: God's image
in the spirit was tarnished, and Adam's intercourse with God
through it was broken; then Adam's spirit thus losing its power
over his soul and body, no longer held the uppermost room in
him to sway from thence his whole being, but it fell lower;
when the soul assumed its place, and then ruled the body of
man and held his spirit in bondage; and Adam became a natural
man, ψυχικὸς ἄνθρωπος.[1] So true is this, practically, that neither
Aristotle nor Plato, nor any philosopher of that age, had any
clear idea of what the spirit—τὸ πνεῦμα—of man is, or of the
place and office it once held. They either identified it with the
breath, or, seeing the soul holding the uppermost rank in man,
they attributed to it gifts that belong exclusively to the spirit,
such as, intercourse with God, and through it, the restoration
of our sinful nature to a better state. It was only later, and
probably through the influence of the Septuagint and of the frequent mention therein of "the Spirit of God," πνεῦμα Θεοῦ, and
of "the spirit of man," πνεῦμα ἀνθρώπου, that 'the spirit' (πνεῦμα)
in man came to be fairly mentioned as distinct from the intellect (νοῦς); as, for instance, by Philo who, though he does not
adopt the same distinction as S. Paul of "spirit, soul and body,"
nor yet "divides soul and spirit," as the word of God does,[2]
expresses himself nevertheless on the subject more clearly than
his predecessors.[3]

[1] 1 Cor. ii. 11.　　　　　　　　　　[2] Heb. iv. 12.

[3] He says, for instance, "every one of us is twofold, ἓν δέ τε καὶ ἄνθρωπος, both
animal and man. To each of these was allotted congenial faculties of the soul;
to the first the faculty of life (ζωτικὴ δύναμις) whereby we live; to the second the
faculty of reason (λογικὴ δύναμις) whereby we are made reasonable. The faculty

VIII. We may thus understand the practical distinction made by the Apostle between (1) "the carnal mind," φρόνημα τῆς σαρκός, when the body with its appetites predominates in man, "which is enmity against GOD; for it is not subject unto the law of GOD, nor indeed can be: so that they that are in the flesh cannot please GOD;"[1] (2) the natural man, ψυχικὸς ἄνθρωπος, that is, man under the sole influence and rule of his soul, and guided only by intellect, reason, will, feeling, &c.;[2] and (3) "the spiritual man," πνευματικὸς ἄνθρωπος, who is being restored to his former estate of intercourse with GOD, "being led by the Spirit of GOD, that bears witness with his spirit."[3]

Hence, on the one hand, the struggle that takes place when the Grace or Spirit of GOD beaming within us, and infusing a new life into our spirit, recalls it to its former estate, and kindles in it heavenly fires that had died out. Our spirit, thus called to a life congenial to itself, to instincts long since dormant or dead, endeavours to resume its energy and also its dominion over the body and the soul; an authority which neither of these will readily give up. It was this struggle that made S. Paul exclaim, "O wretched man that I am, who shall deliver me from the body of this death?" "For we know that the law is spiritual, but I am carnal, sold under sin;" and "to be carnally minded, τὸ φρόνημα τῆς σαρκός is death, but to be spiritually minded, τὸ φρόνημα τοῦ πνεύματος, is life and peace." "I thank GOD through JESUS CHRIST our LORD." So then with the mind—τῷ μὲν νοΐ, that is, with the intellect or understanding and will, under the growing influence and dominion of the spirit in relation with the Spirit of GOD—"I myself serve the law of GOD; but with the flesh the law of sin."[4]

of life received the blood as essence or being, in common with irrational animals; ἡ δὲ τῆς λογικῆς ἀναθέωσεν συγγῆς, τὸ πνεῦμα—ὕπνον τινὰ καὶ χαρακτῆρα θείας δυνάμεως, ὃν ἀνθρώπι κυρίῳ Μωϋσῆς εἰκόνα καλεῖ—τὸ τῆς ψυχῆς ἄρχοντον εἶδος, but the faculty that flows from the spring of Reason, received 'the spirit'—which is by way of being an impression of the Divine power, which Moses calls by the proper name of 'image'—the best form of the soul, described as νοῦς καὶ λόγος, intellect and reason." (Philo, De eo quod deter. p. 170.) This definition of πνεῦμα as τῆς ψυχῆς ἄρχοντον εἶδος, seems to answer practically to Plato's θεωρητικὸς νοῦς, contemplative intellect, as ψυχῆς κυβερνήτης, as guide steering the soul to the presence of GOD—ἀπαντήσασα εἰς τὸ ὂν ὄντως. (Phaedr. 58, 62.)

[1] Rom. viii. 7, 8.   [2] 1 Cor. ii. 14.
[3] Rom. viii. 8—16; 1 Cor. ii. 15.   [4] Rom. vii. 11, 14, viii. 6, vii. 25.

Hence also, on the other hand, the reason that makes the
natural man, ψυχικὸς ἄνθρωπος, assert and endeavour to establish
the supremacy and dominion of his intellect and reason; because
not only does this favour his natural pride, but it involves no
struggle whatever with himself, no surrender of 'self,' soul and
body, to the new and powerful influence of God's Spirit, that
comes to disturb through the spirit of man the good understanding which hitherto existed between his soul and his body.
It is so much easier and so much more gratifying to the natural man to continue such, and to be intellectual rather than
spiritual, that he, like the Pharisees of old with the Law, will
invent and go into all manner of subtilties respecting his reason
and his intellect, rather than surrender them, and receive the
kingdom of God—that is, the rule of God's Spirit within him—
like a little child, and live thereby.[1]   Thus we see clearly the
worthlessness for real practical good, of all moral treatises for
the improvement of man's nature that start from purely natural
principles, apart from the influence and energy of God's Spirit.
They look for a new life where they are told there is death,
since we are by nature " dead in trespasses and sins, and children of wrath;"[2] and they strive to grasp with their natural
faculties things higher than they, and foreign to them.   Therefore does the holy Apostle say, "The natural man"—that is,
the man under the influence of his soul only, ψυχικὸς ἄνθρωπος—
" receiveth not the things of the Spirit of God; for they are
foolishness unto him; neither can he know them, because they
are spiritually discerned.   But he that is spiritual"—that is, he
that is led by the Spirit of God—"judgeth (or discerneth) all
things, yet he himself is judged of no man;"[3] meaning, that
the principles, motives, and wishes wrought in him by the
Spirit of God are so entirely different from those of man in his
natural state, that another man is unable to judge or to discern
them with his natural faculties alone.

IX. How then, and when, does the Spirit of God quicken
the spirit of man, hold intercourse with it, and through it

---

[1] ἀπὸ καὶ ἡ τῆς ἀπλότητος πίστις, " for the faith of simplicity," says S. Athanasius (Contra Arian. Orat. iv. vol. i. p. 451), βελτίων ἐστὶ τῆς ἐκ περιεργασίας
πιθανολογίας, " is better than the plausible talk of meddlesome inquiry."

[2] Eph. ii. 1, 3.   [3] 1 Cor. ii. 11, 15.

so far influence man's whole being, as to 'renew' him, and to
make of him gradually a "new creature?" S. Paul answers:
"In whom (CHRIST) after that ye believed, πιστύσαντες,
ye were sealed with that holy Spirit of promise."[1] It is,
then, through Faith. But what is Faith? Faith, πίστις, consists in receiving with trust and confidence the witness GOD
gives in His Word. By this act on our part we make ourselves
over to GOD wholly and unreservedly, when we believe Him
and His witness true; since Faith, which is trust, implies belief.
"If we receive the witness of men, the witness of GOD is
greater; for this is the witness of GOD which he hath testified
of his SON. He that believeth on the SON of GOD hath the
witness in himself;" this witness being—"the Spirit of GOD
bearing witness with our spirit that we are the children of
GOD,"[2] being "reconciled to him by JESUS CHRIST," "Who
gave power to become sons of GOD to as many as received
him;"[3] to those who "receiving his testimony set to their seal
that GOD is true."[4]   Whereas "he that believeth not GOD hath
made him a liar, because he believeth not the record that GOD
gave of his SON."[5]

X. But, inasmuch as "perfect love casteth out fear, because
fear hath torment," and "he that feareth is not perfected in
love,"[6] we neither can trust GOD, πιστεύειν αὐτῷ, if we are afraid
of Him, nor love Him if we be at enmity with Him. Therefore
the first act of Faith is, as it were, to throw itself into GOD's
arms, saying, Abba, FATHER, through the spirit of adoption it
gives; overcoming all objections, and in token, no longer of fear
or of bondage, but of reconciliation with Him through His beloved SON. And this is done assuredly, not in the intellect, but
in the spirit; since Faith is "a fruit of the spirit," and not of
the intellect, and therefore reaches as much higher than the
intellect as the spirit soars beyond it[7]—even into the presence of
GOD, Who "is Spirit," and Who therefore is to be worshipped

[1] Eph. i. 13.   [2] Rom. viii. 16.
[3] 2 Cor. v. 18; S. John i. 12.   [4] S. John iii. 33.
[5] 1 S. John v. 10.   [6] 1 S. John iv. 18.
[7] " Quia quod credimus ascedit mentem nostram; sed fide suilegimus; et
sic hoc modo totum tenemus fide quod credimus: etsi mente non totam com-
plectimur." S. Athanas. De Fide Sua Lib. ix. Vol. ii. p. 585.

"in spirit and in truth,"[1] albeit no intellect can grasp or understand Him; whence Faith brings back tidings of the good things "that never entered into the heart of man, which God hath prepared for them that love him," and at once kindles in man's heart a hope of them.

This, and this alone, is the starting-point of the renewal of our nature, since "every man that hath this hope in him purifieth himself even as he is pure."[2] Wherefore, "Blessed are the pure in heart, for they shall see God."[3] It is the beginning of our will acting no longer at variance with our spirit, but in harmony with it, under the influence and guidance of God's Spirit, "to fulfil the work of faith with power,"[4] which is, "to work out our salvation with fear and trembling;"[5] "making our calling" through faith, "and our election"—the final setting apart of us unto eternal life—"sure,"[6] through the power of the Holy Ghost "guiding us," by means of our spirit, "into all Truth." But, evidently, nothing of all this can take place, except we be first reconciled to God; not only passively, on His part towards us, but of course actively on our part towards Him. It is not enough He should love us, as He always did in His Son; we must love Him too, if our love of Him in us is to bring us to Him, and make us obey Him. Yet no reconciliation, no love, no obedience can exist in the heart that does not first "believe with the heart" the witness God gives in His Word of His having wrought this reconciliation in Christ. All this structure, then, rests on the foundation of Faith, which is the surrender of our whole 'self' with trust and confidence to God, through "believing" His witness "with the heart;" not merely through the assent of the intellect, which is mere 'belief,' but through "the giving of the heart" to Him,[7] with all its affections, in token of the reality of that belief, and as a necessary consequence thereof. "Not that God," says Hooker,[8] "requires nothing unto happiness at the hands of men saving only a naked belief (for hope and charity we may not exclude); but that with-

---

[1] S. John iv. 24.
[2] S. Matt. v. 8.
[3] Phil. ii. 12.
[7] Prov. xxiii. 26.
[3] 1 S. John iii. 3.
[4] 2 Thess. i. 11.
[6] 2 S. Pet. i. 10.
[8] Eccles. Pol. Bk. i. ch. xi. 6.

out belief all other things are as nothing, and it the ground of those other divine virtues."

XI. In order to make us understand both the nature and the workings of Faith, GOD ceases not in His Word to compare Himself to a FATHER, and us to His children. "Like as a father pitieth his children, so the LORD pitieth them that fear him."[1] "I will receive you and will be a FATHER unto you, and ye shall be my sons and my daughters, saith the LORD Almighty."[2] "Neither pray I for these alone," said He Who suffered and died to reconcile us unto His FATHER, "but for them also which shall believe on me through their word; that they all may be one, as thou, FATHER, art in me, and I in thee, that they also may be one in us."[3] "And if children, then heirs; heirs of GOD, and joint-heirs with CHRIST,"[4] "in the kingdom of CHRIST and of GOD."[5]

Whereon, then, does a child's love for his father and his obedience to him rest? On his belief that such a man is his father. Has he any proof thereof? None, beyond the testimony of his father, or of others respecting his father. Yet this belief acts in him morally, so far as to make GOD compare our relation and duty to Him to that of one of our children to ourselves. For the child trusts his father, and believes in his promises, even if they refer to a long time to come; promises which, therefore, the child can neither know nor understand in detail, but to which he looks forward, hopes for, talks of; in which, in short, he lives in proportion as he believes them.

He therefore waits patiently; patience resting on trust and love; so that if anything should delay the fulfilment of his father's promise, he does not for all that doubt his father, but waits longer. Destroy the child's belief in his father, you destroy at once all his love, his trust, and his obedience to him. Then, comparing things temporal with things spiritual, the same takes place in us spiritually towards our Heavenly FATHER, through Faith in the witness He gives of Himself—first in His works, to which our intellect assents at once; for we cannot picture to ourselves the state of a mind so brutish as to deny the presence of

---

[1] Ps. ciii. 13.   [2] 2 Cor. vi. 18.
[3] S. John xvii. 20, 21.   [4] Rom. viii. 17.
[5] Eph. v. 5.

GOD in Nature as Creator and as Ruler thereof; and which He gives, secondly,—in His Word. For, once His existence allowed, His revelation to man becomes not only possible, but a necessary consequence of His being Creator and FATHER of a creature made after His own image and similitude, which has estranged itself from Him through disobedience and sin, but with which He longs to hold an intercourse of love and of reconciliation, in order to bring it back to His eternal kingdom, whence it had been driven. But, inasmuch as, being estranged from Him by sin, and thus become dead in " trespasses and sins," and "by nature children of wrath, even as others,"[1] we are no longer in our own right His children spiritually; He adopts us back. He is, therefore, said " to have begotten us again unto a lively hope by the resurrection of JESUS CHRIST from the dead, to an inheritance incorruptible and that fadeth not away, reserved in heaven for us,"[2] " GOD having sent forth his SON to redeem them that were under the law, that we might receive the adoption of sons. And because we are sons, GOD hath sent forth the Spirit of his SON into our hearts, crying, Abba, FATHER ;"[3] and hath thus " made us accepted in the Beloved."[4]

We cannot possibly receive this witness of GOD through Faith, —that is, "believe it with the heart,"—without our heart, our whole moral being, feeling at once swayed spiritually by this Faith, and therefore showing it outwardly by our words and by our actions; as children towards a FATHER " who commendeth his love towards us, in that, while we were yet sinners, CHRIST died for us," and " when enemies, were reconciled to him by the death of his SON."[5] Such Faith, once in us, can no more remain idle than fire in fuel. If true and sincere, it must show itself in its works; if it work no works in us, it is neither true nor sincere, but dead.[6] On the other hand, if we do not " be-

---

[1] Eph. ii. 1—3.   [2] 1 S. Pet. i. 3—8.

[3] Gal. iv. 4—6.   [4] Eph. i. 6.

[5] Rom. v. 8—10.

[6] S. James ii. 26. " Quamvis autem dicamus, nihil nobis esse præsidii in operibus et factis nostris, et omnem salutis nostræ rationem constituamus in Solo Christo ; non tamen ea causa dicimus, laxe et solute vivendum esse, quasi tingi tantum et credere satis sit homini Christiano, et nihil ab eo aliud expectetur. VERA FIDES VIVA EST, NEC POTEST ESSE OTIOSA." Apologia Eccl. Angl. J. Juell. p. 23.

lieve with the heart"[1] this witness, not only do we "make him
a liar by not believing the record that he gave of his Son,"[2]
but we shut ourselves out from the promises made in CHRIST,
which are to be inherited by Faith in them, "hoping unto the
end." In very deed then it is true that, "being justified by
faith,"—that is, being accounted righteous for receiving GOD's
witness of His SON,—"we have peace with GOD through our
LORD JESUS CHRIST: by whom also we have access by faith
into this grace wherein we stand and rejoice in hope of the
glory of GOD."[3]

XII. Those, therefore, do greatly err, both as regards themselves and others, who, either through ignorance or conceit,
attempt to make a way for themselves to GOD, and to "come
unto the FATHER" otherwise than through Faith in the reconciliation wrought for us by CHRIST. They either overlook or
deny what the Apostle says, "By grace ye are saved through
faith; and that not of yourselves: it is the gift of GOD: not of
works, lest any man should boast."[4] "By grace"—not assur-

[1] Delitzsch explains Biblische Psychologie, p. 143 ... ... Rom.
x. 10, "with the heart man believeth." to mean that the act of faith ... below
p. 296 takes place in the innermost recesses of man's being. This, however,
was severely be said of καρδια πιστευεται, v. 10 which clearly states the instrument, καρδια although it may be and rightly of v. 9, the καρδια πιστευεται δε εις
works one ... of those who believe in their heart.' All difficulty, however,
disappears, and both passages may be taken literally, if we take πιστευσις, ...
in its right etymological sense of 'τρυστ, believe,' i.e. to allow, or surrender, from
the A. Sax. ᵹetruwan and this from the Goth. ΓΑ·ΛΑΠΒGΑΝ
'to trust in,' from ΛΑΠΒGΑΝ the same, & not originally ΛΠΒ-
GΑΝ 'to love,' being at least related to it. In αccεptance our 'to believe'
means only to accord even with doubt, i.q. to think or 'presume.' Yet it
means in reality 'to allow' or 'to surrender' in another, ... from the A. Sax.
ᵹelyfan but it is more probably i.q. from the Gothic ΛΑΠΒGΑΝ,
ΛΠΒGΑΝ Thus 'to believe' in ... truly answers the truth it implies,
in that well bring out, meaning the popular acceptance of 'to believe,' 'faith,'
'to have, in a better form to ... these facts. For faith is the
... of the heart towards God with trust, ... with belief in Him and
will love for Him, that recognises Him from ... So then to a true that 'faith'
is believing God ' in the heart,' and ' with the heart,' we are dealing of
... is done with confidence and love, proceeds from the heart, and is
... on with the heart, thus ... and ...
  [1] x. vers. 10.   [2] Rom. v. 1.   [3] Eph. ii. 8, 9.

edly for any merit or merits of our own ; for what merits can a creature "dead in trespasses and sins" have, or what claims, but to the free, gracious, and magnanimous pity of the Creator ? So then, "God commendeth his love, in that, when we were thus dead in sins, he quickened us together with Christ, and when we were enemies, we were reconciled to him by the death of his Son."[1]   "Through faith"—for clearly, if we do not believe God's free offer of pardon to us and of reconciliation with us, He in vain makes us that offer ; "and that not of ourselves ;" for "who can bring a clean thing out of an unclean ! and what is man that he should be clean ?" asks Job ;[2] he "in whom dwelleth no good thing."[3]   "Not of works," then—for not only "are we all an unclean thing, and all our righteousness as filthy rags,"[4] but also "whatsoever is not of faith is sin."[5] For there is, and there can be, no merit whatever in our works themselves, since they are acceptable unto God only as a token of our love for Him, wrought by Faith in our being reconciled to Him through His Son. Of course the contrary doctrine, namely, that of self-righteousness, which is false, is far more convenient, and is the only one acceptable to the natural man. Not only does it flatter his pride, but it enables him, by applying to his actions the crooked or pliable rule of 'self,' to shape them, not in conformity to the higher, unflinching, and better will of God, but to his own ; thus obeying no one but himself, and yielding to no one but to himself ; though liable, as he is, to continual aberrations, weaknesses, failings, offences, and sins. Can he, thus halting to the right and to the left, ever reach the end of his course ; and can this save him ? No more than a corpse can raise itself to life. FAITH IS THE GIFT OF GOD.[6]

"If it were not a strong deluding spirit," says Hooker, "which hath possession of their hearts, were it possible but that they should see how plainly they do herein gainsay the very ground of Apostolic faith ? Is this that salvation by grace, whereof so plentiful mention is made in the Sacred Scriptures of God ? Was this their meaning which first taught the world to look for salvation

[1] Eph. II. 5; Rom. v. 8—10.   [2] Job xiv. 4 ; xv. 14.
[3] Rom. vii. 18.   [4] Isa. lxiv. 6.
[5] Rom. xiv. 23.   [6] Eph. ii. 8.

only in Christ? By grace, the Apostle saith, and by grace in such sort as a gift; a thing that cometh not of ourselves, nor of our works, lest any man should boast and say, 'I have wrought out mine own salvation.' "[1]

So also do greatly err those who limit Faith to mere 'belief;' to the assent of their intellect only to what they either see or understand, and go on trying to establish their own righteousness, if not of the law, perhaps, at least of the intellect. For such a faith is not the Faith that is "a fruit of the Spirit," and that "worketh by love;"[2] it is not the Faith that saves us, by keeping our eyes and our heart fixed on God's promises, and thus bringing us safe to the end of our pilgrimage on earth; bidding us "look unto Jesus, the Author and Finisher of our faith," and leading us to "walk even as he walked."[3] But such faith is the barren belief of the intellect, that begets neither love nor trust, but only dread; that works no works, bears no fruit, and is dead. It is the faith "of the devils which also believe and tremble."[4]

"'Ἆρα οὖν ἀρκεῖ τὸ πιστεῦσαι εἰς τὸν Υἱὸν, φησὶ, πρὸς τὸ ζωὴν ἔχειν αἰώνιον; Οὐδαμῶς. Is it, then, enough only to believe on the Son to have life? By no means," says S. Chrysostom.[5] "Yes, hearken to Christ Himself saying, 'Not every one that saith unto me, Lord, Lord, shall enter into the kingdom of heaven.' For even if we believe rightly in the Father, the Son, and the Holy Ghost, yet lead not an upright life, it will not profit us unto salvation." "But rather, begin at once," says S. Cyril of Jerusalem, "to work the works of faith, and abide therein; do not, like the foolish virgins, put off buying thine oil; μὴ θαρσήσῃς ὅτι μόνον κατέχεις τὴν λαμπάδα, ἀλλὰ διατήρησον αὐτὴν καιομένην. Rely not on thy having the lamp only, but keep it burning, that thy light may shine before men, and that Christ be not blasphemed on thine account."[6]

XIII. It is then, assuredly, a fond conceit to assert, as some do, in order to lower Faith to the province of the intellect, that "faith with S. Paul is almost always synonymous with the admission of the Gentiles."

---

[1] Serm. II. 34.
[2] Heb. xii. 2; 1 S. John ii. 6.
[3] Hom. xxxi. in Joh.
[4] Gal. v. 6.
[5] S. Jam. ii. 19.
[6] Catech. xv.

First—it does not appear how there can be two sorts of Faith, one for nations and one for individuals; for Faith must be right or wrong in either case: so that, even if Faith with S. Paul applied to the Gentiles as distinguished from the Jews, the Faith right or true for 'the Gentiles' in general must also be right or true for every individual 'Gentile' in particular.

Secondly—S. Paul makes it plain enough that he did not view Faith in that light, for that "Abraham believed God, and it was counted unto him for righteousness. How was it then reckoned? When he was in circumcision or uncircumcision? Not in circumcision, but in uncircumcision. And he received the sign of circumcision, a seal of the righteousness of the faith, which he had being yet uncircumcised: that he might be the father of them that believe, though they be not circumcised; that righteousness might be imputed unto them also."[1] "For there is no difference between the Jew and the Greek;"[2] "so, then, they that be of faith are blessed with faithful Abraham."[3] "Faithful"—why? because "he believed God," and showed his Faith by his works, "and by works was faith made perfect."[4] This took place, and Abraham became "the father of them that believe," ere there existed any distinction between Jew and Gentile; "but the Scripture hath concluded all under sin, that the promise by faith in Jesus Christ might be given to them that believe;"[5] "seeing it is one God which shall justify the circumcision by faith, ἐκ πίστεως, and the uncircumcision through faith, διὰ τῆς πίστεως."[6]

XIV. Nothing can prove more clearly that there is no distinction, between man and man, Jew and Gentile, but that the righteousness of God which is by Faith of Jesus Christ is unto all and upon all them that believe; "for there is no difference."[7] In other words, "that without faith it is impossible to please God;"[8] but that, in order to please Him, young and old, ignorant and learned alike—since "there is one Lord, one Faith, one God and Father of all, and one hope of our calling"[9]—all of

[1] Rom. iv. 3, 10, 11.
[2] Rom. iii. 22; x. 12.
[3] Gal. iii. 9.
[4] S. Jam. ii. 14—26.
[5] Gal. iii. 21; Rom. xi. 32; iii. 0—31.
[6] Rom. iii. 30.
[7] Rom. iii. 22.
[8] Heb. xi. 6.
[9] Eph. iv. 4—6.

us must "draw near with a true heart," μετὰ ἀληθινῆς καρδίας,
with no selfish or after thought, but with a heart honestly and
wholly turned to GOD in answer to His call to us to 'come,' and
"in full assurance of faith," ἐν πληροφορίᾳ πίστεως, in the reconciliation made for us by His SON.[1] But since, among them
that by GOD are called to believe through His Word—and all
of us are called—some "draw back unto perdition," while
others believe "to the saving of the soul,"[2] it shows evidently,
first—that man's salvation depends wholly on his answer to the
call from GOD, through Faith, as Abraham did; and then on
the active influence of that Faith, which makes him start and
walk towards Him Who calls, and towards His promises, as
Abraham did towards the Land of Promise; not through intellect assuredly, since he understood it not, but in Faith. Yet,
albeit he did not understand all the details of the promise, he
believed it, and trusting GOD, he showed by his works that his
Faith was true, and by his works it was made perfect.

"Our doctrine is," says Hooker, "that a man doth receive that
eternal and high reward, not for his works, but for his faith's sake,
by which he worketh; whereas, in truth, our doctrine is no other
than that which we have learned at the feet of CHRIST, namely,
that GOD doth justify the believing man, yet not for the worthiness of his belief, but for his worthiness which is believed. GOD
rewardeth abundantly every one which worketh, yet not for any
meritorious dignity which is or can be in the work, but through
His mere mercy, by Whose commandment he worketh."[3]

It shows, secondly—that, under such circumstances, Faith is
not optional on the part of man; it is not left to him to believe
or not, as he likes, as if no consequences were to follow; but
Faith is necessary, indispensable, and obligatory on all who
value the salvation of their soul, as the only means thereto,[4]
since we are plainly told to "fear, lest a promise being left us
of entering into his rest, any of us should seem to come short
of it. For unto us is the Gospel"—the Word of GOD—
"preached, as well as unto them, but the Word preached did
not profit them, not being mixed with faith in them that heard

---

[1] Heb. x. 22.   [2] Heb. x. 38, 39.   [3] Serm. II. 33.
[4] "Credere tibi jussum est, non discutere permissum est," says S. Ambrose
(De Fide, Lib. i. c. 5).

it."[1] Faith does, of course, begin with 'belief,' "for he that cometh to God must believe that He is."[2] But that belief is only the beginning, "the foundation of faith," θεμέλιον—πίστεως ἐπὶ Θεόν[3] and the "coming to God," towards His promises, "seen afar off," as Abraham did, through Faith, is to mere 'belief' what a long pilgrimage is to the start for it; what the plodding course of a ship over the trackless deep by night and by day, through stormy and fair weather, making incessantly for one unseen object, is to its weighing anchor and leaving the shore. The sailing and arriving of that ship are the consequence, the working out and perfecting of its leaving the harbour, and starting therefrom. So Faith takes mere belief for granted; it leaves it, as it were, behind, though resting thereon, and reaches unto things that cannot be 'believed,' because they can neither be seen nor understood; but in which Faith trusts wholly and unreservedly, because they are promised by God.

XV. "Salvation," says Delitzsch,[4] "moves from afar towards man. How then is it brought home to him? Through faith. Holy Scripture ascribes sundry energies and conditions of faith both to the spirit[5] and to the soul,[6] yet nowhere is it said that 'the spirit believes,' or that 'the soul believes;' because faith (πιστεύειν, הֶאֱמִין) is an active energy of man's 'self,' distinct from his spirit, his soul, and his body. Holy Scripture indeed says, that 'with the heart man believeth' (καρδίᾳ πιστεύεται, Rom. x. 10), for that faith is an inner, yea, the innermost energy in man; yet, for all that, our believing and trusting 'self,' in us, is distinct even from our 'heart.' For nowhere are the nature and the essence of faith more clearly stated than in Ps. lxxiii. 26, where Asaph says, 'My flesh and my heart faileth, but God is the strength (or rock) of my heart, and my portion for ever.' His 'self' did abide trusting in God, even when his flesh and his heart, that is, his natural (ψυχικόν) and his spiritual being—in other words his outward and his inward man—failed; even then did he hold fast by God, as by the Rock that stands when everything else totters and falls; and as

---

[1] Heb. iv. 1, 2.   [2] Heb. xi. 6.
[3] Heb. vi. 1.
[4] Die Verbindung u. der Glaube. Biblische Psychol. p. 145, 2nd ed.
[5] Ps. cxliii. 7; lxxvii. 8; li. 12.   [6] Ps. cxvi. 7; cxxxi. 2.

by the Portion that he keeps when he has lost everything else.
He held by Him, being himself immortal, because one with Him
Who abideth for ever.   Faith is—to rush for refuge to GOD the
SAVIOUR, through all contradictions, through sin, through suffering, through death and hell; faith is—that earnest, longing
desire towards GOD's free, pitiful love, as manifested in His
Word, and of which this desire lays hold; faith is—that sigh,
heaved in secret, unselfish, and rejoicing only in the promised
grace of GOD; faith is—every ray of light that beams forth
from GOD's love as reconciled to us; faith is—the application
and appropriation to ourselves of the Word of grace, from our
being fully persuaded thereof, and longing for salvation.   Faith
is, in essence, the recipient of the Word of Promise; a means of
again drawing nigh to GOD, which, together with the Word of
Promise itself, is rendered necessary, owing to our estrangement from GOD through sin; since faith has to trust in that
Word of Promise despite all that which man can neither understand, see, nor feel.   All reciprocal actions of sentiment are not
of the essence of faith.   Faith is in its essence *actio directa*, a
direct act; that is, *fiducia supplex*, beseeching confidence."

XVI.   Not only, then, is it impossible in our present condition
of estrangement through sin to draw nigh unto GOD or to please
Him without Faith, but, thirdly—it cannot be otherwise, reasonably speaking.   For it would be derogatory from the majesty
of the Ruler of the Universe that any creature therein should
be free and independent of Him; leastways the creature made
by Him after His own image and similitude.   Yet, if our intellect could span eternity and understand GOD, we should then
walk by sight—for 'to perceive,' εἰδέναι, is 'to see,' vid-ere,
with the eyes of the mind—and as regards the knowledge of
things at present hidden from us, we should then feel independent of GOD.   But our intellect, fallen as it is, lies prostrate,
compared with the height to which it would have to soar into
GOD's presence in order to see and to understand Him.   Yea,
even ere it fell from its original estate, it was subject unto GOD
through oneness of will and through communion with Him.
For within the realms of the ALMIGHTY "by whom and for
whom are all things," He must be, and He is, all in all.   If
man, then, was dependent on GOD when created upright, much

more dependent and subject is be when fallen. And since his intellect can no longer reach unto God, but falls infinitely short of Him, the only way in which he can hold intercourse with his Maker is, through the spiritual energies, and active anticipations of Faith that reaches beyond, turning man's heart and mind on heavenly things, and setting his affections upon them.

XVII. Thus then, he that walks by Faith has no ears for those who, worshipping the gods of this world, ask him to join them, and to come and enjoy with them what they see and touch; instead of as they say, looking ever forward to things unseen, unheard, and which are yet to come. But he hearkens not. His Faith is more precious to him than all that the world offers him; he therefore, like Abraham, leaves behind all that would hinder him from walking forward towards the promises; which being God's promises are more abiding and more sure than the flitting shadows and cheating appearance of a world that soon passes away. And because his Faith bears witness of itself that it is true; as true as the objects to which it looks, and as firm as the promises on which it rests, it is said to be "precious."[1] "Therefore," says Philo,[2] "is faith, which is trust in God, μόνον ἀψευδὲς καὶ βέβαιον ἀγαθόν, the only good that disappoints not, but is solid; it is the comfort of life; the filling up of our best hopes; it wards off evils and secures blessings to us; it keeps evil spirits at a distance, and makes us know what piety means; εὐδαιμονίας κλῆρος, it gives us happiness as our inheritance, ἐν ἅπασι βελτίωσις, and it enables us to make the best of every thing, stayed as it is on the Cause and Author of all things, who is able to do all things, yet only wills what is good." Thus spake of Faith, a man who knew nothing of the ground of Faith —reconciliation with God through Christ.

How much more precious must then Faith be to him who feels that by virtue of his being reconciled to God, "he now has boldness and access with confidence by the faith of him!"[3] But for that, this world would be for him a barren place and his life in it an exile, had he not a home to look to when his race is over, "a house not made with hands, eternal in the heavens."[4] He therefore, studies "to hold that faith and a good conscience,"

[1] 2 S. Pet. i. 1.   [2] De Abrah. p. 387.
[3] Eph. iii. 12, ii. 18.   [4] 2 Cor. v. 1.

walking heavenwards as Abraham did towards the Land of Promise—"hastening thither, not like a man leaving his home for a foreign land, but καθάπερ ἀπὸ τῆς ξένης εἰς τὴν οἰκείαν ἐπανίων, like a man going back from a foreign land to his own home."[1] On his daily walk thither, he proceeds as it were, from "faith to faith"—ἀπὸ τοῦ εἰδέναι εἰς τὸ γινώσκειν—from a mere perception to a greater knowledge;[2] his Faith being to him, in sooth "the substance of things hoped for, the evidence of things not seen." "What can one reckon more profitable and more worthy," says Philo, τοῦ δὲ πιστεύειν Θεῷ καὶ διὰ παντὸς τοῦ βίου χαίρειν καὶ ὁρᾶν ἀεὶ τὸ ὄν, "than to have faith in God, and during one's whole life to rejoice and to see Him that is?"[3]

XVIII. Faith, then, is—definite, in God as FATHER reconciled through the Atonement of CHRIST; it is—unfeigned, it gives up 'self' wholly to God, and embraces CHRIST's Atonement in all its extent and bearings, bringing in naught of 'self,' but gratitude, love, and obedience; it is—firm, it really baffles the intellect, that requires to see ere it yields, and reasoning, that will understand everything. As S. Athanasius[4] says beautifully, οὔτε γὰρ πίστις κατὰ δῆλου φαινομένη πίστις ἂν λέγοιτο, "Faith in what we see cannot be called faith; but that is faith ἡ τὸ ἀδύνατον ἐν δυνάμει πιστεύσασα which relies on the possibility of what is impossible; καὶ τὸ ἀσθενὲς ἐν ἰσχύι, on the strength of that which is weak; on the feeling of what is impossible; on the endurance of what must perish; καὶ τὸ θνητὸν, ἐν ἀθανασίᾳ, and on the immortality of that which is to die." Faith is "the treasure of life;" θησαυρὸς ζωῆς νῦν σοι παρεδόθη, "the treasure of life is given thee in trust," says S. Cyril of Jerusalem, "keep it until the appearing of the Master Who will require this talent of thee."[5] And lastly, Faith is—"most holy." "Our faith most holy!" says Hooker. "O that our hearts were stretched out like tents, and that the eyes of our understanding were as bright as the sun, that we might thoroughly know the riches of

---

[1] Philo. de Abrah. p. 358.

[2] γινώσκειν, h.l. (Joh. x. 14) ut saepius in N. T. sicuti יר habet significationem emendi, &c. Fried. Münter, Symbol. ad Interpr. Ev. Joh. p. 17; and Bp. Bull, Harmon. Ev. vol. iii. p. 213.

[3] De Praem. et Poen. p. 914. See above, p. 785, note 5.

[4] De Salut. Adv. J. Christi, vol. i. p. 642.   [5] Catech. v.

the glorious inheritance of saints, and what is the exceeding greatness of his power towards us, whom he accepteth for pure, and most holy, through our believing !"[1] Such Faith, then, is indeed precious : it stays and bears up the faithful and earnest disciple of CHRIST in his trials,—for when most tried then he is most blessed,—it gives him strength in weakness, patience in suffering, and joy in tribulation ; and it gilds his life with a perpetual sunbeam. In trouble it says : Faint not ; but look unto JESUS the Author and Finisher of thy Faith—He is near ; and in the hour of death, Faith alone has power to say : " I know whom I have believed ; I have fought a good fight ; I have finished my course, I have kept the faith, henceforth there is laid up for me a crown of righteousness, which the LORD, the righteous Judge, shall give me at that day."[2] For " this is the victory that overcometh the world, even our faith ;"[3] —not our intellect. Therefore does Faith leave intellect on the earth to seek the living among the dead ; and spreading her wings heavenwards, exclaim : " Who shall separate us from the love of CHRIST ? shall tribulation, or distress, or persecution, or famine, or nakedness, or peril, or sword ? Nay, in all these things we are more than conquerors through him that loved us. For I am persuaded that neither death, nor life, nor angels, nor principalities, nor powers, nor things present, nor things to come ; nor height, nor depth, nor any other creature shall be able to separate us from the love of GOD, which is in CHRIST JESUS our LORD."[4]

XIX. Such is Faith. Faith hears the call of God's preventing grace, trusts Him that calls, and for His sake believes in His promises ; turns towards Him, walks thitherwards, and thus—saves man, by making him lay hold on and apply to himself, the salvation wrought for him by the FATHER, through the birth, the life, the sufferings, the death, and the resurrection of JESUS CHRIST, His Beloved SON. This belief and trust acts, as it must needs do, on the whole being of man through his spirit turned towards GOD and in communion with Him, the moment the heart has received GOD's witness of Himself in His SON, which He gives in His revealed Word.

[1] Sermon vi. 38.   [2] 2 Tim. iv. 7, 8.
[3] 1 S. John v. 4.   [4] Rom. viii. 35, 39.

But also, the moment this takes place, all the other faculties of man begin to rebel against the intrusion among them of this new principle that overrides them, and sets at defiance all their claims. The first that disputes this authority is the intellect: accustomed to rule in the intellectual though natural man, it says: I yield to none; and I accept only what I can grasp and understand. Faith replies: But thou art fallen, fallen from the height at which are things thou canst neither attain unto nor think; but which I see and to which I look.—Then arises doubt, "the daughter of Satan, a spirit of the earth weak and powerless," as Hermas calls it.[1] But Faith silences every whisper thereof with these words: "all the promises of GOD in CHRIST are yea, and in him Amen ;"[2] therefore "hold I fast my profession without wavering," because "he is faithful that promised ;" "being fully persuaded, that what he hath promised he is able also to perform."[3]—Then reason steps in, and claims its rights: but Faith asks, how is it possible to reason on "things that never entered the heart of man which GOD hath prepared for them that love him," since He says and proves withal, "that the wisdom of this world is foolishness with him !"[4]—After this comes the will, stiff, proud, and unbending, ready to assert its independence and its mastery. But Faith answers: "It is not of him that willeth, nor of him that runneth, but of GOD that showeth mercy."[5]—Then the soul with her affections, asks if she cannot love GOD and hate evil, of herself alone? To which Faith replies: Love GOD from whom thou hast estranged thyself through sin, with Whom thou art at enmity, and from Whose presence thou wast driven for thy disobedience to His will? or, hate sin wherein thou livest? Not alone, indeed; only by the help of His Spirit teaching thine own.—At last the body follows, with its lusts and appetites. But ere it speaks, Faith warns it that it must die, and be remade ere it can enter into the presence of GOD.

XX. No sooner has Faith overcome all these faculties and attributes of the natural man, and gained the mastery over them, than they all receive a new life and a new direction, by being

---

[1] Herm. Vis. V. Mand. 9.
[2] 2 Cor. i. 20.
[3] Heb. x. 23, Rom. iv. 21.
[4] 1 Cor. iii. 19.
[5] Rom. ix. 16.

turned the way Faith has her eyes fixed, heavenwards; and thus placed under the influence, and guidance of the Spirit of God in intercourse with man's own spirit.   Hitherto man was like a ship in a fog without a compass: now he receives a compass that points unerringly to the happy end of his course, with a preserving charm against all dangers and perils of every kind. Then is the flesh crucified with its affections and lusts; the body is "kept under,"[1] and the soul is "kept in life," and " her desire is in the name of the LORD;"[2] the will is brought into subjection to the will of GOD; reason then receives fresh powers; and starting from the only true principles there are, in GOD, reasons soundly and correctly, from premisses that are eternal and true; while doubt hides itself, from the light of the Spirit, and the intellect, instead of roaming aloft as before— like a bubble in the wind, without aim or object, works with renewed energy, with one aim and one object, to know GOD as far as it can and to glorify Him.   Such is the work of Faith.

XXI. And what of the intellect? it is for this world, and for the things of this world, for which it was given to man and in which it works wonders, as being at home therein. Intellect was put into man, as instinct was into animals, for self-preservation, and for the due discharge of the functions and of the work attached to the rank and to the place each occupies in the world: man as a rational being and vice-regent of his Creator over the brute creation, and animals as active inhabitants of this world. Intellect then is in the same relation to man's nature as instinct is to that of animals; and a merely intellectual man does no more relatively to his human nature as such, than an animal does in following its instinct. So true is this, that a man who acts against the dictates of reason fares as an animal would, which acted against the laws of instinct; but when do we see this on the part of animals? And, whereas intellect works as animals apparently cannot work, that is, with reason and with reflexion, and arrives at results in knowledge of which they are incapable, yet their instinct baffles man's intellect, and does in the simplest things, what no amount of intellectual skill could ever do.

Compare, for instance, the fine silken threads of which the

[1] Gal. v. 24; 1 Cor. ix. 27.   [2] Ps. lxvi. 9; Isa. xxvi. 8.

woof of a spider's web is composed, with the finest twist wrought by hand; and try with this, to make a web for a spider, and to make the spider use it. So far then, man as a merely intellectual being is, in the results of his intelligence both above and below the animals among which he lives, and of whose nature he knows so little. Did he teach the bee to frame her hexagon cells, and to place them in the comb the one against the other, so that the flooring of every cell be supported by the meeting joint of the three cells beneath? Or did he not rather learn from this small insect, both how to occupy most room in the least space, and to rear the most solid edifice of the kind? That, however, is only the bee's instinct, though it may surpass man's intellect, both in the gathering of the material—wax, and in the construction of the comb with it; it is only the work appointed to the bee, and to the bee's place in Nature.

Yet the bee has neither man's intellect nor his spirit; the spirit that tends upwards, as originally come from thence; the best part of man, yet enthralled by man's natural will, and thus kept prisoner until Faith in revealed Truth breaks asunder the bands and sets it free to soar on high—to God who gave it. Then is the spirit called " the spirit of the mind,"[1] because the nobler and the better of the two—said to be " renewed," when instead of being chained on earth to things of the intellect, which are foreign to its nature, it wings its flight by Faith to whence it first came, and brings back thence to man, new ideas, new thoughts, new hopes, new joys, and to his soul, a new source of life. This is what Faith does, and what Faith alone can do; this is also what intellect does not, because it cannot; nay, intellect tries to keep man from the Faith, jealous as it is of the power of that Faith, which, being of the spirit, spiritual, reaches up to where intellect alone cannot go. Whence then, comes this Faith, so powerful, so precious? " Faith," says the Spirit, " cometh by hearing, and hearing by the word of God."[2]

XXII. It is then evident, that as regards Him Who is Spirit, and infinite, and past finding out, man's intellect, which is not spirit, but finite and fallen, cannot find Him out. How, indeed, can it rise with its maimed wings, above earth's attraction, into

[1] τὸ πνεῦμα τοῦ νοός, Eph. iv. 23. חֵן מָצָא Job xx. 3.
[2] Rom. x. 17.

God's presence; into the dazzling glare of His light and glory, poor denizen of the earth as it is? There is for it no other way to the realms of the Majesty on High, to the Presence before which even angels veil their faces—than " by the new and living way" which Jesus, the Lord of those realms, " has consecrated for us, through the veil, that is to say his flesh."[1]   None. Man's intellect lives on earth and for the earth which it adorns and beautifies, and in which it delights; but it dares not look earnestly beyond. Either in life it trembles in doubt, or it quails at the gate of death, where Faith and Hope stand, the one firm, the other unmoved; Faith prying into the very lair of the king of terrors, whom THE LEADER of Heaven's hosts did slay for our sakes; and Hope looking across the chasm on to the dawn that glimmers beyond the everlasting hills on our heavenly Home.

XXIII. But intellect alone understands none of all this, and reason is at a loss to think it. Where Faith prevails, intellect doubts; and where Hope is triumphant, reason fails. Ὁ δὲ τελευταῖον ἐφθέγξατο, Ὦ Κρίτων, ἔφη, τῷ Ἀσκληπιῷ ὀφείλομεν ἀλεκτρυόνα, ἀλλ' ἀπόδοτε, καὶ μὴ ἀμελήσητε. "His last words were: O Criton, we owe a cock to Esculapius; mind and forget not to offer it."[2] That was the last effort in death of the intellect of the wisest of men. But here is Faith—

" I know that my Redeemer liveth, and that he shall stand at the latter day upon the earth : and though after my skin worms destroy this body, yet in my flesh shall I see God ; whom I shall see for myself; and mine eyes shall behold and not another."[3]

And here is the Truth—

" I AM THE RESURRECTION AND THE LIFE; HE THAT BE-LIEVETH IN ME, THOUGH HE WERE DEAD, YET SHALL HE LIVE; AND WHOSOEVER LIVETH AND BELIEVETH IN ME, SHALL NEVER DIE."

XXIV. What, then, made such a great difference between the philosopher and the patriarch ? The philosopher, after dis-coursing in a very remarkable manner on death which he saw coming apace, and on the immortality of his soul, had neverthe-

---

[1] Heb. x. 20.   [2] Phædo. 135.
[3] Job xix. 25—27.

less, at the very last, such misgivings in the yearnings of his
own intellect, and in the inklings of his reason, that by his last
act he made his death a warning. Whereas, the patriarch, so
sorely tried as to loathe his life, yet spake, and yet acted as an
example to be followed unto all generations—of Faith that defies
death, and of Hope that " is firm unto the end."

This great difference lay in that, the philosopher had no
revelation, no knowledge of the Truth revealed by God to man,
and therefore had to look within himself for the Truth he could
not find there ; whereas the patriarch had that Revelation, and
with it, that knowledge : " what is man that he should be clean ?
or he which is born of a woman, that he should be righteous ?"
But " I KNOW THAT MY REDEEMER LIVETH !" That Faith in the
Truth revealed was to him in sooth, the substance of things
hoped for, the evidence of things not seen. He therefore believed, hoped and triumphed; while the other could not trust
even his own reasoning.

Δυοῖν γὰρ ἕτερόν ἐστι τὰ τεθνάναι—" to be dead is of two
things one," said Socrates, " either μηδὲν εἶναι, to cease altogether
to exist, or μεταβολή καὶ μετοίκησις a change and a transmigration of the soul hence elsewhere. If death be a state of μηδεμία
αἴσθησις, of no feeling whatever, it is a great gain. If, however,
death be a removal from this place to another καὶ ἀληθῆ ἐστι τὰ
λεγόμενα, and the things we are told be true, that all the dead
are there, what greater boon can there be ? Once in Hades,
and rid of men who here call themselves judges, he will find
real and righteous ones who, they say, sit there in judgment,
Minos and Rhadamanthus, and Æacus and Triptolemus, καὶ
ἄλλοι ὅσοι τῶν ἡμιθέων δίκαιοι ἐγένοντο ἐν τῷ ἑαυτῶν βίῳ, and such
other of the demi-gods as were righteous in their life ; ἆρα
φαύλη ἂν εἴη ἡ ἀποδημία ; will any one say the change would be
for the worse ? What would you think of being in the company of Orpheus, of Musæus, of Hesiod, and of Homer? ἐγὼ
μὲν γὰρ πολλάκις ἐθέλω τεθνάναι, εἰ ταῦτ' ἐστὶν ἀληθῆ. For my
part, I would gladly die more than once, if such things be true ;
for, what a wonderful existence for me yonder, where I should
meet Palamedes, Ajax, and Telamon, and any other of the ancients who may have died the victim of an unjust judgment ;
but where, especially, I might inquire, and, comparing those

that live there with them that live here, be able to find out which of them are wise, and who it is that thinks himself wise, but is not !"[1]

Such was the hope and the consolation the wise man had in death ; this is the hope Faith in God's witness does give :

" O death, where is thy sting ? O grave, where is thy victory ? But thanks be to God who giveth us the victory through our Lord Jesus Christ." "Who shall lay anything to the charge of God's elect ? it is God that justifieth. Who is he that condemneth ? It is Christ that died, yea rather, that is risen again, who is even at the right hand of God, who also maketh intercession for us."[2]

How then, can man any longer halt between intellect and Faith ?

XXV. Yet, that is what the natural man, ψυχικὸς ἄνθρωπος does, who looks within himself for that which nothing can give him, but a firm Faith in certain Truths God sets before him in His Word, as objects on which to fix his eyes, "hoping unto the end," for the enjoyment of them, as Abraham did for the Land of Promise. Conceive Abraham refusing to leave Ur, until he 'understood' what the land was like, which God did promise him ; or, debating within himself whether he had better go thither or perhaps wend his way northwards to the hills of Pontus, or eastward to those of Cardu ! Such halting between two opinions, such doubt would not have been imputed to him for righteousness, neither would he have been called "the Friend of God." He indeed, used his intellect, to find the best and the shortest way to Canaan ; but only when, through Faith in God's promise he had determined to leave his native land, to go "he knew not whither,"—that is, he knew not the details of the promise, and the nature and the features of the land to which he was going ; in other words, he started without 'understanding' the promise God made, but relying upon it in Faith for God's sake.

But Abraham was not a natural but a spiritual man. He did not choose what he would have ; he received and took what God gave him, and as He gave it. Not so, however, with those who call ' Faith,' the mere assent of their own limited and often dull

[1] Apol. Socr. 32, p. 359, ed. L.   [2] 1 Cor. xv. 16, 56 ; Rom. viii. 31—39.

intellect; who thus, will accept only what they see and what
they understand; and who look to themselves and into themselves, for what they call the Truth, instead of receiving what
God gives them as such; forgetting that in "a heart which is
deceitful above all things and desperately wicked,"[1] "there
dwelleth no good thing," save what God puts therein. "But
they, measuring themselves by themselves, and comparing themselves among themselves, οὐ συνιοῦσιν, are not wise;"[2] and thus,
they either gainsay or reject a part or the whole of God's Word,
because there are in it things against which their intellect rebels.

XXVI. But, after all, what does their intellect really understand, that it should take the place of Faith, in things belonging
to God? As regards their own selves, for instance:—as regards
the first beginnings of their existence and formation; the connexion between their soul and the life that throbs in their veins,
and what takes place in all this at the hour of death—does their
intellect go much beyond their microscope and their knife?
The experiments of such men as Bischoff, Pouchet, Carus, and
others, do not seem to prove it. How many men care to inquire
why they are left or right-handed? How then can man's intellect which helps him so little beyond mere experiments, into
the causes of things, pretend to search into those which "eye
hath not seen, neither ear heard, and which have not entered
into the heart of man, which God hath prepared for them that
love him?"[3]

Even as to those that are seen, not only can the intellect not
fathom them, but it cannot even give the causes of a defective
sight. Can it tell, for instance, how and why some men are
more deficient in this sense than even inferior animals, and can
judge neither of colour, of form nor of distance? and thus how
it is that in this as in thousands of other cases, man's intellect
sinks below animal instinct, and his physical organisation below
that of brutes? But if with eyes that can see, and a mind that
can think, we look above—can intellect determine why the earth
and the other planets, revolve so wonderfully, each in its orbit,
as if that orbit were marked out in space, and how they all are
poised there? Intellect answers: by the laws of attraction.
What are these laws? only the uniformity of results observed

[1] Jer. xvii. 9.   [2] 2 Cor. x. 12.   [3] 1 Cor. ii. 9.

by man. And what is 'attraction?' it is only the name we give to the 'result,' to the effect of a 'cause' that can be nowhere but in the wisdom, in the Supreme Intelligence, and in the Almighty power of God.

And, if that be too high, take a leaf out of the hedge and look at it : can intellect understand why it is of that particular shape, and constantly so in the same plant ? and while lost in admiration at the marvellous construction of that leaf, at the several tissues thereof ; at the upper surface smooth and close to let the rain run off, at the under surface open to inhale the moisture from the earth and to breathe thereby ; at the maze of the web, and at the mathematical combination of forces in the form and in the arrangement of the stem and in the so-called nerves of that leaf, can intellect search into the causes of all these things ? The pollen of one tree is wafted over miles of desert land to fructify another tree so distant, and no other ; we notice it, but can intellect explain how or why, and lay bare the causes thereof ?

XXVII. And as to the things we hear—can intellect tell why certain musical sounds affect the ear, and through it the whole being of man, in a particular way ? Why some men are no more capable of appreciating sounds than a blind man colours ; and how the vibrations of the air of musical notes, act upon the nerves of the ear, so that the ear winces at a few vibrations more or less than the just number for every note ? We know and feel it is so ; and we explain it our own way ; yet unless we can enter into the causes thereof, and say why it is so, our knowledge reaches no further than our experiments. Mechanical science and skill, that work wonders around us, are nothing more than the application and combination of certain forces to certain objects. But intellect cannot go into the causes of either the forces or the materials. So also with chemistry, physics, &c., our utmost science and skill are, at the best, only of experiments. So utterly subservient is the intellect and so little has it at command the very forces it handles or the materials it uses so dexterously, that it cannot invent or effect perpetual motion ; and so little does it know of causes, that the aggregate intellect of mankind could not make an oak leaf, nor put in a wing to a fly.

XXVIII. In vain, then, will this poor intellect seek a way to the Supreme Intelligence of Him Who made it ; in vain will

it look into things invisible, spiritual, and eternal, when it is
baffled by the very things among which it moves; things we
see and touch.   What, then, is its office?—The office of this,
the most precious, the most brilliant of earthly gifts, is to make
men intellectual; to raise them above their gross appetites;
above the love of eating, of drinking, and of money; above the
pomps and vanities of this wicked world and other such occupations and pursuits which only tend to lower man, and to hinder
him from rising up to the higher level of his nature.   "That
the soul be without knowledge, it is not good," says the Word of
God,[1] and it is the part of the intellect to find out and to supply
such knowledge; in short, to raise the natural man as high as
he can be raised as an intellectual being in a fallen state; to
give him, therefore, the highest enjoyment of which human
nature alone in its present condition, is capable.

XXIX. But all this does not make a man spiritual; no
more spiritual than instinct makes an animal intellectual. Man's
intellect is of the soul, ψυχικός, but his spirit comes from higher,
and has higher aspirations; it is intended to draw upwards the
soul of man, and with it his body, through intercourse with
Him Who " is Spirit," and Who is to be " worshipped in spirit
and in truth."   This intercourse, as we have seen, however, does
not take place at haphazard; but only under certain conditions.
A man, in order to receive of God's Spirit, must place himself
in active communion with Him through Faith in the reconciliation wrought for him by Jesus Christ, our Saviour; since
we are accepted only " in him the Beloved;" He alone is " the
Way, the Truth, and the Life," and " no man cometh unto the
Father but by him."   Then, but only then, does " the Spirit
bear witness with our spirit"[2]—not with our intellect—" that
we are the children of God; and if children, then heirs; heirs
of God, and joint heirs with Christ;"[3] and thus, by degrees,
and through the intercourse of that Spirit with our spirit, do we
" put off the old man," " cease to be conformed to this world,"
and are transformed in the renewing of our mind, " that we may
prove what is that good, and acceptable and perfect will of God."[4]

XXX. The lawful use of our intellect then, is to lead us to

[1] Prov. xix. 2.   [3] Bp. Bull's Discourse, III.
[2] Rom. viii. 16, 17.   [4] Rom. xii. 1, 2.

seek after God; since the heathens were held "without excuse,"
for not having made that use of it.[1] It cannot bring us to find
God; but it ought to lead us God-wards. If properly trained
and lawfully used, it raises us so far above the earth and the
gross occupations thereof, as to give us glimpses of better things
beyond, which, however, it cannot see, "since they are spiritually discerned." Our intellect is thus used for the noblest
of purposes, as a handmaid to Faith which takes us by the hand
where intellect must leave us, and carries us to the realms of
"things above and invisible which are eternal, where Christ
sitteth at the right hand of God;" and on which it bids us
"set our affections."[2] Such is the lawful use of the intellect,
since it is, as it were, the remnant of a refined instinct that
marks its origin; but few there be that make such use of it.
Small natural intellects are conceited, and pretend that their
wings can bear them upwards. And really great intellects feel
so mortified at finding that there is a world of eternal things
good and holy, higher than that to which they can reach, that
they either gainsay or deny that world, in order to limit the
circle of existence to what their intellect is able to grasp, and
to no more. Thus, at least, may we explain the intellectual
phænomenon, if not rather, the mental aberration, of men who
having all their life long studied the wonderful works of God in
Nature, live as materialists and die as infidels.

XXXI. But with the spiritual man, πνυματικὸς ἄνθρωπος, that
is, with him who allows himself to be led by the Spirit in his
passage through life, the intellect is turned to the most worthy
purpose. It helps his spirit to discern things of daily life—the
spirit spiritually for heaven, and the intellect intellectually as
regards this world; it leads him to search into useful knowledge,
to delight in it and to value it; to be earnest and conscientious
in his studies, not for show, but for reality. Intellect helps him
into the study of the very letter of God's Word. It makes him
say, "The righteousness of thy testimonies is everlasting: O
grant me understanding, and I shall live;"[3] that is, make me to
understand, not the mysteries of Thy law, which are not yet for
me, but the things revealed in it, that I may be an intelligent
servant of Thine, "ready always to give an answer to every man

[1] Rom. i. 20.   [2] Col. iii. 1—3.   [3] Ps. cxix. 144.

that asketh me a reason of the hope that is in me."[1] The intellect rears, as it were, the scaffolding, and the spirit builds
therefrom the spiritual house, a holy temple unto the LORD.
It makes intelligent the man, whom the spirit makes good,
and it adorns with its manifold gifts the worth and the merits
which the spirit imparts; it works and polishes the gem that
shines all the brighter for it.

Intellect, in short, enables the man who is led by the spirit
to judge justly of things of which the Spirit teaches him to judge
rightly. Even as regards the Revelation of GOD to man in the
Bible, whereas the natural or only intellectual man rejects it,
because of the motes he sees floating in that beam of heavenly
Light, the spiritual and intelligent man makes no more of such
πάρεργα, of such accessories, than does that Revelation itself.
And as to the particles of human or of earthly matter which
have clung to it during its stay in the earth, he looks upon such
motes as no part of the Light, but as of the earth, earthy; as
some of the dust of the world in which he lives; and, as independent of the Light he sees, he knows, he loves, and in the
warmth and health of which he ceases not to rejoice. He knows
that in another world that same light will be brighter, for it will
shine alone.

XXXII. Do, then, Faith, love, and obedience forbid or hinder
inquiry? and is the faithful Christian doomed to a vegetative
existence? They indeed forbid a free, fearless, and rash inquiry
into things holy and spiritual; but they expect and require a
modest and respectful inquiry; not once, but always. Can he
who holds, through Faith, communion with Him Who is Light
and Life, be less active, less intelligent, less in earnest, less
hopeful than a man who, yet faithless, aimless, and hopeless,
either gropes among the inextricable mazes of his own fancies,
or is carried hither or thither by every wind of doctrine? But,
inquiry depends on the προαίρεσις τοῦ βίου, on the aim and
choice of the man. The Christian or real philosopher, starting
from the only true principle, GOD, as He reveals Himself in
His Word, as Creator and FATHER reconciled through His SON,
and holding intercourse with him through his spirit, goes forward
in his inquiry, προσιόντα, as Simplicius says; he advances, pro-

[1] 1 S. Pet. III. 15.

ceeds from God down to himself. His inquiry is neither arrogant
nor impertinent; it is therefore neither 'free' nor 'fearless.'
Hence his learning is not empirical, but, as far as it goes, sound
and real. As he beholds the marvellous mechanism of the visible
world, and wonders at the display of boundless love and of settled
design, of immutability of purpose, of almighty power in the
working out of that purpose, of infinite wisdom in devising
things that baffle man's understanding, the Christian philosopher, having begun with Faith, and firm therein, and through
it in communion with God in the spirit, makes his inquiry into
God's nature and attributes, in the light of Revelation—an act
of the profoundest and most devoted worship. Feeling both
how little he knows of the inexhaustible riches of God's love
and attributes, yet how true is the little he knows, "he walks
humbly with his God." "What is man," he says to himself,
"that thou art mindful of him; or the son of man that thou
so regardest him?"[1] and as he thus humbly, at God's footstool,
"acquaints himself with Him, he is at peace."[2]

The sham philosopher, on the other hand, who starts, not from
God as He reveals Himself to us in His Word, as from the only
true principle, but from himself, walks backwards in his inquiry; therefore neither advances nor profits. How, indeed,
can he? He takes himself, his own person and nature, which
he does not, after all, fully understand, and which is not under
his own control—since he knows not the hour of death—and
from this one small bone he makes up a monster of his own
imagination; with this one cog in the splendid machinery of
the visible and of the invisible worlds, he sets about constructing
that marvellous mechanism after his own fancy. Who would
trust him? Who would follow him in such fruitless efforts to
create in his own fashion what He "Whose thoughts are not as
our thoughts" devised and did from everlasting; or to find a
way heavenwards other than the one made and appointed by
Him "Whose ways are not as our ways?"[3] How, then, is it
that those two hundred and eighty-eight sects of philosophers
have tried, and are yet endeavouring to make that way for themselves, if it were to be made by them? And do they not themselves, without God's help, "make their own wisdom foolish,"

1 Ps. viii. 4.   2 Job xxii. 21.   3 Isa. lv. 8, 9.

and ratify the words of the Apostle, that φάσκοντις εἶναι σοφοὶ ἐμωράνθησαν, that "thinking themselves to be wise, they became fools"? There is only one way to God. "I am the Way, the Truth, and the Life," says God, manifest in the flesh and justified in the Spirit; "no man cometh unto the FATHER but by me."[1] He is "the Door of the sheep," and "whosoever climbeth up some other way is a thief and a robber," first of his own soul, and then of the souls of others whom he deludes into free and fearless inquiry respecting that which two hundred and eighty-eight sects of philosophers have not found,—and will never find.

Whereas if, laying down our pride, our vanity, our self-conceit, we, like sensible men, do not run headlong into systems made up by others, but calmly sit down and see how utterly helpless we are of ourselves to find our way to God; and then come to Him through Faith by the way He has made, namely, CHRIST; and then, being thus justified by Faith, have peace with Him; we may start thence on our inquiry, in which we shall have made but little way when summoned to exchange our Faith for the sight of things "eye hath not seen nor ear heard, neither have entered into the heart of man, things which God hath prepared for them that love him."[2] If we look up and lose ourselves among the brilliant worlds of which we learn little else than our own utter mean and frail estate, we rest in the thought that reaches beyond our sight: My FATHER made them all; I shall know about them another day. If we look down upon the earth, and see it full of His riches, stand aghast at His manifold works, all made in wisdom, and find our intelligence baffled by a blade of grass or a tiny fly, again we say: Here He is; only look at His works, how marvellous and perfect! And if we look within ourselves, and can trace a change wrought by His Spirit on our own evil nature, through new feelings, new hopes, new tastes, which He gives, we think the wonder no less. We may then inquire how it is wrought, and find that, plain as the way is, the wisdom thereof is past finding out.

Thus will our inquiry, not free, but guided by Faith—not fearless, but carried on with awe—begin indeed, but never end

[1] S. John xiv. 6; 1 Tim. iii. 16.   [2] 1 Cor. ii. 9.

until inquiry is no longer needed, "and we know even as we are known." We will not then, like some, look for another Truth —there is none; nor for another Revelation—it could not be plainer; nor yet for another Gospel—we could receive no gladder tidings than that we are freely forgiven, reconciled, accepted. We will leave others to try and make things more easy, and to make one world of this and of heaven—that seems to be the object of their inquiry; meanwhile we will walk in the way God has made, and by which He calls us; and we bid them to the same, and come with us to Him.

XXXIII. It is not, however, likely that questions or matters of such vital importance as these should, if I may use the expression, have been left to take care of themselves; and that man, though fallen from his first estate, yet still the masterpiece of his Creator's work, should alone be subject to no rule of government, but be left to wander uncared for in the world. For in the realms of Him "Who spake the Word, and the worlds were made," and Whose will they follow ever since; Who spangled the heavens with brilliant worlds in patterns they dare not break, since more than once He took them as witnesses of His unchangeable purpose—independence and self-will cannot be. He receives homage and subjection from the whole of Nature; but from man, created by Him after His own image and similitude, He requires, what such a being is bound to yield—love, obedience, and worship.

Yet, since neither love, obedience, nor worship could be rendered to an authority only either fancied or absent, "He left not himself without witness, in that he did good; and gave us rain from heaven and fruitful seasons, filling our hearts with gladness."[1] And He makes His Presence known not only through such tokens of His visible power as Ruler of the universe, but through His government of man, suited to man's being, both moral and temporal. By moral government we understand the immutable, uniform connexion between certain causes and their effects affecting the moral being of man, that may be noticed by the least intelligent minds in what happens daily; so that they are without excuse who do not notice such things : as, for instance, crime and punishment, vice and misery, &c., and who

[1] Acts xiv. 17.

do not draw thence the existence of the moral government of
GOD. But, in like manner as man's moral being is practically
inseparable from his body while he is in life, so also we may
safely think that, generally speaking, the broad, universal features of the laws drawn for the well-being of civil states, whatever be the details of features ascribed to each severally, do
attest the Presence of GOD as Temporal Ruler of the world, because He is also the Moral Ruler of it.

XXXIV. Every part of man, then, is placed under control by
GOD. His body, as temporary abode of his soul and spirit, is
liable to the laws of health and of disease, and is at GOD's mercy,
Who alone has power over life. And, in order to prevent his intellect from running riot, and from setting for itself its own fancies
as objects of pursuit, GOD laid on it the stern, unflinching rule and
iron yoke of the universal principle of 'that which is,' τὸ ὄν, as
regards everything on which it is capable of thinking. This
principle asserts its authority by its own laws of Truth, τὸ ἀληθές,
in the abstract; to which man's intellect is made to bow, to
yield, and to obey, under the penalty of rebellion or folly. And
this applies to everything of the bare intellect, τὰ νοητά, considered as subjects on which the intellect is able to work until
it has ascertained the Truth regarding them.

XXXV. But as regards things spiritual, which are not of the
intellect, because they are of the spirit, it is evident that τὸ ὄν,
the reality of these is beyond the scope and reach of the understanding alone, which on that account can ascertain, τὸ ἀληθές,
Truth as regards them, only so far as they concern the intellect—that is, of course, very little, since their sphere lies far
beyond it. This Truth regarding things spiritual—that is, the
idea and the perception of them suited to our present earthly
state—must therefore of necessity be transmitted to man from
beyond the range of his intellect; in other words, it must be
made known or revealed to him. But since Truth in this case
is not about matters of the intellect and for the earth, but about
matters of the Spirit and for heaven, wherein our supreme happiness consists, it therefore is 'the Truth' ἡ ἀλήθεια κατ' ἐξοχήν—
"that principal Truth," says Hooker, "in comparison whereof
all other knowledge is vile."[1]   It is the highest Truth of all,

[1] Eccles. Pol. Bk. iii. ch. viii. 9.

the Truth of things spiritual, invisible, and eternal. Thus, while the part of man's intellect is to find out Truth in the abstract, as the expression of that which is, τὸ ὄν, in things within the range and compass of its faculties, the spirit of man taught from his home, heaven, receives by revelation, and through Faith in it, the Truth, τὴν ἀλήθειαν, as the expression and will of ὁ Ὤν, of Him Who says of Himself, "I AM."

XXXVI. It is, then, evident that man only shows his weakness and his vanity when he pretends to look within himself for the Truth. He cannot make it, for it exists independently of him; he cannot reach it, for it lies far beyond his conception and the grasp of his intellect. All he can do is to receive it by Faith, and to act upon it. Therefore have we yet to learn, as regards our salvation and our own active part in it, what 'subjective Truth,' of which some men talk, can possibly mean, beyond the witness which the Truth when received—not made—bears of itself in the heart that has welcomed and received it. For, if there could be such a thing as Truth either made by man or to be found within him—"wherein dwelleth no good thing"—apart from GOD's Truth revealed in His Word, and imparted through the Spirit of Truth, which is given by GOD as a seal[1] of acceptance with Him through Faith in His promises; and if man were thus really able to find within himself 'the Truth' to which he is bound, at the risk of his soul, to give allegiance, all obedience to GOD, all need of a Revelation, and therefore all Faith in Him, and with it all hope in His promises, would cease, and man would walk on earth, no longer by Faith, as becomes him, poor, fallen creature as he is, but he would then walk by sight—a state of things as regards him, in his present dependent condition, utterly at variance with the majesty of GOD's spiritual rule. But "matters of Faith," says S. Cyril of Jerusalem, "were not arranged according to the fancy of men;" ἀλλ' ἐκ πάσης γραφῆς τὰ καιριώτατα συλλεχθέντα, μίαν ἀναπληροῖ τὴν τῆς πίστεως διδασκαλίαν—"the principal Articles were gathered from the whole Scripture, and make up the one doctrine of Faith."[2] In other words, in order to keep man's eyes fixed in the same direction towards his home, GOD has set before him, as before Abraham, certain Truths as objects pointing that

way, to which he is to look steadfastly as to the end where his
course on earth will finish—objects and promises made known
to us in His Word.

XXXVII. Thus are we told that, of old, those whose hope was
set on high "died in faith, not having received the promises,
but having seen them afar off, and were persuaded of them, and
embraced them, and confessed that they were strangers and pil-
grims on the earth." If men did so "of whom the world was
not worthy," and who, though "having obtained a good report
through faith, yet received not the promise; GOD having provided some better thing for us, that they without us should not
be made perfect"—what else ought we to be than "followers of
them who through faith and patience inherit the promises?"[1]—
the promise of His heavenly kingdom, to which He brings us,
in fulfilment of His promise to send His Spirit, "the Spirit of
Truth, to guide us into all Truth," on our way thither. But
His Spirit does not come at random to all. He is sent as Guide
and as Comforter only to those who, keeping their eyes fixed on
the Truths He sets before them, walk with humble but firm
Faith "as their provision by the way during life,"[2] towards the
better country they seek. "Wherefore GOD is not ashamed to
be called their GOD, for he hath prepared them a city."[3]

XXXVIII. We then see clearly, first—that it is impossible
either to come to GOD or to please Him otherwise than through
Faith; and secondly—that Faith cannot exist except in objects
set before it on which to look, and for which to hope. And
this makes it necessary that these objects should be shown and
pointed to by GOD Who wrought them. Therefore is a Revelation from GOD to man not only possible according to GOD's
nature, but it is, as we have seen, rendered necessary through
GOD's love towards man, who is estranged from Him and fallen
through sin, and thus unable to find within himself the means
of returning to GOD, or the way thereto. The very first ray of
GOD's light into man's heart shows him his real state; and
from that moment Faith receives not only thankfully, but also
most humbly, the message sent from GOD, and embraces the
Truths and the Promises revealed to us in His Word. Whereas

---

[1] Heb. xi. 13, 39, 40 ; vi. 11—15.
[2] ἐφόδιον—S. Cyril. Hier. Cat. v.   [3] Heb. xi. 14—16.

the intellect, ere it yield obedience to Faith, and be governed
thereby, will naught of revelation, because it does not either see
or feel its natural fallen estate; but, self-sufficient and self-
willed, it attempts to assert its own independence; and flaps
its broken wings in order to fly upwards—but only to fall back
with its own weight to the earth.

REVELATION AND THE BIBLE.

XXXIX. Those, then, do indeed wander away from the Truth
who, through either conceit or ignorance, deny their dependence, and pretend to put their reason and their understanding
in the place of God's revelation to us. The whole tenour of
Plato's deep, solemn, often touching language, shows that, like
Columbus, he felt there was a land of realities (not Atlantis)
beyond the reach of his splendid genius, which made him sigh
for that which he felt he could not reach. When, for instance,
he describes the soul as led by the best part thereof, which he
calls νοῦς κυβερνήτης, the intellect guiding her nearer into the
presence of God, whence, ἀνακύψασα εἰς τὸ ὂν ὄντως, looking upwards into Eternal Truth, it looks down, καθορῶσα, upon the
things of the world,[1] he could hardly go further with his unaided intellect; but he seems to speak as of what he had seen,
though how dimly, he was the first to acknowledge, since he
longed to have the film, ἀχλύς, removed from the eyes of his
understanding, that he might see more clearly, and be made a
better man.[2]   And he has left on record, in the most touching
words, "that since, τὸ μὲν σαφὲς εἰδέναι ἐν τῷ νῦν βίῳ ἢ ἀδύνατον
εἶναι ἢ παγχάλεπόν τι, it is either impossible, or at least most difficult, in this life to know what concerns our future existence,
none but the most craven or the weakest of men, πάνυ μαλθακοῦ
εἶναι ἀνδρός, would either refute or deny what was said on the
subject, without having first well considered it in all its bearings.   For, concerning such weighty subjects, of two things one
must be done: ἢ μαθεῖν ὅπη ἔχει ἢ εὑρεῖν, either to learn or to
find out how the matter stands; or if this be impossible, then to
take the best opinion of men, and the reasons least likely to be
gainsaid; and thus carried, to risk oneself on that ὥς περ ἐπὶ

[1] Phædr. 62. sq.   [2] Alcib. sec. 23. sq.

Y

σχεδίας κινδυνεύοντα, as on a raft, and so cross the ocean of life; εἰ μή τις δύναιτο ἀσφαλέστερον καὶ ἀκινδυνότερον ἐπὶ βεβαιοτέρου ὀχήματος ἢ λόγου θείου τινὸς διαπορευθῆναι, unless one might be transported more safely and with less danger on a more solid craft, or on some divine word."[1]

We Christians have this "Divine Word," the Word of God revealed to us from heaven. What, then, are we to think of those who wish to set it aside, and to bring us back to Plato? Plato himself would none of us; he was much too wise for such folly. He indeed was wise in what he did, because he made full use of the light he had, and reached upwards as far as his understanding could go; though "by his wisdom he knew not GOD," as GOD is, and fell short of what he sought after. But what was wisdom in a man without revelation is folly in men who have it—since through it "GOD hath made foolish the wisdom of this world;"[2]—and who practically, setting aside that Revelation, attempt to do, with only a portion of Plato's ability, what he could not accomplish with his mighty mind. If, however, such men be honest, they must either deny the Revelation come from GOD, and thus abandon their claim to Christianism, or they must receive that Revelation, and abandon the ridiculous pretensions of their Rationalism—of all 'isms,' the most unreasonable.

XL. Our own sense, then, tells us, that whatever message of reconciliation GOD sent to man must be so plain, that "he may run that readeth it," and he that readeth may understand. And such is revelation; it reveals, draws aside the curtain that was between man and GOD, so as to make known to man what GOD is, and what man's position and duty are towards Him as a fallen, sinful creature, "dead in trespasses and sins," yet freely forgiven, reconciled and restored to the state whence it fell, and even higher.

---

[1] Phædo, 78. This λόγος θεῖος, "divine word," has been explained away by some to mean 'divine reason;' but the unsoundness of this shews itself in that although Plato had more 'reason,' and more of the so-called 'divinity' thereof, than other men, he yet found it insufficient. By others this passage is thought to be interpolated. But first—it is much too good Greek to have been written by any one else than Plato; and secondly—Plato could not write otherwise, having arrived at the uttermost limits of his reason; whence he heard, it seems, echoes from a better world.

[2] 1 Cor. i. 20.

Like the light of the sun, God's Word bears witness of itself, and the same witness also to all alike, whether high or low, ignorant or learned; for again, "with God there is no respect of persons." It shines, it warms, it quickens. It does not require of all those who come under its influence that they should be able to analyze it, and to reason thereon; it leaves this task to those whose special office is to search into its constituent parts and properties, so that they may, first for themselves and then for others, learn and know the wonders of this Divine Light revealed to us from heaven. But, practically, these men, however learned in it they be, benefit no more from the brightness, the warmth, and the life this Light gives, than do those who know no more about it than that it is light. They see it, they admire it, and they rejoice in it; it bears witness of itself to them, it lightens, it warms, it comforts them; and they would rather behold the light of that Sun, and bask in his beams, than shut themselves out from it. They do not care whether it reach them through undulation or through irradiation; when it reaches them they at once feel it is 'true Light,' and they neither can understand the existence of another light, nor even wish for it. It is "the Word of God that worketh effectually in them that believe."[1]

XLI. Yet so true and so searching is the witness of that Light revealed from heaven, that its presence alone convicts those who try to go from it. Yea, "this is the condemnation, that light is come into the world, and men loved darkness rather than light, because their deeds were evil. For every one that doeth evil hateth the light, neither cometh he to the light, lest his deeds should be reproved. But he that doeth truth cometh to the light, that his deeds may be made manifest, that they are wrought in God."[2] And this is the only reason that makes men either reject altogether or gainsay the Bible: they hate the light it brings, by which their works are reproved. Were it not so, they would receive it, and gladly come to it. But the 'argumentum ad hominem' brought by light to weak or sore eyes, is a convincing witness at once of the brightness of the light and of the soreness of the eyes.

XLII. But, those who gainsay Revelation on the ground that it is supernatural—that is, above natural reason and in-

<hr/>

[1] 1 Thess. II. 13. [2] S. John iii. 19, 20.

telligence—outwit themselves in so doing. Real philosophy
teaches us that there is, and that there can be, nothing in itself
supernatural; since what we, owing to our limited intelligence,
call 'laws of nature,' are only the result of our own observation,
and the effects of causes which we can find nowhere else than in
God. Assuredly not in matter itself; where else, then, than in
Him Who made all things, and " by Whom all things consist ?"
Nothing good can be above God's nature and attributes; and
since He is Almighty, there can be for Him nothing either
supernatural, wonderful, or miraculous. These are only terms
relative to ourselves, and to our fallen estate.

The miracles wrought by our Lord, then, were proofs, not of
His Divine Nature only, but also of our human nature before it
fell through sin, and thereby lost powers, energies, knowledge,
and an intimate acquaintance with the spiritual world, and with
these said 'laws of nature,' which, being only the obedience of
matter to the supreme will of the Creator, may be stayed, hindered, enacted by Him, and followed by that matter at His
bidding, and thus appear sometimes as if out of the track we
call 'natural.' Real philosophy, therefore, knowing this, wonders at none of the so-called signs and miracles; because these,
while they attest the power of God, also tell us of what our
own power might be, if, instead of being degraded from what
we originally were, we now enjoyed the state of existence of
Adam before the fall. Neither does real philosophy stagger at
a Revelation; since it looks upon it only as the making known
to man things which are above his nature thus fallen, and which
on that account appear to him supernatural. But they are natural to God.

XLIII. So-called philosophers, however, who try to explain
away miracles as supernatural, do not see that, by so doing, they
deny to their human nature the superior condition which it once
had, and of which it will once more be rendered capable in a
future existence. On the one hand they affect to doubt or to
deny everything they do not understand; and sooner than admit
the possibility of agencies to us apparently supernatural, yet
within the capabilities of our human nature restored to its original state, they would readily deny these capabilities to that nature,
and thus lower it to the standard of their limited and often misty

understanding; and this only in order to gainsay Scripture. We, therefore, who believe the Bible and the miracles told therein, honour human nature more than they; and we do not explain away what appears to us supernatural or miraculous, not only because we think nothing impossible to God, but also because we like to be thus reminded of some of the powers which of right belong to our nature, which it once had, and which it will once more possess.

So true is this, that when these philosophers set about explaining away direct interpositions of God's will and power,— as, for instance, in the passage of the Red Sea, they fail not to make themselves ridiculous by their inconsistency. We saw erst how some will insist on the 'east wind' having been a 'north wind,' and how others say it can have been no other than a 'south wind;' but I did not then mention the fact, that one of them, who will explain away the miracle so as not to disturb 'the laws of nature,'—which he must then think inherent in matter,— gravely tells us that the neap-tide, which he says Moses consulted ere he led the children of Israel through the sea, was felt all along the Red Sea as far as the Straits of Bâb-el-mandeb; this disturbance, in the opinion of that philosopher, being less than the staying of the tide during a few hours in the comparatively insignificant gulf of Suez; especially at the place where the passage probably took place. If such men were more consistent with themselves, very far from denying or explaining away miracles or wonders, and thus dooming their human nature to no greater capabilities than it now possesses, they would rather multiply tokens of what we now call supernatural agencies. But, in fact, miracles are only one of the many pretexts such men choose in order to gainsay Revelation. They would sooner lower their own nature and themselves with it, than not do what they can to revile the Light they hate.

XLIV. As we might expect, they of course deny, or explain away the mode of revelation adopted by God towards us; that is, through inspiration; through the Holy Ghost teaching certain men what to say and what to write, as a record of God's Will and Counsel. Some deny it altogether, others only in part. They parcel out the Bible according to their fancy, into what they think 'inspired' and what they do not; but even the

portions they consent to call 'inspired' must suit their ideas of
what inspiration is, in order to have a claim to such distinction.
This is not the place, neither is it my intention to discuss or to
refute the tenets of such philosophers; for time and labour would
be wasted in noticing the various absurdities by which men, who
thought themselves wise, have at sundry times laid open their
folly. But, as I am writing plainly for plain people, I will only
mention two or three considerations which common sense alone
suggests, as regards the revelation of God to man in His Word.

XLV. First—this message of reconciliation, become necessary through man's estrangement from God, must, in order to
be understood by man, be written in man's words, with man's
ideas, but not with man's mind; for then it would be man's
message, and not God's, and it could then reveal to man nothing that was not human. Neither could it be written by
angels; for if so, another Revelation would be required, in order
to explain the first; but it must be written by the Spirit of
God with the pen and with the words of men.

XLVI. Secondly—although this Revelation must be written
in human words, yet, as it is addressed to all men alike, its pur-
port and meaning must be independent of the idiom and of the
form of words used to express it.

I mean that—whereas the oracles of God were dictated by
the HOLY GHOST to men, who wrote them either in Hebrew or
in Greek, if God sanction the translation of those oracles into
any other language, as He evidently did in the case of the Septuagint, He shows clearly thereby that He never meant to restrict inspiration to the form, to the sound, to the etymological
meaning, or to the grammatical construction of the Hebrew and
of the Greek words in which the originals were written. Otherwise either no translation of them would be allowable and effec-
tual, or all men who are to be benefited by the inspired words
should have to read them in the Hebrew of the Old Testament
or in the Greek of the New. Since, however, we see that translations are multiplied, and that all, even defective ones, do
more or less the work whereunto they are sent, in carrying to
the heart of man the power of God's teaching unto salvation;
and, since we may hold as an axiom, that no language can fully
render another language, translators not being inspired, some

of the inspiration of the original terms never reaches those who use translations.

Neither does it altogether reach those who read the original texts, which are written in languages now dead; for no dead language is ever fully understood. Yet the proportion of the original inspiration of the Hebrew and of the Greek texts which is transmitted through whatever language, is sufficient to bring salvation to those who hear or read it. This evidently shows that, if God's inspired Word were addressed only, or chiefly, to the intellect of man,—that is, with mathematical precision,—it could be so only through the languages of the original autographs of the sacred writers; languages which, on this account, must have continued living languages; for none but a living language speaks accurately and fully to the mind of them that speak it; since it is only in proportion as we identify ourselves with a people that we understand the language thereof. But, since we find that this Revelation, written in languages now dead, nevertheless accommodates itself to every idiom, we see plainly that it is addressed chiefly to that part of man which is bound by no such formulas as the etymology, form, and construction of words, namely, to his spirit, and through that to his moral being; the nature and constitution of which is the same in all, whatever be their language.

It is well to bear in mind this important fact, that seems generally overlooked, because it explains at once several circumstances which have been seized by gainsayers as arguments against the Bible.

XLVII. Considering the scope and object of the Bible, we must see that it may be quite consistent with the teaching of the Holy Ghost, that men taught by Him what to write with regard to the aim and intention of the whole Book, should mention by the way, things that were and that could be true, only at the time they were written; things, therefore, as regards ourselves, irrelevant to the main object. Likewise, and for the same reason, many words and ideas may be inspired that lead neither to salvation nor to any particular good for man; because they were intended only as collateral information necessary, at the time the Book was written, for the credibility of that Book.[1]

[1] "The several books of Scripture having had each some several occasion and

Thus, passages like: "And Gera, and Shephuphan, and Huram,"[1] and thousands more such, are practically, to us, of no use whatever, though necessary as links of evidence to entitle the writing to credit at the time it was written. Yet, being inspired, and forming part of the Sacred Canon, they are for us 'sacred.'

XLVIII. For men, writing in human words and with human ideas, though under divine influence and control, wrote, of course, so as to be understood in all the details of their writing, by the men who lived at the time they wrote, and to whom their words were immediately addressed: but, on that very account, likely to be understood, by men who were to come after them, or who lived in other countries, only in the portions of those writings which impart information, or Truths, intended for all time. Thus, for instance, Job alludes to a custom of his day, but that no longer obtains, when he says: "Oh that my words were now written! that they were graven with an iron pen and lead in the rock for ever!" words, however, that convey a Truth which is our comfort in death, and the warning of our Church to her children around the grave: "I know that my Redeemer liveth, and that he shall stand at the latter day upon the earth!"[2] Thus, it is, also, quite consistent with inspiration that Joshua, relating the slaughter of the five kings of Canaan, who were cast into the cave at Makkedah, should say that the stones rolled at the entrance of the cave, "remain there until this very day,"[3] though it be no longer true.

Likewise, it was apparently true and according to the notions of the time, but of no importance whatever to the main object of the Bible, that "the sun did stand still;"[4] and it could not have been stated or written otherwise. Had Joshua been taught by inspiration the actual fact, that the earth and not the sun must have then stood still, and had he so stated it, no one would have either understood or believed him; because it would

particular purpose which caused them to be written; the contents thereof are according to that special end whereunto they are intended. Hereupon it groweth that every book of Holy Scripture doth take out of all kinds of truths, natural, historical, foreign, supernatural, so much as the matter handled requireth." Hooker, Eccles. Pol. Bk. I. ch. xiv. 4.

[1] 1 Chron. viii. 5, &c.   [2] Job xix. 23—27.
[3] Josh. x. 27.   [4] Josh. x. 12, sq.

have been, not only against the notions of the time, but also
against the appearance of the miracle, wrought, as much for the
appearance as for the reality; as much in order that the sun
should be seen standing still, as that Joshua should have time
to achieve his victory. The question at issue was not, of course,
whether the earth or the sun stood still; and it might be believed
or not according to the times of those who heard or who read
the account. In this case, as in that of the defeat of the five
kings at Makkedah, the question was, to give instances of God's
power when fighting for His people; and this shall remain true
as long as His Church is militant in earth; however differently
His power and deliverance may be both displayed and described
according to the times in which He acts.

XLIX. So also, as the Bible was not intended to give us
lessons in geography, in geology, in physics, in astronomy, nor
in any of the sciences which depend on experimental knowledge,
and that improve as knowledge increases, according to the prophecy of Daniel,[1] in all such matters[2] the Bible speaks, as it must
needs have spoken, after the manner of the times in which its
several parts were written. And this, very far from invalidating
its witness in the slightest degree, is an internal evidence of the
authenticity of its several Books. Were they all written exactly
alike, speaking precisely the same language, with no traces
whatever of the human hands that wrote, though under the
guidance of God's overruling Spirit, yet purposely, as of necessity they must have written in them, according to the notions
of the several ages in which they wrote, things to us apparently
irrelevant—then, indeed, we might suspect collusion and imposture. Whereas, the very discrepancies we find in the style, the
words, the ideas, and the expressions of the several writers of
those Books, attest the genuineness of their writings, however
much these peculiarities may differ one from the other, and all
of them from our own way of thinking. All this simply forms
a plain proof of the oneness of intention, of aim, of object, of
purpose in the writers, who while writing at times distant from

[1] Dan. xii. 4.
[2] It is evident that this holds good only in matters of custom, opinion, notions, &c. In matters of faith, as for instance, in that of the creation, as we
shall see below, the case is different.

each other, wrote so as to be understood by their own countrymen, at the time they wrote; and so as to convey information
and to impart Truths that were to remain true for those who
came after. The human element,—and by this I mean, for instance, the difference of style, of ideas, of handwriting, &c., of
the several writers, therefore attests the guidance of the Spirit
which did not allow these human forms of style, of ideas, and of
expressions, to affect the general even tenour of the whole Book,
which centres on one subject—the call of God's Church from
out the world, and the Redemption of that Church through the
Blood of Christ.

L. But this view of the subject which is correct, because
consistent with common sense and with Truth, does not, of
course, suit those whose object is to find fault with the Bible,
in order, by all means to gainsay it. They wilfully shut their
eyes to the fact, that these differences of style, ideas, &c., are
not only consistent with the economy of inspiration which is
addressed to the spirit rather than to the intellect of man, but
that they are so many proofs in favour of it. And assuming
the sophism that, 'if the Book is inspired it can contain no
discrepancies of any kind whatever,' they take advantage of every
one of these details irrelevant to the main object and independent of it, in order to impugn the whole; and this argument
specious as it is, though unsound, succeeds in deceiving many.

Such men act the part of a hodman who, while carrying mortar
upon the scaffolding around S. Paul's, would run down the skill
and the genius of Sir Christopher Wren, because he discovers a
crack or a flaw in one stone or another. He argues, plausibly
to himself, that Sir Christopher Wren could not be the man
people think, otherwise there would not be this flaw or that
crack in this stone; that, in short, he does not think such an
architect did ever live, whatever they may say; for that, he,
hodman though he be, would be more careful of his work, if
they would but give it him to do. So reason many philosophers
of the day. We who are more simple, however, look upon this
flaw or that crack in the stone only as a proof of the perishable
nature of that stone; and we conclude, as we think, rightly,
that—since after such a length of time this crack or this flaw is
no worse, the workmen who chose the stone, and the architect

who overlooked the whole, must have been, the one very careful
and the other very clever. So that, reasoning only according to
our own sense, we say: Sir Christopher Wren must have made
use of the materials he had; so that, but for his presiding genius
all the stones in the building, and not a few only, would show
signs of decay. He therefore deserves great praise for his work.

And it would be contrary to common sense, when applying
this reasoning to the edifice of God's Word, to say—that God
might have used what materials He pleased. So, of course, He
might; as He might have chosen to cause His Word to be
written by Angels; but that Word being addressed to men, it
was to be written after the manner of men, though by the wisdom of God. Therefore, do these touches of humanity in the
writings of the Prophets and of the Apostles, attest the means
used and the presiding and overruling Spirit of Him Who used
them. These apparent defects are allowed to remain as tokens
of the hand that stayed them from affecting the beauty and the
solidity of the whole.

LI. This, I ween, is the view to take of the passage often
misunderstood: "All Scripture is given by inspiration of God,
and is profitable for doctrine," &c. We all admit 'inspiration'
to mean: 'the HOLY GHOST teaching or moving men to speak
or to write;' and we also admit that whole chapters of genealogies, rolls of Levites, &c., were thus 'inspired;' but we cannot
say that such chapters or verses are "profitable for doctrine, for
reproof," &c., for anything, in short, but to fill up a list of
names, which to us however are of no service whatever. It is
clear, therefore, that S. Paul could not have such chapters or
verses in view in applying the latter part of this and the following verse (v. 17) to "all Scripture is given by inspiration of
God." But he evidently said Πᾶσα γραφὴ θεόπνευστος of the
whole, and ὠφέλιμος πρὸς διδασκαλίαν, κ.τ.λ., only of portions
thereof; using πᾶσα in this case, as πᾶν in πᾶν τὸ ἐν μακέλλῳ
πωλούμενον ἐσθίετε, "Whatsoever," or, all that, "is sold in the
shambles, that eat;"[1] for all that is sold there is not eatable,
though it be lawful to eat it. S. Paul then, leaves a wide
margin for what is not "profitable," &c., in "all Scripture
given by inspiration," as he leaves out many things that cannot

[1] 1 Cor. x. 25.

be eaten, in "whatsoever is sold in the shambles," &c.; which is precisely what I meant to express. He, therefore, that would deny the inspiration of these rolls and genealogies, &c., because they are not "profitable," would be as far from right, as he who would allegorise or spiritualise them, because they were written by men inspired; in the same way as he who would abstain from certain meats as unlawful, would be as far from understanding S. Paul's meaning as he who would undertake to eat the whole and everything sold in the shambles, because it is said, "Whatsoever is sold, that eat," &c. In the words of Archbishop Laud, already quoted in the preface, "all propositions of Canonical Scripture are alike firm, because they all alike proceed from Divine Revelation; but they are not alike fundamental to the Faith ;"[1] being all equally " given by inspiration," though not all equally "profitable for doctrine, for instruction," &c.

There is a wide gap from this clear and true statement of the actual fact to the sophistry that "some Books of the Bible are less inspired than others," as some men assert who arrogate to themselves the power and assume the right of deciding for themselves and for others also, 'the much' or 'the little' of this inspiration; thus evidently making a Bible for themselves, instead of bowing and of submitting themselves to the Bible as God gives it. For unless we receive it whole and in its integrity, our obedience to it is a pretence, and our obedience to our own 'self' is a reality; since we practically choose for ourselves those parts of it that suit us, and reject the rest. But real philosophy teaches otherwise. It teaches that the inspiration is the same, whether of the Books of Ruth, of Esther, Ezra, &c., or of the Psalms, the Proverbs, or of the Song of Songs; whether in the burden of Nahum, in the narrative of Jonah, or in the prophecies of Isaiah or of S. John; due regard being had to the time, to the purpose, to the object for which these Books were severally inspired and written.

LII. This touches another question, that of 'verbal inspiration;' which is, also, I fear, mistaken by many. Strictly speaking, 'verbal inspiration,' as some people understand it, no longer exists. The only documents that might with justice be said to

[1] Relation of a Conference, &c., p. 37, sq.

be "verbally inspired," that is, every word of which was inspired—were the autographs of the holy men who wrote, as
moved by the HOLY GHOST. But the very first copy made
from those autographs, introduced some mistakes, and so far,
destroyed the 'verbal inspiration' of those copies; that is, the
inspiration of every word in them. These mistakes increased
more or less in after copies; so that their number is now considerable. And yet, considerable though it be, in the originals
both of the Old and of the New Testament, their aggregate
influence on the sense, meaning, power, and authority of those
texts, amounts to little or nothing; to no more than to the
effect the spots on the sun have in lessening its bright light
and genial warmth, that is—not at all. The light of both the
sun and of the Bible outshine all spots or other supposed defects
in them.

Secondly—as we have remarked when alluding to the Septuagint,[1] the undeniable fact, that no language can be fully and
adequately rendered into another, does away at once with
what, strictly speaking, can be called 'verbal inspiration,' by
which is also understood,—the whole amount of the inspiration
contained in the words of the original texts, transmitted through
translation; a thing simply impossible. As an example of this,
I went into detail—but, now-a-days, few care for such details—
in the Notes to my Translations of the Gospel of S. John,[2] in
order to show that, for instance, in these words—'Εν ἀρχῇ ἦν ὁ
λόγος, καὶ ὁ λόγος ἦν πρὸς τὸν Θεόν, καὶ Θεὸς ἦν ὁ λόγος—not
only is ἀρχῇ not well rendered through "beginning," but the
def. art. 'the' used with it in the translation gives a meaning
very different from the Greek; since 'the' points to a beginning
that never existed. Eternity has no beginning; and since the
WORD was GOD, and was with GOD from all eternity, it was so,
not 'in the beginning,' but rather 'on principle'—that comes
nearest the Greek. I also pointed out that in this verse ἦν is
not fully expressed through 'was;' nor λόγος through 'word;'
nor yet καί, πρὸς, Θεός through 'and,' 'with,' and 'GOD,' respectively; to say nothing of the use of the definite article with

---

[1] See p. 17.
[2] The Gospel according to S. John, translated from the eleven oldest Versions,
except the Latin, &c., Notes p. 1—14.

'God' in Greek, which has precisely the contrary effect in English; so that, the only two words in this verse that may be said to render the original correctly are perhaps 'in' for ἐν and 'the' for ὁ. This may apply, more or less, to every verse in the Bible; and that too, on the supposition of only one Version in the same language.

But in most countries that have not the advantage of an Authorised Version, and even in this, there is more than one translation from the originals; how then shall we measure the relative degree of inspiration transferred into one or the other rendering of the same original words, since those renderings differ; and to which will the term 'verbal inspiration' apply? As an instance of this I quoted[1] from among many other passages: ἐγὼ γὰρ ἐκ τοῦ Θεοῦ ἐξῆλθον καὶ ἥκω· οὐδὲ γὰρ ἀπ' ἐμαυτοῦ ἐλήλυθα, S. John viii. 42, and asked which of these two renderings—".for I proceeded forth, and came from God, neither came I of myself," A. V., or "for I proceeded forth, and am come from God, for neither am I come of myself," R. V., is best, since both are incorrect, and can hardly be made better; for ἥκω and ἐλήλυθα convey, each, a very different idea to the mind, and should not both be rendered alike. Where, in this and in thousands of other such cases, is the 'verbal inspiration' in the English rendering of the Greek? Nowhere.

LIII. Yet, let no one be startled at this. These apparent flaws and imperfections are, nevertheless, a strong argument to show the real divine origin and inspiration of the Bible, and the presence of the HOLY GHOST in it, as proved by the work He does in the heart of man through that Book, and in spite of such apparent defects. Seeing the Word of God—and by 'Word of God' I mean the whole Sacred Canon of Scripture—brings to man a Revelation of things "which never entered into his heart," and which, therefore, are not to be either found out or attained by his intellect alone—the subject as well as the object of that Revelation are both spiritual rather than intellectual. The subject—God "is Spirit," not 'Intellect,' and "they that worship him must worship him in spirit and in Truth," and not in 'intellect,' since intellect alone cannot reach Him. And in His Word He reveals Himself to man, as "mani-

[1] Preface to S. John, p. xiii.

fest in the flesh, justified in the Spirit;" not in the 'intellect;' as "CHRIST crucified, to the Jews a stumbling-block, and to the Greeks foolishness." But unto them that are called—the power of GOD, and the wisdom of GOD. "Because the foolishness of GOD is wiser than men." "For it is written: I will destroy the wisdom of the wise, and will bring to nothing the understanding of the prudent: where is the wise?—hath not GOD made foolish the wisdom of this world?" All this shows how little the burden of this Revelation is in accordance with human wisdom, that is, intellectual; so that both cannot hold together the same place. Therefore, "Let no man deceive himself. If any among you seemeth to be wise in this world, let him become a fool, that he may be wise. For the wisdom of this world is foolishness with GOD. For it is written: He taketh the wise in their own craftiness." And again: "The LORD knoweth the thoughts of the wise, that they are vain. Therefore let no man glory in men."[1]

There is in all this, assuredly, very little room left for man's intellect, reason and philosophy, as substitutes for Faith, because—

Secondly—the object of this Revelation is not man's 'intellect,' but man's 'spirit;' it is addressed to the spiritual and moral part of man, and to his intellectual faculties only in so far as his intelligence is connected with his spirit, and thus with the beginning of his Faith. However it may tax our intellect either to study the very letter of GOD's Word, and to seek to understand the whole economy of His love towards us, of our redemption by our LORD CHRIST, and of our sanctification by the HOLY GHOST, the object and intention of the Bible is not to make of us learned or scientific men, clever engineers or profound naturalists; but it is to make us better men morally,—to transform us from being natural men, ψυχικοὶ ἄνθρωποι, who, however intellectual perhaps, yet "receive not the things of the Spirit of GOD," which they cannot know naturally,—that is, intellectually,—"because they are spiritually discerned," into men spiritual, who may discern all things and judge of them; being guided into all truth by the Spirit of Truth. Now this Spirit is, we are told,[2] the seal set by GOD on our Faith in the witness

[1] 1 Cor. i. 18—28; iii. 18—21.   [2] Eph. i. 13; iv. 30.

He gives of Himself in His Word. "For by a like Faith,"
says S. Cyril of Jerusalem,[1] "are we reckoned children of Abraham; and like Him also do we, through Faith, receive τὴν πνευ-
ματικὴν σφραγῖδα, the seal of the Spirit, being circumcised by
the HOLY GHOST, διὰ τοῦ λουτροῦ, by means of the washing"
(of water, or of regeneration)[2]; since "the fellowship of the
Spirit is given to every man, κατὰ ἀναλογίαν τῆς πίστεως, in proportion to his Faith,"[3] which Faith rests, as we have seen, "not
on the wisdom of words, ἀλλ' ἐξ ἀποδείξεως τῶν θείων ἐστὶ γραφῶν,
but on the witness of the Holy Scriptures, and on proofs drawn
from them,"[4] whose infallibility, as Word of GOD, is, Archbishop
Laud says, "a Prime Principle of Faith."[5] For while "the
things of GOD knoweth no man, but the Spirit of GOD," yet "as

---

[1] S. Cyril, Catech. iv.   [2] Eph. v. 26; Tit. iii. 5.
[3] Id. Catech. I.   [4] Id. Catech. iv.

[5] Relation of a Conference, &c., p. 28, and 46, sq. "To the question in
hand then: Suppose it agreed upon, that there must be a Divine Faith, cui
subesse non potest falsum, under which can rest no possible error. That the
Books of Scripture are the Written Word of God: If they which go to the testimony of the Holy Ghost for proof of this do mean by Faith, Objectum Fidei,
the Object of Faith that is to be believed, then, no question they are out of the
ordinary way. For God never sent us by any word or warrant of His, to look
for any such special and private Testimony to prove which that Book is, that we
must believe. But if by Faith they mean, the Habit, or Act of Divine infused
Faith, by which virtue they do believe the Credible Object, and thing to be
believed; then their speech is true, and confessed by all Divines of all sorts.
For Faith is the gift of God, (1 Cor. xii. 3, 4,) of God alone, and an infused
Habit (dator coelis a Deo, &c. S. Aug. in Ps. 37); in respect whereof the soul
is merely recipient; and therefore the sole Informer, the Holy Ghost must not
be excluded from that work which none can do but He.—So that Faith, as it
is taken for the virtue of Faith—though it receive a kind of preparation, or
Occasion of Beginning from the Testimony of the Church, as it proposeth, and
induceth to the Faith; yet it ends in God, revealing within that which the
Church preached without. For till the Spirit of God move the Heart of man,
he cannot believe, be the Object never so credible." (The capitals and italics are
Abp. Laud's.)

"In Scripture," says Hooker, (Ecclas. Pol. Bk. III. ch. iii. 3,) "hath God
both collected the most necessary things that the school of nature teacheth unto
that end (the knowledge of salvation) and revealeth also whatsoever we neither
could with safety be ignorant of, nor at all be instructed in but by supernatural
revelation from him.—All such things if Scripture did not comprehend, the
Church of God should not be able to measure out the length and the breadth of
that way wherein for ever she is to walk, heretics and schismatics never ceasing
some to abridge, some to enlarge, all to pervert and obscure the same."

many as are led by the Spirit of GOD, they are the sons of GOD;"[1] and thus, through "the Spirit of GOD bearing witness with our spirit that we are children of GOD," our mortal "body is quickened by that Spirit," and then offered as "a spiritual" and a "living sacrifice, holy and acceptable unto GOD, which is our reasonable service,"—that is, the service which, according to reason, it becomes spiritual creatures to render to a spiritual GOD.[2] And this service is not only reasonable, but also rational; for, says Hooker:

"As it were altogether bootless to allege against the impious adversaries of the Church, what the Spirit hath taught us, so likewise even to our own selves it needeth caution and explication how the testimony of the Spirit may be discerned, by what means it may be known; lest men think that the Spirit of GOD doth testify those things which the spirit of error suggesteth.—Wherefore albeit the Spirit lead us into all truth and direct us in all goodness, yet because these workings of the Spirit in us are so privy and secret, we therefore stand on a plainer ground, when we gather by reason from the quality of things believed or done, that the Spirit of GOD hath directed us in both, than if we settle ourselves to believe or to do any certain particular thing, as being moved thereto by the Spirit."[3]

Thus only can man be sanctified wholly, and his "whole spirit, soul and body, preserved blameless unto the coming of our LORD JESUS CHRIST."[4] And this is the intention of GOD's Revelation to us.

LIV. Therefore "to the poor is the Gospel preached,"—to those who, whatever be their 'intellect,' are equally endowed with "the spirit of man that goeth upward,"[5] and are, therefore, fit subjects for the spiritual and moral influence of a spiritual and moral teaching. Therefore did S. Paul remind the brethren at Corinth "of their calling;" "how that," in the midst of that large, intellectual, and refined city, "not many wise men after the flesh, not many mighty, not many noble, were called," from among her illustrious people.[6] Therefore,

[1] 1 Cor. ii. 11; Rom. viii. 14.
[2] Rom. viii. 16, 11; 1 S. Pet. ii. 5; Rom. xii. 1.
[3] Eccles. Pol. Bk. iii. ch. viii. 15.   [4] 1 Thess. v. 23.
[5] Eccl. iii. 21.   [6] 1 Cor. i. 26.

z

also, did our SAVIOUR say to His disciples, "Verily I say unto
you, whosoever shall not receive the kingdom as a little child
shall in no wise enter therein;"[1] for He did not then mean baptism, which He had not yet formally instituted as a Christian
rite; but He meant the childlike simplicity and ready faith of a
child, as applicable to the kingdom of GOD.[2]

LV. Therefore, also, since the main business of Revelation is,
if I may so speak, with the spirit of man, and not with his intellect, which is for the earth, earthly, the spirit and power of
that Revelation, which are one and the same for all and unto all,
must yet be such as to adapt themselves to the circumstances
and to the peculiarities of all nations; and thus far be independent of the peculiar features of race or nationality of the intellectual channels through which they are conveyed to man.
Thus, whether the Greek—

Ἐν ἀρχῇ ἦν ὁ λόγος, καὶ ὁ λόγος ἦν πρὸς τὸν Θεόν, καὶ Θεὸς ἦν ὁ
λόγος·

or the English—

"In the beginning was the Word, and the Word was with GOD,
and the Word was GOD;"

or yet the Mandchu—

"Toktan de Giaun bihe; ere Giaun apkai Etchen de bihe; ere
Giaun utkbai apkai Etchen inu;"

all convey the same Truth, though it be through different ideas,
and by means of words etymologically wide apart. How then
shall we measure the relative degree of inspiration in these two
translations? In no wise; neither need we. They are each a
fair and conscientious rendering of the original words—even
"in the beginning" has long done duty for ἐν ἀρχῇ—and although they are not the originally inspired Greek words, yet
they impart enough of the same Truth to do the same good as
they. Since, then, both the English and the Mandchu minds
receive the same Truth, though not in the same way intellectually, the inspiration of the words lies, for each, in the Truth
conveyed, and in its influence over the spirit of man, which is
the same in all; and not in the form of ideas or of the words,

[1] S. Luke xviii. 17; S. Matt. xviii. 3.   [2] See p. 289, note.

which differ more or less in all nations and in all languages. For if it lay in these, it either would vary with the language, or require always the same language to convey it to the mind and to the heart.

LVI. And if we be told that such is the case with every kind of knowledge that is thus conveyed through translations, whether of natural, physical, and other like sciences, we reply, that all these differ altogether from the kind of knowledge to be conveyed through translations of inspired words. In purely intellectual knowledge, as that of certain branches of mathematics, the numbers and the formulæ convey their own witness, independently of words: in other branches of mathematics applicable to physics, astronomy, &c., experiments and demonstration supply the lack of words; and in natural history, no knowledge is worth much that does not rest on personal experience and observation. Whereas, as regards the knowledge of spiritual things to be conveyed through translations of inspired records, as they are matters of Faith, and not to be mathematically or experimentally demonstrated, the knowledge of them imparted or received depends entirely on the words used; the chief difficulty being in either finding, or coining terms and expressions in every language, as the Apostles did in Greek, capable of transmitting the inspired Truth. Yet, with all this, the result is all over the world the same; and in every part of the earth the same moral good and transformation of the natural man into one spiritually minded is wrought through the same means.

LVII. It is therefore, but natural to think, that since even at the present day the inspired Truths contained in the Canon of Scripture, adapt themselves, not in substance only, but even in the outline of words, to peoples of all manner of languages, and of a greater variety of habits, customs, and associations, than ever they did before,—that the Canon itself, written at different times and by different men, though in the same languages—the Old Testament in Hebrew, and the New in Greek—may show signs of the same adaptation to times and to circumstances in the letter thereof. And so it is. We find in it, and consistently with the economy of Inspiration, collateral statements, things of secondary importance, others of no importance to us at present, yet necessary at the time they were written for a right

conveyance of other important or vital Truths. We therefore
must expect to find, and we do find, as part of those several
inspired records, matters of mere belief, as distinct from Faith;
statements of opinion, allusions to customs and to a state of
knowledge which altered with the times; of necessity mentioned
by the writer or writers without comment, in order to be understood by those for whom he or they wrote; but assuredly not
intended as rules of either opinion, customs, or knowledge for
us to follow. Thus do we frequently find polygamy and other
social abuses mentioned in connexion with the best men of old,
though without remarks thereon; because they are simply alluded to as customs, and stated as facts, and remarks on them
would often be foreign to the subject in hand. But when directly
treated, God institutes and blesses marriage with one wife only
to every man, and curses whoredom and adultery.

LVIII. Practically then, our position towards God's Word,
the Canon of Holy Scripture is this:—To look upon it as
"all given by inspiration of God," and to venerate, love, and
worship every word of it for His sake; not blindly, but admitting
that there are in it many things irrelevant to the main object
but relevant to the object the several writers had in view, to
the persons for whom, as well as to the times in which they
wrote; the whole being for us both holy and sacred. The
parts which belong unto our spirit and unto the life thereof,
being by comparison 'holy;' and those which are only collateral
and complementary being also 'sacred,' by reason of the Book
in which they are found, and of Him at Whose bidding they were
written. Very far from wishing it otherwise, we take such features as additional proofs of the authenticity of the several
writings contained therein, as showing unity of object and of
purpose without combination on the part of the writers. We
know, of course, that the several parts thereof have suffered
from the wear and waste of time, because the words though
inspired, were written on perishable materials; yet less so than
any other Books of the same ages, extant: the authenticity and
the credibility thereof also rest on a foundation laid deeper and
firmer than those of any other Book or Books of the same respective age or ages. This so far satisfies our intellect, as to
make it assent to the credibility of that Book, and receive it,

even on that ground alone. But when opened, it bears witness of itself and of its origin; it finds its way straight through the spirit to the heart, as objects in the light do through the eyes to the mind. It speaks for itself; it says: I am the Truth: as light says: I am light; and we feel it.

It is, if I may use such an expression, the Bread of Life; the bread is so far not pure, as there are mingled with it particles of earthly matter that have clung to it during its stay in the earth; but it is suited to this our present earthly state. When we are fitted for the company of angels, we shall have food suited to that state also, the same Truth, but brighter and clearer; because we shall then understand all things, know God as we are known of Him, and see Him as He is. For the present, and seeing we can find spiritual food nowhere else, we receive this bread with thanksgiving, and as we eat it we subsist thereby. Some of our fellow men, will none of it as it is given them, but attempt to do what no man can do, and insist on extracting from it, after their own fashion, what they call the 'flour' alone whereof they say that bread consists; meanwhile they starve themselves, because they refuse to eat; but we live, because we partake of it. Others treat it even less reverently, and as if it were no bread. All we can say with our MASTER, is: "FATHER, forgive them; for they know not what they do."

But, for our part, we receive it whole as it is; we will not, and we dare not, lay hands on any one part or parts thereof, because the whole is holy and sacred; and because it is not for us to pretend to know better than it does, things which we do not understand. We then receive, love, and worship, the Bible, as "all given by inspiration of God," and we bow to it as such; feeling persuaded that as regards that Book and things pertaining unto God, in Whom we believe, although we neither see nor understand Him—we shall sooner be forgiven for having believed too much of things we cannot know at present, out of love, trust and worship for Him, than too little, from lack of Faith, and from self-conceit or unbelief.

LIX. Time would fail in rehearsing the several objections raised at divers times by philosophy against the Bible. But some of them are more popular, because better known, than others. Among these are the Creation as recorded in the first

chapter of Genesis; which is either cavilled at, or often entirely
set aside by "modern science and philosophy."

But, it was not God's good pleasure to give us a treatise on
geology, otherwise we should have it, for ever to lay the dust of
man's reasonings on the subject, and to teach true science; that
is, things as they were and as they are, and not as we fancy
them to have been or to be. Whereas we are left in a matter of
this kind, of very inferior importance compared with the object
of God's Revelation to man, to gather our information from
facts that fall under our observation. These, however, are so
few, and the space on which we can observe them, is so limited
in comparison with the size of the globe on which we must bring
to bear the conclusions we draw from our slender premisses, that
no prudent or sound-headed man will think himself justified in
hastily forming his judgment on the subject.

God tells us plainly what He would have us know with certainly, and what we should never have known unless He had
told it us, namely—that in the beginning He "created the
heavens and the earth;" and that He alone, "is worthy to receive glory, and honour, and power; for He hath created all
things, and for His pleasure they are and were created."[1] So
true is this, and so necessary was it to establish it as a fact
against all the fanciful systems of philosophy both old and new,
that it is made a matter of Faith: "through Faith we understand that the worlds were framed by the Word of God, so that
things which are seen, were not made of things which do appear."[2] And as the Spirit of God foresaw that this teaching
would be doubted and gainsaid, we are further warned that—
"there shall come in the last days scoffers—willingly ignorant
of this, that by the Word of God the heavens were of old, and
the earth standing out of the water and in the water."[3]

When, then, was "the beginning?" God does not say. If
we are to believe in the successive convulsions that brought
this earth to its present state, and made it fit for man, these
several formations must have taken place between the first and
the second verse of Genesis; without for all that, destroying
the witness of Scripture; and "the beginning" must be thrown

---

[1] Gen. i. 1; Rev. iv. 11.   [2] Heb. xi. 3.
[3] 2 S. Pet. iii. 5.

back to an indefinite period. But if we adopt the far more probable system of the Flood having caused the phænomena we notice in the crust of the earth, then "the beginning" would be far more recent.

However this be, the argument sometimes brought forward that since "by man came death" the animals we find in a fossil state in strata which might thus be younger than the first and older than the second verse of Genesis, cannot have then existed—will not hold good. For, the same authority tells us, that brute beasts "were made to be taken and destroyed;"[1] whereas man was created after the image and the similitude of God, to live for ever; therefore does "the spirit of man go upward; and the spirit of the beast downward to the earth."[2] Death brought in by man, could not, then, be said of the cessation of existence of creatures made 'a priori' to be taken and destroyed; but it must refer only to the death of man as "wages of sin." There is then, nothing to hinder one who will not swerve from the word of Scripture even in matters Scripture was not intended to teach us—from admitting, if need be, the possibility, or even the probability of these anterior creations, until he, with his own eyes, see lying in rocks, shells, fishes, reptiles, trees, and quadrupeds, which existed ere the last time when "the earth was without form and void." Then may have followed this, the last creation and arrangement of the present system. Night was before light, and light was before the sun, which only on the fourth day was made the centre of light, and possibly, also of our system. And, only after that, began the appearance of life on the earth; first the animal world; and then, at last, man.

LX. Albeit there is nothing said in Scripture to hinder us from carrying back the first verse of Genesis, if not to an indefinite period, at least to a time anterior to the second and the following verses of the same chapter—yet it seems illogical to argue, as some do, from what takes place on the surface of the globe, now in a settled state, to what did take place when the earth was being prepared and moulded into its present shape—nearly that of a mass either liquid or plastic, revolving on its axis, as does the earth.[3]

[1] 2 S. Pet. ii. 12. [2] Eccles. iii. 21.
[3] Since the earth is an oblate spheroid, it is clear that its shape is in relation

Yet, after all, what does our real knowledge of the conformation of the earth amount to? If we take a lump of clay, shape it like a sphere eight inches in diameter, $\frac{1}{16}$ flatter at the poles than at the equator, then bake it; paste on that a strip of brown paper one-third of the circumference wide, on each side the equator, so as to cover two-thirds of the sphere between the poles with brown paper; then paste on it a hair, and a grain of sand; these will be to that sphere what the highest mountains are to the earth. Then mark out on the brown paper a spot the size of a penny, and riddle it with holes made with a pin, —that will answer to Europe and to the mines and coal-pits in it; make also a few hundred more pin-holes elsewhere on the brown paper, and these will answer to the mines, &c., out of Europe, as the brown paper will represent the earth's crust known to geologists, through those pin-holes. Would anyone argue deliberately from the accidents of wear and tear to that hair, or from the knowledge of the crust derived from those pin-holes, to what took place in the mass ere it was being finally moulded and baked? or would he measure the time it took to mould and to bake that mass, from the time it would take wind and rain to leave traces on that grain of sand or on that hair? So then, when we hear from trustworthy observations, what alterations have taken place in the diameter of the earth at the equator within the last six or four thousand years, we may then begin to think this globe is in a gradual state of either formation, transition, or decay. Till then, we must consider the present state thereof as stationary; as the state of the period "when

to its rotation. If after having calculated accurately from the data we have, the probable density of water at the depth of 3960 miles, the mean half-diameter of the earth, the centripetal and the centrifugal forces acting upon a liquid decreasing in density from that depth to the surface, and then describe the exact shape such a mass of liquid the size of the earth would take; then compare that with its actual shape, and with the influence both sun and moon would exercise on the liquid mass in rotation, we might possibly come at some data as to the time the earth, which seems to have experienced greater nutations of the poles than at present, was made to revolve regularly round the sun. If it were also possible to ascertain whether the primitive formations by fire or by water, such as gneiss, granite, &c., partake of the exact shape of the globe, or whether the secondary formations have a share in swelling the diameter of the earth at the equator, it might be possible perhaps to form some definite theory respecting the Deluge and other questions relating to it.

GOD gave to the sea His decree, that the waters should not pass His commandment"[1]—a fact we see proved by every map we look at—until the final overthrow, for which, according to the Word of GOD, it is reserved.

LXI. Still, we cannot look up on a clear night, to the brilliant worlds that spangle the firmament of heaven, and think that this our earth, which is invisible from the nearest of them, is, after all, but an atomic speck in the Universe, without our mind at once attempting to soar above and ramble among those worlds, wondering what they and the state of them can be. Yet, if such thoughts do aught else than raise us higher towards GOD who rules over those countless worlds, they only tend to raise within us questions which can never be answered in this world. We may be sure that if it were necessary for the better knowledge of our present or of our future existence, that we should know more of the condition of those worlds, that knowledge would have been granted. As it is, however, the sight of GOD's glory which the heavens declare, and the language they speak, bid man " walk humbly with his GOD."—" O LORD, our LORD, how excellent is thy Name in all the earth! who hast set thy glory above the heavens."—No observations will penetrate beyond that; no thought even, can reach it.—" When I consider thy heavens, the work of thy fingers, the moon and the stars, which thou hast ordained; what is man that thou art mindful of him, or the son of man that thou so regardest him ?" " For thou hast made him a little lower than the angels, and hast crowned him with glory and honour—thou hast put all things under his feet." " I have created him for my glory," saith the LORD, " I have formed him; yea, I have made him."[2] This is the task set us by our Creator—to glorify Him; and whether or not He have done the same for other worlds, is idle for us to inquire; inasmuch as we shall answer for ourselves and not for them.

LXII. So also as regards the pre-Adamite existence of man, as it is called. It is diametrically opposed to the words of Scripture that " in Adam all die." Our local knowledge of the crust of

<hr />

[1] For the local trifling encroachments of the sea or of the land, are of no account, when compared with the whole surface of the earth and of each continent.
[2] Isa. xliii. 7.

the earth is as yet so limited, and we are thus so far from being
able to draw safe and settled conclusions from the little we know,
that no cautious mind will be in a hurry to do so, and to commit itself to the fallacy of judging of a period of catastrophes by
a period of rest.   When, as was said just now, we have ascertained to what extent the diameter of the earth has either increased or altered during the last six thousand years, we may
then make up our mind as to whether or not we be in a transition state, as regards the formation of this earth.   And when,
moreover, undoubted human remains proved to be anterior to
the Adamite period—nay, to the Noachic Deluge—are found,
it will then be time enough for men to decide, who wish to hold
by the Bible, without shutting their eyes to matters of fact.
For, indeed, we cannot be expected to put faith in pre-Adamite
specimens and in pre-Adamite speculations, of which we know
nothing, until we see brought forward well authenticated remains of the human race which we know to have existed ere it
was destroyed by the waters of the Flood.   Let us first have
this well established by proofs which ought to be forthcoming
somewhere, in recent strata or even in the 'diluvium;' and
when we have set before us one whole and perfect fossil human
skeleton to every thousand human beings who lived in the days
of Noah, we may then proceed to consider the other so-called
remains of another period several thousand years older.

We have all the more right to claim such undeniable proofs
of the assertions of geologists, ere we change our mind, as
"modern science" as it is called, argues for a local Deluge.
Since then, even under this supposition the whole race of man
which was then destroyed, must have been limited to one country
of no very great extent, human fossil remains of that date,
cannot be past finding out, if all the theories, the assumptions,
and the systems founded on modern discovery be correct.   On
the contrary ; if everything were so sure and so clear as certain
theorists affirm, and if results were logically deduced from the
causes or premisses they pretend to have established, fossil
human remains ought to be at least as plentiful and as well
preserved as those of plesiosauri and of iguanodons, said by
them to be immeasurably more ancient, or as the delicate fresh-
water molluscs in a fossil state, which they tell us are more recent.

LXIII. The truth is, that geology which of all sciences is one of observation, is as yet in its infancy, and from the very nature of its subject matter and of the circumscribed limits of its observations, it bids fair never to grow up to childhood. It is easy to make diagrams of small localities,—but to reason on these, and to infer from these particulars to the whole is too illogical to suit a well constituted mind. Hence the infinite variety of theories, and the yet greater variety of deductions from them and of opinions about things which after all, we cannot know with any certainty.

And lest I should be thought prejudiced in favour of my own way of thinking, I will give a better opinion than mine, that of a very able naturalist who, while he denies 'creation' by God as we who receive the Bible believe it, and attributes the formation of vegetables to the bare and accidental combination of ' natural causes' independent of the Creator's will—nevertheless bears unconsciously witness to the record of Holy Writ.

" As long," says M. Raspail,[1] " as geology limited itself to the study of the nature and of the order of the strata that cover the crust of the earth, it brought about results which cannot be gainsaid. But, the mind of man does not long tarry in the study of details; it soon wearies of mere classification—and not only wishes to know what every being is, but also whence it comes; and here it is that difficulties in geology increase.— Every step it makes must be first dug by hand ; and science, that does not create but only observes, had not a sufficient number of hands able to dig into this immense labyrinth ; whence it happens that the amount of our knowledge in geology is next to nothing, compared with what we do not know, which cannot even be guessed at. We have found that the surface of the earth known to geologists, is to the globe, as a pin's head is to a sphere sixteen feet (seventeen English feet) in diameter. Now, if one gave a chemist a fragment the size of a pin's head, broken off a sphere sixteen (seventeen) feet in diameter, and asked him to tell the substance of the whole from the analysis of this one fragment, he would assuredly answer, that the inference from the one to the other would be very rash. And if instead of only one fragment, we gave him three, broken off at

[1] Nouveau Système de Physiologie Végétale, vol. ii. p. 320, sq.

various parts of the sphere, and all these fragments differed
in some respects the one from the other, he certainly would say
that the process by which one would pretend to judge of the
whole sphere from these three specimens, was wrong.

"Modern geologists, however, have not been so wise and so
cautious in their theories about the successive catastrophes of
the globe. A somewhat hasty survey of about twenty quarries
in the neighbourhood of Paris was enough for Cuvier to enable
him to tell us the history of the primitive world.[1] There is
nothing algebraical in his calculations, and his demonstrations
are plain enough. He counts the number of species found in
each layer, and enrolled in our lists. When a certain number
of species occurs constantly in several layers or strata, one over
another, he makes a formation of these several strata; and thus
divides the series of geological strata into several formations,
characterized only by the presence of the same animal species.
Then, finding that, according to his view of the case, the species
found in an upper formation do not occur in a lower one, he
concludes that, at the time of the lower formation, the animal
species of the upper formation did not exist. On this hypo-
thesis he held in his hand the genealogical table of animals, and
the order in which they had appeared on the surface of the
globe; and he showed that oviparous animals preceded the vivi-
parous, since the crocodiles of Honfleur lie under the chalk,
the seals and grampuses in the shell limestone; while land mam-
malia appear only in strata above the coarse limestone, that is,
in the gypsum or 'plaster of Paris' formation, in fresh water and
alluvial deposits.

"Thus zoophytes, molluscs, and crustaceous animals, with
trilobites, appear in transition strata; from the old red sand-
stone to the lias the strata contain vertebrated animals, saurians, turtles, &c. Then come the ichthyosauri, and in the
chalk sharks' teeth, encrinites, &c.; as in tertiary formations
remains of birds and of mammifers. Then, however, salt and
fresh water covered alternately the same soils; in flowed the
sea, slowly to deposit the chalk; and after that fresh-water
lakes to line it with plastic clay. Back came the sea to cover
this with coarse limestone, and then it retreated before the fresh

---

[1] Ossemens fossiles, Discours prélim.

waters that deposited the gypsum. These again withdrew before
the sea that brought the thin layer of oyster-clay of Mont-
martre; and at last fresh waters returned, and remained there
to leave calcareous marls and millstone grit, with fresh-water
shells analogous to those of our own lakes: and last of all came
man. Such was the system of Cuvier. Astronomers, into
whose hands the sea did not play as into his, laughed in secret
at his system, which only in 1829 was declared to rest on false
premises."—" He wrote as if nothing could happen to upset
his fabric; whereas every day tended to contradict it. The vertebrated animals of the gypsum have been found in plenty with
fresh-water shells in coarse limestone, as they had before been
found in chalk; and sea and fresh-water shells were found together elsewhere frequently. All this tended to modify the
system, which, however, many would not give up; and fossil
botany, like fossil zoology, at first thought settled, has since
been repeatedly taken to pieces.

"This comes from our trying to measure the vast and overwhelming catastrophe to which we succeeded from the paltry
results of our local meteorology. We have seen the whole
world in the small corner of earth we scrape with our feeble
hands; we have drawn up the geography of the primitive world
after the scale of a few square miles; we have rebuilt the ancient
world with four or five specimens brought from the museum
of the Geological Society; in short, we, as it were, witnessed
' en famille' what took place at the Creation. But let us return
to facts recorded in Nature, and to logic.

1. "Were the geological strata deposited on the crust of
granite, according to laws different from existing ones?—No;
for we may reproduce them over a few feet square of ground,
with all their characteristic features. Yea, even in a tumbler
we may trace from the same liquid as many as five distinct
layers or deposits, always in the same order—that of the specific
gravity of their respective particles. These layers may again be
multiplied through the reaction of some ingredient likely to
produce it, and as it would take place in still water. But the
waters of an overflow, that would sweep everything before them,
stirring up the mud of such a sediment, and carrying it thus
distributed within them down to a lower level, when, meeting

with some obstacle, and thus for a moment being at rest, would deposit their contents according to the relative gravity of these, the sand at the bottom, and organic matter at the top; and if, the moment the sand was deposited at the bottom, the waters again brake through their temporary obstacle, they would then leave as deposit only the layer of sand perfectly clean, and carry with them every other particle of mud. Only look at the sand left by the tide on the strand, and at the mud the same tide deposits when at rest, in docks or in a close harbour. Moreover, since the laws of physiology are dependent on physical laws, and inseparable from them, if beings either identical with those which exist at present, or like them, existed then, the conditions of the atmosphere, &c., must have also been the same as now.

2. "Does the greater or less thickness of strata overlaying one another imply a longer or a shorter time for their respective formation?—By no means. It is of course evident that the deepest layer was deposited first, and the next after it, and so on; but it is easy to conceive that the greatest number of strata observed on a given point of the globe might have been deposited within the narrow space of one astronomical day; all that is required is, to grant to the wave or waves that brought them adequate power for it. Count, on a vertical section, the various strata left one over the other by an inundation, such as those which often occur in France; you will frequently find the number of them equal to that observed on the highest mountains, only you will find the substance and the proportions of them infinitely smaller. Nevertheless, the aggregate of this *diluvium* will sometimes amount to several metres. Now consider: this torrent which has just overflowed the land in one of these inundations was hardly one hundred metres in length; and, admitting that its deposit would be one metre thick, how many metres thick of deposit would such an overflow two hundred leagues (six hundred miles) in length leave after it? Nearly thirty thousand feet in depth; that is, considerably higher than the highest peak of the Himalayas, or of the Andes. Yet such an overflow would hardly cover the country that stretches between the Pyrenees and the Alps; and the geology of pre-historic *diluvia* implies much more extensive and more

powerful currents. Still, that geology hardly likes to face such a mass of water and the results thereof; it finds it easier to make a world after its own fancy, than to explain the one that is on a scale too great for its narrow sight.

3. "Does the difference in texture and in chemical nature of the several strata imply that each is the deposit of a distinct current, or of a special overflow ?—No; since from the same liquid we obtain deposits in several layers of different thickness and of a different chemical nature. It is true that we find in the earth the same layers separated by thick strata of a different kind; but the same occurs in every inundation. Such a torrent is not like a river flowing quietly in its bed; it is rather a tumultuous concourse of currents, of counter currents, and of eddies, which are less and less rapid as they are further from their starting point. Meanwhile the counter currents tend to quiet the effect of the overflow, until a fresh wave come to put again the whole mass in motion. Since the deposits depend on these several causes, the eddies and the counter currents will leave deposit over deposit in a spiral shape, if followed from end to end, although in a vertical section they look as if they were overlaid; while on each side of the eddies currents will have left deposits of a different nature and texture. When we think of currents and of counter currents six hundred miles in length, we cannot wonder at regular and homogeneous stratifications of more than a hundred and twenty miles in extent.

4. "The fact of a layer being without organic remains does not prove that it contained none when formed, inasmuch as there are numberless organic beings, both animals and plants, with a soft skeleton which rapidly decays; as we see it take place in certain soils and in lime. Thus vegetables soaked in water, and deposited in a limestone or chalky formation, would decay as completely as zoophytes, worms, molluscs, &c., in the course of a few years. Whence it follows, that the number of organic remains found in geological strata does not represent anything like that of the beings that were then overwhelmed. At one and the same time the same wave of the overflow might both cover a space with sand or gravel and bury a forest, the remains of which are seen in our coal-beds.

" Hence it appears that all the animals and all the vegetables

found in the strata of the earth existed at the same time, and
all perished in the same overthrow, from the ox, the elk, and
the elephant, to the belemnite and the trilobite, and to man
himself. Man was witness of this catastrophe, and his remains
must be found some day, as well as those of the horse and of
the camel that did him service in those days."

LXIV. I regret that I cannot, in these few pages, give at
length the whole of a very clear and logical statement, wherein
the writer evidently considers Noah's flood as the catastrophe that
produced the geological phænomena of the crust of the earth. At
all events, and without adopting the cant phrase of "adapting
geology to Scripture," he accounts satisfactorily for facts respecting which men the most versed in the science differ from
each other widely and essentially. We can quite well understand, according to his view of the subject, the formation of
certain intricate deposits, their breaking asunder by their own
weight, and thus presenting the appearance they do, which it
is vain to attribute to general upheavings after formations made
by water in a state of rest. We really have, on the whole, so
very little knowledge of the subject that is not empirical, that,
amid the confusion of systems, of opinions, of assumptions, of
doubt, and of absolute ignorance of the real state of the case,
we may at least adopt the most simple as well as the most
plausible explanation of the phænomena we see, in the small portions of the surface and of the eight thousandth of the diameter
of our globe, accessible to us. This system at least gives us a
rational idea, almost in the words of Scripture, of the awful up-
turning and overwhelming catastrophe, which we cannot picture
to ourselves apart from our faith in "the fountains of the great
deep being broken up,"[1] and in "the windows of heaven being
opened;" when the waters of the great deep mingled with those
of heaven in chaotic confusion, to leave after-traces of their currents, counter currents, and eddies rushing from north to south,
in the ridges of mountains, the outline of continents, and in the
principal currents of the sea, now comparatively at rest. The
words of Scripture are of course explained away by many theorists in their own way; nevertheless the most reasonable study
of the present physical aspect of the world brings us back to

[1] Gen. vii. 11.

those very words, which tell us very briefly of the most awful convulsion our planet ever experienced, and explain the causes of certain results which, apart from those sacred words, we cannot account for.

LXV. With this question is connected that of the formation of species, lately revived in this country, and, like that of the Creation and of the Diluvial overthrow, treated at variance with the letter of Scripture. This is not the place to enter fully into the subject. I will only state what appear to me to be objections to such propositions.

First—we have no warrant in Scripture for such a formation or filiation of species as that proposed.

Secondly—the fact that certain species which we know to have existed before they were fossilized, both among molluscs and crustacea, fishes, saurians, and mammals, as well as among the vegetables of the then world, being lost, and no longer existing, is against the supposition of the development of an indefinite number of species from the same type, apart from the overruling will and wisdom of the Creator. For if, in the space of four thousand years, this pretended endless formation of species, though always formed with regard to the one original type, which is like the centre from which they start, and around which their successive formations are said to revolve, has not returned to the type or species lost, we are indeed reasoning in a circle, to no purpose whatever. Whereas certain species, we see and know, do disappear, yet not to return; despite the type of them, said to exist.

Thirdly—our experience only goes to show that the very, very rare instances in which this mixture of species, or this growth of one species out of another, may, perhaps, be said to exist in nature, are only exceptions that prove the rule of God's infinite variety of design, as well as of immutability of purpose in Creation. Not only is this evident to our senses, but we have monuments thereof in the drawings of plants and in the mummies of birds upwards of three thousand years old—the same then as we now find growing and alive. The insignificant proportion of from forty to fifty hybrids in nature among plants, to the myriads of known species, and the fact of such a case hardly ever occurring in the animal world, are assuredly sufficient proofs of the Will

A A

and of the Order that reign throughout; especially when we descend as far as we can from the mere outward appearance of Nature into the marvellous harmony and incomprehensible wisdom of its most minute and hidden details.

Fourthly—the influence of climate alone may, and does, affect the growth and physiological functions of plants and of animals, but does not change one species into another; although it may effect varieties which do not propagate by seed. On the contrary, facts show that plants depend mostly on the soil and on the temperature, without which they cannot live. Thus may we draw a line across a continent north or south of which the vine or the olive will not grow. On the other hand, the same species may reappear in totally different climates and localities; showing how little there is of accident and how much of wisdom and of Providence in the distribution of both vegetable and animal life all over the world, according to the requirements of every climate or country. Thus the curlew does not become an ibis in Egypt, neither does the *Ibis falcinellus* become a curlew in England. The hooded crows I fed every morning in Bengal were the same species that I see in the North of Scotland; the *Alcedo Smyrniensis*, which I kept for weeks in India, in company with the *A. Bengalensis*, is precisely the same species that I shot on the banks of the sea of Galilee; the kite of Bengal, the kite of Palestine, and the kite of England are the same species; the *Pieris Daplidice*, *Pol. Phlæas* and *Virgaurea, Corydon* and *Alexis* I caught at Tyre, and on the hills of Galilee, were exactly the same one may catch in England also; the silvery tufts of *Bry. argenteum* and *Grim. pulvinata* I often noticed at the Cape certainly struck me as the same I had found in this country, until I discovered a slight difference in the leaf; likewise the *Ophr. Apifera*, or bee-orchis of Galilee and of the neighbourhood of Jerusalem, is the same as that of the chalky neighbourhood of Dorking; so also specimens of *Papaver, Echium, Lycopsis,* and several other species are found the same in Palestine, on the banks of the Tigris, in the South of France, and in England.

LXVI. When we see instances of this in Nature, side by side with plants that would die under the same circumstances, and wheat, which, being necessary to man, not only is of most climates and soils, but also preserves its vitality for thousands of years, while other seeds, not so useful, lose it by the mere touch of the hand, we see therein no accident, but a reason, even if we cannot always find it out.   Yea, orchids, the very plants chosen as an example, show, by the rare instance of hybrids among them when growing wild, despite the complicated mode of their fecundation, that, but for the overruling Will of the Creator, Who gave a place and Who set a work to do to every member of His wonderful household, the Universe—which for us especially, is the earth—hybrids and all manner of such confusion would be the rule, instead of being the very rare exception.   And, to reason from what takes place in plants in the artificial state of cultivation, when God's laws are thwarted by man's fancies, to what takes place in Nature when such plants are left free to obey those laws, or to what might happen if things were different from what they are, is really to reason about ' ifs' and 'ands' to very little purpose.   We might as well argue that, since certain plants, like certain animals, may be propagated by cuttings, that depend entirely on their physical organisation, therefore cuttings are the normal and general mode of reproduction, instead of the seed made for that purpose, and common to all vegetables— as to reason from the capabilities of organic bodies tried and proved in a garden, to what is found in Nature, acting in obedience to her Creator's Will.   But such reasoning is neither logical nor sound. Nay, such a generation of fictitious species, as a general rule, is not only shown to be impossible by facts, that prove such abnormal beings to be seldom capable of reproducing themselves and their confusion of species, but it seems also to be a theory—it is no more—against the words of Scripture, " that the worlds were framed by the Word of God, so that things which are seen were not made of things which do appear,"[1] as well as in direct contradiction to the positive statement that at God's bidding " the earth brought forth grass, and herb yielding seed after his kind, and the tree yielding fruit, whose seed is in itself, after his kind : and God saw that it was good." " And God made the beast of the earth after his kind, and cattle after their kind, and every thing that creepeth upon the earth after his kind : and God saw that it was good."[2]

So true is this, and so inherent in every organic being is the

[1] Heb. xi. 2.   [2] Gen. i. 11, 12, 20—25.

A A 2

law by which it perpetuates its existence, according to the general type or pattern set to it by GOD, that, no sooner has man through cultivation succeeded in destroying the order and harmony of Nature by, for instance, transforming necessary organs into superfluous ones, as in the case of double flowers, than the plant ceases to be able to reproduce itself naturally. And when no organs are thus destroyed, but only a variety of either fruit or flower is produced by gardening, the seed of the fruit or flower thus treated tends to reproduce the original type of the tree or of the plant; as in the case of grafted trees, the seed of which yields wild fruit-trees, that require grafting ere they can be available for man. Yet, in the face of such, and of other like facts that prove the truth of the words of Scripture, which alone explain the common phænomena of organic Nature, "modern science and philosophy" tell us that, at first, and ere the rock of which the surface of the earth consists became coated with soil, it got gradually covered with vegetable substance like unto green mould, wrought by natural causes, such as damp, heat, and other agencies; and that this rudimentary vegetable gradually developed itself into all the various plants and trees that adorn the earth! Animals then grew by 'a similar process,' something like the rats of Herodotus, half rat, half mud; and as to man, he was originally, according to an Italian 'philosopher,' a fish that swam ashore, where its fins and tail gradually altered into hands and feet; while others find in monkeys and gorillas types of themselves! Rightly, perhaps; since 'philosophers' of this sort not only prove the words of the Apostle true, that, "professing themselves to be wise, they became fools,"[1] even humanly speaking, since they argue for a fact psychologically impossible, but they also, says a higher authority than mine,[2] besides being infidels, "muss sich selbst erst gründlich verthiert haben," must have thoroughly brutalised themselves ere they can arrive at such a conclusion.

We may, indeed, smile, or perhaps feel interested, when we read in Tibetan annals of the sweet, cream-like substance which at first covered the earth, and out of which the Lha-mas of Lha-sa grew like so many sugar-canes. But when the same sort of

---

[1] Rom. i. 22.
[2] Delitzsch, Der Mensch als Ziel, &c. Bibl. Psychol. p. 59.

lore is taught in a Christian country, in the full blaze of revealed light and knowledge, one hardly knows whether most to pity the ignorance, or to wonder at the folly of men who seem bent on stultifying themselves, by ascribing to what they call "natural agencies," '*natura naturans*,' facts and results which cannot be, apart from the Will and the Wisdom of an overruling and Almighty CREATOR. But when, further, we are told to reconcile this "modern science and philosophy" with the Bible, —that is, to bring the Bible to it, and not it to the Bible,— we are at a loss to know what those who may that think of their intellect, ability, and learning, or of our own. We will examine, search, discover, and admire the marvellous wisdom of GOD in His works, as an act of worship; but shut our eyes to His Presence among them, and ascribe them to chance, and with "modern science and philosophy" to reconcile darkness with Light. Not as long as we retain our faculties; when bereft of them, possibly we may. Till then, we will keep to the words of Scripture, as to the only true, sensible, and intelligent statement of existing facts.

LXVII. It is also, I may add, against my whole experience to see aught in Nature but the working together in perfect harmony of the Almighty Will, Infinite Wisdom, Absolute Rule, and Supreme Intelligence of Him Who made all things good. Taking pleasure as I do in the study of GOD's works, I collected very many birds, insects, plants, and other inmates of this beautiful world, and I observed wherever I went, East or West; but never, as far as my observation goes, have I found a feather out of place in a bird, so as to confound one species with another, nor a hybrid among insects I caught, nor yet among the flowers I gathered. I have always found the characters of the species and those of the genera constant. Only once did I see a *S. hippophaes*, a *B. pudibunda*, and a *Noctua*, exhibit a 'lusus naturæ'; but they had been reared in captivity, and the mode of transformation of insects may render such cases less impossible than in other orders of animals. Yet these amount, of course, to no more than to monstrosities of double birth in animals, or of abnormal excrescences in sundry umbelliferæ, ferns, mosses, &c., allowed as examples to show what a scene of confusion Nature would be, but for the Ruler thereof. I have,

like everybody else, met with accidental varieties, chiefly in the
want of colouring matter of the tissues, as among certain animals
and often among birds ; as, e.g., a white pipit, a starling speckled
with white, &c.; and I had last spring a black and white black-
bird on my lawn, that reared in the adjoining shrubbery a nest of
four young ones, all, however, of the orthodox brown and black.
It certainly never occurred to me to look upon these as upon
the beginning of a new species ; any more than one white egg
among four other blue ones in a dunnock's nest struck me as
introducing a new colour among the dunnocks, or the winter
dress of ptarmigans, &c., a new fashion among those birds. But,
when I invariably found the grey variety of the cuckoo's egg in
the nest of the common wagtail, and the brown variety in the nest
either of a land or of a wood-lark, so that these birds might sit
without suspicion upon the egg, not their own, introduced into
their nest, I saw therein neither chance nor accident, but a singular proof of sagacity in the bird that lays the egg, and then
carries it to the nest of eggs best agreeing in colour with its
own ; and one of the innumerable instances of God's Presence
among His works, shown in the instinct He gives to His creatures, from the least even unto the greatest, and which is past
finding out.

With Eusebius,[1] then, with Linnæus, and with many more
great and sensible men, we may look upon the constancy of
species, as an evident proof of God's Rule, and of His Presence
in Nature. We can only wonder and adore, and with the Psalmist say, " O LORD, how manifold are thy works ! in wisdom hast
thou made them all; the earth is full of thy riches."   And we
may safely leave philosophers who pretend to know better, to
find out and tell us, for instance, by what law of Nature inherent
in matter the same kind of oak grows year after year out of the
same kind of acorn, and does not gradually become either a
beech, a hazel, or a chesnut, all of the same family; also why
the feet of the bee, like those of the wood-louse, are always all
of even length, and as perfect in all their parts as their own feet,
or as those of the elephant.

LXVIII. In fact, life is too short to enable us to go deep
into the marvels of this visible world, on which God has written

[1] Theophan. Syr. Book I. 10, sq.

His Name in a wonderful manner, and which He alone rules and governs. Our intellect has more than enough to do, baffled as it is almost at every effort, to study and try to understand the things we see, and hear, and touch, without turning from these, its first object, to raise itself against the Word and the Wisdom of Him Who says to man : Understand these things of to-day first, then try to understand Me, Who am past finding out. For the intellect, we have seen, cannot enter into the very commonest things of life; neither has it yet discovered anything of positive knowledge that proves any important record of the Bible untrue. All that sound reason can do as regards geology is to collect specimens, class them, observe and study the order and formation of strata. Yet so little do we know positively even of this, that to reason thence to the whole is unsound and empirical. We know it not ; and, most assuredly, shall never know it in this world. How far may, for instance, geology expect to penetrate into the interior of the earth ?—at the utmost, say two miles. Even then, what is that to the three thousand nine hundred and ninety odd miles left of the half diameter of the globe ? And when will those who talk so big of "modern science and philosophy" know anything at all of the rocks underlying the mighty deep, that they should have the assurance to raise their discoveries and their knowledge—which are as 'nothing' to what yet remains to be discovered and known—in opposition to Holy Scripture and to the Faith, reverence, and worship we poor weak human beings, creatures of a day, owe to that Word of God ? So, then, neither geology nor any other theoretical or empirical science, nor yet questions belonging thereto, put and answered thereby, that bind God's power with human cobwebs, need disturb the Faith of any one man in the Bible. He may collect his fossils in peace, and gather his plants with delight ; they are intended as a link in the chain that binds him to God, for they are His work.

LXIX. But enough of this. The truth is, that if the Bible were any other book—if it did not bear witness of itself and of its divine origin ; such witness, too, that a man must either love or hate it—men would worship it for the beauty of its diction, for the sublimity of its ideas, for the purity of the precepts it teaches, for the greatness of its morality, for the glory of its promises and for the value of the history which it alone imparts. They would grant it all the respect which the proofs of its authenticity and the marvellous agreement of the whole command, written as it has been at various times, extending over nearly two thousand years, by men of different countries and of different minds. All this combined would lead thinking men to conclude that such a Book cannot be human, but that its origin is from a higher region than mere human intellect, and that there must have been some divine element at work in it.

For we may well ask, where is there a book to be compared with it, even in a literary point of view? We admire some of the Vedic hymns, as well we may, at least in their own unrivalled idiom; some of the oldest parts of the Avesta have a peculiar beauty of their own; some also of the Egyptian hymns sung to Atum or to Osiris, in the days of Abraham and of Joseph, are invested with a mixed feeling of wonder and of veneration, owing a little to their beauty, but chiefly to their being, as it were chanted from the tombs. Many passages in Confucius, in Lao-tsze, and in Manu, are beautiful and touching, as are also very many found in Plato. But they are all lifeless and dead. They attempt to describe a GOD they know not, and they cannot impart a life they have not; and however we may and ought to admire them as relics of olden time, and as reflecting, to a certain extent, the glimmer of refracted Truth, yet they are in themselves helpless for real good. They speak, some to the intellect, others to the imagination, and some to neither; but they are one and all powerless to reach the heart.

How is it then, that the Bible should be singled out even by some of those who profess to believe it, as the butt of their bitterest invectives and of their untiring hatred and aversion? Simply for this reason—that the other books, being helpless and harmless, assert no authority, and exercise no real influence over man; whereas the very sight of the Bible exercises its own silent influence and asserts its own calm authority over the heart and mind, even of him who hates it and who tries to gainsay it. But with what success and with what result, besides an evil conscience, and remorse at having done so, those enemies of the Truth may confess, who are not yet past feeling. There is no better practical proof—and one worth a host of arguments—of

the Divine origin and spiritual authority of the Bible, than the
untiring efforts of its adversaries to gainsay it. A Bengalee
proverb says: "No one throws stones at a tree that bears no
fruit;" no 'philosophers' would throw their stones at the Bible
if it did not bear fruit which they dislike, because of the pride
and of the conceit of what they call their "intellect, their ability,
and their learning;" as if the intellect were such that does not
lead man towards GOD; as if his ability deserved the name,
unless it helps him the better to study GOD's Word; and as if
that was good learning and real, that is not fit to be laid as
an offering at the foot of our SAVIOUR's Cross!

The same man, for instance, who expatiates on some commonplace remark of Plato or of Cicero will call the Book of Proverbs
"the work of an apostate king who was in advance of his age."
In advance so far, that he never has been reached by any of his
followers. It may be, that, quite apart from Faith or no faith,
one mind cannot enter into the ways of thought of another mind
differently constituted. One may not therefore understand,
how a man, who calls himself a Christian and may be, holds a
high office in the Church, can bring himself to express such a
sentiment. My experience, I must confess, leads me to the
very opposite conclusion. I have invariably found when comparing the sayings of heathen philosophers with the Proverbs,
that these were, to use the words of an Indian poet, like "a
topas, giving lustre to bits of glass brought close to it."[1] One
has real worth, and carries authority and conviction; the other
only gives pleasure in proportion as it coincides with its model
or prototype in Eternal Wisdom. For as there is only one
centre of light in our system, so also there is only one Truth,
one Wisdom, one Faith; and nothing is wise or true that does
not come from thence and return thither.

LXX. The Christian philosopher then, whose principles ἀρχαί,
whose elements or articles of Faith στοιχεῖα are in GOD, and

---

[1] During the course of my reading I have collected several thousand passages
from Mandchu, Chinese, and other Asiatic writers, to illustrate parallel passages
of the Proverbs. If this should meet the eyes of the dignitary who is reported
to have made use of the expression above quoted, and he happens to have travelled over the same road I have as regards that Book, I shall feel greatly
obliged to him for allowing me to compare his notes with mine, that I may see
how it is we arrive at such opposite results of the same experience.

who, by means of the Spirit of GOD brought into communion
with his spirit through Faith—ἀνάκυψας εἰς τὸ ὂν ὂντως—looks,
as it were, into THE TRUTH as regards himself and his position
towards GOD, understands both. As regards himself—his own
consciousness tells him he is a fallen creature; and his intellect,
striving to grasp that which ever escapes it, confesses itself
limited, weak, and as helpless to find the way to GOD, as his
unaided moral being is powerless to keep to it. He therefore
admits honestly, that "in him dwelleth no good thing." And
his position towards GOD, is—that of a creature wholly dependent on its Creator, whom it had offended past reconciliation on
its part, but to whom it has been reconciled freely, frankly, and
fully on GOD's part through His Beloved SON.

And he feels, and indeed sees, that the part and duties of this
dependent condition are, to obey without saying a word or even
thinking it; it is, therefore, to trust without after thought or
misgiving; and as proof of this filial love, to await the FATHER's
orders; to receive them unconditionally, and to yield to His
will in all things;—it is his FATHER's will; that is enough.
This begets, if I may so speak, mutual confidence between the
FATHER and His child; and this confidence is the reward of
Faith and of obedience, through which the child proves the love,
the faithfulness, the mercy, the pity, the justice and the wisdom
of his FATHER;—and this is to him the source of a "peace that
passeth all understanding," that keeps the child's heart under
his FATHER's smile, and gives him a foretaste of Heaven. His
FATHER's Word "is a lamp unto his feet and a light unto his
path." He does not question that light; it is his only real comfort in sorrow, his peace in trouble, his guide in difficulty, and his
hope in distress. True, there are in it things which he does not
understand; but, what else does he really understand in this his
earthly state, as yet away from his home, a pilgrim heavenwards?

His eyes are dim, and he is now dull of understanding; he
will therefore, judge nothing before the time, but he will wait,
until his fallen nature be risen again glorious, until he see what
he now hopes for; until he know as he is known. Meanwhile,
his FATHER's Word is for him holy and sacred, ἅγιος. He respects the things in it which he does not yet understand out of
love for those he knows; and from a firm Faith in his FATHER's

kindness, wisdom, and faithfulness, at no price will he lay an impious hand on so sacred a trust; it is holy, unto the LORD. He might question, inquire, doubt,—but no; never, as regards his FATHER, or His Word. He knows his place is, to walk by Faith, that is—to obey, making his FATHER's will his own, trusting in His promises, and in a sure hope of eternal life—and he does it. Such is his philosophy; it is reasonable, for it is the philosophy of Faith; it is true, for it begins with GOD, it rests in GOD, and it ends in GOD; and it is enduring; for the end thereof is Everlasting Life.

LXXI. Far from this are philosophers whose wisdom is their own, whose philosophy begins with them, rests on them, and ends in them; whose will is to follow their own; whose obedience is, practically, to themselves alone; whose only light is the glimmer of their own intellect; whose hope is ill-defined because it is not sure. No wonder; they will none of Faith. If ever they acknowledge themselves fallen creatures, they certainly do not act as if they did; but they are evermore striving after what they never will obtain with their own efforts; they are, as the Buddhist tells them, "like bees buzzing in a glass case," yet thinking all the while they are flying upwards. In reality, the GOD they seek, is the GOD they fancy; not the Personal and spiritual GOD who reveals Himself in His Word; for they gainsay or doubt, or despise this Word. They acknowledge no guide but what they call their Reason; they obey no laws but those of their own will; they cast off all Rule of Faith, all creed, all dogma, as not made for them; they are, in reality, and whatever they may think, like men sailing in a mist, without compass, chart, or time-keeper.

As our Faith, so is our Hope. Ask them what hope they have? Whether they "have confidence towards GOD," or that peace of mind and of conscience which nothing gives but the surrender of 'self' and of 'self-will' through humble Faith and obedience to GOD? Therefore do such philosophers ill brook to see others who, knowing how utterly helpless is their own intellect, their ability, or their learning, to secure them a moment's happiness, seek it elsewhere, and find it in walking by Faith; in studying to forget themselves and in actively placing themselves at GOD's mercy. The dry, lifeless philosophy of intellect has nothing in common with this. What then can such men do? Too proud or too vain to acknowledge either their error, or the utter inability of their intellect to satisfy the natural cravings of their spirit after better things—they set about trying to destroy the Faith and the Hope of those whom they see happier than themselves, so as to bring them into their own ways; as a quieting thought to their uneasy conscience—that when so many either think or walk alike, they must all of course, be right. Such philosophers strive to raise themselves, not by rising higher, but by lowering others to their own level; for a man lowers himself who descends from Faith to mere belief—from the child's Faith to "the faith of the devils who believe in God and tremble"—and from belief to Reason; since Faith is, as we have seen, a fruit of the Spirit; but mere belief is of the intellect, and Reason, that is, Rationalism, is of neither.

Such philosophers must of course make disciples, but among whom? Certainly not among the really intelligent who make the best use of their intellect—which is to learn to know themselves—and who are thus brought by their intellect alone, well directed, to seek God otherwise than through themselves. Neither among the really able is this philosophy successful; for real ability consists in making the only right use of the powers we have received from God, to grasp as much of His Truth, as human nature can hold; nor yet among the really learned will the mean scholarship of some of these men carry much weight; for scholarship does not depend on the man that deals it, neither is it mere opinion; but it consists in certain facts brought together with judgment to bear on one subject; and learning is the knowledge of those facts.

LXXII. Learned or really well-informed men, then, who will think—have, therefore, nothing whatever to fear from such philosophy. But the effect of it is great for evil on the ignorant, the thoughtless or careless, on the clever intellectual artisans, who seldom perhaps hear of Faith, of Hope, and of Charity, and whose spiritual good has been, or is, neglected. Such are too glad to follow any leaders whom they can make responsible for their opinions, be these what they may. But as the multitude is led by feeling and by opinion either for good or for evil, and neither by scholarship, by learning, nor by reasoning, it is evident, that if they see the Bible attacked or gainsaid, the worship of God and His Church lowered before them by men to whom they naturally look up as to their guides—they lose at once, there and then, the only guarantee for their individual, and thus also for their national good conduct and morality—the fear of God and reverence for His Word. The multitude stands, practically, towards the Bible as towards a clock. Not one in a thousand of those who look at the town-clock to guide them in their daily business knows anything of its construction. Watch-makers and a few others know it, and may reason upon the combined forces of the mechanism of that clock. Yet, after all, even these derive no greater practical benefit from it than those who even, perhaps, think the clock alive—and that benefit is—to know the time. What should we think of one of these watch-makers, not only stopping the town-clock, but taking it to pieces, and throwing the works at the feet of the people, saying: We have all been wrong in keeping time hitherto; we had better go by the sun—whether it shines or not? Those who had watches or clocks in their own homes, might be independent of such wanton mischief; but what state would the people of the town be in? To say the least, would it be sensible, judicious, kind, and considerate towards them?

LXXIII. Likewise does the Bible guide and influence the multitude unto salvation by teaching the Truth, right feeling, and morality, never taught by intellect and philosophy. This is its work, whether with the learned or with the ignorant; and the work it does, is its own witness. There is not much intellect at work in the poor cottager who opens the Word of God, and reads out of it to his children around him. The amount of understanding brought to bear on the reading, whether from the father or from the children, is very small indeed; yet who will deny that the moral effect thereof is great,—the greatest,—for good? But if they be told by men whom they trust that it is not the Word of God, what will become of the moral good it might have worked on those souls? To the poor the Gospel is preached, "and to the poor in spirit belongs the kingdom of heaven;" and whosoever directly or indirectly robs them of that inheritance, has a Judge who will judge him, when He avenges their rights, and sifts every man's work to reward him accord-

ingly. God has entrusted the people to His Church, and in
the Church to her pastors and teachers, and He will require at
their hands the souls who perish either from want of knowledge,
or through false teaching. These pastors and teachers ought
to discuss certain things among themselves, as their duty is to
do, and as indeed they may, with profit to themselves: but
there is a wide difference between this and acting without remorse the part Ham acted to his brothers. If those who
boast "of their intellect, ability, and learning," choose so
far to waste these good gifts in turning them from their lawful
use—the service of God and the salvation of their own souls
and of those of others—the fault is theirs, and they will either
receive or not the reward of their works. "But these sheep,
what have they done ?"—Why should the poor, the ignorant,
the careless, who ought to be taught aright, be further led
astray, by the worse than careless doings of many of those who
are set to watch over them, but who seem to take pleasure in
the mischief they do, by raising doubts which neither they nor
wiser men than they can settle ? Apologues are not wanting to
teach us that division among the chiefs is the death of the
people. Especially in matters of Religion. For, as Locke says:

"Most of the people reason thus: 'The founders or leaders of
my party are good men, and therefore their tenets are true;—it
is the opinion of a sect that is erroneous, therefore it is false;—it
hath been long received in the world, therefore it is true;—or, it
is new, and therefore false.' These, and many the like, which are
by no means the measures of truth and falsehood, the generality
of men make the standards by which they accustom their understanding to judge. And thus they falling into a habit of deter-
mining of truth and falsehood by such wrong measures, it is no
wonder they should embrace error for certainty, and be very positive in things they have no ground for."[1]

Such being the case as regards by far the majority of men,
by which we understand the people or society—it is little else
than suicidal folly to teach or to preach aught either untrue,
or which from being, perhaps, only partly understood, will sap
in them the only foundation there is of moral worth—"The
fear of the Lord which is the beginning of wisdom, and the
knowledge of the Holy which is understanding." And this

---

[1] Cond. of Underst. Sect. vi.

foundation must go if God's revealed Word is gainsaid in the ears of the people, and His Truth wantonly disparaged.

LXXIV. The practical unsoundness of such philosophy, however, is nowhere so apparent as in the sophisms and in the illogical shifts to which its advocates are driven in order to defend it. A favourite argument with them in behalf of themselves is, that they have made assertions which no one has answered; but they do not say whether it be owing to the wisdom or to the folly of the assertions. We know, for instance, who may throw into a well a stone, which many wise men may not draw out. Does this prove the wisdom of the action or the folly of the wise men ? Likewise a man may think himself very clever in talking of, or in making plausible assertions respecting, things about which no one either knows or can know anything, and which, therefore, no one can contradict ; and because no one can deny facts no one knows, but only the greater or less, πιθανόν, probability of them, he in his wisdom thinks them proved. Yet who will think so, but he and friends equally wise ? So also with regard to the Word of God, by which I mean the Canonical Books of the Old and of the New Testaments ; a child, or one even less wise than a child, may ask questions and make assertions which no one can answer, simply because it pleased Him Who caused those Books to be written for a particular purpose, that such questions or assertions should be unanswerable, consistently with His own counsel respecting both the Bible and those for whom it was caused to be written.

Thus, for instance, a man may say he will not believe in the Pentateuch, or, at least, only in certain portions of it, because he believes that, very far from Moses having written it, it was written by from five to fifty different writers. The futility of such argument appears in that, whereas all these philosophers are one in saying they will believe what Moses wrote, hardly two of them agree as to what portions Moses did actually write.[1] This plainly shows that since their assumptions can be neither

[1] " Verum, ô Deus bone, quinam isti tandem sunt, qui dissentiones in nobis reprehendunt ?—Cur Albertus Pighius a Cajetano, Thomas a Lombardo, Scotus a Thoma, Ochamus a Scoto, Allirensis ab Ochamo, Nominales a Realibus dissentiunt ? Vix enim unquam inter se convenient, nisi forte, ut olim Pharisæi et Sadducæi, aut Herodes et Pilatus, contra Christum.—Eant ergo sane, et pacem potius inter seos domi sanciant."—Apologia Eccles. Anglic. auctore Joh. Juello, olim episc. Sarisb. p. 27, sq.

proved nor disproved, even by themselves, there is no reality, no
truth, in such assertions. They must, of course, have been
foreseen, but at the same time also deemed worthless, and thus
unlikely to shake the Faith of sensible men in these Books;
otherwise they would have been answerable. For even such
inquirers grant that Faith is due to certain portions of those
Books; only they can neither tell nor agree among themselves
as to which they be.

LXXV. But, in sooth, a man of sense will reason otherwise.
He will at once submit himself to the evident, tangible fact that
moral being created for another and a better existence, is under
the immediate, temporal, moral, and spiritual government of
his Creator. Even the beasts of the field and the birds of the
air acknowledge God's government as regards themselves and
their condition. Is it, then, reasonable to admit the moral and
spiritual government of a spiritual Creator over His creature,
partly earthly and partly moral and spiritual, without admitting
at the same time that this Creator, Who is Spirit, infinite, invisible, eternal, has a full and unconditional right not only to
do with His creature what the potter does with the clay, but
also to govern that creature after His own will and judgment?

Yea, rather, it is reasonable to think that such a government
exercised, as it is, over a creature both natural and spiritual, in
which "that is first which is natural, and afterwards that which
is spiritual,"[1] should be temporal for the natural part of that
creature, and spiritual for the moral and spiritual part thereof?
And so, indeed, it is. This creature is governed, that is, placed
partly under the influence of temporal things that are seen,
being themselves overruled by God, and partly also under the
guidance and influence of things spiritual, which are not seen,
and eternal. But, since these are, like the Spirit that created
and that guides the spirit created and guided, as yet invisible,
this moral and spiritual government therefore, also unseen, is
acknowledged on our part only by Faith in Him that is invisible; since such a government of necessity implies mutual in-

[1] οὐ πρῶτον τὸ πνευματικὸν, ἀλλὰ τὸ ψυχικὸν, ἔπειτα τὸ πνευματικόν, 1 Cor.
xv. 46. Ψυχικὸν δὲ καὶ πνευματικὸν οὐχ ἕτερον δείκνυσι σῶμα. τὸ μὲν πρῶτον,
ἐν ἰδιότητι καὶ φύσει ψυχῆς, διὰ ψυχικὸν τὸ δὲ δεύτερον, ἐν ἰδιότητι καὶ φύσει
πνεύματος, διὰ πνευματικόν. S. Athanas. De Incarn. Chr. vol. I. p. 620.

tercourse and relation. If we be reasonable, then, we must either deny the existence of a spirit in us, and that of the Spirit Who made and guides us, and thus degrade our nature through our own folly; or else we must admit both the existence of this temporal, moral, and spiritual government, and that we can be duly ruled thereby only through Faith in Him Who governs.

And GOD reminds even the dullest intellect of His supreme and absolute Rule, and that, even in every-day life, man must feel he is not his own, but under authority. He knows not the hour of his death, nor yet how long he has to live, because his life is in GOD's hands; so that he cannot even make plans for the morrow without saying, "GOD willing," since no man may "boast of to-morrow, for he knoweth not what a day may bring forth."[1] How could GOD better and oftener teach man that he is to walk by Faith, in trust, and in hope, even as regards his daily ways, than in making him feel he is in GOD's hands for them? But men heed not such warnings. They live, and traffic, and make plans, as if they were their own masters, until death takes them unawares as a fowler in his net. But the earnest Christian, far from forgetting that he walks by Faith, loves to be reminded of it, so as to trust his FATHER in all things, "without Whose Will not a sparrow falleth to the ground;" asking Him to give him strength unto his day, to teach him the way he should go, and to make it plain before him.

LXXVI. But it is also very clear, first—that, consistently with this moral and spiritual Rule through Faith, had GOD made all things plain for us, there would be no room for the exercise on our part of Faith in Him, and through Faith, of trust, and through trust, of obedience, and through obedience to Him in things which He alone sees and knows, of the surrender of our will to His will in all things, as becomes creatures to their Creator. If we saw and read everything as it was, as it is, and as it is to be, we should then no longer be governed spiritually and morally by Faith, but altogether by intellect and sight; and thus as we have already seen, we should be raised above the position of entire dependence which alone befits the fallen creature of a pure and holy Creator. Neither is this dependent state in which it reasonably befits us to live the result of mere

[1] Prov. xxvii. 1.

B B

accident, or the simple consequence of the relation between the
creature and the Creator, for we might have been created independent of Him if He had willed it so.   But this our state of
dependence, and therefore, this evident call for the exercise of
Faith, of trust, and of obedience on our part, is a further proof
of His moral and paternal government, through which He con-
tinually reminds us how thoroughly "we live and move, and
have our being in Him," both temporally and spiritually; so as
to straiten the bonds of protection and of love that unite us
together.   Even the heathen, looking up to heaven said :

"Mad'hu Disu-r-astu na: Pita!   May Heaven, Father, be gracious to us!"[1]

  Ζεῦ πάτερ—
  —χάρτη λοιβῆς σὺ δίδου φρεσὶν αἴσιμα πάντα,
  καὶ βίον εὐθύμοισιν ἀεὶ θάλλοντα λογισμοῖς,[2]

as an echo of prayers long since forgotten ; and as an instinct of
prayers once more to be offered in the bond of filial affection, whereby we are taught to say: OUR FATHER WHICH ART IN HEAVEN.

LXXVII. Therefore, we conclude, that it is reasonable to expect—because it is in accordance with GOD's spiritual government of us—that there should be things connected with His Revelation to us, which we do not and cannot yet understand, as well
as questions which we cannot and shall not answer this side the
grave ; so that, unless we receive GOD's Word on His own
terms, we must reject it altogether ; since He alone has a right
to make the conditions relating thereto.   But, if we reject it,
we must also with it deny our spiritual nature and GOD's
spiritual government of us.   For, things that should be plain
are made so plain in the Bible "that he may run that readeth
it."   "The secret things," said Moses to the children of Israel,
"belong unto the LORD our GOD: but those things which are
revealed, belong unto us and to our children for ever, that we
may do all the words of this law."[3]   On the other hand, things
that should be kept hidden for the present, and until we exchange Faith for sight, are so told and so hidden as purposely
to try our patience to the uttermost.   "For who hath known
the mind of the LORD? or who hath been his counsellor?"[4]

[1] Rig-V. L 6, xvii. 7.   [2] Orph. Hymn. 19.
[3] Deut. xxix. 29.   [4] Rom. xi. 34, 35.

And God is not bound to reveal unto us as much as we wish; but He reveals to us as much as He thinks proper, and as much as He knows to be necessary for us in this our present state.

The whole tenour of His dealings with His Church, from Abel to our own selves, and as exemplified especially in Abraham is—that we should walk by Faith. Were it not so, our Saviour would not have said to His disciples, "In patience possess ye your souls ;" for patience which "must have her perfect work," is made up of Faith; therefore of trust, and of love. However impatient our natural intellect may often feel at being thus kept in suspense, or at being denied so much it wishes to penetrate; our place is nevertheless—to wait; to wait in Faith, and patiently, until the scales fall from our eyes at the revelation of Jesus Christ. Until that day, or rather, until we rest in sure and certain hope of that day, we can, we shall, understand very little of "things which never entered into the heart of man," but we shall have to dwell on them by Faith; not only in the promises themselves, and on the Truths revealed to us, but we shall have also to take in Faith even the very Word that brings us tidings of those promises by teaching us those objective Truths.

LXXVIII. True, we might wish to have the autographs of the Prophets and of the Apostles. We may imagine what sensation would create the news that Moses' autograph of the Pentateuch, or even of one of the Books thereof, was at last discovered, as well authenticated as Papyri of his age or anterior to him. Or if even one of S. Paul's autograph epistles were brought to light, would not the Faith of some in those Books, and through them in the whole Canon of Scripture be strengthened ? Why then, were those autographs, written on durable materials, and held in greater veneration than any other Books ever written before or after, allowed to perish and our Faith be deprived of that stay, while documents inscribed on most perishable substance, and others even recovered from their own ashes, were allowed to subsist ? The reply to this is very plain. "My word," saith the Lord, "that goeth out of my mouth shall not return unto me void, but it shall accomplish that which I please, and it shall prosper in the thing whereto I sent it."[1] Once uttered, the Eternal Truth of that Word could never die; it defies time, waste, wear and decay, and even if the letter of it perished the

¹ Isa. lv. 10, 11.

B B 2

spirit thereof would live evermore. But it may also be, that comparing the weighty burden of the Scriptures with the light matter of other works, documents of no importance whatever compared with the writings of the Apostles and Prophets, as regards them it matters comparatively little whether our belief in them be weak or strong. Whereas, we are told by revelation—yea, we feel our own selves, that our calling is so high and so spiritual, and the promises set before us so far above our intelligence, that, it could not be that we should be allowed to walk towards them by sight. Faith is for us, as it was for Abraham, our first motive; once held, it begets in us as it did in him, Hope; yea "a Hope that maketh not ashamed;" all which, Faith and Hope, for us, as also for Abraham, rest entirely on God's Word; and which in us, as in him, bear witness of the immutable Truths that are the subject of the one and the object of the other; making Faith "more precious to us than gold that perisheth" since "the end of it is the salvation of our souls;"[1] and giving us Hope as "the anchor of the soul sure and stedfast," through all the storms of life; until we reach our Father's home.

But Faith is an act of submission to the witness God gives us in His Word; an act which implies 'self-denial,'—the self-denial of letting Faith take the first rank and intellect only the second. 'Self-denial,' however, is the last act to which the natural man will consent. Thus it happens that "all men have not faith;" and that so many go on trying to establish their own intellectual righteousness—and fail. Therefore also does S. Paul after having shown to the saints of Achaia that "the wisdom of the world is foolishness with God," give them this solemn charge: "Examine yourselves, whether ye be in the faith: prove your own selves. Know ye not your own selves, how that Jesus Christ is in you, except ye be reprobates?"[2]

THE CHURCH AND CLERGY.

LXXIX. And lest, either through dimness of intellectual sight, or through some other individual frailty, man should mistake some of the objects thus set before him by God, as landmarks on his way to Heaven, and as beacons thitherward, God has

¹ 1 S. Pet. L. 7, 9.   ² 2 Cor. xiii. 5.

made His "holy Catholick and Apostolick Church" warden of those plain, distinct, and objective Truths; Truths on which rests His Church both in earth and in heaven. Whatever a man may build thereon, whether he, as a wise master builder, build with gold, silver, and precious stones, or with wood, hay and stubble—yet "other foundation can no man lay than that is laid, which is Jesus Christ."[1]   On this foundation rests the household of God; built upon the foundation of the "Apostles and Prophets, Jesus Christ himself being the chief corner-stone; in whom all the building fitly framed together groweth unto an holy temple in the Lord; in whom we are builded together for an habitation of God through the Spirit."[2]

This Church, ἐκκλησία, "the blessed company of all faithful people"[3] is in the Earth like leaven which is to leaven the whole lump, and to spread in the mass, until the Church has called all her members from out of the world into one flock—the flock of Christ, and that flock into one fold—the fold of Him who is the Good Shepherd.

She is in the world, yet not of the world; and as being distinct from it, she makes her members also separate therefrom. They are called, by virtue of their rights to that call, as being before chosen of God to it; so that their call from out of the world, like that of Abraham out of Ur, is a token of their election, ἐκλογή, to eternal life;—for since "the gifts and calling of God are without repentance,"[4] we cannot understand their being called by God without an intention and purpose of salvation on His part. In token of this they are washed with the water of Baptism—a seal of their death unto sin and of a new birth unto righteousness, and thus made one with the Body of Christ the Church, in order to draw thence both His Spirit and His Life.

---

[1] 1 Cor. iii. 11, 12.

[2] Eph. ii. 19—22. "Credimus unam esse Ecclesiam Dei, eamque non ut olim apud Judæos, in unam aliquem angulum aut regnum conclusam; sed Catholicam atque universalem esse et diffusam in totam terrarum orbem ut nulla nunc natio sit quæ possit vere conqueri, se exclusam esse, et non posse ad Ecclesiam, et populum Dei pertinere. Eam Ecclesiam esse Regnum, esse Corpus, esse Sponsam Christi; ejus regni Christum solum esse Principem, ejus corporis Christum solum esse caput; ejus Sponsæ Christum solum esse Sponsum."—Apologia Eccl. Angl. J. Juell. p. 13.

[3] Second Collect before the Doxology in the Communion Service.

[4] Rom. xi. 29.

Yet this is only the beginning of their struggle as members of
the Church militant. But as their ultimate safety, or salvation,
depends on that struggle being honestly carried on by every
member for himself against sin, the world, and the devil, and
on his enduring unto the end—the Head of the Church, Christ,
is present in her through His Spirit, the Comforter, the Spirit
of Truth, to guide her sons into all Truth, to help them in their
infirmities, and to enable them to "make their calling and
their election sure"—so as not to fall from grace, nor to grieve
or quench the Spirit in them, but to be so faithful to Him and
to her, as that at last, they may be chosen as fit inheritors of the
kingdom of Heaven.   In other words, that Spirit so trains
them, that they may be found worthy to enter with the Church
triumphant into the joy of her Lord, as having been faithful
soldiers and servants of that Church militant here in earth.

Yet, inasmuch as among those who are thus called into the
Church, many faint in the struggle, fall off and go back to the
world—"draw back unto perdition," says the Apostle, while
others " believe to the saving of the soul ;"[1] and thus many make
their latter end worse than their beginning, while others make
it better : her Lord provides for them in the Church to which
He calls them, channels through which He communes with
them, if I may use the term,—officially ; means of grace through
sacraments, through the ministry of the Word committed to
men duly appointed thereto according to His will ; through
offices and in a worship which the Church, as a family, renders
Him together. The spiritual life of all these means of grace,
however, is imparted only to those who open their hearts thereto,
through Faith in Him who is present in His Church, and
through Faith in the Sacrifice of Himself once offered for her
redemption from the world.   In like manner then, as "they are
not all Israel, which are of Israel," "for he is not a Jew that is
one outwardly,—but he is a Jew which is one inwardly;"[2] and
since the "Israel of God"[3] is "that which is of the faith of
Abraham, who is the father of us all,"[4] in vain shall we say :
" We have Abraham to our father,"[5] unless we bring forth fruits
meet for repentance ; in vain shall we say, We are of the Church

[1] Heb. x. 39.   [2] Rom. ix. 6; ii. 28, 29.   [3] Gal. vi. 16.
[4] Rom. iv. 14, 16.   [5] S. Matt. iii. 9.

of Christ, unless we be members of it inwardly, by having the
Spirit of Him "whose words are spirit and are life,"[1] and
without whose Spirit in us we are none of His.[2]   In vain,
then, shall we, in this country, claim to have for a whole life
enjoyed the priceless blessings of the purest, and of the most
faithful of all Churches built on the foundation of the Apostles;
of having had the daily use of her Ritual made up of the best
and simplest portions of others, yet free from their dross; and
in vain shall men say they were bred, brought-up, and buried
in this Church; all these invaluable privileges will only add to
their condemnation, unless they lived by Faith in the Truths
held by the Church, and in the Spirit they had the best means
of receiving through her from her Head, Christ.

LXXX. To His Church has Christ given in trust certain definite Truths, Rules and Articles of Faith, drawn out of His Word
revealed to man; Truths without which neither Faith nor Church
can be said to exist.   The Church holds, keeps and defends
these Truths, but does not make them; she has the authority,
but not the power to enforce them beyond the power inherent in
the Truths themselves; for as her Lord said: "My kingdom
is not of this world," albeit His Church is militant in it, He
clearly meant to give her no temporal nor secular power, beyond
the resistless influence of the Truth she holds and teaches.

Hence the struggle she has had to sustain from the first with
the world without; and often within, from men who called
themselves her sons.   The Truth like light, bears witness of
itself.   And the Truth held by the Church Catholic is, if I may
use such an expression, so true, and it is so impossible it should
be otherwise, that those who will not receive it, feel themselves
self-convicted thereby.   And that feeling of inward conviction
from which they cannot flee—since conscience follows us everywhere—has always shown itself, in various ways, indeed, but
with the same spirit—that of hatred for the Truth.   This spirit
is the same, whether in the taunts, the revilings, the open enmity
or the persecution of the world without in olden and in modern
times, or in the attempts of her sons from within, to throw
down her fences, setting at naught her teaching or denying
her doctrines.   The Truth is hated, because it is the Truth;

[1] S. John vi. 63.   [2] Rom. viii. 9.

and because, like light, it convinces and bears witness of
itself, and thus asserts its authority, whether over the intellect
which pretends to set aside all dogmas and to look within itself
for the Truth, so as to shake off allegiance to the Truth that is,
and to be master of itself—or, over ignorance and prejudice,
both of which do precisely the same thing, though from different
motives. Yet, all this is no more than the Church militant has
a right to expect. Her LORD went not up to joy but first He
suffered pain; and she too must suffer affliction ere she can
enter into the joy of her LORD. But, the very gates of hell
shall not prevail against her. In Him and through Him she
lives, "Who gave Himself for her," and who said to her at the
beginning of her struggle: "YE SHALL HAVE TRIBULATION
TEN DAYS; BUT BE THOU FAITHFUL UNTO DEATH, AND I WILL
GIVE THEE A CROWN OF LIFE."[1]

LXXXI. If we turn from these general facts to what is taking
place at our own doors, we find the Church of this country at
present on her trial—yea, even sorely tried; yet, perhaps no more
than she has often been before. Error is abroad in the land, and
scepticism is on the increase; and if we were to judge of the
public feeling towards the Church from certain publications said
to represent it, we should say it was hostile and not friendly to
her; but the real feeling and sense of the nation are so often
better than what they are said to be, that we believe the
Church and the nation to be one. Then, free, loose, and rationalistic opinions put forth by writers more self-sufficient than
either able or wise, and eagerly taken up by men fond of novelty,
or by others who would rather let go the anchor of the soul,
Hope, than be bound by the Faith that holds it—already begin
to bear fruit in the swerving of many from the Faith, in the
estrangement of some, in a growing indifference to religion, and
in the disaffection of the youth of England from the Church, as a
profession. While the minds of very many of her worthy sons,
whom neither the State nor the Church can spare, is so rudely
shaken by the late Judgment of the Privy Council, as perhaps

[1] Rev. II. 10.

to take a needlessly gloomy view of the present state of things, and to overlook the wonderful reaction for good produced of late years in the Church, through fresh energy, devotedness, and life. We will try and look at it calmly.

LXXXII. Whatever view men may take of that Judgment, there remains this fact which a hundred columns of newspaper homiletics, or any other kind of reasoning will not alter—that the Church of England has received a blow at which her enemies rejoice. Whether it was aimed or intended, seems irrelevant to the question, and is for those alone who ruled the Judgment, and not for others, to determine; but that the blow was given, there is no doubt. Neither will any quibble or other specious writing succeed in convincing sensible men that—a judgment that practically makes neither error nor heresy amenable to the law of a State that legislates for the Church, can be otherwise than important; explain it as you will. It does not, assuredly touch, affect or reach the Truth, the Spirit and the life of the Church; it cannot do that; for the Truth were not itself if it could be touched by men; yea Truth and the Truth exist, stand and will ever abide, in spite of all that men may say or do against it.

But, if the late Judgment does not injure the Spirit of the Church, it certainly affects her humanity. It affects deeply— and more so, probably, than the framers of the Judgment ever dreamt of—the minds of many members of the Church. It sanctions the holding of error, even among teachers whose heads are not clear enough to distinguish error from the Truth; and among others who are weak enough to leave their conscience in charge of their friends. It weakens the confidence of earnest, able, and good men, who are as loyal subjects as they are good Churchmen, in the intentions and in the rule of the State; it makes others doubt whether they may continue in a Church thus treated; it has, in short, so rudely shaken the whole fabric of the English Church, as to crack some of the stones thereof, and to loosen the joints of many more. It has created a general deep feeling of grief, of disappointment, and of distrust, which nothing but a ' Judgment reversed' would allay; while the effect of that Judgment on other countries which are unable to form a correct idea of the ' ins' and ' outs' of the case, is the broad fact,

damaging to the English Church, that—as they interpret it—
the Church does not believe in hell, and denies everlasting punishment. In vain will any Society try to lengthen her cords
abroad, or to seek fellowship with other Churches, in the face of
such an opinion of her present Creed as by law allowed; and
the effect thereof on the good opinion of the English name
among men abroad whose friendship is worth having, and who
used to say, "Surely this great nation is a wise and understanding people"—cannot be denied.

LXXXIII. It is not therefore to be wondered at if, in a
Judgment which engrosses the minds and the hearts of so many,
some should have inquired into the ἕξις—into the habit of mind
likely to have influenced such a Judgment; yet one cannot but
regret that there could be some show of reason for such a question to be raised, not by a few thoughtless individuals, but by
thousands of grave and earnest men. For whatever one's private
opinion may be, it seems very undesirable to discuss publicly a
matter of this kind, which is, to say the least, derogatory from
the dignity of an English tribunal and from the importance of
the case. Besides, the fault lies less, perhaps, with the judges,
than with the anomalous constitution of the tribunal set up to
decide such matters. There is a wide difference between up-
holding the Royal Supremacy in such a case, of which there
can, of course, be neither doubt nor even a wish to doubt, and
paying the same respect to the Judgment of the heterogeneous
Court into which that Royal prerogative in such matters has
practically dwindled. One cannot but think that it must have
been an oversight, and that it has only to be noticed in order to
be rectified—like, for instance, the law to which Townley owes
his life—not from any particular love to the Church, but from
a mere sense of justice and fair play, that allows appellants to be
judged by a tribunal and by judges suited to their appeal. It
is the principle that has made English justice and fair play
famous over the world; and which could never be abandoned,
especially in matters of such paramount importance as Faith and
Doctrine, except by an oversight, to which the best heads and
the best intentions are everywhere liable. A court wholly ecclesiastical, to decide on such matters, would be neither advisable
nor practically beneficial; for the best legal advice and opinions

as regards mere technicalities and points of law could not be dispensed with. But we may easily understand how a tribunal set up to judge of Faith and Doctrine, should in all fairness have Ecclesiastical Judges, with legal assessors; and not, as at present, Civil Judges with or without any Ecclesiastical assessors at all.[1] It is therefore, needless to attempt a defence of the present system of appeal; we can only look at the Judgment as a matter of fact, which cannot, at present, be undone; and briefly consider both its bearings and our own conduct under it.

LXXXIV. Granting, then, to some, that it is an affront to the Church; beyond that, what does it amount to? To this—that a Clergyman may hold and preach error freely and with impunity, so far as the State is concerned. The mischief of this is, of course, practically, very great; but it lays no blame on the Church—it is entirely a civil act. It does not force any one to teach and to preach erroneous doctrines; it does not affect in one tittle the real teaching of the Church, neither does it fetter the conscience of a single Clergyman, nor impose upon him the burden of holding anything that is not in strict accordance with the Formularies and with the Faith of the Church. The Church, therefore, is left untouched by this Judgment, since it does not alter either her Creed or the Articles of her Faith. How could it, indeed! It is simply a civil act on the part of the State, whereby it affects to loosen, as more convenient, instead of straitening, as more wholesome, the bands of Religion and its hold on the conscience. The consequences of this, whatever they be—and great they will and must be—will recoil on the State. The Church is in no wise to blame; she only suffers from it as a State Church.

LXXXV. Yet, perhaps, even less than she thinks. If it be an affront, her LORD was treated so when arraigned before the High Priest;[2] but how did He bear it? He bore it, not only as forgiving it at once, but as showing that such an affront recoils on him that offers it; and as having, therefore, taught His disciples, when they are smitten on the one cheek, to offer also the other.[3] It is a blow, and we feel it: how, then, shall we act

---

[1] See a temperate and sensible article on the subject of Final Appeal in the *Saturday Review*, Dec. 17.

[2] S. John xviii. 22, 23.　　[3] S. Luke vi. 29.

under it? Resent it? No; bear it. Bear it as a trial of our
Faith and of our patience; and "hear the rod, and him who
hath appointed it." Surely it was allowed to be, and to create
all the grief, all the sorrow it has caused in thousands of honest
and true hearts, for some good reason. Therefore ought we to
check every feeling of anger or of irritation towards the instruments of the trial. Hezekiah did not revile the messengers sent
by Rabshakeh, but he "received the letter at their hands and
read it; and then went up into the temple of the LORD, and
spread it before the LORD, and prayed before the LORD."[1]

We know the issue, let us do the same; we have the same
Throne of Grace, the same help at hand, in our need. But we
must nevertheless "read the letter" sent. Are there not many
grievous sins of worldliness among the chiefs of the Church, of
worldly-mindedness among her dignitaries, to be visited? No
nepotism, no filthy lucre, no abuses, whereby thousands of her
children are denied their bread, and are left to starve, while
others are over-fed? None of her servants, honest, hard-work-
ing, and devoted, whose life, however, seems to be to grapple
day by day with the woes and with the throes of a bare existence at the gate of richer, though perhaps, less worthy brethren,
who do little or nothing, and yet fare more or less sumptuously?
No conformity with the ways of the present world, beyond the
necessary requirements of society, for fear of being seen bearing
the Cross—although it be the honour and badge of a servant of
THE CRUCIFIED? No sins of idleness, of indifference, of lazi-
ness, of intemperance, of carelessness as to Truth and error, and
of ignorance among servants who ought to eschew these things,
and "endure hardness as good soldiers of JESUS CHRIST?"
If there be none of these things in the Church, then the blow is
harmless, and the letter sent has no meaning. If, however,
there be such things in the Church, then the blow should be
felt, and the letter should be read and understood.

And the burden of the letter is, "Be watchful, and strengthen
the things which remain, that are ready to die; for I have not
found thy works perfect before GOD. Remember, therefore, how
thou hast received and heard, and hold fast, and repent."[2]

LXXXVI. But seeing that, from the very constitution of the

---

[1] 2 Kings xix. 14, 15.   [2] Rev. iii. 2, 3.

Church and of the parochial system, the amendment where
needed, and the healthiness of the whole, depend chiefly on the
individual life, energy, and work of every member of that
Church in particular, but especially of her Clergy—let us set to
and correct what is lacking in every one of us individually; let
us show by our greater union in spirit and greater unanimity of
purpose, by our renewed attention to studies likely to furnish us
unto our work, by fresh efforts in doing good for our MASTER's
sake, by our honest and humble conversation, and by our devotedness to the people committed to our charge, that we have
"heard the rod, and him who hath appointed it;" and that no
Judgment can either touch or harm us, because we be followers
of that which is good.

LXXXVII. Those, then, do greatly err, I ween, who in their
grief, or in their zeal, would either advise or look to a schism in
the Church on account of the Judgment of the Privy Council.
Such a step would be unconstitutional, unphilosophical, and
unwise.   It would be unconstitutional—for, since the Church is
by the Constitution joined to the State, as the State is to the
Church, a schism in the Church, however little cared for, perhaps, by the State and by the world in general, would nevertheless be as much against the Constitution as a schism in the
State itself.

Secondly—a schism in the Church would be unphilosophical,
in that, a nation is but a multiple of persons, each individually
consisting of body and spirit.   As the body is dead without
the spirit, so also is the nation dead without a Church, that
should hold in the body of the nation the place of the spirit in
that of man.   But, inasmuch as a spirit without a body is a
being not intended for every-day life in this world, so also a
Church existing alone and independent of all humanity is at
best a vision of the Church, not as it must be here on earth, but
as it will be when all error and all divisions have ceased.   The
mission of the Church on earth is to bring souls to CHRIST by
gathering them from the world; not by absorption, but by fetch-
ing them, by blending herself with the body corporate of society, not in grave State matters only, but in small matters of
every-day life; exactly as the spirit influences, in great and in
small things alike, the soul and the body of man.

To sever the Church from the State, then, would be to part asunder our body and spirit; thus dooming the one to death, and the other to uselessness in the world. The Church here in earth has, and must have, a human side; she must be practical, not merely as a spiritual hierarchy, but as a body militant, since she cannot do her work without having to fight against her spiritual enemies; and there is nothing so matter-of-fact as warfare. It is her lot; therefore does she need the help, the support, and the countenance of the civil powers as much as the spirit of man requires the help of the body to do aught good in life. Even heathens made their worship a part of their State duties, from Egypt that raised her high-priests almost to the throne, to Greece and Rome, downwards. So also in Christian States; and so wise is the combination, and so much according to what is suitable for the present state of things in earth, that no other arrangement succeeds. Only look at a State, if I may so say, all Church—Rome, which after having flourished only through clerical tyranny, ends at last in effete decrepitude. And look on the other side, at a State, with no Church—America; and see to what lengths a nation can go with talent, intelligence, energy, and enterprise, but without National Religion, because without a National Church.

Then look at England; and think of the twenty thousand churches and more, in which on the same day, at the same hours the same inspired words are read, and the same solemn and earnest prayers are offered by the same intelligent people and orderly congregations, worshipping according to the same Ritual —the purest and best of all, East or West—in strains understood of the people, who learn from childhood to love, to respect, and to breathe them for the same object, to the same FATHER—and say those supplications can rise into Heaven and not be heard nor answered in blessings on those who pray, and for their sakes on the nation at large? Is she not at peace and prosperous? Things are so here, but here only; because here only do the Church and the State walk together; because here only the enlightened, innate good sense, the reverential and religious feeling of the better part of the nation is that it should be so. Who then, in his sober senses would wish to substitute for this time-honoured, holy and venerable Church, a voluntary system of chance-preachers—every one coming with his own words, and turning the House of God and of prayer, into the house of man and of preaching? and who would thus wish to give to this great nation a multitude of sprites instead of her one Good Spirit? Let us, then, if we can, learn to value our blessings ere we have lost them.

LXXXVIII. And since in our present human state, we can hardly suppose the possibility of a Church so constituted as to benefit a whole nation, and yet be independent of the State—an 'imperium in imperio' that would not last long—so also, thirdly —a schism in the Church on account of the Judgment of the Privy Council, would be most unwise, and would, probably, do more harm than ever that Judgment can or will do. Does any one think that a Free Church would in reality be purer, more orderly, more at unity with itself, and more free from human infirmities? At first, perhaps it might look as if it were; while her own, forgetting our Lord's warning to let tares and wheat grow together in His field until the reapers come to sever them, worked hard at plucking one by one every suspicious blade of grass—thus making many, many mistakes. But a man must know very little either of human nature or of Church history who thinks that such a Church should long continue to stand. Yea, rather, it might happen, as it has happened more than once already, that human passions being under little or no control, would exert themselves within that Free Church with a freedom that would lead to anything rather than to good and to edification. In such Establishments, despotism often takes the place of government; and tyranny that of rule; and being clerical—not to say spiritual—they are of all the most absolute.

Practice in this case, too often differs from theory; and some of the clergy may often forget the words of S. Paul of which S. Chrysostom[1] reminds us, saying: Τοῦτο γὰρ καὶ ὁ θαυμάσιος ἐκεῖνος ἀνὴρ συνιδὼς Κορινθίοις ἔλεγεν· οὐ γὰρ κυριεύομεν ὑμῶν τῆς πίστεως, ἀλλὰ συνεργοί ἐσμεν τῆς χαρᾶς ὑμῶν. Μάλιστα μὲν γὰρ ἁπάντων χριστιανοὺς οὐκ ἔξεστι πρὸς βίαν ἐπανορθοῦν τὰ τῶν ἁμαρτανόντων πταίσματα· "That wonderful man understanding all this, said to the Corinthians: 'Not for that we have dominion of your faith, but are helpers of your joy.' For to Christians

[1] De Sacerd. Bb. L. 3.

especially, it is not lawful to redress the failings of sinners by
force;" the less so, as very few sensible men, who will not be
driven, will refuse to follow a leader whom they can trust. In
short, so great would the harm be to the nation from another
schism in the Church, that we could not reasonably expect a
Free Church formed under such circumstances, to be likely
either to inherit or to vouchsafe a blessing. It will be time
enough for such a separation when we are by law made to preach
or to teach error; then let us break off at once. Meanwhile,
let us abide faithful. A schism in whatever shape, is oftener
than not, a cloke for much of human pride and self-will, in-
dulged under the pretence of conscience. We do better work,
both for ourselves and for others, in bearing and forbearing
much that we dislike—so that it be not against GOD's will and
the Truth—than in breaking asunder, because we chafe under
the rod. We shall not escape it by so doing: our only way is
to "bear it, and him who hath appointed it."

LXXXIX. At present, then, the duty of every earnest servant
of the Church lies before him. It is not, assuredly, to forsake her
in her trial; but it is to rally round her, to stand by and to defend her. However much we may feel it, we must, nevertheless,
lay to our account, that her lot is to be tried, and ours is also,
to be tried with her. We may, of course, picture to ourselves
how pleasant it would be if all relationship between the State
and the Church were on a friendly footing; if instead of being
often attacked she were always befriended; if the arm of the
State instead of being shortened, were always stretched towards
her, either to support her, or effectually to mend her abuses;
to see that all her revenues flowed in their rightful channels,
and that at least a crumb of her loaves were given to every one
of her children; so that, instead of being as she is practically,
to a great extent, a stranger to her people, she were indeed,
what she was meant to be, the nursing Mother of it; making
that people yet better and greater, by being one with it through
her spirit and through the life that is in her; living in the
people, and the people in her.

We can easily fancy what such a state of things would be;
and how easy her warfare would prove under such happy circumstances. But that would be a time of rest; which is not

yet. Meanwhile we, her clergy, may do much to bring about
such a state of things, by "making full proof of our ministry"
—"giving no offence in anything that it be not blamed : but in
all things approving ourselves as ministers of GOD in much patience, in afflictions, in labours ; by pureness, by knowledge, by
long-suffering, by kindness, by the HOLY GHOST, by love unfeigned, by the word of truth, by the power of GOD, by the
armour of righteousness on the right hand and on the left, by
honour and dishonour; by evil report and good report ;"[1]
"for in doing this we shall both save ourselves and them that
hear us."[2] The more earnest we are in our work, the more
also do we receive as our first reward, the respect, the good-will,
and the confidence of all in the land that are right-thinking,
sensible, and worthy ; while in the narrow little sphere of our
several parishes, our poor live in us; their affection and their
love cluster around ' their clergyman,' if he but do his duty by
them, and love them as he ought for CHRIST'S sake ; and what
little good he may do them, is amply repaid into his bosom,
not only by his MASTER, but by the very work itself. It keeps
him up to the mark of reality in his own religion, while he
rallies his people around the Cross, to the blessed Name of
JESUS; giving them Faith in Him, Hope of Heaven, and Charity
towards men; and thus sprinkling with salt the mass of the
nation, that the good therein may not perish, and that what is
worse in it be made better.

XC. In this only is the real strength of the Church, and
with it of the nation. Though "it be not for us to know the
times and the seasons which the FATHER hath put in His own
power,"[3] yet we may see around us signs of "the time of
the end;" when "many shall run to and fro, and knowledge
shall be increased ;" when "many shall be purified, and made
white, and tried, but the wicked shall do wickedly ; and none of
the wicked shall understand, but the wise shall understand ;"[4]
when "many false prophets shall rise, and shall deceive many ;
and because iniquity shall abound, the love of many shall wax
cold ;"[5] so that he alone "that shall endure unto the end shall
be saved." We already hear of wars and rumours of wars,

[1] 2 Cor. vi. 3—8.   [2] 1 Tim. iv. 16.   [3] Acts i. 7.
[4] Dan. xii. 4, 10.   [5] S. Matt. xxiv. 11, 12.

c c

though we are told "the end is not yet;" and nation rises against nation, as if the foundations of the earth were out of course. Yet, in the midst of these rumours of wars all round, this little island is living at peace, and thriving with unparalleled prosperity. Who gives her peace? Who sends her prosperity, but "he that sitteth upon the circle of the earth, that taketh up the isles as a very little thing, before whom the nations are counted as the small dust of the balance, and who bringeth the princes of them to nothing?"[1]

But if, in order to try what life and strength there really be in the Church,—and if, in order to visit the nation for the great, the special, yet ill-requited blessings of which she is the object,—"for to whom much is given, of him shall much be required"—He were to give the word, to blow against her ships; and if, instead of speeding them to the ends of the earth, He were to bring those of other nations to her shores, and the hand were seen writing against the wall, "Thou art weighed in the balance, and found wanting,"—how would certain writers alter their tone; how would senators, perhaps, recall to their memory sundry councils both public and private, and certain laws enacted, perhaps, as if He, like Baal, were absent, and as if His Word were not true! How would the affrighted nation, on bended knees and with trembling lips, beseech Him again to cover her island with the broad shield of His protection! Since, then, peace, prosperity, and plenty are His gifts, and are national blessings, the only sure way to secure them is, as a nation, to fear and to serve Him; to give all honour unto His Name; to worship Him; to give Him thanks; to reverence, and not to slight or to gainsay His holy Word, but to show Him, as a nation, that His blessings are received at His hands, and are used with a thankful heart. As long as England does so, no foes shall prevail against her.

With us Clergymen, then, and in the full discharge of our work, lies the duty of reminding the people of these things; of teaching them how to secure these blessings, and to acknowledge them when received; to love and to fear God, and thus to lessen among them the woes of immorality and vice. At all events, let us see that we do our duty, "as having to give account."

[1] Isa. xl. 12—23.

But that duty is often far from easy. We have not only to
teach the poor and the simple-minded, who receive all we tell
them; but now especially we may have to contend with error,
and with " the opposition of a science falsely so called," because
it opposes itself to the Truth. Error will ever be in the earth;
yet it prevails only as long as Truth is not brought face to face
with it. Still, unless we acquaint ourselves with that Truth,
and search into it, not instinctively, but earnestly and learnedly,
we cannot compare it with error; neither can we think ourselves furnished unto every good work of our ministry, and ourselves " workmen that need not be ashamed, rightly dividing
the Word of Truth."

The days of dry moral essays in the pulpit, 'all for GOD, and
against the devil,' as the common saying is, are gone. Our
preaching should be, of course, suited to our congregations, yet
always plain—so plain, as to leave a distinct impression on the
mind of our hearers; and it should be more intelligent than
intellectual. It should be to teach them the Truth intelligently,
showing, first, that we know and understand it for ourselves;
and secondly, that we are able to impart it to them: remembering what Aristotle tells us (R. vi. a. p. 3), that our being able
to teach is a proof of our own knowledge. Then, let us think
less of ourselves, and of the impression we are likely to make on
our audience, than of the burden of the message we bring, and
of the good we ought to do. We cannot, indeed, think too
humbly of ourselves, or too highly of our office, as messengers
of GOD to the people; ever bearing in mind that we are ourselves beset with infirmities, and that " we have this treasure in
earthen vessels, that the excellency of the power may be of GOD,
and not of us,"[1] and that as shepherds of the flock we are servants of our people for our MASTER's sake. Therefore, "if any
man speak, let him speak as the oracles of GOD; if any man
minister, let him do it as of the ability which GOD giveth."[2] Nothing will be required of us but what was given us; but that much,
at least, will be required. Surely it is enough to keep us active
and humble in teaching and admonishing, " not as being lords
over GOD's heritage, but as being ensamples to the flock ;"[3] and
in preaching, not as into the air, but as we ought "to preach the

[1] 2 Cor. iv. 7.   [2] 1 S. Pet. iv. 11.   [3] 1 S. Pet. v. 3.

Gospel; though not with wisdom of words, lest the Cross of CHRIST should be made of none effect."[1]

XCI. But "who is sufficient for these things?"—"Not that we are sufficient of ourselves to think anything as of ourselves; but our sufficiency is of GOD."[2] This is our strength for our daily work, according to the promise, "As thy day, so shall thy strength be;" a promise that never fails. Even he who was taken to the third heaven, "where he heard unspeakable words, which it is not lawful for a man to utter," was kept from being exalted above measure on that account, and ever reminded of his own weakness by Him Who said, "My grace is sufficient for thee: for my strength is made perfect in weakness." "Most gladly, therefore," says the holy Apostle, "will I rather glory in mine infirmities, that the power of CHRIST may rest upon me."[3]

With such promises and with such an example, how can so many as we hear of, halt between two opinions, and hesitate in their choice to enter the Church and to serve CHRIST therein? No ability, says one—but we are "to minister as of the ability that GOD giveth." For with our MASTER, if there be first a willing mind, "it is accepted according to that a man hath, and not according to that he hath not;"[4] and He is sure to find work for a willing mind to do. No interest, says another—but make interest with Him Who sends His workmen to His vineyard, and Who allots to every one his work. If He give the work, He will also give the wages; for He is faithful that promised. He "that hath ordained that they which preach the Gospel should live of the Gospel,"[5] will not think of it for some and forget it for others, whenever the service of Him in His Church is undertaken for His sake.

XCII. But the cause of disappointment in this respect is owing to this—that Holy Orders, being a sacred profession and a spiritual calling, and secular only in so far as the Church is militant in earth, those who look upon her service only in a secular point of view make a great mistake. Then, either they are allowed to reap from her only the secular advantages of slender means,

---

[1] 1 Cor. i. 17.   [2] 2 Cor. ii. 16; iii. 5.   [3] 2 Cor. xii. 4, 9.
[4] 2 Cor. viii. 12.   [5] 1 Cor. ix. 14.

albeit with a better social position than any other richer profession would give; or, if they have taken upon them the sacred vows of their office from family motives, convenience, or interest, apart from a real calling thereto from within, disappointment follows even then; not from want, perhaps, but from regret,—from a feeling of utter unfitness for the work,—from a distaste for it, and, worse than all, from the inward, crushing weight of an awful responsibility, lightly undertaken and never discharged. On the other hand, no man ever yet entered the Church from conscientious and devoted motives, who felt disappointed at having done so. The work well done brings its own reward, even for this world—in the esteem and in the respect of our fellow-men; in a social position which very many covet as a lift into society; in the affection of the people, and in the conscience of doing good in our generation; may be, unknown of men and uncared for by the world, but known of our MASTER, and cared for by Him. He watches over His faithful servants, and sees that, according to His promise, "they shall want no manner of thing that is good" for them; while their reward in Heaven is to be, that those whom they had made "wise, shall shine as the brightness of the firmament;" and themselves, "as the stars for ever and ever," for having made others wise "by turning them to righteousness."[1]

XCIII. But the chief reason which at present thins the ranks of the Clergy is, perhaps, the strife of tongues and the clashing of opinions abroad in society. Yet, if they find themselves thus, like children "tossed to and fro with every wind of doctrine by the sleight of men,"[2] it is all the more important they should see to it, even for themselves; lest haply, "having swerved from the faith and turned aside to vain jangling"[3] about matters of greater moment than the things of this world, and regarding which every man will have to give an answer for himself, they slight that which they ought most to mind, and at the last, "concerning the faith, make shipwreck."[4] As we should not know light but for darkness, so also we should not be able to value the Truth as we ought, if it were not for error waging war against it. Is it, then, the part of wise and understanding

[1] Dan. xii. 3.   [2] Eph. iv. 14.
[3] 1 Tim. i. 6.   [4] 1 Tim. i. 18—20.

men to think lightly of things on which hang either their eternal life in GOD, or their eternal death away from Him? It will not do to leave it to others to settle such things for us, seeing that on these things rests all our hope; and that they alone are to be either "the prize of the high calling of GOD in CHRIST JESUS;"[1] "the salvation of the soul;" the wreath of immortality given "to every one who will so run that he may obtain"[2]—or the woes of the bitterest disappointment for every one who, bent on gaining this world and the praise of men, finds at last, that for it he has lost his own soul.

Very far, then, from turning away from the Church as a profession, and leaving the defence of the Truth, that requires Faith, intelligence, learning, ability, courage, and manliness, to men who may lack these gifts—

> ὁ μέγας δὲ κίνδυ-
> νος ἄναλκιν οὐ φῶ-
> τα λαμβάνει·

some of the generous and manly youth of England ought to set themselves with a good heart to what will make their country yet greater and yet better—to the service of GOD in the Church and to the defence of the Truth as taught by this Church; making full proof among the people of the Spirit of CHRIST breathed in her formularies, in words which, being His, "are spirit and are life;" and thus working as wise master-builders, or as good workmen, at strengthening the only foundation there is for the real and lasting greatness of the nation. The service is not hard; it is that of a good Master, CHRIST, Who, wishing to show Peter how best he could prove his love for Him, said to that Apostle: "FEED MY SHEEP;" and the reward is great, both here and hereafter. Χαλεποὶ ὁ καιρός, "these are hard times," said S. Basil to S. Chrysostom, when advising him to take Orders,[3] οἱ ἐπιβουλεύοντες πολλοί, τὸ τῆς ἀγάπης γνήσιον ἀπόλωλεν, ἀντεισῆκται δὲ ὁ τῆς βασκανίας ὄλεθρος. ἐν μέσῳ παγίδων διαβαίνομεν, καὶ ἐπὶ ἐπάλξεων πόλεων περιπατοῦμεν. οἱ μὲν ἕτοιμοι τοῖς ἡμετέροις ἐφησθῆναι κακοῖς, εἴποτέ τι συμβαίη, πολλοὶ δὲ πολλαχόθεν ἐφιστήκασιν· "many there are that plot against us; genuine

---

[1] Phil. iii. 14.   [2] 1 Cor. ix. 24.
[3] De Sacerd. lib. i. 4.

love has perished, and malice and envy reign in its stead ; we walk in the midst of snares, and watch night and day on the parapet of our walls; many there are ready to rejoice at evils that may befall us, should anything happen ; and we are surrounded by them on all sides; there is no one to take our part, few as these are at all times.   Beware then lest, if we be disunited—we cause the adversary to rejoice, and we ourselves suffer loss even greater than their rejoicing."

Words almost written for the present time.   For we are, it seems, threatened[1] probably by men who seek their own and not the nation's good, with a kind of "wide, all-embracing worship," which will do away with all dogmas, all Truth; with everything, in short, except what each individual thinks and likes for himself.   God, Revelation, the Truth, the Church, Faith, Hope and Charity, Heaven and Hell, are too old-fashioned, it appears, for the "intellect, the ability, and the learning" of the present generation, that installs Reason and 'self' in their stead. If the heart did not sicken at such folly, one would smile at the sight of poor human beings—not one of which can with all his philosophy lengthen one moment the short span of his life, or tell what will befall him on the morrow,—attempting to arrange as they like the immutable counsels of the Most High, and to set up their wisdom above His !   Yet, that they should go so far as even to think of such a thing, is enough to set us on the watch, to abide by the Truth, and to defend it at all events. The struggle, let us remember, is not of our own seeking: we were enlisted for it "by Him who called us to be soldiers" of His Church militant here in earth, and to be with her humbled, tried, reviled, and even hated for His Name's sake—but after that, also "glorified with him."

"Wherefore," says the Holy Apostle, "take unto you the whole armour of God, that ye may be able to withstand in the evil day, and having done all, to stand.   Stand therefore, having your loins girt about with Truth, and having on the breastplate of righteousness ; and your feet shod with the preparation of the gospel of peace; above all taking the shield of faith, wherewith ye shall be able to quench the fiery darts of the wicked.   And

[1] See Mr. Keble's letter in *The Times* for September 27, compared with the last article in the same paper for March 9.

take the helmet of salvation and the sword of the Spirit, which is the word of God : praying always with all prayer and supplication in the Spirit, and watching thereunto with all perseverance."[1]   THE CAPTAIN OF OUR SALVATION sets us the example ; He leads the way, and holds our reward.   Let us then look unto Him, the "author and finisher of our faith," and fight under His banner "the good fight of faith ;" not as beating the air, but as with Him and for His Church.

The struggle is short, but the rest is—for ever.   Yet, no fight, no victory ; no victory, no triumph ; NO CROSS, NO CROWN.

[1] Eph. vi. 10—18.